DEVI

By The Same Author

Felicitavia
When the Time Comes
The Ashram
Anandamurti: The Jamalpur Years

DEVI

Devashish

InnerWorld Publications
San Germán, Puerto Rico
www.innerworldpublications.com

Copyright © 2010 by Devashish Donald Acosta

All rights reserved under International and Pan-American Copyright Conventions. Published in the United States by InnerWorld Publications, PO Box 1613, San Germán, Puerto Rico, 00683.

Library of Congress Control Number: 2010905197

Cover Design © Lourdes Sánchez (Mukti)

ISBN: 9781881717096

The greatest obstacle in the collective progress of the human race is the ignorance of the individual mind.

— Shrii Shrii Anandamurti

PART ONE

KALI

1

THERE ARE DREAMS THAT dance so lightly on the surface of our consciousness that they slip offstage without leaving any trace of their passage. Others remain to trouble our waking hours, though they be of little real consequence. Then there are the dreams that lead us inward, past the shadows thrown up by our present life, and into an encounter with the self that never sleeps.

It was the last of these that woke the sleeper that morning, though he did not know it, and turned his life in the one direction it was always meant to go. But for now, all he was aware of was an immense sadness at the end of a long and fruitless life for which he had no one to blame but his own wrinkled and tired face in the mirror. Still dreaming, he fought back the impulse to close his eyes, to look away, to do anything but acknowledge the face he saw and the silent recriminations that stared back at him from the glass. Then the shadow on his mind began to dissipate. A few fleeting moments later, his waking consciousness returned. He still felt the sadness in his body, a tightness in his chest that made it somewhat difficult to breathe, but the dawning realization that it had only been a dream brought with it a great measure of relief. He sprang off the bed and sat down at the small table where he had left his laptop, the only thing he had bothered to unpack before collapsing on the mattress, tired and aching after the long, uncomfortable bus ride from Dharamsala. He turned it on and clicked the file entitled "Dream Journal."

Rishikesh
8/7
7:15 AM

I just had the most surreal dream—though no more surreal than spending fourteen hours in an Indian bus being tumbled like sneakers in a dryer. I woke up dreaming that I was looking at myself in a mirror, but in the dream I was an old man with dark, wrinkled skin and only a few strands of white hair to cover my bare, blackened scalp. As I stared at that face—my face—I felt a bone-deep weariness, a kind of sad and bitter sense of resignation. Tragic is the word that comes to mind. At the same time, I was conscious that I had no one to blame but myself. I had thrown away my life, and now all I could do was endure the pain and wait for death to liberate me. The emotions were so strong they woke me up. When I opened my eyes I could hardly breathe. I had this terrible constriction in my chest, almost like I had a knife lodged there. It passed quickly, once I was awake, but I can still feel the aftershocks. In fact, I don't think I've ever had such a vivid dream. That's one thing Leiris mentions: your dreams become more vivid when you start writing them down—or rather, you remember them more vividly and more readily. Maybe my subconscious is finally starting to catch on. While I was waiting for the bus in Dharamsala, I was reading some of his *Nights as Day, Days as Night*. It struck me how mundane my own dreams were in comparison to his. I began to worry that I wasn't even creative in my dreams. But this was different. It was short but powerful, like a cameo appearance from some tragic figure hiding out in my subconscious. Who knows, I may even be able to use it in my book. Isn't that, after all, the whole point of this journal—to get material for my book? I have no idea yet where I might fit it in, but it's here if I need it. At the very least, it bodes well for the future. If my dreams start getting creative, then maybe my conscious mind won't be far behind.

Rodrigo closed his laptop, satisfied that he had gotten down the salient points of his dream. He opened his trolley bag, laid out some clean clothes, and went into the bathroom to take a shower. There was no shower stall, only a single showerhead protruding from the wall in one corner of the white-tiled room. Above it and to one side was an ancient, rusted water heater. A thin plastic strip glowed red next to the on-off switch. Who could possibly want to use hot water in this heat? he thought. Late summer in the foothills of the Himalayas might not be what it was on the plains, but it was still enough to make a body long for a cool shower. He unwrapped the bar of soap that he found lying by the sink, and turned on the cold-water faucet. The pipes creaked momentarily, and then the water came flowing out of the showerhead in a cool, refreshing stream.

As the water poured over his back, he became aware that the dream had not completely faded from his consciousness. The image of the old man's face still troubled him. Behind it lay a shadow, an uneasy feeling, not entirely vanquished, that he had willingly thrown away his life, a burden that tasted thickly of guilt. Funny how our dreams can remind us of things we'd just as soon forget, he thought. It was the same feeling that had assailed him when he'd finally signed the divorce papers some three months ago and slid them over to Beth across the kitchen table they had bought at the Salvation Army eight years earlier, both of them stunned to see a solid mahogany table wearing a fifty-dollar price tag. He remembered sitting there after she had gone out the door for the last time, feeling precisely this same feeling: that he had wasted eight years of his life on a dream that had slipped through his fingers like water. By then she was already living with another man. He was angry about it, as by rights he should have been, but he couldn't free himself from the feeling that he had somehow brought it on himself. He had considered dragging her through the courts, but his guilt wouldn't let him. There were just too many times when he had said or done the wrong thing, fully knowing that it would add fuel to a fire that she had set blazing. Too many times when he had failed to recognize the warning signs and turn back. He thought he had put those feelings behind him, but obviously he hadn't. Some residue still remained in his subconscious. But what did it mean that he had dreamed himself to be an old man, still beset by the same unresolved feelings? Could he be afraid that he was going to carry this with him for the rest of his life?

"Probably gave it away because it didn't match their new marble countertops," Beth had said, as they laid their hands on the table to feel the grain. He had accepted her indignation as his own. A world full of greed, of crass consumerism and superficial pleasures, and only the purity of their art to save them. He shook his head at how naive they had been. There had been no guilt then. They had been soulmates, pure and simple. They had seen the world very nearly through the same set of eyes. The same ironic glances at the folly of humankind. The same aspirations to be great artists, her behind the lens of her Pentax D-50, he enveloped by the luminous aura of his iMac. The same certainty that the future was waiting for them to arrive—breathlessly, if the truth be told.

As he started soaping his shoulders and arms, he thought back to their very first conversation—in his office, one hour after she had walked into his English composition class by accident, sized him up with a single glance, and decided then and there that she was going to transfer into his section. They talked for nearly an hour, and he barely noticed a word she said, his senses numbed by her graceful, willowy figure, two inches taller than his own, and her impossibly round, impassioned, nut-brown eyes that cleaved through him like a finely honed blade. He signed her entrance form without a moment's hesitation, barely aware of what he was doing, though his section was closed and he had already turned away two students earlier that day. It was only when he got home that evening that he was able to clear her fragrance from his senses. "Cupid's arrows and Jupiter's thunderbolt, flanking me on either side," he wrote in his journal that night, but there was no ironic sleight of words that could downplay the volcano that had erupted in his soul, spewing forth its deadly lava, its fires fed by every romantic notion that had been planted in his febrile brain by the stories and songs he had consumed throughout his life like manna from heaven. She had arrived in his office with a China-crepe shawl draped over her bare shoulders and a wide, pleated cotton skirt that hooped as she walked like a dervish's, a throwback to the sixties who gave no hint of the goddess within who had swooped down from her Olympian perch to have a little Dionysian fun with an unsuspecting mortal. He resisted, of course, but how long can a mere mortal hold out when the gods are determined to have him as their plaything? His fledgling sense of professionalism held fast for a few weeks, then wavered under the onslaught of her perfume and the artful lines of mascara that encircled her eyes, not to mention the snapshots she took of him coming in or out of class and then slipped under his office door with snatches of poetry scribbled on the back. It was abandoned altogether when she convinced him that his professional etiquette was not only boring—it flew in the face of everything a true artist held sacred. Not that he needed much convincing. By then, he had already painted her into his image of the ideal woman out of the fantastical colors supplied him by the architects of the Western literary tradition. She was his Isadora Duncan, the carefree, visionary artist, as graceful as a Nordic fairy, destined to be his muse, to open the door in his garden wall and lead him into the spirit land of artistic immortality. He was her Byron, the dark-haired, faintly myopic, post-romantic poet who was chosen by fate to sketch her portrait in words that would enable her to live forever. They both acknowledged the other to be their destiny, and despite the university's baleful frowning on college professors who got involved with their students, neither of them saw any point in making destiny wait.

Again he shook his head. Could he really have been that naive? But of course the answer was yes. He remembered the late nights talking about the books he planned to write, debating whether her photos showed more influence of Mapplethorpe, as he divined, or of Warhol, as she insisted. Year after year, locked into a dream, until the slow deterioration of their once beautifully scripted fairy tale became so obvious that even his obtuse eyes could see it. Long conversations about how much of his own life he planned to fold into his books somehow morphed into short diatribes about how he had sold out to the capitalist machine. Imagine that! Somewhere along the way, she had turned him from a Byronic figure into a pusillanimous university functionary who had become so enamored of his academic prestige, his fawning students, his faint but safe reputation as a literary critic, his tenure and the addictive pleasures of a regular paycheck, that he had forgotten the pact he had made before the sacred altar of everlasting art. How had they gotten so turned around? The easy answer was sabotage, the saboteur asleep in the bed beside him. In the last months, he had clung to that notion as tightly as he could; yet, while it assuaged his anger, it did nothing to stifle the sadness and the guilt, or hold back the fear he instinctively knew was at the root of the pain that had followed fast upon their separation.

No, there was no mistaking the source of his dream, no mistaking whose ancient face he had seen in that mirror. Not even two oceans and a foothold in the Himalayas could separate him from his failures. But why the aged wrinkles? Why the dark skin? Why the recriminations of a tired old man, instead of the fresh sorrows of his waking face? Could the dream be a message from his subconscious that he was afraid she might be right? That he might one day come to the end of his life without ever having set foot on the road he had always dreamed of walking? Was this the fear that was stalking him, the added knife that had made the pain of losing her so difficult to bear?

He took his loofah and started scrubbing vigorously his back and shoulders.

The course, fibrous matter of the natural sponge shucked the dead flakes of skin and sent them rushing toward the drain, along with the last of the dust and grime that had settled on him during the course of the long bus ride. He bent down to scrub his legs and then bent each knee, one after the other, and scrubbed the soles of his feet. Satisfied with his ablutions, he shut off the water and reached for the towel.

So what if it was? His subconscious was pushing him, that's all, the same old litany he had hoped to leave on the other side of the ocean. If so, then he would push right back. He had not come to India to run away. His marriage might be lost but he was not. The only image that a mirror in a dream can reflect is the ghost of a sleeping mind's fancy. He was flesh and blood and at the beginning of his road, not the end. He was thirty-five years old. Proust had been thirty-seven when he began work on his great novel. The past might be his enemy but the future was his friend. History was full of great writers who had begun their careers at his age or later. No one knew that better than he. He still had two years on Proust and every intention to live decades longer than the French master's fifty-one years. He may have had Proust's slight build and his jet-black hair, but he was healthy and took good care of himself. Who knows how much he might accomplish before he was through? He would make her see the day when she would tell her friends with pride that she had once been married to Rodrigo Arroyo. And if they hadn't heard the story already, they would gasp and beg her to tell them what the legendary master had been like when he was young.

As he stepped out of the bathroom and began putting on his clothes, he glanced at his watch. Breakfast was at eight, still ten minutes away. He took his small collection of books out of his luggage and placed them on the night table. Then he sat down on the bed with his back against the headboard and tried to picture Le Gentil approaching the shores of South India. The French astronomer would be feeling the spray of salt water in his face. The smell of approaching land would be in his nostrils. What emotions might he be feeling as he came within sight of Pondicherry for the second time? He would be hopeful, certainly—aware that finally, after eight long years and much hardship, he was in sight of his goal. He would have no inkling of the failure that awaited him and the severe depression that would follow as he saw his life literally be eclipsed by clouds. But that depression was coming. It was held in trust by his creator. Suddenly, Rodrigo realized that the dream and its tragic sadness was exactly what he needed for the scene that would immediately precede the climax of his book. It might well be that his subconscious was merely throwing back at him the despair he refused to acknowledge in real life. It might indeed be trying to frighten him with his unacknowledged fears of how he might end up. But what of that? Van Gogh had turned his despair into art that would vie with eternity for longevity. Proust had taken his emptiness and given it a voice that reached across continents and spoke for an entire generation. He would take his dream and his failed marriage and do the same. Let his fear come at him. He would turn it against itself and from that battlefield conjure forth the genie of transcendent, enduring art.

Rodrigo had little difficulty finding his way to the guest dining hall. There he found a buffet of steaming silver pots and three rows of low tables about a foot high along the other three walls with mats for the diners to sit on. He spooned out some porridge from one of the pots and helped himself to two slices of toast from a basket and a cup of tea from a large silver dispenser. Then he found a seat in one corner from where he could watch the other diners.

Almost all of the twenty-five or thirty people who came and went while he ate were westerners. He heard French, Spanish, German, English, and a language he couldn't place, but which, from the Latinate words, he guessed to be Romanian. How many of them had come to India on some sort of spiritual quest? All, most likely, after one fashion or another. What else would bring a wandering westerner to an ashram in Rishikesh? In this respect he was an outsider. His quest was artistic, not spiritual, but the milieu was exactly what he was looking for: a quiet place with clean rooms where no one would bother him. Where better than a Himalayan ashram? He had started his sabbatical in Dharamsala, to satisfy a long-standing desire to meet the Dalai Lama, whom he admired for his lifelong efforts to save a unique and endangered culture, but now it was time to immerse himself in traditional Hindu culture, knowing that it was the only way he could give his book the authenticity it would need. Pondicherry would still be too hot at this time of year—he had not planned to reach there before November. In the meantime, Rishikesh seemed a likely place to begin his quest: cool enough that he wouldn't be overly bothered by the heat; small enough that he wouldn't be suffocated by the crowds; and, most importantly, steeped in centuries of Hindu culture with only the barest contamination from the irreverent West.

He would have liked to sip his spiced tea a while longer, but they had asked him to register as soon as he was done with breakfast. He finished a second cup, savoring the pungent flavors of cardamom and clove, and walked over to the office, which was housed in the same building. As he entered through the open doorway he saw a thirty-something Western woman in a white sari sitting on a mat in front of a low glass-topped counter. She was talking on a cell phone and working at a computer with her free hand.

Rodrigo sat on a mat in front of the counter and listened curiously to the woman's speech. Her accent was unmistakably New York City, born and bred. Not only New York, but New York Jew, he thought, judging by the wavy black hair that hung untamed over her shoulders and her distinctly Semitic features. And yet she was speaking Hindi into the phone without any trace of hesitation or awkwardness. She even laughed at what might have been a joke she had made. Who could joke in a foreign language if they weren't completely fluent? Rodrigo was impressed. After a few minutes, she snapped shut her cell phone and acknowledged him with the same smile that had been present throughout her conversation.

"I was told to come here and register after breakfast?"

"Name?" she asked, glancing down at a typed list under the glass.

"Rodrigo Arroyo."

"Arroyo. Here it is. American. Do you have your room already?"

"Yes. I arrived about four thirty this morning. They put me in room 242."

Rodrigo showed her the heavy brass key with the room number engraved on it.

"Nice room, overlooking the Ganges." She handed him a registration form. "Fill this out. I'll also need to see your passport when you're done."

When he had finished filling out the form, she checked it against his passport and then turned back to the computer and rapidly typed in the information.

"I'm Bhagavati," she said when she was done. "I oversee the office work and take care of Swamiji's engagements and whatever else he needs me to do. If you need anything while you are with us, just come and see me and I'll try to take care of it. How long are you planning on staying?"

"I'd like to stay a month, if that's possible. I wrote that in my email when I made my reservation."

"Ah yes, I remember now. You said in your email that you were interested in studying yoga and Hindu philosophy. This is your first time in India, right?"

"That's right." Rodrigo shifted his position, uncomfortable at the thought that his letter had been somewhat misleading. "I'm also working on a novel that's set in India. I thought this would be a perfect place to get started."

Bhagavati appeared intrigued. "You're a writer?" she asked.

"Yes. I'm also a professor of literature at the University of North Carolina. I'm taking a year's sabbatical to work on a book."

"Really? How interesting. Well, there's nothing like regular spiritual practices in a good environment to unleash the creative juices, and in my experience there's no better place for that than Rishikesh. I'm sure you'll get a great start on your book while you're here. Anyhow, I'll just run through a few things you need to know and we'll be all set. The suggested donation is five hundred rupees for rooms overlooking the Ganges and four hundred for rooms on the inner courtyards. You're welcome to change rooms at any time if you decide the one you have doesn't suit you. Just let me know and I'll arrange it. The donation includes meals, but we do ask that you let us know at least one meal in advance if you plan on missing a meal, so that the kitchen can know how much to prep are. We also ask that our guests attend the *arati* program at dusk."

She reached under the counter and handed him a small folder.

"Here is a brochure that explains the arati and gives some more information about the ashram. The arati starts a little after five on the steps of the ghat—that's directly in front of the main entrance. Yoga classes are at seven AM in the yoga center. That's at the far rear of the ashram. Philosophy classes are at ten, also in the yoga center, but if the weather permits, Saraswati usually likes to teach her classes outside under the banyan tree. Let's see. There's chanting and meditation each morning at five in the main hall with the *brahmacharis* and the rest of the ashram residents. That's right behind this building. There's another collective meditation in the main hall after arati. You're welcome to attend these sessions any time you like, but they're strictly optional. When Swamiji is in residence he often leads them personally."

As she said this, Bhagavati pointed to a large portrait hanging on the wall behind him. A handsome, dark-skinned man dressed in orange robes and *rudraksha* beads stared out at him. He had long black hair, a thick black beard streaked with gray, red markings on his forehead, and a smile that seemed to grow out of the twinkle in his eyes. The picture felt imposing, perhaps only because it was so large, but the expression on his face made him seem immensely likable. He wouldn't mind meeting this swami, Rodrigo decided, whoever he was.

"Well, unless you have any questions, I think that's about it."

"No, no questions."

"Good then. Enjoy your stay. I think you'll find that the ashram is a very special place."

It could have been a conversation with the reception staff at a New York spa, if it were not for the sari and the fact that they were both sitting on mats on the floor. Bhagavati had that practiced, pleasant, efficient New York air that he had not failed to appreciate on his few visits to the city. Though it felt odd to meet with such a reception at an Indian ashram, it bolstered his confidence that this was a place where he would be left alone to write.

As Rodrigo stepped out of the office and into the bright morning sunshine, he took his first good long look at the place he had planned on making his temporary home. It had still been dark when he'd arrived that morning. All he had seen from the back of the rumbling three-wheeler that had taken him the two kilometers from the bus station to the foot of the Ram Jhula Bridge was a wide expanse of gray sand and dim boulders on one side, bordering the black waters of the Ganges, and the looming shapes of one- and two-story concrete buildings on the other, huddled tightly together in the dark. He had felt the mountains more than he had seen them, but even then they seemed to impose their will on the shadowy, desolate surroundings where everything appeared to be brooding motionless under the cover of night. The only sounds he'd heard, other than the discordant braying of the three-wheeler, were the wind whipping off the water and the lone bark of a dog, far in the distance, plaintive and mournful. They had gotten out, himself and the four other passengers, at the foot of Ram Jhula, a narrow, swaying, four-hundred-foot steel suspension bridge that hung over the shallow, rapid waters of the Ganges. As he crossed the bridge on its walkway of wooden planks, barely wide enough for two people to walk abreast, he had kept one hand on the wire-mesh siding to steady himself against the wind, which was strong enough, as it swept down from the mountains upriver, to chill his bones despite the balmy summer air. A young tout had accompanied them, diligently handing out hotel cards to each of the new arrivals. The boy had walked him to the ashram gate, some three hundred meters downriver, and then complained mightily over the ten-rupee tip, until another ten rupees brought a yellowed grin to his small, dark face and sent him scurrying off into the engulfing silence.

Now, as he looked around in the daylight, Rishikesh seemed anything but mournful. From where he stood, he could see the blue-tinted waters of the Ganges framed in the arch of the ashram entrance. Beyond the river rose the foothills of the Himalayas, green forested slopes glinting under the glare of the morning sun. He turned slowly and followed the mountains as they encircled the ashram on three sides, loosening their grip on the sky only in the direction in which the Ganges flowed, south toward the plains of Northern India. He could sense an air of quietude hanging over the grounds, a hushed solemnity that he hoped would favor the writer as much as it did the devout meditator.

Rishikesh, as he had learned from his well-thumbed travel guide, was a hill town, quiet, sturdy, industrious, but the ashram was not situated in Rishikesh proper. It was part of a separate enclave on either side of the river that consisted mostly of ashrams and temples. This small settlement began just south of the Ram Jhula Bridge, about a kilometer and a half from the edge of town, and continued up to the nearly identical Lakshman Jhula Bridge, two kilometers upriver, where, legend had it, the god-king Rama had crossed the Ganges in his flight from Ayodhya. According to the guide, yogis and spiritual seekers had flocked to this picturesque Himalayan setting for hundreds, perhaps thousands of years, to pursue their meditations and chant the holy names passed down to them by the sages of antiquity. Even today, few people came to Rishikesh who were not seekers of spiritual enlightenment or religious absolution, since there was little else to do in this graceful warren of spiritual ashrams, other than attend yoga classes or chanting sessions, visit temples, or listen to lectures by spiritual teachers. There was no cinema hall, no nightclub, no live music that was not devotional in character, and no restaurant that served non-vegetarian food, this mandated by local law long before the government had begun advertising Rishikesh as the world capital of yoga.

As Rodrigo stood there, drinking in the majestic sight of the encircling mountains, he heard the sounds of distant mantras carried to his ears by the wind that was gradually dying down, as it did each morning just about the time the town's residents were getting ready to start their day's activities. Feeling his spirits quickened by the music, he decided to make a short tour of the ashram before setting out to explore the town. As he walked through the grounds, it reminded him of an elaborate maze: compound after compound of colorful, two-story buildings wrapped around courtyards of various sizes, each of these crisscrossed by concrete pathways lined with well-tended shrubs, shade trees, and flower beds, one compound snaking into another through covered and uncovered passageways, then suddenly and unexpectedly opening up into a wide, two-acre lawn presided over by the spreading canopy of an ancient banyan tree. Most of the buildings had verandas on both floors where the residents could recline and gaze upon the mountains. The courtyards were decorated with meticulously painted alabaster statues representing scenes from Hindu mythology, carefully labeled in English and Hindi. Here and there a fountain splashed by the side of the statuary. Together with the abundant greenery, they served to lend the ashram a curious air of gaudy religiosity and understated beauty.

When he completed his round, he headed out the main gate and crossed the lane to the ghat that faced the ashram entrance. He entered through the small swinging gate and slipped off his shoes, following the protocol outlined in the pamphlet Bhagavati had given him. The ghat was built of marble—the smooth, polished, off-white slabs so closely fitted together that the ghat seemed to be fashioned from a single piece of stone. The spacious upper landing was some ten meters wide and forty in length. To the right stood a small temple, also made of the same polished stone, and to the left a gazebo. A series of wide steps descended to a lower landing by the edge of the river, followed by two final steps that the water lapped with a gentle scudding music. Some seven or eight meters into the river stood a beautifully sculpted statue of Shiva on a bed of stone and concrete boulders. Five meters high, its brilliant white surface reflected against the pale marble of the ghat. The crescent moon on his forehead glinted in the sun, and the look of profound contemplation on his face seemed so real, so sunk in eternity, that for a few moments he caught his breath and held it before he was aware of what he was doing.

A dark-skinned child was at the bottom of the steps, leaning out into the water. He extended a flower in his tiny hands and dropped it reverently into the steady current while his mother looked on solemnly a few paces away, wrapped tightly in the folds of her sari. Rodrigo took out his camera, adjusted the viewfinder, and took a picture of them. But when he looked up again, he felt uneasy, as if he were profaning a sacred moment by endeavoring to preserve what was both ephemeral and timeless.

From there he headed up the lane that ran alongside the river, walking in the direction of Ram Jhula, slowly enough that he would not miss anything. He saw mendicants and orange-robed sadhus huddled by the side of the lane, begging alms; others were walking along in either direction with their begging bowls and staffs. Several of them glanced toward him with a curious look of disinterest as he passed, then extended their begging bowls a few inches and intoned the ritual *hari om*. There were numerous westerners as well, ambling along in clothes that seemed to be a mixture of hippie and mendicant. He noticed one of them squatting on the ground next to a sadhu, sharing a cup of tea and a bidi cigarette. Bookstores, curio shops, and dingy restaurants with wooden tables and benches lined both sides of the lane. Flies darted around the baskets of fritters and sweetmeats, heedless of the owner's lazy attempts to shoo them off. Near the foot of Ram Jhula, a CD stall blared out Hindu mantras on a boom box, while just across the road pilgrims were ringing bells at a small temple. A little farther on, the shops ended and the path skirted above a large expanse of white sand that reached down to the edge of the graceful waters. On the far side of the river, the thickly forested foothills gradually gave way to taller and taller mountains, the colors shifting from greens to browns to grays as the vegetation became sparser and sparser, until they became blue, snow-capped shapes fading into the distance.

He spied a shaded empty bench overlooking the river and sat down to marvel at the natural beauty that had so enchanted the British when they began making their summer homes in the hill stations of the Himalayas. How they must have felt like emperors, he thought, when they first came here, knowing that all this was theirs for the taking. Little wonder that so many of them balked at the idea of going home when their years of service were over. Where in Britain could they have found a place this beautiful, this peaceful, blessed by so hospitable a climate? How they must have felt the lure of these tranquil waters sliding underneath the bridge, lulling their minds to rest, and the sight of the mountains behind them, receding toward a sky so blue and so vast that it seemed only fitting to refer to it as the heavens. Yes, Bhagavati was right, he decided. This was the perfect place to begin writing his book.

As he sat and looked at the river, he mused about what it might be like to live in such a place for an extended period of time and write. Proust had spent almost all his productive years imprisoned behind the walls of his apartment. Imagine what he might have done had he been in Rishikesh, resting his eyes on this enchanted scenery, dipping into the springs of memory for his material. Certainly, he would have lived longer and been happier. An immortal work might have been made even richer, if that were possible. It certainly would have been longer.

For the last several years, Rodrigo had taught a class on expatriate writers in Paris in the 1920s, the so-called "lost generation": Fitzgerald, Pound, Hemingway, Dos Passos, Gertrude Stein—all of them Proust's contemporaries. The Paris of that time had been teeming with notable writers, not to mention the streams of painters, sculptors, musicians, and dancers from diverse countries who flocked to the city like pilgrims to Mecca, a list that began with Pablo Picasso at the height of his creative powers and ended with Isadora Duncan in the twilight of hers.

"There was a symbiosis between these writers and the city they had adopted as their home, between the artist and his environment," he had lectured to his students. "By the time that *Swann's Way* went to print, centuries of cultured aristocracy, revolutionary turmoil, French philosophy, and a blend of architectural styles had conspired to give birth to an artistic explosion that was uniquely Parisian, though its practitioners came from all over the globe. Without Paris, Hemingway would not have become the Hemingway that we know today; nor Henry Miller, the Henry Miller."

Would Proust then have created such an enduring work of art had he been liberated from his Parisian apartment and transported by Scheherazade's magic carpet to the banks of the Ganges? Undoubtedly, he reasoned, for Proust still would have been Proust, but the masterpiece he gifted to the world would have been a different masterpiece. It would have been more spacious, less Parisian, exhaling the clear air of these mountains by which its creator would have revitalized his spent lungs. It would have carried in it—hidden perhaps, but unmistakably present—the scent of Himalayan pine, the fragrance of centuries-old incense, the mystic overtones of a culture far older than his own.

As he had stood there in front of his students, exploring the ways in which a writer is shaped by his environment, thus making it the most important of the conscious choices he can make, he had been dreaming of his own Paris, still unsure where it lay, that as-yet-unexplored territory where he could stoke the creative fires that were sleeping in his dormant soul. There would perhaps be many a Paris for him before he was through, as many as the different currents of his writing necessitated, but first he needed one, just one, before he could call himself a writer, rather than a literature professor who dabbled on the side. As he looked out at the river, he hoped that in some way Rishikesh might become to him what Paris had been to the lost generation, a spark to ignite his literary fire. The university was certainly not the place. That was one thing Beth could never understand, one of many. All she saw were the long vacations and the house in the suburbs. What did she know of teaching full-time to students who sucked your energy and distracted your attention? When had she ever had to go to war with the capitalist machinery that dominated every aspect of university administration and left him with headaches that it took all summer to get rid of? Every morning, she put her easel and her paints into the back seat of the red Dodge Neon he had bought her—a private dig at her loud and outdated apparel— and drove off to wherever her fancy directed her. Or else she took her cameras and spent the day snapping black-and-white photos of the shoppers strolling down Franklin for the Chapel Hill Magazine. Had he ever objected when she took off for weekend or even weeklong excursions to photograph seascapes or the march on Washington or the everglades? Had he ever once mentioned that she was free to follow her artistic dreams because he had struggled for years to establish a secure financial and professional base, starting in graduate school and then working toward his tenure? He had put up the money to have her first photography collection privately printed in a local press and had helped her with the text. And yet she complained that he was suffocating her with his bourgeois lifestyle, that he had sold out to middle-class complacency, that he was stifling her artistic aspirations instead of inspiring them as they had both promised to do years before, that it sapped her will to see him waste his talent like this. Had she forgotten Wallace Stevens? The Connecticut poet had spent nearly twenty years working his way up the Hartford Accident and Indemnity ladder until he became a vice president so he could then dedicate himself to his art without having to expend long hours and precious mental energy trying to make his two ends meet. Could she not have afforded him the same leeway? Granted, Wallace Stevens's wife never appreciated him either. No, Beth had never given him credit for having scratched and clawed to become a respected scholar, had never done anything more than turn up her nose at the regular paycheck and the faculty dinners—in between her expeditions up and down the coast where she stayed in chic hotels and ordered room service on his credit card. The woman could no more understand the writer's quest than a monkey read Shakespeare. And then to betray him like that with a no-talent capitalist because he promised to jump-start her career? It just didn't make sense.

He felt his heart tighten, a residue of the anger he thought he had put behind him. He blinked back the suggestion of a tear and pictured her walking up to

Quail Ridge Books with her no-soul, no-account lover, clutching her chest when she saw his book in the showcase window: *The Venus Transit*, by Rodrigo Arroyo, huge stacks of hardcover volumes on display, each one a weight on her heart. A pleasing sense of triumph eased the constriction in his chest. No great artistic journey is without its obstacles, he thought. This was part of the cross he would have to bear until he made it across his Calvary. He thought of Fitzgerald and Hemingway and how they had folded their personal setbacks into their stories, how their private tragedies had helped to give their work its universal character. He hoped to do the same. Certainly, he had Beth to thank for his being here. It was the disintegration of their marriage and the sight of her on the arm of Raleigh's most prestigious gallery owner that had convinced him to apply for his sabbatical, already several years overdue, propelled by an overwhelming urge to flee the scene of her crimes. How many times had he vowed to himself since then that he would show her? How many times had he envisioned himself coming back from India with a completed manuscript, his passport into the land of the immortals, knowing that it would prove her wrong every time she picked up a newspaper and saw his name in print? It was not the best of motivations, he knew, but it had gotten him on the plane to Paris. After that, a far deeper urge had taken over, the urge to prove to himself that he was indeed a writer, born to the noblest of callings, as he had always told himself he was. He had published a few short stories, to be sure, and a score of critical articles on his favorite writers, enough to earn him the reputation Beth had so facilely derided, but the simple truth was that he had yet to embark on his true calling. He could not yet call himself a novelist, as he longed to, a practitioner of the one supreme art form that had commanded his undivided attention since the age of ten.

It was Beth, in fact, who had given him the idea for the book he had finally settled on to be his first after numerous false starts. They had been sitting on the back porch one evening in the beginning of June, two years ago, looking up at a sky studded with stars. It must have been close to the new moon since there was nary a whisper of moonlight, nor any hint of the usual haze that tended to contaminate the summer sky in the triangle area. She had bought a telescope the previous summer and set it up on a tripod behind the house. Every night without fail for almost a year she would go out there and spend at least an hour with her eye fastened to its lens, a development that never ceased to surprise him, given her incurable penchant for flightiness and her hitherto total disregard of any aspect of science that didn't impact directly on the creation of art.

"Are you aware that Tuesday is the Venus transit? There hasn't been one since 1882—122 years ago. Imagine that."

She was staring through her refractory lens at the glowing orb of Venus hanging low on the horizon, just above the trees that bordered the back of the property. He was grading papers, silently annoyed at the intrusion on his thoughts.

"Uh huh. And why exactly should I be interested?"

"Well, for one thing, the Venus transit was only the object of the single greatest adventure in astronomical history, that's all. I'm surprised no one's ever written a novel about it. Maybe if they had, you might consider it worthy of your attention."

"So enlighten me then, now that you're such an accomplished astronomer."

The look she shot him could have scalded milk, but it didn't stop her from prattling on with a supercilious edge to her voice.

"In 1677, Edmund Halley—you may have heard of his comet; I believe it has appeared in a novel or two—yes, well, he traveled to the island of St. Helena to measure the Mercury transit. That's the time it takes Mercury to cross the face of the sun. Afterward, he realized that if he could measure a Venus transit, then he could use it to determine the solar parallax—Venus being much closer to Earth than Mercury—and hence the geometric distance from Earth to the sun. Is that clear so far?"

"Okay, I'll bite," he said, setting his papers down on the recently oiled redwood planks. "And what would he stand to gain from that?"

"He would then be able to measure planetary distances in units of the Earth's orbit. In other words, he would be able to accurately map out the solar system. This was the great pursuit in astronomy in the seventeenth, eighteenth, and nineteenth centuries. The only problem was that Venus transits are very rare. The next one wasn't going to be until 1761. Obviously, he wasn't going to live that long, so he started working on a plan to send observers to different parts of the globe to measure the transit, the farther apart the better for their calculations. The entire international community of astronomers took up the challenge in the next century and dispatched expeditions to some of the most inaccessible places on earth: South Africa, the Indian Ocean, the South Pacific, Siberia, North and Central America. Remember, this was the eighteenth century; they couldn't just hop on a plane. There were no five-star hotels where they were going and very few detailed maps. In fact, they had more chance of dying of disease or shipwreck en route than they had of getting back to Europe with their calculations. But that didn't stop them. They went all over the world, funded by different governments. It was like a joint space program nowadays. With the help of the transit, they were able to measure the distance to the sun as 149.59 million kilometers, almost exactly what it was proven to be in the twentieth century with modern radar techniques and Doppler telemetry.

"There was this French astronomer, Le Gentil. He was sent to Pondicherry, but when he got there, Pondicherry was under siege from the British. The harbor was filled with British warships. He couldn't get off the boat, so it was impossible for him to measure the transit. But instead of going back, he decided to stay in Southeast Asia till the next transit—they come eight years apart, you see, and then they don't come around again for more than a century. He didn't even know if the other astronomers had been successful or not, but he stayed anyways. Talk about dedication to science. So he goes back to Pondicherry seven years later, after exploring Southeast Asia, and on the morning of the transit it clouds over and he can't see a thing. Poor guy. And that wasn't the half of it. He had to wait nearly a year to get a ship back, and in the meantime he got sick and almost died. Then, when he did finally get out of Pondicherry, his ship got wrecked in a storm; he had to find another one. That one also nearly got shipwrecked. In the end, he was gone almost twelve years, and when he finally makes it back to Paris, he finds that his relatives have declared him dead and looted his estate, and the French Academy of Sciences has given away his seat. He did marry a wealthy heiress, though, so at least he died rich."

"Well, now I can see why nobody ever bothered to write a novel about it."

And then that look of hers, as if to say, "Why do I even bother?"

But something about the unlucky Frenchman caught his attention. Maybe it was the fact that he was heading for his own shipwreck, his marriage at the point of splitting open on the rocks, and his artistic life floundering in the shallow waters of his comfortable profession. The next day, he went looking on the Internet for information about Le Gentil. He made no mention of this to Beth, of course. It would have only furnished ammunition for her verbal arsenal, and she had enough of that already. The truth was, historical fiction had always been his favorite popular genre, ever since he began reading Edgar Rice Burroughs's Tarzan books as a child. When he graduated to literary fiction in high school, he was pleased to discover that serious writers favored the genre almost as much as popular writers did. The appeal of such a story was obvious. One need not look any further than Shakespeare. The scope it afforded to play with events already written by history was nearly endless. You could subvert their meaning or bring to light what the outward face of history had hidden. In popular historical fiction, if well done, an entertaining tale was lent added richness by offering the reader a peek into a bygone era, transporting him back in time to sights and sounds that were otherwise barred to him. But in the hands of a literary master, the retelling—or, more often than not, the reinvention—of history could open a window into the hidden meaning of the journey of the human race. It could lay bare the ancient prejudices, whether tacitly accepted or bitterly opposed, that have made us who we are today. There was no doubt that a literary mind had to truly understand the past before it could successfully point to the future. He had often thought of finding such a vehicle for himself. Two of his discarded ideas for a first novel had been modern deconstructions of historical tales. But one roadblock or another had always derailed him before he could effectively get going. Maybe it was just as well. When he first read Le Gentil's story on the Internet, he was certain he had found the vehicle he had been waiting for. To be sure, it was only the skeleton of a story, but it was enough for him to strike his sails in a sea of possibilities. He saw Le Gentil immediately as a Tom Jonesian figure: the brilliant, good-natured rake and his comic misadventures, his mind so far ahead of his contemporaries that it laid bare the failings no one else could see. Then, as now, it was a timeless theme, ancient follies always being the antecedents of our own.

A flash of ochre distracted Rodrigo from his thoughts. He glanced downward from where he sat and saw a sadhu taking off his tunic by the riverbank. Tall and very dark, the sadhu stepped into the river in his orange loincloth and began splashing water over his dense matted locks. Then he leaned backward and started floating on his back. The translucent waters lapped around his nearly motionless body, rippling his hair outward in the direction of the current.

Rodrigo had never seen a single bather in the Seine during the three weeks he had spent in Paris on the first leg of his journey. A century of pollutants dumped into the river from upstream factories had freed it of bathers. Here, however, the water was so clear, it was very nearly like looking through glass. The various shades of pebbles on the riverbed were visible even from a distance of twenty meters. He remembered gazing into the murky waters of the Seine and laughed. If ever a seat by the river afforded the poet a chance to look into his soul, as the common conceit had it, then what troubled waters the Parisian poets must have spied in the depths of their unconscious when they sat by the banks of that muddled river. Maybe that had something to do with the dark visions he had so admired in the poems of Rimbaud and Baudelaire without ever managing to feel comfortable in their company. Though he loved the Rive Gauche and his night-time walks through the Quartier Latin where he had taken a room in a *pension*, pleasantly aware that he was just around the corner from where Henry Miller had shacked up for five francs a night while he poured his soul into the pages of *Tropic of Cancer,* in no place had he felt as at home as he had in the Sorbonne during those weeks of Parisian summer, leafing through Le Gentil's journals, his scientific writings, and all the biographical references to the astronomer he could find in that august institution. The Sorbonne housed the original handwritten copies of Le Gentil's journal that he had submitted to P. Sonnerat in 1781 for publication. An attractive, dark-haired librarian had waited patiently by his side one morning while he carefully admired the fourteen hundred immaculately penned pages. The same librarian had helped him in his research, patiently unearthing information on the intrepid astronomer that he never would have found on his own. It was she who allowed him to photocopy the library's priceless first print of *Voyage in the Indian seas, on order of the king, on the occasion of the passage of Venus across the Sun on the sixth of June, 1761, and the third of the same month, 1769, by M. Le Gentil, of the Royal Academy of Sciences*, a long-winded title characteristic of Le Gentil in his best moments. She had also brought him their best French-to-English dictionary so he could annotate his copy with translations of the unfamiliar words. He must remember to send her an autographed first edition of his own book once it was published.

His book! The monumental significance of the moment did not escape him. Tomorrow he would begin his life's work in earnest. A month or two in Rishikesh would see him well into the first draft. Then he would move on to Pondicherry, maybe find another ashram there to stay in. By the time spring arrived, his first draft would be finished. The second draft would take him back into summer, the draft that he would shop around when he returned to the states. One revolution around the sun. He took a long, deep breath, the pure mountain air as heady as any wine he had ever tasted. Suddenly an idea occurred to him. He rapped himself on the forehead. Of course! He needed something to commemorate the occasion. An image flashed in his mind of the Tibetan Buddhist ritual he had witnessed in Dharamsala, the day after his long-awaited audience with the Dalai Lama, a privilege afforded him due to his work with the Chapel Hill chapter of Students for a Free Tibet. There had been fifteen of them ushered into the room by a small retinue of ochre-robed, shaven-headed monks. The Dalai Lama was no different in person than he seemed to be on TV: candid, personable, warmly effusive, to the point where it seemed like they had been close friends their entire lives. His Holiness said a few words about Tibet and their efforts to save its cultural heritage. He shook hands with everyone in turn, asking them their names and where they were from and thanking them for their efforts on behalf of his embattled country. Then he gave them his blessing—not from on high, like the pope might have done or a head of state, but more like a kindly, bright-eyed uncle, wishing you all the best from the bottom of his heart. Before they left, he invited them to the Tibetan ritual that would begin the next morning—the Kalachakra Initiation. They all went, along with more than ten thousand other residents and visitors. The Dalai Lama conducted the ritual, decked out in an exotic headdress and ceremonial robes. Rodrigo found it incomprehensible but fascinating: the chanting of mantras in those strange, guttural voices; the clouds of incense; the ringing of bells and the interminable bowing. His head was spinning by the time he left McLeod Ganj that afternoon to catch his bus, tipsy and disoriented from a long day of exotic sights and sounds.

Yes, considering where he was, there absolutely had to be a ritual. Nothing like what he had witnessed, of course, but one of his own invention. His gods were the gods of literature. Why not propitiate them before he started his book? What harm could it do? Who knows, one day a young professor might stand up in front of a crowded lecture hall and start describing how Rodrigo Arroyo had begun the writing of his classic first novel with an offering to the gods of literature in the foothills of the Himalayas. He might even try to point out to his students the influence of Rishikesh in the artist's work.

This last thought brought a smile to Rodrigo's face. Pleased by the idea, he lay down on the bench, crooked his arm to serve as a pillow, and decided to take a short and pleasant nap in the cool, leafy shade. Soon he was immersed in a daydream about his long-envisioned protagonist. He saw the French astronomer approaching the shores of Pondicherry for the second time, seven years after a spate of British warships had forced him to watch the first Venus transit from the pitching deck of a French frigate, despite the letters of free passage that he carried in his breast pocket, signed by representatives of both the French and British crowns. He pictured him standing in the foredeck, watching the same strip of land inch slowly toward him that he had failed to reach when it most counted. He heard him cursing that ridiculous war that had forced him to remain at sea where it was impossible to make any useful calculations. A string of French imprecations singed his ears. There was something defiant in the Frenchman's posture as well, a physical reflection of the undaunted spirit that had convinced him to remain another eight years in the South Asian seas without a moment's hesitation, refusing to accept his defeat at the hands of nature and mischance, and with it the defeat of his race's efforts to tear down the barriers that stood between man and an unclouded knowledge of the universe he lived and dreamed in.

The Frenchman's vehement defiance was still fresh in Rodrigo's mind when he opened his eyes and bolted upright on the bench. He cursed himself for not having brought his laptop. Not even a notepad! Taking a cue from his soon-to-be-born character, however, he refused to let this little indiscretion faze him. He began reprising the daydream so that it would still be fresh in his mind when he had a chance to write it down. Plunging even deeper into his character's head, he parsed through Le Gentil's memories as he stood on deck, the hardships he had undergone while trying to make it to Pondicherry that first time with the sounds of warfare whirring in the salt air around him, the despair that followed on the heels of the realization that his long voyage from France had proved futile. Suddenly, Rodrigo realized that this was exactly what the opening scene needed. It was the obvious place to start filling in the events of the previous seven years: his decision to stay on and wait for the next transit in defiance of nature and whatever imaginary gods the Orient had thrown at him; selected images from his nearly five years in Mauritius, happily spent pursuing his secondary occupation as a naturalist, cataloguing the local flora and fauna; the failed trip to Manila and his run-in with the Spanish governor; the near shipwreck while trying to make it back to Pondicherry, which had recently returned to French hands. Chronologically, this was all extraneous to his tale, but the reader needed Le Gentil's memories to understand how important this second transit was to him. Without them, the climax would lose its emotional appeal. This was the perfect place to start introducing the forces that had led him to Pondicherry Harbor on this twenty-seventh of March, 1768. Let him review those seven years in brief episodes as his ship approaches the shore, the emotions pouring through his head as he realizes that he is finally drawing near his long-sought goal. Then, and only then, can the reader know and feel what is at stake when he reaches land and the untold story begins, the one Le Gentil left out of his journals, the one Rodrigo had come to rescue.

Tomorrow two quests would begin: his and Le Gentil's, creator and created. He would set out on the road to becoming a great writer—an immortal, if things went as planned—and Le Gentil would reach the shores of South India in his quest to solve the age-old problem of measuring the distance from the earth to the sun, thereby entering his name in the annals of astronomical immortality. They needed each other if either was to succeed, although Rodrigo was well aware that a fundamental divide separated him from his nascent character. Le Gentil's fate was already known to him; it had been two years in the planning. His own fate was much less certain, a fact that did not seem to bother him as he headed back down the Ganges toward lunch.

2

THE FIRST THING RODRIGO was aware of when he awoke the next morning was the sound of chanting floating in through the open window: *Hare Krishna, Hare Krishna, Krishna Krishna, Hare Hare,* the words faint but distinct. He listened for a few minutes without opening his eyes, his ears gradually differentiating the sounds of cymbals and hand drums marking time for the voices. The slow, steady pulsation had an almost hypnotic effect: for a few moments, he felt as if he were floating out the window, born aloft by the music to the other side of the river from where it seemed to be originating. Then thoughts appeared and began to drag him back to earth. Fragments of a dream surfaced. He reached for them anxiously but they slipped away, occasioning a brief gust of disappointment. He wondered if he might have lost something valuable for his dream journal. Then he remembered what morning it was. He sat up in his bed, instantly wide-awake. Today he would begin in earnest his journey as a writer, leaving behind all the disappointments and failed hopes of the past years. Today he would start bringing Le Gentil to life with his careful brushstrokes, leading him out of the depths of his mind to walk down the alleyways of Pondicherry and through the markets and fields of the world. Today was the dividing line that would separate who he had been from who he was meant to be. And it would all begin with a ritual, a symbolic beginning toward a very real end.

He got out of bed and walked to his second-story window. A slate-gray vapor was rising from the river, making it appear as if the statue were sitting on some Himalayan peak among drifting clouds. The sun had yet to crest the mountains, and the lane in front of the ghat was empty. Nothing was moving anywhere that he could see, other than the silent waters that glided steadily along without ever changing place. The only sound he heard was that of the pilgrims on the other side of the river sending their reverent mantras toward heaven. Heedful of the solitary setting, Rodrigo decided not to waste any time. He spent a few quick minutes in the bathroom and then grabbed the items he had prepared the previous night when he had designed the morning ritual. It was not much: an anthology of American poets; the five novels he had chosen to take with him to India, one each from his five favorite writers; and a single sheet of paper, blank except for the words "The Venus Transit" written out in block letters at the top. He left his room and made his way to the ghat in the balmy morning air. He walked down to the edge of the flowing water and sat cross-legged on the marble step, thankful that he was alone, accompanied only by the sky, gradually turning blue as the mist thinned, and the mountains that sought their shelter there. He arranged the five books in a semicircle in front of him, touching each one to his forehead before setting it down, as he had seen the Hindus do on a couple of occasions. Then he picked up his book of verse and began intoning the poems he had chosen for the occasion, the spare and sonorous syllables of Wallace Stevens, a poet whom he had struggled with for years, never quite sure if the poet was mocking him for his lack of understanding or simply living in a rarefied air that few mortals ever visit. He began with his favorite modern rendering of an ancient tale, one he felt he finally had the right to claim as his own:

> *Under the shape of his sail, Ulysses,*
> *Symbol of the seeker, crossing by night*
> *The giant sea, read his own mind.*
> *He said, "As I know, I am and have*
> *The right to be." Guiding his boat*
> *Under the middle stars, he said:*

> *"If knowledge and the thing known are one*
> *So that to know a man is to be*
> *That man, to know a place is to be*
> *That place, and it seems to come to that;*
> *And if to know one man is to know all*
> *And if one's sense of a single spot*
> *Is what one knows of the universe,*
> *Then knowledge is the only life,*
> *The only sun of the only day,*
> *The only access to true ease,*
> *The deep comfort of the world and fate."*

When he finished intoning the eight long stanzas and six pages of this nearly epic poem in his best imitation of the Buddhist monks he had listened to in Dharamsala, he ended his sacred recital with the last stanza of "A Clear Day And No Memories." He hadn't originally intended to add this stanza to his long recitation of "The Sail of Ulysses," but it had felt right the moment his eyes glanced upon the verse just before falling asleep. He wanted to start his journey free of the past—that was the whole point of the ritual—and he could think of no better poem to sum up that fervent wish.

> *Today the air is clear of everything.*
> *It has no knowledge except of nothingness*

And it flows over us without meanings,
As if none of us had ever been here before
And are not now: in this shallow spectacle,
This invisible activity, this sense.

When he was done with his recitation, he closed his eyes and rested his hands on his knees. Rodrigo had never practiced meditation before, but here, in this place and at this time, it was what the ritual required. He visualized himself floating in the middle of the cosmos and silently began invoking the gods of literature, offering them his obeisance and calling on them to fill him with their sacred fire. His book, and those that would come after it, would be his offering to them, theirs in perpetuity for the gift of making him their medium. For at least ten minutes, he repeated his silent prayers, gazing into the vastness within his mind and trying to feel the presence of the silent watchers who heard his prayers and received his offering and looked into his soul to see if he was worthy of the boon he was asking. Then he opened his eyes and looked straight into the dispassionate eyes of the statue. He did not know what kind of a god Shiva was, or what he represented in the Hindu imagination, but at that moment Rodrigo accepted him as the symbol of all gods—the gods of literature, the gods of creativity, whatever divinity, real or imagined, that humans prayed to and called upon for guidance. He lifted the single sheet of paper, blank except for the title of the book that was yet to be born, and offered it to the flowing waters, as he had seen the Indian child do the previous morning. The page was blank because he himself wanted to be empty, to let the gods of literature fill him with whatever words they willed. He set it in the river to let it merge in the current of all literature, offering it up to the river of life in whose waters his book would take birth and in whose current it would continue to flow long after he had passed away.

When Rodrigo returned to his room, he was still tremulous with emotion from the ritual, which had proved more powerful than he had expected. He spent the rest of the morning in front of his window overlooking the Ganges, staring into his laptop as if into a crystal ball, summoning forth the omniscient narrator that he had chosen as apropos to the period he was describing. It was slow work, almost painful at times, trying to find words to fit the pictures that flitted in and out of focus within his mind. Chapter one began as planned, with Le Gentil standing on the deck of the Portuguese ship that was bringing him back to Pondicherry, cursing the war that had kept him from recording the first Venus transit in 1761. As the astronomer came within sight of land, a surge of exhilaration coursed through him at the thought that the end of a long and trying odyssey was now in sight. The emotions of the moment sent his mind careening back through the previous seven years, revisiting the hardships and the sacrifices he had willingly endured in order to remain in Southeast Asia for the second transit, now little more than a year away, knowing that Venus would not return to visit the sun for more than a century. He had almost completely lost touch with Europe, apart from a few letters and some unreliable tales that had reached his ears in the Isle de France and Manila. At times, he had lain despondent or angry in his bed, shaken by thoughts of the discoveries that might be passing him by, but he had known that this was part of the price he would have to pay for the greater glory of science and the laurels that would await him when he returned. It had been seven years since he had last seen the only French protectorate in these waters, and then only from a great distance as the missiles of war whirred overhead. Seven long years marooned at the edge of the world by his own volition, years that, nevertheless, had been anything but unprofitable, no matter how far removed he might be from the seas of civilization. Nearly five of those spent on the Isle de France. Five thick, hardbound journals filled with his observations of wildlife that he was sure had never before been studied, much less catalogued, by any civilized scientific eye. Hundreds of carefully preserved samples. When he arrived back in France, he would be bringing a new and unseen world with him, locked safely into his four felt-lined trunks and the folds of his brain, a world that was sure to dazzle the eyes of his compatriots, even if their only window into that world was through the spidery script in the pages of his journal.

One by one, Rodrigo sketched out the fragments that he drew forth from Le Gentil's memory: a shouting match with the Spanish governor, who accused him of being a French spy; his trysts with a Mauritian maiden who came to trust him enough to lead him to the hidden spawning grounds of the soon-to-be-extinct Rodrigues Giant Tortoise; the near shipwreck and near mutiny during the voyage from the Philippines. It was difficult for him to decide just how much of Le Gentil's ruminations to add. Too much and the reader would lose himself in the quicksand of the past, sacrificing his sense of the present moment and the all-important forward motion of the story. Too little and the reader would be just as much at sea as Le Gentil, lacking the necessary incentive to invest in the story. He had taught these concepts to his students in graduate seminars, but it was far easier to point out the adroit strokes of a Thomas Mann or a Gabriel Garcia-Marquez than to make those same brushstrokes yourself with an unformed story and no actual experience to draw upon.

By lunchtime, he had written over five pages, a feat that afforded him no small measure of satisfaction, though it was accompanied by an uneasy feeling that what he had written was far too unwieldy to pass for anything but a very rough draft. Even then, he knew that the gods of literature were smiling their favors upon him. He was on his way, as sure as Ulysses when the Argonaut weighed anchor and set out for Troy. Somewhere his single blank page was surging toward the Bay of Bengal, and in its stead, the gods were filling him with their written words. What was important was not how the journey began, but the very fact that it had. The gods themselves had planted the obstacles in Ulysses's path. It was thanks to those obstacles that Ulysses was able to prove himself worthy of his place among them, as the most immortal of the mortals. By calling on those same gods, those that walk untamed through the human imagination, Rodrigo had assured himself of tests no less trying. He knew he might get discouraged, as had happened with the Greek hero on the isle of Calypso, but he would not lose faith. Minerva had not abandoned Ulysses and she would not abandon him, even if he had to call her into existence from the archetypal sea that swam within him.

After lunch he went for a short walk, making a note to himself to set aside some time to explore Rishikesh—"field research" was the phrase that came to mind—as well as time for studying Indian culture and Hindu beliefs. It was still monsoon season, the clouds thick against the mountains now, gathering with a rapidity that reminded him of battalions massing for an attack. He returned to his room when he felt the first drops of what proved to be a short but heavy shower and spent the rest of the afternoon navigating through Le Gentil's memories, accompanying him up until the point when his ship was about to set anchor and receive the governor's longboat that was to take him to his destiny. His eyes were tired by then. A long day's work had left him a little tense, but rather than relax, he took the time to read what he had written. As he suspected, it bore little resemblance to the prose of his favorite writers. The language was clumsy in places, stilted in others. The episodes from Le Gentil's seven years in Asia lacked the coherence he knew they would need to bring the character to life for the reader and create that sense of urgency and anticipation he wanted for his protagonist's quest. But the raw material was there. At this point that was all that really mattered. He would have time to shape it later on. For now, he would concentrate solely on getting the story down. At this rate, he should be able to finish the first chapter sometime tomorrow. Then he would move straight on to the second, in which Le Gentil would go ashore and receive his grand welcome from the French governor. The writing would no doubt get better as he got his sea legs, to borrow a phrase that had come out of Le Gentil's mouth a couple of hours earlier. Everything in its time. Somewhere his Penelope was waiting for him, but first he had a sea to cross.

Rodrigo leaned back in his chair and interlaced his hands behind his head. His unfocused eyes rested on the bluish haze hanging above the mountains outside his window. Relaxing now after the day's labors, his mind wandered down well-trodden roads to some of the favorite resting places of his imagination: the official book launching, which he usually visualized taking place in the Times Square Borders, unusually well attended for the work of a first-time novelist; the first magazine reviews—*Publishers Weekly* and the *New York Times Book Review*, of course, followed by the watershed review in the back pages of *Newsweek*; and his most recent favorite: his first interview on national television. He couldn't quite decide which would be better: a seat at Charlie Rose's round oak table involving a tasteful intellectual discussion about the social themes in the book and his primary literary influences, or a satellite relay on *Larry King Live* where he could talk from the comfort of his own living room about whether or not he planned on leaving his teaching gig for the life of a full-time novelist—this only after satisfying Larry's curiosity about the by-now-well-known ritual in front of the Shiva statue. The first would be more literary; biographers might refer to it someday and draw useful quotes. The latter would help sell more books, but as an interview it would be quickly forgotten. In the interest of thoroughness, he rehearsed them both. Midway through the second interview, the unmistakable sounds of someone testing a loudspeaker intruded on his reverie. He straightened up and peered through the window. Down at the ghat, a group of monks and lay disciples from the ashram were setting up the sound system on the lower landing for the evening arati. Others were covering the marble steps with strips of thin red carpet. He remembered that he had not attended the program the day before, as was expected of guests. It would not do to create unnecessary waves. Semi-regular appearances were definitely in order. Moreover, this was part of his research. It was why he had come to Rishikesh in the first place: to have a chance to immerse himself in traditional Hindu culture without having to rely on the mediation of the written word.

Hurriedly, he closed his computer and got ready to attend the program. By the time he reached the ghat, the steps were teeming with people all the way down to the water. The air was fresh from the afternoon shower. A small group of instrumentalists were tuning their instruments in front of the microphones on the lower landing. To the right of them in a semicircle sat a large group of school-age monks in saffron robes, the youngest of whom couldn't have been more than seven or eight. The swami was sitting on the other side along with Bhagavati and several other Indian women in saris, each with a microphone in front of them. Rodrigo left his sandals just inside the small gate alongside scores of others and found a seat at the top of the steps at the far edge of the crowd. In the meantime, more people continued to arrive, searching for a place to sit. Across the river, the last rays of sunlight faded and the sun solemnly dipped below the horizon. He took a couple of photos, hoping that his camera would catch the fading glory of sunset, and then opened his notebook to add a few descriptive notes. The music started while he was in the middle of a sentence comparing the swami to the Buddhist lamas he had seen in Dharamsala. It was much louder than he had anticipated. He finished the passage with a cursory note about God not being deaf and turned his attention to the scene in front of him.

The music was similar to the other religious chanting he had heard since his arrival in India: harmonium, hand cymbals, and tablas; a syncopated, driving beat; and scores of people singing at the top of their lungs, often skirting a fine line between singing and screeching. The swami, who had a surprisingly rich baritone, was leading the chanting, accompanied by the Indian women seated next to him, their voices shrill by comparison. The young monks acted as a chorus for the traditional call and response. The swami would intone a line and they would repeat it, joined by those in the audience who knew the chant. Everybody clapped time to the music, irrespective of whether they knew the words or not. How could they do otherwise? The beat was hypnotic, irresistible. Rodrigo followed along, his loud, staccato thunderclaps clearly audible amid the controlled, zealous cacophony. He had no idea what the words meant but the tribal pulsation made him feel as if he were participating in a ritual that might be thousands of years old—if it were not for the intermittent static of the loudspeakers. When the first chant ended, he pulled out the brochure from his small satchel and discovered that the chants were devotional hymns in Sanskrit and Hindi dedicated to different aspects of the Divine, such as Shiva, Krishna, and the Divine Mother. Here and there, he recognized a word from the examples in the brochure, but he needed no translation to understand the devotional fervor taking hold of much of the gathering. By the time the second chant was underway, most people had their eyes closed. Many of them were swaying from side to side, as if intoxicated; some were stretching out their arms toward the statue like a child toward its mother. It was quickly obvious who was a spectator and who was a devotee, a fact that made him thankful he was sitting on the outside of a circle to which he did not belong.

The chanting lasted about forty-five minutes, by which time darkness had fallen and the first stars had begun to appear above the mountains. After the penultimate chant, two middle-aged women stood by the water's edge in front of the statue. They held a large golden platter between them laden with burning incense and camphor that sent fragrant plumes of smoke into the air. As the music started up again, they began tracing slow, solemn circles with the tray, their eyes never wavering from the flames. The audience joined in for the singing of the final hymn, a steady, dirge-like chant that rose and fell like a boat making its way toward the horizon over a gently rolling sea. Rodrigo regretted that he could not understand the words. Again he glanced at the brochure and saw a picture of the ritual and a short explanation. The song, the brochure explained, was a hymn of praise and reverence to the Divine Mother in the form of the goddess of the river.

As the hymn continued, his eyes drifted to the deepening sky. A vague sadness began to rise like an invisible mist from the shadowed mountain peaks. In the midst of all these people, at the end of a sustained outpouring of devotion and reverence, he began to feel alone and adrift, disconnected from the world and its inhabitants. He noticed an emptiness in his stomach that could not be confused with hunger. The sky, slowly filling up with stars, grew cold and unwelcoming. It was a feeling he was familiar with, an old melancholy that in the recent past had come dangerously close to despair, but he was determined not to give in to it, despite the uneasy suspicion that not even India was far enough to get away from himself. He turned his eyes back toward the arati and made a conscious effort to focus his attention on the sonorous syllables rolling like a wave toward the shore.

When the chant ended and the crowd began to disperse, he opened his notebook and took up his best line of defense, the bulwark of words raised upon the empty plain of a blank page, a vantage point from which he could see his thoughts in relief and thus vanquish their power to creep up on him unnoticed in the night. With a few firm strokes of his pen, he began describing the arati, and along with it, the sadness and loneliness that seemed to trail behind it. By doing so, he gradually started to put some distance between himself and his emotions. As the people filed out, a sense of stability slowly began to return. A young monk, who was rolling up the carpet on which he was sitting, stopped just short of him and made a smiling, impatient gesture. Rodrigo moved aside and then sat back down on the marble step, almost without breaking contact between the paper and the ball of his pen. He continued writing under the soft illumination of the lights from the temple on the upper landing, drawing strength by connecting himself to an unbroken line of great writers who had kept journals of their experiences, thoughts, and feelings, and turned those journals into literature.

A few minutes later, a shadow fell over his notebook; Rodrigo was interrupted by a female voice with a New York accent.

"Ever the writer at work, I see."

He looked up to see Bhagavati smiling at him. The ghat was almost deserted now, apart from a few young monks sweeping off the marble steps and the white folds of her sari, ghostlike against the night.

"How did you enjoy the arati?" she asked.

"Very much; it was…very powerful."

Bhagavati nodded. "Good choice of words."

"I wish I could have understood the songs, but even then, I could still feel a little of what everyone was feeling when they were singing. Devotion, I guess you might call it."

Bhagavati laughed softly. "That is what we call it. The Sanskrit word is *bhakti*. In Hinduism, bhakti is considered the best and the quickest path to God. The path of work and the path of knowledge, karma and *jnana*, are the other two principal paths, but the scriptures say that in this age of Kali Yuga, the age of spiritual darkness, those two paths are too difficult. Few people have the stamina or the mental clarity to be able to follow them successfully. But bhakti is easy. The mind naturally becomes concentrated when it's filled with love. When we sing to the Lord and invoke his name through the sacred mantras, it becomes easy to feel that love. We automatically feel connected to the Divine Presence. Do you know Tagore?"

Rodrigo shook his head.

"He was a poet and a musician, among other things. He has one song that explains it better than I ever could."

Bhagavati paused for a moment and then began reciting the lyrics in a slow, lilting cadence, no longer looking at Rodrigo but at the sky behind him.

"I know that only as a singer I come before thy presence. I touch by the edge of the far-spreading wing of my song thy feet which I could never aspire to reach. Drunk with the joy of singing I forget myself and call thee friend who art my master.

"Beautiful, isn't it? For me it sums up the whole essence of devotional singing."

"That is beautiful. Who did you say wrote it?"

"Rabindranath Tagore. T-a-g-o-r-e. It's a song from his best-known book, Gitanjali."

"I'll have to read him."

Rodrigo got to his feet and the two of them started walking back toward the ashram.

"Tagore's poetry is a great place to start if you want to appreciate the beauty of Hindu thought. He was not only a great poet, you see, he was also a great saint, a great yogi. He used to meditate for four hours every morning before he started his day. What I love most about Tagore is that even though virtually all his poems are about some aspect of spiritual experience, you mostly wouldn't know it unless you were doing spiritual practices yourself. You might think they were about nature or worldly love. It's a little like Hinduism. You can understand it at different levels, depending on where you're at. The arati, for instance. You wouldn't know it, but every gesture, every word has a special spiritual significance. There's a whole philosophy behind it. Some of the Hindu rituals may seem a little strange at first, especially to a westerner, but they're actually a kind of symbolic language that the ancient sages used to describe the ultimate reality and our relationship to it. Once you understand them, you begin to see that they actually teach you how to tune yourself to the Divine, even before you realize that that's what you're doing. It's a wonderful process—amazing, really. Everything in Hinduism has a way of pointing us down the path toward realization. The more you get into it and the more you understand, the more fascinating it becomes. At least that's how it was with me. That's why I'm still here after ten years. No better place on earth, as far as I'm concerned."

"Really?"

"For a spiritualist? Absolutely. But Swamiji can explain these things far better than I. He has a gift for making even the most complicated philosophy seem simple. If you're interested, there's a group arriving from South America in a few days; Swamiji's going to give a private talk for them about Hindu practice, arati, and so forth. You're welcome to come if you like. It might even help you with your book."

"Absolutely. I'd love to."

"Good. We haven't fixed the time yet, but I'll let you know once we do."

After Bhagavati disappeared into the office, Rodrigo took a seat on a bench in the courtyard outside the dining hall. Dinner was not due to be served for another half hour. He rummaged in his satchel for his notebook, but instead of opening it right away, he took a few minutes to collect his thoughts. Just in front of the bench there was another statue of Shiva. The great god was sitting atop a mountain peak on his favorite tiger skin. Water was running off the mountain and splashing down into a small pool. Rather than being immersed in contemplation, Shiva was looking out on the courtyard, just as Rodrigo was doing. What Rodrigo saw as he scanned the grounds reminded him of a sylvan bower from an ancient India that he had never seen but which must have seemed familiar to the god looking down from his alabaster mountain. The statuary glimmered in the soft light, looking like ancient Hindu gods walking through their celestial gardens. It was a balmy evening, the stars appearing and disappearing as thick clouds drifted slowly across the sky. A few people were moving along the path. The only sounds were the low murmur of their muted conversations and the steady splashing of the water. It was certainly beautiful, enough perhaps to still his heart had he come here at another time and under other conditions. But on this evening, he could feel the loneliness pressing against him, haphazardly buried emotions stirred back into his blood by the pulsations of the music. For a few moments, he felt envious of Bhagavati's calm assurance and unquestioned convictions. He thought of Sartre's famous quote: "To believe is to know you believe, and to know you believe is not to believe." He wondered if this applied to Bhagavati or the swami or any of the closed-eyed, swaying devotees who were able to lose themselves in their devotion the moment the swami's basso voice rose up above the tablas in the religious fervor of his ancestors. Were they aware of the absolute and unquestioned nature of their beliefs? Were they in any way capable of stepping back and examining them with the dispassionate eye of an impartial observer? Did they have the courage to see those beliefs for what they were: artifacts of the human imagination? Or would that knowledge have stripped them of their devotion? "Every man is condemned to freedom," Sartre had said. Had anyone ever summed it up better, the unremitting loneliness that seemed to be the fate of any truly aware human being? In the final analysis, every human being is alone in this universe, he thought, face to face with the uncomprehending and the incomprehensible. Most of us do whatever we can to avoid staring down that cold fact. We run to our ideal lover and huddle up against the cold, as he had done. But in the end the cold bears down upon us, implacable and unfeeling. And if we reach for knowledge as a stanchion, or as a last resort, or even out of the sheer necessity of knowing, then we pay the ultimate price: We are condemned to awareness of our fate.

He opened his notebook and again made his best efforts to stave off his loneliness by forcing it into a prison of words from which it would be hard pressed to escape. "Was that what Beth and I were trying to do?" he wrote, his pen strokes far more confident than his words. "Trying our best to ward off the cold?" In the last months, there had been a touch of desperation about it, as if the closer they got physically and the more friction they created, the more the heat they generated would create an illusion of warmth. But no matter how much they clung to each other at night, during the day the cold seemed to seep back into their bones, and from there no amount of effort could keep it from their tongues. "So how much didn't you write today?" he remembered her saying one evening. "A whole chapter, part of a chapter? No, let me guess: The critical scene in which the heroine pledges her undying love to the hero after saving his ass from mediocrity. I'd share with you all the photos I didn't take today, but I have to get into the darkroom and develop the ones I did. Sorry." As usual, she sashayed straight from the kitchen to the converted maid's room under the stairs that she used as a darkroom without waiting for an answer, mostly because there never was an answer forthcoming. If she would have waited there for him to fetch a notebook and write down what he wanted to say, then maybe they could have had a truly creative argument, something straight out of *The Taming of the Shrew*. Perhaps then the raising of the bridge could have been arrested. The river that rushed between them could still have been crossed. But he could never come close to matching her gift for caustic repartee. So he tried to pass off his silence as indifference, drawing it about him like a cloak to keep out the chill that followed her across the tiles. It never worked. He just slid deeper into the loneliness, and so did she. At night, they tried to claw their way out with passion, but whatever temporary relief it afforded could not withstand the glare of daylight. And so it had gone, month after month, until he found himself waiting for the dinner hour in the courtyard of a Hindu ashram while she was getting ready to open up her lover's gallery for another day of unsold paintings. Two blind travelers floundering in the dark. But were they so different from everyone else on this boisterous planet, whipping its way through an icy void? Were they not simply defending themselves as best they could from the onslaught of the unknown? That was what he wished to know as he perused the half smile that never lifted from the Shiva's blue-tinted face. Is it not the best anyone can do, to glide downward to darkness on extended wings? So much better than flapping furiously in a futile effort to stave off the inevitable, turning an elegant descent into a frantic, frightened fall. Could this be what the ancient Hindu sages had realized? Might not their colorful rituals and sonorous mantras, their philosophy and their symbolism, be nothing more than a concerted and fundamentally artistic effort to turn a fateful, fiery crash into a beautifully choreographed swan dive? Certainly Proust had something of this in mind when he chose the name "Swann" for his most important character. Unlike his fellow Parisians, bickering and backbiting their way toward the grave, surfeiting themselves on bourgeois prejudices and self-infatuation, Swann glided through a lifetime of disappointments and tragedies into the velvet shroud of a painful and premature death with the elegance of one of nature's most beautiful creatures. It was an artistic life, a life well lived, despite all its tribulations, despite the fact that its only certainty was that of a cold grave. Perhaps all this talk of devotion and enlightenment was just the ancient Orient's way of pursuing an elegant life by freeing it from the burden of consciousness, from the knowledge that we are alone in the universe. Was this so different from the artist's quest? Was this not the ultimate goal of Stevens's Supreme Fiction? As long as we are alive, there must be an art of living. Anything less would be unforgivably pedestrian. No matter how profound Sartre's philosophy, he was never a great artist. The darkness is still the darkness, Sartre might have argued, and he would have been right, but perhaps the flight is more important than the ultimate destination. He must take a closer look at what the Hindu sages had to say. Would they not have wanted human beings to live well, above all other things?

Rodrigo clicked his teeth on the end of his pen as his thoughts gyrated in the night air. He glanced at his watch and saw that dinner was only a couple of minutes away. He would have liked to follow his thoughts further to see where they led, but he knew he did not think as well without a pen in his hand and even less well on an empty stomach. He padded into the dining hall in his bare feet after parking his sandals just outside the entrance and helped himself to a generous serving of rice pilaf and curried vegetables. The dining hall slowly filled up as he ate, but rather than listen to the low conversations, he opened his notebook beside his tray and busied himself with stray thoughts about the following morning's scene. Tomorrow his astronomer would go ashore; he would have his first real look at India. But after that, only the muse knew where the book would take him. A few ideas popped into his head and were scribbled down, but nothing solid enough to distract him from his dinner.

He was still musing over where his story might go when he drifted off into sleep that night. His last thought, however, before he crossed the border into the land of dreams, was not of his astronomer or where his adventures might lead him. His last thought was of the arati. He heard again the lilting melody, but this time his somnolent mind was pondering the words he had read in the brochure, wondering who might this goddess be whose hair flowed over her shoulders and down the mountains in rivulets that joined together to stream across the plains of Northern India until they emptied, serene and mighty, into the Bay of Bengal. *Jai Devi Ganga Ma*, "victory to the Divine Mother in the form of the river Ganges." To whom was offered all this adulation? This was the last thought that played in his mind before he was carried off by the eddies of forgetfulness.

3

Rishikesh
8/9
7:40 AM

Moments ago I was in the middle of a dream so vivid it feels like it's still going on, and so unusual I can barely believe I dreamed it. I can still feel the goddess's eyes on me, imprisoning my heart with her fathomless glance, telling me without words to be patient, to trust that she is guiding me, whether I see her or not. And yet, at the same time, here I am, sitting in front of my computer, moments after leaping from my bed, my forehead and neck covered in sweat. It is still relatively cool on this Himalayan morning, but in my dream the weather was oppressively hot. And still the sweat pours, like these monsoon rains that come like clockwork almost every afternoon. But I am forgetting my dream journal discipline. Let me first write down all that I can remember, before it disappears.

In the dream I was a priest, a Hindu priest. I was in a temple, kneeling in front of an ornate stone statue that was almost as big as I was. It was an idol of some Hindu goddess, a fantastic creature that commanded every drop of my attention. She was jet black from head to toe and had a bright red tongue sticking out, like a flame in the night, and four outstretched arms—not unusual for a Hindu goddess, from what I gather. In her upper left hand she held a bloody sword. I'm pretty sure she was holding things in the other three hands as well, but I can't quite remember what they were. She was decked out with an exotic headdress, something similar to the tall crown I saw the Dalai Lama wearing in Dharamsala during the Kalachakra Initiation. Around her neck she wore a garland of skulls that hung almost to her feet. All in all, quite fearsome looking.

The idol was standing on a marble slab in the center of an intricate diagram. I remember now that I had drawn that diagram with some colored pastes when I entered the temple. It was a set of triangles of different colors, one inside the other. Around the triangles was a circle ringed with flower petals, then another circle, then a set of concentric squares. After I drew the diagram, I knelt down and offered the idol some food on silver plates: some lemons, I believe; some chili peppers; and some dark green leaves. I remember distinctly that I did this with a sense of reverence, which is what most surprises me, for I have nothing of the devout in me. She was real to me, not simply an idol but someone—or something—with whom I had had a long and profound relationship. I lit some incense and started waving it around. After that I offered her flowers—roses maybe, at least they were red. Then I started chanting in a low voice with a peculiar rhythm. It was some kind of mantra that I knew almost as well as I knew how to breathe. The words were so familiar, it seems like I should be able to remember them even now, but I can't quite catch them. Anyhow, I must have recited this mantra a few hundred times. Of course, dream time doesn't flow at the same speed as real time. I may have only recited it a few times. The point is, it seemed like forever. When I was done chanting, I showered the idol's head with flower petals; then I bowed down and touched her feet. After that I sat in front of her, cross-legged, and started praying. I don't exactly remember the words, but for some reason I was deeply frustrated. I was praying for the goddess's help in this matter—or rather, I was hoping with all my heart that she would be pleased with my efforts and grant me this boon in return. I had my eyes closed at this point (it was a kind of meditation, I guess). And then it happened, without a moment's warning, as if I had stepped through a magic doorway into another world: I saw the goddess appear within my mind, no longer an idol but a living, breathing presence, as if the statue had heard my prayers and suddenly come to life. I guess I was in some kind of trance. She was smiling, like she was happy with me, or perhaps amused. Then she began to communicate—not with words but mentally, as if our minds were linked, only hers was infinitely greater than my own. She was telling me to wait; she had something planned for me; I needed to be patient and let her guide me. When I heard her thoughts, I was filled with a kind of ecstasy, as if I were surrendering to some kind of benevolent cosmic force. Then the vision ended. She disappeared to wherever she had come from—the cosmos, I suppose. I opened my eyes and found myself back in the temple, sitting in front of a stone idol once again. Moments later, I was back in my bed, aware that I was waking up. And yet, I was still dreaming. Part of me was still in the temple feeling the shock of that vision, remembering how the goddess had come alive before my eyes, while the rest of me was lying in bed, knowing it was a dream and that I had to write it down. What a strange feeling! Like I was alive in two places at once, in two bodies at once. It's gone now, but the thought of it makes me shiver.

Anyhow, that's all I remember of the dream, at least its outer surface. There are still some inner details to add. During the dream, I was completely convinced that the goddess was real—strange indeed, since I have been irreligious since my mother died. I was aware that it was a stone idol, but even then I knew somehow that the image was a window to something beyond it that could hear me and respond to my prayers. It wasn't a belief or a hope but rather a kind of powerful certainty, maybe something akin to what the swami and his followers felt during the arati yesterday. There was no question in my mind about her reality. She was the goddess, as real in her incarnation of stone as she was in my vision. The only question or doubt in my mind concerned myself. Would I be able to communicate with her? Would she consider me worthy of her favors? I can still feel the emotions that I felt when the vision ended: exhilaration, because the goddess came alive in answer to my prayers; but fear also—or maybe anxiety is a better word—because I knew that whatever was going to happen would be totally out of my control. She was the puppeteer and I was the puppet, and it had always been that way. Indeed, what other relationship can a man have with the gods that rule our universe and our destinies? That was the feeling I had as I came out of the dream and woke up to my real self.

So, then…how do I explain this? I guess the arati must have had a stronger effect on me than I realized. That and the mere fact of being in India, surrounded by an alien culture thousands of years old. Perhaps I should avoid drinking the water. Who knows what these Indian goddesses are like? If they're anything like the Greek goddesses, then I could be in real trouble. Just look at what Ulysses had to put up with with Minerva, what to speak of Calypso. Of course, it may be only in our sleep that the mind is free to respond fully to its surroundings. Either way, this is exactly what I want—what I need—if Le Gentil is going to respond to the heady reality of finally being in India, a land more mysterious than his eighteenth-century mind can possibly imagine. There is no doubt now that this dream journal is starting to bear fruit. Some of this material is sure to find its way into the book, in one form or another. Venus is also a goddess. In a way, Le Gentil has dedicated his life to her—is not science a kind of religion and an astronomer a kind of priest?—and she is playing him like a puppet. Maybe I can work in these allusions as he gets exposed to Indian culture. She can become a nemesis for him as well as an objective, not just a planet or a scientific challenge but a worthy adversary that tempts him and taunts him from the heavens. A bit of the mythic imagination creeping in due to the influence of his surroundings. East meets West and each leaves its mark on the other.

Rodrigo closed his laptop with a sense of satisfaction. He had gotten down the salient details of his dream in one sustained burst, and if he were right, it would add something new to the book. He had never thought about Venus as a goddess, never considered the possibility that Le Gentil could have a relationship with her based on anything other than the dispassionate eye of a scientist looking out on an icy orb shining from an unimaginable distance, a relationship built on calculations and observations, the cold facts of science. But the hero of his tale was to be anything but dispassionate. He would have read the Greeks and been far more familiar with them than an astronomer from our own time. Would he not play with the idea of Venus as his adversary, especially after that disastrous first transit, personifying her in his mind as a way of entertaining himself or spurring himself on in his quest? Would he not find her much more interesting and challenging in the robes of a Greek goddess, wearing a smile that both enticed him and mocked him? What could be more natural to his eighteenth-century mind, especially the longer he spends on Indian soil where everything in nature has a soul?

Noting that it was almost time for breakfast, he slipped off his pajamas and stepped into the bathroom. As he began his shower, he noticed how fresh the dream seemed. He could still recall the images almost as clearly as if they had been real experiences. This rarely happened. Generally his dreams slipped away moments after he was fully awake, resisting his best efforts to detain them. Since he had begun his dream journal, he had noticed that his ability to recall his dreams had increased, but even then the greater part of his nighttime voyages disappeared into his unconscious within seconds after he stepped away from the computer. This was different. Not only could he still see the image of the goddess in his mind—a living, breathing presence that was only human in appearance, if that—he could still feel the resonance of her thoughts. Something was about to happen, something monumental and unavoidable, subject only to her whims; and though he knew it was just the lingering aftereffects of the dream, he could not entirely shake that feeling. All he could do was remind himself that it was a dream, grist for the writing mill, an opportunity to take those emotions and transfer them to one or more of his characters. Suddenly he stiffened; his eyes lost focus and he became oblivious of where he was, of the water cascading down his back, of the soap waiting to be lathered. This was the challenge! How does one take an emotion from real life—or in this case, dreamed life—and write it into a fictional story with so much authenticity that the same emotion reappears in the reader, brought back to life by the power of the author's words and the magical spell of shared experience? That is the artist's Everest! From what other well could the writer draw the waters of emotion, other than from the well of his own experience broadened by the generous employment of empathy? His thirty-five years of experience was the book from which he must write. His imagination might shape it any way it willed, but at the bottom of that well lay the fruits of his own living—all of it, dreaming or awake, for better or for worse. It may have been a dream but the emotions were real. They were his emotions, and now they were stored away in his subconscious, waiting to be resurrected at the appropriate moment. As were all his experiences, good and bad, mulching in the fertile soil that would give birth to his creations. A wry smile appeared on his lips. What would Beth say if she knew that at this moment she was busy being converted into fertilizer, pushing up the daisies of his first novel? At least she could say that she had played her part.

The aftereffects of the dream were gone now, turned to ash by a single flash of creative insight. This is what he had been longing to feel, why he had set his sights on becoming a writer: this surge of energy, this flood of life that comes rushing in when one pursues a creative truth down into the caverns of the subconscious. It was not that he had never come across this idea before. But it had been nothing more than that—an idea, a twitching of brain cells that had left no trace upon his life. This was his own blood coursing through his veins, heated to a fever pitch by the flames of insight. Suddenly he could not wait to get back to his computer and write. Take breakfast at a canter and let the adventure continue!

When Rodrigo sat back down at his desk and looked over what he had written the day before, he realized that he was going to have to do a better job of communicating Le Gentil's emotions. The man had spent seven years in the Indian Ocean waiting for the next Venus transit. Seven years away from his family, his friends, his colleagues, his native France. Imagine the emotions that would be running riot in his head as he got set to disembark, knowing that the end of his journey and the goal of his scientific aspirations was little more than a year away. As a writer, he must find those emotions somewhere inside himself and infuse them into his character. He remembered the exhilaration he had felt when the goddess came alive inside his dreaming mind. Le Gentil would be experiencing something similar—perhaps not as acute, but far less transitory. Seven years was a long time to nurse a single hope. There might be some anxiety also, well hidden, an indistinct presentiment that tempers his excitement with its uneasy hue. There is no guarantee that he will accomplish what he has set out to accomplish; subconsciously, he knows that his mission is subject to the whims of nature, of fickle Venus, just as he himself, disguised as a priest in his dream, knew he was subject to the whims of the goddess whose favors he was trying to court.

Working his way backward, he began revising Le Gentil's approach to Pondicherry Harbor, drawing upon the fresh emotions of his dream as a way to see and feel himself into the astronomer's state of mind. Some of these emotions he put into a dialogue with the ship's captain, adding a few important bits of information as he showed the astronomer's excitement bursting through his words. The remainder he put into his character's thoughts. By mid-morning, Rodrigo had reached the point where he had left off the day before, the dropping of the anchor a half league from shore. By this time, Le Gentil was already busy assembling his possessions on deck: the three trunks filled with the naturalist's samples from the Isle de France and other ports of call; a fourth trunk with his astronomical instruments, diaries, and scientific texts; and three valises with his clothes and personal effects. Shortly thereafter, he spied a small boat approaching the ship containing representatives from the governor's office. He, the first mate, and several ship hands were the first to disembark. It was thus that at nine o'clock on the morning of March 27, 1768, Guillaume Le Gentil set foot for the first time in the land where he would be fated to etch his name into the annals of history.

His first act after stepping on land was to make the sign of the cross. Lifting his eyes above the silhouettes of the mountains far in the distance, he thanked God for his good fortune, grateful for the blessing of having been safely delivered to his destiny. He sent forth a silent prayer to the Maker of the lands that spread out before him, asking him to help him fulfill his purpose in coming here. At the same time, the beauty of the harbor did not escape him. Its pearl white sands traced a gentle curve against the blue lapping waters, lightly striated by the falling shadows of a wide ring of coconut palms. Even when he had worn the abbé's robes as a young man, he had been far more moved by the beauty of God's creation than by the words of praise and of menace that he recited each day in a forced voice during his theological studies. It was perhaps this, more than anything, that had convinced him to spend his evenings observing the heavens rather than adorning the benches of the theological seminary disputing vain arguments.

Satisfied that he had given his Maker his due and received his blessings by way of the spectacle of beauty that presented itself to his eyes amid the balmy tropical air, he moved on to more practical concerns. Judging from the costly cut of his Parisian-tailored waistcoat and his aristocratic bearing, the man who was now stepping out of the elegant open carriage was quite likely the governor, coming to meet the boat. After a whispered inquiry confirmed this, he presented himself to Monsieur Law, Governor-General of all French possessions on the Indian subcontinent, which at the moment was limited to Pondicherry and its immediate surroundings but would not remain so, not as long as the eye of Providence found favor with their efforts and their obeisance, and the French navy finally proved the equal of its infantry.

"Monsieur Le Gentil, savant of the French Academy of Science, I have been waiting a long time to have the honor of making your acquaintance. Your reputation precedes you, good sir."

The governor was a large, affable man with a healthy, well-tanned complexion whom Le Gentil immediately took a liking to. The governor gave orders to disembark the astronomer's possessions with the utmost care and carry them to his offices in the city. Then he invited Le Gentil to spend the day with him at his country estate so that he could get acquainted with the best that French India had to offer. The journey lasted the better part of an hour, during which the governor kept up a lively commentary that did not suffer in the least for the lack of space it afforded Le Gentil to join in, apart from a couple of brief questions that spurred the governor on to even greater heights. It was both entertaining and informative, and even had it not been, he would have forgiven the governor his effluence on seeing a new face so far from the tides of civilization. It was a phenomenon Le Gentil had met with on a number of occasions these past seven years, though he himself found the company of nature to provide sufficient fellowship and the best of all stimuli for his imagination. Before the hour was up, he had acquired a thorough grasp of the uneasy accord with the British. "Bastards, all of them, except for that Henry Fielding—now he can turn a tale worth a best bottle of Bordeaux—but they rule the seas for the time being, no denying that—a pox on every British warship south of the channel—so until good King Louis empties more of the royal coffers into our shipyards, we'll just have to live with the devils and like it. It's enough to turn a young man's hair gray, though, knowing they could swoop in with their forty-cannon frigates and take back Pondicherry any time they damn well please." But what most interested Le Gentil was the governor's intermittent description of the countryside they were passing through—a world of flora and fauna entirely new to him, waiting to be catalogued—and the natives who inhabited it, with their quaint superstitions and their ebony faces that stared out at him from the villages they passed along the way, half hidden among the luxuriant thickets and sculpted rice fields that decorated either side of the road.

Soon Le Gentil could feel his mind divided between the land flowing past his eyes as the carriage rattled down the packed-dirt road and the voice of the governor, bright and effusive in his ear. The governor's voice spun a lively story in his head, replete with images that ranged backward to the founding of Pondicherry and out across the seas to Europe and the clash of cultures that he had embraced since his childhood, but the scenic pleasure of his eyes was even greater. The love of nature that had given him the brightest of his boyhood memories vied for his attention in a voice infinitely more seductive. His imagination raced far ahead of the carriage, spinning out images of the future: the year he would spend here feasting his senses and filling up his journals, the land by day and the sky by night. It was the renewal of a romance that had its beginnings in Coutances, when his father would take him to the seashore on Sundays after church, where they would wander collecting seashells and memorizing the names of birds from a copy of Buffon's *Natural History* that his father carried in his satchel when they walked. Every summer they would go off by themselves for several weeks, exploring the hills and forests of Normandy, his father making up for his lack of money with an endless willingness to satisfy the boy's curiosity about all they saw there. It was a love affair that was still as fresh as his first spring, forty-two years earlier. When his colleagues sometimes remarked that he had never taken a wife because he was wedded to science, or else that he had never really taken off his abbé's cloak, he would tell them the truth: for him nature was all that a woman could be and more.

Rodrigo leaned back from his computer and furrowed his brow. But wasn't his astronomer a rake? The imagined one, not the real one, who might have been but in any case had never mentioned women in his journals or his memoirs. What he had just written didn't fit the image of the astronomer that he had set down in his character sketch. But he couldn't bring himself to hit the delete key and hold it down until his fancy was erased. Could this be a side of Le Gentil that he hadn't seen before? Odd thought. What he meant was, a side of Le Gentil that he hadn't thought of adding before. He had wanted to give his character a decidedly romantic nature, but might it be that until this point in his life what Le Gentil's romantic predisposition best responded to was nature in its widest sense, not solely limited to a woman's form, even that of a Venus, whatever gallivanting around he may or may not have done when he was not observing the heavens? For his part, Rodrigo admired nature, though usually from the window of a book, but what he was sensing here was a finer sensibility that he had never devoted to nature, though he considered himself a romantic in both the modern and Byronic meanings of the word. His romantic sensibilities had been awakened by the best lyric prose and verse, and by Beth's willowy sensuality that had left him breathless during the first few years of their poetry-laden courtship. He remembered the impassioned journal entries he would pen in the morning while he watched her sleeping figure—Beth never rose before eight and he had to reach the campus by seven thirty to find a parking place and get ready for his eight o'clock class—and the notes that he would append to her easel on pink or blue Post-its, scraps of free verse that he never bothered to turn into completed poems, or aphorisms that he would copy from antiquity and then subvert to immortalize the tangle of her dirty blond locks sprawled across the pillow or the almost imperceptible freckles that hid in her face like grottos on the isle of Capri. Often when he came home, he would find the same Post-it as the subject of a watercolor framed by flowers, or in the center of a black-and-white print that she had propped up against his computer with the scribbled title "Post-it among roses." She would almost always be out when he came back in the afternoon, but the imagined fragrances of these tender missives would buoy his spirits until she came home in the evening to a meal that he cooked and served to her like an offering to a princess. He had even wondered sometimes if he were too much in love to be a successful artist, ceremoniously quoting Balzac's famous quip at the end of another amorous night: "Well, there goes another novel," a facetiousness that Beth did not always appreciate. Yet, no matter how developed his own romantic sensibilities were, they were not what Le Gentil was feeling as he looked out the window at the luxuriant wonders of the Coromandel countryside, though they could have been a close relation, perhaps sisters of different fathers.

For the rest of the morning, Rodrigo worked on Le Gentil's almost rapturous reaction to the vistas passing by the carriage. When he broke for lunch, however, he had a vague feeling that his character was somehow getting away from him. Amorous adventures with beautiful Indian maidens were what he had planned, if the unformed ideas that crowded his mind and his journal entries could be called a plan. Add in some intrigue with the French administration, encounters with wise old Brahmin astrologers who looked askance at his gallivanting about and warned him cryptically about unscrupulous relatives fleecing his estate, and other such spicy dollops, and he would have a modern-day *Tom Jones*, or something very nearly like it. But would the Le Gentil of his second chapter be interested in those types of adventures? This Le Gentil seemed closer to the original in his passion for science and the wonders of nature, and different from any—real or imagined—in the subtle sensibility with which he greeted his arrival in Mother India. But wasn't that what all great writers had always talked about, that the unexpected was to be expected?

Rodrigo began his afternoon session with Le Gentil's arrival at the governor's estate—though by the astronomer's reckoning it was barely ten o'clock. It was a Sunday. The estate was full of guests who had arrived the day before to enjoy the governor's generous hospitality. Among them was a curate, a jovial, ruddy-faced man a bit younger than himself named Père Le Duc, but there was no sign of a Sunday service. Perhaps the good curate had already said a mass for the penitents before Le Gentil's arrival, to sanctify their day of leisure. As for himself, he was thankful that the ship's chaplain had held a short service just after daybreak from which he had emerged to find a distant coastline hugging the horizon. It was a revelation to find himself in the cultured company of French citizens after fifty days aboard a Portuguese ship, although among them were two Englishmen and a Spanish count who was on his way to Manila, the three of whom spoke near-perfect French. The governor set an excellent table, which the guests enjoyed not only during the early afternoon meal and a late dinner, but at every hour in between, since the governor's servants made sure its stocks of wine, confections, cheeses, and breads were constantly replenished. In the evening, a string quartet played the latest light dance numbers from France while the guests supped, and afterward, a trio of Rameau suites. It was as pleasant a day as Le Gentil had passed in quite a while, highlighted by the plentiful and varied conversation of a group that included not only a curate, a governor, and a count, but a shipwright, the city marshal, the owner of Pondicherry's one newspaper (also its local poet laureate), the four young musicians, a horse-breeder, who was founder of the Pondicherry hippodrome, the dean of the lycée, two military attachés, and a number of wives who had merits of their own, not the least of whom being Madame Law, who had been an opera singer in her younger years with a stout chest to back up her reputation of having been able to shatter glass at fifty paces. And yet, despite the patrician luxuries, the engaging company, and the fine music, Le Gentil could not help but feel that the bright gas lamps in the governor's garden were little more than a desperate attempt to ward off the encroaching darkness, to keep out the alien eyes of a land that would have engulfed them had they let down their guard, even for an instant. He remembered a story he had heard when he was young of an explorer in an African jungle huddled by his fire, wary of the savage eyes that watched him from behind the dense foliage, unsure whether they belonged to man or beast, or which he should be most afraid of. India, he knew, was still largely an unexplored continent, apart from a certain number of British, French, and Portuguese enclaves, almost all of them clinging close to the safety of the sea. It was inhabited by a mingling of races that all claimed to be far older than his own. Its jungles boasted of elephants and tigers, some of which had made their way to European zoos, and other creatures that might yet be mythological, though his people had once thought that of elephants when the tales of these mythic beasts first reached their ears. Its towns and villages filled the holds of British ships with the finest ivory, whiter and smoother than porcelain and a thousand times as strong, a host of aromatic spices and perfumes that befuddled the senses, and enchanted jewels that ignited the greed of the crown heads of Europe. The sky above his head was the same sky that reflected its impassive beauty on the spires and cathedrals of Paris, but the world outside the walls of the governor's country estate was one that few men with his color skin had ever seen, and one which he might never see again once petulant Venus finished her transit across the sun and the billowing seas carried him and his eight years in the Indian ocean back to French waters. For all that he appreciated the governor's welcome and the ease with which he had passed the day in the fellowship of his countrymen, it was that world he now had his sights set on. What did Venus see as she gazed down on the Indian subcontinent? How many of its secrets would she allow her votive to discover in the coming fifteen or so months that she had consigned to him?

It was eleven o'clock when he made it back to Pondicherry in the governor's carriage, the plenipotentiary asleep beside him throughout the journey, dozed by the goodly port that had comforted his evening. Le Gentil spent the entire journey peering into the night, aware of Venus low on the horizon, teasing him with her soft, almost purplish light. He could hear drumming from a distant village, and now and then he caught the light of small fires among the trees or beyond the rice paddies. India! The name itself was enough to make him shiver. He had finally made it. The thought of the mysteries she would yield up to him lifted his spirits far more than the day's revelry had. The secrets of the earth unlocked by the man who sought the key to the secrets of the heavens.

Rodrigo looked up from his computer and gazed out the window. It was late afternoon now. The light was softening. The sun was edging past darkening clouds toward the tops of the nearest peaks. There was no jungle to be seen, only a stately pine forest winding its way up the mountains until it thinned and evaporated in the higher altitudes, but he could feel India looming nonetheless, as Le Gentil had minutes earlier in the warm forests of the south. The dream certainly had something to do with it. The water and the air had begun to affect him, dropping him in the temple of an Indian goddess while he lay defenseless in his bed. India was getting underneath his skin, and what was underneath his skin was bound to come out his fingers. When he read over his afternoon's work, he was glad for the dream and the overtones it had added to this, his second chapter. Though he felt unsure about the direction in which it was pushing him, the mere fact that he was being pushed seemed like an unexpected boon. This was to be a long journey he was embarking upon. He needed his subconscious if he was to avoid crashing on the rocks when he rounded the Cape of Artistic Aspiration and made his way for home.

He picked up his story the next morning in the governor's mansion in the city. At this point, Le Gentil's journals gave him little to go by. The only thing the astronomer had mentioned about that meeting was that the governor had told him to look for a spot to build his observatory and had promised to send him masons. Rodrigo was counting on his muse to guide him from there, but he was not yet sure what name to give her. Venus belonged to Le Gentil. Moreover, knowing what a fickle dame she would prove to be, he thought it prudent to choose another, more constant source of illumination. He thought momentarily of the Shiva who had presided over the inauguration of his voyage, but weren't the muses always women, and of Greek or Roman descent? Perhaps he didn't need to give her a name as long as he could hear her voice. But at this hour of the morning, that was precisely the problem. It was still dark in Europe and the goddesses of the Mediterranean isles had not yet deigned to put in an appearance. Other than a vague outline, dozens of possible scenes and subplots, and his character sketches, he had no idea what regions his book would travel through between its beginning and its climax—which was exactly how he had envisioned it. He wanted his writing to be a journey of discovery rather than a pre-planned trip to familiar tourist destinations, a prodigious outpouring from the creative fires within that would surprise and overwhelm him before he could give it shape and share it with his readers. The only problem with this, he realized, as he led Le Gentil into the governor's office and found both the astronomer and his host at a loss for words, was that he had no idea where to go next.

He slid his chair out and started pacing back and forth between the door and the window, the two opposite poles of his writer's hermitage, a distance of five meters that he covered with seven carefully measured strides. As he passed by the bed, he thought again of his dream and the direction in which it seemed to be pushing him. Could it be that his subconscious would not be satisfied if his book were merely a tale of Le Gentil's comic adventures in an exotic country during his quest for scientific glory? What if it were intent on adding a further modicum of depth, slanting it more toward his encounter with an alien culture that would work on his psyche and help him to see the world in a different, deeper, richer way? This would not obviate the need for adventure—the book would still need a surface means of capturing the reader's interest—but it would add a more meaningful substrata, flowing underneath the obvious like a subterranean river. A clash of cultures, then, a chance for Le Gentil to examine his core values and those of his race, to call into question the whole Western way of looking at the world. This would present a significantly greater challenge, but it would make for a more substantial book, and substance was what he was after.

The thought excited him. He quickened his pace, trying to catch a glimpse of the possibilities that seemed to appear before him like sails on a distant horizon. He glanced at his watch. Little more than an hour to go before lunch. There was no sense in sitting in front of the computer now. First he needed to settle his thoughts; he could return to his writing later. He needed some sky to help him think, space for his thoughts to roam. The four walls of his room were far too confining for the rapid flights that his mind demanded. A walk, then, in the open air. Perhaps this was what his muse was waiting for before she would show her face. Instead of going down to the grounds, however, he decided to climb the single flight of stairs to the roof directly above his room. Like most of the ashram roofs, it was a flat concrete slab surrounded by a parapet, about forty meters long and a dozen meters wide, more than enough room for him to roam untrammeled and unheeded. One side looked out over the Ganges; the other kept company with the rest of the ashram, forming part of the outer edge of a small ocean of turrets, parapets, and platforms nested among the palm fronds and the leaves and branches of the larger trees, some of which towered well above the rooftops. As he crested the stairs, he noticed a small troop of monkeys gliding lazily along the parapet at the far end of the building. They looked at him briefly, with a largely disinterested air, and then sat up on their haunches and started grooming one another. He looked up momentarily at the ponderous, bluish-gray clouds that hid the sun and added a note of appreciation for the foresight of nature. It was hot on the roof at this hour of the day, hotter than a Carolina afternoon at the peak of summer, but somehow the veil of clouds and the breeze off the river made it reasonably comfortable, as if he were out strolling by the sea after an afternoon shower.

As he walked, his thoughts flittered between what he remembered of his dream and the different paths that his story might take. He remembered the implicit faith he had felt for the goddess. If he had still been dreaming, he would probably pray to her now to reveal to him where the book should go next. If he were still a priest, then she would be his muse, the mother of all muses. But fortunately—or unfortunately—he was awake now. Reality, as he knew it, did not work that way. He changed his tack and tried to approach the problem analytically. If he were going to expose Le Gentil to Indian culture so that it could clash with his own worldview, then he would need one or more characters who could articulate that culture to him and argue intelligently their point of view when he challenged it. Somebody like Bhagavati, who could speak his own language and yet be a true spokesperson for an alien culture. Suddenly he stopped, opened his eyes wide, and sent a clenched fist soaring toward the heavens. Of course! Le Gentil would need an interpreter. Why not make her a woman? Beautiful, young, intelligent, proud of her culture, and out of bounds to him as far as his romantic conquests go. He could add an undercurrent of attraction, grab the reader's interest with the surface of her smile. Brilliant! So then, how to introduce her? Obvious. He asks the governor for a translator to help him with his work; or the governor suggests it, either way. A day or two later, the governor introduces him to the girl and explains why she's by far the best person for the job. Educated in a convent school, from a noble, well-connected native family, fluent in at least two native tongues. . . .

Rodrigo's mind leapt forward to possible scenes and backward to the character sketch that was now pending. Moments later, he took the stairs at a trot and raced back to his computer. When the lunch hour appeared on his watch, he was still typing his notes at a furious pace into a file that he had opened up for his as-yet-unnamed interpreter. He closed his laptop but brought his notebook with him to the dining hall and continued scribbling as he ate, filling out the character between bites. If she had studied in a convent school, which would explain her fluency in French, then she should probably be Christian, a fact that would win the confidence and patronage of the governor. So she's familiar with Western culture, but she is still proud of her own, though she keeps that pride under wraps. She hides it from the governor and the other French officials, but she can't hide it from Le Gentil, not for long. And this will spur their discussions.

As Rodrigo ate, he was barely aware of the food, though the fragrant spices enriched his senses and made the act of writing even more enjoyable. His mind teemed with ideas, one leading to the other by an unconscious logic, cascading through the landscape of his story, outracing the rapid strokes of his pen. While Le Gentil is busy bedding the native wenches, he can unwittingly and unwillingly be falling in love with her—why not give her a mind the equal of his own, if not better?—and that impels him to actually listen to what she has to say. Through her, he discovers that Indian culture is not all barbaric superstitions and primitive rites. She can lead him into the soul of her people, thereby transforming forever his own soul. But if he were going to go in this direction, he would have to do some serious research. He would have to learn as much about India as Le Gentil does, if not more. This was the challenge. He had the girl but not the thoughts to fill her mind. Though he still had to find a body for her and a name, her thoughts and her words would make her who he now realized she was: the heroine of his tale.

Rodrigo decided to spend the afternoon browsing through the bookstores near the ashram. The closest turned out to be the best. Apart from a small showcase window by the side of the door, all four walls and the two center islands were crowded with books on Hinduism, Buddhism, yoga, meditation, Indian mythology, and so on, thousands of brightly colored volumes that drew him like a moth to a flame. It even had a small literature section to which he promised himself regular visits, as if he were a child with money in his pockets staring down an aisle of candy and cookies. He spent most of the afternoon scanning the titles, section by section, with methodical deliberateness and a great deal of stamina. Those titles that drew his attention, he pulled off the shelf, fingering the pages delicately after an informed glance at the back cover and the table of contents. He sampled the opening pages of several chapters to see how informative, well written, and well researched the book was. If it warranted a second and decisive look, he added it to a steadily growing pile on a low bench at the end of one of the center islands. Otherwise, he returned it to its native spot. When he finished his long sojourn through the titles of the relevant sections, he sat down on the bench and carefully winnowed his bulky pile down to an eclectic selection of twenty books that promised to provide most of the information he would need to make Le Gentil's encounter with Indian culture as authentic as one could hope for in a fictional encounter 238 years in the past. To this, he added one travel book by a writer who had been on his reading list for the last couple of years, a literary wanderer through the Orient who had just come out with a book about the two months he had spent backpacking in India.

After he safely deposited his trove of treasures in his room, he set out to explore the town. He had already learned that Rishikesh's spiritual settlement was divided into two main enclaves, one on either side of the river, with most of the buildings lying between the Ram Jhula and Lakshman Jhula bridges. On the far side, a reasonably good road hugged the slopes well above the river. It ran past Lakshman Jhula and then wound its way north into the Himalayas. On his side of the river, a smaller, sparsely traveled road fronted the lower, forested hills that began behind the ashram; this road joined up with the river just before Lakshman Jhula, though the pedestrian traffic invariably kept to the dirt-and-gravel path that paralleled the river until it joined the paved road. Almost all the buildings close to the river were either ashrams, temples, or meditation huts, apart from a few shops and restaurants near the foot of either bridge, but the further one got from the water, the more one came across residential dwellings nestled among the trees.

Rodrigo decided to make a complete circuit of the settlement. He began by crossing the Ram Jhula Bridge. From there, he turned left and followed the river past a series of small shops that sold items of interest to spiritual pilgrims—beads, holy pictures, spiritual books—but also Ayurvedic and Western medicines and basic grocery items. After a couple of hundred meters, he came to the Muni-ki-reti taxi stand where he saw some cafés that catered mostly to westerners, just opposite the entrance to the huge Sivananda Ashram. From there he turned right and started walking up the road that led to Lakshman Jhula, resisting the urge to hop in one of the three-wheelers that ran up and down between the two bridges for a one-rupee fare. There were very few buildings along the way, for which he was thankful, since the view was stupendous. To his right, as he walked, the river snaked through its narrow valley some forty meters below, half hidden by the towering pines that bordered the road, its clear waters gliding past smooth gray boulders and stretches of immaculate white sand. The river's swift current trailed wisps of white foam at intervals like strips of tinsel in the goddess's hair. To his left, the forest sloped upward, an endless, undulating series of foothills that seemed to terminate at heaven's door where the distant snow-capped peaks shared their azure tint with the sky whose stately lower regions they inhabited. Behind him, toward the plains, he could see the heavy rain clouds gathering on the horizon, but when he looked in front of him, toward the upper Himalayas, the sky was clear and as iridescent as mother-of-pearl.

As he approached Lakshman Jhula, the buildings reappeared, clustered together. He was soon thrust into a bustle of activity: long rows of shops and restaurants; music blaring from CD stalls; groups of tourists and pilgrims with cameras slung around their necks, peering into the shop windows or eyeing the wares on the hawker's tables; the ubiquitous Internet cafés. To get to the bridge, he had to descend a long, narrow flight of stone steps. Near the bottom, he encountered a gauntlet of beggars and mendicants squatting by the edge of the stairs, one to a step. Each of them held out his begging bowl to him as he passed, aluminum coins jingling faintly at the bottom of the metal bowls. He fumbled in his pocket for coins and dropped one each in as many of the bowls as he had coins for. When he ran out of coins and saw the angry looks on the faces of the last few beggars, he wondered if he had made a mistake by his unplanned generosity. He quickened his pace and felt better once he stepped on the swaying footbridge, some 150 meters long. The bustle behind him faded into a low hum as he hung suspended high above the river. It coalesced once again into a tapestry of voices when he approached the other side, fed by the pilgrims streaming in and out of the thirteen-story Trayambakeshwar temple that towered above the foot of the bridge like a conical wizard's hat of orange and white.

From there he turned back toward Ram Jhula. The shops quickly petered out and he entered the enclave known as Swargashram, heaven's ashram. Here he saw only small ashrams and hermit's huts half hidden by the trees to his left and an occasional stone pathway leading down to the riverbank to his right. There was no one else on the dirt-and-gravel path. Soon all he could hear was the breeze ruffling the trees and the muffled sound of his own footsteps. Dusk was fast approaching. As he rounded a small bend shaded by trees on either side, he caught a glimpse of the Ram Jhula Bridge, perhaps half a kilometer downstream. Not far beyond it, the arati would soon be starting. He quickened his pace. A short ways ahead he heard the sound of low voices. When he passed the next bend, he saw a group of fifteen to twenty people dressed in white standing in a clearing. Only one of them was talking, a diminutive elderly woman in a plain white sari who was pointing through the trees to the river while her companions looked on.

Feeling slightly self-conscious, Rodrigo slowed his pace and walked as noiselessly as possible as he approached the group, his eye drawn by the elderly woman. Her hair was snow white and hung down well past her shoulders. Judging by the wrinkles on her face, she looked to be in her late seventies, perhaps older, but she exuded a surprising air of health and vigor. Her musical, animated voice sounded more like it belonged to a young girl than to a woman of her age. As he was about to pass the group, she said something that made everyone smile. Abruptly she turned around, looked directly at him, and addressed him in Hindi. He froze for a moment, aware that everyone in the group had turned to stare at him. Before he was able to apologize that he didn't speak Hindi, a tall, light-skinned woman in a saffron sari stepped to her side and addressed him in English with a light but distinct German accent.

"The Mother is asking if you are lost."

Rodrigo was startled by the question and even more startled to discover that there was a European in the group. He looked at the old lady, who was now grinning like a mischievous child, but for some reason he couldn't think of anything to say. Again she spoke to him in her high-pitched, musical voice.

"Mother is asking again if you are lost. She says that you should not feel bothered about being lost. It is a necessary condition for being found."

What an odd thing to say, Rodrigo thought as he recovered his composure. "No, I'm not lost," he said. "I know where I'm going. But thank you for asking."

The old lady smiled. Crinkles appeared around her eyes. Rodrigo realized that she must have been very beautiful when she was young. She began talking again, while the German woman translated quickly and effortlessly.

"Almost everyone is sure they know where they are going, but that doesn't stop them from getting lost. If the path were so easy to walk, we would not need a light to guide us in the dark. Where are you from?"

"I'm from America."

"You have come a very long ways to get here. May the Lord guide you and help you to reach your destination. In the meantime, if you do find yourself lost along the way, remember one thing: The road is always right underneath your feet and it leads in only one direction. God has given you two eyes in the front of your head so that you can look forward, not backward."

The old woman's gaze seemed to bore into him, as if she were looking through him to something beyond or behind him that he could not see. He felt his mind grow foggy, his vision hazy, as if he were slipping into a kind of confused suspended animation. When the old woman spoke again, her eyes half closed now, the sound of her voice seemed to be coming through the fog in his mind, as if from an unseen speaker whose distance cannot be determined.

"The Divine Mother has commanded me to give you a message. She says that you will not be able to find her by your own efforts, but do not worry, she will find you. She is walking the path beside you. First make yourself ready to receive her; once you are ready, she will appear. And do not delay. Though she has infinite patience, you have kept her waiting a long time."

The old woman folded her palms to her chest. "Good luck to you, pilgrim. *Namaste.*" With one final smile, she turned away and started moving down the path toward Lakshman Jhula with the rest of her entourage. Rodrigo stood there transfixed, staring after her, unable to take his eyes from her small, ghostly figure until she disappeared around the bend and the muffled voices of her and her companions faded softly away. It was only then that the fog cleared. He shook his head, as if he were shaking off the aftereffects of a powerful dream. Yet this had been no dream. What had caused him to suddenly become so disoriented in that woman's presence? What was there in her gaze that had transfixed him so, leaving him rooted to the spot until she passed out of sight? It was said that the holy men and women of India had supernatural powers. He could almost believe it. Undoubtedly, she was some kind of holy woman, out walking with her disciples. Now that his head was clear, he suspected that she possessed a kind of magnetic aura that he had never before come across in another human being. Perhaps some of the power these Indian fakirs were said to possess was the pure, hypnotic force of a powerful personality that attracted disciples to their side and left idiots like himself gawking on the road after a single glance. And yet he had looked into the Dalai Lama's kindly eyes and seen nothing like this, for all their soulfulness and contagious warmth. What was it she said? She had asked him if he were lost, and it was clear that she was not talking about whether or not he knew the way to his hotel. He had told her that he knew where he was going? Did he really? Wasn't he just as lost as everyone else, struggling to gain a foothold on this slippery planet? If this were not the case, Rishikesh would not be filled with seekers looking for a magic vial to rescue them from their existential angst. Neither he nor anyone else needed an Indian holy woman to point out this simple fact. It was the human condition and he was a human being. There was nothing more to it than that. You either stood your ground and got the most you could out of your life, or else you caved in and let the emptiness overtake you.

He started walking again in the direction of the ashram. The first couple of stars had already started to appear above the treetops, the blue of the sky now deepening its way to black. He might be lost, he thought, but at least he knew the road he was on, the one he had been waiting all his life to take. It was, as she had said, the one right underneath his feet. Perhaps he had dallied much longer than he should have. He had let too many excuses get between him and his dream of becoming an accomplished writer, someone whose words people would still read years after he was dead. So much time had been wasted in meaningless rituals, the hours slipping through his fingers so fast that he could not account for a fraction of the ten years that had gone by since he had received his PhD with distinction and accepted an associate professorship at the university. Too many mistakes to even bother trying to account for them all, too much heartache to waste time shedding any more tears. But that was all behind him now. He was certain of it, or at least as certain as he could be, even without the two chapters under his fingers as confirmation. There is a difference between being lost and not having any idea where you are going. He would admit to being lost but he certainly knew where he was going. It was only a question of finding his way. Could that be what she had meant by "being lost is a necessary condition for being found"?

He approached the foot of the bridge and thought again of attending the arati whose rollicking sounds he could hear rising above the river, but his encounter on the road had left him in no mood for the revelry of an alien culture. Instead, he turned left and ducked into one of the two restaurants that lay just up the road. He ordered a cup of spiced tea and some savories and climbed the stairs to the empty balcony seats. A young waiter in a white shirt and an old vest brought him his tea and his snacks a couple of minutes later. While he sipped the sweet, pungent brew, he tried to remember the rest of what the old woman had said, her words still tinged with the fog that had stolen over his mind. He remembered something cryptic about the Divine Mother waiting for him, that he would not find her, she would find him. He thought about it for several minutes, brief images of his dream that morning dotting his reflections. Finally he decided that if it did make sense, he was not the person to make sense of it. The only divine mother he knew was the one who had given him birth, with the possible addition of his aunt, her elder sister, who had taken over that role after his mother died when he was twelve. He could still remember the shock of her death after she had battled the cancer for six months, a hopeless campaign that the entire family suffered with her. He had been there by her bedstead when she died, but he had been asleep. He remembered being swept up in a bear hug by his aunt, her tears wetting his cheeks as she pressed his face to hers. Then his father's hug, his eyes dry but full of scars. Sadness was too delicate a word for what he saw in them. Then he looked at his mother's inert form and realized what had happened. He, too, started crying. He had known that she wouldn't last out the day. Everyone had known. He had been preparing for that moment for weeks, for months even. They all had. But still, when it came, he was not ready for the pain that seared through him like a rusty sword, which, rather than cauterizing the wound, left it gaping open. From that moment on, his life was divided into two halves: the joyous, careless days before she fell sick, in which he could no longer find any difficult memories; and the painful days that followed, those bottomless days that seemed like they would never end. He had escaped into books after that with a vengeance that was almost preternatural. He sometimes liked to say that it was literature that cured him, but the truth was that his mother's absence was an ache that had dimmed but never completely faded. Was that why he had failed so miserably in love, why his marriage was a longer version of the failed relationships that preceded it? They say a man unconsciously searches for the image of his mother in his lovers, and, until he matures out of this infantile and illusory pursuit, he will never find true happiness in his conjugal life. It seemed to him that his problem was that he had never looked for his mother at all, but rather for an image from the books with which he had filled his teenage head to get over the pain of her absence. He couldn't think of anyone more unlike his mother than Beth. Where his mother was constant, she was fickle. Where his mother's feet never left the ground, Beth's feet never touched it.

"Do I remind you of your mother at all?" she had asked him on the plane when he took her to California to meet his father for the first time.

"Babe, you are from Venus and she was an Earthling. She would have died of asphyxiation in two minutes flat had she landed on your planet without a life support system."

"And what the hell does that mean?"

"Nada. I just mean that she was a traditional Mexican-American mom. Family first and family last and in between a steady job and lighting candles during Semana Santa. She would never have understood a free-spirited artist who doesn't want to have children before she's forty. She would have adored you, don't get me wrong, but I can just see her rolling her eyes and making the sign of the cross the minute you went out the door. *!Dios nos proteja!* She wasn't one to hang out with artists, my dear."

"But you're an artist."

"Ah, but I wasn't then. Remember, she died when I was twelve. Sometimes I think I got my PhD and my teaching gig just to keep her quiet in the hereafter."

By the time he went away to college, he had begun running from his mother's image, and the still-present loss it evoked, into the arms of whatever free-spirited girl would have him, the more unconventional the better. If he had actually found someone like his mother, he thought, he would almost certainly still be married, though he doubted it would have saved him from the existential malaise that had not quit him since the moment he began to dimly realize that what he was searching for in books was truth. No matter how far he went in that direction, there was always a nagging suspicion that dogged his steps after he came back to earth from his latest mind-altering literary journey, a suspicion that the truth was, in fact, nowhere to be found. Kick as he might, that dog never left him alone. Whatever classical author he was reading at the moment would seem to him like the wisest human he had ever encountered, especially the further back in time he went. Who could argue with Shakespeare being the wisest of writers? Until you read the ancient Romans and the ancient Greeks and realized that his entire work was one long disquisition on ideas that had already been plumbed to their depths by the best minds of antiquity. And who knows to what extent their wisdom was molded by contact with ideas that had flowed into the Mediterranean from India and China? But even then, no matter how deeply he read, what he ran into at the bottom of all great works of art were questions—the greater the work, the more profound the questions. Was that not what Sartre had been driving at, the realization that staring into the universe was like staring at a question mark of infinite dimensions? Was this not the essence of the long history of the human race? Man goes searching for answers, but in the end all he finds are questions. It was why he found *Steppenwolf* more convincing than *Siddhartha,* and Mann more convincing than Hesse. Mann had the courage to end his greatest works on a question mark. It was this that he considered the hallmark of the race's greatest achievement, its literature: the courage to end the human quest at the place where it begins, with the only answer that a conscientious human being can acknowledge as the truth: I don't know.

Staring into his tea, Rodrigo was aware that he was in the land that historians readily acknowledged to be home to the planet's oldest civilization. If one wanted to come looking for answers, it stood to reason that this would be the place. The road to antiquity did not lead back any further than these mountains whose reflected light cast a faint, silvery shadow over one corner of his little table. Unless you wanted to believe in a mythical Atlantis that had taken the highest wisdom to the bottom of the sea with it, as Beth had claimed to believe ever since she underwent a past-life regression and discovered that she had been—what else!—an Atlantean princess with mystic visions and great artistic sensibility. At least she didn't believe she was from another planet, like some of her friends did—on loan to earth to help raise the consciousness of our otherwise backward race with their otherworldly vibes. He shook the last bit of tea in the bottom of his cup and drank it down. What else had she said about the Divine Mother? That she would find him when he was ready to receive her? It sounded like that line out of *Field of Dreams*: "Build it and they will come." The problem with being the world's oldest civilization was that it had thousands of years of easy answers to lull it to sleep, like a heavy soporific in the water. He could not let himself be taken in so easily. This was a choice that human beings had always had to face, and most likely always would: accept the easy answers—and there were plenty of them at hand, whether your tastes ran to religion or to science or to consumerism—or take the high road into the mountains and come to grips with the unanswerable questions with nothing between you and the empty sky but your eyelids. And should you choose to keep them open...

Rodrigo was beginning to feel more confident now. Perhaps his chance encounter with the old woman was a simple test from the gods to see if he were willing to keep to his road. Minerva dusting off one of her old saris to make sure her acolyte was not getting cold feet. Or else an indication of what was up ahead. Perhaps Le Gentil would have his own existential angst, the natural byproduct of a young culture not yet put to sleep by old answers. The girl challenges that angst with the wisdom of a far older culture that has learned to be comfortable with man's seemingly ephemeral place in this world. Rodrigo reached for his notebook and started scribbling down some ideas. Almost immediately, the ground began to feel solider underneath his feet. The old woman and her cryptic words were soon forgotten. He pictured himself at his writing table the next morning, the mist rising off the river outside his window. The image brought a smile to his face.

As long as he was writing, all was right with the world.

4

THE NEXT DAY'S SESSION began briskly. Rodrigo opened the third chapter by having the governor give Le Gentil the use of a small house in Ville Blanche, the quarter reserved for French officials; he also promised to carefully consider his request for a translator. The following day, the astronomer received a message to meet the governor in his office at five PM When he passed through the door at five minutes to five, his eyes were immediately drawn to the striking young woman standing demurely to one side of the governor's desk. She was taller than the Indian women he had seen, nearly as tall as he was. She was wearing a blue-and-gold silk sari whose sheen seemed to heighten the glow of her smooth ebony skin. Her long black hair hung down in a single braid to the small of her back. She returned his gaze briefly and then lowered her eyes, but not before he saw that they were lit with a similar curiosity.

The governor greeted him with his normal effusive smile. "My good astronomer. Please, take a seat. How do you like the house? It's not a mansion, I know, but it was the best I could do on short notice. This is not Paris, much as I lament the fact. So, have you found a spot for your observatory yet?"

"I've looked at a couple of possible sites. So far the most promising is on a hill a little south of town. I was told that it was once a citadel and then after that a kind of palace. I don't know if you are familiar with it. It had two pavilions, but they are both in ruins."

"Of course. I know it. It was the mansion of the late Monsieur Dupleix. It did not survive our little disagreement with the English, I'm afraid. We have been using the basement of one of the pavilions as a powder magazine."

"So I was informed. I was thinking of using the other pavilion, if that meets with your approval, unless I can find a better site in the next day or two. The foundation is still intact and what remains of the walls looks to be quite sturdy. I was thinking that would help to limit the expense."

"Capital idea. I think it's just the place. I'll see if I can find time tomorrow to go and look it over. Now, as to that second piece of business. You asked me for an interpreter. I've thought about it carefully and I've decided to give you—on loan, mind you—our very best, as long as she remains available to me whenever

I have any pressing engagement that requires her presence. I'm loath to part with her, but I'm aware how important your work is to the greater glory of France. Let it never be said that I didn't do all I could to further the progress of science, especially when that scientist comes as a direct representative of the king."

Le Gentil had been acutely conscious of the girl's silent presence as they spoke. The moment the governor said "she," indicating the girl with a slight movement of his head, his heart had given a little leap. As the governor made the introductions, Rodrigo made Le Gentil's heart race even faster, especially when she reached out her hand and brushed his in a fleeting handshake accompanied by a restrained smile that instantly convinced the astronomer that the native girls were thoroughly enchanting. Le Gentil had not imagined that the governor might find him a female translator, much less one with her looks and obvious intelligence, but once he got over his surprise, the increased oxygen to his brain made him acutely aware that this was a singular stroke of good fortune. With the governor's permission, he asked her to meet him the following morning at his house so he could explain to her his plans. She agreed and then excused herself. As soon as she had left, the governor started filling him in on her background, making it clear that he considered her his protégée and the pride of the colony, a Christian native who, he was quite sure, could acquit herself as well in Paris as she could in Pondicherry.

"I mean to see that she has the chance one day. Give them a taste of what we're producing in the colonies. Maybe even find her a good husband while she's there, a military man perhaps. Wouldn't be the first to have a native wife. The family is first rate. The father is a doctor; he has an estate that would turn a duke green with envy. I've known her since she was seven, ever since she entered the convent school. I've known her father even longer. She speaks French better than I do, English better than half the blaggards in England, and three or four native languages to boot. Quotes the Bible better than Père Le Duc. Yes, if I had a daughter, it would be her. Only sons though. Three of them. The youngest you met. He sails back to France next week. The other two are in Paris busy eating through their inheritance. I wouldn't mind marrying her to the eldest. Right age and all, but he's in court service; it wouldn't do. He hopes to be an ambassador one day. A native wife is out of the question. I bet she'd keep him in his place, though. You may not know it, but she's got some spunk, that girl. Hell, if I were twenty years younger..." The governor took a short, rueful glance into the full-length mirror affixed to the wall to the left of his desk. "Well, no turning back the clock, is there?"

The girl did not yet have a name, but she was starting to acquire a personality. Rodrigo worked on the scene for the rest of the morning. Just before lunch, he reread what he had written and declared himself satisfied. His newly minted creation, still fresh from the creative fires, would serve as Le Gentil's conduit into the heart of Indian culture. With a little luck and a lot of craft, the attraction between them would continue to smolder until it erupted into one of the memorable love stories in Western literature: the Indian maiden and the French aristocrat; the barbarian princess and the famous astronomer; the pupil who deftly but imperceptibly turns the tables on her mentor and becomes the teacher that he could not see coming, but which he needs more than he can imagine. What a pity he would have to wait weeks, perhaps months, before he could arrive at those love scenes—scenes that would be repeated again and again in the minds of his readers for years to come. The girl would resist, of course. After all, Le Gentil was a foreigner, and at forty-two, he was nineteen years older. Didn't Indians at that time secretly consider westerners to be barbarians? Who knows, maybe some of them still did. But this was her destiny. There was nothing she could do to fight it, not so long as Rodrigo was holding the pen—or in this case, the keyboard of his computer. The heart has powers that not even the best of minds can overcome, fictional or otherwise. For his part, Rodrigo was determined that their hearts would remain intertwined for as long as literature could keep them alive. And he intended that to be a very, very long time indeed.

Rodrigo returned to his desk in the afternoon, determined to maintain a strict writing discipline of at least six hours a day—the four hours between breakfast and lunch, and two more in the afternoon after a short rest and some reading. John Gardner, whose book *On Becoming a Novelist* had become a kind of surrogate bible for Rodrigo, had once said that anyone was capable of becoming a published author if they were willing to work at it twelve hours a day, year after year. Though the discipline Gardner called for was more than a little extreme—to Rodrigo's mind six hours was both reasonable and manageable—there was no doubt in his mind that the main obstacle between him and his dream of becoming a great writer had been his full-time duties as a professor of literature. All that the afternoon produced, however, was a couple of paragraphs that he read and then erased and a nagging suspicion that the girl's lack of a name was one of the principle factors that was slowing him down. Dissatisfied with his lack of progress, he decided to cut his session short and dedicate what was left of the afternoon to his research. He rummaged through his books and selected a couple of them to bring down with him to a secluded courtyard bench that lay resting in the afternoon shade.

The first book he opened when he got there was a thick tome on the pantheon of Hindu goddesses; it was entitled *Devi*, the Sanskrit word for "goddess." He browsed through the table of contents, alert for any name that might catch his eye, and then did the same with the index. Several names caught his attention. He put pencil marks next to them and then flipped to the section on Ambika. This goddess was described as an astonishingly beautiful woman who made a practice of luring demons to their deaths. First, she would tell them that she would not go to bed with anyone who was not able to defeat her in battle. Dazzled by her beauty and maddened with desire, the demons would throw caution to the wind and rush into battle with their demon hosts behind them. As soon as they drew near, Ambika would kill their followers with a supersonic hum and then transform herself into the fearsome Kali and slay them.

Rodrigo laid down the book and flashed a triumphant smile to the vacant courtyard. Need he go any further? She was his girl. He had recognized her on the spot, the proud, beautiful, intelligent Tamil girl who was fated to be Le Gentil's match, and more. She would dazzle him with her beauty and defeat him with her mind. He was not the demon that she was luring to his death, though. Not at all. What she would slay would be the demons within him—his arrogance, his pride, his selfishness—the entire host felled by the supersonic hum of her articulate and penetrating speech. She was the goddess who would set free the greatness hiding inside the rogue. He rolled the three syllables on his tongue. Am-bi-ka. A mellifluous beginning; a sharp, powerful end. She would do what Minerva had done with Ulysses: she would recognize the hero sleeping inside him and use her goddess's wiles to awaken him. But beware the goddess who makes her project the salvation of a mortal man. All too often she is caught in the mesh of her own snares. If it had happened to the Greek goddesses, why not to an Indian goddess as well?

Thrilled by his discovery, he walked up and down a few times in front of the bench to discharge the kinetic energy that had built up inside him. Arati was nearly an hour away, so he sat back down and turned to the table of contents to find the page number for the section on Kali. He noted in passing that more pages of the book were devoted to Kali than to any other goddess. When he found the page and saw the full-color image, he was so startled he nearly dropped the book. It was the same image he had seen in his dream. The jet-black skin, the disheveled hair, the bright red tongue thrust out menacingly, or mockingly, from her mouth, the four extended arms, one clutching a bloody sword, another a severed head, her body naked except for the gruesome garland of skulls that hung around her neck and a skirt of dangling arms—every detail was just as he remembered it, all graphically depicted by the artist. How had it managed to leap from the book into his brain? The shock was only momentary, however. Of course, he must have seen it somewhere—on the Internet, in a poster, browsing through a book in the oriental arts section—and left it lodged in his subconscious. For a minute or two, he tried to rack his brain to discover where that might have been, but then he abandoned his efforts as immaterial. It didn't really matter where he had seen it. What mattered was that his subconscious had taken the image and worked it into his dream as deftly as a playwright who knowingly slips the necessary symbols into the early acts of his play so that their resonance will make the reader tremble when the climax looms. The adroitness of his subconscious astounded him. The goddess Ambika turned herself into Kali when she was ready to slay the demon. He had dreamed himself a priest worshipping at the altar of that same Kali, begging for her favor, just at the moment when he was ready to introduce his heroine. And that favor had been granted. She had come into his dream so that she could come into his story and slay the demons inside Le Gentil, thus leading his character to the brink of greatness.

He read on, eagerly now, taking it as a sign that his muse had been at work, playing with his mind so that she could then play with his fingers. Kali, he discovered, while often thought of as the goddess of death and destruction, was actually the goddess of time and change. Her name was the feminine form of *kala*, a homonym meaning both "time" and "black." Black as the night shrouding the cremation grounds in which she dwelt, Kali was the female symbol of the one cosmic force that no living being can withstand, the inexorable tide of time that leads all beings to the funeral pyre where the goddess awaits them. Wild and untamed, her disheveled hair represents her defiance of conventions. Her nakedness represents nature, unencumbered by the norms of culture. With her outstretched tongue, she teases and mocks her devotees. Her garland of skulls is a grim reminder that we all come before the goddess one day. Was this the goddess to whom he had prayed in his dream? He smiled, proud of his subconscious for having chosen such an unforgiving deity, so representative of the stark, unforgiving nature of reality. Kali was fierce yet playful, heedless of convention because she knows that all conventions are annihilated by time. These were all qualities he could give in some measure to Ambika, who would hold within her the potential to transform herself into Kali at a moment's notice should the demon appear and attempt to best her in battle.

Reading further, he came across a picture of Kali dancing on the outstretched body of Shiva, a picture of wild abandon. In the explanation that followed, he discovered that in the Tantric texts she was considered the causal matrix of the universe, a symbol for the creative power of absolute consciousness. For that reason, she was depicted dancing on the motionless body of the god. It was Kali who transformed the pure, undifferentiated consciousness, Shiva, into the three worlds, creating form out of the formless; and it was Kali who withdrew those forms into the darkness of eternal night in the cosmic dance of dissolution. The more he read, the more surprised he was to learn that each of her features and characteristics was symbolic of something that seemed to belong more to the domain of serious philosophy than folk religion. He found himself having to reread some of the concepts several times in a mostly unsuccessful effort to understand them. Undoubtedly, his astronomer would run into the same difficulty when the time came. With his naturalist's eye and his scientist's thirst for knowledge, he would almost certainly ask Ambika to show him the local temples and religious ceremonies. He would consider it all very primitive at first, but she would quickly disabuse him of that notion, and he would have no choice but to listen, drawn on by her beauty, her exotic allure, and her ability to challenge his mind in ways that continually surprised him. If Ambika were going to play her role successfully, however, Rodrigo would have to become versed in the philosophy she had been raised on. He might find fault with it. He might scoff at some of its notions, compare it to the way of all religions—at worst a dreamy opiate for the masses; at best an attempt to lead a happy, restful life by inventing elegant answers to unanswerable questions—but he had to understand it before he could successfully argue her side of the romantic and cultural equation. From the looks of it, this was not going to be an easy task.

He now turned to his book on Tantra, a thick and highly philosophical text that had attracted his attention in the bookshop by its erudite English and its puzzling concepts—Kant on steroids, he had told himself at the time. Thankfully, it included a long section on Kali rituals and their symbolism that he hoped might go a long way toward solving the demands of his character. Now, if he could only understand it. He took a deep breath, preparing his mind for what he knew was going to be a difficult undertaking. Just then, however, he heard the sounds of the ashram residents on the ghat setting up for the arati. With a mixture of relief and reluctance, he closed his book and went to his room to get ready for his own ritual.

After dinner, Rodrigo retired to his room for an evening of serious reading. He propped up the two pillows against the headboard, turned on the reading lamp, and picked up the heavy volume on Tantra with its bouquet of indecipherable runes splashed across the cover. He hefted it in his hand for a moment before deciding that such heavy reading was not good for the digestion. Instead, he reached for his travel book, its cover graced with the exhaust fumes from a Delhi taxi rattling its way down a cacophonous and crowded city street. He raised an eyebrow and then plunged in. Soon he was immersed in a world that was Rishikesh's polar opposite. He had spent all of twelve hours in Delhi before leaving on the train for Pathankot, a short bus ride from Dharamsala. The book immediately reacquainted him with those disagreeable first impressions: the dirt, the smog, the crowing human voices, the touts trying to shuttle you into a taxi or a shop or a hotel, if they couldn't sell you something first. Delhi was an explosion, both human and profane. It had knocked him off balance before he had even gotten out of the airport, trying to shoulder his way into a cab, and kept him off balance until he had finally fallen asleep on his overnight berth, the metallic rumbling of the wheels and the swaying of the carriage seeming like a blessing after a long day spent walking those hallucinogenic streets. Now, however, from the safe distance of his ashram bed, he found the madness full of a strange, disarming charm. Part of it was the writer's satiric gift, but a greater part was the literary cast Rodrigo gave to his own memories. Time and the act of reading gave him a chance to process that truncated slice of life that he had experienced less than two weeks earlier and returned it to him wrapped in the bright tinsel of a writer's encounter with life in all its mad, exasperating richness. He felt a momentary flare of disappointment when the writer boarded the train for Jaipur, but the journey proved to be so interesting that he ended up sharing his relief to be out of Delhi.

It was nearly ten o'clock when he put aside the book and fulfilled his pledge to do some serious research before he went to sleep, though after ten minutes he began wondering if it were at all prudent to give himself a headache before retiring for the night. He found the beginning of the section on Kali symbolism as tedious and as difficult as he had found Kant and Hegel in his one undergraduate philosophy course, and only slightly less imposing than Derrida and Foucault, whom he had tackled in graduate school and learned to appreciate without ever learning to like. This shared some of the same flavors, full of floating signifiers that would have drawn some hearty admiration from the French philosopher-linguists. It was also heavy in Sanskrit terminology, which, it explained, was unavoidable since many of the Sanskrit words had no equivalent in English or any other language. Much of it had to do with the creation and dissolution of the manifest universe, the work of Kali in one or another of her myriad forms—*shakti, prakriti, bhairavi,* and so on—all signifiers for different aspects of the creative principle or causal matrix as it works upon consciousness, gradually transforming it into mind and then into matter by introducing *kala,* or curvature (an additional and more philosophical meaning of the word), into what is fundamentally beyond conception—the pure, unmanifest consciousness. The explanation went on for pages, every outgoing and incoming manifestation of consciousness, each symbolized by different facets of the Dark Mother's cosmic dance. He was about to put the book down when it began explaining the symbolism of the fifty skulls. While the surface meaning was obvious, with its overtones of death in the Mother's arms, it also had a deeper, more philosophical meaning. Each of the fifty skulls represented one of the fifty letters of the Sanskrit alphabet; they, in turn, represented the fifty primordial sounds out of which the creation arises, beginning with *a,* symbol for the seed of creation. He read on, fascinated now by the thought of an alphabet whose every letter signified a different aspect of creation.

The book called the fifty letters "acoustic roots" and claimed that they were the seeds of all manifest expression. Whether there was any truth to this claim did not interest him. After all, he was not looking for truth in these texts but artistic resonance, something he could use in his book—or rather elegance, a word he kept coming back to over and over again. There was something supremely elegant about this idea, the conception that there is an acoustic vibration at the root of any manifestation, and that these acoustic vibrations can be distilled down to a combination of fifty primordial sounds that later find expression in the human mind in the form of language. He had made his way through most of Derrida and Foucault's work, kicking and screaming most of the way but a prisoner to the quality of their thought, no matter how dry and convoluted he found their language. He had accepted their fundamental linguistic premise, that we conceptualize our universe through language. Without words to give meaning to our mental conceptions, there would only be white noise in our minds. The image of an ocean would be meaningless if we did not transform it into a concept by appending the word "ocean." If this were true—and he had spent enough time grappling with the idea to accept its validity—and if the Tantric premise were true that every manifestation was vibratory and all vibrations emitted sound—and this accorded with what he knew of physics—then it stood to reason that human language and thus human thought would also arise out of the same sounds that constitute the universe, and that these sounds would make up the compendium of conceivable sounds that we call the alphabet. Whether there were 50 or 30 or 130 was immaterial. It was the logic, the subtlety, the artistic flare of the idea that he loved. He wasn't sure yet how he could use it, but the sophistication of the thinking was something he knew would greatly impress Le Gentil when he heard it coming from his young interpreter's lips. On the strength of these ideas, her mind would be sword enough to slay his arrogance and thus lay open the road to his mind, and thereafter to his heart.

He lay the book face down on his lap and tried to imagine a scene in which he could make use of these ideas. Perhaps Le Gentil could hear something about Tantra that piques his interest. Ambika expounds upon it, inflaming his interest even further; when he asks for the source of her information, she offers to translate an ancient text for him—one, of course, that Rodrigo could find in the bookshop. But when Le Gentil fails to understand the text, she has to lead him through it. His pride is dealt a blow, but he is scientist enough to recognize her worth and that of the difficult text she elucidates for him. A hitherto fragile respect for what he had thought a primitive culture begins to undergo a fundamental change, helped along by the woman who is its symbol and its most refined manifestation. Rodrigo rested his chin on his hand and stared at the wall. It could work. But he would have to be careful to keep the actual philosophy to a minimum. Otherwise, there was a risk of boredom, not to mention how difficult it would be to write.

He picked the book back up and turned to the section on Kali worship. A number of different rituals were described there, many of them accompanied by quotes from different Tantric scriptures. He was about to close the book for the night when he was stopped short by the final two lines at the bottom of the page. "While the traditional offering to the goddess is a blood sacrifice, most often a goat, in many of the Tantric rituals blood offerings are shied away from. Instead, different non-traditional foods are offered, most commonly sour lemons, hot chili peppers, and bitter neem leaves, unlike the more traditional sweets that are offered to other goddesses." He would not have been able to recognize neem leaves had he seen them, but he remembered that in his dream he had offered lemons and chilies on a silver plate. Could the leaves that accompanied them have been neem leaves? He was ready to swear they were. He sat bolt upright in the bed and furrowed his brow. How could his dream have been so precise? Had he read this somewhere before? Had he seen it in the same picture that had taken up residence in some hidden compartment of his brain? He could have come across an image of Kali anywhere, he supposed, but he had never knowingly read about Tantric rituals. A quick search through his memory yielded nothing further, so he continued reading, plagued now by a vague apprehension about what he might find there. Two pages later he had an even greater surprise, one that sent a sudden cold shudder down his spine: a colored diagram more or less identical to the one he had seen in his dream. Below it was a quote from the Kali Tantra:

"First I speak of yantra, the knowing of which conquers death. At first draw a triangle. Outside, draw another. Then draw three more triangles. Draw a circle and then a beautiful lotus. Then draw another circle and then a square enclosure with four lines and four doors."

The triangles were each of different colors. Though Rodrigo could not remember the colors of the triangles in his dream, he was prepared for the probability that they were identical. A yantra, he read, was an abstract geometrical symbol of the ultimate reality, a figure used for both meditation and ritual worship. So it was a yantra he had seen. He had drawn it himself at the base of the idol before he began his worship. Wherever he had seen the Kali statue, it must have been sitting inside a similar yantra on a similar pedestal. That was the only possible explanation. And beside it in that same picture had probably been a plate or plates containing lemons, chilies, and neem leaves. His vague apprehension faded, replaced by a sense of amazement that his subconscious could have retained such a fleeting impression—as it almost certainly had been—with such remarkable precision. Then he remembered reading somewhere that every imprint on our senses leaves an impression in our brain, which, while quickly buried, is never completely erased. This was the supposed explanation behind some of the remarkable feats of recall by subjects under hypnosis. That he had proof of this through his dream was remarkable enough, but what was even more remarkable was that it was exactly the kind of input he was looking for. How much had his environment to do with this memory surfacing in his dream? Probably everything—that and his subconscious need to find material for his book. As he had told his students on many an occasion, the choice of place is among the most important decisions a writer can make, one that inevitably shapes his work. It had taken a lot of heartache to get him on a plane to India, but now it was starting to look like it was all paying off.

5

HE FOLLOWING MORNING, RODRIGO began the slow process of getting acquainted with his new character. The next chapter began with Ambika arriving at Le Gentil's house precisely at ten, as they had agreed upon the previous day. Rodrigo paused to wonder how acceptable this would have been in the Indian society of the time. It was quite possible that unmarried girls from good families would not have done such a thing. He would have to find out. Still, she was a government employee and he was a member of the ruling class. The English and the French did as much with their employees and servants in Europe. They would have almost certainly expected the same in a backward land that they were in the process of bringing to heel. Nevertheless, he would not give himself license to indulge in scenes or situations that were not entirely plausible. *Le bon dieu* was in the details, as Flaubert had famously said. If he wanted his work of historical fiction to emanate an aura of authenticity, he would have to carefully think through each and every detail, no matter how much extra work that implied. He nodded briefly to his muse in acknowledgment, wherever she might be, and made a resolution to spend some time in the Internet café after lunch running down this information and whatever other question marks might arise in the meantime.

As he had planned, Le Gentil was slightly nervous and the girl surprisingly self-assured—surprising, that is, to Le Gentil. Rodrigo knew that her confidence stemmed from a firm conviction that her culture was far older and wiser than his, a conviction she had prudently chosen to hide from her foreign employers. All he would know at this first meeting was that she was a confident young woman who did not seem at all thrilled to be assigned as his translator, a surprising commodity even in the upper reaches of Parisian society but especially so in an Asian colony where a dark-skinned woman was an inferior among her betters and always would be. For now, Le Gentil would simply be surprised and curious, but eventually that curiosity would lead him to become aware of the real reason for her confidence. There was something in her bearing that could not be hidden, a proud light in her demurely downcast eyes that defied the veil she drew across them. Despite her best efforts at dissimulation, Ambika exuded a natural sense of superiority that his unusually perceptive eyes, trained to ferret out the secrets of nature through careful, continued observation, could not help but pick up on. Her efforts had been more than enough to fool the governor, with his good-natured, slightly oafish patronizing of a conquered race, but Le Gentil was a breed apart from any European she had ever met. She would answer his questions on this morning and pretend not to notice the nervousness that he was doing his best to hide, a fillip of nature brought on by his being around a beautiful young woman who spoke his own language for the first time in over seven years. But she would fail to recognize that the mind that inhabited that ghostly pale body, so ill suited to the South Indian sun, was trained to read from the book of nature; and she, despite the seventy centuries of culture at her back, was written into that book in a language he had taught himself to decipher.

Suddenly, it seemed incongruous to Rodrigo that she should be a Christian if she felt this strongly about her culture. He lifted his hands from the keyboard, leaned back in his chair, and strove to picture her slender brown limbs and thoughtful expression draped inside the folds of her sari while she listened quietly to Le Gentil pontificate about the importance of the Venus transit. Then it struck him. His beautiful Ambika was no Christian at all, just an accomplished actress and a pragmatic emissary of her people. Of course! How could he have not seen it before! She was from a well-to-do, highly cultured and influential Tamil family, the type of family that would never sell their soul to the oppressors. But they were pragmatists. They knew there was no way they could defeat the occupiers through force of arms. India had endured invaders before. Had they not always defeated them by letting them be browned by the Indian sun, lulled to sleep by its tainted waters, and finally swallowed by the shifting sands of its seven-thousand-year-old culture? They had succeeded in the past by being wiser and more patient than the naive foreigners who mistook them for half-naked primitives, whether those foreigners came from the familiar lands just beyond their borders or from the unknown ones across the seas. Her family would have placed her in the convent school on purpose, knowing that the enemy one does not know is far more dangerous than the enemy one does. And even more pliant still is the enemy who thinks you have become one of them—an eager, albeit inferior disciple—and lets you into their inner sanctum, and thus into their thoughts and plans. Now it made sense. Ambika was the best of these silent, smiling spies, because she was not only intelligent, she was beautiful. She knew that beauty was a weapon that can be used without the victim ever becoming aware of the blow. Le Gentil would discover most of this in time, but by then it would be too late, for by then he would be on her side, whether he realized it or not.

Now her quiet confidence made sense. Rodrigo set his hands back on the keyboard and listened in as Le Gentil explained to her about the construction of the observatory.

"There is no need to worry on that account," Ambika assured him. "I will find you the best masons and metal forgers in Pondicherry, as good as any India has to offer. And I will make sure they use the highest quality materials. The governor has extended you a line of credit. I will do the rest."

"I want workmen who will be able to follow my exact instructions. I am very particular about these matters, I will have you know."

"As I said, monsieur, there is no need to worry. I will find you masons and forgers who are capable of executing any design you might give them."

"Well then," Le Gentil said, relaxing now, "I suppose all that is left for the moment is to take a run out to the site. It is one thing to see it on paper. It's quite another to stand out there with the wind at your back and what remains of the foundation in front of you. You'll be able to visualize my design much better then. Once the observatory is finished and my telescope mounted, it will be the pride of South India. What am I saying? There will probably be no better observatory in all Asia. I just hope it doesn't go to waste after I've gone. That reminds me. I was thinking of researching the works of Indian astronomers in my free time. Who knows, maybe the governor will even allow some native astronomers to use the observatory after I leave—that is, if there are any. You wouldn't know anything about that, I suppose?"

"We also have astronomers in India, monsieur. Astronomy has been a subject of study here for thousands of years."

Le Gentil lifted an eyebrow, but the girl gave no evidence that she was aware of his unspoken doubts. Thousands of years? Well, it was an old culture, older than his own, however primitive it might be. It was possible.

"I would like to have a chance to go through whatever texts are available while I'm here. There might be something of interest there. At least it will give me a chance to see how much they knew of the universe, what conceptions they had of the planets and their motions, that sort of thing. See how close they might have gotten on their own to our modern understanding."

"I see."

Could that be skepticism he saw in her face? It was hard to tell. Her tone had become even drier, if that were possible, but she was exceedingly difficult to read. Her face didn't seem to betray any expression at all, yet there was no mistaking the intelligence that shone forth from her dark eyes.

"Would you know at all where I might be able to get some information about any works of astronomy that Indians might have written over the past—what was it you said?—thousands of years?"

Finally, the appearance of a smile on that lovely face, faint but captivating. What's more, he was sure it wasn't involuntary. It was not his wit that elicited this unforeseen thaw but her willingness to recognize it.

"I can consult a Brahmin astrologer I know and make a list of some representative works that might interest you. I doubt that any of them have been translated into either French or English, but if you like, I can begin translating portions of them, time permitting. If you find any of it interesting, I should be able to arrange a meeting with one of our astronomers."

There was little wonder why the governor had been so enthusiastic about his young interpreter. It was not simply that she was beautiful, though with the governor that might have overridden all other considerations. This was a competent and intelligent young woman. Surprising to see a native girl who spoke French—as the governor had implied—better than half the students he had gone through the seminary with. He had a feeling she might prove as competent an assistant as any he had ever had, despite her sex. But it certainly didn't hurt that she was young and beautiful. His blood had calmed down by now, back to flowing at its natural pace, but a little added fervor was good for the brain. Makes you more alert, he thought, livens up the senses.

All in all, Le Gentil was extraordinarily pleased with his new assistant. Rodrigo, even more so. He liked this Ambika—better with every passing minute. It was nearly lunchtime now, time to close the computer at the end of a short but promising scene. He got up and began to stretch his body, still picturing her at the table across from Le Gentil, her lithe limbs hidden by the smooth grain of the tabletop. Yes, she would not only be his first but perhaps his greatest heroine. For Le Gentil, the attraction was at least partly physical. Not so for Rodrigo. In his case, it emanated from the depths of his soul. She was what Beth had never been: courageous, visionary, charismatic, the missing part of Rodrigo's psyche, the girl he would have chosen for himself had she been able to step off the page and into his life. That first conversation in Le Gentil's house was short, but it made a powerful impression on him, as well as on his main character. It wasn't so much what was said, but what he now knew was coming, though the dreams he dreamed of her were still too vague to see in terms of scene or plot, just a smoldering of possibility that seemed to him at that moment like a full-grown fire. He was not sure where to take the story next, but for now that didn't matter. For now, his dreams of his heroine had him walking in rarefied air.

After lunch, Rodrigo walked over to the Blue Hills Travel cybercafé, some fifty paces from the ashram gate. He found it virtually empty. Behind the desk, the lone employee was enjoying a siesta, reclining in a swivel chair with his back against the wall. The twenty or so computers were unoccupied except for a pair of young westerners who sat at adjoining monitors in one corner of the room. Rodrigo cleared his throat softly; moments later he cleared it again, this time a little louder. The man behind the desk opened his eyes briefly, motioned lazily in the direction of the computers, and then closed them again, but not before glancing at the clock on the far wall.

Rodrigo chose a computer on the other side of the room from the whispering couple and logged into his email, something he had yet to do since he'd arrived in Rishikesh. The connection was quite a bit slower than he was used to, despite the sign on the wall that read, "hi-speed broadband internet." He waited somewhat impatiently for his inbox to open. When he noticed the untitled message from Beth near the top of his list of messages, his heart rate began to accelerate. He took a few slow, deep breaths to calm his nervousness and then decided to leave her email for last. None of the others turned out to be of much importance, with the possible exception of a letter from his lawyer, which he saved to a folder to read later. The rest he skimmed over as fast as he could, dashing off a few quick replies. By the time he got to Beth's email, he was feeling much calmer. He opened it up and began to read.

Dear Rodrigo,

I hope you are well. You probably know by now, but if not, the final divorce papers arrived in the mail last week. I suppose this is as good a time as any to tell you: Ralph and I have set a date. We are going to be married in November. I'm sorry to have to tell you this in a letter, but as you can see, it is either that or not tell you at all. To be honest, I thought about not telling you at all after I got your email from Dharamsala. It really upset me. Anyhow, I'm not going to go into that here. All I will say is that I am happy you feel that you are changing. I hope this time it's for real. But our relationship is over; it is time for you to get on with your life. I've told you this before but I will tell you one last time: I tried as hard as I could to make our marriage work, I really did, but you kept pushing me away with your criticism, your coldness, and your need to always be right. There is only so much that a woman can take and then something inside her dies. It took me a long time to feel good about myself again and about my work, and I don't know if I could have done it without Ralph. He taught me to respect myself again and have faith in who I am and the path I have chosen. After years of criticism and lack of support, I think I had forgotten how. Anyhow, I don't want to reopen old wounds. I don't think that helps and I don't wish to hurt you. I honestly hope you are making the changes you say you are, although I would be less than honest if I didn't say that I find it a little difficult to believe. It sounds too easy to me, and I know from bitter experience that it is never that easy. Still, I wish you all the best. I hope that when you become whole yourself, you can meet someone with whom you can share your life. I hope she is someone whose company fulfills you—not because you need her, but because you have so much to give her. In the meantime, please don't write and don't call. I'm sorry if that sounds harsh, but the wounds still hurt and your last letter made me realize that it is better this way. I hope one day we can be friends, I truly do, but that time hasn't come yet. Good luck with your novel. I've been waiting for years for you to write it. I hope to see it in the bookstores before long.

Sincerely,
Beth

P. S. Your lawyer should be contacting you with the details of the settlement, specifically the sale of the house.

By the time Rodrigo finished reading the letter, tears were clouding his eyes; he had to brush them away to read the postscript. For a few moments he had difficulty breathing, the air entering his lungs in fits and starts. He wiped his eyes and started reading the letter again, slowing almost to a standstill as a painful flood of memories prevented him from concentrating on the computer screen.

How he wished he had never written that letter! Not that it would have made any real difference, but still, he knew when he was writing it that she wouldn't like it, that the effect would likely be the opposite to what his fevered imagination was hoping for. Something had warned him he should erase it—the feeble voice of reason, no doubt. His finger had even shaken for a few moments while he vacillated over whether or not to click the send button. He had had an uncomfortable sensation in the pit of his stomach, a warning, perhaps, from his conscience that no good could come of it, and likely a good deal of harm, but he had ignored it. Something had been driving him at that moment, a madness such as that which had sent Ahab after the whale, a similar false prophet of a voice whispering in his ear that this might be his last chance to tell Beth how he felt, his last chance to salvage what he could of their love. Foolish was far too kind a word to describe it. Idiocy was closer to the truth. Grasping at a piece of straw dangling from the edge of the cliff instead of preparing his parachute for the long hard fall. That voice had driven him to the end of the three torturous pages, goaded him into spending nearly an hour revising it—as if his words could accomplish what years of selfishness could not—and then pressed his finger to the mouse to click the send button while his conscience covered its eyes, thrusting him over the precipice with a jammed parachute and no time to fix it. He had walked out of the Internet café in Dharamsala soaked in sweat, too proud of his last heroic effort to realize that he had just divested himself of his last shred of dignity. The next day he had his brief audience with the Dalai Lama. What a contrast between the clear eyes and benign smile of that supremely ethical man and his own bedraggled countenance that had stared hesitantly at him from the mirror that morning.

And now, what was it she had said? His eyes skipped to the end of the letter. He refocused them yet again, blinking away the watery film that covered them. "Please don't write and don't call…it is better this way." The finality of her words seemed overwhelming and irrevocable. Measured against them, her contention that she hoped they could be friends one day fell like an empty, weightless platitude. Perhaps it satisfied her conscience, but it did nothing to soften the blow. What the divorce could not accomplish, or even the sight of her in another man's arms, these words had. I hope we can be friends one day, but not now. So that was it. It was over. He remembered the day he had come home to find her house keys dangling from the front-door lock. He became so disgusted with her flightiness and lack of responsibility that he refused to open the door for her when she came home that evening. Nearly half an hour he made her wait, walking up and down in front of the house in obvious anger, before he opened the door and went back to his computer without saying a word. Would it have made a difference if he had been more understanding then? Or the time she went to bed with tears in her eyes and he pretended not to notice, knowing that it was his own coldness she was reacting to, but justifying it to himself for some slight of hers that he could no longer remember. Could a single embrace have turned their destiny around? Opened his heart and diluted the acid with which she wounded him in return? Perhaps not. Perhaps they were just two ill-matched people who had clung to each other in the dark and then blamed one another for the blindness in their eyes.

One by one, the questions assaulted him in the blue-tinted semi-darkness of the cybercafé. Fragments of the past that cut him with their jagged edges. Shards of regret, of embarrassment, of anger. His past was a ghost that haunted him in the daylight. It whispered in his ears with a mocking voice that sounded eerily similar to his own: It's over; she's getting married; she's lost to you forever and it's your own damn fault, your own failing, your own dark face in that mirror.

One more image: sitting in his office reading Eliot when a colleague called to say that he was sorry to have to tell him this, but he felt it was his duty—he had seen Beth kissing some man in a Raleigh nightclub the week before. The initial shock. The disbelief followed by the nauseating certainty that it was true. Confronting her that evening, quietly, knowing the answer that was coming, preparing himself for the pain, then feeling it knife through him with a force for which he was totally unprepared. Then remembering his mother just after her death and realizing that it was the very same feeling, the man unable to escape the fate of the child.

Now, as then, he could not stand to remain sitting. He had spent the better part of an hour doing battle with her letter, but now he no longer had the stamina. When he finally signed out of his email client and paid for his time, he felt as if he had spent an entire day in a warehouse hoisting heavy boxes and breathing secondhand smoke. He set out along the Ganges in the direction of Lakshman Jhula, walking quickly and paying only the barest attention to his surroundings. The hot August sun with its coterie of thick, ominous clouds huddled above the mountains went unnoticed, as did the signs of an afternoon downpour. All his attention was directed toward his thoughts—or rather they forced their attention on him with the rude, rough, in-your-face directness of a dockworker, and he did not have the strength to resist or look the other way.

Eight years they had been together, more than five of those married, and it all ends with one last accusatory letter and a don't-call-me-I'll-call-you. Cruelty, thy name is woman. Was this now all that was left of those eight years? This and a house on the market, the proceeds to be divided equally once it is sold? Was that what she thought, that it could be summed up so easily, so trenchantly? What had become of their dreams, the ones they had dreamed together? Had they simply vanished, winked out of existence? Or had they gone into hiding, waiting for a chance to reappear? Would she fasten them onto the new guy, the rebound guy? Would he? What then would become of those eight years of hope that had given way to disappointment and discontent? Unless it was the residue of experience distilled down to the persons they had become. He could not say at this moment that he liked either one of them all that much. They had failed each other, and in the process they had failed themselves. She as well as he.

The blaring of the CD stall near the foot of Ram Jhula interrupted his thoughts. He quickened his pace and soon put the harsh, discordant sounds behind him. The pavement ended and he found himself bracketed by trees on either side, sparser to his left where the river rushed along in the opposite direction. The sun passed behind the clouds, a welcome relief though his mind barely registered the relative comfort it brought to his body.

Of course, he had made his mistakes. He had admitted as much, though perhaps less than he could have. But how could she claim that she had tried as hard as she could to make the marriage work? What about her moodiness, her almost total disregard for his writing, and that not-so-subtle way she had of pointing out that everything he did was not quite good enough? No, she was the martyr and he was the obvious choice to take the fall. For Beth, life was a morality play, all black and white, no in between, no shades of gray, not even an ounce of suspicion that there might be some validity to his way of looking at the world. Well, beware what you wish for. She had closed the book on him, packed up her paints and wrapped her shawl around her gallery owner's size sixteen neck. Does he have any idea what's in store for him? Just wait till the smoke settles on this little passion play. She'll get him in her crosshairs soon enough.

Rodrigo smiled weakly and added some firmness to his step. As he passed the clearing where he had talked to the old holy woman, he began visualizing a scene designed to combat the despondency that assailed him. He pictured Ralph coming home late one evening after a date with his bowling league. Beth is slumped in a plush recliner, thumbing through her first collection of photos, the one Rodrigo paid to have printed and whose text he had helped to write. She mutters a thinly disguised insinuation that he prefers the company of his beer and his bowling buddies to hers, something Ralph is not yet ready to suspect will soon prove true. Her mind is filled with nostalgia, wondering why she left a critically acclaimed, soon-to-be famous author for a capitalist with a fondness for art but no real understanding of it. He sits, listens patiently to her all-too-familiar martyr's monologue about how undervalued and underappreciated she is, forced to live in a world in which men have been indoctrinated since childhood to subconsciously consider their wives to be domestic slaves and trained to treat them accordingly. When he goes up to the bedroom, she sinks back into her chair and realizes that nothing has changed. Her complaints are the same complaints. The disillusionment and discontent are back. They had, in fact, never gone; they had only been masked by the novelty of trading one husband in for another. Meanwhile, upstairs in the bedroom, Ralph is staring at the ceiling, wondering why his wife seems to be so irritated with him these days when all he has ever done is support her in style and give her the freedom to follow her dreams.

This final thought gave Rodrigo a peculiar sense of satisfaction. Though it was only a fantasy, he felt in some way vindicated for the lack of appreciation he had endured these past few years. That, at least, he would not miss. Caught up now in the vividness of his imagination, he went back over the scene again, polishing it as he walked. He added a sense of despondency to Ralph's final thoughts, easy enough to do in his present state of mind, then a touch of remorse to Beth's as she stared straight ahead in a darkened living room, the book they had collaborated on open on her lap, thoughts of their early halcyon days flitting by like shadows on the wall. By this time, he was passing through the bustle of Lakshman Jhula. As he passed the entrance to the enormous Trayambakeshwar Temple, he became aware of where he was. He glanced for a moment at the entrance to the bridge. A small group of tourists was gathered around a popcorn vendor who had a monkey on his shoulder. Their laughter and animated conversation brought a scowl to Rodrigo's face. He stopped to buy a bottle of water from a street-side stall and continued straight ahead, quickly leaving the last of the buildings behind, and with it the bustle and bluster of human activity.

The road now passed under a thick canopy of trees. To his left the foliage obscured his vision of the river some twenty meters below; to his right the forest climbed steadily upward into the Himalayan foothills. Soon he was far enough upriver that he could see no sign of Rishikesh, neither before him nor behind him. Nor could he hear anything other than the sounds of the forest and the steady churning of the waters. Thoughts of Beth's letter once again forced their attention on him, but he had no more heart for his fantasy of her future remorse. The quiet purposefulness of nature would not allow it. Instead, he was thrown back again into a river of fragmentary episodes of their life together, rushing along like the water beyond the trees: their early days when he had sometimes felt so exhilarated to see her asleep in the bed beside him that it made him dizzy; the poetry readings, painting exhibitions, and evenings at the jazz club; the mounting conflicts that never turned into all-out war but rather a protracted siege in which they both felt themselves to be confined within the walls of a beleaguered castle, grateful for the temporary truces but knowing they would never last. Round and round like a kaleidoscope the images turned, whirling among the trees as if they were part of his natural surroundings.

A loud rustle broke in among his thoughts. He turned his head and was surprised to see a cow foraging in the forest to his right, picking its way stolidly along the slope. He stopped and looked behind him. How far had he come from Lakshman Jhula? One kilometer? More? He was tired. His feet, with only thin sandals between them and the asphalt road, were beginning to ache, though the shade felt cool and refreshing. If he went on, every step would be an extra step he would have to cover coming back. He looked to his left and saw the river glinting through the trees. He caught a glimpse of large boulders by the water's edge and a stretch of white sand. A short way ahead, he spied a path that appeared to lead down through the trees to the banks of the river. He made for it and carefully picked his way down, grabbing on to the overhanging branches to steady himself. When he reached the sand, he stopped and scanned the riverbank. Looking upriver, he was momentarily startled to see someone standing motionless on the sand about fifty meters away. He had pale skin, blond hair curled up into a topknot, black pants, and no shirt. It seemed odd, the way he stood there without moving, staring straight ahead at the river with his fingers interlaced, palms downward, his arms extended slightly away from his body. Then he gradually started lifting his arms until they were extended straight over his head, palms upward. He remained in that posture for a full minute and then slowly brought his arms down to their original position. Rodrigo watched curiously as he repeated the same movement over and over again, his gaze never wavering from the river in front of him.

Turning his eyes from the unusual sight, Rodrigo walked over to the nearby outcropping of boulders that extended out into the water. One of the boulders had a relatively flat, smooth surface that he found to his liking. He sat down and within moments his thoughts returned to Beth and her letter, quite possibly the last he would ever receive from her. Once more, he glanced over at the odd, motionless figure, and then he forgot him entirely, blinded by the warring motions of his mind. He had made many mistakes—they both had—but the most serious mistake of all she had never mentioned, because she had never known about it. They had been sitting at the kitchen table, a table they both loved. She had been voicing once again her dissatisfaction with their marriage. He could hear the bitterness in her voice, the accusatory tone he so detested. Then, all of a sudden, without any premeditation, he suggested a trial separation. Why had he done that? He still couldn't explain it. The thought had never even occurred to him before that moment. Had he said it out of frustration, as a dare? He didn't know, not then, not now. He had repeated his words as if he had been deliberating the possibility for weeks. As if he were sure of what he was saying. As if he had reluctantly come to the conclusion that it was the only option that could give him back his peace of mind. And yet he was just as surprised at what he was saying as she was; it was as if he were listening to a stranger speak. What was not surprising was the look of disbelief on her face that quickly mutated into anger. His stomach went queasy, but he also felt a sense of triumph at the look on her face, a spiteful reaction that now filled him with revulsion. Had he simply been trying to get back at her for accusing him of being cold, cynical, controlling, and cut off from his emotions, four *c*'s as scimitar-like as the letter itself, though he knew all too well that there was a lot of truth in the things she was saying? All he could remember of his psyche at the time was a feeling that he was being impelled by an unknown force, as if something alien to him in his unconscious wanted to ensure that the worst would happen, just to see what it would feel like. Thinking about it afterward—was it that very night, when she grabbed some clothes and left for a friend's house?—he had remembered Freud's death drive, a primordial urge for self-destruction that was supposed to be hidden deep within every human psyche. In his case, it was not an impulse for physical self-destruction but for emotional death, a deep-seated, unconscious desire to sabotage everything he clung to and depended on to keep his psyche secure. The death drive! It could not have been more aptly named. After that, there had been no going back. Even though he consciously regretted what he had done, that impulse still drove him and held him back when a kind word or a hug or a simple admission of the truth could have tipped the balance. And then it was too late. One day, he felt a hardness in her that became a distance he could never bridge. "Something inside a woman dies" was the way she had put it in her letter. She became lost to him on that day, and deep inside he had known it, even then, though he hadn't been conscious of the fact. A few weeks later Ralph came along, but if it hadn't been Ralph, it would have been someone else. Anyone but him.

Yet not even Freud could explain why a human being would seek out his own destruction. He had documented this tendency in certain patients and postulated that it was an instinctive drive, usually held in check by social conditioning and the other, opposite urges that also inhabit the human psyche. But why should it even be there at all? Why had Rodrigo been unable to avoid actions and words that he knew would only make him miserable, and Beth along with him? Was there some kind of perverse satisfaction to be gained from sabotaging one's own life? There are enough things to make life difficult that are out of our control. What could he have done to forestall his mother's death, or the pain that followed in its wake and still resided in some seldom-visited corner of his mind? Nothing. This was the price one paid for being alive, the blood offering required in exchange for a human body, our forty pieces of silver. Why then do we compound our misery by making a mess of the only thing we can control—our own actions? Was this part of the ultimate life sentence, our being condemned to freedom, that we are also free to ruin the good and the beautiful that life offers us along with the sufferings she requires? He had loved Beth, loved her with all his heart at one time. If he was to be perfectly honest, he loved her still. There was a time when she had been the best thing that had ever happened to him. Their finest moments were so beautiful, they had made him tremble, and even the ordinary pleasures of life had taken on such a heightened existence in her company that he had sometimes shuddered at the thought that it might not last. And yet, when the wheel turned and their happiness started slipping away, he had poured fuel on a fire that might have easily been put out with a little attention and a few buckets of water. How could he have done that? How could he have let things get so out of control so fast? It didn't make sense. Why would any human being do this? And yet they did it all the time. He and Beth and over six billion other planetary waifs. Somewhere, somehow there should be an explanation, but he hadn't come across one yet, and he doubted he ever would. This was the universe he lived in, the one he would die in, as cold as the space that separates the stars. All he could do was swallow his pain and move on, and hope, perhaps, that his art would see him through to a happier, if not a more meaningful, life.

Rodrigo shrugged and looked at the river rushing past the boulders. What could he do? Here he was, his sorrow and he. They were no strangers to each other. His eyes focused and for the first time he noticed how transparent the water was, despite, or perhaps due to its speed, every inch of its pebbly bed open to scrutiny. There was a metaphor here, he suspected, for what he was experiencing—there always was—but for the moment it seemed to be out of reach. The water moved swiftly on, never pausing, inexhaustible, tireless, infinitely more transparent than his murky thoughts. He stared at it for several minutes, observed how its sliding currents formed shifting patterns in the light of the waning sun that slanted off its surface. At the end of those several minutes, he thought he detected a quietness that he knew he did not and had never possessed. Perhaps there are metaphors that never grow old, he thought, precisely because they are metaphors for lessons we have yet to learn. He didn't need a guru to tell him that this was one lesson that had escaped him, one he hadn't even begun to understand. He thought of the old woman and her cryptic comments, but her words seemed as slippery as the water that slid past his dangling fingers. He withdrew his hand and shook his head. The light was fading fast, the last sliver of the sun having just disappeared behind the mountains across the river. He remembered that he had a long walk back, though he had nothing to look forward to there other than dinner and a bed. He finished off what was left in his water bottle and started making his way toward the trees. When he reached the ascending trail, he remembered the silent figure upriver. He looked over and saw him sitting on the sand in meditation, his back perfectly straight, his body as rigid and as still as a stone statue. Rodrigo stopped for a few moments and watched him. Would that he were able to shut out the world like that, the world without and the world within. For an instant, he thought he detected the same momentary quietness that he had felt while looking at the river, a fleeting glimpse of something sculpted out of air and falling water, but it lasted only a moment and then it was gone. Was that what the silent figure felt, sitting there motionless on the sand? He looked impervious to the ills of the world, but was that even possible? Perhaps. Perhaps it was. But not for him.

6

THE FOLLOWING MORNING, RODRIGO sat dutifully in front of his computer and tried to work on his novel, but he could not force his sluggish thoughts away from his troubles and into his story. Every time he tried to picture the next scene in his book, he ended up getting lost in a scene from his own life, almost always with him and Beth as the principal characters. Often it was their dialogue that fateful day at the kitchen table, only now he had an opportunity to revise the scene until he got it right. Instead of asking for a trial separation, he resisted his destructive impulse and made a gallant, almost heroic effort to admit where he had been wrong. He had made too many mistakes, he told her, but he was going to make up for them. What he had done, he was capable of undoing. He listened to her complaints with stubborn attention, overcoming his resistance and trying to put himself into her shoes. When he made the ill-conceived slip of mentioning that she had made mistakes as well, setting off a reaction in her that he was all too familiar with, he erased his remark and rewound the scene. Swallow your pride, he told himself, before it swallows you. Soon his efforts paid off. Each time he played through the dialogue, Beth got up from the table with a wider smile and fewer regrets. The separation that never was became a marriage that would endure long after they were both laid in their graves, immortalized in the memoirs that he would write in his sunset years. Who knows, there would probably even be a movie, though he might prefer to defer that until after he was gone.

Eventually, he recognized the futility of trying to reverse the past, regardless of the satisfaction it gave him. This grudging realization was not enough to propel him back into his writing, however, but rather a just motive for shifting the scenario to one of future reconciliation. Two months after divorcing Ralph, they meet by accident—or is it design?—in a poetry reading. She has gone there out of nostalgia, remembering the many happy hours they had spent together in similar readings. In the back of her mind, she knows there is a possibility he might be there. When she sees him come in the door, alone—she was afraid that if she did see him, he would be on the arm of a beautiful young coed, his student—her heart leaps. Her feet are rooted to the floor, but she is unable to stop staring. Is the longing showing in her face? He reads something there, but he is too polite to interpret it. He goes over to her, says hello with an artless smile, full of confidence, as if she were an old friend that he was surprised but glad to see. He asks her how she's doing; she shakes her head wanly. *Comme çi comme ça*, she says with a fair accent. He asks how Ralph is—generously, sincerely. That is when she frowns, the barest glistening of a tear, and tells him about the divorce. I'm so sorry to hear that, he says, genuinely moved. I hope it hasn't been too difficult, he adds. She shrugs, says it was for the best, and changes the subject to his writing, how proud of him she was when she saw his book in the bookstore. Yes, she's read it. Loved it. Knew all along that he would be a success. Slightly embarrassed, he changes the subject to the well-known poet who has just arrived and is about to start the reading. One thing leads to another. Three hours later they are sitting in a jazz club, sipping Don Perignon and laughing about old times. She wonders if he might be free for lunch one of these days, and from there the fantasy spirals out of sight and into his bed.

Though Rodrigo broke off his reverie at intervals with a girding of his artistic loins and an arsenal of grimaces that varied from self-reproach to grudging resignation, he still could not find a way to catch the runaway carriage of words. Every time he forced himself to concentrate on the screen in front of him and direct his thoughts back to eighteenth-century India, the only images he saw there were himself and a certain willowy blond who looked more and more winsome and beautiful with every passing moment in that imaginary landscape. When he looked at his watch—for the first time since he sat down—he was startled to see that nearly four hours had passed and he still did not have a single line that had made it all the way to the period at the end of the sentence. Regretfully, he discounted the morning as a waste of time, but he consoled himself with the thought that it was something he needed to get out of his system.

After lunch he returned directly to his computer. It quickly became evident, however, that whatever it was, it was not out of his system. He realized then that as long as his own story kept getting in the way, he would not be able to concentrate on Le Gentil's story. And as long as that held true, he might as well write about what he was going through, anything to keep his fingers moving and perhaps thereby free his creative juices to flow once again. He opened up a blank file and began venting onscreen until he could see his thoughts and emotions peeking out at him from behind the clouds. He started by listing all the slights, real or imagined, that he had suffered during his relationship. The mere act of writing them down was enough to show him how petty much of his anger had been. He went on to make a list of all the things he had done that he regretted, starting with moving in together while she was still his student in freshman composition and ending with the letter he had written her from Dharamsala, now an embarrassment that he was sure turned his ears red even if the bathroom mirror didn't show it. After each of these, he added a colon and a few sentences about what he would do differently were he able to turn back the clock with the help of quantum physics or Wells's time machine. As he scrolled down the page, regret changed to sadness and sadness to resignation. It was only when he felt his eyes beginning to ache that he closed the laptop and threw himself on his bed, exhausted but still not free from the emotionally charged images of his marriage that spilled in noisy torrents down his frontal lobes like water over a dam. When he heard the ashramites setting up for arati, he welcomed it as a godsend, a chance to distract himself with music from the voices and images that would give him no peace.

The next day unfolded in precisely the same manner, only this time Rodrigo was not willing to sit like a piece of driftwood in front of his computer, carried away by his rampaging thoughts. He spent a dutiful hour trying to focus on the not-as-yet-begun scene and then gave it up as a waste of time. There were better ways he could make use of his day until the emotions evoked by Beth's letter faded and he could get back to work. He could explore Rishikesh, do his research, read a novel. He was a writer. Writers needed time to read, time to study, time to explore the world they wrote about. When better than when the writing runs into one of those unavoidable mishaps on the road. It frees the wheel, replenishes the tank. He closed his computer and sat down on the bed with his books on Indology arrayed around him in a tight semicircle. He picked up one and then another, but after a few minutes, he pronounced himself psychologically unfit for any serious work. What he needed was the reprieve of a novel, his best and truest relaxation, a chance to draw some sustenance from the roots that had set him writing in the first place. He remembered the novel he had picked up in Dharamsala and removed it from his trolley bag, where it had lain untouched since he had bought it. It was written by a Tibetan lama and was supposedly the first novel ever written in the Tibetan language. He spent the rest of the morning and most of the afternoon lounging on his bed reading. With the novel's themes of reincarnation, meditation, Buddhist rituals, and the like, it seemed perfectly fitted to his surroundings. In the late afternoon, after the rains stopped, he took a long walk, making it back at dusk for the beginning of the arati.

The following morning, he again found himself unable to stretch his mind past a single sentence. He tried some freewriting to get the language lobes functioning again, but when he returned to his story, he sat there and continued to stare at the chapter heading until it was well on toward lunch. When he called it a day and returned to his Tibetan novel and the prospect of another long walk, he felt even more frustrated than the day before, when he had to some extent felt relieved to have some time off. It reminded him of similar dry spells when he had tried to write during the afternoons he didn't have to teach, but at least on those occasions he had had a steady supply of good excuses at hand. Here he was not so fortunate, unless you considered the dying pangs of a jilted lover's grief to be a good excuse. When the same scene was repeated the next day, he finally took the reluctant but radical step of diagnosing himself with writer's block. This, at least, was something he could deal with, unlike Beth's letter that had arrived like an ICBM from across the sea and then dissolved into smoke after doing its damage. He had a plethora of suggestions at his fingertips on how to overcome writer's block, all neatly assembled in a folder that included his collection of writer's tips, a compendium of inspiring quotes, and PDF copies of books on his chosen craft. The first and most oft-repeated strategy was to take a break: a day, a week, even a month, if necessary, until the juices started flowing again. Much as this appealed to him, he knew he couldn't afford the vacation, not if he wanted to finish his book before his sabbatical was over. Corollary strategies included taking a research break to replenish the well of ideas; a reading break (good novels to inspire you to write better, bad novels to assure yourself that you can do better blindfolded); and a planning break—in essence, giving yourself license for a prolonged daydream until the story begins to revive. The next set of strategies was better suited to his deadline and his history of never quite getting started. They were based on the maxim "writers write; everyone else makes excuses," and included writing with the monitor off; not allowing yourself to do anything else that day until you write a certain number of words, no matter how bad they may seem; writing a letter to yourself about how you are unable to write and how frustrating and depressing that is; forcing yourself to sit at your computer for a certain number of hours, even if nothing comes of it; and writing a two-page list of excuses at the end of any day in which you haven't written. Over the next couple of days, he tried each of these in turn; and at the end of both days, he wrote up his list of excuses for why he hadn't been able to get anywhere with his story. Finally, he went back to his grab bag of suggestions and pulled out one more bit of advice that he had somehow overlooked. "Tension, agitation of mind, and doubt in oneself," it read, "are what prevent a writer from writing. Anything that allows you to clear your mind, free it of tension, and trust in yourself will work. If all else fails, do some yoga, meditate, check into a Zen Buddhist monastery for a few days. I am told this never fails." The irony of where he was when he read this piece of advice did not escape him. He wondered if he could legally substitute an Indian ashram for a Buddhist monastery and then decided it would be okay. It would save him the highly uncomfortable bus ride back to Dharamsala. That evening he asked Bhagavati about the yoga classes, and she, in turn, extended him an invitation to the Swami's forthcoming talk.

Rodrigo reached the yoga hall precisely at seven the next morning. He left his Birkenstocks on the veranda beside an orderly row of assorted sandals and stepped cautiously into a spacious hall with marble floors and a high, concrete ceiling supported by round pillars at seven-meter intervals. A dozen students, none of them Indian, were limbering up on thin foam yoga mats arranged in rows at the front of the hall. He walked over to an empty mat at the back and sat down. At the front, an attractive young blond dressed in white yogi pants and a white long-sleeved blouse was sifting through a small stack of CDs. She selected one and inserted it in a portable CD player. Moments later, the soft strains of a harp and acoustic piano began filtering through the hall. The girl closed her eyes and sat cross-legged facing her students with her hands on her knees, palms upward, the thumb and index finger of each hand curled to form a circle. The rest of the students followed suit. Rodrigo imitated them as best he could, conscious of the fact that his knees were sticking up in the air, unlike nearly everyone else whose knees hugged the ground in more or less perfect meditation posture. After a minute of silence, the girl began to intone om in a stately, gravelly vibrato while the rest of the class joined in. The sound they made reverberated in the mostly empty hall for a full thirty seconds before it faded and died out. After a few seconds of silence, she began again, and then a third time. Rodrigo felt the chant not only in his throat and chest but throughout his body as the low-pitched drone reflected off the hard, unadorned walls and filled the room with its almost tactile presence. The sensation was strange but not at all unpleasant. She followed the oms with a short Sanskrit verse that most of the other students recited along with her. Then she brought her folded palms to her chest and opened her eyes. Once again he was greeted with an American accent.

"Namaste. Good morning. We'll start today with some *surya namaskar*, sun salutation, to get the *prana* flowing and generate some heat in our bodies. Everyone to their feet—*tadasana*, mountain pose. Feet together, hands by your side, fingers open, spine perfectly erect. Fix your gaze directly in front of you at a single point. Now, without letting your gaze waver, bring your attention to the soles of your feet. Feel them planted firmly on the surface of the earth, as solid as the base of a mountain ... Now feel your center of equilibrium passing in an axis from the soles of your feet to the crown of your head. Lengthen your spinal column, your head reaching for the sky, your feet sinking into the earth ... Now direct your attention to your skin. Your skin is alive, intelligent, infinitely perceptive. Through your skin, you are aware of every centimeter of your body. Through your skin, you are able to feel your body occupying the space around it ... Now direct your attention inward. Feel the space within you, as your body lengthens and opens, starting from the center of your being and reaching outward toward the Infinite. Inhale, bring your hands upward, palms together .... "

She started leading the class in some measured but vigorous repetitions of the sun salutation. Rodrigo had found the opening chant calming, almost mystically suggestive, but by the third repetition of the sun salutation, he was starting to sweat profusely as he tried the best he could to follow the challenging sequence of postures. It was early and not yet particularly hot, but there was little air circulation in the room, despite the open windows and doors. He noticed that the few ceiling fans were switched off. After the first repetition, the instructor began walking around the room, correcting people's posture.

"Extend and expand," she intoned cheerfully as she passed from one student to another. "You are an expanding being. Open up space in your body. Space brings freedom. Allow your energy to flow."

When she got to Rodrigo, she guided him with her hands through the entire sequence while still continuing to call out the movements for the rest of the class.

"Shoulders down ... more, more."

She leaned over him and pushed his shoulders down, aligning his arms and back in the downward-facing dog, forcing his musculature into a position he was sure it had not been designed for. He let out a muffled grunt of pain as his shoulders and legs began to burn as they had never burned before.

"Don't run from the pain. It is there to teach us. Embrace it. Let the pain teach you tenacity and perseverance."

Finally she took her hands off him and moved on to the next student. He came out of the posture like a drowning man reaching for a life-giving breath.

"Relax, people, relax. Remember, asana is the practice of achieving perfect calm in your body, mind, and spirit. Relax your body as you hold the posture and let the serenity of your soul shine through. Relax your tongue, relax your neck, brea-ea-the … Okay, next repetition."

Relax! How did she expect him to relax when his body was on fire? What was that she said—be one with the burn? What the hell did that mean? He glanced over at the person nearest him, a thin, limber girl with short black hair and slightly Asian features. She smiled at him, a buxom grin that could have been either sympathy or laughter. He returned a grimace that he hoped would pass for a smile and launched into the next repetition.

The practice continued for an hour but it felt more like two. The girl's voice hounded him from one posture to the other, commanding him to perceive with his skin, think with his heart, and see from behind his temples, but all he could think about, in between furtive glances at his watch, was somehow making it to the end of the class. When she announced that they had come to the final posture, he felt a surge of relief that bordered on pure, unmitigated joy. The thought that he would never have to put himself through this again felt like a soothing balm to his aching muscles.

The class ended with five minutes of silent meditation and three more oms. Rodrigo was as worn out mentally from the practice as he was physically. He spent those five minutes massaging his legs and wondering how yoga had ever gotten the reputation that it was relaxing and calming. After the oms, he lay down for a couple of minutes and stared at the ceiling. He noticed the Sanskrit writing that ran in a circuit around the room at the top of the hall and mentally compared it to the Tibetan script he had seen in Dharamsala. By the time he got up, folded his mat, and left it in a corner with the others, the instructor was in the doorway, saying goodbye to the last of her students.

"I hope you didn't find it too difficult," she said when he reached the veranda and began slipping on his sandals. "Was this your first time?"

"No, not exactly."

"Second time?"

"More or less."

"I thought so. My name's Amrita." She shifted the CD player to the arm that was cradling her yoga mat and extended a hand.

"Rodrigo."

"So how did you like the class?"

"To be honest, I found it pretty challenging. I was expecting something … I don't know, a little more relaxing?"

Amrita laughed softly as they started walking in the direction of the main compound. Her husky voice seemed to fit perfectly with her lightly freckled skin and the dirty blond hair that hung loosely over her shoulders.

"There are many different styles of yoga. Each has its own approach, its own philosophy. The style I teach is mostly Iyengar. I don't suppose you're familiar with Iyengar?"

"No.

Amrita was walking at a leisurely pace, as if she had nowhere in particular to go, so much so that Rodrigo had to make a conscious effort to curb his urge to speed up.

"Iyengar is a yoga master from South India. He's all about challenging his students—among other things. The idea is that if you don't push yourself, you'll never be able to get past your limitations. One of the great things about this practice is that it brings you face to face with your own resistance, right off the bat. The challenge is to push through. Once you do, you realize that what was stopping you was not your body, it was your mind."

Amrita halted, as if to emphasize the importance of what was coming next.

"What really stops us is that voice in our head that tells us we can't do it—it's too hard, it hurts, when is it going to stop?" As she said this, she made her voice sound like that of a whining child. Rodrigo couldn't help but find it comical.

"I'll bet you heard that voice during the class. Admit it."

"Well, maybe a little."

Amrita raised an eyebrow.

"Or more than a little."

"You see?" She resumed walking at the same leisurely pace. "So the idea is that you push yourself, or I push you, until you break through and realize that it is your own thoughts that are holding you back. You're not that old, you know. You should be able to do these postures without any problem; all they require is a little practice and a bit of determination. But your mind's getting in the way. I can tell. The next step, once you learn to push through, is to train your powers of attention. As long as your mind is agitated, you'll never attain perfect relaxation in the posture. You can't divorce your body from your mind, or your mind from your spirit. Fortunately, it works both ways. If you can train yourself to keep your body firm and still and relaxed, then your mind automatically becomes calm. The practice begins with the body but in the end it's all about the mind. You're not a vegetarian, are you?"

"No, not really," Rodrigo said, surprised by the question. "What makes you ask?"

"Just the obvious. Your joints are really stiff, for one. Meat is really acidic. It causes a buildup of uric acid in the blood and that leads to mineral deposits in the joints. Meat eaters lose their natural flexibility while they're young, something that doesn't happen with vegetarians. There are some other things I noticed as well. Of course, you don't have to be a vegetarian to practice yoga, but it helps. Anyhow, as long as you're in Rishikesh, you're a vegetarian."

"Come again."

"You do know that Rishikesh is vegetarian by law?"

"Now that you mention it, I do remember reading that in my *Lonely Planet*."

"It's the only municipality in the world I know of that doesn't allow non-vegetarian food. Plenty of great restaurants and every one is vegetarian. Yogi paradise." She let out a low, tinkling laugh. "How long are you planning on staying?"

"At least a month, maybe two."

"Wonderful. You'll feel the difference, I promise you. Especially if you keep coming to yoga class. Judging by what I saw today, you really need it. Same time every morning, except Sundays."

Amrita turned off for her room just before they reached the main courtyard. Rodrigo returned her over-the-shoulder wave and headed for the dining hall. He had no intention of taking her class again. He was looking for some way to relax so he could start writing again, and her class was anything but relaxing. It had been a good workout, though—that he had to admit—as good as he'd had in a long time. He could use some form of exercise, and he doubted he would find a gym or an aerobics class in the yoga capital of the world. If he did go back, though, it wouldn't be on a regular basis. Once or twice a week was about all he could take. Either that or find a yoga class in one of the other ashrams that was a little less challenging. It didn't hurt to have such an attractive teacher, though. That was one way to distract yourself from the pain. And this one seemed interesting, despite all the mumbo jumbo—be one with the burn, think with your heart—but definitely someone better enjoyed in small doses. One of those women who is sure she knows what's best for you and is not shy about telling you so—like someone else he knew. At least Amrita didn't seem to take herself so seriously.

One yoga class, however, was not enough to liberate Rodrigo from his writer's block. He did feel a little less agitated, perhaps because he was worn out from the practice, a little less preoccupied with his ex-wife, but he still could not get untracked when he sat down in front of his computer after breakfast. He tried following Flannery O'Conner's advice of sitting at his desk for a fixed number of hours, even if nothing came of it. Nothing did. By mid-afternoon, he had managed to write seven different versions of a single paragraph, none of which he saw any reason to keep. Each of them took the story in a somewhat different direction, and the only thing they had in common, other than being torturously difficult to write, was that the direction somehow felt wrong. The only positive was that he didn't feel any discomfort in his back, which he usually felt after sitting for a long period of time. He counted at least seventeen places where he could feel aches of one magnitude or another but his lower back was not one of them. He knew those aches would be even more acute the following day but they were the right kind of ache, the kind that comes from exercising muscles that have been neglected for so long, atrophy has begun to set in. Yoga did have its benefits, he decided, even if peace and harmony were not among them.

He went to bed earlier than usual that night. When he woke up the next morning, shortly after dawn, he was in the midst of another remarkably vivid dream. He rushed to the bathroom to relieve himself, trying to hold on to the images still fresh in his mind, afraid they might slip away with a moment's inattention, and then went to his computer and started typing at a furious pace.

Rishikesh
8/19
6:15 AM

What a dream I just had! It was so intense it feels like it is still going on, as if I can't quite differentiate which is real: this room where I am writing, or the room that I was dreaming. Both feel real in ways I can't quite define. But the dream world, at this moment, seems so much more vivid than my actual surroundings. I can feel its allure commandeering my attention, whereas this room—and I guess, by extension, my life—seems drab and uninviting by comparison. Once again I was dreaming that I was a Hindu priest (an interesting disguise). The last thing I remember was sitting on a bed, my bed. It was more of a cot really, a hard wooden cot with a thin mattress in a small, dimly lit room that served as my bedroom. I was frustrated, tense, mad at the world, mad at my fate, but mostly mad at certain people. Does this sound familiar? There were some books lying on the bed in front of me. One of them was open—I had been reading from it—and there were some more books in a small bookcase. I seem to remember a small altar by the head of the bed with an idol on it. I was complaining to the goddess about these narrow-minded people who were forever standing in my way and doing their best to make my life miserable. I was furious, actually, like I haven't been in real life for a long time, if ever. It was a long dream, I don't remember all of it, but earlier I had been sitting in a larger room at a table with a group of old men. I think they were also priests—rather, I'm sure they were. They were the temple elders, or something of that ilk. They had called me there to reprimand me for not following temple protocol, not maintaining the temple traditions like I was supposed to. I remember I had to sit there and listen to them without opening my mouth while they lectured me like wise old scions giving sage instruction to some wayward young disciple who was still wet behind the ears. So condescending, so smug, so totally unaware of what fools they were. At least that was how I thought of them. The more they talked, the more outraged I became at their ignorance, but I couldn't show it. My position in the temple wouldn't allow it. When they finished their admonitions, I tried to argue my point of view but they wouldn't listen. Like I said, smug and crotchety. That, I think, is when I left and went back to my room. Or else they dismissed me, more likely. So I sat on my bed complaining bitterly to the goddess, venting my frustration to the one being who could understand me. Was the book some sort of scripture that I was reciting to calm my mind? I think it was. Anyhow, strange as it seems, I'm pretty sure I was talking out loud to her. What's more, I knew she was listening. It was like she was there in the room with me. Not the idol exactly, but the living presence that the idol represented. Even when I wasn't talking out loud, I was sure she could hear me, sure that she could hear my thoughts. To me she was a real being, not in any way a figment of some religious imagination. I was utterly convinced that she could help me, like some kind of powerful, righteous mother figure who could get back at my enemies if she took up my case. Strange that I would once again dream something so out of character. It might have something to do with these books I'm reading.

Anyhow, that is about as much as I can remember. It reminds me, though, of a recurring dream I had when I was maybe eight or nine. I kept dreaming I was Superman, flying around saving people. I don't remember how long it went on for, but it could have been a month or two—two or three times a week, maybe. Of course, I had a collection of Superman comics, and I had probably just seen the movie—the first one, with Brando, long before Christopher Reeves had his accident. It's the only other time I can remember dreaming repeatedly that I was someone else. I wonder if this is a side effect of the writing? (Leave aside the fact that I haven't actually written anything for a full week now.) Is this how a novelist dreams? In scenes with a central character? Maybe not, but I suspect the writing does have a role to play. The frustration is easy enough to explain. I haven't been able to write, and my subconscious mind is understandably mad at whatever is holding me back and blocking me from accomplishing what I was put on this earth to accomplish. Beth, her renewed rejection and her lingering criticisms? Undoubtedly. She fits nicely into the role of an old priest afraid to admit anything new into her temple. But I suspect it's not only Beth that my subconscious is railing at. My conscious self is also a likely target. Just look at the role I played in the demise of our relationship and the fact that I still haven't gotten over my grief after all this time and have let it affect my writing. After all, it's been months since I've seen her and a week since I got her letter. Enough is enough! If I were my subconscious, I'd be frustrated too. And then there's the university. All the stuff I had to put up with: the conservatism, the hidebound and often downright stupid administrative policy, the "elders" who cared a whole lot more about keeping their comfortable jobs than actually educating anyone. Definitely a traditional temple, not at all the kind of place for a living, breathing artist. Much too suffocating. In the end, though, I think the dream is mostly about my general frustrations as a writer, the writer's block, my worries over whether I'll ever become the writer I long to be—though I can't leave Beth out of the equation. I wouldn't be in the situation I'm in today if it weren't for her letter. Funny how our dreams take our worries and our aspirations and weave them into an entirely new story. It's very much like literature. You have to face your own stuff in your dreams and deal with it, except that now you're somebody else all together in a fictional setting that often has no connection with your daily reality. But, of course, you are not somebody else. You're you and it's your stuff. What the imagination does is give you another platform on which to work things out. Real life, by comparison, seems rather stingy in this regard. Literature does the same thing, which makes sense because it's the same imagination at work. Whether you're the reader or the writer, it's still you in the guise of the characters (through the process of reader or writer identification), dealing with your own fears and inhibitions and challenges and whatnot. It is interesting also how the practice of keeping a dream journal sharpens your recall. When I first started keeping it, I could only remember small fragments. Now I can remember whole dreams, or at least huge chunks of them, not to mention the fact that the vividness and immediacy of my dreams has been on the upswing ever since I started writing them down. Which only brings me into more direct contact with the demons that are hiding out in my subconscious.

It occurs to me now that this dream may also be a sign that my imagination is getting ready to break loose again and start writing. Vent, get it out of your system, and then get back to work. That may be what's happening here, and if so, then my subconscious might as well play its part. So damn Beth and her letter, her divorce, her new husband, and all of it. I might as well come right out and blame her and her letter for my block. I won't complain to the goddess like the priest in my dream and summon hellfire down on my enemies, but it's the same "damn, damn, damn her." Feels good, now that I've said it, nice and cathartic. I hope it works. We'll have to wait till afternoon to see, however. The pujya swami is giving his talk this morning and I promised Bhagavati I would go. It wouldn't look good if I didn't show up, and it will probably give me something I can use in the book. I'm assuming he won't mind if I take notes. Let's see if Venus wakes up and starts transiting again after lunch. I hope she's had a good nap, she and my sleepy-eyed muse.

Rodrigo showed up at the office at nine thirty as agreed upon. From there, Bhagavati escorted him into a small private inner courtyard where a group of middle-aged Western women were sitting on blankets on the lawn in front of a fountain formed of small boulders and surrounded by flower beds. They reminded him of a knitting circle or a group of housewives getting together for their weekly book club, but even then they didn't seem out of place.

"This is the group I told you about," Bhagavati said, as she led him in. "They're from Argentina. I'll just go and tell Swamiji that we're ready for him."

The women greeted him with friendly smiles, seemingly as comfortable as they might have been in their own living rooms. One of them unfolded her blanket and motioned for him to sit down. The woman just in front of her turned around and extended her hand.

"I'm Lara. I'm the translator. A couple of the girls speak a little English but not enough to follow the swami's talk. Are you also staying at the ashram?"

"Yes, I've been here for almost two weeks now."

"It's beautiful, isn't it? We're going to be here for a week, and then we'll be going to Benares...."

Bhagavati returned with the swami and the conversations ceased. She placed a folded blanket on the ground in front of the fountain for him to sit on and then introduced him to the group.

"Namaste. On behalf of everyone I want to thank Swamiji for being so kind as to spend some time with us this morning."

The swami bowed his head slightly and folded his hands to his chest.

"As you may know, being the head of the ashram, Swamiji has many duties that take him all over the world. Last week, he met with the ambassador from China, and next month he will be addressing the United Nations. While he is in New York, he will also be receiving the Mahatma Gandhi Humanitarian Award in recognition of his charitable work. Yet Swamiji always tells us that no matter how many awards he might receive, or how many dignitaries come to see him, there is nothing he enjoys more than sitting with a group of simple devotees and talking of God. It is where he feels most at home. So let us then enjoy our chance to sit with Swamiji and talk of the Lord."

"Thank you, Bhagavati. Please, sit."

It was the closest Rodrigo had been to the swami since arriving at the ashram. He had listened to him almost every evening leading the arati, and on one of those occasions the swami had given a brief talk afterward thanking one of the ashram's benefactors for a recent, generous donation, but it was his first chance to observe him at close quarters in the daylight. Tall and robust, the swami had the same beaming smile on his face now that Rodrigo saw each evening during the devotional singing, the same smile that stared out at him from the picture that he passed each time he made his way to the guest dining hall. He was dressed in the thin saffron robes that he always wore, with an orange shawl draped around his shoulders and a single strand of prayer beads strung around his neck. Now, as before, Rodrigo had difficulty judging his age, despite being only a couple of paces away. He had the exuberant vitality and healthy skin of a man in his late thirties or early forties, but the white streaks around his temples and in his thick bushy beard, and the aura he exuded of having lived and seen much more than other men, made Rodrigo suspect that he was a good deal older than he looked.

What was most striking, however, was the air of happy serenity that shone forth from his rugged but handsome features.

When Bhagavati had taken her seat, the swami folded his hands again.

"I am very happy to see you all. Welcome to Mother India and welcome to the ashram. Bhagavati has told me that you are interested in learning more about Hinduism while you are here, so why don't I say a few words about Hinduism and then I can take your questions. Is that okay?"

Lara translated quickly and effortlessly, allowing the swami to speak naturally, with only a short pause between sentences. When she translated his question, the rest of the women nodded or said, "*si, si.*" The swami smiled and tilted his head from side to side a couple of times in the graceful Indian gesture that, as Rodrigo had discovered, lay somewhere between a Western nod yes and a shake no, and could mean either depending on context, and many other things as well.

"*Accha.* Let me start by saying that the word 'Hinduism' was coined by the British to refer to the religion of the Hindus. We ourselves prefer the words 'Sanatana Dharma,' which is the original name for the spiritual traditions of this land. *Sanatana* means 'eternal' and *dharma* literally means 'one's true nature,' but here it refers to spirituality or religion. In other words, the way or the path. So we can translate 'Sanatana Dharma' into English as 'the eternal way' or 'the eternal path.' Of course, we also use the word 'Hinduism' for convenience, but only when speaking English. The words 'Sanatana Dharma' are much more accurate. There are many sects and many religious institutions in India—this ashram, for instance—just as there are outside of India, but there is only one eternal path."

The swami lifted his hand as he spoke these last words to emphasize his point and paused as he glanced earnestly from face to face. Then he continued in his confident basso voice.

"This path existed before there was any India, and it will remain after India is no more. Gravity did not come into existence when human beings discovered it. It existed before we knew about it, and it will continue to exist even when we are no longer here. In the same way, the spiritual laws that govern the universe are eternal and unchanging. Sects and institutions come and go. Great spiritual teachers also come and go. But the spiritual truths they teach do not change, whether you are from South America or from India, whether you are living now or lived thousands of years ago in the time of Shiva or Krishna. What we call Sanatana Dharma, then, is nothing more than the collective endeavor of the human race to seek that divine truth and bring our life into harmony with it. For this reason, you cannot say when Hinduism began. It has no beginning. You cannot center it around any one saint or avatar. There are many saints and avatars and they all belong to the same eternal way. It cannot be limited to any particular group of people or particular scripture or particular religious personality. If it could, then it would not be eternal. It would not be *sanatana.*

"So this is the first and foremost teaching of Sanatana Dharma. There is only one universal truth, one universal spirit, a uni-verse—one song, beginningless and endless. Anyone who sincerely seeks to know that Divine Spirit follows the

Sanatana Dharma, whether they come from Buenos Aires or from a small village in the Himalayas. If you want to understand Hinduism, then you must first understand this.

"There is a verse from the most ancient of our scriptures, the Rig-Veda. No one knows how old it is, but our anthropologists place it anywhere from twelve to fifteen thousand years back. It is so old that the language is not even Sanskrit but a form of Old Vedic."

The swami raised one hand, palm upward, and intoned a long Sanskrit verse with his eyes closed, a solemn, in-drawn expression on his face. When he opened his eyes, he flashed a bright smile, his countenance changing from solemn to playful.

"I will try to translate it for you. Please forgive me if I cannot do justice to the original."

The swami spoke slowly now, half chanting, half speaking, looking at Lara and waiting for her to finish each phrase before moving on to the next.

"There was neither death nor immortality then. No signs were there of day and night. The One was breathing by its own power, in infinite peace. Only the One was. There was nothing beyond. Darkness was hidden in darkness. The All was fluid and formless. Therein, in the void, by the fire of fervor arose the One. And in the One arose love. Love is the first seed of the soul. The truth of this the sages found in their hearts. Seeking in their hearts with wisdom, the sages found that bond of union between Being and Non-Being."

After finishing, the swami nodded his head slowly and carefully scanned his audience.

"Just see. The Rig-Veda is the oldest surviving record of human thought. The oldest book of the world's oldest culture. One hundred and fifty centuries old, if we accept the word of our modern-day historians. And even then, there were sages in this land who intuited the existence of the Supreme Spirit, the 'One' as they called it in this verse. They saw the Eternal Spirit in their own souls and perceived the truth that the creation arises out of love. But now, listen to the next verse."

Again the swami slowed his speech and began intoning the words in a measured cadence, waiting for Lara to finish before moving on to the next line.

"Who knows the truth? Who can tell whence and how arose this universe? The gods are later than its beginning. Who knows therefore whence comes this creation? Only that god who sees in the highest heaven; he only knows whence came this universe, and whether it was made or uncreated. He only knows, or perhaps he knows not."

The swami laughed softly. "You see? They found themselves face to face with a mystery. How does the One become the many? Who can possibly answer this? The seed of creation is beyond the mind. How can the mind know the source of its own creation?"

The swami looked around as if he were asking a simple question and waiting for an answer from his pupils. The women looked at one another, but mostly at the translator, who looked at the swami, smiled, and shook her head.

"The whole of our Hinduism, the whole of our Sanatana Dharma, its fifteen thousand years of history, is one long endeavor to answer this question and the others that naturally arise out of it. What is the spiritual nature of the universe? Who or what is that Spirit from which all arises? What is our relationship to that Cosmic Spirit? And, most important of all, how can we discover the truth of who we are? We Hindus have made this the focus of our culture for fifteen millennia. The answers to these questions and an unbroken lineage of saints and sages who have embodied those divine truths are India's true heritage and her greatest gift to the world.

"So we begin there. What is Hinduism? It is fifteen thousand years of one culture's search for the truth: What is this universe and who is this human being who looks out on it and wonders?"

The swami fell silent, looking, as he sat cross-legged on his blanket, like one of those ancient sages he had just finished talking about, serene yet intensely present. After a minute of silence, Bhagavati asked him if he would take some questions. He nodded and several hands went up. The swami motioned toward one of the women and Lara translated.

"Could you please talk about the meaning of the arati?"

The swami nodded, as if he were expecting the question.

"There is a verse from the *Brihadaranyaka Upanishad* that we chant before we begin the arati proper. We chant it in Sanskrit, of course, but in English it goes like this: 'From delusion lead us to truth. From darkness lead us to light. From death lead us to immortality.'"

Several of the women nodded, obviously familiar with the verse.

"In this verse, we ask the Supreme Being to guide us to the truth. We ask for his guidance because we know that on our own we will never be able to reach there. We are walking in darkness, the darkness of spiritual ignorance, unable to see where we are going. Knowing this, we ask the Supreme Lord to shine his light in that darkness, so that we can find our way to him who is the truth and the light. The arati, then, is a ritual in which we act out this prayer in a spirit of reverence and surrender. We wave our small little light in unbroken circles, symbolizing the unbroken cycle of creation, and then we offer our little light to him who is the source of all light, the eternal One who is beyond all seeing and who guides us on our way. We offer the light of our little lamp to whatever manifestation of the Supreme we choose. Thousands of years ago our sages realized that everything in this universe is a manifestation of one eternal consciousness. The One has become the many, but the many does not cease to be the One. Or rather, the many is not separate from the One, just as the waves of the ocean are not separate from the ocean. The One has become this river, which flows from the mountains to the sea and passes by this ashram. So the sages honored this river as sacred, because all things are sacred. They called her 'Ganga Ma,' the Mother Ganges, the goddess who carries our boats and gives us the water without which we cannot live. So when we offer our arati here in the ashram, we offer it to Ganga Ma, knowing that we are offering our light to the Supreme Giver of all light in the form of the

Mother Ganges. You can offer arati to whatever aspect of the Divine you wish, whether it be a god or a goddess, a saint or a guru, or an avatar, such as Krishna or Rama. Either way, it is the same. What is important is that you light the lamp of love in your heart and offer it to the Lord who dwells within you, praying with all sincerity for him to lead you home. From delusion to truth. From darkness to light. From death to immortality."

As the swami intoned the verse in English, an image flashed in Rodrigo's mind of the devotees swaying in their devotional fervor and afterward walking reverently down to the edge of the flowing water to float a flower or a small leaf lamp on the river and watch the current take it, their heads bowed and their hands folded to their chest. At that moment, a similar image interposed itself: other pilgrims at other rivers, thousands of years ago, repeating the same gestures. What were the words the swami used? An unbroken lineage? For a moment or two, he could feel the depth of their reverence and their yearning. It astounded him to think that the same human urge had been alive since the beginning of human memory, burning like a flame that could not be put out.

Another woman wanted to know what the relationship was between Hinduism and yoga.

"The essence of spiritual endeavor lies in the answer to a single question: How can a human being know the Supreme Truth? Not through the mind, obviously, because the Supreme Spirit is beyond the mind. The mind cannot know its creator any more than the person you dream of can know the dreamer. There is a verse in the *Kenopanishad*: 'What cannot be thought with the mind but that whereby the mind thinks, know that to be Brahman, the spirit, and not what people here adore; what cannot be seen with the eye, but that whereby the eye can see, know that to be Brahman, the spirit, and not what people here adore.' So what is the answer to that question? The answer is that the mind must be brought to perfect stillness. It must become like a lantern without wind, perfectly calm. In the Gita, it is said that when thought resides in quietness, then by the self one sees the soul. Yoga is the discipline by which you learn to bring your mind to perfect stillness. When you can achieve this, you will perceive the Supreme Spirit out of which the creation arises. So how then did those ancient sages discover the hidden truths of the universe? By peering into the depths of their own being, which can only be done when one attains perfect control over body and mind. The discipline that enabled them to attain this self-mastery is called 'yoga.' Yoga means 'union,' union with the Divine. It refers to the discipline developed by those ancient Hindu sages to achieve this spiritual union or spiritual perfection. Anyone can practice yoga, even an atheist, though I very much doubt he can remain an atheist if he does. People of every religion practice yoga nowadays and many people who do not subscribe to any organized religion. However, since this practice was developed by those ancient Hindu sages, there is a special connection between Hinduism and yoga. You can say that yoga is the soul of Hinduism, but really yoga is the soul of all spirituality. It is the supreme achievement of the human race."

Rodrigo raised his hand, bothered by this last statement, which sounded a little too chauvinistic for his taste. When the swami nodded in his direction, he worded his objection as cautiously as he could.

"But what about people who don't practice yoga? Can't someone who doesn't practice yoga be just as spiritual in his own way, as for instance people from other cultures with different beliefs, different practices?"

"Good question. I would say there are two answers. Yes and no. Yes, because anyone who loves God and makes a sincere effort to lessen the proximity between him and the Lord is a spiritual person. And that is a kind of yoga—bhakti yoga, the yoga of devotion. However, on the highest level the answer becomes no, because in order to realize the highest truth, you must attain perfect mastery over your mind. There is no other way. You must learn to close your eyes and still your thoughts if you wish to see the Divine. And that is yoga, whether you stumble upon it on your own or learn it at the feet of an Indian sage. There is a reason why seekers have been coming to India for thousands of years in search of spirituality. It is because the spiritual tradition on our planet began in this land. While the influence of yoga and Indian spirituality has been felt all over the world for many, many centuries now—whether people are aware of it or not—it is still here that the tradition is maintained in its purest form. Thousands of years ago, people came in caravans to India in search of its sages; now they travel in airplanes, but still they come. All of you have come here for this same reason. You are spiritual seekers. You want to drink from the fountain at its source, where the water is purest. Of course, some of you may not know that this is why you have come."

The swami paused and looked directly at Rodrigo as he said this, smiling and lifting his eyebrows, his intent so obvious that everyone turned and glanced at him.

"At least not yet. But that doesn't matter. You will. It is not a matter of if, but only of when. Remember what I said at the outset: we are all walking the same path, the Sanatana Dharma. The only difference is that some of us are still asleep, some are waking up, and a very few are wide-awake. When it is time for you to start waking up, that is when you go looking for yoga. That is when you begin to realize that it is your own mind that stands between you and the truth, and that without finding a way to attain mastery over your mind, you cannot reach the truth. That path we call yoga."

Rodrigo nodded and thanked the swami for his answer, trying to keep the discord he felt from appearing on his face. The unequivocal pronouncements of religion had always struck a discordant note in his mind, which had been trained by literature to distrust in absolutes. If pushed to it, he probably would have said that the pursuit of artistic truth was the first and highest of his goals, but if asked to explain what he meant by artistic truth, he would have had to admit that the words themselves were a paradox, for in his estimation the true task of art was to extract meaning from the mystery of living while knowing that all such endeavors were ultimately doomed to end in a question mark. The swami had no such problem. He exuded absolute certainty when he spoke. He did not leave any open doors to the uncertainty that seemed to haunt even the greatest of artists, the uncertainty that for Rodrigo was an inescapable part of living. It was that certainty that bothered him most, more even than the unfounded insinuation that he had come to India in search of its sages and its wisdom. The certainty that no one can realize the truth without practicing some form of yoga to still the mind. The certainty that all existence arises from a Divine Consciousness and that the goal of human life is to realize that Consciousness. How could anyone ever be so certain and at the same time be sure that it was not just another form of blindness? Had the swami himself not said that the mind cannot know what is beyond it? Who or what was speaking those words, if not his mind? Did the swami believe and not know that he believed, or was there something that Rodrigo was missing?

Afterward, Rodrigo accompanied the women to the dining hall where they chatted as they ate. He pretended to share their enthusiasm over the talk, but all through lunch the swami's tranquil certainty continued to stir the turbulent waters of his mind. He had never lived with such a conviction, but he suspected that it must be a powerful intoxicant. Why else did religion still hold such a sway over the human imagination? But a lingering doubt continued to assail him. Was there something there that he was missing? In a mind raised on doubts and the need to question all that society taught, it was hard to get past this one question mark. What if? What if, despite the lack of visible evidence, that certainty came from a source that had nothing to do with belief?

7

Contrary to what he was hoping, Rodrigo's dream did not herald the freeing of his literary genie. He tried to work on the novel in the afternoon, but the results of his endeavors only made his frustrations mount. Adhering faithfully, almost religiously, to the adage that a writer writes, he sat at his computer and forced himself to place one word after the other. Though he stalled over and over again in the middle of sentences, the words accumulated in fits and starts, crawling down the backlit screen like a swarm of ants trying to sludge their way through a pool of honey. The metaphor stuck with him, for when the ideas did come, they seemed to ooze out of his mind covered in a thick syrup of mental lethargy. Somehow, by the end of the day, he had managed to elaborate a short scene in which Le Gentil went for a walk to acquaint himself with the French areas of Pondicherry, his curiosity about the natives and their living conditions piqued by the relative luxury and isolation in which the citizens of the French crown lived. Mentally exhausted by his efforts, Rodrigo went back and reread what he had written. When he was done, he almost wished he hadn't. The words felt awkward and lifeless; the scene rambled and ended up nowhere in particular. "Gratuitous" was the word that came to mind. Had he really wasted nearly three hours of his life apparently trying to prove to himself that he couldn't write? A computer-generated text would have appeared no less dead on the page. Disgusted, he copied it to his scrap heap, that mountain of false starts, scene fragments, and exercises that he knew were of no value but which he couldn't bear to completely erase. Then he tried to put it out of his mind as he got ready to go to arati, telling himself that he would do better tomorrow, a mental pat on the back whose insincerity he well recognized.

The next morning, he rescued the scene from his scrap heap and spent a couple of hours trying to revise it, still hopeful that it might have some value that he had overlooked in his frustration and his self-pity. But no, it was clearly worthless, so he retired it permanently to the land of eternal exile and began a new scene wherein Le Gentil would get acquainted with some of the other prominent French citizens living in Pondicherry. Through them, he would learn about the affairs of the realm and the squalid conditions of the natives. The writing proved no easier.

He grew more and more tense as the day went on, struggling with his inability to harness the wild horses of his thoughts, which insisted on dragging him away into purposeless daydreams or bitter lamentations about his failed marriage. He got up at intervals to pace the room or nibble on the snack food he had stocked up on from the small shops outside the ashram, seeking in this way to discharge his nervous tension and free his thoughts to find their way back into the story, but at best they would reel a few drunken paces before coming to a slow and lifeless halt. When the afternoon waned, he gathered his courage and forced himself to read the scene, knowing full well what he would find there. If anything, it was worse than what he had written the day before. Again it went to the scrap heap and again he went to the arati feeling depressed, latching on to the energy of the singers like a shipwrecked sailor to the side of a lifeboat.

Rodrigo had been a professor of literature too long not to recognize bad writing when he saw it. That night, as he lay in his bed, he pondered the necessity of a new course of action. His confidence had eroded too far, he decided, to subject it to another day like the previous two. Already he had begun to admit suspicions that he might not have what it took: the talent, the discipline, the calling. He could not allow himself to go down that road. Without a firm belief in himself, a belief he had never lacked, even though he had nothing objective to base it on, he might as well give up and go back to being a literature professor who had once hoped to be a writer. Sometimes it was better not to tempt one's fate, especially when he might well be teetering on the edge of something far more serious than he realized. After all, some of the best writers had found it prudent to take time off when they were blocked, rather than feed their frustrations and waste hours that could be put to better use. Writers write, no doubt, but they also need time off like everyone else. As great a writer as Tolstoy, who would sometimes be blocked for months at a time, had packed his bags and taken a vacation when he found his writing stalled. Rodrigo's time might be limited, but he was not going to risk a serious setback to his career for the sake of an imaginary deadline. At the very least, he would take a few days off to see if it helped. In the meantime, he would read and walk. He would explore Rishikesh and study his books on Indian culture and beliefs. Give his mind a vacation from itself and then hopefully come back to it fresh.

A couple of mornings later, Rodrigo took his books to the shade of a pipal tree in a secluded courtyard near the rear of the ashram. He had not opened his computer for two days. As he had hoped, he was starting to feel a little better, if not about his life then at least about his writing. After all, how could he be expected to tap his creative powers when he was still dealing with the breakup of his marriage? Beth's letter was the final chapter in a long and difficult odyssey, but it was almost over now. All he had to do was get through the epilogue. Once he did, he was sure to get back into a productive flow. In the meantime, he was doing his much-needed research, delving into the colorful oddities of Hindu culture. He had finished his book on Indian goddesses the day before and bought another one dedicated to Kali. The more he read about her, the more familiar she seemed, and the more the blurred edges of his dreams seemed to sharpen and come into focus. The question that most intrigued him about this mistress of the cremation grounds was why human beings would invent a goddess of death and destruction in the first place—terrible to look upon and even more terrible to think about—and then worship her. What would make them feel so drawn to the night and the terror that hides behind it? What peculiar fascination the shadow side of life held over the human imagination! But then he looked at his own life and it became easy to see why he had been drawn to her, rather than to any of the other gods or goddesses he had read about. She fit his prevailing mood perfectly. Only someone who has not been scarred by life could fail to recognize the terror hiding behind the painted smiles we wear. Behind our health, sickness lies in wait; behind youth, old age, then infirmity and death—if death does not catch you tomorrow around a corner you have walked every day of your life without ever once thinking what might be lurking there. Death, destruction, the annihilation of everything we hold dear and cling to in the hope that we can steer clear of the storm. This is the precarious reality of human existence. Only someone fast asleep could fail to see it.

This, then, must have been what his subconscious had been trying to tell him. Though he might not remember where he had seen or read about Kali, he knew that dreams didn't lie. They might dissimulate, but only in the manner of a playwright inventing a drama in order to imbue his very real convictions and feelings with a power that mere telling could never hope to convey. It occurred to him that the ancient Hindus might have propitiated the goddess as a way to deal with their fears without having to directly confront them or acknowledge them for what they really were. Perhaps this was the mythic imagination at work. You unearth your deepest fears and aspirations and fashion them out of clay into an external image that you can venerate or placate or beg for favors. Maybe in this way our fears become easier to understand, or at least to keep at bay. Imagine a graphic image of your fears sitting on an altar staring at you when you wake up in the morning, getting ready to leap into your dreams when you go to bed at night, a kind of primitive psychoanalysis where the idol reflects back at you what you would almost certainly avoid looking at otherwise. He could not see himself running off to find a Kali temple to see if a few flowers or lemons and chilies could help him understand why his life seemed to be falling apart, but he couldn't fault his dreaming self for trying. He certainly needed something.

Rodrigo leaned back against the tree, picked up his notebook, and began jotting down some of his thoughts. There must be some way he could work Kali into the book. One possibility was to have her be Ambika's family deity. Another would be for Ambika to bring Le Gentil to a Kali temple and introduce him to the temple priest. Either way, he could take parts of his dream and insert them directly into the narrative. Ambika at home performing her private worship. The camera pulls in. We see her thoughts, her fears, the hopes that she places before the Dark Mother's feet. We listen in as she begs the goddess for an answer to her prayers. Thus becomes evident the contrast between her private pagan beliefs and her public Christian self, a growing divide that Le Gentil must bridge before he can understand this exotic maiden who beckons from the shores of another culture. Or else, we witness a heated discussion between Le Gentil and a Brahmin priest at a Kali festival while Ambika translates, as unobtrusive as a shadow. He feels an initial sense of shock at the strange ideas, then a grudging appreciation for the brilliance of this half-naked, alien mind, two opposite wills pitted against each other and neither giving way, though one is a primitive and a pagan, and the other, the intellectual flag bearer of a conquering race.

As he was debating the various possibilities and their respective merits, he noticed Amrita walking along the path in her trademark white cotton blouse and billowing yogi pants. They exchanged waves. She changed direction and started toward him at her normal leisurely pace.

"Namaskar, Rodrigo," she said when she was close enough not to have to raise her voice. "Am I interrupting?"

"No, not at all. I was just jotting down some notes."

Amrita sat down on the grass next to him, sliding one leg underneath the other with the ease of an accomplished yogi. Rodrigo envied her flexibility, though not the many hundreds of hours it must have taken for her to achieve it.

"I was wondering when I was going to see you again. I keep expecting to see you in yoga class."

"I'm still planning on going. I just haven't been waking up early enough. Maybe I need to go to bed earlier."

"Well, your mat is there waiting for you, whenever you come. The Lord knows, you need it." Amrita flashed a quick, mischievous grin and then cast a sideways glance at the books lying on the grass. "So, what are you reading?"

"Right now, I'm reading about Kali. That's what these notes are. I'm looking for material I can use in my book."

Amrita opened her eyes a little wider. "And what book would that be?"

"I'm writing a novel; it's set in India."

"You're writing a novel? Really? I didn't know you were a writer."

"I am. That's actually the main reason I came to India. I wanted to write it here so I could make it as authentic as possible. I suppose you could call it writing on location."

"Cool. So what's the story about?"

"It's about an eighteenth-century French astronomer who comes to India to record the Venus transit. That was the greatest astronomical undertaking of that age. While he's here, he has a series of adventures. He meets this Indian girl, falls in love, and things sort of take off from there."

"So is it historical fiction then, like *The Girl with the Pearl Earring*?"

"Exactly," Rodrigo said, surprised at the reference and happy to be talking about his book. "It's historical fiction. Le Gentil was a real guy, just like Vermeer in *The Girl with the Pearl Earring*. The setting is real, his work on the Venus transit is real, but the story is fictional. It's whatever my imagination decides to do with it. So, do you like literature?"

"Oh, I do. I love to read. I'll read whatever I can get my hands on, especially if it has anything to do with spirituality. So, what about your novel? Does it have to do with spirituality?"

"I suppose that depends on what you mean by spirituality. One of the main themes of the book is the clash between cultures, between the Western and Indian ways of looking at the world. Naturally, Indian religion and Indian philosophy factor into it in a major way. They challenge the main character's way of seeing the world. What comes of that challenge, I'll have to wait and see. That will depend on the needs of the story. And on the needs of the characters, especially. In a certain sense, they dictate where the story goes. I'm still in the early stages of the book, so even I don't know exactly where it's going yet. Some of it is just as much a mystery to me as I hope it will be to my readers when they get into the first few chapters. These books are part of my research. When you walked up, I was just thinking about how and where I could work Kali into the story, and the ideas she represents—you know, the impermanence of life, and all that."

Rodrigo handed her the other two books he had brought with him, one on Tantra and one outlining the major Hindu scriptural texts. Amrita flipped through the pages, first of one and then of the other, nodding here and there and furrowing her brow.

"That's some serious reading you have here."

"I have a whole collection in my room that I bought for my research: yoga, meditation, Hinduism, Buddhism, a book on Hindu saints, the whole gamut."

Amrita pursed her lips and nodded as she set the books down on the grass, her habitual smile giving way to a more sober expression. "I always thought that writing must be pretty hard work. But you know, if you want to learn about Indian spirituality and Indian culture, you can't just read about it. You have to experience it for yourself."

"Oh, I know. Like I said, that's why I'm here. I want the book to be as authentic as possible. Rishikesh is my first stop."

"In other words, you're making your own journey into the heart and soul of India so your character can follow after you. Is that it?"

"More or less."

"Far out. Well, Rishikesh is the perfect place to start. It's not only the capital of yoga, you know, it's also one of the most important Hindu pilgrimage sites. You didn't know that, did you? Thought so. Some of the important stories in Hindu mythology are supposed to have taken place in Rishikesh. There are a number of famous temples here, both in town and in the nearby mountains, like Kunjapuri and Nil Shankar. Hundreds of Hindu pilgrims pass through here every day to make an offering in the temples and take back some Ganges water with them. And then you have the ashrams. I don't know how many there are exactly, but it's got to be close to a hundred. There are some famous spiritual teachers who live here year-round, like Swamiji, and there are many more that come here regularly to teach. To be honest, you'd probably need a year to take it all in, but even in a month or two you'll get a very serious dose of Indian spirituality. I wouldn't be surprised if you get all you need for your book, and more. Have you visited the Sivananda ashram yet? No? Well, you have to go there. It's probably the most important ashram in all Rishikesh. It's certainly the most famous. Swami Sivananda was the best-known saint to have lived here on a permanent basis. You see his books everywhere you go, not only here but all over the world. He attained enlightenment meditating in a little hut on this side of the river, not too far past Ram Jhula. I can take you there to see it sometime, if you like."

Amrita's voice had grown more animated now; it was obviously a subject that fascinated her.

"After he became enlightened, his disciples built an ashram for him on the other side of the river, across from Muni-ki-reti. That was in the late twenties or early thirties, I forget exactly. He lived there until he died in '63. By that time, it had become one of the most famous ashrams in India. Since then, several of his disciples have also become famous gurus, especially in the West. His successor, Swami Chidananda, still lives in the ashram, but he's rarely seen in public anymore. There are some other direct disciples, though, that you could meet. They give talks sometimes. In fact, they have public lectures at the ashram every day, all year long; they also have collective spiritual practices twice a day and a kirtan that's been going on continuously for more than fifty years, if you can believe it, twenty-four hours a day. It's a very vibrated place. You really should talk to some of the swamis there. You'll get a lot of material for your story, things you won't find in books. Oh, and the ashram also has a wonderful library, perfect for your research. I go there sometimes in the afternoons to read. Which reminds me, I have a friend who lives at the ashram. She's a sannyasi, from Australia. She'd be a good person for you to talk to. Would you like to meet her?"

"Sure, that'd be great."

"How about this afternoon? I'm going to a program at the Andrew Cohen Center—meditation and a video. She'll be there. There'll also be other people you might want to meet."

"Sure, that sounds interesting."

"Why don't I meet you outside the office at one thirty, then. We can have some apple pie at Lakshmi's on the way and drop by the Sivananda ashram."

Rodrigo was glad for the invitation. As long as he wasn't able to write, he might as well learn a little more about Rishikesh and meet some of the people who lived there. Though he suspected he might feel out of place at a spiritual gathering, he also knew that he needed the experience if he was going to learn what drew a constant stream of Western seekers to Rishikesh and the other spiritual Meccas that dotted the Indian subcontinent. Some of those seekers might even be his readers one day and recognize something of their own experience in his writings. Though his book was set nearly two and a half centuries in the past, his readers belonged to the twenty-first century. Whatever struggles Le Gentil would have as he tried to peer through the unfamiliar prism of Indian culture, though imbedded in the understanding of an eighteenth-century Frenchman, would have to resonate strongly with the modern-day confrontation between the Western and Eastern minds if his story was to be successful. The people he would meet that afternoon would likely be more or less ideal representatives of that ongoing encounter, people raised in his own culture who had somehow developed a peculiar fascination for Indian spiritual ideas, more specifically those that had grown out of the Hindu tradition. From what he had seen of Hinduism in these past couple of weeks, it seemed far more alien than anything Buddhism had to offer. Buddhism was somehow cleaner, more logical, more philosophically oriented, all qualities that appealed to the Western mind. Hinduism was gaudy, chaotic, much like India itself, full of unruly devotees and strange beliefs that defied logical explanation, many of which exuded a strong odor of superstition. But as much as he felt a certain affinity with Buddhism, it was the Hindu mind that would need to flower in his book and assault Le Gentil with its ancient prejudices and whatever wisdom Rodrigo could find there. Both, however, were known for the practice of meditation. He had not forgotten the advice to clear his mind and free it of tension. He had never meditated before, but he wondered now if it might not be time he tried.

Amrita was waiting for him when he finished his lunch. Instead of crossing the Ram Jhula Bridge on foot, they took the small ferry that transported pilgrims across the river for a two-rupee fare. True to her word, she started filling him in on the history and principal spiritual attractions of Rishikesh. It was not Paris, by any means, but he was surprised to hear about the huge variety of spiritual programs that were available in the different ashrams, the Ayurvedic clinics, the yogis who lived in forest caves furnished with televisions and sofas, the scholars who preserved manuscripts of unbelievable antiquity, the great musicians for whom their music was a yoga. For someone who was interested in such things, Rishikesh did indeed seem like a place that would take a year to explore, despite the fact that it was, in reality, nothing more than a small town in the mountains.

Their conversation brought them to the Muni-ki-reti taxi stand near the entrance to the Sivananda ashram. There she led him to a small café that served hot apple pie and other dishes that catered principally to Western tastes. Amrita ordered two apple pies and two hot ginger lemon honeys. While they were waiting for their order, Rodrigo asked Amrita what had brought her to Rishikesh.

"Not what but who. I met Swamiji in Los Angeles about a year and a half ago. He was invited to inaugurate a new Hindu temple there, an incredible place in West LA. The entire structure is made of marble brought over from India and fitted together by Indian masons. One of the directors of the temple was my student, so I got an invite to the inauguration. When Swamiji found out I was a yoga teacher, he practically insisted I come back with him. I don't know why. He said he was looking for a yoga teacher for the ashram and for some reason he was convinced that I was the person he was looking for. What could I say? LA is great. I was pretty successful there. I had a lot of students. But I couldn't pass up a chance to live in Rishikesh and be close to Swamiji. I've been here fifteen months now and I still feel like I'm dreaming sometimes. It's the closest thing to paradise I know of—I mean if you're into yoga and meditation and such things. If not, I imagine it might be pretty boring. There's not much else to do here. There's not even a movie theater, which is surprising since there is no country in the world where the people are more fanatic about their movies. I guess that shows how seriously they take their spirituality in Rishikesh. But you came here to write a book?"

"That I did."

The owner of the café, a smiling, portly middle-aged woman in a faded cotton sari, arrived with their drinks and placed them wordlessly on the table. Amrita stirred the honey, sitting an inch thick at the bottom of the glass, until it dissolved and her drink took on an amber color. She took a sip, puckered her lips, and set the glass down.

"So, let me venture a guess. Just a shot in the dark, mind you, correct me if I'm wrong, but you haven't actually ever practiced meditation or yoga before, have you, or any other kind of spiritual practice?"

"Didn't I mention that I took a yoga class once when I was in college? But I suppose that doesn't really count, does it?"

Amrita flashed a good-natured smile and shook her head.

"Wait a second, I did see the Dalai Lama a couple of weeks ago. That must count for something. He even asked me my name and gave me his blessing. But no, I suppose you could say that and it wouldn't be too far from the truth. However, seriously speaking, I think that depends a lot on what you mean by spiritual. I would say that I have my own kind of spirituality. It just has nothing to do with religion, that's all."

"Of course. Religion and spirituality are two entirely different things. So what do you mean when you say you have your own kind of spirituality? What do you mean by spirituality?"

The pie arrived at that moment, fresh from the microwave, gaining Rodrigo a temporary reprieve from having to answer what was for him a very difficult question. They each took a bite of their pie and commented on how tasty it was. Amrita looked at him expectantly as she broke off a second piece with her fork and put it thoughtfully into her mouth.

"You don't have to answer if you don't want to," she said when she had finished chewing her mouthful and taken another sip of the still-fragrant brew.

"No, no, it's not that. It's just a hard question to answer, that's all. I mean, how do you put that kind of thing into words? You know what I mean?" He paused for a few moments, trying to collect his thoughts. "I guess I would say that for me spirituality is a kind of feeling that comes over me when I'm in the presence of a great work of art, or sometimes when I've been sitting alone in nature, a feeling of being connected to something greater than myself. I don't know how better to put it. Maybe it's just a sense that I belong to something beyond me: the human race and all its traditions, the earth, life itself. That's about as near as I can put it into words."

Amrita leaned back and eyed him as if she were surprised. "I'm impressed. That's rather poetic. But I guess that's to be expected from a writer."

"Thank you. So let me ask you. How would you define spirituality?"

"Much the same, actually. I think religion is about what you believe in and spirituality is about what you experience, or what you are trying to experience. For me, it's the experience of feeling connected to spirit, to the whole of existence, to God. Feeling one with the universe instead of feeling isolated and separate. In other words, yoga. Do you know what the word *yoga* means?"

"I do, actually. I went to swami's talk the other day. It means 'union,' right?"

"Exactly. Union with the Divine, the realization that we are one with the universe. That's the fundamental spiritual experience."

"Now, this is where we disagree. I can admit that might be true on some abstract level, but the real truth of the human experience is that we are separate, separate and alone. That's the human condition. We may have these flashes of feeling that we belong to something greater, but in the end we are still separate beings moving between two finite points, birth and death. If you are really, truly honest with yourself, you can't deny that. You're there and I'm here and never the twain shall meet, to paraphrase Mr. Kipling. Not the greatest of poets, by any means, but a pretty profound line."

Amrita shook her head perfunctorily. "It might be nice-sounding poetry, but if that's what your Mr. Kipling means, then he doesn't have a clue when it comes to the meaning of life. I have another line for you: Let those who have the eyes to see, see." Amrita flashed a quick, defiant smile.

Rodrigo threw up his hands in a gesture of mock surrender. "Look, everybody is going to believe what they believe. And that's fine. Whatever works for them. I'm just trying to be honest with myself. I think it's very difficult for an intelligent human being in this day and age to believe in God without being aware that it's just a belief. There's just no way we can ever know for sure if there is a God, or if this is all there is." He made a sweeping gesture with his hand. "What you see in front of you. I think most people don't want to face the possibility that they might be all alone in an incomprehensible universe that is carrying them toward the end faster than they can run. It's just too scary. It's much easier to believe in religion and all that goes with it, life after death and all that."

"It's only scary if you're scared. And that's on you. It has nothing to do with what's out there. It has to do with what's in here." Amrita tapped herself twice on her chest. "And you're wrong when you say there's no way we can know for sure. You don't have to look any further than the lives of any of the great saints to know we can. They all had the same experience, every last one of them, regardless of their culture. They all experienced this universe as an expression of a Divine Consciousness—call it God, nirvana, the ultimate reality, whatever you want. They all realized that each of us is nothing more than a drop in that ocean of consciousness. And the moment the drop becomes aware of the ocean, it is the ocean. It loses its separate identity. That's why they called it yoga, union, because it's all one. Separateness is just an illusion. It wasn't a question of belief for them; it was a question of experience. Not only that. They taught anyone who was interested, how to achieve that same realization. Study the lives of the great saints and that's what you'll find, Rodrigo. What you're talking about is just fear. All the great saints had to conquer their fear before they could achieve enlightenment. That's what made them the heroes they were."

"It's not fear, Amrita, it's reality. It's being honest enough to face what is. There is a quote from Sartre that sums it up far better than I ever could: 'Life has no meaning the moment you lose the illusion of being eternal.'"

"And you think Sartre was a wise man?"

"Wiser than most. Have you read Sartre?"

"No. I don't think I would have much patience with him."

"He is difficult, I admit, but well worth the effort, if you are up to the challenge."

By now they were both finished with their pie. Amrita asked for the check and paid for it above Rodrigo's strenuous objections.

"Rodrigo, you're a nice guy. You're probably a hell of a lot smarter than most people I'll ever meet, but on this point you are totally out to lunch. I'll make a deal with you. You said you want to make your book as authentic as possible, right?"

"Right."

"Okay then. You make an open-minded effort to understand Indian spirituality and I'll read Sartre—every last word he ever wrote, if you want."

"I'm already doing that. You saw the books."

Amrita slung her cloth bag over her shoulder and got up from the table. "Yes, I saw the books. But those are just words printed on paper. Spirituality is a practice. If you really want to understand the Indian spiritual tradition, then you have to practice it. You have to meditate. You have to have your own experience. Spirituality is not the kind of thing you can understand from the outside looking in, no matter how many books you read."

They left the café and started walking past the parked taxis toward the main gate of the Sivananda ashram.

"So let me get this straight. What you're saying is that you'll read Sartre if I learn to meditate?"

"Not just *learn* to meditate. Meditation is a practice. You have to do it every day, week after week, month after month, before you can even begin to know what it's about. And until you do, you will never understand Indian spirituality. It's not something you can learn about with your intellect. You have to experience it firsthand. A month or two is much too short a time, but at least it'll be a start. Who knows, you might even make that book of yours as authentic as you hope."

Both of them remained silent as they entered the ashram gate and started walking up the long, steep flight of whitewashed concrete steps, though for Rodrigo the conversation continued within the precincts of his mind. He congratulated himself for having more or less held his own in his first spiritual argument and then began debating over whether or not practicing meditation regularly while he was here was a fair exchange for reading Sartre's collected works. Amrita was convinced it was, but he was not. The hours and the effort required tipped the scales heavily in her favor, as he was sure she was aware of. Still, he had already thought about learning, though he didn't want to be bullied into it, and there were other factors to consider. First and foremost was the impact on his writing, and it was there that Amrita's main argument weighed most heavily. If he wanted to fully understand the culture he was writing about, then he needed to fully immerse himself in that culture. He needed to understand it from the inside, as she had rightly implied. If, as the swami had claimed, the essence of India's ancient culture was their fascination with spiritual experience, then perhaps he would not be able to understand it properly unless he knew what it was like to meditate. As they passed the landing, midway up the flight of steps, he held a brief consultation with his characters. Would Le Gentil have agreed had Ambika put the same challenge before him? The astronomer assured him that he would have. He was a scientist and no scientist could come to a trustworthy conclusion without having first performed the necessary experiments. Ambika was even more emphatic on this point, but of course she would be, since it was her culture and her pride in that culture that was at stake. This brief consultation proved to be the deciding factor. Whatever difficulties it might entail, the demands of his story came first. If he was going to write the tale of a Frenchman and an Indian maiden, then he would have to become part Indian himself, at least for as long as it took him to write the book. Wasn't that why he had boarded a plane for India in the first place? And if, along the way, it helped him to overcome his writer's block, then that would be a more-than-welcome side effect.

"Okay," he said, as they reached the top of the stairs and paused to catch their breath. "It's a deal. I'll learn to meditate and you promise to read Sartre, once you can get hold of his books.

"Deal. The swami will be happy to initiate you. But just be ready. There is an old Sufi saying: if you don't want an elephant in your living room, don't make friends with the elephant trainer."

"And what exactly does that mean?"

Amrita smiled. "Don't worry, you'll figure it out. I promise. Once you've been meditating for a while, it will be as clear as a day without clouds. But if it isn't, you can always ask me then."

They spent the next hour wandering through the ashram grounds, a sprawling complex of ornately decorated brick-and-plaster buildings set on the slopes north of the river and enclosed on all sides by a thick, high wall. They slipped off their shoes and spent a few minutes in the temple and then in the meditation hall, where Amrita described in hushed tones the different activities he could participate in should he be willing to enter into the spirit of both Hindu and yogic practice. Then she brought him to the library and turned him loose to browse the stacks, which he did with unfeigned delight. Though many of the books were musty and most dealt with topics that would not have interested him had he not been researching his novel, the mere presence of a sizable collection of leather- and cloth-bound volumes was enough to make him feel more at home than at any time since his arrival in the subcontinent. The fact that Amrita liked to spend an occasional afternoon there helped to dispel the mantle of quirkiness that he had draped around her, if their conversation in the café had not already done so.

He was glancing through a book entitled *Myths and Symbols in Indian Art and Civilization*, an intriguing, scholarly looking volume, when Amrita touched him on the shoulder and whispered that they needed to leave, otherwise they would be late for the program. Rodrigo made a mental note to add the book to his research list and followed her out the door and down the long flight of steps to the street. From there they caught a three-wheeler that took them upriver toward Lakshman Jhula. They got down halfway between the two bridges, in an area where no buildings could be seen except for those visible through the trees on the far side of the river. From there they followed a narrow dirt path that wound up into the woods. A few minutes later, they came to a two-story house nestled in the shade of the forest, fronted by a neatly kept lawn.

A half dozen people were milling about on the veranda, talking. A brunette in her mid-to-late forties, wearing jeans and a t-shirt, waved to Amrita as they walked up. She greeted them politely with a musical New Zealand accent. The two women hugged each other. Amrita turned and caught Rodrigo lightly by the elbow.

"Linda, I want you to meet Rodrigo. He's a writer from America. He's been staying at the ashram for a couple of weeks now, working on a novel. Rodrigo, Linda."

Linda extended her hand. "Glad to meet you, Rodrigo. Welcome to the center."

"Linda and Paul run the center. That's Paul over there on the right." Amrita pointed to a tall, thin figure with a balding head and a serious look on his face who was standing a few paces away conversing with a sturdy, sandy-haired man about Rodrigo's age. "They are two of the best hosts in Rishikesh and dear friends."

Linda's ruddy cheeks reddened even more at the compliment. "Well, I think we should get started. Sulabha and a few others are already in the meditation room. Let me call everyone."

Linda made an announcement that they were ready to start. Rodrigo and Amrita followed her into a spacious room with a blue carpet, white walls, and thick, blue, half-drawn curtains in front of the two windows. A dozen chairs had been set up in the center of the room and in front of them were several rows of cushions, some of them already occupied by meditators. At the back of the room there was a table with books and magazines on display and at the front a television with a VCR and separate speakers; alongside it was a small bookshelf filled with VHS tapes. Amrita nudged Rodrigo in the arm and pointed to a tiny woman on one of the cushions who sported the saffron robes and shaved head of a monastic.

"That's my friend Sulabha," she whispered, "the one I was telling you about. Why don't you sit here? I think you'll be more comfortable on a chair for now. I am going to sit on a cushion."

Once everyone was seated, Paul knelt down in front of the television while Linda drew the curtains, plunging the room into shadow. "I'd like to welcome you all to the Andrew Cohen Center for our regular Wednesday program," Paul began. He had an English accent and spoke with pleasant, measured cadences. "Today we will be watching a video of Andrew's entitled 'Being and Becoming,' but first we'll begin as usual with a short meditation session. As Andrew tells us, meditation is the portal to the fourth dimension, the door to the realization of limitlessness."

Paul asked everyone to close their eyes and straighten their backs; then he began leading a guided meditation. He spoke slowly, leaving ample space between his sentences, until finally his voice faded out altogether and the period of silent meditation began.

"Be still. Relax. Allow yourself to be completely at ease. Take a minute to be aware of your breathing. Watch your breathing as it slows and deepens, flowing in and out like the rising and falling of a wave. Let your attention begin to expand and flow freely until it becomes as vast and as open and as clear as the sky. In that open space, thoughts will come and go, along with emotions and physical sensations, but you don't cling to any of them. You let them pass by like birds tracing an invisible path across the sky. Your attention keeps expanding until your awareness itself becomes the object of your attention. Everything else falls away, until you discover yourself in a place beyond the manifest world, the radiant void out of which everything arises. In this limitless place, you discover the unqualified freedom that is the true ground of being. Merge into that self and let everything else disappear."

Rodrigo kept his eyes closed and tried to keep his back straight without leaning against the backrest, but apart from this he found the instructions difficult to follow. He was able to watch his breathing for a minute or two, but what did it mean to let his attention expand and flow freely, to observe his thoughts without clinging to any of them? Wasn't this simple daydreaming, except with his eyes closed? And what did it mean to make his awareness the object of his attention? It was an intriguing concept but difficult to grasp. He struggled with it for a few minutes, but no matter where he looked, he found no trace of a place beyond the manifest world. What he found instead was a desire to slump back in his chair, and a parade of thoughts that seemed far more interesting than a radiant void, despite the promise of unqualified freedom. Soon he found himself back in the world of his novel, eavesdropping on Le Gentil, who was sitting in his new home, unpacking his books and arranging them in alphabetical order on a small wooden shelf. Le Gentil's thoughts turned to Ambika and her next visit, which the astronomer was looking forward to with a noticeable undercurrent of excitement. Rodrigo could hear his thoughts and feel his excitement, but he was not yet sure of the reason for her visit. Was she simply reporting for work at her regular hour, or had she been given some special assignment that Le Gentil was waiting for with anticipation? No matter. He could figure that out later. What was important was the fact that Le Gentil was gradually becoming caught in the quicksand of a powerful attraction that he could not dismiss as merely physical. Rodrigo would need a scene or two first, however, to gradually build up the effect, to lay the groundwork for the onset of romantic desire. Not the garbage he had thrown on the scrap heap the last time he had tried to write, those gratuitous bits of folderol that he had wasted two days over, but scenes with a purpose, scenes that would set up the reader for what was coming later. He felt a sense of giddiness, the same tingling that Le Gentil had just been feeling. This was a scene he could look forward to writing. For a moment he savored the feeling. Then it occurred to him that it had been a while since he had felt this good. Was it because while he was immersed in the astronomer's world, he had no recollection of his own problems? The world seemed brighter and more alive than it had only minutes before when he had still been tied fast to the plodding melodrama of his own life. This was a kind of freedom, freedom from himself. Could it be the meditation? But how could it? He had no idea what he was doing, other than slipping into an unusually vivid daydream. It might not be meditation, but whatever it was, it felt good, and it certainly seemed like it might benefit his writing. In fact, it was very much like writing, except that his eyes were closed and his fingers still. If this was meditation, more or less, then the deal he'd made with Amrita might turn out to be relatively painless after all, certainly a lot less painful than wading through thousands of pages of Sartre. There were some gems to be found there, no doubt, and a brilliant intellect to grapple with, but what a headache it had given him, not that he had gotten anywhere close to wading through even half of the writer-philosopher's prodigious output....

Rodrigo's reverie was interrupted by a sharp pop, followed by the static of the speakers. He opened his eyes and saw Paul manipulating the buttons of a remote control. The blue light of the screen turned black; moments later the credits flashed. A handsome man of medium stature not much older than himself appeared onscreen standing in front of a small audience and pointing to a diagram on a whiteboard fixed to the wall. He had a shock of thick black hair, streaked with gray, and was wearing black slacks and a black shirt, not exactly his stock image of a spiritual teacher. The video began with a question by a member of the audience that Rodrigo found more or less incomprehensible, something about timelessness and an authentic self. But the answer intrigued him. Not the words but the speaker. He spoke rapidly with an American accent and American idioms that made it seem as if he might have been one of his fellow professors holding a graduate seminar and fielding questions from his students. A philosophy seminar, of course, since his discourse was too abstract for Rodrigo to follow and was peppered with words like "being" and "consciousness" that he had trouble finding a context for. After a couple of minutes, when Rodrigo had gotten accustomed to the velocity of his speech and the uncanny sense that he was back in the university with one of his colleagues, he gradually started paying attention to what he was saying. Slowly some of it started to make sense, though not enough to alleviate the feeling that he was wandering in a foreign land where everyone spoke the language but him. What exactly did he mean when he pointed to a blue area at the bottom of the diagram and talked about entering the ground of being and thus freeing oneself from all conceptual structures? Rodrigo had no idea. He had struggled to get through Heidegger and Kant and had retained enough in his short-term memory to get a decent grade on the final exam, but he had never claimed to have actually understood them. This was not as abstruse, that much he could tell, but without a set of Cliff Notes he could only understand bits and pieces, as if he were floating in a raft from iceberg to iceberg. One of those icebergs was something about being caught in the world of the ego, alienated, cutoff, and confused. Was that what he meant by a "negative relationship to life"? Now that was an experience he could relate to. Just about anybody could. Another was his comment that our culture was oriented around "what's in it for me" rather than acknowledging any connection to a higher paradigm. It seemed clear that he was talking about a sense of ethics, something Rodrigo was quite familiar with from his own field where the depiction of a moral imperative was at the heart of all classical literature until the early twentieth century, when the ground began to permanently shift under the artist's feet. Another concept that engaged his attention was the notion that he was teaching a new type of enlightenment that was postmodern rather than premodern. His ears pricked up at the words "postmodern" and "premodern," ideas that were fundamental to contemporary literary criticism, but what they had to do with enlightenment, he could not quite understand, perhaps because he had no real idea what was meant by enlightenment.

After the video, Paul invited everyone out to the patio for tea and biscuits. Linda arranged a number of plastic chairs around a round metal table, and Paul emerged from the house a couple of minutes later carrying a silver tray with a steaming kettle, tea bags, cups, and several packets of biscuits. While everyone was helping themselves to the tea and biscuits, Linda introduced Rodrigo to the group. After a few pleasantries, Paul asked everybody what they thought of Andrew's idea of a new postmodern understanding of enlightenment. Sulabha, her shaven head and pale hands the only parts of her petite body not covered by the generous folds of her saffron robes, was the first to offer her opinion.

"I think Andrew is absolutely right when he says that the highest realization is not to be found by escaping from the world but by engaging with the world from an enlightened perspective. What struck me was the similarity with Swami Sivananda's teachings, though he expresses it very differently. Sivananda always placed a lot of emphasis on social service, not just with his words but by his example. As I think you all know, Sivananda was a doctor before he became enlightened, but the interesting thing is that even after he became a famous guru, he still worked in his clinic and treated people on a daily basis. That was his way of showing how important service is. He also placed a lot of emphasis on following a code of ethics in one's life, which is something Andrew really emphasized in his talk. Of course, that's always been part of the yogic tradition, ever since Patanjali. So if I understand Andrew correctly, he is basically saying the same thing as Swami Sivananda. Instead of going off to the mountains or to your room to pursue your own enlightenment, a spiritualist should engage with the society, help people, try to lift them up, spiritually and materially. It's an ethical stance. If we want to be truly moral beings, then we have to confront suffering in whatever form it appears and do whatever we can to relieve it. A sense of ethics implies a commitment to helping others. Only I don't know about this distinction between premodern and postmodern. As I understand it, this has been part of the traditional yogic teaching as far back as Krishna and the Gita."

Paul nodded slowly as she spoke, his brow slightly furrowed, as if he were trying to restrain himself from expressing some unspoken objection. Ron, the robust man with whom Paul had been speaking before the program, now entered the conversation in a soft-spoken American voice that carried traces of a southern drawl.

"Exactly. It's more like Andrew is giving a modern slant to an ancient teaching. The way I see it, it's basically a devotional perspective. The more enlightened we become, the more we consciously fashion ourselves into vessels of the Divine. The idea is that eventually we become like a bamboo flute where the wind of God blows through us. That wind is the creative urge that Andrew was talking about. Even though it flows through us, it is the Lord who is playing the music. You find this idea a lot in medieval Vaishnava poetry—Jaya Deva, Chandidas, and those people. So in other words, yes, we should engage with the society, but we should do it from an enlightened perspective, as Andrew rightly says. If we do, then it is not the ego who's working but God who is working through us. It's the Divine Consciousness expressing itself through our bodies and minds, and the fundamental impulse of that consciousness is to free all living beings from the bondage of the ego. That's the evolutionary impulse."

There was a brief pause. Paul took advantage of the momentary lull to step in, looking around earnestly from face to face as he spoke, slowly and precisely, each word appearing to have been carefully chosen. "I don't know if you quite understand all of what Andrew is getting at. If you remember back to what he said about Eckhart Tolle and others who teach this premodern idea of enlightenment, their answer to suffering is to transcend existence and enter into pure being. But when you transcend existence, you disconnect from the world, you cease to actively participate in the creation. This has been the traditional spiritual teaching for thousands of years, both Eastern and Western. What Andrew is saying is that this teaching has traditionally ignored the world and our potential for becoming an enlightened conduit for the creative impulse. If you look into traditional Buddhist teachings or the Upanishads or Christian mysticism, you see the same thread of transcendence running through all of them. They all emphasize transcendence rather than immanence."

Ron nodded in agreement, "Of course, the Buddhists have always taught that."

"Exactly. And their modern-day followers and most spiritual teachers. That's what Andrew is getting at. But now evolution has brought us to the point that that paradigm is about to change."

Vikram, a short, stocky Indian man, the only Indian present, lifted his hand.

"Not all Buddhists, and not all Vedantists, either. Remember the Bodhisattva vow. I refuse to take enlightenment until all beings are liberated. In Vaishnavism, and especially in Tantra, the approach is quite different."

Paul formed his spidery fingers into a triangle and leaned forward. "Andrew is not saying that no one has ever understood this before. Please don't misunderstand. What he is saying is that an evolutionary shift is taking place. For thousands of years, this was the dominant teaching all over the world. There were exceptions, but they were exceptions to a general rule. Now, as Andrew says, we are becoming too smart for that. The evolutionary impulse is maturing and that will bring a new understanding of enlightenment into the mainstream."

Vikram looked doubtful but he didn't add anything further.

"Hasn't the evolutionary impulse always been the same," Amrita asked, "even before there were human beings on the planet?"

Paul flashed an eager smile, the first Rodrigo had seen from him. "Absolutely. The impulse has always been there, but the human race was not evolved enough until this point to fully recognize it. It's a process of collective maturation. The Buddha taught that life was suffering, desire was the cause of suffering, and the path of extinguishing desire was the path to freedom. Naturally, people accepted that the easiest way to do this was to escape society and its temptations. You see the same idea in Christian mysticism and Christianity in general, which is no surprise since Christ and Christianity were deeply influenced by Buddhism. And Buddha's teachings didn't arise in a vacuum, either. Remember, he was part of a group of ascetics who lived in the forest and renounced practically every aspect of mundane life so they could attain enlightenment. That was the dominant teaching in the society he was born into. He gave it a new shape, but it was there long before he came along. What Andrew is pointing out is that the evolutionary impulse has advanced to the point where this approach has become passé, or is about to."

"Well, I for one hope Andrew is right," Amrita said. "As long as most of the great saints keep hiding in the mountains or the forests—Rishikesh excluded, of course—it's going to be business-as-usual on planet Earth and that's not very inspiring."

"There is a school of thought," Ron said, "that says that the saints who live in seclusion also play a critical role in the spiritual evolution of the planet by purifying the psychic atmosphere with their thought waves. You may remember that from *Autobiography of a Yogi*."

"Yes, yes," Vikram said. "Babaji and his circle of disciples. You're exactly right. They uplift the world through the power of their meditation."

"Paul," Sulabha asked, "has Andrew ever mentioned anything about this, that you know of?"

"Not that I know of, but even if such people do exist I think he would definitely consider them as belonging to a premodern understanding of enlightenment. Personally, I doubt that whole line of thinking. If such people were uplifting the planet to such a degree, would we really be in the mess we're in today?"

Ron handed a plate with biscuits to Rodrigo. He took one and passed the plate to Amrita. "So Rodrigo," Ron asked, "where do you situate yourself in this whole discussion? Are you a postmodern or a premodern?"

"Well, I've always considered myself pretty postmodern," Rodrigo answered, uncomfortably aware that his definition of postmodern and the one they were using were probably miles or even light years apart.

Ron put down his tea and rested his chin on the back of his hands. "So can I take it by this that you agree with Andrew's contention that the teachings of Eckhart Tolle and Adyashanti are premodern interpretations of enlightenment?"

Rodrigo froze at the question. He could feel everyone's eyes on him, waiting for him to answer, but he couldn't think of a single thing to say, nothing that wouldn't totally embarrass him. Several awkward seconds passed before he felt Amrita patting his knee.

"I think that before we can convince Rodrigo to join our discussion, we first have to get him to admit the existence of God. That's something he's not ready to do yet—'yet' being the operative word. He's here to learn about Indian spirituality but he's just beginning. You'll have to go easy on him, Ron. I know that goes against your grain, but it will be good practice for you."

"I think, my dear, you will find that I am just as tactful as the next person, at least when the situation warrants it. So let me ask you this, Rodrigo, do you admit to the possibility that God might exist?"

"Of course," Rodrigo answered, still two shades from mortification but feeling better now that Amrita had made an effort to rescue him. Ron's question put his footing back on solid ground, one that he had trodden many a time, as recently as a few hours earlier in the café. "How can anyone definitively say whether or not God exists? It's a matter of belief or disbelief, and I try to keep myself free from both."

"I can understand where you're coming from, Ron said. "I've been there myself. But I think you'll have a hard time finding anyone in Rishikesh who will agree with you. Or most of India for that matter. You see, in India it is not a matter of belief but a matter of practice and experience, and in the end, direct perception. This is the world's oldest culture and the first to intuit the truth that God can be perceived by the awakened mind. I don't know if you are aware of it, but the word *buddha* means 'the awakened one.' Until you awaken to direct perception of Consciousness, you are asleep, asleep to reality; you are a prisoner of your mind and its conception of the world. In short, you're a prisoner of your ego. It's the ego that condemns us to the feeling of separateness, and the ego, as all awakened beings have discovered, is essentially an illusion. But of course, until you gain that experience and have the direct perception of reality, it doesn't hurt to keep an open mind. It doesn't hurt at all. However, if you do keep an open mind and you follow a rigorous process of logical philosophical inquiry, then you will have no recourse but to accept the existence of a Supreme Being. Doubt, in the end, must capitulate to certainty."

"I must warn you, Rodrigo," Linda interjected. "Ron is our resident philosopher."

"Yes," Sulabha added, "and once he gets a captive audience, he doesn't let them go very easily. The monks at Sivananda's have been known to turn around and walk the other way when they see him coming. I have witnessed it myself. In fact, I'm one of them."

Ron flashed an indulgent smile and lowered his head briefly, as if he were acknowledging a tribute. "They exaggerate, I assure you. I'm just the poorest of yogis who likes to keep his mind sharp, and there is nothing better for that than philosophical inquiry. But to return to the point, being an agnostic is fine for starters, but if you wish to keep an open mind, then you have to make room for the wisdom of the saints. If you approach their work honestly, with a truly open mind and a sincere effort to understand—which is not easy, by any means— you'll discover that they all had the exact same experience, the direct perception of the Godhead. It doesn't matter whether they were Indian or Western, ancient or modern. Once you get past the differences in language, you'll see that they're all talking about the same thing. And if one person can experience it, then all persons can experience it. Am I not right, Paul?"

"Absolutely. What is capable of happening once in the universe is capable of infinite repetition. It's simple physics."

"And so," Ron continued, "if the best and the wisest minds throughout history, regardless of culture, tell us that they were able to perceive the reality of a Divine Consciousness out of which everything originates and into which everything merges, and thereafter show us a path whereby we can also achieve that same experience, then where does that leave an agnostic?"

"On the defensive, I suppose," Rodrigo answered, "at least as long as said agnostic is in Rishikesh."

Though Ron's tone was good-natured enough in its challenge, Rodrigo felt like he had just taken a broadside, not much different than the one Amrita had hit him with earlier. This time, however, he was not so unprepared.

"I would point out, though," he said, "that the etymology of the word doesn't have anything to do with belief. *A – gnosis*, from the Greek, 'without knowledge.' It simply means that one does not know for sure whether or not God exists, and one is honest enough to admit it. Assuming for a moment that this direct perception is possible, wouldn't any spiritual seeker who hadn't attained to that experience also be an agnostic by definition?"

Ron smiled and clapped his hands lightly. "Bravo. Well said."

Paul raised a hand to object. "Not so fast. One doesn't need to be a Buddha to have direct experience. Even an ordinary meditator has some direct experience long before he reaches enlightenment."

"Okay, that's enough you two," Linda said. "I'm sure we can find a more suitable subject that won't interfere with our digestion. Paul, Ron, you may be interested to know that Rodrigo is a writer."

"Really?" Ron said. "Have you written anything I might have read?"

"Probably not. Up until this point I've written mostly articles of literary criticism for different literary magazines: *The Antioch Review, Kenyon Review*. A few short stories. I'm working on a novel now while I'm on sabbatical."

"*Kenyon Review, The Antioch Review*. I'm impressed. Where do you teach?"

"The University of North Carolina. English literature."

Ron's face lit up with surprise. "You're kidding! I teach at Duke. Philosophy, both Eastern and Western. From Kant to Krishnamurti. Yeah, I teach summer session and usually fall semester. Occasionally spring semester, but never both in the same year. I like it here too much. Six months in the US of A is about my limit. We'll have to get together sometime when we're both back in the States." Ron turned to the group. "The schools we teach at are only seven miles apart."

"You spend the rest of the year here then?" Rodrigo asked, after acknowledging a bevy of polite exclamations.

"At the Sivananda ashram." Ron leaned back in his chair and sipped his tea, looking very much the professor on vacation. "Drop by any time. I'm also working on a book, contrasting the Eastern and Western philosophical traditions. We can talk shop. Derrida, Foucault, Proust, Joyce, the whole nine yards."

"So, Rodrigo," Linda asked, "how did you find Andrew's talk? Was it too esoteric? "

"I found it interesting, actually, though I must confess, I didn't understand all that much of it. I think I'd need to listen to it again before I could really digest it properly. Or better yet, see it written out. A lot of the ideas were new to me—as you can imagine."

"Andrew's teaching is very innovative. I think you'll like it. We have a lending library here of his books. Would you like to have a look? I could use a break from all this philosophy."

Rodrigo was glad for the respite and Linda's affable, easy chatter, both of which helped to ease his discomfort. The conversation had reminded him of his first semester in graduate school when he had struggled to stay afloat in a sea of critical discourse that seemed unforgivingly alien to him. He had made a determined effort then to master that discourse and leave everyone else in his wake. It had cost him most of his free time and a boatload of frustrations, but he accomplished what he set out to do, so much so that he had secured a professorship right out of graduate school and had been on safe ground ever since—until now. Once again, he was in a place where the inhabitants spoke a language he could barely understand. This was not going to be a matter of reading a few books, he realized. If he was ever going to stand his ground with these people and their esoteric notions, then he was going to have to really apply himself to his studies. And yes, that would have to include learning their practices, at least to some extent. This appeared to be the price he would have to pay for acquiring a firm grasp of the world's oldest culture.

When the gathering broke up, he headed down the path alongside Amrita and Sulabha, only half listening to their happy chatter. Though he still felt embarrassed by the experience, he was determined that he would do whatever it took to understand this culture and its philosophies, even if that meant sitting on a cushion day after day and staring at his navel. It was a matter of pride as well as a matter of art.

When they reached the road, he took advantage of a momentary lull in the conversation to thank Amrita for her timely intervention.

Amrita patted him on the shoulder and winked at Sulabha. "You know I couldn't let your nose be completely rubbed in the ground. Not yet. There will be time enough for that later." Both she and Sulabha had a hearty laugh at his expense. "There is a little matter of an elephant in your living room," she added. She turned to Sulabha. "I made a deal with Rodrigo. He's agreed to learn meditation and to practice it regularly as long as he's here."

"Oh, I see," Sulabha said. "*That* elephant. Good luck to you, sir. I hope you are not keeping anything of value in your living room."

They both laughed, over and over again. After that, Rodrigo could get nothing more out of them about elephants.

8

S RODRIGO LAY IN his bed that night, he noticed the chipped paint on the ceiling and the missing knob on the headboard post, subtle signs of neglect that he had failed to pay any attention to before but which now seemed indicative of a general disregard for the material world that could no doubt account for a good deal of India's centuries-long poverty. Why, he wondered, if they were so good at philosophy, so good at splitting hairs between two differing shades of enlightenment—ideas so subtle they defied the words used to explain them—could they not see the disorder of their daily living? He remembered his shock at seeing the swarms of beggars in the streets of Delhi, many of them young children, some either cruelly maimed or emaciated to the point that it took away his appetite and made his eyes water. There had been one young boy in particular with withered hands—he must have been no more than ten or twelve—whom he had watched dragging himself by his elbows down the sweltering asphalt of a crowded marketplace, his bent and twisted legs writhing behind him like the tail of a mythological serpent vomited up from some subterranean cavern. People flowed by him in a steady stream, peering into shops, fingering the cloth of brightly colored saris or the gleaming yellow skins of ripe mangos, but no one seemed to notice he was there, looking up at them with his eyes blinking away the glare, waiting stone-faced for the possibility of a coin before slithering to another spot a little further down. They paid no more attention to him than they did to the trash swept up haphazardly into fetid piles on the sides of the road or to the pockets of mud and slime they sidestepped without a downward glance, behaving as if it were perfectly normal for human beings to live this way. One beggar followed another, each pile of trash had its neighbor, and still the shrill, grating voices rushed along with their owners in the chatter of unconcern. This was the holiest of lands? The cradle of spirituality on planet Earth? Rishikesh was the only place in India he had seen so far that was relatively well-kept—its beggars received coins with their daily diet of neglect— but it was also a place of privilege that carefully kept alive thousands of years of spiritual discourse and material disregard. He might not be able to keep up with their thinking, he might be a stranger in a land where he could barely read the signboards, but his instincts made him distrust flurries of brilliance that belied the evidence of his eyes. Of what good was all this talk of enlightenment and direct perception of the Godhead if it meant having to face one's hell here on earth? Perhaps he was overstating the case, but he wished now that he had put this question to Ron or Paul.

And yet, despite his suspicion that India's fascination with a world beyond the senses had blinded it to the afflictions that this material disregard engendered, despite his supposition that the spiritual tourists with whom he had sipped tea that afternoon were just as badly out of touch with the very real ills of the world they lived in as the Indian gurus they emulated, he was aware that they possessed something he did not, and this made him feel uneasy. It was not the absolute certainty of their convictions that bothered him now, the unquestioned beliefs he had always looked upon with distrust, but rather the unremitting smiles that accompanied their doctrinaire assertions and the sense of quietude that seemed to envelop them. Could he be so prosaic as to give it the name "happiness"? He had long prided himself on his intellectual honesty, but at the moment this seemed an empty standard alongside these easy smiles that he could not distrust. They were, after all, very much like him—well-educated westerners. He would have seen any sign of pretense the moment it appeared. No, their smiles were not feigned, nor the tranquility in which they were wrapped. No one knew this better than he, for he had neither of these qualities. Of what good, then, was his intellectual and artistic honesty, other than as a fagot for his pride? It had kept his eyes open to the maladies of his civilization, but it hadn't enabled him to do anything about them, not even when he had witnessed those same maladies festering in his own life. No, there was some fundamental discord with the picture he was trying to piece together. These were intelligent people Amrita had taken him to meet, as was she. They shared his cultural history and likely many of the same hopes and aspirations. They could not be totally blind to what they saw around them, and yet they championed their spiritual ideas like they were the only things on earth that really mattered. They talked of saints and enlightenment and overcoming the ego like his colleagues talked about the latest Jose Saramago novel, only with more conviction and less pride. He could dismiss those spiritual ideas as the opiate Marx had famously considered them to be, but there was no sign of the poppy-induced dream in their eyes. None whatsoever. In fact, their eyes had seemed as clear as any he had ever come across. What was it about them, then, that eluded his understanding?

Quietude.

He kept coming back to that word. Did it have something to do with India, with the fact that they had adopted this culture's spiritual perspective as their own? At first glance, it didn't seem possible. India seemed the essence of chaos, but he was beginning to see, in the middle of the maelstrom, the unmistakable signs of quietude everywhere around him. For Rodrigo, there had always been three possible options open to a human being when faced with life's unanswerable questions: You could believe in God and an afterlife, hand your conscience over to some extra-sensorial entity who absolved you of responsibility for the hard decisions and often harder consequences of life and offered you a warm cozy place to emigrate to when the final curtain came down. That was the easy way out. Was it any wonder that nine-tenths of humanity went down that road? Or you could stare your own mortality in the face without the comfort of an imagined eternity to shield you from the terminal nature of reality. You could be like Sartre, unflinchingly honest. No belief to comfort you, only the evidence of your eyes and your intellect. This had been the road he had chosen, called to it like a priest to the church by the voice of his conscience and the whispered counsels of the writers he admired most—the modernists, his own holy trinity of Joyce, Beckett, and Proust, they who had questioned the unexamined precepts of classical literature the way Sartre had questioned the theological underpinnings of Western thought. But artists and philosophers aside, there were few who ever went down this road. It was too difficult, too painful, too lonely, though it also had a beauty that passed most people by. It was obvious that here in Rishikesh it was an option worthy of full-throated deprecation, but it was to his mind the most honest of roads. And then there was always the third alternative: you could stick your head in the sand and not think about such things. Otherwise known as the bliss of ignorance, the joy of sleep. Blessed are those who make no effort to wake up, for theirs shall be the glory of the dream-laden bed, for ever and ever. Not a road open to an artist or a thinking man, but that didn't stop him from feeling jealous sometimes of people whose minds were free from any preoccupation with the meaning of life.

As he felt the first welcome traces of sleep clouding his vision, his mind flashed to the two times he had dreamed he was a Hindu priest. Both times he had believed wholeheartedly in the reality of a Divine Presence, as much, or perhaps even more so than any of the spiritual seekers he had seen. Strange that this should be. He recoiled from such a belief in his waking hours, offended by what often seemed to him to be nothing more than willful blindness. Was the desire to be comforted by the belief in eternity so strong in human beings that even he could not avoid it once he was submerged in the depths of his subconscious? Was this attraction we feel for its easy answers so powerful that we are ready to do anything in exchange for its promise of happiness, even if it means making peace with our finite existence by pretending it to be infinite? In a matter of minutes, he would relax conscious control over his mind and give himself up to the fictional world of sleep. Once he did, would his consciousness turn away from Sartre, pronouncing him cold and impersonal, and instead hold out its arms toward the comforting embrace of the goddess, hoping to find in her imagined eyes the impassioned gaze of a lost mother or a long-awaited lover? He wondered. His life at this point seemed short on meaning and even shorter on happiness. But no, he could not see himself putting on white yogi pants and writing odes to enlightenment. There was too much at stake. He had spent too many years moving down his chosen path to give up now and take the easy way out. He would rather bleed tears if necessary to find whatever truth there was to be found in art. Where else could the human mind go to look beyond itself and into the mystery that surrounds it? Had not the pursuit of art always been the noblest pursuit of the human race, an effort to tear the veil from before our eyes? Since time immemorial, it had been art that had called forth the visionary powers inside the human being and put them on display so that all could partake from their healing waters. Could not art serve the same function as religion? Could it not give meaning to life, as Stevens had proposed with his supreme fiction, without the need to take on faith what could not be known, for all that Ron or Paul or Amrita might insist otherwise?

The last thing Rodrigo was aware of before he fell asleep that night was the ambient music wafting from sonorous fragments of a Wallace Stevens poem drifting among his thoughts. The first thing he became aware of in the morning was his unspoken laughter as he presided over his long-awaited vindication. For the next several minutes, he remained in a translucent state midway between the bright colors of his dream and the drab light of morning that filtered in leadenly through the open window, gradually becoming aware that he did not want the dream to end, that he did not want to be extricated from this strange but exhilarating new world and transported back to the dull weariness that awaited him in the old one. It was only when his waking consciousness fully asserted itself, and his eyes, unable to sustain their inward glance, blinked open against his will, that he roused himself with a sudden liquid purpose, threw off his covers, and took two long strides to the desk where he opened up his computer and began to type.

Rishikesh
8/23
7:25 AM

What an enjoyable dream! I wish I could savor it a little longer, but first I must write. For the third time I dreamed I was a Hindu priest. It seems that my subconscious is rather fond of this scenario, or else it is easily influenced by its surroundings. It was a long dream, whatever that means, and so enjoyable that as I was waking up I found myself instinctively struggling to remain there, for I did not want to exit from a stage on which I was winning—literally winning, though perhaps everything that happens in our dreams is figurative in nature. But let us to the details, before they slip away:

First, the setting: I was sitting on a makeshift wooden stage somewhere inside the temple grounds. There was an awning over the stage to afford protection from the daytime sun. I was sitting on a cushion and beside me was another priest sitting on an identical cushion. The audience was sitting on the grass in front of us. We were bare-chested, both wearing the traditional white cloth they call a dhoti and both with a single thin chord slung over our right shoulder and across our chest, the Brahmin's sacred thread. The other priest had his pate shaved and the rest of his hair tied back into the Indian topknot. Was my hair tied in the same fashion? I have no way of knowing. This seems to be a detail that my subconscious did not take into account. Anyhow, the action was as follows: We were having a debate, a scriptural debate, and I was winning. I remember my emotions clearly: elation, power, a bit of arrogance, perhaps. While I cannot remember what I said while under the influence of my subconscious mind, I remember that I was thoroughly convinced of my brilliance. The audience was clapping and vociferating their agreement, a veritable balm for my ego. Wait, I do remember one thing I said: it was about how the goddess represented the creative urge of consciousness and the first seed of that impulse. If I remember correctly, I even used a special name for her in that state (something out of my readings, most likely). Yes, we were debating how the seed of creation first sprouts and I was quoting various scriptures to back up my point. It was a long argument and there were many others that followed, but the details escape me. There is no forgetting, however, the feeling of elation I had when the debate ended and the judges declared me the winner by popular acclaim. It was a case of summary vindication. I had just shown myself to be the master of my domain. I had shown everyone in a public forum that no one else in the temple could match me in philosophy—or dare I say wisdom, since that is how I thought about myself in the dream: the wisest among them, by popular acclaim. The same old men that had so irritated me in my last dream were also present, sitting by the side of the stage. The temple elders is how I thought of them, but there was no reverence in my thoughts. When I looked over at them after I had won, I felt that my victory was a vindication of my ideas over theirs, for who should dictate temple policy but the man with the sharpest mind and the deepest understanding, no matter what his age. And then, amid the congratulations and the admiring looks, I began to wake up, feeling quite pleased with myself. A feeling that still persists.

Can it be that this dream is my subconscious's way of bolstering my ego after what happened yesterday at the Andrew Cohen Center? It seems the obvious explanation. I was out of place there, adrift in alien waters, and everyone knew it. I was embarrassed, to put it plainly. So now in my dream I get the upper hand. I debate on their turf, spiritual philosophy (only in the dream it is also my turf, since I am temporarily a priest), and since it is my dream, I win. It makes perfect sense. And actually I do feel better, much better. Thank God for dreams, which in this case is pretty much the same as saying thank God for fiction. In this improvisational theater, I redeem what I could not in real life (not yet, at least). Am I then inching toward a supreme fiction through my dreams? "How simply the fictive hero becomes the real." Is this how the mind works in its shadowy interiors? We slip and we stumble and we scrape our knees as we make our way through the fog of our so-called "real" life. And then in our dreams, our mind goes back and replays those episodes, correcting our mistakes as a writer revises a scene that doesn't quite work. If I can redeem myself in this way, am I then a better man when I awake? Are these lessons that are learned through trial and retrial, or just a sound and a fury signifying nothing? And if it is the mind's subconscious self-correcting mechanism at work, am I doing the same thing when I write or read fiction? It is an intriguing thought. Is life first lived on the rough surface of the earth and then polished in the imagination? Is one a rehearsal for the other, and if so, which is the true performance? "Soldier, there is a war between the mind and sky, between thought and day and night... It is a war that never ends." So says Stevens. But is it really a war, or just a necessary skirmish so that we can test and hone our skill with the blade (in this case, our mind, our awareness)? One further question: Is the apprehension of reality, then, the real reality, rather than it being a question of how material the substance? Now that would be a question for these Indian philosophers and their Western wannabes. "How gladly with proper words the soldier dies, if he must, or lives on the bread of faithful speech." It is obvious where Stevens's sympathies lie. And mine as well. My real life seems painfully inadequate to me, but every time I turn to fiction, I feel a renewed sense of hope that my failure can be redeemed and turned to glory. Once again, thank God for dreams. And perhaps today, finally, I will be able to write and let my fictive hero fight my battles for me. Lord knows, I need his help. I have been doing quite poorly lately in this "real" life.

Nota bene: It has been more than a week since I have written anything of consequence (with the possible exception of this journal entry), but after this dream I feel a renewed sense of confidence.

Rodrigo's confidence was, however, short-lived. It accompanied him through breakfast and a short conversation with a girl he recognized from the one yoga class he had taken, but it did not make it back up the stairs with him to his room. Once he sat in front of his computer, he ran into the same roadblock that had brought his writing to a halt more than a week earlier: he had no real idea where his story was going and no inspiration to which he could turn for directions. His muse, if indeed he had one, was deathly silent. He had wanted his book to be a journey of self-discovery, a free-spirited adventure with no fixed itinerary, relying entirely on the unpredictable creative fires of the imagination. For that reason he had sketched out only the barest of an outline. But what do you do when your imagination fails you? What do you do when the voice you had counted on to guide you takes you to the borders of an unfamiliar land and leaves you there without a map or bus fare to the nearest settlement? He had no provision for such an eventuality, though in truth it tasted too much like the many lost hours he had already wasted in previous attempts at starting a novel, none of which had ever gotten past the first few desultory chapters. By rights he should be used to this. The only difference was that previously his life had been full of distractions: his teaching, his relationship, the scholarly articles he had to turn out on a regular basis to maintain his privileged position at the university. He had had no end of excuses to explain why he was never able to get past this stage: lack of time, stress, the wrong environment, the wrong partner, a whole string of albatrosses around his neck. Now that he had none—no wife, no class to prepare, no faculty meeting to attend—it was getting hard to successfully disregard the suspicion that this was a pattern, a habit, perhaps even a fundamental and insoluble flaw. How many times had he read that a writer needed to maintain confidence in his abilities, even if no one else did? What would happen to him when his confidence was completely gone?

He remembered how a couple of years ago Beth had accompanied him to a reading by a German author who was in town to read from a translation of his latest novel, a work of historical fiction that Rodrigo hoped could serve as a model for the book he wanted to write. It was witty, controlled, and irreverent, yet at the same time it found a way to be poignant and sympathetic to the follies of the human condition. "Now *he* can write," Beth had said matter-of-factly as she leaned down to pick up her coat just after the author had closed his book and thanked everyone for coming. A dismissive resonance hung over her words as she edged her way sideways between the too-tight rows of chairs to the aisle, turning left toward the exit without bothering to turn around and see if Rodrigo, who had wanted to stay and meet the author, was still behind her. He felt his stomach clench when he heard her words. He had to struggle to keep the flush from his cheeks in that noticeably overheated library conference room. Throughout the drive home he remained silent, waiting for her to notice his indignation as he sat in the passenger seat and stared fixedly ahead. But it wasn't until they were pulling into the driveway that she offered him a momentary, unexpressive glance and said flatly, "You're pretty quiet tonight…for a change." That was when he realized that she had not been putting him down for his failure to live up to his aspirations. She had long ago dismissed the possibility of his ever doing so. There had been no irony in her remark, and that in itself was far crueler than the sarcasm that had been only imagined.

It had been one in a long litany of slights that had served to erode his confidence. Beth had a catalogue of ways to show her disappointment in him as an artist. She would pull out whichever fit the occasion with the insouciance of a housewife sending off to Sears & Roebuck for a new set of stainless steel mixing bowls to replace the plastic ones that no longer fit her newly redecorated kitchen. She would sigh after they made love with just the right tone of resignation and repeat his own words from the days when they had not yet gotten the stars out of their eyes: "Ah, there's another book that will never get written." When she came home and saw him sitting in front of the computer surfing the Internet, she would shake her head and then shrug her shoulders ever so slightly, as if to say, "Why do I keep thinking that I'll come home and find him writing?" Then she would pat him on the shoulder and ask him politely if he were planning on cooking, or if he were waiting for her to do it. In earlier years, when he accompanied her to her friends' parties, she had introduced him as her husband, the writer. Recently it had become, "He teaches American Lit at Carolina—could you be a good boy and go get me a drink?" She now wore her once-long hair short and stylish—though her clothes remained stubbornly out of tune with the latest fashions—and her husband as an adornment that had long since become passé.

As he thought about these deliberate slights, he wondered if Beth had perhaps not been right, she who claimed to know him better than anyone after sleeping in the same bed and eating at the same table for eight long years. He had always dismissed her sarcasms as a way of getting back at him for imagined injustices, or as just plain ill temper triggered by runaway hormones. He had never stopped to consider the possibility that they might contain some glimmer of truth. That would have been too scary a possibility to admit, too disheartening. Who would he be if stripped of his image of himself as a writer? A terrible disappointment was the only answer he could come up with, a failure, no matter how successful he had become as a teacher and a literary critic. Not that he didn't value those accomplishments, but their value for him lay in their ability to prepare him for the writer's life, both financially and intellectually. If they were all that lay ahead of him, other than an early retirement and a library full of books, then he was sure the joy would go out of living entirely. He had lived with his dream of being a writer since his early teens. Not simply a writer but a literary master, his place on the bookshelf coming before that of Proust and Joyce and Beckett—and not merely due to his prior position in the alphabet. Strip that from him and what did he have to live for?

Every morning for the next week, Rodrigo stationed himself in front of his computer and tried to fashion a scene out of mere words and an unwillingness to give up. Every afternoon he read what he had written and came away convinced that it was just as dull and as empty as it had seemed to him while he was forcing himself to write it. Finally, at the end of these seven torturous days, he had no other recourse but to admit that it was he who was dull and empty and who had therefore nothing with which to fill the page. Even his initial few chapters no longer seemed full of the promise he had seen there when he had first written them. Though the screen of his laptop stilled glowed with the same bright sheen, the words they revealed lay insipid and bedraggled within the gray box of his word processor. Barely able to contain his anguish, he looked at the light that entered through his window and realized that it was advising him of the probability that he had not been born to be a writer after all but simply a literary critic and a teacher of other people's work. Some people were just not meant to scale the mountain. If they still persisted when all common sense told them to desist, they ran the risk of dying on the upper slopes, gasping for their last breath in the thin air before the cold and the snow sealed their bones into an eternal, icy grave.

That afternoon, Rodrigo ducked into the Blue Sky cybercafé to check his email, something he had not been able to bring himself to do since he had received Beth's caustic and terminal missive. As he sat down, he felt a sense of oppressiveness crowd him, as if the already shabby walls were leaning his way, baring their teeth with a hint of their immanent collapse. His neck itched under the collar of his t-shirt and beads of sweat started to slide down his forehead, angling for his eyes, unaffected by the lazy circles of an overhead fan. He looked out the window toward the river, unable to concentrate, wondering why he was still in Rishikesh. Yes, it was the end of August and still hot in Pondicherry, but what did it matter if he could not write? He had no other purpose in being here. Despite the clear mountain air and the transcendent scenery, Rishikesh was starting to be peopled with ghosts, self-created phantoms that were now turning round to haunt him. He could go on to Pondicherry as planned and brave the heat, but would Pondicherry be any different? If he could not write here, under what he had to admit were the best of conditions, what was there to make him think he could write in Pondicherry? The impenetrable wall that loomed in front of him with its cackling, wraithlike voices told differently. How much longer could he ignore it?

An old impulse to escape leapt out at him. Suddenly the thought that he could simply pack his bag and head for the train station seemed like a liberating wind forcing its way through the closed shutters of his prison. He savored the thought for a moment, caressed it like he might a child. In six hours he could be in Delhi. In twenty-four, he could be halfway over the Atlantic, heading for home. But what then? Would he not be coming home to his same tired self, to the same prospect of resigning himself to a fate that he might deserve but could never appreciate? He looked out the window of the cybercafé and saw the river pushing outward toward the blue hills on the other side. He remembered the Shiva statue and his ritual offering; the bookstore, which still drew him like a magnet every time he walked by, forcing him to resist the urge to step in and pick yet another volume from its shelves; the bench near Ram Jhula where he had gotten an idea for an early scene. And he saw that the war that never ends was still raging. Among its fires, he saw the hope that still lived inside him, the hope that a change of scenery might help, might, in fact, be all he needed—but at the same moment, he knew that the only scenery that mattered was the wind-swept, overcast vistas within him, that a change of place would be merely a change of place and not a change of story. He leaned back in his chair, oblivious of the screen flickering purple and blue in front of him, and wiped the thin film of sweat from the nape of his neck. If he could just clear his mind, if he could just free himself from these images that plagued him, then maybe he would be able to see where he was going. But when had he ever seen clearly? Not during all the years he had been with Beth, to be sure. Before then? Not if he was truthful. As he turned and looked back at his life, all he saw was a dense fog hiding all but the barest glimmers from his downcast eye.

At that moment, a young woman in jeans and a black sleeveless blouse opened the door and asked the man behind the desk about train tickets to Delhi. Her strident, tinny voice distracted Rodrigo from his thoughts. He glanced at her momentarily, then noticed the signs on the wall behind the desk advertising whitewater rafting, visits to mountain temples, and a trip to the nearby elephant preserve. He turned, flicked the mouse, and tried to concentrate his mind on the list of messages still sitting unread in his inbox, but he found it much easier to listen to the conversation taking place just behind him. The girl was going to Delhi. Her accent sounded Italian. Would she take a plane from there and be back in Rome in a few days, staring at the opulent facade of the Vatican as she goes out to buy a newspaper and sip a caffè latte? Perhaps she would soon be savoring a gelato in a Firenze side street, whipped chocolate and hazelnut edged by the thinnest of wafers. He would have liked to follow her to the counter and book his own ticket to Delhi, perhaps they could even travel together, but no, he was not yet ready to give up on his life and go crawling back to the tired comforts of mediocrity. Despair was simply not a good enough reason—not yet, at least. He turned around again and looked at the signs on the wall behind the desk. Beside one of them, there was a small picture of what looked to be a temple staring out from a Himalayan peak. When the girl had paid her money and left, he got up and asked the man about the picture.

"Kunjapuri. Four hundred rupees." The man's eyes were expressionless, except for a vague hint of resentment for being put to so much bother. It took several more questions from Rodrigo and a stitching together of the short monotone replies before he understood that Kunjapuri was a temple on a nearby peak from where one could see all the way to Annapurna and the Great Himalayas. Apart from being one of the major attractions for Hindu pilgrims, it was also a favorite of westerners, both for its unobstructed view and for the eleven-kilometer, four-hour hike down the mountainside and back to Rishikesh. The picture and its description reminded him that he was, after all, sitting in a cybercafé cooled by the shadows of the world's tallest mountains. Suddenly it occurred to him that there might be no better way to clear his mind than to spend a few hours hiking the slopes of some solitary peak.

"I won't get lost?" he asked.

The man blinked and shook his head lazily. "Only one road. Down."

It seemed like a metaphor for his life, but rather than be discouraged, he booked a taxi for the following morning. He would carry with him a couple of books, some water, and a light lunch. Hopefully, the invigorating air of a mountain temple and the sight of the highest peaks the world had to offer would help him see his way through to what he should do next. Maybe he would even know his next destination by the time he hiked down the mountain and made it back to civilization—if one chose to call Rishikesh civilization.

His mind made up, Rodrigo returned to his computer and managed to finish going through his email. He may not have known what he was going to do with his life, but at least he knew what he was going to do with the following day. It was not much, but it was all he had for the moment.

9

RODRIGO CONTINUED TO FAITHFULLY record his dreams each morning when he woke up, but none of the disjointed fragments that accompanied the return to his waking world could compare in either literary or psychological appeal to the vivid textures of his three visits to a Hindu temple. Each time he realized that he was swimming back to consciousness out of a sea of banal events jumbled together in chaotic fashion, he experienced a twinge of disappointment. Such dreams did not spur his mind forward in a mad rush to know itself. They did not confront him with questions that would trouble him throughout the day, questions both uncomfortable and exhilarating. They were simply bubbles from his subconscious rising up in a fine vapor, discharging the pent-up energies that roamed restlessly in his brain. But on the morning of his hike to Kunjapuri, he returned once again to those increasingly familiar temple grounds that shifted and dissolved and re-formed like the scenery of any other dream but which always seemed to return to a more and more precise rendering of the same landscape. Again his emotions were the first thing he became aware of, rocking him back into wakefulness like the tossing of a boat in a summer storm. Elation and pride mixed together with guilt and self-deprecation in a fervent brew that drove him to his computer in a sudden leap from his bed, anxious to expiate his sins with the sacrament of the written word.

Rishikesh
8/30
7:12 AM

Once again my recurring dream has returned me to my favorite landscape. This time I was sitting in a small garden patio. I seem to recall that it was behind the main temple building—I remember the temple looming over our conversation and the felt presence of the other priests worshipping in its interiors. I was sitting on a bench with one of the elders. There was a trellis above us covered with creeping vines thick with yellow flowers. The air was heavy with their scent and mildly intoxicating, so that I felt a little giddy. But perhaps that had something to do with his words. He was admonishing me to hold my tongue and stop criticizing the other priests. I remember his words clearly: "You will be high priest one day, and sooner than you think. Why do you insist on jeopardizing that by criticizing the very people who hold your fate in their hands? Don't be a fool! Bide your time and hold your tongue. Accept what they say. There is more wisdom in it than you think. When the time comes for you to be high priest, you can change what you like. What will it matter to us then? Our bodies will be mere ashes in an urn and our spirits one with the great Brahma, unless our penance and our sacrifice have been insufficient and we are destined to come again as his servant." These may not have been his exact words, but they convey the essence of what he said. The moment he told me I would be high priest one day, I knew he was speaking the truth. He was telling me in his oblique way that it had already been decided. The only thing that could stand in my way now was my own stupidity. This indirect admission filled me with pride and elation, though I did my best to keep it from my face. I nodded humbly while he talked and kept my eyes respectfully lowered, but all that time I was visualizing how I would change things the moment I became the keeper of the inner sanctum. The elation didn't last, though. While I was assuring him that I understood now, that he was right, I grew more and more uneasy. I began to feel that I was betraying myself with these saccharine words, betraying my ideals and the goddess herself. To put it plainly, I felt like I was selling out, giving up my beliefs in exchange for position and power and a supremely comfortable life. I could feel the prestige associated with being high priest playing with my desires as he talked. I wanted it, wanted it badly, so much so that I was ready to do whatever it took, but at the same time I knew that in order to fulfill that ambition I would have to compromise the ideals that were burning inside me. Elation, pride, disgust swirled together in the air above my head, mixing with the heady perfume of those bright yellow flowers, while I sat there on the bench and listened to the prattle of this old man whom I clearly despised, nodding humbly like I was an acolyte in front of some great sage. When I woke up, I could feel the pretense curdling my blood, even as the elation washed over me in receding waves.

So what is my fictive hero up to? Is my subconscious punishing me because deep inside I feel like I have sold out and not been willing to admit it? It is a suspicion I have entertained from time to time in recent years, helped along by Beth's not-so-subtle insinuations. Have I not always seen myself as a writer first and last? Was not becoming a professor of literature just a means to an end, a way to make money and survive while I practiced my craft without having to stray too far from what I loved and dreamed of doing? It has been ten years since I got my PhD and landed the job at Carolina. I've bought a house and two cars, gotten married and divorced, and taken three trips to Europe. And what have I published in the meantime? A few short stories in a campus rag and a score of scholarly articles that have won for me my tenure and a middling reputation among my own kind—English professors who write literary criticism with both eyes on their professional security. That and a few unpublished poems, a few unfinished short stories that I locked with a password so Beth couldn't read them, and the half dozen or so false starts on a novel, the same unwritten novel that I had somehow convinced myself would be the beginning of an oeuvre that would rival Proust's. But I have my job, my wedding pictures, and my Altima. No wonder I feel so terrible! No wonder my subconscious is beating me up about it by casting me as the brilliant but ambitious priest trading his soul for prestige and power! I remember telling myself that I had to be practical. The old guy was right. First become high priest and then you can do what you like. But how many years will go by before you finally follow your passion? And when, or if, you do, you run the risk of it being too late. You run the risk of looking for your soul and finding that you lost it one night while you were grading papers, the same night you finally accepted your mediocrity. Should I have remained poor and unsuccessful and dedicated myself to my writing right out of college? Or gone into a writing program instead of a PhD program and lived in a loft for the next ten years eating peanut butter sandwiches and banging away on an old PC because I couldn't land a job or afford a decent computer? Maybe I'm afraid the answer is yes, and that at the end of this sabbatical I will have found out that it's already too late. It's been two weeks since I've written anything that didn't end up in the trash, and there's no evidence to suggest that anything I wrote up until then is worth the sliver of a megabyte it takes up on my hard drive. Or else, if I have not yet crossed that point of no return, is my subconscious telling me then that it is fast approaching, that I now face a final decision between pursuing my art or returning to a lifetime of comfortable mediocrity? I doubt I can finish this book in a year. The whole idea of doing so is bitter comedy in light of what I'm going through. And what will happen when I do go back? Does my book go back on an electronic shelf and remain there until my next sabbatical? Perhaps I am reading too much into this dream, but somehow I feel that I should pay attention. It is my life that is hanging in the balance, the life I want versus the life I have gotten stuck in. I ask myself if these dreams will continue. And if they do, what, then, will the priest do? Excuse me, what will *I* do? Our decisions in the present are what decide our future. Wallace Stevens was right. This is a war. I can only hope that the fiction I am moving toward is a supreme fiction and not a Harlequin romance in the checkout aisle of my local supermarket.

A couple of hours later, Rodrigo found himself in the back seat of a taxi winding his way up the steep slopes of the Lower Himalayas, his camera pointing out the window toward the stunning vistas that swept past him with a velocity that made him dizzy. His driver did not appear to be much interested in the scenery. He was gripping the wheel tightly and staring intently ahead, leaning forward as if he were trying to peer around the next bend and anticipate the traffic. With every turn, they climbed one rung higher. The view became more and more spectacular, deep forested ravines spilling over to the next slope in a downward spiral to the Gangetic plains, the lower altitudes gradually receding into a haze that made him feel like he was leaving the world behind and climbing into the lower reaches of heaven. From time to time, they passed small villages perched precariously on the slopes, enchanted clusters of brick-and-plaster houses that disappeared at the next bend in the road, as if by the flourish of a wand, plunging him back again into the crisp, cool solitude of the incipient mountains.

Rodrigo dutifully took pictures of each noticeable change in the scenery, intent on having a visual record of the trip, but he found it difficult to keep his mind on the gradually expanding vistas. His dream continued to bother him. Images of the temple interiors interposed themselves over the widening landscapes that occupied his eyes. Why had he nodded so obsequiously to the temple elder? Was he really so enamored of his prestige and his comfort? The sense of disappointment seemed to grow as the altitude increased. Granted, it was just a dream, as insubstantial as the air flowing past his window, but his emotions were real, and he knew they reflected the stunted motion of his life and the string of poor choices he had made that had led him to this impasse in the mountains. Beth had made her own thoughts on the matter painfully clear. In her eyes, he had let himself be swayed by the easy attractions of his comfortable, privileged position, until the man she had married was no more to be found. He had stubbornly refused to see himself in the mirror she held up to him. It was merely one of her creations, he had told himself, a photoshopped image that bore no real resemblance to the original, but could it be that his subconscious had compared the two and declared the artist to have captured the true essence of the man?

Some forty minutes after they had set out, he saw the temple appear through the trees on the top of the peak up ahead, jutting into the sky like a jagged set of ramparts aimed toward heaven. The sight of it distracted him from his thoughts. It reminded him of a castle in an old fairy tale: impossibly remote, brooding, full of portents and lurking dangers. The forest here was not as dense as it was in Rishikesh, but if anything it was more imposing—less luxuriant but endowed with more character. The struggle of each individual tree was more evident to the eye as they fought for a foothold in the craggy slopes, bent and striated by the wind, stubborn in their refusal to let the difficult conditions strip them of their dignity. Fir, Himalayan Oak, Bel, European Nettle, and others whose names Rodrigo would soon read on a signboard at the foot of the temple steps, each adapting itself to the mountain solitudes with a tenacity that made it seem as if they had fed themselves on stone, drawing it up through their roots and into their sinews to furnish them with the strength and the steadfastness they would need to endure the centuries of silence that awaited them.

The taxi moved cautiously now along the narrow strip of road carved into the mountain like a series of broad steps. Ten minutes later, it arrived at a small landing below the temple where a few tiny shops were selling green coconuts, incense, and trinkets for the pilgrims to offer to the deity, as well as small images of the goddess for anyone who wished to bring a semblance of the Divine Presence back with them to their homes. Rodrigo paid the driver, who looked at him with a noticeable air of disbelief when he told him he could go, as if this pampered, thin-limbed westerner's claim that he intended to walk back to Rishikesh were just an idle boast that he would think the better of once he had a chance to look back down the mountain slopes and see the enormous gulf that separated him from his warm bed, his milk toast, and his tea. Rodrigo smiled, but as soon as the driver had taken the four one hundred rupee notes and turned back toward his taxi with a dismissive shrug, his resolve began to waver. He felt a sudden urge to tell him to wait after all, in case he changed his mind. Only his embarrassment at his own weakness stopped him. Before he could overcome it and err on the side of prudence, the driver had turned his taxi around and taken off without a further glance for the foolish westerner whom he had left stranded on the edge of an eleven-kilometer descent.

Rodrigo stared for a few moments down the now-empty road, shaking his head at his own foolishness. Then he turned and stared up at the temple nearly a hundred meters above him. Only a bare glimmer of the whitewashed walls of the temple compound could be seen through the trees that clung to the steep slope. Above a rampart, he could see the orange flutter of a small triangular flag. Directly in front of him, there was a white archway and a long flight of white concrete steps that climbed steeply upward and disappeared into the foliage. He took a picture of the steps and the signboard beside the archway that detailed the local flora in both Hindi and English. Then he began climbing the 408 wide steps that turned left at one landing and then right at another until they brought him to a second archway that led into the temple grounds. This one was presided over by two golden lions that glared imperiously at him from either side of the entrance. A few feet above them, two gray elephant heads lifted their trunks toward the sky. A large iron bell hung down from the middle of the arch to a height just above his head. He remembered the Buddhist monks in Dharamsala ringing similar bells as they entered their temples. He wondered if the Hindus did the same; for a moment, he was even tempted to give it a gentle ring, but he hesitated to disturb the silence before which even the sound of his footsteps seemed like an imposition.

Rodrigo passed under the arch and entered a spacious courtyard framed by an odd assortment of buildings that reminded him of the Tibetan temples he had seen, only sparser and less colorful. The buildings were painted white with orange borders, doors, and window shutters. Only the temple stood out from the rest. It had vertical orange stripes on the walls and on the pillars of the veranda, and a large, pyramidical cupola that shot up from the roof like a gnome's hat announcing the fairy-tale character of its owner. He went up for a closer look and peered through the open doorway. The temple priest was performing a ritual for the benefit of an Indian family that was crowded into its small interior. He inched forward, intrigued by the similarity between this and the dream he had had some three weeks earlier. The priest had a shaved head and a red stripe in the middle of his forehead. It made Rodrigo wonder momentarily if he would have seen that same stripe had there been a mirror in his dream. The priest turned and looked at him quizzically. Suddenly self-conscious, Rodrigo backed away and walked over to the next building, a small concrete gazebo with iron mesh walls, also painted orange; inside it was a blue statue of Shiva sitting in the same meditative posture as the much larger statue in front of the ashram, his silent presence blessing the temple compound. Dozens of bright tinsel ribbons, orange, red, and yellow, fluttered gently from the iron mesh that enclosed the statue. Rodrigo guessed that they had been tied there by pilgrims hoping for favors from the great god. He took a picture and then completed his circuit of the grounds. There was not much more to see. It was a small mountain temple, and from the looks of it infrequently visited. The pilgrims might curry favor with the goddess by their visit, laying green coconuts and burning incense in front of her image, but for Rodrigo the main attraction was the clear mountain air, the solitude, and the immense panorama of the Himalayas rising up beyond the compound wall. The pictures would go into his collection, but he had come there to think, and it seemed like the perfect place for that.

He walked around for a few more minutes, trying to decide on a place to sit, until he noticed a concrete platform at the back, just outside the compound wall. There was a small opening in the wall and a few cracked steps that led to a dirt path that ran down past the platform and into the brush. He clambered down and stepped onto the platform, his eyes drawn like a magnet to the magnificent vistas that stretched out to the north, ridge after ridge of Himalayan fastness, the mountains closest to him covered with trees and brush, those that succeeded them barren and rocky, those in the far distance shrouded by a veil of snow. Looking down, he could see a highway snaking like a silver ribbon across the face of the nearest slopes. It looked so close, it seemed as if he could reach it with a well-thrown stone, but the trucks that were inching their way along it like tiny ants, barely visible to the naked eye, made him realize that this was just an illusion brought on by the altitude and the clarity of the thin mountain air. How much farther would the snowcapped peaks be? Forty miles? Eighty? It made him wish that he had brought an atlas with him or had at least read up on the Himalayas in preparation for his journey.

By now it was mid-morning. He had come there to take advantage of that Himalayan clarity in the hope that it would help him bring some clarity to his life. Still, he had at least three hours before he needed to start heading back. In the solitude of these mountains, three hours seemed like more time than he could measure, a distant way station between where he stood and eternity. He decided to lie down and read for a while, anything to put off this uneasy rendezvous with his thoughts. He had brought with him a couple of books: one on the local gods and goddesses that included a short section on Kunjapuri, and another on Kashmiri Tantra, whose influence was said to extend throughout the Himalayas. The sun was slanting across the platform, carving it into separate triangles of light and shade. At this altitude the warmth felt good on his skin. The scent of pine and wildflower mingled with the barest whisper of a breeze. He lay on the edge of the sunlit portion, facing the mountains, and pulled out his book of gods and goddesses, hoping for an extended dose of oblivion to escort him within sight of the noon hour.

He thumbed through the index looking for the reference to Kunjapuri that he had noticed earlier and then turned to the designated page. It belonged to a longish chapter on the wives of Shiva. He flipped back to the beginning of the chapter and began reading. According to tradition, Shiva had three wives: Kali, Ganga, and Parvati, who was also known as Sati. It turned out to be Parvati who was associated with the temple. Her father, the Aryan King Daksha, considered the non-Aryan Shiva to be his enemy and forbade his daughter to marry him. Parvati, however, strong-willed and very much in love, defied her father and wedded the great spiritual master who would be known in later years as the father of Tantra. This enraged Daksha. He mounted a slanderous campaign against Shiva that culminated in a great sacrifice to the god Vishnu from which he deliberately excluded his daughter and her husband. At the entrance to the hall in which the sacrifice was to take place, he set up a statue of Shiva and openly defiled it. Parvati went to attend the ceremony, hoping she would be able to make a dent in her father's enmity. She assumed rightly that the daughter of the king could not be refused entrance, but when she saw the shameless insults heaped upon her husband in his absence, she could not contain her grief and committed suicide by throwing herself into the sacrificial fire. When Shiva learned of the tragedy, he hurried to the site of the sacrifice and decapitated Daksha, replacing his head with that of a goat. Then he carried Parvati's body on his shoulders back into the Himalayan solitudes. According to the legend, the places where the parts of her dead body fell became known as Kunjapuri, Surkanda Devi and Chandrabadni, thereafter worshipped as *siddha piths*—holy pilgrimage spots filled with *shakti*, the divine energy of the goddess. The temples erected on those sites became the holy triangle of the Himalayas for all who worshipped the devi.

The story was nothing if not colorful. It had a literary rightness that Rodrigo could not help but appreciate. He wondered if the Hindus had ever actually believed in these myths. Or had they always been literary abstractions to them, passed down by their tongue-in-cheek forefathers who had amused themselves with these fantastic, wildly entertaining tales—tales that could hold both the attention of their children, who peopled their dreams with these bright, mythic figures, and their students, who were convinced they held the symbolic key to the deepest philosophical truths of the universe? He made no effort to decipher the secret meanings of the myth but instead flipped avidly ahead to the next one and then the next, increasingly absorbed by these brash stories of divine and semi-divine beings who leapt over mountains and sent forth mighty rivers when they unbraided their hair. Soon he was no longer aware of the mountains in front of him but only of the mountains within, peopled by sometimes heroic, sometimes petty, beings who amused themselves by interfering in the affairs of humans, springing traps for them and delighting when they somehow wiggled free, then quickly forgetting these short-lived creatures when faced with the far more serious matters of internecine conflicts and epochal jealousies with others of the divine blood. One thing was clear: fiction had been alive and at work since the beginning of human history, even up here in these mountains where the earliest human citizens carved out a meager existence by day among the thistles and the thorns and by night dreamed of piercing the stars with their thoughts and giving birth to the natural wonders of the world that awed them as they worked. Did they also use their dreams to rewrite the unsuccessful dramas of their daily lives and then write them down as the myths that would govern their children's understanding of the world? Were these goddesses the wives and daughters of their ancestors writ large and chastised into perfection by a mind that was ever yearning to better the reflection it saw in the mountain pool? A lifetime devoted to literature convinced him that they were.

Rodrigo found himself growing drowsy as the sun grew warmer. His thoughts began to drift lazily in the nearly motionless air. Shifting over into what remained of the shade, he turned onto his back and slid the book under his head as a makeshift pillow. The sky at its zenith was as blue as he had ever seen it, despite the proximity of the sun. He draped his right arm over his eyes, untethered his mind, and let it drift off into what he hoped would be a short and pleasant nap. He began his reverie by imagining what it would be like if Ambika introduced Le Gentil to the myths of the different gods and goddesses as she began her deliberate efforts to educate him about Indian culture. He would balk at first, but soon he would see the similarities to the stories of the Greek gods and goddesses that he knew so well. This would lead him to wonder if the same stories had made the rounds from culture to culture in the ancient world, changing their faces but not their purpose. Myth was as far removed from science as one could get, but Le Gentil had always maintained an interest in cultural anthropology. To his way of thinking, nothing reflected better the psychology of a people than the myths that governed how they interpreted the world. Just look at the Christian myths and how they had prejudiced the medieval world against the practice of his profession. The study of a culture could not be complete without an understanding of its myths. Ambika would share this way of thinking, but for her the myths of her people fulfilled an even greater purpose: they were a creative means of conveying the deepest philosophical truths to the masses, whose long hours in the fields did not allow them to cultivate the study of books.

Ambika and Le Gentil tossed their ideas back and forth, leading Rodrigo further and further from the temple. As his conscious volition waned and daydream turned to dream, the scenery began to change. Ambika's face metamorphosed into Beth's, still in a sari, still with her nut-brown skin, at the age that Beth had been when he first met her. A door opened and he stepped in for Le Gentil like a well-trained understudy. But the part was not the one he had prepared for. He was still the astronomer and she his secretary, but now he was writing his book, the great account of his voyages in the Indian seas and his heroic efforts to record the Venus transit and thus determine Earth's exact place in the solar system. "There is just one problem," he heard Beth say, her skin sporting the same dark sheen as Ambika's. "You're a terrible writer. Do you actually think anyone will want to read your book, much less publish it?" The scenery shifted again. Now they were sitting in their comfortable suburban house, ten minutes from campus. She was still in her sari but her skin was growing paler and the expression on her face more foreboding. She fixed him with a stare and told him that she was moving out and would be filing for divorce. All he could do was to stammer out the words he had stammered out in real life: "But you love me." Her reply was the same as it had been: "I can't say that's true anymore." As he felt once again that terrible sinking feeling in his stomach, the visible portion of the whirlpool that had sucked the joy out of his life, he felt the concrete pressing rudely against his shoulder blades. He realized that he was no longer dreaming but remembering. Again he felt the same anguish he had felt that day and every day since, but instead of arriving piecemeal, held off by his confusion, it fell on him all at once like a huge hooded wave falling from a great height onto an unprotected shore. In its wake it left the taste of salt in his mouth and the certainty that he was alone and adrift, abandoned by the woman who was supposed to have been his Beatrice. Reeling from the impact, he felt a spasm in his stomach and the wet trail of tears on his cheeks. He had loved her and now she was gone. All his life he had been longing to find the love that had been denied him since his mother died. He had looked for that love in one woman's face after another, as he had looked for it in the stories that lit up his imagination, searching their eyes for some sign of an eternal bond that would see them safely across the hard stones of their lives, warmed and protected in one another's embrace. The one woman who would know his innermost heart and find her solace there, whose enchanted gaze and musical laughter would melt his hard exteriors and turn the world's sorrows into joys. And then one day she had walked into his classroom, in answer to the prayers he had offered to the void, only to declare him unworthy of her love, abandoning him to his fate.

Rolling over onto his side, Rodrigo curled up into a fetal pose. His last trace of hope, and with it the last of his ambition, escaped him with a tremor and dissolved into the circumambient air. The tears continued to stream, unimpeded. Though he knew he would have to get up soon and walk back to Rishikesh, it no longer seemed worthy of his attention. Nothing any longer was worthy of his attention. Whether he continued working on a book that no one would ever read or cast it aside, whether he stayed in Rishikesh or left, whether he remained laying there outside the Kunjapuri temple compound or made the trek back to his ashram room. What would it matter if he could not fill the void that gaped inside him?

No matter what he did, he could not get away from himself—and that was the whole of his problem.

For nearly two hours, he remained lost at the edges of the world. The sun started falling in a western slant toward the tops of the furthest peaks. The faint whisper of a breeze drifted past unnoticed. Rodrigo slipped in and out of dreams that he could not remember, aware only of the heaviness in his limbs and the deadened, hopeless quality of his thoughts. The sun was well past its meridian when he entered a dreamscape that seemed more real to him than the stark facade of a world that had robbed him of his will. He saw a figure walking through a somber wood. It was a young woman in a sky blue sari. He saw her from a distance and only in profile, but even then he could see that she was achingly beautiful. She made no sound as she padded through the underbrush. The gracefulness of her step made it seem as if she were gliding. Then the sound of ankle bells came rippling after her, a fluttering tintinnabulation that was more music than any ordered collection of notes he had ever heard, a sound that seemed to rise from the depths of the ocean of air around her until it washed over him and carried away his tears. The image made his heart ache with longing and with sorrow, but at the same time it seemed to awaken him to the possibility of hope, as if the wind had changed direction and brought with it the first salty inkling of the nearby presence of the sea. He awoke with a strange fragrance in his heart. He blinked away the moisture around his eyes and sat up. Directly in front of him the mountains loomed as immense as ever, though now a faint haze made them seem more opaque, less substantial than they had been. Just then, he heard the sound of ankle bells again, distinct and unmistakable. It startled him. He looked around. There behind the wall of the temple enclosure, about ten paces away, he saw a young woman in a pale blue sari gazing at him with a familiar smile. She had dark skin and long dark hair that spilled over her shoulders. Her smile made the open wound within him throb. He lowered his gaze, struck by a sudden, confused timidity, and then looked up again a few moments later. She was still there, looking at him with such fond familiarity that he now wondered if he might not have seen her before, in the ashram or wandering the streets of Rishikesh. She lifted her hand and beckoned to him. A bevy of golden bangles on her wrist slid toward her elbow with a shivering sound like that of a rainstick, making the gesture seem like a brief musical interlude. Rodrigo was momentarily confused. He didn't recognize her and the gesture seemed so out of place in that setting that he distrusted his interpretation of what she meant. Again she beckoned to him. He pointed to himself. The girl laughed, her voice more musical than any he had ever heard. She turned around and started walking away with one last glance over her shoulder and a final wave of her hand. As if possessed, he scrambled to his feet, stuffed his book and his bottle of water hurriedly into his knapsack, and clambered up the path toward the opening in the boundary wall. When he entered the courtyard, the girl was halfway to the temple, walking slowly over the brown, stubbled grass in her bare feet, her ankle bells rustling like wind chimes in the still air. She walked leisurely up to the veranda of the temple without looking back, while Rodrigo followed hesitatingly some twenty paces behind. She stepped onto the veranda, glancing sidelong at him with a look he could not decipher, and then ducked into the open doorway.

Rodrigo approached the temple slowly, unsure of himself, still weary from the emotions that had depleted him while he lay curled up on the concrete, held fast in the throes of an incomprehensible, impetuous momentum. When he reached the veranda, he removed his shoes and peered in through the open doorway. The priest was sitting by the side of his priestly paraphernalia, his head bent over a book. Rodrigo hesitated, fighting his embarrassment. Then he stepped inside, expecting the girl to be sitting in a corner where she could not be seen from the doorway. When he didn't see her, his confusion reared up and mocked him.

"Yes?" the priest asked, lifting his head and waiting for him to speak.

"I was looking for a girl," Rodrigo said awkwardly, trying to look around without being impolite. "I thought she came in here."

The priest smiled indulgently and shook his head. "No, no girl. But please, come. Do you wish to make an offering?"

"No, no thank you."

Rodrigo folded his hands to his chest and inched back from the doorway. The priest inclined his head ever so slightly and returned his attention to his book. Rodrigo slipped on his shoes as he scanned the empty courtyard. He took a quick look behind the temple but there was no one there. He peered over the back wall, thinking that she must have slipped away down the path that ran outside the wall, but again he saw no one. A crushing sense of disappointment filled him, a certainty that his last hope had just slipped away, barefooted. Then he realized that it didn't matter. A chance encounter with a young Indian woman was not going to change his fate. A few minutes' conversation, if she even spoke English, was not going to alter who he was. At that moment, she was probably headed down the stairs to the landing, but the idea of following her now seemed patently foolish. What he had lost, he had lost long ago. He would not find it in the folds of a young woman's sari on the steps of a Hindu temple hidden in the mountains.

Chastised by his thoughts, he walked over to a whitewashed concrete platform to the left of the entrance in which was imbedded the trunks of two large shade trees. It was well after one. He knew he should be starting back, but the ache in his heart seemed to paralyze him. He sat down with his back against one of the trees. From where he sat, he could see the Shiva statue gazing back at him, half hidden by the orange mesh and the bright tinsel ribbons that sparkled in the afternoon sun. He remembered the ritual he had performed on his second morning in Rishikesh. He had felt the presence of the statue then as a living witness to his offering, a symbolic representative of whatever gods might have been watching over him as he set out on his journey toward becoming a great artist, someone capable of reaching deep into the human heart and bringing to life its aspirations and its disappointments, its joys and its fears, casting aside the veil that hides us from ourselves. Now he looked into that impassive, unblinking eye of stone and felt that the great god, whoever he might be, was presiding over the disintegration of his dreams, the end of everything he had ever hoped for. In the absence of those dreams, he felt the immanence of his own mortality, and he knew that after he was gone this statue would still be there, a mute witness of his absence. Was this, then, the only image of eternity he could muster, this lidless eye of stone? For several weeks now, he had been surrounded by pilgrims, each in their own way sure that eternity lay at the far end of their journey. Their faith kept them on their feet and gave meaning to a life that to him seemed to be forever slipping into shadow. He could not share their trust in an enduring truth that lay beyond what the eye could see, and his reward for this was a gnawing emptiness that was as close to the Infinite as he would ever get. He had relied on his love for a star-crossed woman and his destiny as an artist to give his life meaning, but his destiny had left him stranded in the Himalayas, tottering on the edge of the world's highest peaks, and the woman had vanished into the shadows of his past. His words had failed him. They had proved as empty as the thin mountain air. His companion for the journey, the soulmate who was to share his dreams and help to fill his life with meaning, had vanished into the same vapid air, as insubstantial as his words. One glance from an unknown Indian girl had been enough to show him that his desire had not died. What had died was the illusion that such a love existed, or if it did, that he could find it. If he had been an ancient Greek, perhaps he would have accepted the girl as a divine apparition, come to mock him for his folly, but he was not an ancient Greek. He was a modern American agnostic, one step removed from the cradle and two from the grave. He had no faith to comfort him and no illusions now to cover up that void. Nowhere to go that would not be the same empty place, and no way to change his fate.

He closed his eyes and slumped against the trunk of the tree, his mind plunged into shadow. A half hour later, he opened them again and headed mechanically for the stairs. The temple was deserted now. When he reached the bottom of the steps, the landing was empty of taxis. He bought a green coconut from one of the small shops, drank the water, and verified the path back to Rishikesh. Then he set off on his four-hour trek down the mountain, passing through the village just below the road, the firmly packed soil of its one street echoing his footsteps, and then out into the fields and down the slope toward the trees that he could see about a half a kilometer farther on. He walked as briskly as he could, knowing that he would still be in the forest when darkness fell if he did not hurry. True to what he had been told, there was only one path, winding down the mountain in meandering but graceful loops. He saw no one on the path until he had been walking for a couple of hours. Then he heard voices, the high, clear notes of children. Minutes later they rounded a bend coming toward him, a group of ten or twelve youngsters in faded clothes that would have been used for rags in his country. The oldest could not have been more than ten. They were carrying bundles of sticks on their heads tied with vines, balancing them with one upraised arm. When they saw him, they stopped and stared and then almost as quickly broke into laughter. One of them shouted, a tiny boy of perhaps seven or eight. The boy dropped his bundle and darted into a sparse thicket by the side of the path. Rodrigo thought for a moment that he might be afraid of the pale stranger, but then he saw him climb into a tree and start throwing down small yellow fruits that he plucked from its branches. The rest of the children dropped their bundles and rushed after him. Soon they were all happily digging their teeth into their unexpected treasure. The strange white man was forgotten. A couple of them glanced briefly at him as he started walking again, but only briefly. The fruit was an elixir and they were drunk on its ambrosia, impaled by the moment and rooted to the ground on which they sat. Rodrigo shook his head, wondering if he had ever been like them, so unquestionably one with who and where they were. He thought not, but if he had, it had been long, long ago. At this point in his life, there was no escaping who he had become, and the thought of it was almost unbearable.

It was dark when he saw the lights of the first houses appearing through the trees. He was only fifteen minutes from the Muni-ki-reti road, but rather than feeling any anxiousness to get back, he found himself hesitating. He sat down on the path for a few minutes to massage his aching calves and feet. Behind him the forest was growing invisible. Even his own body seemed like a shadow that would fade out of sight when the last traces of sunset could no longer find passage through the trees. When his legs felt better, he found it difficult to overcome his reluctance to go on. A desire came upon him to melt into nothingness along with the contours of the wooded slopes that were fast disappearing. What a relief it would be to feel and be nothing. To simply disappear, as if he and the world had never been. But then he remembered that the morning would come and he would be revealed once again for who he was. He shook his head and rubbed his calves one last time. Then he got up and started walking, knowing that he had no real choice but to go on.

PART TWO

SARASWATI

10

RODRIGO DID NOT SLEEP well that night, despite the weariness that had seemed like a blessing to him when he went to bed. Rather than bring oblivion, his sleep merely showed him that there was no escape from his troubles. Where his conscious mind forgot, his subconscious mind held vigil. He woke up several times during the night, and each time he could remember fragments of dreams that took little or no effort to connect directly to his sorrows. One was of the girl he had seen at the temple; it was accompanied by an ache in his heart, a longing he was loathe to put a name to. Another time he woke up dreaming of Beth; this time the longing was even more acute, for his dreams admitted what his waking mind would not: how much he missed her, how deep the wound left by her absence. Early in the morning he awoke for a third time, dreaming that he was back at Carolina teaching "Introduction to American Literature" for the forty-fifth time, inching toward retirement, every student's face in the spacious hall a reminder to him that those who can write, write; those who cannot, teach. When he woke up for good, shortly after dawn, he was dreaming of the old lady he had met on the road. The scenery was vague and inconstant, as if the cameraman of his imagination could not quite decide between Matisse and Cezanne, but despite the distorted shapes and the odd colors, the reds and purples superimposed on mountains that could not sustain them in real life, he recognized the road that paralleled the river. The face and voice were unmistakably hers. He did not bother to transcribe the dream when he finally sat up in his bed because the details were too similar to the ones that were still fresh in his memory. Once again, he had heard her tell him that he was lost, only this time he had agreed with her and cried a few silent tears while she looked at him with a great tenderness etched into the wrinkles of her face. He sat there for a long time, revisiting that chance encounter, remembering her words, the admonishing "God has given you two eyes so that you can look ahead and not behind" and the enigmatic "Being lost is a necessary condition for being found." He remembered the way her eyes crinkled when she smiled and it made him smile, almost in spite of himself. Then he remembered what the swami had said in his talk, and it was as if the two of them were talking in tandem, the words uttered weeks ago directed specifically to this moment in time. Had he really come to India in search of its sages and the wisdom they had to offer, lost but willing himself to be found? It was a difficult idea to entertain, but here he was, undeniably lost but suddenly unwilling to turn back.

He looked around the room now. For the first time since he awoke, he became aware of the sounds of chanting floating in through the open window. Everywhere in Rishikesh, devotees and yogis, Eastern and Western, were sending their words and their thoughts toward God. Many of them, no doubt, were sitting in silent meditation at that moment as the sun inched above the horizon. They had been doing the same thing in the same place for thousands of years. It was difficult to comprehend. For thousands of years, these yogis had crossed their legs and closed their eyes and sent their minds in search of peace—the one thing he did not have and the one thing he most needed. He might not believe in God, but he certainly believed in peace of mind. If there was one thing he could thank his troubles for, it was the firm conviction that the opposite of peace was hell and that no amount of outer peace was enough to douse the inner fires. For a few minutes he listened to the chanting. It was too faint to pick up more than an occasional word, but there was a feeling he caught that was not plaintive, as he had once thought, but soulful in the best, most literal meaning of the word. Then a thought struck him, so hard and so evident that he felt momentarily blinded by its plainness. He was in Rishikesh, the world capital of yoga, surrounded by people in hard pursuit of the one thing he most needed, most desired, and most lacked—happiness and peace of mind. Was he not a fool if he didn't take advantage of his time here to learn what he could? Of course he was. Perhaps he would still be a fool, even if he did, but there was no helping that and no sense looking behind, as the old lady had rightly said. He had nowhere else to go and certainly nothing more important to do. For some reason, an image of Hemingway appeared in his mind, the one of the youthful angler standing proudly by a ten-foot marlin in Bimini. This was followed by an image of the writer's white-bearded head slumped face first on the floor, a still-warm shotgun just beside it, the air acrid with the odor of gunpowder. Is that what he wanted to do with his life, to chase the perfect story but lose sight of the hunter, to court oblivion in the name of art? No, it was not. He would have none of Hemingway's depressive depths, no matter how much material it might furnish for his art. He could still become a writer one day, if that was his destiny, but first he had to become a healthy human being.

Rodrigo got up and went into the bathroom to take a shower. In the time it took him to cross the seven tiles from the bed to the bathroom door, he made up his mind. He would start with Amrita's yoga class, and this time he would not complain about how difficult it was. He would begin by putting himself in her hands and then take it from there. Rishikesh was full of teachers. In fact, it was full of nothing *but* teachers and students, not that much different than the university campus where he had spent his entire adult life, no matter how esoteric the subject matter. The difference was that now he would be on the other side of the educational divide. He was starting from scratch, with hopefully no way to go but up.

In the days and weeks that followed, Rodrigo became Amrita's best student. Whereas the other students came and went, he never missed a class. He set his alarm to get up early and was almost always the first to arrive, sometimes waiting on the veranda to catch her before she entered the hall so he could ask whatever questions were pressing on his mind.

Despite the physical discomfort that came from having gone so long without exercising, he struggled doggedly to master the postures. Soon he even found himself looking forward to the pain, almost as if this form of low-grade torture were a means of expiating his sins. If Amrita was surprised at this sudden, determined devotion, she didn't show it. She treated all her students with the same studied informality, although at times Rodrigo could catch her looking at him out of the corner of her eye, a quick, penetrating glance that made him suspect that she was just as aware of his presence as he was of hers. She corrected his posture at intervals, but soon she started dedicating more of her time to the newer students, though many of them were far more flexible than he was. He took this as a silent indication that he was making progress. Indeed, as the days went by, he found his range of motion increasing to the point that some of the simpler postures began to feel comfortable and relaxing. At times, he started to notice a certain sense of calm invading his experience. These brief moments of inner quiet, even more than the satisfaction he felt from being able to steer his body into places it had never gone before, gave him a new-felt appreciation for the practice. He knew that his nature was not calm, apart from these infrequent but welcome moments. Rather, as a rule, he felt more agitated than he had ever felt, wandering through a labyrinth of self-regrets, frustrations, and sadnesses that fell on him like a wind whipping down an open valley, inexplicable gusts that seemed to change direction every time he looked up to see where they were coming from. But those few moments were enough for him to glimpse the possibilities, to hold on to a growing hope that his future might be different from his present and entirely separate from his past.

One day after class, Amrita caught up with him just before he made his customary turn in the main courtyard to head up to his room before breakfast. She had come up behind him as silent as a rising tide and startled him with her voice, that husky, rasping resonance that had seemed at first to be at such odds with the mellifluousness of her gait.

"Rodrigo, I've been meaning to ask you. Have you forgotten our pact?"

"Our pact?" Rodrigo furrowed his brow, aware that there was something he had forgotten but unable to remember what it was.

"Yes, our pact. You promised you would learn meditation. Or perhaps you thought that I'd forgotten?" She turned a wry smile toward him and shook her head in that peculiar Indian fashion that had so many shades of meaning, one could give it whatever meaning one liked.

"Oh, that. No, no, I haven't forgotten. I've just been a little preoccupied, that's all."

"Good. I took the liberty of setting up an appointment with the swami for you this afternoon. He came back last night and he's only here for a couple of days before he goes out on tour again."

Rodrigo had indeed been thinking about it. He had been thinking that he would love to be able to sit completely motionless, like he had seen the monks do, and let his mind sink into a peaceful oblivion, but he didn't think he could ever be successful at it. His mind was not like theirs. He could see the peacefulness etched into their faces. It even showed in the way they walked, now that he was looking for it. It shrouded them like a fine mist on an early winter morning. His mind, on the other hand, was like a wild boar tearing through the underbrush, rooting rudely in the earth in search of some temporary sustenance and then charging boisterously into a thicket. The idea of making it sit still and think of nothing seemed preposterous. Indeed, it was precisely his imagination that was his strongest suit, even if he could not harness it fully with words or make its hidden colors intelligible to another's eyes. It would never sit still for him and wait idly while he traveled to a world it could not enter or even understand. He knew it would not accept its banishment under any conditions, however temporary they might be. But he had promised, and Amrita's tidy proclamation seemed like a directive from some royal authority that he had hoped would never come, but which, once having come, he had no choice but to obey.

That afternoon he sought out the swami in his private chambers after receiving some brief instructions in the proper protocol from Bhagavati. The swami received him graciously, gave him a mantra, and taught him how to meditate with it. He now belonged to the twice-born, the swami told him when they were done, not in the religious sense, as many Hindu Brahmins understood it after their investiture with the sacred thread, but in its secret esoteric meaning of having died to the dream of materiality and awakened to a life of spiritual pursuit. Rodrigo did not feel any different. He could not see why he should, but the swami assured him that the mere fact of trying to meditate twice a day on the sacred sounds of the mantra would change the very ground of perception on which he stood. He would not realize it at first, that change being as gradual as the changes in one's features when seen each day in a mirror, but before long it would completely alter his understanding of who he was and the world he lived in. A change of perspective, the swami said, was a change of existence. When practiced properly, meditation had the power to reveal the universe—not as we think it to be, but as it actually is. He would understand this once he had climbed high enough to get free of the clouds that now obscured his sight and tasted free air and an unobstructed vision for the first time.

Rodrigo was intrigued by the swami's words. The idea of seeing deeper and more clearly into the nature of reality appealed to his artistically sensitized mind. So he practiced his meditation twice a day as instructed, but he saw little to show for it, other than a recognition of the enormity of the struggle that lay before him, trying to tame a mind that paid no heed whatsoever to his efforts at instilling discipline and instead went on its merry, chaotic way, searing him with his failures and reveling in its capacity to inflict punishment. He gave up, temporarily at least, his fruitless efforts at writing. He even all but abandoned his journal and instead gave himself over to his reading and long walks through the streets of Rishikesh, occasionally venturing upriver and into the forest solitudes that acted like a temporary balm, soothing the edges of his frustration. He studied the books he had bought on yoga and meditation as he had once studied for his PhD, with a voracious appetite and a steadily increasing curiosity, determined to ferret out their secrets. He borrowed others from Amrita and made a habit after lunch of browsing through the shelves of the nearby bookstore. But he also read novels with something close to his former regularity; while he had been right in assuming that he would not easily be able to lose himself in a peaceful oblivion through meditation, he was able to slip away into the world of the novel with the barest of efforts, a habit long cultivated that now came to his aid and gave him the only lasting respite he could find from the lashings of his mind.

One morning after yoga class, Amrita asked him how his meditation was going. "Not well," was his immediate reply, a rapid, hard-edged retort that carried more of his frustration in its tone than he wanted to let on. Rather than commiserate with his difficulties, as he might have expected, Amrita smiled, her face brightening as if she were glad of this development. She nudged from him a few explanatory details, and with each answer she nodded knowingly, beaming with satisfaction.

"Good. You're making progress."

"Progress?" Rodrigo said, more than a little annoyed at her determined cheerfulness and her refusal to show any sympathy for his struggles but making every effort not to let his annoyance show.

"Yes, progress. You have to take it step by step, my dear. There's no jumping ahead, so you can just check your well-conditioned American impatience at the door. This is going to be a slow process; you might as well get used to it. But believe me when I tell you, you're on your way. Everything you've just said proves it, clear as day. You see, the first step is to become aware of how out of control your mind really is. Until we start meditating, most of us have no real idea of what's going on inside. Which only stands to reason because we've never actually sat down, closed our eyes, and taken a good long look. We spend our whole lives worrying about the outside world: what we have, what we don't have; what we want to achieve or what we've already achieved or what we regret not having achieved. We're so identified all the time with what we are doing out there that we never take the time to really understand what's going on in here. But when you start to meditate that all changes. Your whole focus shifts. You start actually looking at your mind, observing it, seeing how it functions; and when you do, you begin to find out what a mess it is. And I don't mean that in a bad way. It just means you're a normal human being with the normal untrained mind. It was the same way with me. I still remember. Oh, yes. Anyhow, the point is, you shouldn't get discouraged. You're not going to reverse a lifetime of habit in two weeks. It takes time, but if you keep at it, you'll get there. You told me a few minutes ago that your mind has become more agitated since you started meditating. Actually, that's not true. Your mind was always like that; you just weren't aware of it until now. And that by itself is a huge step forward. It means you're becoming more conscious. It's like Gurdjieff said: Before you can get out of a cage, you first have to realize that you are in a cage. Understand? You're finally starting to recognize what it means to be behind bars. It's like you're in *The Matrix* and you just took the red pill. 'Oh my god, is that who I am? You mean my whole life has been an illusion? How did I get into this mess? Who did this to me?' Yes, it feels terrible, I know, but it's totally necessary. It's the first step in the process of awakening. You can't begin the search for freedom until you realize the nature of your predicament. First you have to understand that you're a prisoner. You have to understand what that really means—and not just with your mind; you have to feel it in your gut. Then you can start trying to figure out how to open the door of that cage and escape. That's the next step. How are you going to get out of the matrix? That's when it starts to get interesting. In other words, you've discovered how out of control your mind is. Well done. Now, the next step is to start working on getting it under control. Fortunately, the world is full of people trying to get free and they are all there to help you. That's how you got the red pill in the first place."

Their conversation took them to one of the ashram benches, just to the side of a mythological scene depicting Rama fighting the demon Ravana. A small shisham tree cast the bench in a dappled morning shade, gently highlighting the golden tints in Amrita's hair. For some reason, her immaculate white cotton clothes and the streaks of sunlight that fell across her shoulders made Rodrigo think of Athena out for a stroll among the mortals. He might have felt more at ease had she actually been an immortal. He felt out of practice in the art of talking to other human beings—other than the customary small talk, tidily confined to the surface of things. But Amrita was not one for small talk, as he had already discovered. She was blunt and unapologetic by nature, seemingly convinced that truth was a virtue and that all virtues were better in larger doses. She asked him a few pertinent, probing questions, and like a pie bursting from the heat of an oven, Rodrigo soon found his past spilling out in front of him in hot, lava-like flows. He lamented his inability to write, revealed his fears of never becoming the writer he dreamed of, and drew a painful sketch of his relationship with Beth and its ignominious end. Amrita's gaze never faltered. But rather than frown or shudder at appropriate moments, or gently touch his hand in a show of sympathy at his mounting failures, she maintained the same steady cheer and airy lack of preoccupation, though her gaze gradually grew calmer and more intent. Her reaction disconcerted him, but the mere telling of things he had bottled up for so long with only himself for an audience generated a cathartic sense of relief that felt long overdue.

"Well, you've certainly gone through quite a lot, Rodrigo" she said, continuing to look at him with the same intensity. "But sometimes that's what it takes to open our eyes. Otherwise, we would just end up sleepwalking through our lives. In the end, we get what we deserve, neither more nor less, but it's all good because those just desserts are what motivate us to search for freedom."

"We get what we deserve?" Rodrigo felt a hot rush of blood to his face, but he made an effort not to let his indignation sully his voice.

"Don't pout my dear. I am not dissing you. The furthest thing from it. But compassion is sympathy with its eyes open. There is a reason for everything that happens in our lives. You can't escape that, even if you don't understand it. Everything that has happened to you has happened because it's your *samskara*, no one else's. You brought it on yourself due to your past actions. I know that can be tough to hear sometimes, but that's karma, baby. That's samskara. It is what it is. The key is to recognize that the whole mechanism is designed to lead you down the path of liberation. There's a divine purpose behind it. That's what you have to look for. Samskara is the real ghost in the machine; it's what turns the gears."

"What was that word you used? 'Samskara,' right? I've come across it a few times but I don't remember exactly what it means."

Again Amrita shook her head in that maddeningly ambiguous gesture that Rodrigo was still having trouble deciphering.

"Bery, bery important," she said, turning the *v* into a *b* with a mock Indian accent. "I would explain it further, but that takes us into philosophy and that's where I get off the bus. If you want to understand samskara—and sooner or later you have to—then you should talk to Saraswati. She's the dean of philosophy in this ashram. You haven't met her yet? Well, then you're in for a treat. You'll like her. If she weren't a yogi, she'd probably be a college professor, like you. Her class is at ten o'clock, Mondays, Wednesdays, and Fridays, under the banyan tree— unless it's raining, and then it's in the yoga hall. Whatever questions you have, bring them; she'll have the answers, believe me. She's that good. In fact, I heard she's starting a new class on the Yoga Sutras in a couple of days. It'll be perfect for you. There's no better place to begin than at the beginning. And if you don't mind me pointing it out, my dear, you are a beginner."

Rodrigo did not buy Amrita's implication that she wasn't good at philosophy. The sparkle in her eyes as she made that remark suggested otherwise. For some reason, she didn't want to share with him what she knew. Maybe she thought he should attend Saraswati's class, and that by withholding something he wanted, she could condition his response—shades of Psych 101. What had sounded on the surface like a suggestion had felt more like an order, one he could disregard at his own peril. Or perhaps she simply didn't have the patience to deal with his ignorance and preferred to leave it to a trained professional. Whatever the reason, he did not insist. By the time he reached his room, he had decided it was a good thing. Much of what he was reading he found confusing. He needed a teacher to guide him through ideas that lay in what were, for him, uncharted waters. As a teacher himself, he knew there was no better place to clear up these confusions than in the classroom and no better guide than someone who not only knew her material but knew how to communicate it to others. In other words, he had already known he needed a philosophy teacher, even if he had yet to articulate it to himself. He only hoped she would be a good one.

Rodrigo had not dreamed of his Hindu priest since his descent from Kunjapuri, but the temple grounds of his imagination were never far from his thoughts. He remembered them at times during the day, especially when his mind grew more reflective. Sometimes those lucid fragments seemed more concrete and more immediate than his real memories. At such times, he wondered if his fictive hero might not be better equipped to deal with his current frustrations and sadnesses than the real Rodrigo, who had very little of the hero in him that he could see. From what he had seen, his priestly self could meditate without losing control of his unruly mind, the same mind that ran away from Rodrigo every time he closed his eyes. His priest shared his ambitions, but with less of the self-doubt that had paralyzed Rodrigo's artistic aspirations. He was not troubled by Beth's rejection or by his inability to write a convincing scene. He was at home in a world of faith and at ease in his own skin, at least by comparison with his flesh-and-blood counterpart.

Now, on the morning after his conversation with Amrita, with the sun still below the horizon but already casting a pale light among the mountain peaks outside his window, his dreaming mind picked up the thread once more and brought him back to the same sanctuary where he had first seen the image of the goddess on her marble pedestal. When he awoke, he felt a surge of recognition as he became conscious once again of those strikingly vivid images: the cold marble, hard against his knees; the scent of incense filling his nostrils; the looming presence of the goddess wrapping herself in the mortal folds of a stone statue. He lingered in the bed as his mind raced backward through the dream. A doorway opened and another scene emerged, just prior to the one he had been immersed in when he woke up. A dark, sultry face floating in front of a bed of flowers, challenging him with her eyes. And then nothing more could be uncovered. He sat up, reached for his laptop on the night table where he had left it, and let his fingers draw him down into the pools of memory.

Rishikesh
9/14
5:35 AM

I am back in the temple. Or was just moments ago when I woke up. The exhilaration I feel is not difficult to account for: it is as if I had been longing to go back there and have just had my wished granted. And indeed I had been longing to go back. These dreams are far more interesting than my real life, if the truth be told. They seem to take place in vibrant, living colors—pungent reds and bright yellows, deep purples and dark, luminous greens—while my actual day is filled with innocuous shades of gray and an occasional dull yellow or washed-out green. I have missed waking up to find that I am someone else, temporarily freed from the cage in which I spend my days plucking at seeds on the papered floor and frilling my plumage. But today, for at least one more morning, I can say with conviction that my life is a dream.

When I woke up, I was in the inner sanctuary kneeling in front of the image of the goddess, as I had been when I first dreamed of her. The silver plates of lemons and chilies and neem leaves were there at the goddess's feet where I had placed them (now I recognize them as neem leaves, having seen the tree), occupying strategic points within a maze of painted triangles. I was making the ritual offering of flowers and incense, throwing handfuls of pink and red petals over the idol's head; I can almost swear I saw her smiling as the petals careened off her wild corn-silk hair and fell down to her feet like manna showered from the heavens. I can still hear parts of the verses I chanted. The syllables slip away from me as I reach for them, but the meaning remains like a fine mist that lingers, having risen from the waters of sound: 'I am the dance of death, the ultimate horror and the ultimate ecstasy, the dance of destruction that draws all beings into the timeless void that is my bosom and sends them back again into the dance of rebirth.' I can still feel the devotion I felt when I was reciting those syllables. There was no trace of the unbeliever that I am. I was kneeling in front of the mother of the universe with full, unquestioning faith, staring into the eyes of the creator. As I looked up into those black irises of painted glass, I believed I could see galaxies opening up beyond her head and stretching out into infinity. She was withdrawing these galaxies into her bosom, and I knew that one day she would withdraw me as well. It was a conviction, a belief, that is totally foreign to me, something that in real life I might label holy ignorance, the lamentable scourge of blind faith; yet in my dream it was as natural as a mountain spring, bubbling out of the depths of my being—in fact, it seems to have been the source of my strength. After these verses, I recited a prayer, asking her to lead me to the light. Then I sat cross-legged for meditation. I closed my eyes and started reciting the same mantra the swami gave me, but in the dream I was adept at this practice. It was a talent I had honed over the course of a lifetime. Within moments, I could see an ocean of light opening up inside me, but for some reason a lingering agitation remained. I kept seeing this face, a beautiful dark-haired, dark-skinned woman's face, much like the face of the girl I saw that afternoon at the Kunjapuri temple. She kept floating into my consciousness and distracting me from my meditation. Then I remembered why:

It had happened just before I went into the deity's room to perform my worship. I had been walking in the temple gardens, thinking over some point of philosophy from one of the scriptural texts I had been reading. Some point in the text had me puzzled and I was trying to figure it out. Then I noticed a girl standing there watching me. She was a servant girl with ebony skin. Her hair was very straight and very long, drawn into a single thick braid. She was wearing a threadbare sari of very poor quality. Her feet were bare and she was balancing a large earthen pot on her head. She was, I knew, one of the girls whose job it was to draw water from the well and fill the vessels in the various rooms. She was looking at me expectantly, so I asked her if she wanted something, thinking that she might be having difficulty with one of her assigned tasks but did not want to speak before spoken to, not to a priest. She put down the pot on one of the stone benches by the side of the path and asked my permission to speak. She was very humble about it—she could not have been otherwise, a low-caste servant and a woman talking to a Brahmin priest—but there was a gleam in her eye that was anything but humble. I wouldn't call it proud, but I had a distinct sense that she did not feel any sense of inferiority, despite her tone of voice and the way she bowed her head and averted her eyes. I was a bit impatient, not wanting to be disturbed from important thoughts, but she surprised me with what she had to say. Instead of asking me if I needed water in my chambers, or if the veranda outside my room needed sweeping, as I had expected, she told me that she had greatly appreciated my debate the other day but there was one point I had made that had puzzled her; she wondered if I could clarify it for her. I was somewhat taken aback. It was not a question a servant would ask, much less a woman, but I was intrigued, so I told her that she was free to ask her question. What she said, as far as I can remember, went something like this: In your analysis of so-and-so's commentary on the Gita, you defended his interpretation that salvation is attained by knowledge alone, but does not the sacred text on which he based his arguments also teach that since the ultimate reality is beyond the mind, it is also beyond the purview of knowledge, no matter how elevated that knowledge may be? I knew exactly what passage she was referring to. I was about to say something dismissive when I suddenly realized what she was implying. Salvation could not be attained by knowledge alone. The argument I had made in the debate was fallacious. She said it so coolly, so matter-of-factly, as if it were just some little something that had confused her, but she was not confused at all. It was I who had not thought it through properly. I had missed this all-important point. No one else had seen it. Neither the other priest, nor the elders who were judging the debate, nor anyone in the audience. No one, except this water girl who must have been standing off to one side unnoticed under a tree. She was telling me in an oblique way that I had been mistaken, that I had better think it through again.

Think of it! A low-caste servant girl who was nothing more to me than a shadow on the temple grounds! She had probably been working there for years and I had never noticed her, and probably never would have, had she not dared to talk to me as no other servant would have dared. I didn't know what to say, I was too shocked for words. I tried to cover my embarrassment and excused myself, telling her that it was time for my worship, but the agitation she set off followed me into my meditation. And it follows me still.

What a dream! I still feel surprised, shocked, dumbfounded, but most of all exhilarated. Is this excitement a residue from the dream, or am I excited because my Hindu temple has called me back, and in most dramatic fashion? Either way, my blood is racing. Something seems to be awake in me that's been asleep these past weeks. Does this mean I may soon be able to write again, or does it go deeper than that? I have been profoundly unhappy for some time now. I thought I had hit bottom when I signed the divorce papers and boarded that plane, spurred on by my anger and an all-consuming urge to escape. But I did not know what bottom was until I climbed to Kunjapuri and opened my eyes to who and what I have become. True disillusionment, they say, is when you are finally stripped of your illusions, only to find that they were all that was keeping you afloat. That, I believe, is what happened to me on that mountain. Funny that I had to climb up to reach the bottom—and to a temple no less. Within sight of the worldly icon of heaven, I was ushered through the gates of hell. Fitting for an unbeliever like me, I guess. Then I climbed down from my mountain and back into the world (or up from Hades, if you prefer), and reached for a lifesaver to keep me from drowning—yoga and meditation—in the hopes that it could carry me to dry land. Thus I join myself to the stream of seekers who are my only company in this lonely outpost. But it is hard, this practice, harder than I could have imagined, and I am just as much at sea now as when I first went to graduate school—even more so. I've been confused by what I've been reading and by what I've been practicing, hopelessly confused at times. Though I have long prided myself on my intellectual acumen, the more my mind insists that I should be able to understand what I am getting myself into, the more it seems to slip away from me, like this mind that evades my grasp every time I try to meditate. Maybe my alter ego, the priest, was also sure he had a thorough grasp of things, that he was the master of his domain, as I had long fooled myself into believing, but the part of me that knew better borrowed a woman's form (image supplied in part by the girl I saw at the temple) and disabused me of that notion. In the open courtroom of the subconscious, my ego felt the blow, absorbed the shock, and registered its dismay, but it also became excited, because if there is a girl who can see so easily what I cannot, then maybe she can also teach me. Which leads to hope, the same that Pope assures us springs eternal. So will this Saraswati, whom I will meet tomorrow in philosophy class, be like a vision that steps out of my dreams and gives voice to the wisdom that is hidden inside me in some inaccessible region? Rather far-fetched, my waking self insists, but at least my imagination is active and perhaps even on the high road to recovery. Maybe something has been loosened, finally, like a floe of ice breaking free from the polar mass. Maybe the dream is the harbinger of that, if not the catalyst. Only the morrow will tell, the morrow that is today and the rest of my life. Now I will meditate, or try to. Then I will practice yoga with Amrita. Then I will sit in front of my computer and find out if it was only a dream or the rumbling of my imagination as it gets ready to rouse itself from sleep. Ah, words, words, words—be they a prison or be they an open sea, they are my destiny. For better or for worse.

That morning after breakfast Rodrigo sat in front of his computer and found that his prayers had been answered. At least he thought of it in that way, though all he knew for sure was that he started writing again. And though what he wrote was not the literary wizardry he dreamed of, he found that he could read it and not be totally dismayed. That, by itself, was a great step forward. At first the words came slowly. He had to force himself not to criticize what he had written at the end of each sentence; time and again, he had to will himself to resist the urge to blot it out and start over. But the wheels creaked forward. One sentence stumbled into another, until at some point—he never knew quite when—he slipped through the garden wall and became lost in what he was seeing, the hesitant interplay between Le Gentil and Ambika. Soon the words ceased to matter as the images in his head began to flow from his fingers to the keys.

It was mid-morning when Ambika showed up at Le Gentil's house. She still had no semblance of a routine, no clear idea of what her new employer expected from her. This she found disconcerting. Annoying, in fact, since she herself had had a clear sense of exactly what she wanted from her life since before the age of ten. Each morning since her early teens, after her daily worship and before her breakfast, she would draw up a list of what she planned to do that day and spend at least fifteen minutes ordering those tasks and thinking about the most efficient way to complete them. Le Gentil, on the other hand, as she discovered to her dismay, was a man with no fixed routine and no idea of what he was going to do from one day to the next, despite claiming to be a man of science from the intellectually conceited West, a decorated citizen from one of those countries that monopolized the seas and considered it their manifest destiny to colonize "primitive" nations like her own for their own good and a sizable profit. He started each morning with both eyes on his cup of coffee and his fresh baguette. Then he would sit silent in his recliner, reading a few pages out of one book, then several out of another, both drawn from scattered piles on the floor near his feet, until an idea dawned of what he wanted to do that day. Then he would bound up with a frenzied energy that Ambika found indecent and start shouting orders at his servants to get his carriage ready or set up his instruments on the veranda. He had one house servant and a gardener, both provided by the governor, neither of whom spoke more than a couple of words of French, plus a driver who understood the colonizer's language but was careful not to let on. The first thing Ambika invariably did when she arrived each morning was to translate orders that had not been carried out—Le Gentil's attempts at sign language did not translate well into Tamil. The one job that had been decided upon, the construction of the observatory, was delayed because Le Gentil had not drawn up the plans yet, despite his daily assurances that they would be done in the next day or two, and so Ambika had wasted a number of good hours during the previous days waiting for her boss to make up his mind what he wanted her to do. These were days, of course, that Rodrigo had wasted himself, and the parallel between his life and those of his characters seemed perfectly fitting. Neither did art imitate life, nor did life imitate art. They simply ran hand in hand, both prisoners to the same active or inactive imagination.

On this morning, however, something was percolating, about to reach a critical mass that would send the story spinning off in an unexpected but perfectly inevitable direction. Rodrigo could feel it coming, though he still wasn't quite sure what it was, just as he could feel that morning by the weight of his dream that something inside him had awakened. He stalled for a few paragraphs, waiting for it to appear. Ambika put on a pot of tea. Le Gentil blew the dust off a leather-bound book. Ambika brought the tea to a boil while Rodrigo watched patiently, well aware of the subtle symbolism at work in her simple act. She and Le Gentil eased into a conversation between rooms that began with her giving directions to the servants about the vegetable garden he wanted started in back of the house and segued into an impassioned discourse by the Frenchman about the principles of modern astronomy. And then it happened, the turning point Rodrigo had been waiting for, like the sudden appearance of the sun when it slips its cloud cover for the first time during a late spring morning. Ambika had brought the tea in on a platter and calmly poured out two cups while Le Gentil paced up and down as he talked, gesticulating with broad sweeps of his hand, pointing toward the ceiling as if the stars were clearly discernible there. She took a couple of sips of the steaming brew and sat back, looking at him in total silence. Finally he slowed his discourse and looked at her, as if he had just become aware that he had an audience he had failed to account for.

"You are very quiet," he said. "Have you been able to understand any of what I said, or have I been going too fast for you."

"Of course I understood," Ambika replied with an indulgent tone. "These things have been known in India for millennia. I'm just surprised that you Europeans are only just discovering them now."

This remark stopped Le Gentil in his tracks. He looked at her with an expression of disbelief that lasted for a full half minute before he opened his mouth. Ambika pretended not to notice, savoring her tea and adding a bit more sugar.

"What exactly do you mean?" he said, continuing to stare at her through the same narrowed set of eyes.

Ambika looked up at him with an innocent expression to which she added a delicate and deliberate touch of bewilderment. "But didn't you tell me that your expedition has been organized in tandem with England and several other European nations?"

"Yes."

"Well, I just assumed that the level of astronomical knowledge was the same among your different countries. Was I wrong? Is it only France that is so far behind India?"

She said it with such an air of innocent purity that he was completely taken in; he failed to recognize that a gauntlet had been thrown down. It was a mistake he would make on a number of further occasions, before he finally learned never to underestimate her again.

Le Gentil left off his pacing and sat down to question his beautiful young translator about matters of astronomy, incredulous at first as she detailed the feats of Indian astronomers who had studied the heavens long before the Gauls traveled south to the sacking of Rome, but increasingly vexed and agitated as she refuted his assertions of European preeminence with references to Hindu texts he had never heard of.

"You say that Copernicus was the first astronomer to advance a scientifically precise heliocentric theory of the sun and moon's motion? Less than three centuries ago? Nonsense. That knowledge has existed in India for at least six thousand years. Thirty-five centuries ago, Yajnavalkya wrote a detailed analysis of the motions of the sun and the moon. He explained the apparent retrograde movements of the other planets, how the spinning of the earth on its axis as well as its motion around the sun affects our perception of the motion of other planetary bodies, all these things. Really, you surprise me. I had no idea you Europeans were so backward in this respect."

It was a deliberate attempt on Ambika's part to put this brash barbarian with his enormously inflated ego in his place. But rather than simply making him mad, it inflamed his curiosity. For Le Gentil was not merely a brash, loud, and resolutely reckless member of an uncultured and egotistical conquering power, as she initially assumed him to be. He was also a scientist whose chosen discipline was not only a vocation but a calling. If there were any truth to what she was saying, then he would turn back heaven and earth to find it. And if he found it, he knew, without yet being able to articulate that conviction, that he would rescue that knowledge from the oblivion to which it had been consigned and broadcast it to the four corners of the earth. Though he was a Frenchman and a European, his true allegiance was to science, a domain that recognized no cultural or political borders. The riches he sought, the treasure trove of knowledge, were pearls that he would just as soon scatter from continent to continent so that anyone might pick them up and benefit from their luster.

Ambika could not see this yet. She had no idea of the depths that lay hidden in this brash Frenchman, no inkling of the changing tides that would soon invade her resolute heart. She did not yet have the tools she needed to interpret the fire suddenly ablaze in his eyes. It was a situation, Rodrigo realized, that needed to be nurtured if the story was to possess the tension and the hidden depths it required. There would be time enough for romance later. First he needed friction, and now he knew where he would find it. Her unshakable conviction that India's fifteen millennia of cultural history and single-minded pursuit of knowledge dwarfed any achievements the impudent European civilization could boast of, coupled with her inner calm and her ability to mould or withhold her speech in the service of her intentions, put her on a collision course with Le Gentil's impulsive, extroverted nature, so characteristic of the vastly younger culture into which he had been born, a culture full of creative energy but naive to a fault. Rodrigo had no idea yet how this nascent conflict would play itself out. It was going to require a lot of research and would undoubtedly lead him to discoveries he could not foresee. But play out it would. Already he could sense that here was something that would not only round his characters but enrich his readers—that is, if he ever had any.

Rodrigo left the scene hanging on the hook of Ambika's verbal lash, the unexpected force of her I-had-no-idea-you-Europeans-were-so-backward stunning Le Gentil into a mute but fervent silence and thereby providing Rodrigo with his cue for exiting offstage. He went to lunch feeling cautiously exultant, even more so than when he had awoken from his Hindu temple and poured into his journal what he remembered of his dream. He was writing again, and that was cause for celebration, but the feeling only lasted a few minutes. By the time he reached the dining hall, he had given himself over to the calming, sobering waters of reflection. Did he really want to make that same mistake again? Did he really want to get carried away by his illusory dreams of becoming a famous writer, only days after the collapse of those same illusions? He listened for the answer, and when it came back no, he felt a sense of relief. There was no reason to believe he would ever be a literary success, and even if he were, what would it really matter? No amount of external success would make him any happier. Fame was not a gateway to mental peace. If he had learned anything these past few weeks, it was that. As he finished his lunch and set out for a walk along the river, he examined his feelings, watching for any sign that they might be getting ready to trick him into believing that he was something he was not. He saw that a sense of satisfaction still lingered from his morning session, but the more he examined it, the more he realized that it had little to do with his dreams of becoming a great artist. Gradually it dawned on him that it had felt good—and still did—to actually have something to say. What difference did it make if he had an audience of thousands or an audience of one? He turned this over in his mind as he crossed the bridge and decided in a brief instant to head for the Sivananda library reading room. None, really, was his conclusion. Was it not enough to be satisfied with himself? With who he was and what he had to say? The difference might be subtle, but at the same time it felt like a fundamental shift. In some way, he had always seen himself through other people's eyes: Beth's, his students', the disembodied writers and literary critics who crowded his imagination. What would happen if he drew a curtain between him and them? What would happen if he limited his literary conversation to a dialogue of one?

As he reached the top of the steps, it suddenly struck him. The satisfaction he was feeling stemmed not from the idea or the hope that he was on his way somewhere. Rather, he was excited over where he had been. This realization took on so much the character of revelation that he had to stop and sit down on an empty bench near the top of the steps, unwilling to let anything get between him and his thoughts, not even his wandering feet. He sat there for a long time, peering into his experience, before he finally went into the reading room and left the solitude of his thoughts for a dialogue with the author of a book.

Could this feeling of internal satisfaction, he asked himself, unrelated to what other people thought or any external success it might presage, have something in common with the encounter with the self that the yogis talked about? Could it be a prelude, an entrance pass into the beginnings of the interior life? He had always thought of the novel as something outside himself, a magic apparition that the novelist conjures up from thin air. But what he had written this morning had felt more like a private conversation between him and his thoughts. In a way, it was as if he had taken them down just to see what they were. A chance to see what his mind was made of. It was a new feeling to him, a strange feeling. He had lived all his life with the idea that what he was searching for lay outside—in the accolades, the recognition, the place in literary history that would serve as his everlasting home. Today, however, had felt like a first good look at the home he already inhabited. He began to feel excited, this time to find what else he might discover there. He decided to take it as a sign, if not from the gods or from his muse, then from the self that was waiting to make his acquaintance, a sign that his fortunes were changing, a slight but significant shifting of the wind.

11

T HE SKY WAS PERFECTLY clear as Rodrigo walked up the path the next morning, making his way toward the huge banyan tree that cast its dense, cool shade over a wide amphitheater of lawn directly across from the yoga hall. The mid-September sun was warm on his shoulders as he walked but not oppressive. It reminded him of Carolina in the summer, an invigorating heat that made it feel like a crime to remain indoors. Above the cathedral-like canopy of leaves, two long-winged black birds circled in convex loops, one slowing as it reached the apex of the loop, the other gathering speed as it fell. A group of seven or eight people were sitting in a loose semicircle near the edge of the shade, about fifteen meters from the enormous bifurcated trunk that delved into the ground like a huge hammer splitting open the earth. Its roots crisscrossed the lawn, rippling in and out of the soil like a family of serpents whose slender, slithering humps belied their commanding presence beneath the surface.

Rodrigo looked at his watch before sitting down at one of the open ends of the semicircle. Three minutes to ten. He looked around, wondering if one of those sitting there might be Saraswati. All but two of them he recognized, either from yoga class or from the dining hall. Then he noticed a short Indian woman in a pale saffron sari walking up the path. She had short-cropped black hair and was cradling several books in one arm. As she approached the group, everyone folded their hands to their chest to greet her. When she had put down her books and sat at the open end, facing everyone, she returned their silent greeting with a solemn, almost grave expression on her face. Then she closed her eyes and folded her hands in her lap. The rest of the students followed suit, except for Rodrigo, who used the time to study her face. It was far from what he would call attractive. She had a sharp nose and one eye slightly askew; her short hair added to a mannish look that was accentuated by the seeming sternness of her expression. But there was also a sense of character in her face. Looking into the blemish-free sheen of her wheatish skin he could easily imagine her having royal bloodlines, forgotten but not diminished by the years. When she opened her eyes a couple of minutes later, her expression softened, but it wasn't what he would call a smile; it was rather a sense of welcome that was seen more in the eyes than on the lips. When she began to speak, he found her voice melodious and pleasant but very deliberate, as if each word were carefully chosen in an effort to convey her meaning with a minimum of ambiguity, like a well-oiled miter saw dipping into a block of wood along the fine pencil lines traced on its surface.

"Good morning. I see a couple of new faces. Welcome." Again she touched her folded hands to her heart, nodding her head ever so slightly in Rodrigo's direction and then toward the other side of the semicircle. "Today we begin a series of classes on what is arguably the single most important text on the theory and practice of yoga. The name of this text is *Patanjali Yoga Darshan*, which translates literally as the 'the yoga philosophy of Patanjali'; however, it is more popularly known as the 'Yoga Sutras,' since the text, as indeed all traditional philosophical treatises in India, is written in the form of *sutras*, or aphorisms. Before embarking on our study of the text, however, we begin with a little history, since everything that exists, exists within a context. The greater our understanding of that context, the better we can understand our object of study."

Though Rodrigo was only sitting a couple of paces from Saraswati, closer than anyone else, he had the uncanny feeling that her words were coming from a great distance, as if she were sitting atop an elevated peak surrounded by clouds. Her speaking voice was not flat or unnatural in any way—it had a soothing, steady modulation—but she did not seem to be talking to her audience but through it. She sat perfectly still as she talked and her eyes did not focus on anyone but seemed to be turned inward, following her thought with only a minimal awareness of her surroundings. It was an unsettling feeling, accustomed as he was to lecturing professors who filled their lecture halls or classrooms with equal amounts of passion and indifference, both tributes to their professorial egos. He had seen one or two who might have been labeled as abstracted, but they had a way of filling the room with their quirkiness, while she seemed to be on the point of disappearing, leaving only a disembodied voice with a volition of its own. The effect was to make him retreat within his thoughts, within the act of listening; like most of the other students, he found himself naturally closing his eyes while she spoke.

"Little is known about Patanjali, other than that he lived approximately 2900 years ago and was a brilliant grammarian as well as a philosopher. However, a great deal is known about the context in which he lived. At that time, yoga already had a history that stretched back four thousand years. What had begun as a small seed forty centuries earlier had, by the time Patanjali was born, grown into a huge tree with thousands of branches that extended all across Southeast Asia. In the forty centuries before his birth, countless systems of yoga had sprung up, taught by a myriad of different masters, each adding their own unique understanding, each introducing their own modifications and innovations, until the body of yogic teachings had become so vast and so varied that no one could see what unified it. Patanjali's brilliance lay in his ability to recognize that these were all variations of a single practice, one river of thought emanating from a single source and proceeding on to a single destination. Rather than lose himself in a maze of tributaries and rivulets, he was able to see through to the principle current and trace its passage from source to destination. In other words, he was able to extract the essential from the non-essential, the enduring and the timeless from the ephemeral and the transitory, and codify it into a single unified system that when analyzed was recognized to have been there all along. This was his great contribution. He was not an innovator. It is not even known if he was a realized yogi or merely a highly advanced practitioner, but he did what no one before him had ever done: He removed the veil that blinded and revealed yogic practice to be what it had always been: one unitary system.

"Patanjali wrote his work in the form of sutras. The word *sutra*, while it can be conveniently translated as 'aphorism,' literally means 'thread.' It is the thread, the kernel, the core or linking thought at the center of a nexus of ideas. The tradition of writing texts in the form of sutras arose in the time before the invention of written script, when texts had to be memorized in order to be passed on. The core of any one argument or idea would be stripped down to its barest essentials, without any concession to grammar, by which one could then remember the entire argument or idea or teaching. The teacher would sit with her students and expound upon the aphorism until they had understood the argument and memorized the sutra. They, in turn, would teach their students in the same way, expounding upon the sutra in their own words and adding their own insights, if any, but making sure that the sutra was memorized so that the original text and the essential teaching would remain intact. Even after the invention of written script, this traditional method of teaching and learning through sutra and commentary, aphorism and exposition, remained. Why? Because the ancient yogis learned through practice that it was an excellent means of developing the mind and its thinking capacity, for it lays equal emphasis on the two principal faculties of the intellect: *smriti*, or memory; and *manana*, or discursive thought. What was true then is still true today. So this morning we will carry on that tradition, beginning with the first three sutras. You will learn the sutra and I will pass on to you the traditional explication of its meaning. In time, by memorizing the sutras and understanding their explanation, you will not only gain a deep and precise understanding of yoga, you will be able to retain that understanding in your mind and pass it on to others."

Saraswati took a few sips from a small thermos and opened one of her texts, placing it on the grass in front of her. Her motions were slow and deliberate but graceful, echoing the careful passage of her voice. But at no time did she exchange glances with anyone or offer more than the whisper of a smile. She simply placed her hands in her lap, closed her eyes for a few moments, then opened them again and continued on in her quiet, steady way.

"*Atha yogánushásanam,* 'now begins the instruction in yoga.' This first sutra acts as an introduction to the subject. The only thing that needs be mentioned here is the literal meaning of the word *yoga*. Yoga means 'union.' It is derived from the Sanskrit root verb *yunj,* 'to unite,' which is also the source of the English word 'yoke.' Remember now, Patanjali was addressing his book to a community of practitioners with four thousand years of tradition behind them. They knew what the word *yoga* meant. They would not ask the question, union between what and what?

"In the next sutra, Patanjali gives his definition of yoga. Rather than providing an etymological definition of the word, however, he gives us an analysis of the conditions that are necessary for yoga, or union, to occur. *Yogashcittavrittinirodhah*, 'yoga is the cessation of the thought waves of the mind.' Now, Patanjali's audience was well aware that the word *yoga* referred to the union of the individual soul with the Divine Soul, the achievement of the state of oneness with God—what we commonly call 'enlightenment' in English. In Christianity, it is sometimes called 'mystic union'; in Buddhism, 'nirvana.' Patanjali's definition, however, refers to the psychological conditions required to achieve that state. And what are those conditions? The waves of the mind must be brought to perfect stillness. By implication, then, yoga is not only a state of mind, it is also the practice or the discipline through which one achieves that state of mind. What is yoga, then, according to Patanjali? It is the practice of bringing the thought waves of the mind to perfect stillness. And what happens when one achieves the state of yoga through the practice of yoga? Patanjali tells us in the following sutra: *Tadá dristhu svarupevasthanam*, 'then one abides in one's real nature.' And what is our real nature? Our real nature is consciousness; we are all expressions of one infinite and eternal consciousness.

"Now, let us take a closer look at the second sutra, quite possibly the single most famous sutra in the history of spiritual discourse. *Yogashcittavrittinirodhah*. The sutra is composed of four words: *yoga, citta, vritti,* and *nirodha. Citta* means 'mind'; *nirodha* means 'cessation'; *yoga,* you already know. That brings us to the word *vritti. Vritti* has several different meanings. The most common meaning is 'occupation' or 'livelihood.' Another is 'mental tendency' or 'mental propensity.' A third meaning is 'vortex.' A few minutes ago, I translated it as 'thought waves.' Why? Because thinking is the sole occupation of the mind, its sole means of livelihood. The mind thinks. That's all it does. If there is no thought, there is no mind. And what form does this thinking take? It takes the form of mental tendencies or mental propensities, and these propensities are, in fact, a kind of subtle energy vortex. So in simple terms, *vritti* means 'mental activity.' It may express itself as emotion or as abstract thought. It may involve visual images or auditory images, or it may simply be a sense of self. Any type of thought wave, be it perception, emotion, or abstract thinking, any mental activity of any kind is known as *vritti* in Sanskrit. And so, Patanjali tells us at the beginning of his exposition that the word *yoga* refers to the complete cessation of these thought waves, the complete cessation of all mental activity. Now this begs the question: what happens then? In order for the mind to exist, it must think. When thought ceases, the mind disappears. So what is left? What remains when all thought comes to a halt?"

Saraswati paused and slowly scanned her audience; nothing in her expression betrayed the fact that she was waiting for an answer. As the pause lengthened, those who had their eyes closed gradually opened them. Finally, a plump, thirtyish blond, wearing jeans and a t-shirt, raised her hand. Saraswati nodded in her direction.

"Consciousness?"

"Yes. And what are some other words for consciousness?"

"Soul," offered another young woman.

"Spirit?" said another in a tentative voice.

"God," added a stout, sturdy man with a German accent who raised his hand before he spoke.

Each response brought an affirmative nod from their teacher.

When no more answers were forthcoming, she continued. "Exactly. In Western philosophy the single most famous phrase—I cannot quite call it a sutra—is *cogito er sum,* 'I think, therefore I am.' René Descartes. Many consider this statement to be the basis of Western philosophy. In fact, it is not only the basis of Western philosophy, it is the basis for how most people understand their existence, whether they live in the East or the West, whether they are alive today or lived a thousand years ago, even so-called religious people. Who are we, if not our thoughts? This unspoken understanding—an understanding we all share—reflects the fundamental nature of the human condition. We are identified with our thoughts, totally and unconditionally. There is nothing unnatural or remarkable about this. Unless and until we achieve the state of yoga, all we can know of this world and of ourselves is what our mind tells us. We are what and who we think ourselves to be. In other words, our ego, our sense of individuality, arises from our thoughts and ends with our thoughts. What we know of our existence, we know through this sense of individuality. But that individual existence only remains as long as there is thought to sustain it. What happens when all thought ceases, and along with it, the individual ego? The answer to this question is the starting and ending point of yoga, and the fundamental basis of all spiritual understanding. But it is not a question that can be answered by the intellect. The most the intellect can do is form an idea or a belief about the nature of that state. This question can only be answered through direct experience, since the mind, in that state, is absent. And what is the nature of that experience? *Cogito tamen ego sum non meus sententia,* 'I think, but I am not my thoughts.' In Patanjali's words, *Tadá dristhu svarupevasthanam,* 'then one abides in one's real nature.' In other words, when all thought ceases, one abides in the state of oneness with the Divine, what the yogi calls 'consciousness.' One experiences yoga, union."

Again Saraswati paused to take several slow sips from her thermos. Rodrigo opened his eyes and looked around at the other faces in the circle, wondering if anyone else found this last idea as difficult to comprehend as he did. He took comfort from the puzzled looks and blank stares that passed from one face to another as if they had been handed off like a baton in a relay race. Saraswati did not seem to notice, however. She put down her thermos with solemn deliberateness, almost as if it were a ritual in some Oriental ceremony, and once again resumed her lecture with indrawn eyes.

"There are several analogies that are commonly used to explain this sutra.

Perhaps the most common of these is the comparison between the mind and a lake, or any such similar body of water. When the water of the lake is agitated, the mud rises and prevents us from seeing through to the bottom. At the bottom of this lake shines the pure light of consciousness. But because the water is cloudy, that light cannot be clearly perceived. We see it only dimly. When the lake becomes still, however, the mud settles; the water grows transparent and allows the light to shine through unobstructed. All of us have within us the light of pure consciousness, the soul, infinite and eternal, whose very nature is infinite bliss and perfect tranquility. It is this eternal, immutable consciousness from which the mind arises. But we cannot perceive it or experience its nature as long as the mind is active. We can catch glimpses; we can feel or intuit its presence at times, when the mind becomes relatively quiet. And when we do, we feel great happiness, peace, a feeling of being connected to the universe. But these are only glimpses, a glimmer of light that sneaks through to the surface. Ordinarily, the activity of the mind veils that light. If we want to experience it, we must turn the water of the mind transparent. In other words, we must bring the mind to stillness. There is a line from a poem by Shelley that you may have heard: 'Life, like a dome of many-colored glass, stains the white radiance of eternity.' Substitute 'mind' for 'life' and you have a poetic description of this spiritual truth.

"Another common analogy is that of a pot of water in which we see reflected the light of the moon. If the water in the pot is agitated or cloudy, then the moon's reflection is distorted or indistinct. But when the water becomes still and clear, then the moon is perfectly reflected. Each of our individual minds is like a pot of water that reflects the one moon, the one Divine Soul. There are many pots but only one moon. If we can make the water of our mind still and clear through the practice of yoga, then we will find within us the perfect reflection of that light. We will know God and know that we are God.

"Now, even in Patanjali's day, and even in a country whose entire history is the history of spiritual endeavor, there were people who did not believe in the soul, who did not believe in God. But part of the beauty of this sutra lies in the fact that it requires no belief. It is purely psychological and experiential. What he is implying is that this is a demonstrable truth that anyone can verify in the laboratory of her own existence. Still your mind and you, too, will experience the existence of a Divine Consciousness, the ultimate reality. Perform the experiment and you will get the results. The rest of his treatise is, in fact, simply an elaboration of this sutra. It details how to achieve this cessation of thought and what happens along the way. But all we really need to know of yoga is encapsulated in this one sutra.

"Now, before we move on to the discussion, I want to read to you a passage from the book *A Search in Secret India* by Paul Brunton. In this passage, the author, an English journalist, is interviewing the sage Ramana Maharsi; he asks Ramana a question about this very point."

Saraswati picked up one of the books that were lying next to her and opened it to a bookmarked page.

"The first and foremost of all thoughts, the primeval thought in the mind of every man, is the thought 'I'. It is only after the birth of this thought that any other thoughts can arise at all. It is only after the first personal pronoun 'I' has arisen in the mind that the personal pronoun 'you' can make its appearance. If you could mentally follow the 'I' thread until it leads you back to its source, you would discover that, just as it is the first thought to appear, so is it the last to disappear. This is a matter which can be experienced."

"You mean that it is perfectly possible to conduct such a mental investigation into oneself?"

"Assuredly! It is possible to go inwards until the last thought 'I' gradually vanishes."

"What is left?" I query. "Will a man then become quite unconscious, or will he become an idiot?"

"Not so! On the contrary, he will attain that consciousness which is immortal, and he will become truly wise, when he has awakened to his true Self, which is the real nature of man."

"But surely the sense of 'I' must also pertain to that?" I persist.

"The sense of 'I' pertains to the person, the body and the brain," replies the Maharsi calmly. "When a man knows his true Self for the first time, something else arises from the depths of his being and takes possession of him. That something is behind the mind; it is infinite, divine, eternal. Some people call it the kingdom of heaven, others call it the soul, still others name it Nirvana, and we Hindus call it Liberation; you may give it what name you wish. When this happens, a man has not really lost himself; rather, he has found himself."

Saraswati closed the book and smiled, the first real smile from her that Rodrigo had seen. It amazed him how much it lit up her face.

"Beautiful, isn't it? *Patanjali Yoga Darshan* is philosophy, and no matter how illumined or how profound that philosophy is, it doesn't come alive until it is brought to life by a human being. When you listen to Ramana talk, you can feel the truth of his experience. Remember, this is not just philosophy we are discussing. This is real life, the why and wherefore of the human condition. Okay, now we can open it up for questions and discussion."

One by one, people started asking questions and making comments. Some were simple questions that Saraswati clarified quickly. Others required more involved explanations. The pudgy blond girl with the familiar American accent had a complaint more than a comment. "Patanjali makes it seem so simple and so straightforward, but the truth is, it's impossibly difficult." Her tone of voice and the grimace on her face made it clear that she considered Patanjali's academic concision a direct affront to her sensibilities.

"Impossible it is not, Clara, but very difficult? Without question. In a sense, this is a war we are engaged in. We are trying to conquer our minds; and no war is without its sufferings, its setbacks, and its struggles. Patanjali knew this as well as anyone. That's why he wrote his book. To provide us with a map or a manual that will help us to eventually win that war. And it should be difficult. We are talking about the greatest achievement possible for a human being: complete mastery over oneself. Doesn't it seem fair that the greatest achievement should also require the greatest effort?"

Clara nodded her head reluctantly. She started to say something else, but cut herself off mid-sentence. Saraswati waited for her to go on. When she didn't, Saraswati looked at her watch. "There is time for one more question."

Rodrigo raised his hand. "I'm a little confused by what you mean when you say 'consciousness.' Are we not conscious *because* we think?"

Saraswati nodded, as if she had been expecting the question. "Some people, of course, use the word in that sense, but it is a very imprecise, if not incorrect, use of the word. Yogic psychology is very precise in its terminology—extraordinarily precise, in fact. What the word denotes, however, is so subtle that any confusion is understandable. First, let me try to explain what we mean when we use the word *consciousness* in yoga, and hopefully that will make it clear why we prefer it to more ambiguous terms such as *soul* or *spirit*, which are so laden with religious and cultural connotations.

"Patanjali based his work on Samkhya, the world's oldest philosophy, from which he borrows much of his terminology. Samkhya divides the mind into three parts: *manas, aham,* and *buddhi. Manas* is the content of the mind, the images, feelings, abstract thoughts, and so forth. *Aham* is the Sanskrit pronoun for 'I.' *Aham gacchami,* 'I go.' *Aham* is the ego, our sense of individuality, what almost all human beings think of as their self. I am Saraswati; I am hungry; I am thirsty; I am happy; I am sad; I see the world. What is it that links all these sentences? It is the pronoun 'I,' *aham.* Behind *aham* lies *buddhi,* the pure feeling of existence. Before you can feel that you are somebody, you must first feel that you exist. This feeling of existence is not differentiated. It is not individualized. It has not yet confined itself to the prison of 'I am Saraswati.' It simply *is.* There is no difference between my feeling of existence and your feeling of existence. As Ramana rightly said, this 'I am' is the primordial thought from which all other thoughts arise. However, there is something in us, even subtler, that is aware of this sense of existence. What is that? When your mind is at its quietest, if you pay attention, you will be aware of your feeling of existence. What is it in you that is aware? What is it in you that knows that you exist, that witnesses your presence on this planet? As it says in the *Kenopanishad,* at whose behest does the mind think? This witnessing entity we call *atman* in Sanskrit; it is often translated into English as 'soul.' The nature of this witnessing entity is pure awareness, a simple undifferentiated, unmodified, eternal and unchanging field of awareness. We call it 'consciousness' because that is its nature. It is conscious; it is aware. Not thought, but awareness of thought. When thought recedes, that awareness remains. It is what lies behind the curtain of thought. In the final chapter of the Yoga Sutras, Patanjali discusses this in detail, as shall we when we get to that chapter. But let me just quote one sutra from that chapter for you to reflect upon. *Citterupratisamkramáyástadákárapattao svabuddhisamvedanam.* 'Consciousness is unchangeable; as the reflection of consciousness falls upon the mind, the mind takes the form of consciousness and appears to be conscious.' To use an analogy, imagine a stage lit by a spotlight. The actors come onstage and act out the drama. We are only able to see that action and those actors by virtue of the light that illumines the stage. That light is consciousness and the actors are our thoughts. If the actors are absent, then the light illumines an empty stage. Or, to use a more modern analogy, think of a movie screen. Light passes through a film and breaks up into color and form, creating a series of moving apparitions on the screen. Those figures are transitory, ephemeral. But the source, the light itself, is unchanging. Remove the film and the light continues to shine on an empty screen. Consciousness remains, though there are no thoughts for it to witness. But you will only be able to truly understand this through deep meditation. Until then, your mind will only get in the way.

"And *that* is the problem."

Saraswati looked at Rodrigo, apparently waiting for this last remark to sink in. The expression on her face did not change, but the light in her eyes seemed to grow more intense. He let a few seconds of silence go by and then he asked another question.

"I wonder if you could explain about samskara?"

She tilted her head in typical Indian fashion. "We will get to that, but on another day. Our time is just about up for today and we still have to memorize the sutras from today's lesson."

When the class was over, Clara came up to Rodrigo and introduced herself. They were surprised to discover that they had grown up only two towns away from each other in Southern California. This led to a long conversation that continued all the way through lunch. It was Rodrigo's first extended conversation with anyone other than Amrita since he'd arrived in India, and he was glad for the company, especially since Clara didn't seem to be your typical spiritual seeker. She was heavily involved with Amnesty International, for whom she had worked for many years as a volunteer before being hired on the year before as a full-time staff member in their Ottawa headquarters. She was on her way back from an extended trip to Burma monitoring human rights violations in that embattled country and was eager to share her indignant assessment of the situation there. They talked for well over an hour with no mention of yoga or spirituality before Rodrigo finally asked her what had brought her to the ashram and how long she was planning on staying.

"I've been coming here off and on for the past eight years, whenever I get a chance. It's my favorite place to decompress, and believe me, I really need it after this trip. I've been here five days already and I'm still struggling to let go of the experience. It had my stomach tied up in knots. You think I'd have learned by now not to let it get to me, but it's just not that easy for me, not yet at least. I guess I'm just a terrible meditator sometimes. I could hardly meditate at all in Myanmar. I just couldn't concentrate with all the stuff that was going on. I was there for three weeks and I doubt I sat more than three or four times. Which, of course, is why I got so stressed in the first place. Meditation is the one thing that keeps me sane, so of course, when I needed it the most, I didn't do it. Anyhow, I've gotten back in the swing of things now. I'm finally starting to feel better about the whole thing. Thankfully."

"So how did you get started?"

"I started doing TM when I was in high school. I think I was born with an agitated mind, so when I heard about the benefits of meditation, I couldn't wait to learn. And it helped. Been doing it ever since. It even helped me with my grades. Then, when I graduated from San Diego State, I came to Rishikesh for an advanced meditation course in the TM center here. It's just down the road. That was just before they closed it to westerners. Afterward, I stayed in town for a while, took some yoga classes, got to know the ashram, and eventually it became a kind of home away from home for me. I think this is my eighth or ninth visit already, I'm not exactly sure. Anyhow, I'm here for another eleven days and I plan on savoring every minute of it. I'm not expecting enlightenment, but I do plan on feeling good and mellow before I leave."

Clara let out a laugh and took a final sip of her tea. She put her cup down with a flourish and leaned confidentially toward Rodrigo. "I decided long ago I was going to leave enlightenment for my next life, but I'm usually pretty blissed out by the time I leave this place." She patted herself on the folds of her stomach. "I'm also usually a few pounds heavier with all the oil and the *dal*. Everything has its pluses and its minuses, I suppose."

"So you must know Saraswati pretty well, then?"

Clara's jovial expression brightened even more. "She's probably the biggest reason why I'm here. I think most of what I've learned about spirituality, I've learned from her. She's probably the most yogi of all the yogis I know."

"She certainly seems to know her philosophy, that's for sure. She does seem a little cold, though, don't you think?"

"Cold?" Clara appeared surprised. "No, I wouldn't say that. She can be pretty serious, but I consider that a strong point. It's a serious world out there, in case you hadn't noticed. She probably knows that better than anyone I've ever met. If there's one yogi on the planet that doesn't have her head up her navel, it's Saraswati. No, she's friendly enough once you get to know her, and I highly recommend making the effort. I don't know, maybe with you being a guy, it might be a little different, with her wearing the saffron robes and all, but I've never gotten that impression from her."

"Well, it's just a first impression. I'm probably wrong."

Whether Saraswati was cold or not was beside the point. She was unquestionably a brilliant woman and to all appearances a kind of expert in her field. Though she hadn't answered his question about samskara, her introduction to Patanjali's work had already cleared up some of the doubts that had been bothering him these past couple of weeks. The thought of studying with her on a regular basis excited him. There was simply no substitute for having a first-rate teacher, especially when the subject matter was as abstruse as the study of human consciousness as seen through the lenses of the great yogic masters. He could just imagine her on the faculty at Carolina, this brilliant Indian import who combined a rapier-like intellect with the tranquility of a yogic adept. The counterculture youth would be lining up to get in her Oriental philosophy classes, and they'd probably be joined there by some of the more straight-laced students from the Psych department. Wasn't the Psych department known for its studies on meditation? He might have even been tempted to sit in on some of her classes himself, and he could see some of his cohorts from the English department joining him.

When Rodrigo went to bed that night, surrounded by an assortment of esoteric books, he had already decided that as long as he was in Rishikesh, he did not intend to miss a single one of Saraswati's classes. He was finding his reading more and more interesting, but even more interesting was the prospect of being able to take his questions to someone who would be able to illumine for him what he was unable to decipher on his own. He fell asleep feeling more hopeful than he had in a long time.

When he awoke early the next morning, he was dreaming once again of his Hindu priest, a role he was now becoming quite familiar with.

Rishikesh
9/16
5:30 AM

When I awoke this morning, I was back in the temple. Again! I know I should be surprised that I continue to dream in sequential fashion like this, but why then does it feel so natural, almost inevitable? Is it only because my subconscious mind has grown quite fond of this scenario—little wonder when I compare these dreams to my real life—or is it, perhaps, because I know that there are lessons hidden here that I can no longer avoid? In a sense, it seems as if what I am witnessing in these dreams is a drama staged by my subconscious for my benefit—for education as well as entertainment—and now that I am hooked, I can't wait to see what will happen next.

This time I was sitting on a lawn in the temple grounds. It must have been late afternoon, since I was aware of it growing darker as the time passed. In front of me sat a group of young men, some of them merely boys. They were acolytes in the temple, young Brahmins, and I was giving them a class. A few of the older priests were also present, but I was doing all the teaching; they were simply sitting there, looking bored but very important, as if my students and I should consider ourselves twice blessed that they were even there at all. That wasn't what annoyed me, however—I had lived with their arrogance long enough to be used to it. What annoyed me was that these people were my elders, a fact they made sure I didn't forget, and yet they didn't know half of what I knew and were too blind to realize it. I was explaining to the boys their duties in one of the forthcoming temple rituals that would take place later in the year. Then I began explaining the symbolism and the philosophy behind the ritual. That, I believe, was when the older priests stopped making any pretense of paying attention. The students were attentive, but I could see the looks of confusion on their faces. I kept having to repeat myself and search for simpler and simpler analogies to get my points across. As I did, my frustration began to mount. Here I was, surrounded by priests and acolytes, students and teachers of the sacred texts, and yet there was no one who could understand those texts as I understood them, no one who could understand or appreciate my thoughts. As I taught the class, I was grumbling to myself about the decline in the standard of the students entering the temple in this age of ignorance. Then I remembered the girl who had startled me in the gardens with the pointed subtlety of her question. Could it be that the only soul in the entire temple complex capable of understanding my thought was a low-caste servant girl whose very shadow I should be careful to avoid? The irony fell on me like a weighted shroud. Here I was, isolated and unappreciated, in the one place that should have been my haven, my sanctuary, my castle keep. I even glanced behind me a couple of times to see if she might be loitering by a jar that she had come to fill, listening to what I had to say and turning it over in her mind. When I didn't see her, I felt a pang of disappointment, a feeling for which I could find no justification, and yet there it was.

Such were the feelings I had when I woke up. Frustration, perhaps a whiff of desperation, the saddening realization that I had no one whom I could really talk to, no one who could challenge me like I was trying to challenge these students with the dull and uncomprehending looks on their faces. When I opened my eyes, my head was hot and I felt some throbbing in my temples, as if my frustration had been taking a physical toll on me while I was dreaming.

One more detail: It is not often I can recall the words I spoke while I dreamed. Sometimes I wake up dreaming that I have just said something brilliant, but I can never remember what it was. This time, however, I actually remember some of things I said while I was teaching this class. I remember telling my students that all external rituals were symbolic reenactments of the spiritual techniques we use to help us get rid of our accumulated samskaras (there is that word again!), or rather pre-enactments, since the external ritual trains us to be conscious of the internal practices we need to perfect. I told them they should not think that the performance of the *karmakanda* by itself can expiate our sins (I have no idea what *karmakanda* means, but I must have read it in one of my books). Instead, we should realize that the real benefit of the external sacrifice is that it gradually teaches us about the internal sacrifice through which the samskaras are actually burned. I can remember my words, I can even write them down in this journal, but I have no real idea what they mean. That is the difference between dream and reality, although the two may seem reversed at first blush. In my dream I understood it perfectly. Not only this—I was convinced that it was a monumental insight, though obviously beyond the capacity of my students, or even my fellow priests, to grasp. And now the same is true of my waking self. Anyhow, I will look at it later and see if there is any meaning to this madness, or if it is just a piece of dreamed gibberish. Perhaps I can even ask Saraswati about it.

So there it is, what I can remember of my dream, although I am sure there is much I have forgotten. What does it mean? Obviously, the content must have been sparked by Saraswati's class. Do I detect some envy leaking out? Do I, the professor, feel that I should be able to teach this philosophy and teach it as well or better than she? Perhaps, or perhaps I am simply identifying with her at some gut level due to our shared experience as teachers. Her class was intriguing and challenging; I think the dream shows that I have a desire to understand this philosophy and master it, as she has, as I have mastered the teaching of literature. I am beginning to understand now that this yogic philosophy is far deeper than I had imagined. Is my fictive hero even now straining himself to wrap his mind around these difficult concepts that I have failed to understand thus far? If so, then good luck to him. But I think the frustration is just as important here. I can still feel it lodged in my bones. No one understands me; no one appreciates what I have to offer. These are feelings I have had for a long time, feelings that Beth heartily reinforced. Maybe Saraswati's class brought them to the surface again; maybe it also reminded me how much I thrive off my imagination and my thoughts, how I have no one to share that part of my life with (the hidden mass of the iceberg). Here in Rishikesh I am very much alone, just as my priest feels himself to be very much alone in his Hindu temple. And though my solitude has been self-imposed, my conversation with Clara made me realize how much I long to have someone I can really talk to. The only company I've had up until now has been Amrita, and I don't know how far that can go. She is a good deal younger and doesn't seem to be one for intellectual discussions of the kind I favor, though perhaps I shouldn't jump to conclusions. Saraswati, on the other hand, has a mind I can truly admire. Any secret envy I might have would not be entirely misplaced; I'm sure she would be very much at home as a professor on a college campus. But I don't know if I will have any opportunity to talk to her outside of class, or get to know her as anything but my teacher in a classroom setting. Shades of a certain priest and a certain water girl?

12

*I*T ONLY TOOK ONE class for Rodrigo to become a permanent member of Saraswati's thrice-weekly study circle. Up until this point, he had preferred to keep himself relatively aloof from the communal life of the ashram, a wayfarer looking in through an open window at the life lived indoors. But that began to change the moment he took on the role of a student in pursuit of knowledge. His new teacher and her imposing intellectual discipline fed a dormant hunger within him that had never been completely clouded over by the mental routines of being a college professor. Soon he found himself diving into his spiritual studies with the same eagerness he had once shown as an undergraduate, his head turned by the romantic images he had formed of the great writers whom he worshipped like an acolyte, and by their texts, toward which he felt the same reverence the ashram residents felt toward sacred scripture. His newly adopted studies joined him to the current of seekers that flowed through Rishikesh and through the ashram, and caused him to begin to share the sense of community that people share when they find themselves companions in the things that matter most—conscious travelers on the path of life. This sense of camaraderie began with the other students in his class. Though new faces were forever passing through like water underneath a bridge, there were five of them those first two weeks that formed the center of the circle: himself, Clara, and three others who had been religiously attending her classes for several months and who considered themselves students of hers in the truest sense of the word: Ely, a short, swarthy Argentinean in her late twenties with a protruding hook nose that marred what otherwise would have been a classically beautiful face; Marlena, an introverted French woman in her early forties who spoke little and smiled less; and Georg, a big-boned German in his mid-fifties with a barrel chest who came to each class toting a list of questions inscribed in an exercise book in which he took notes as assiduously as Rodrigo's best graduate students. Rodrigo had recognized their faces from the ashram dining hall, but he had failed to notice that they invariably sought out each other's company for meals. Now he found himself a member of their group by default. He no longer had time to scribble in his notebook while he ate or leaf through the pages of a book. Instead, he became a de facto participant in their conversations, which never seemed to stray far from wherever Saraswati had left off in her previous class. Their obvious adulation of their philosophy teacher was mostly left unspoken, but it was clear to him from the weight they seemed to give to every word she spoke.

These conversations were a welcome addition to Rodrigo's life. At some point—he never knew quite when—the idea of moving on to Pondicherry subsided like froth upon the sea and made no signs of reappearing. Though he still assumed he would have to go there eventually to add some verisimilitude to his book, that prospect was, for the time being at least, a necessity too distant to consider. Though it was inertia that had kept him in Rishikesh, he began to notice the growth of roots fixing him to the ashram soil. There were faces he grew accustomed to seeing at certain times and in certain places; their familiar greetings became a compass for his day, marking the passage from one part of his daily routine to another. Soon he became so used to waking up to the gray light of his spare room and the whistling of the wind above the river outside his open window, accompanied by the sounds of cymbals and chanting voices, that the thought of Carolina gradually began to fade from his mind, both the life he'd left behind and the life that awaited him on his return. He wrote, he dreamed, he struggled with his meditation and his yoga, and he poured through his books on spiritual philosophy with an urgency that he described in his journal as a craving to make up for lost time.

In the succeeding classes, Saraswati's little circle slowly made their way through the first chapter of Patanjali's masterpiece. The sage's analysis of the different types of thought waves and the means of controlling them far surpassed any understanding of psychology that Rodrigo had been exposed to in his undergraduate psychology courses. Not only did it amaze him to discover such a subtle and detailed understanding of the workings of the human mind, the emphasis that Patanjali placed on attaining mastery over these mental processes seemed so logical and so obvious that he couldn't quite understand why he had never seen anything like this before. It was during Saraswati's explanation of the twelfth sutra—"these are controlled by practice and non-attachment"—that a light seemed to go off in his head. In a matter of minutes, yoga went from being a useful but strange, esoteric practice to being the most logical, most fundamental, and most necessary of the sciences: the science of self-mastery. Clara had prefaced the discussion with some reservations she had about the word *non-attachment* and the all-too-easy tendency to confuse it with indifference. Saraswati agreed with her that it was a common confusion, but rather than address her question immediately, she asked her to hold it in reserve until they had gained a firm understanding of the sutra in its entirety.

"There is always a certain imprecision that arises when we try to translate these sutras into English. Many of the Sanskrit words have no true English equivalent. If you only learn the English, it becomes difficult to avoid confusion. Our only recourse then is to try to understand the original Sanskrit word. Remember, these are sutras. Every effort has been made to compress an entire argument into a few words. So it is absolutely incumbent upon us to properly understand each word. Perhaps in time, as interest in yoga grows in the West, many of these words will be absorbed into the English language, as has happened with words like *yoga*, *karma*, and *nirvana*, but for the time being, we have to make an effort to learn and understand the Sanskrit terminology.

"Let us now analyze the sutra, word by word. *Abhyasavaerágyabhyam tannirodha. Tan*, 'that' or 'these,' referring to the five types of thought waves described in the previous five sutras, are 'controlled' or 'restrained,' *nirodha*, by *abhyasa*, 'practice,' and *vairagya*, 'non-attachment' or 'dispassion.' Let us start with the word *nirodha. Nirodha*, you may remember, is the same word Patanjali used in the second sutra to define yoga. There we translated it as 'cessation' and here we translate it as 'control' or 'restraint.' Both are correct. A more accurate translation, however, might be 'non-arising.' If the mind is left to its own devices, it will think incessantly. That is the nature of the mind. Thought waves rise and fall continuously on the surface of the ocean of consciousness. The only way for those thought waves not to arise, that is, to cease, is for us to restrain them, to exercise control over their arising. So *nirodha* refers both to the act of restraining the thought waves as well as to the state of perfect restraint, that is, cessation, an ocean without waves. It is the same word, but we are forced to translate it differently into English to make the sutra intelligible.

"Now let us look a little more closely at this idea of controlling our minds. And for the purposes of this discussion, let us now retranslate the second sutra as 'yoga is control over the thought waves of the mind.' In other words, yoga is the practice of controlling our minds. There is a common analogy used in the yogic tradition to describe the normal state of the human mind, the untrained mind. Yogis compare it to a drunken monkey stung by a scorpion."

Saraswati permitted herself a slight smile and a suitable pause. There was a smattering of smiles and some soft laughter, occasioned no doubt by everyone's recognition of the aptness of this analogy.

"In its normal untrained state, the mind is incredibly frenetic; it jumps incessantly from one thought to another in chaotic fashion like a crazed monkey stung by a scorpion. Ordinarily, we are not aware of the vast majority of these thoughts. For that reason, they are called subconscious—lying below the surface of consciousness. Suppose we are sitting in the office, listening to our boss give us instructions. We think we are attentive, but while we are listening to him, our mind is carrying on a dialogue with itself. Commenting on something he did last week, debating whether or not we like him, noticing his smell, what our mother told us the night before, the itch we have in our leg—a host of different thoughts in the space of a single minute. And on and on, all day long. One famous yogi once said that if our thoughts were open for all to see, then most of us would appear to be muttering madmen, not much different than those poor souls we see on the street sometimes. As you learn to meditate, you gradually become aware of this incessant flow of thoughts, and as you do, you begin to see that it is this flow of thoughts that determines your experience. This can be very disconcerting at first, and often downright unpleasant. It is no wonder that many people get discouraged at this stage. They start to realize that their minds are controlling them rather than the other way around, and this shakes their confidence. A runaway mind is as dangerous to our welfare as a team of runaway horses is to a crowd of innocent bystanders. In the words of Swami Vivekananda, the mind makes a very good servant but a very poor master. Behind this lies a very simple truth: The quality of our lives depends on the quality of our thoughts; and the quality of our thoughts depends on our ability to control them. Fearful or anxious thoughts drain our sense of well-being; they carry us against our will into depression or despair. Elevated thoughts—if we can cultivate them and harness them—lift our spirits and fill us with hope and inspiration and understanding. When our thoughts become agitated and superficial, we lose our inner peace and innate happiness; when our flow of thoughts grows calm and deepens, when it becomes more like a gently flowing river than a set of raging rapids, our sense of well-being and fulfillment deepens. In short, those who control their minds, control their lives, and vice versa.

"In Sanskrit, the word for human being is *manush*, which literally means 'mind-preponderant being.' We are primarily mental beings, not physical beings. Our experience of the world, our sense of happiness or unhappiness, well-being or despair, depends principally on our minds. Even when we are physically unwell, our experience of that illness depends on our mind, not our body. One person falls sick and gets depressed. Another person suffers the same illness but she laughs it off. One person suffers an external setback and it crushes her spirit. Another person suffers the same setback and she shrugs her shoulders and moves on. Long before the first yogis started dreaming of enlightenment, they realized that the quality of their human experience depended entirely on the extent to which they were able to control their minds, and so they developed the *brahma vijnana*, the intuitional science of yoga. They developed a practice that enabled them to gain control over their thoughts and thus the ability to turn life from a tragedy or an empty farce into a masterpiece of meaning. I have known some people, especially westerners, who think that discipline is an obstacle to happiness. Nothing could be further from the truth. True discipline is the ability to make your mind do exactly what you want it to do. Without it, no human being can ascend to the unobstructed heights of the human spirit where one enjoys wisdom, peace, and fulfillment. This is *nirodha*, control. In its highest expression it leads to enlightenment, but long before that, it gives you the ability to become the master of your life."

Later, Rodrigo would look back at that moment and consider it a turning point in his life. He had been so focused for so long on the dream of creating a great work of art that he had never stopped to consider the possibility that his life could be a canvas. He had spent so long with his attention turned toward the words he dreamed of writing that he had never turned back to look at the dreamer, as if he had unknowingly draped a black cloth over the looking glass and for that reason had failed to find his own reflection in the mirror. But with a small nudge from Saraswati, that particular veil drooped and began to fall away. For the first time, he began to truly understand that art was a reflection of the artist, that it was only by harnessing the wild, untapped power of his mind that he could direct its creative energies where he willed, that it was only by developing the ability to see himself that he could leave something worthy on the page for others to see.

Both Ely and Georg had questions for Saraswati, but Rodrigo barely heard them. His mind was spinning with what he considered a revelation that undermined everything he had been taught and led to value by his culture. It was only when Saraswati segued into the next word, that he forced his attention back from the airy heights where it had wandered, admonishing himself that if he wanted to learn to control his mind, then now was a good time to start.

"Next comes *abhyasa*, 'practice.' The following sutra clarifies what is meant by *abhyasa*: 'Practice is the repeated effort to follow the disciplines that give permanent control of the thought waves of the mind.' That is followed by sutra fourteen: 'Practice becomes firm when it has been cultivated uninterruptedly for a long time with earnestness.' In short, *abhyasa* is repeated earnest exercise or effort cultivated over a long period of time. What Patanjali is telling us is that there is no substitute for effort; there are no shortcuts. It is only by long, sustained, and arduous practice that a person can attain mastery over her mind. This is both the greatest adventure and the most difficult task that a human being can undertake. It would be naive of us to expect that we can get there without running the gauntlet. For those of you who know the story of the Buddha, you will remember that on the days and nights leading up to his enlightenment, he was assailed by a host of demons whom he fought off by an act of will. You may have seen the colorful Tibetan paintings of demons and dragons attacking him as he sat? Those demons are our fears, our attachments, our desires, and our ignorance. They are the obstacles that stand between us and our goal. They can be quite fierce and quite terrible, or alluring and insidious. But the task is not impossible. After all, they are only thoughts. They can be defeated, but only through long and arduous practice. It is not a battle, swift and soon forgotten, but an epic, the stuff of legends, the stuff of heroes."

Saraswati's voice slowed, taking Rodrigo to the edge of what seemed to be a great vista. He caught a glimpse of an indomitable will hiding behind that calm and steady gaze. Her tone of voice did not change. Her seemingly expressionless features remained as difficult to read. Her customary measured pace with its quiet modulations never wavered, but behind that gentle motion Rodrigo felt the force of a powerful, unseen current that could not be checked. He looked at her and felt as if he were seeing her now through new eyes. The self-assurance she radiated was not just confidence; it was conviction, a conviction born from her own experience. What he had mistaken for coldness was something else entirely, something he could not quite make out. The word "strength" seemed much closer to the mark, an intimidating aura of self-control that sprang from a source that could not be seen. In fact, the world she lived in seemed submerged so far below the surface that any judgment on his part was forthwith rendered trivial. No wonder Clara and the others talked about her in such glowing terms. She was not simply teaching them an ancient school of thought that she had unearthed from the pages of a book but daring them to see what she could see, a sight bequeathed her by generations of seers receding back into a past shrouded in mists but never forgotten, not even for a moment.

"And now we come to the last of the three principle words, *vairagya*, commonly translated as 'non-attachment' or 'dispassion.' Sutras fifteen and sixteen expand upon the idea of *vairagya*, just as sutras thirteen and fourteen expanded upon the idea of *abhyasa*. Fifteen: '*Vairagya* is self-mastery; it is freedom from desire for what is seen or heard.' Sixteen: 'When, through knowledge of the atman, the soul, one ceases to desire any manifestation of nature, that is the highest kind of *vairagya*.'

"Etymologically, the word *vairagya* comes from the root verb *raga*, or attachment—literally, the act of coloring or dying. When the mind is colored by passion or desire, thus giving rise to attachment, we call this *raga*. The prefix *vi* denotes opposition or negation. When the mind remains unaffected or unassailed by the colors of the world, when it is not subjugated against its will by the surging waves of attraction or repulsion—that is *vairagya*. So, what does Patanjali mean when he says that *vairagya*, the ability to remain unaffected by the outside world, is fundamental to self-mastery? Why is it so absolutely fundamental to success in yoga? Anyone?"

Saraswati looked around the circle but there were no answers forthcoming.

"Okay, Clara, suppose you go into a restaurant and someone whom you've never seen before starts insulting you. How do you think you'd react?"

"I'd probably get angry; in fact, I think you can count on it."

"Okay then. And what happens when you get angry? You lose control of yourself. Not only do you lose your peace of mind, your ability to react effectively in that situation diminishes. If you totally lose control, you could even end up in jail or end up hurting yourself or somebody else. Now, suppose someone who wants to get something out of you decides to flatter you. What happens if their flattery gets to you and inflates your sense of ego?"

"I'd be putty in their hands."

"In other words, you lose your judgment. You get drunk on pride or vanity, which can be just as intoxicating as alcohol. Now I ask you all, who is greater, the person who doesn't get affected when she is insulted or flattered, or the person who gets carried away with anger or vanity? Which of the two is the greater master of herself?"

The answer was obvious. It was not something Rodrigo had ever thought about, but now that he had, it could not have been more self-evident.

"Even if we cannot remain unaffected at that moment, when we calm down later on, we wish we had. We know in our hearts which is the greater path. The second person is a puppet of her emotions. She has no control, and because she has no control, she has no freedom. She is a prisoner of the moment, a prisoner of the situation, often acting against her own true interest. Something happens in the world outside to provoke her and she loses her balance; she loses her peace of mind, her happiness. A strong wave comes and her boat capsizes. Why? Because she has not yet learned how to control that boat. She drowns in a sea of suffering because she is a slave to her reactions rather than the master of her inner life. A person who is a slave to her emotions can never be her own master.

"So now, finally, we are in a position to address Clara's question about the difference between non-attachment and indifference. It is not that a yogi becomes indifferent to the world or lacks passion. Rather, her attention and her passion are hers to bestow or withhold as she chooses. Such a person is far more aware of what is going on in the world than the person who is blinded by her passions. That awareness allows her to choose the best course of action in any given situation, rather than being forced into a corner by her lack of self-control. What is that line of Keats you like so much, Clara, from 'The Second Coming'? 'The best lack all conviction, while the worst are full of passionate intensity'? From a spiritual point of view, the worst are certainly full of passionate intensity, a passionate intensity over which they have no control, but the best do not lack all conviction. Rather, they are full of conviction. Their conviction comes from the fact that they are not blinded by their runaway minds. They see clearly and that fills them with certainty. Think of it in this way: If we compare our mental propensities to a keyboard, then a person who lacks control over her mind is only capable of making noise. Think of a monkey at a piano and remember the yogi's analogy. The keys ring out with little rhyme or reason and the sound is full of discord. No one can make great music without great artistry and great control. There are times when anger is the appropriate response, just as there are times when we wish to summon forth a passionate intensity. But a person who is the master of herself decides when and where and to what degree. She uses her mind as an instrument, which is, after all, what the mind is and was meant to be. It is an instrument, nothing more, nothing less, and yoga teaches us how to master that instrument. The highest mastery comes, as the next sutra tells us, when we fully identify ourselves with consciousness, when we free ourselves from the bonds of the ego. *Tatparan purushakyatergunavaitrishnayam.* 'When, through knowledge of the atman, one ceases to desire any manifestation of nature, that is the highest kind of *vairagya*.' When we realize our oneness with the soul and taste its infinite bliss, then we attain perfect freedom. Then and only then can we watch each and every manifestation of nature from a state of perfect clarity, tranquility, harmony, and bliss, unaffected by what we see. This is what is meant by freedom. No longer are we puppets with our hands and feet tied to the strings of nature, forced to dance against our will. We are free to act as our conscience instructs us. We remain in bliss and at peace, even as we act, even in the most difficult of situations. We are free to appreciate the world, its beauty and its depths, the perfection that lies at the heart of all things, precisely because we are not caught up in it."

Again Saraswati paused, querying the faces that, like his own, were struggling to assimilate her words. Georg looked at his notes, started to say something, but then shook his head.

"Let us take a different analogy," she continued. "Imagine you are an actor in a play. Suppose you are so caught up in your role that you feel the sadnesses and triumphs of that character as if they were your own. For the duration of the play you are that person. You have become lost in your role. If the events are tragic, then your life for those two hours is a tragedy. As long as you are identified with that character, you suffer her sorrows and her anguish. Now contrast that with an actor who is fully conscious that she is playing a role. She may play a scene in which her character suffers a great loss, but the sorrow she acts out doesn't affect her. That sorrow is only the visible surface of her person; what you don't see from the outside is the actor making sure she plays that role as artistically, as authentically, and as convincingly as she can. Her *vairagya* is far greater than that of the first actor. To the degree she is detached, she can perfect her role; and at the same time, she can appreciate the artistry of her fellow actors and delight in the unfolding of the play. Finally, contrast her position with that of a dispassionate connoisseur of the arts sitting in the audience. Every nuance of the play is revealed to that connoisseur precisely because she is not caught up in the individual triumphs and tragedies. She is aware of them, she feels their resonance, but as brushstrokes in a painting. It is not in the individual brushstrokes that we see the transcendent beauty of great art. It is in the painting as a whole. It is only when you are not enmeshed in the individual triumphs and tragedies of the actors that you can truly appreciate the greatness of the play. Only one who sits in the audience of pure consciousness can fully appreciate the transcendent beauty of the play of life. This is the highest form of *vairagya*. Is it a little clearer now?"

It was to Rodrigo. The idea of transcendent bliss was still foreign to him, but the practical value of maintaining his internal balance and peace of mind in the face of external vicissitudes could not be overstated. It was the difference between a lasting happiness and an intermittent hell. He thought of Beth and recognized immediately how much he had been blindsided by his own reactions. When he thought of how much he had blamed her for his own unhappiness, it made him feel ashamed. He remembered Amrita and her once obscure reference to elephants in the living room, and he realized that the great beasts had been camping out in his living room all along. He had simply been too blind to recognize the mess they were making. He did not know what elephants Amrita and Saraswati had had to deal with in their lives, but it was obvious that they were both warriors in the truest sense of the word. They had taken up a battle that he had unknowingly run away from. Rodrigo began to feel a new ambition stirring inside him now. He still wanted to be a writer, even a no-talent writer, if that was as far as his destiny would take him, but perhaps he could be both a writer and a yogi. His greatest heroes had always been artists and writers, almost as far back as he could remember. They had inspired him and given direction to his life. But had the world ever seen a greater hero than Patanjali or the Buddha or the other yogi-saints whom Saraswati had mentioned in her classes? Those who had achieved complete mastery over their minds, who had conquered their internal weaknesses? He doubted it, doubted it now as much as he had ever doubted anything. If, as a grown man, he was going to emulate anyone, why not emulate the Buddha? Why not Patanjali?

The next day the members of his class skipped their usual lunch at the ashram and went to an Italian restaurant near Lakshman Jhula to hold an informal going-away party for Clara. The restaurant featured a wood-burning stove and authentic Italian recipes presided over by its Italian owner, a midlife matron from Parma who had married an Indian man and settled down to idyllic days of imported pastas in the rarefied atmosphere of the Himalayan foothills. The talk turned swiftly and inevitably to Saraswati. Clara's eyes moistened when she expressed how much she was going to miss her beloved philosophy teacher and her daunting thrice-weekly classes. Her understated emotions, echoed by the other members of their party, only increased Rodrigo's growing admiration for that short, plain, and overly serious woman who rarely allowed any visible emotion to register on her angular, cautious face. If she had a fan club—and she certainly did—then it was time for Rodrigo to inscribe his name as a member in good standing. When Georg asked him if he had decided how long he would be staying, his answer was "indefinitely," and the sound of his voice carried a conviction he had not known he'd felt until that moment.

It was during those first few classes on the Yoga Sutras that Ambika showed up at Le Gentil's house with her first translations of the promised texts on ancient Indian astronomy, knowing full well that he had been growing impatient to see evidence of the claims she had made. Not that he had said anything, but the Frenchman could not hide his growing agitation from someone with seven thousand years of Indian culture at her back. She had read his efforts to conceal his impatience like she might have read the simple wishes of a young child who is eager for sweets but afraid to show how much he wants them for fear of their being withheld. And withhold them she did, waiting until she had exacerbated his anticipation to what she considered a sufficient pitch before gliding into his house one morning with a stack of handwritten pages tucked underneath her arm. She put them nonchalantly on one corner of the desk he had given her and set to work with her back to him, translating a set of instructions he had written out the evening before. She could sense him looking at those pages from his chair across the room, his fingers tapping the cover of the book he held in his hand. She could almost smell his curiosity riding on the fragrant morning air that wafted in through the open windows; so she bent her head over her work as if nothing in the world could break her concentration. Her pen scratched its fine lines across the page, dipping now and then into the small pot of Indian ink, until he finally called out to ask her what those papers were.

"Oh, yes," she said, without looking up. "I almost forgot; they're translations of some of those ancient astrology texts you wanted to see."

The tapping stopped. "Don't you mean astronomy?"

Ambika could almost hear his grimace. "No, astrology. Why do you ask?"

"Why do you think?" Le Gentil blurted out, as an inadvertent smile crept across her face. "I'm an astronomer; I'm interested in astronomy, not astrology. Haven't I made that clear enough? If you remember, our whole conversation that day was about astronomy. The conversation where you claimed that Indian *astronomers* had supposedly made many important discoveries before our Western astronomers?"

Ambika continued writing with the same deliberateness while she answered him, as if his outburst was only worth a fraction of her attention. "In India we do not differentiate between the words *astronomer* and *astrologer*," she said, in the same tone of voice she might have used when speaking to a child. "All of India's great astrologers were also astronomers; they conducted their studies of the heavens with the scientific precision they needed to ensure the accuracy of their calculations. No Indian astrologer ever made the foolish mistake of taking the earth to be the center of the solar system, like your Western astronomers have." As she said this, she wagged her pen suggestively and then returned it to the page. "But our astronomers are also astrologers; after all, what is the utility of studying celestial bodies and their movements if not to arrive at an understanding of the impact they have on our human lives? Of course, they were curious to find out when the next eclipse would occur, or how long it took a certain planet to complete its orbit, but they were far more curious to map out the destiny of human beings, and their investigation of the stars did them great service in this regard. There is a universal principle at work here: Everything that exists in the microcosm has its reflection in the macrocosm, and vice versa."

Ambika put down her pen and turned around to face him. "An astronomer who was not also skilled in astrology would have seemed a fool to them. He would have been like a person who can read aloud from a book but has no idea what it means, or like a poet who is skilled in meter and rhyme but whose words are trite and ugly."

She picked up the sheaf of papers and brought it over to him. Le Gentil took them without saying anything, still smarting from the insult, but not entirely sure if it were meant as such. He was puzzled by her distracted air and her lack of visible emotion, not recognizing the confident sense of superiority it reflected. He was, Rodrigo now realized, a man who had yet to learn the value of *vairagya*, unlike Ambika who would have absorbed the essence of Patanjali's teachings from her parents and her culture, even before she became consciously aware of it. As long as he did not, she would continue to have the upper hand, something Rodrigo now saw as indispensable to his tale.

As Le Gentil was making a quick perusal of the first couple of pages, his annoyance at Ambika clouded his perceptions. He recalled with pride that his was among the first generations of astronomers who had left behind the medieval superstitions that had dominated his profession only a scant century before, when Western astronomers had also been astrologers. Copernicus and his contemporaries had been studying the heavens rather than the cosmos when they began to suspect, to their surprise, that the earth revolved around the sun. They had been studying God's heavenly creation in order to see how the mind of the creator worked and to substantiate with science the dictums of the church. Only it hadn't worked out that way and astrology had gradually fallen into a state of disrepute, deservedly so in Le Gentil's eyes. His indignation rose to the point that he was barely aware of the words he was reading. He laid the papers on his desk and said, "You're a good Christian, from all that I can see. How can you believe in this sort of superstition?"

"I would not be a good Christian if I did not accept the primacy of a spiritual reality. It is our lives that matter, not dead stars. Indian astrologers are quite accurate with their predictions. They know how to read the book of nature—that, by the way, is the real science. Can you say the same?"

Le Gentil wanted to scoff at her insinuation, but her look disconcerted him and he stayed his tongue. Her eyes were neither vacant nor vapid; they shone with an intelligence that suddenly seemed to him uncommon in any land. Intelligent people, he knew, had been known to subscribe to some very unintelligent notions. They could even be gullible to a fault, though he had trouble reconciling such weaknesses with what he considered refined intelligence, the prerogative of a scientifically trained mind. But there was nothing in her look that suggested gullibility. If anything, there was the clear suggestion of a challenge, not only to him but to his culture. A challenge he could not dismiss. "I will look at them tonight," he said, before turning the conversation to a different topic.

After Ambika had left for the day, Le Gentil settled down to read her translations in the quiet of his comfortable recliner. He did not stay in it for long. Though his agitation had abated, he soon found himself pacing up and down in his living room, vaulted into orbit each time he came across a passage that intrigued him—and there were many, some that even astounded him. He knew scientific thoroughness and precision when he saw it, and he saw it on each and every page. The excerpts Ambika had copied out made it clear that he was reading from the works of astronomers who would have been labeled as geniuses had they been born in eighteenth-century France. There was no mention of astrology or astrological interpretation in those pages, other than a few oblique remarks—more than likely, these would come in the as-yet-to-be-translated pages—but instead of being glad that they were missing, he began to feel a sort of incongruous curiosity growing, a willingness-turning-eagerness to know how these prescient geniuses would interpret their findings. He was proud to belong to an enlightened age, free from the superstitions that had crippled previous generations of European thinkers and scientists, but in these pages he could detect none of the intellectual debility that he associated with superstition and dogma. Would they suddenly fall prey to superstition and imaginative fancy at the end of a long odyssey of difficult calculations and disciplined thinking? It was like a puzzle that he could not put down until he had figured it out. And he could not figure it out until Ambika translated for him the many missing pages.

In the meantime, what he held in his hands seemed like a treasure rescued from the bottom of the sea. Its value was sure to prove incalculable to his profession. Even though they were only fragments, those fragments were as precious as any gem ever extracted from the earth.

It was late at night when Le Gentil finally got to sleep, and the short sleep he had was troubled—as Ambika had been counting on.

13

ONE AFTERNOON, RODRIGO WAS on his way out of the ashram for what had become his habitual walk along the Ganges when he crossed paths with Amrita in the front courtyard. They exchanged a bit of lighthearted banter, the kind that had made the ashram feel increasingly like home, but as usual Amrita quickly steered the conversation toward his practices. Despite the fact that he was at least ten years older than her, she seemed to have deliberately assumed the conscientious air of a doting teacher. When she asked him how his meditation was going, Rodrigo was ready with the signs of progress that he had been tracking so eagerly and so assiduously over the past few weeks. He was sitting longer and without discomfort—at least half an hour, sometimes as long as forty-five minutes. He was now able to stay somewhere in the vicinity of his mantra for the duration of his practice, unlike at the beginning when his mind would wander where it willed, refusing to be tied down by the bonds of concentration. While he had yet to experience what it was like to drown in an ocean of bliss—as one of his books had quaintly put it—he had noticed that no matter how much he struggled during his practice, he almost always felt calmer afterward. It was starting to get addictive, this feeling. He would savor it after he got up from his meditation like he had often savored a good meal in the past, but in this case the taste lingered much longer. It had begun to color his moods with its calming hues, and for that, he was thankful. They might be small steps he had taken, but it felt like he had turned a corner.

"You turned that corner the day you started meditating," Amrita said emphatically. "You may just be starting to become aware of it, but you've been well on your way for a while now. That's usually the way it goes. Most of the time other people notice the changes before we do. Like me, for instance."

"You mean you've noticed that I've been making progress?"

"Oh yes, my dear. Not only me. Saraswati has also. She tells me you've followed my advice and become a regular in her philosophy classes."

Rodrigo was surprised. He wasn't entirely sure that his reclusive philosophy teacher even remembered who he was once she left the confines of their morning circle, much less that she might be charting his progress. Be that as it may, the mere mention of her philosophy classes served to loosen his tongue. One by one, he shared with Amrita the most important of the insights he had gleaned from Saraswati's teachings, his tongue tripping over itself as he tried to find words to express thoughts that were still unclear to him, despite the dazzle they had left in his mind. His inability to express himself clearly only made him appreciate Saraswati even more, especially the precision with which she used language to clothe ideas that evaded any ordinary mortal's attempts to corral them. It was, no doubt, a skill she had imbibed from Patanjali during the hundreds or perhaps thousands of hours she had spent dissecting his impossibly condensed text, turning it over and over in her mind looking for the one facet in the diamond that reflected the light of consciousness.

Amrita listened silently as he talked, her smile an open invitation for him to be as voluble as he wished. He finally stopped himself when it occurred to him that his brilliant insights were probably no less elementary than "See Spot run" for a girl who had been a serious yogi since the age of sixteen. Amrita, as he might have expected, refused to make light of his experience.

"Remember, Rodrigo, the fact that other people have experienced what you've experienced or understood what you've understood doesn't make it any less profound. Every time a human being takes to the spiritual path, it's a cause for celebration. Each person's journey is an entirely fresh and unique re-creation of the eternal journey. Didn't some writer once say that there are really only seven basic plots? That doesn't make a new novel any the less interesting, not if it's well written and imaginative. Spiritual awakening is the greatest drama ever staged. It never gets old and it never gets trite. If it did, God would probably wrap up this show and invent another."

Then I'm not completely boring you to death?"

Amrita laughed. "Not at all. I would caution you about one thing, though, now that you seem to have caught the yogic philosophy bug. I think you need to be careful not to get too caught up in your head. Philosophy is great and all, but the spiritual path is more about the heart. It's really easy to remain in your head, especially for some people, but that can be a trap, a really big trap. Don't get me wrong; the intellect is helpful, but only to a point. After that, it can make your ego grow and dry out your spiritual juices. If your practice doesn't get centered in your heart, then it's difficult to get far on this path."

"You think I'm too much in my head, then? Or is my head too big?"

Amrita paused for a moment before speaking. "If you're asking me if I think you're a head case, then the answer would be both yes and no. Can I be blunt?"

"Somehow I think you will be, no matter what I say."

Amrita shrugged and nodded. "Probably true. I never was much for pulling punches. So if you don't mind me going straight to the point, I'd say that you're one of those people who are very good at living in their heads but have a hard time coming down into their hearts—I think most intellectuals I've met are like that, to one degree or another. You're making good progress, but you still have a wall around you. It's one of the first things I noticed when we met."

Rodrigo was a little stung by her words, which had an uncomfortable ring of familiarity. "I suppose that may be true, to some extent" he said, "but I've been through a lot recently—you know, with my divorce and all."

"I know, but this is something that takes years to build up, maybe lifetimes. It's nothing to be ashamed of, though. Almost everyone on this path has to make a conscientious effort to open her heart. It doesn't just come naturally. Part of it is our culture. It's the way we grow up, the way we were raised, the ideas that get pounded into our heads. Personally, I think fear is a big part of it. A lot of people resist making the effort because they're afraid of the pain involved, but there is no way around that, not if you want to grow spiritually, or even emotionally. You know, the Sufis call the spiritual path the path of the bloody heart. They have it exactly right. I can't think of a better way to describe it."

Amrita reached out and grabbed his hand. "I haven't made you feel bad, I hope?"

"To be honest, it's not the easiest thing in the world to hear."

"Remember the elephants, Rodrigo. Whenever the going gets tough, just remember the elephants. The minute you start walking this path with sincerity, your living room starts filling up with the beasts. All the ones that were hiding in your basement start coming up the stairs. But it doesn't mean they're going to stay around forever. And anyhow, in your case, it's too late to turn back. You've already made friends with the elephant trainer. Now you just have to make friends with the elephants. If you can make friends with them, then you can tame them; if you can tame them, then eventually you can put them out to pasture. Well, maybe not out to pasture exactly. Let's say, you can send them back to the forest where they belong."

"And they'll go?"

"Oh, they'll go. It will take a while, but they'll go."

"But in the meantime...."

"Exactly. In the meantime, you've got a lot of cleaning up to do in that living room of yours."

By the time Rodrigo passed the ashram gate, he was so preoccupied with Amrita's observations that he barely noticed his surroundings. A few hundred meters past the Ram Jhula Bridge, he spied an empty bench overlooking the river and sat down so he could give full attention to his thoughts. He had no doubt that Beth would have agreed with her. She might have even stood up and cheered, had she been present. Had she not said the same thing in different words on a number of occasions, though with nowhere near the compassion? He remembered those words all too clearly, at the kitchen table or stalking off to her darkroom: "What's the use of talking? You put up this wall around you and after that there's no getting through to you. I've got better things to do with my time than stay here and pound my fists against the wall." Or other words to that effect. When she first brought that complaint to him, it was more of a lament. He had listened then— somewhat. Had told her she had it wrong. He wasn't shutting her out; he was just tired from a long day at school, or frustrated with his writing, or else she had put him off with something she had done or said. She would apologize or console him and they would work out the awkwardness—in bed, if all else failed. But toward the end of their marriage, her lament had morphed into a calcified, resentful caricature of a man whom he did not recognize, as if she had painted him into an imaginary corner, signed her name at the bottom, and declared the painting finished and inviolable. By then he no longer bothered to refute anything she said, though more often than not she left her opinions carefully unstated, preferring scantily disguised insinuations to direct conversation. He had dismissed those poorly concealed barbs with the belief that if she had him so wrong, if she could not see through the jaundice in her eyes, then that was her problem, though the acid in his stomach and the silence that had grown between them told him otherwise. Had she seen something in him that he had steadfastly refused to look at? Undoubtedly. Perhaps it had even been the main reason for her disillusionment with him, rather than the suburban life that supposedly disagreed with the idealized image of the artist she so cherished. It was not as if she had no walls of her own, no secret spaces that she was afraid or ashamed to let him see—he had often felt them, though he never tried to scale the ramparts as she had done. But that was entirely beside the point. Maybe if he had brought down his walls, hers would have come down as well. And even if they hadn't, he still would have been freed from his share of the burden of isolation. What if what Amrita had said was true? What if his wall were not merely a product of the hurts that his failed relationship and his frustrated dreams had wrought, but something he had carried with him from childhood—or beyond—something imposed by his culture and with which he had unknowingly conspired? This would not absolve him, he knew, but somehow that bit of perspective gave the fear and the shame a space into which they could begin to dissipate. He could feel something begin to release itself as he sat there, looking out over the water flowing inexorably on its way south and east toward the ocean. Was this not an inescapable part of the human condition that Sartre had referred to in the cool logic of his writings that now sounded more to his ears like an impassioned lament? "The freedom to do what you can with what's been done to you…this creeping pain that gnaws and fumbles and caresses one and never hurts quite enough." He had been born into a culture that had left its weight upon his back and thrust its nails into the soles of his feet, flowing around him and past him toward a destination he could not see. How could he have been expected to fight off its influences without the knowledge of how to do so, without the tools to enable him to recognize what was happening to him? Beth had been caught in the same unforgiving undertow. Both had been swept away by the current. Neither of them had ever been taught how to look into their own hearts or how to open their hearts to others so that others could look into them as well. Maybe if they had, the society that cradled them would not be submerged in such dire pains of its own.

The next morning, Rodrigo caught up with Amrita after yoga class, once her other students had taken their leave. "So tell me," he said, "if I wanted to open up my heart, what would I do?" Amrita's canny grin made him think that she had been anticipating the question.

"Like everything else in yoga, you work on it. You do the practices, especially devotional practices, and gradually you get better. The best place to start is devotional singing: kirtan and bhajan."

"You mean evening arati?"

"Yes, although I was thinking more of collective chanting and meditation in the morning. Five o'clock in the main hall."

"Five o'clock?" Rodrigo repeated, wincing slightly.

"Yes, five o'clock. The hour before sunrise is called the *brahma muhurta*, the hour of God. It's the best time for concentration and spiritual practices. At that hour your mind is naturally quiet and the vibration in the outside world is at its subtlest; it's very conducive to meditation. You may be sleepy at first, but once you get used to it you'll love it. We chant for thirty or forty minutes, a few bhajans, a few kirtans, and then we meditate. There's nothing like it. You spend the early morning communing with God and the rest of your day just floats along like a blissful dream. It's guaranteed ecstasy, more or less, once you get in the flow."

Amrita tossed her long blond hair back with one graceful sweep of her head. "I'll help you; it'll be fun. The thing is, you have to learn the songs; you have to know the meaning of the words so you can really put your heart into it. But they're easy to learn. They're the same songs we sing during arati. Once you learn them, then it's just a matter of singing with all the feeling you can muster. You don't just sit there like you're listening to a concert. I've seen you in arati. That's what you do. You're not attending a concert. You're the singer; God is the audience. You pour out your heart to him. He's listening, not you. Give it a try. Your heart will do the rest, I promise. We could even start this afternoon, if you like."

The confident, gravelly texture of Amrita's voice and the warmth of the spontaneous hug she gave him when he left her at her door broke down whatever resistance he might have had. As he was getting ready for breakfast, he found himself looking forward to their afternoon appointment with an eagerness that surprised him. Here he was, a confirmed agnostic, looking forward to learning Sanskrit chants and songs in praise of God—not only learning them but hoping that the sentiments they induced would enable him to bring down the walls that had long encased his heart. A month ago he likely would have scoffed at such an idea. What had changed? For years, in fact, the mere mention of God outside the ambit of pure speculation was likely to occasion in him an uncomfortable reaction. To his surprise, that reaction was nowhere to be found. Instead of going straight down to breakfast, where he was almost always among the first to enter the dining hall, he sat on his bed and examined this unexpected development.

Rodrigo had grown up in a Catholic family, the fond son of a devout mother, but even as a child he had begun to grow uncomfortable with the beliefs that were expected of him and the rituals in which they were imbedded. He remembered his confirmation, twelve years old, two months before his mother died. Though she was terribly sick at the time with the aftereffects of the chemo, nothing short of an earthquake would have prevented her from attending his confirmation, and then only if the earthquake had taken down the church. He remembered how proud and how happy it made her. Helpless as he had felt in the face of her illness, he was glad that he was able to do something to brighten the spirits of his frighteningly sick mother, but apart from that, the ritual meant nothing to him. After she was buried, after the *velorio* had been completed and the nine nights of *tercios* had been faithfully observed, after the tears had abated but while his father was still wearing the black mourning clothes that he would wear for a full year, he went to him and told him he didn't want to attend mass any longer. His father put up little resistance. He had far greater problems to worry about, with two college-age children testing the limits of the ultra-permissive Southern California sun and a difficult bereavement that had his children wondering where their unconquerable and domineering father had disappeared to. The last time Rodrigo entered a church was for the mass that was performed in his mother's memory on the one-year anniversary of her death. But by then he had already ceased to believe in God. If he had any belief at all, it was that he would never believe in God again, not this God who had watched in silence while his mother lit the votary candles, year after year, with the simple, unquestioning faith of her Mexican forefathers, and then maintained that silence while he put her through ten months of relentless suffering and an agonizing death. But Amrita's God and the God he had been raised to fear and never question were not the same God at all. There was no fierce expression on his face, no great, menacing beard, no bejeweled throne rising above the seas, surrounded by angels and great beasts of prey (from the time Rodrigo read Humberto Eco's *The Name of the Rose* at the age of fourteen, he could never dissociate in his mind the Christian image of God from the magnificent and appalling description of Jehovah seated on his throne that appears early in the book, as seen through the eyes of the young Adso when he enters the Abbey's church for the first time). The yogic deity was no deity at all but rather a playful personification of an infinite and eternal consciousness that was beyond any attribute the mind could give it. "The ground of being," one yogic writer had called it. This was a God Rodrigo could approach with his intellect without suffering the deceptions he had suffered as a child, even if he had yet to develop the quietness of mind necessary to perceive him. Amrita had told him weeks ago in the café that religion and spirituality were two entirely different things. He understood now exactly what she had meant and why she had said it. As a college-age man, he had realized that his youthful discomfort with the religion he had grown up with had stemmed from a child's untutored awareness of the hypocrisy that ran rampant in the sacred halls of blind faith. As a child, he had not had the necessary concepts to be able to identify these feelings, but even without them he was aware that the lay brother who indoctrinated him in the Christian dogmas every Sunday after mass did not actually know if what he was saying were true or not. All he knew was that it was written in a book and testified to by his forefathers. Saints had experienced the presence of God and taken down his commandments; that was good enough for him. But it was not good enough for anyone who practiced yoga. This was the one thing, more than any other, that had turned Rodrigo's mind in a direction he had once been certain it would never take. Yogis had never been interested in belief. They were only interested in experiencing for themselves what the great saints of the past had experienced: the direct, blissful perception of the ultimate reality. For them, someone who had no experience of Divine Consciousness was at best a beginner, no matter how many years he had been unrolling his yoga mat or studying the yogic texts, and at worst, a pretender. Yoga was a science; its object of investigation was the self; the knowledge it sought could not be gleaned from books but could only be achieved by opening a window within one's mind to the eternal source of being. The people he had met in Rishikesh were proof of this: the swami, Saraswati, Amrita, the different seekers he had met in the two months he had been there. There was something in their eyes and in their bearing, to a greater or lesser extent depending on the depth of their practice, that he had never seen before, not before coming to India and having his brief audience with the Dalai Lama. Call it wisdom, peace of mind, fulfillment, call it what you will, this was what he wanted. And if devotional practices would help him get there sooner, then he was not going to let a little thing like lifelong agnosticism get in his way.

For the next few days, Rodrigo barely opened up his computer. Instead, he sat in one of the inner courtyards with Amrita under the shade of a spreading pipal tree and learned the popular bhajans and kirtans, the devotional songs and chants, that were sung at the ashram—line by line, Sanskrit word by Sanskrit word. Most of them were quite simple, as Amrita had promised. The chants consisted of short phrases containing one or more of the many names of God sung over and over again in a melody and a rhythm that seemed designed to induce a hypnotic state. *Om Namah Shivaya*, "I bow to Lord Shiva"; *Hare Rama, Hare Krishna*, "Lord Rama, Lord Krishna." Nothing could be simpler. But each had its own special charm. Each name of God viewed the Divine from a different vantage point that Amrita patiently explained. As he practiced the chants with her in a low voice, he began to feel the richness evoked by the exotic juxtaposition of syllables, the way each slid mellifluously into the next and from there into the meaning, which opened up before him and leaned toward the horizon. The bhajans, or devotional songs, were more complex. He had many more words to commit to memory and more difficult melodies to deal with, but the poetic richness of the ideas they expressed more than compensated him for the effort. As he got a feel for each line and began to sing it as if he were singing in his own language, he began to feel the devotional sentiments they expressed as if they were his own. When he sang to Krishna of his longing to hear the sound of his flute, to lose himself in the bewitching curves of his smile, he began to feel his own heart tugging at him, begging him to lead it to Krishna, to seek out his hiding place—as the song directed—"in the luminous depths of his soul." When another couplet evoked the pain of separation between his soul and his beloved, he could feel the tears wetting his eyes and a burgeoning desire gathering force within him like an approaching storm. Poetry had always had this effect on him, the ability to rouse emotions he would never have experienced otherwise, but he had never come across poetry infused with these kinds of devotional sentiments. Strangely enough, the fact that they were in a language entirely foreign to him only seemed to heighten the effect, as if there were some mystical allure hidden in these exotic syllables that cast a spell over him the moment they began vibrating in his vocal cords. The words of Tagore that Bhagavati had recited for him came ringing back into his mind as if they had been engraved on a silver plaque and set there to remind him why he was singing: "I touch by the edge of the far-spreading wing of my song thy feet which I could never aspire to reach. Drunk with the joy of singing I forget myself and call thee friend who art my master."

After a few days of this dedicated study, Rodrigo started accompanying Amrita each morning to the collective practice. There he joined the monks in their bright saffron robes and the many other ashram residents, all of them so intently inward at that hour of the morning that no one even seemed to notice his presence. He did not feel the ecstasy Amrita had promised—not that she had promised it so quickly—nor an outpouring of love for a God he still could not recognize, but he felt a loosening in his chest, as if a mesh of tightly wrought cords were being probed by an unseen hand searching for a means to unravel a hitherto insoluble knot. It only took a few days of this for him to realize that Amrita was right. Somewhere along the way he had barricaded himself into his room and fashioned of it a prison from which he now found it nearly impossible to escape. But impossible it was not. Difficult certainly, arduous perhaps, but not impossible. He knew she was right when she had said that he would not get far on this path unless he could bring down the walls he had put up to protect himself but which now held him prisoner; he knew he would not be happy until the knot in his chest finally unraveled and set him free. And though it disheartened him at times to see how far he had to go, it also gave him hope to see that the path was transitable. Whatever elephants were blocking his way could be tamed, lulled into docility by the chanting and the meditation. Until then he would get used to being an early riser. So long as he remained in Rishikesh, he did not want to miss a single morning session. He had a long road to travel and he wanted to get started as soon as possible.

A few mornings later, Rodrigo awoke with a cry of despair on his lips and a song of longing in his heart. He had been lying in his bed with his eyes open, but it was not the one in which he had gone to sleep. There, by the head of the bed, stood a small altar with an image of the Divine Mother on it in the form of Kali Ma. His despair and his longing were both directed toward her, she who was the architect of his destiny and the object of his adoration. She had not forgotten him, he knew, but he could not fathom her designs. Why had she stranded him, her devotee, in the middle of a desert, surrounded by people who could not understand her, did not try to understand her, and so could not understand the man who spoke for her and led them in their worship? Her skin was as dark as the moonless night, and darker still was the veil that hid her intentions. He would follow her wherever she led—he had given his vow long ago and it was so much a part of him now that he could not imagine taking a single breath without it—but he had lost all sense of where she was leading him, and to what end. The gray tint of despair lingered on as a dim glow made its impress felt against the one bare windowpane. And then he felt the constriction in his chest, the stiffness of limbs that have been too long in one position; suddenly, he became aware that he was dreaming. Even then he continued to lay there, unable to shake the heaviness. When he finally opened his eyes, he saw that it was four o'clock. He sat up, feeling drained and anxious at the same time, and reached for his computer.

Rishikesh
10/14
4:00 AM

This early morning hour seems to blur the divide between sleep and waking, between what we take to be real and what we assume to be purely imaginary. But are we not the same person in both instances? Is our experience not just as valid, just as real to our inner senses, to the self that none of us truly knows?

In my dream I was lying on my bed, my imaginary body in the same identical position as my physical body, only in the dream I was awake and unable to sleep—a testament to the reality of the imagination. It was my now-familiar temple room. I had performed my nightly worship of the Divine Mother there in front of my little altar, followed by a long meditation that seemed to continue even after I lay down on my wooden cot. During my worship I had cried out to the Mother, cried out in anguish, knowing that she heard me but not knowing if my anguish moved her in any way, if she were pitiless in her transcendence and her omniscience. I cannot remember what had happened to bring me to that point, but I know that as I sat there to perform my worship, I could feel the walls closing in on me. The temple felt like a prison, and my room an isolated cell; this temple-prison an island in the middle of an arid desert. There was no sympathetic soul in that place, no one who loved the Divine Mother as I loved her, no one who cared about her teachings as I did. Why had she consigned me to such a fate? Such were my thoughts as I performed my worship, and afterward as I tried to meditate. Was it my karma, a product of forgotten misdeeds? Or was it a sacrifice that she was asking of me, her servant? Had she put me there to bring light into the darkness of these befuddled, self-serving minds, eager only for comfort and the pleasure of the senses? Was she asking me to forego my own desires for the good of a world gone blind, no matter how pure and spiritual those desires might be? I was pledged to her service, but what good did it do, I wondered, when no one listened to me or appreciated what I had to offer? At the same time, I was filled with a longing to see the Mother in the flesh, to have her inhabit my thoughts in vision so that I could converse and commune with her. That was my prayer and my despair when I lay down after my meditation. I prayed for her to step out of the shadows and be a companion to her devotee, to accept my worship—not as an idol but as a living image, more real to me than the ignorant souls with whom I was forced to spend my days. But in the gray light of that sleepless room, I feared that the years would go by and she would continue to hide herself behind this veil of stone. The feelings rolled like a river, on and on, as I lay there staring vacantly at the ceiling, trying to ease the stiffness in my nagging limbs, longing for her presence, fearing that she might never come, despairing for the dry days that lay in front of me, stranded in a temple full of strangers who mistook me for their brother. It seemed that sleep would never come that night, the same thoughts revolving round and round like a Ferris wheel with the lights extinguished. And all this time my waking self had fooled my body into thinking it was asleep. Until I recognized my ashram room and gave a little cry, having woken up somewhere in between—between a temple alcove and an ashram room above the Ganges, between reality and the imagination, between sleep and the illusion of sleep.

And now, in the aftermath of a dream that seems difficult to separate from my waking life, I am faced, as always, with questions. Recently, I have been reliving these dreams during my afternoon walks, taking myself back consciously to memories that I know are imaginary but which have the texture and fragrance of reality. As I walk, I wonder how my alter ego would put into practice the things that Saraswati and Amrita are teaching me. Would he struggle with them, as I do, or is this a wisdom that is already known to him, a wisdom he unearthed long ago from his dusty texts or learned from the temple elders or from the Mother who inhabits his dreams and his desires? I compare myself to him and find myself wanting, especially now that the things I seek have drawn so much closer to the things he seeks. Somehow, some hidden portion of my mind is speaking to me through him—I feel an urgent need to understand what he is saying.

When I stand back and try to look at it objectively, I have to wonder how much of this dream has been triggered by what Amrita said to me. Is it the cry of a closed heart longing to be opened? Is the desert that I have fashioned for a home as arid as the one the priest decries? Is devotion, then, what I have been secretly longing for all along as I hid out from myself in my agnosticism? In my priestly garb, devotion seems to come easily to me, as easy as breathing. I felt it even in that very first dream, though it seemed exceedingly strange at the time. Now, as I look back, I suspect that this desire must have been sleeping inside me all along, all through the long years since my mother died. Where else could these feelings have come from, if not from me? In this latest episode, my devotion was fraught with pain, the pain of separation from the beloved. It had been so long since I had seen the Mother that I feared I would no longer remember her face or recognize her voice. Amrita warned me that this was a part of the devotional path I needed to be prepared for: the state of absence, the anguish that comes from feeling separated from the beloved, coupled with a longing to be reunited, a longing that is always fraught with pain. It seems that my dreaming self is dealing with these very questions, and perhaps has been all along, dealing with the long-overdue work of opening up my heart. If, in the process, it bleeds, then it may be that this blood is what is needed to nourish the parched soil inside me. Part of me fears, I think, that I will not emerge from this without ugly scars, or worse—a cripple's gait, my eyesight permanently clouded over. Saraswati told us that this path is not for the fainthearted. It is time to take her at her word. What choice do I really have? As Amrita said, it is too late to turn back now. Somehow, that makes it easier. If there is nowhere to go but onward, then one might as well keep walking.

For several days afterward, Rodrigo's afternoon walks were vaguely troubled. He continued to revisit the scene of his priestly despair, hoping to decipher the message that his subconscious had hidden in the shadows, but the best he could do was extract a warning that the path ahead would be a rocky one, as befitted the Sufi epithet of the bloody heart. Now that he had learned the songs and chants and gotten used to his new routine, he felt eager to pick up the threads of his writing. Before he could do so, however, he needed to do some reading. A determined trip to the bookstore netted several excellent volumes on Hindu astrology, two works on Indian history that included chapters on the development of Indian astronomy, and two more books on yoga that contained extensive explanations of samskara and karma, concepts that he now knew he needed for the upcoming scene. By this time, he already owned two versions of Patanjali's Yoga Sutras, each with very different commentaries, and had successfully memorized the sutras that Saraswati had covered in her classes. But they had yet to talk about samskara, and he did not want to wait any longer to work in ideas that he knew would be fundamental to his story. Finally, over the weekend, he began sketching out the next scene in earnest.

The scene began with Ambika walking through her employer's door, her next set of translations cradled underneath her arm. This time she handed him the thick handwritten sheaf directly upon entering. The new translations contained some of the astrological deliberations that she had purposely left out on the prior occasion. While Rodrigo had been busy learning the chants and getting used to rising at such a godly hour, she had been seeding some careful comments, dropping them into her conversations with Le Gentil at appropriate moments. By these, and by not answering certain of his questions, she had succeeded in fanning the flames of his curiosity about what these Indian astrologer-astronomers had to say regarding the esoteric meanings of the heavenly bodies that he had devoted his life to studying. What she could not know was that the astronomer needed no extra prodding from his subtle-minded secretary. The writings themselves had stimulated all the curiosity he needed. He had met their minds on the level playing field of their written calculations and found that they were men who had something to say that was worth paying attention to. He might not subscribe to their beliefs, but he would hear them out. Their obvious genius demanded no less.

This time they sat on the back veranda, in front of the newly planted vegetable garden. Le Gentil sat motionless in his chair, reading rapidly and with intense concentration, somewhat awed once again by the artistry of her penmanship. Ambika brewed their customary pot of tea and set it on the table between their two chairs. She sipped her tea in silence, waiting for the comments she knew were coming and the ensuing conversation, which she had already rehearsed in her mind the previous night. Nearly an hour passed before Le Gentil finally leaned back in his chair and took a last cold sip of tea.

"Are you sure about the dates of these manuscripts?"

"The Yajnavalkya manuscript is an approximate date. It is generally given as 1800 BC, but some historians dispute that; they cite evidence that shows that he lived more than a century earlier. The others are publication dates from existing manuscripts: 1350 BC for Lagadha's text and 498 AD for Aryabhata's. One of my father's friends, Professor Sandip, is a well-known astronomer and astrologer. He helped me to choose the texts for you. The professor told me that Lagadha's book is generally considered to be a compilation from much earlier texts, some thought to be as much as two millennia older. He also asked me to inform you that Indian astronomers had developed a theory of gravitation, predicted solar and lunar eclipses to the minute, calculated the radius of the orbits of the other planets around the sun, and accurately determined the earth's circumference long before the earliest Greek astronomers. In fact, he said that there is evidence that shows that the early Greek astronomers were heavily influenced by Indian texts. I don't know if you are aware of it, but there was a lot of trade in those days between our two countries. And, as you can see, their work is all heliocentric, right from the beginning."

"You know, I've actually heard of Aryabhata's text, but I'd never seen a copy of it," Le Gentil mused out loud, shuffling through the papers. "It's been translated into Latin, I'm told."

"In the thirteenth century, from the ninth-century Arabic translation."

Le Gentil looked at her in surprise. "Is astronomy another of your hidden talents?"

"No. But history is. My father taught me when I was a girl that if I wanted to understand people then I needed to learn their history. How people think and perceive the world is a product of their history. So I started with the history of my own people. Astronomy is a part of that history, as is astrology. In Sanskrit we use the same word for both, *jyotish*, like Lagadha's book, *Vedanga Jyotish*. *Jyotish* means 'light'; it also refers to the heavenly bodies and their movements. Astronomy is *jyotish siddhanta* and astrology is *jyotish samhita*. *Siddhanta* means 'theory' and *samhita* means 'a collection of texts.' In other words, in the *siddhanta* you make calculations about the movements of the celestial bodies and extrapolate theories from those movements, and in the *samhita* you interpret and explain them. That is where your Western astronomy falls short."

Le Gentil chose his next words carefully, acutely aware now that the alluring young woman seated a few feet away from him had a mind like a double-edged sword, a fact that made her appear even more attractive to his eyes, if that were even possible given the luster of her bronzed skin and her almost perfect features.

"What I would like to know is why such obviously brilliant men insisted on looking for meanings beyond a simple objective understanding of how the universe works. Why fall back on superstition?"

"Why do you say men? Some of the ancient masters of *jyotish* were and are women."

Le Gentil nodded, waiting for her answer, still convinced that these ancient Indian scientists had crossed an invisible line when they ventured into the fairy-land of astrology, forcing them to leave their objectivity and their careful thinking behind. He considered it a shame, since he felt an unspoken connection to them, as if the bonds of their common profession were far stronger than the cultures and the centuries that divided them. But there was something about Ambika's almost imperceptible smile that stopped him short in his conviction. It made him wary, even as he tried to dismiss the possibility that there could be more to the universe than what could be perceived by the aided eye and analyzed by the mind.

Ambika began slowly, also choosing her words carefully, knowing that she was about to venture into territory that was difficult to navigate. She was not at all sure if Le Gentil could follow her, but she was curious to find out.

"Like all scientists, they wanted to know how the universe worked, but being Indian, they knew that there were spiritual laws that governed the cosmos, from the subtlest manifestation of thought to the crudest motion of matter. Our ancient sages teach us that everything is linked together by the universal law of cause and effect. The fabric of time and space is all interconnected. It's like a stretched-out piece of cloth. If you twist one end, then you will see its effect all the way through the cloth. Or else you can compare it to a pond. You throw a stone in any part of the pond and the ripples travel clear across to the other side. The linking principle, from one end of the universe to the other, is cause and effect. In Sanskrit we say *karanakaryabhavat*. There is no effect without a cause, and that cause is the effect of a previous cause. The science of *jyotish* is based on this principle. The movement of any heavenly body sends ripples across the fabric of time and space. The moon not only affects the tides. It affects the water in your body; it affects the water of your emotions; it affects the flow of your life. Nothing is disconnected. Anyone with a little intelligence and some perseverance can measure the movement of a planet. But only a profound intelligence can decipher the chain of cause and effect that binds you to that planet—and to everything around you. The great practitioners of *jyotish* were not mere scientists. They were sages. They could see into the truth hidden by the veil of appearances. Of course, my explanation is rather simplistic, I know. I don't do them justice, but it is very difficult to do so. They were very profound thinkers. Should I go on?

"Yes, please. I cannot say that I am convinced, but I am certainly interested."

"Well, the law of cause and effect extends to every thought and every action in the life of a human being. In my country, we call this 'karma.' In Christianity, we say that you reap as you sow. Every action creates a reaction, and that reaction cannot be avoided or escaped. Our destiny, then, is a result of the sum total of all our thoughts and actions and the reactions that accrue from them. And because everything is connected by the law of cause and effect, the universe becomes a reflection of who we are. It's like looking in a mirror. The map of the heavens at the exact time of our birth from our vantage point in space accurately reflects our karma, and our karma determines our destiny. As that map changes over time, it reflects our own journey through time and space. So you see, in my country a practitioner of *jyotish* can never be satisfied with simply mapping out the movements of the stars. He wants to know what those stars tell us about our destiny, about who we are and the meaning of our voyage through life. The more accurate his calculations, the more accurate the map, but the best map in the world cannot help us if we don't know how to read it."

Le Gentil fell silent, uncomfortably aware of her growing magnetism but even more intrigued by the riddle she had posed. At this point Rodrigo paused as well, growing more and more enamored with the supple figure of his female lead and her finely etched Dravidian features as he watched her grow solider and sharper, almost by the moment, like a diamond turning toward the light. He detected something of Saraswati in her discourse, and it pleased him that his heroine had borrowed something from his teacher, if only in this one instance. But there the resemblance ended. There was something wild in Ambika that brooded just below the surface, setting her far apart from the carefully restrained, coolly controlled master of philosophy. Le Gentil had yet to see it. He felt the attraction but failed to recognize the fire that lay behind it, the fire that was sure to burn him if he came too close and sure to pull him in if he tried to keep his distance, the same fire that gave her mind the brilliant edge whose first thrusts had caught him off guard. But the greater part of it burned well out of sight, fueling her hidden ambitions and the dreams that only her father suspected, for it had been he who had planted them there and nurtured them well before she was old enough to have ambitions of her own.

While Le Gentil was not yet ready to be convinced, Rodrigo was well on his way. From the moment he had accepted the challenge of becoming the master of his mind, it was only a short leap to the realization that a lawful universe based on cause and effect was the only universe that could give meaning to the life of a human being. It was, as Ambika had said, a universe in whose mirror one could see the reflection of one's own face. He had heard many times the new age platitude that everything happens for a reason, but it was only now, aided by the voice of philosophy, that he had begun to pay it any heed. He left Le Gentil there for the moment, unsure whether or not he would have the perspicacity to notice that Ambika's contention could only hold true if she accepted the doctrine of reincarnation. Le Gentil needed time to ponder her arguments and the new translations she had brought him, and Rodrigo needed time to think more about samskara, and, if possible, a chance to ask Saraswati to clarify his doubts. The next morning was a Monday, and Monday meant philosophy class. He would come with his questions, every bit as prepared as Georg but hopefully faster to raise his hand.

14

ORDINARILY, SARASWATI DID NOT like to jump ahead when teaching any of the traditional texts. It offended her love of order and reminded her too much of the era she lived in. Nowadays, everyone seemed to be in love with speed. Everyone seemed to have their eyes fixed on the future rather than the present, always eager to find a shortcut, to avoid the effort and the hardship that was part of any worthwhile endeavor. Unfortunately, even many spiritual people shared this mentality. She had once thought that it was primarily the westerners, but lately she had to admit to herself that she no longer saw much difference between them and her compatriots. It was the age they lived in, leaving its imprint on them all, the dark clouds of the Kali Yuga gathering on the horizon—everyone, everywhere was affected. She herself had had to shake that compulsion when she first arrived in Rishikesh, chomping at the bit because the Mother—in her eyes—had sent her into exile. She had not dared to argue with her in person—no one would have—but the moment Saraswati left Benares, she started complaining to the Mother in the privacy of her mind, initiating a conversation that had yet to falter, having become as much a part of her daily experience as the weather.

It was during those first few weeks and in that ongoing conversation that she realized how much she had come to measure herself by her accomplishments, too many of them external to her spiritual life, and how those accomplishments always seemed to inhabit an imaginary future rather than the damp, musty soil of the present. How many times in those first weeks had she poured out her frustrations in front of the Mother's picture on her altar and received in return the same enchanting smile that kept shifting in the light, coaxing her to look deeper into the mirror, to pick up the trail of samskara that had led her to this point in her journey. Every time she did, she could hear the Mother's laughter and feel her invisible hand dabbing her tears. She had been in Rishikesh a couple of months when she finally realized that the mountains were there to protect her, not to imprison her, that the Mother had chosen them to be her teachers as well as her guardians, though recently every time she lifted her eyes and let them linger on those cloud-capped peaks, they seemed more and more fragile. How much longer would they be capable of keeping the outside world at bay? How much longer did she want them to?

This time, however, Saraswati broke with her long-standing practice and agreed to skip ahead, despite the fact that they had yet to finish the all-important opening chapter. The determining factor was something she saw in Rodrigo's eyes, not just impatience but determination—determination to gain a grasp on what might well be the single most important concept in all spiritual philosophy. If she had been in his shoes, put off by her philosophy teacher for several weeks now, she would have done the same: ask and ask again until she got an answer. And so she paid respect to his determination by asking those who had brought copies of the Yoga Sutras with them to open their books to chapter two, sutra twelve: *kleshamulah karmashayo drishtadrishtajanmavedaniyah*. First she explained the meanings of the individual Sanskrit words. Then she had them repeat the sutra after her until they had memorized it. As expected, they struggled with their pronunciation, especially the subtle difference between the dental and palatal consonants in *drishtadrishta*, typical among westerners, who were forever being caricatured in the Indian media for their stubbornly faulty pronunciation. All except Rodrigo. He had caught on to the difference in his first week of class and now reproduced these consonants and the rest of the Sanskrit alphabet as flaw- lessly as if he had been born to it.

It was one of a number of things that had surprised her about him. The first had been his unexpected appearance in her class. She had recognized him immediately, of course, the moment she saw him sitting among her students, so close she could have reached out and touched him. He was the clueless tourist the Mother had stopped on the road during her last visit to Rishikesh, the one who had looked so bewildered when she had asked him if he were lost. It was not entirely unprecedented for the Mother to talk to passersby. She had seen it happen several times and had always assumed there was a reason, some special blessing that these lucky wanderers had merited due to their past actions. But she had never seen any of them again. They had disappeared back into the ocean of humanity, carried off by the swells of an unseen fate. This one had wandered into her class more than a month later, looking just as lost as he had when the Mother had stopped him on the road. She was immediately curious, wonder- ing what samskara he might have that had caused the Mother to reach out of the transcendental blue and send him to her. There was no coincidence in this world. If he was there, sitting in front of her, it was because the Mother had willed it so. As the class progressed, she could not help but notice his absence of inner calm and the thin veneer of skepticism that he wrapped around him like a shawl, so common among Western intellectuals who didn't meditate and could not shake their complex of cultural superiority. Such persons rarely had the patience for a serious study of spiritual philosophy, but he had been marked by the Mother—she had seen it—and great sages like her never did anything out of chance or happenstance. He was there, she knew, because there was something the Mother wanted her to teach him. Whether it would be just a passing lesson or an extended tutorial was beyond her capacity to know, but as long as he was there, she told herself, she would honor the Mother's unspoken wish and teach him whatever it was he was supposed to learn.

She was not surprised, then, when he didn't miss a class in the month that followed. What did surprise her was the rapidity with which she had seen the jagged edges smoothing out, the facile skepticism replaced by flashes of eagerness and uncommon insight that impressed her almost against her will. Indeed, she had come to look forward to his questions. They were not the questions of someone who had been reading a lot but rather of someone who had been thinking a lot. Perhaps most of all, his question about the *karmakanda*, whether or not the Hindu rituals had been intended as a kind of symbolic external rehearsal for the subtle internal practices. She had lost some sleep that night wondering how he might have arrived at that conclusion—his vague reply when she had asked him about it after class had done little to satisfy her curiosity—but one flash of the Mother's smile in her mind was enough to remind her that her guru's whimsical sport was beyond human comprehension.

When she was satisfied that they had memorized the sutra, she began her explanation.

"Suppose you have a rubber ball and you press your finger into it. It creates an impression in the ball. What happens when you remove your finger? Ely?"

"The ball goes back to its original shape."

"Exactly. In other words, the original action generates a reaction. You take out your finger and the ball becomes round again. The purpose or the nature of that reaction is to return the ball to its original state, that is, to counteract the effect of the original action. And what happens to that impression, Ely, as long as you keep your finger there?"

"It stays there."

"Correct. In other words, the reaction can only take place once the appropriate conditions have been created. In this case, the finger has to be removed. Until then, the reaction remains in abeyance; it's an energy or a momentum that is waiting to be expressed. The mind is like that ball. Whenever any impression is created in the mind, its inherent nature is to return back to its original, unmodified state by undergoing the requisite reaction. Any action that our ego performs, whether mental or physical, distorts our mind; it leaves an impression. That impression or distortion creates momentum, and this momentum is the root cause of the reaction. In Sanskrit, the action is called *karma*, and the reaction is called *pratikarma* or *vipaka*. However, as long as the reaction remains unexpressed, as long as it remains in potential form only, it is called *samskara*. The sum total of all our unrequited reactions is our samskara. One of the literal meanings of the word *samskara* is 'purification,' because it is by undergoing these reactions that the mind is purified or liberated from its karma. Sometimes the reaction is obvious and immediate. Suppose you stick your hand in a fire. You burn your hand and you feel the pain. But suppose you steal someone's jewelry and become the cause of her suffering, but the law fails to catch you and you go unpunished. That doesn't mean you've escaped the reaction. It just means that it is held in abeyance until the necessary conditions are created. That distortion remains in your mind, whether in the form of guilt, arrogance, indifference, whatever it may be. Sooner or later, you will have to suffer the reaction. It may be after five years, it may be after twenty years, it may be in your next life. In the end, it doesn't matter. You cannot escape. You are bound by the law of cause and effect. The manner in which you suffer may vary, the hour may vary, but you will have to pay your debt.

"Now, over the course of many lifetimes, we have all accumulated a storehouse of unrequited reactions. That bottled-up momentum is the cause of rebirth. After death, it propels the bodiless mind in search of another body so that it can have the opportunity it requires to express its samskaras. This is not a conscious process, of course. Without a brain the bodiless mind cannot think. It is propelled by nature and by its own momentum. This momentum draws it like a magnet toward a suitable body with which it can maintain parallelism and begin a new life. The child is born into a new environment, but its fundamental character has not changed. Even though it does not have access to the memories of its previous life, it is the same mind with the same tendencies, the same unrequited reactions, the same destiny. The environment is different. The conscious experiences are different. But the child perceives and reacts to that environment and those experiences according to the samskaras that it brought with it from the previous life. As the ego develops and starts acting independently, the child begins to earn new samskaras and its character slowly gets modified depending on the choices it makes. So when we talk about a person's character or personality, we are really talking about that person's samskara. It is samskara that determines our character and thus our destiny. In effect, the effort to achieve enlightenment is synonymous with the effort to liberate ourselves from our samskaras."

Saraswati noticed the puzzled looks. They were not unexpected. This was a difficult concept, she knew, but she also knew that no matter how dry or intellectual it might seem to them, a proper understanding of this fundamental, universal law would be critical to their future spiritual progress. She paused for a moment to search her mind for an example to illustrate her point, one that would speak more intimately to their experience.

"Okay, Ely. Suppose you attend a gathering and someone you don't get along with particularly well insults you for no obvious reason. How would you react?"

"Knowing me, I'd get angry. I'm not real fond of insults. I'd probably give them tit for tat, say something I probably shouldn't say."

"Okay. Marlena, how would you react in the same situation?"

"I'd be offended. I probably wouldn't say anything, but I'd be hurt. Maybe wonder what I did to deserve that."

"Okay. Same situation, two different people, two different reactions. One person gets angry and lashes out. A second person feels hurt; maybe she feels unfairly victimized. Now let's put a third person in that same situation, but let's make this third person a yogi—not just any yogi, an accomplished yogi. She doesn't react at all. It doesn't bother her; it doesn't disturb her peace of mind; she shrugs it off as easily as a piece of lint from her shirt. Instead of getting angry or feeling hurt, she feels compassion for the person; she knows that only someone who is unhappy would act that way. The difference between these three persons is their samskara. The sutra says, 'A person's latent tendencies have been created by her past thoughts and actions; these tendencies will bear fruit, both in this life and in lives to come.' These tendencies are your samskaras; you take them with you from life to life, and they determine how you react to any given situation. We don't see the samskara, like we don't see the movements of the earth's plates at the bottom of the sea. But we know we've had a seismic event when we see the tidal wave bearing down on us. For one person, that tidal wave may be anger; for someone else, it may be anguish or depression. But in each case, the reaction is not an isolated event. It has a history and we call that history 'samskara.'

"But it doesn't stop there. Our samskaras not only determine how we react to different situations; they also determine what situations we have to face. Why did that person insult you? Why did you fall sick or lose your job or meet that person out of the blue and later end up marrying him? The answer is that all these external events that you may consider random are actually reflections of your samskara. The universe has an inherent self-correcting mechanism, and that self-correcting mechanism is action and reaction, cause and effect. You are placed in these situations according to your samskara. If it is your samskara to suffer for actions you have done in the past, no matter how distant that past may be, then sooner or later the universe will create the necessary conditions for you to undergo that suffering. Nothing is random. Nothing is accidental. Everything is lawful, and the law that governs this universe is cause and effect."

Saraswati scanned the eyes of her students, alert for any sign of a blank stare. Though she didn't see any, she decided it was a good time to add a traditional aside that she slipped into her lectures from time to time.

"Now I know Patanjali's philosophy can sound very intellectual; it can be daunting at times and also a little tedious, but I assure you, there is a practical value to what we are studying. It's not just a mental exercise or some kind of entertainment for our minds. The understanding of the world that we gain from philosophy serves to guide our actions. It teaches us how to walk the spiritual path. So then, what does an understanding of samskara teach us? First and foremost, it teaches us to take responsibility for our lives—not only for our actions but for all our experience—and in doing so, it eliminates the victim psychology that so many people suffer from.

"Let's say you walk across the street and a car comes barreling around a corner with a drunk driver at the wheel and puts you in a hospital. If you don't understand the theory of cause and effect, you may feel that you have been unfairly victimized. If you are a religious person, you may bring your complaint to the Lord. 'Why did you allow this to happen to me, Lord? I've always kept your commandments. I didn't deserve this.' But of course, you did. If you understand samskara, then you understand that you get exactly what you deserve. In other words, you know that somewhere in your past, whether in this life or in a previous one, you caused suffering to others through your actions, and now the universe has created the necessary conditions for you to pay that karmic debt. You are not a victim. Rather, you are balancing your account, paying off your debt. And despite what some people may think, this realization sets you free. How so? Because once you understand and accept this, you also realize that you are the architect of your destiny. One of my favorite Buddhist verses is 'Sow a thought and you reap an action; sow an action and you reap a habit; sow a habit and you reap a way of being; sow a way of being and you reap a destiny.' Every thought, every action, is a building block in the temple of our destiny. We have gotten ourselves into this mess, but we can also get ourselves out. Every elevated thought, every enlightened, compassionate action, generates a good reaction, and those good reactions will speed our progress. We cannot escape the samskaras we have already accrued. All we can do is burn them by going through the accumulated reactions—and the faster the better, if we are serious about our progress—but in the meanwhile, we can create a luminous future for ourselves by seeding our path with good actions and good thoughts. To quote the Buddha, the opening lines from the Dhammapada, 'We are what we think, having become what we have thought.'

"So now, let us return to our original example. A person insults us and our mind reacts in a certain way. That is determined by our samskara, both the insult and our immediate reaction. In most cases, that initial reaction sets off a chain reaction. We shout, it feeds our anger, we shout some more. We've all been through this. All of us have our own reactive patterns. But we have a choice in the matter and that choice will determine our future. There is nothing you can do about the initial reaction; it has already occurred in accordance with your samskara. But then you remember that you are a spiritualist and that the winds of your samskaras are blowing you in a direction you don't want to go. So you make an effort to control yourself. You remain silent, or you make some conciliatory remark, whatever is appropriate to the situation. You don't allow the situation to control you. You accept the suffering it entails, knowing that you are paying your debt, and turn your attention to your own reactions. The next time you are faced with such a situation, you do the same, and each time it gets a little easier. Once you are able to control your actions, you stop creating new samskaras of that type. Eventually your old ones get exhausted and you are no longer the person who reacts in that situation. You become the person who doesn't lose her mental balance. And when that happens, you find that the world around you has changed. The universe no longer needs to put you in such situations in order to satisfy your samskara. You've learned your lesson, so you move on to new ones."

Marlena raised her hand, something she had rarely done in the nearly four months she had been attending Saraswati's class. Saraswati acknowledged her with a nod, feeling as always a sense of fondness for this quiet, restrained woman with the beautiful French accent. She was someone who seemed to be nursing a deep wound. This was not uncommon in her classes. Saraswati had seen many people over the years turn to yoga and meditation to heal them from their past when all else failed. Desperation was often a worthy adversary and a fine motivator, if the person could summon enough determination to stick with their practices. Marlena had proven to be one of those persons. Behind the sadness that often expressed itself on her face, Saraswati could detect a quiet resolve and a steadiness that she was sure would carry her through the vicissitudes of her emotions. She suspected that most people missed this about her; it was one of the reasons why she never failed to respect her habitual silence. Another was that when Marlena did speak, it was always with a purpose.

"Could you explain a little more about the relationship between samskara and fate?"

"From the yogic point of view, samskara *is* fate. You were born in France at a particular time and into a particular family due to your samskara. And where you go from here, both in this life and the next, will depend on whatever samskaras you have yet to exhaust and the new ones you create. We are born into a particular family and a particular culture in order to satisfy our samskaras. If you were a yogi in your past life, then you are born into a situation that allows you to resume your spiritual practices from where you left off. India might be a likely destination, though from what they tell me, California has also become a popular landing place. If your samskara requires you to suffer a terrible illness at the age of ten in order to pay for something terrible you did, then you will be born into a family where the parents have a samskara to suffer the illness of a young child. The same of any brothers or sisters you might have. It is an intricately interconnected web of unimaginable complexity. The web of universal relations revolves around samskara. There is an old Chinese saying: marriage is debt. In other words, marriage, like everything else, is also a samskara, usually a very strong one. You marry someone because you have a debt to pay, and that person provides you with the necessary opportunity."

"You mean the necessary suffering," Marlena added, with one of her few smiles.

"Either pain or pleasure," Saraswati replied, allowing herself a little smile as well but wondering if the allusion was to something specific in Marlena's past. "It all depends on your past. In either case, the net result is the same. We learn the lessons we need to learn so that we can move along the path of liberation, and in the process we have to pay off our debts. In short, your accumulated samskaras have brought you to this point, and that, coupled with the samskaras you create from here on out, will determine your future."

Georg raised his hand. "Are there methods in yoga to speed up the burning of samskara?"

"Certainly. In fact, you could say it's an art form. The most important, as you might imagine, is meditation, but there are a lot of other things we can do as well to speed up the process. However, in the end I believe it all boils down to a question of will. Let's say you have a certain amount of suffering that you have to pay back in the form of karmic debt. It's like a loan you owe the bank. You can pay it all back in one year, or you can spread it out over ten years. If you pay it back in one year, then your experience during that one year will be extremely intense. You will have to undergo great hardship in a short amount of time trying to raise the money. If you pay it back in ten years, then it's much easier to handle, but you have to wait a longer time to be free. Instead of being in bondage for one year, you are in bondage for ten. If a yogi wants to advance as fast as possible, then she asks the Lord to give her the fire as hot as she can take it. Why should I wait ten years when I can get it over in one? That's the mentality. I'd rather suffer the hardships and earn my freedom as soon as possible. But you have to have the strength to endure those hardships. So you build up your strength through meditation and the various other practices, and then you ask for the fire. If you ask for it—sincerely—you will get it. This is a spiritual law. But you must be prepared. This is something we will come back to later in our studies."

Saraswati saw Rodrigo's hand go up. As usual, she was curious to see where he would take the discussion.

"Can you burn samskaras through your dreams?"

The question caught her off guard, not the first time this had happened with him. She paused to visualize the Mother floating in the air in front of her, her ancient smile as bewitching as ever, even in this insubstantial form. As she invariably did when she didn't know the answer to a question, Saraswati asked her guru to supply her with the words. After all, she was nothing more than a conduit for the Mother, at least to the extent that she could keep her ego out of the way. The Mother was the real source of wisdom in her classes. Her only duty was to let the Mother work her magic. Moments later, an answer came, as it always did, one that she found herself listening to just as much as her students.

"To be honest, that is a question I've never heard before. But let us think about it logically. If your experience in the dream were sufficiently intense, then the answer would be yes. Intense mental experience, whether suffering or joy, means that a samskara is being expressed. Something in your past is being released. However, the emotions we experience in most dreams are fleeting. They have no lasting impact, so in most cases the answer is no. According to yoga, most dreams serve as a simple discharge of psychic energy by our subconscious mind. There is another kind of dream, however, that arises from the deeper layers of our mind. Such dreams are very rare, but they do happen, and they are directly tied to our samskara. For the most part, though, samskaras are expressed through our conscious experience. We win the lottery or lose our job or get hit by a car, and we react to these experiences with suffering or joy. Meditation ripens those samskaras; thus, it speeds up the process. Usually this translates into a heightened intensity of experience in our daily life, something experienced by most meditators, but sometimes we experience those ripening samskaras purely at the subconscious level while we meditate; in other words, while we meditate we undergo some form of intense mental experience. If the same thing were to happen to you while you were dreaming, then you might well be exhausting samskara in your dreams."

That evening Saraswati took a walk on the roof above her room. She remembered the interchange with Rodrigo and hoped that she had been pure enough in that moment to let the Mother's wisdom flow through her unimpeded, though she would have preferred to have had time to meditate on the subject beforehand. The question still intrigued her. She could not remember having had dreams of her own that she would classify as requital of samskara, but she had had a roommate in college for the better part of a year whom she had sometimes heard weeping or laughing in her bed at night while she slept. She knew of one lady in her village, a friend of her mother's, who had nightmares strong enough to wake her from sleep, shaking with fear. The woman's family had taken her to the local *ojah*, thinking that she might be possessed by a malefic spirit. Certainly this was the play of samskara; everything was subject to its inexorable laws. While such dreams might not be intense enough, compared with our experiences in the waking state, to unburden us of any significant portion of our karmic debt, they undoubtedly had some minor role to play in the process. But what of Rodrigo's dreams? From the look on his face, his question was related to something he was going through. The yogic psychologist in her would have liked to know what it was. Was it in some way related to his ongoing spiritual awakening? she wondered, unconsciously querying the Mother in the hidden chambers of her mind, her conversations with herself having long since become conversations with her guru, whom she saw as the pure reflection of her inner self. She suspected that the Mother had bestowed her blessings on him to help relieve him of some heavy karma from the past. Could his dreams have something to do with this unseen burden?

There was something about Rodrigo that still made her feel uneasy—wary was perhaps a better word—despite his keen intelligence and the marked changes for the better that she had seen in him. Something in him had made her hackles rise when he first joined her class and ignited her mistrust, though it was lessening now. She had been surprised at her reaction, well aware that the Mother would not condone it. At first, she had shrugged it off as a minor annoyance, the human mind being what it is, but when he continued to attend her classes and her feelings persisted, she had made a conscious effort to examine those feelings and trace them to their source. On the surface, there didn't seem to be any obvious reason for it. He was well behaved and courteous. He was intelligent and obviously sincere about his spiritual studies and his practices. There was a time when she might have felt that way simply because he was a man, but those days were long past. Thousands of hours of meditation had burned those feelings out of her, attested to by the fact that she had had plenty of men in her classes these past few years and had never once experienced a similar reaction. No, she could not believe that she had regressed in this one area after all this time. There was something specific about him in particular that the Mother was choosing to veil from her conscious perception but not from her intuition. It might very well be something in his past that had put her subtle senses on alert, some heavy samskara that had triggered her unconscious defenses. Whatever it was, it had made for some interesting introspection and a worthy challenge. To be alert, but not let that state of heightened vigilance betray your calm or lessen your compassion. To listen to your intuition, but to remember that behind the play of good and evil there was one Divine Consciousness amusing itself with itself in an endless sport. This was just another of the Mother's tests, one more in a gauntlet that would only cease when she herself had ceased by merging herself into the Mother's waiting heart.

15

T HAT NIGHT, AS RODRIGO lay in bed, he opened his book on Indian goddesses and read for the first time, with amusement and interest, the chapter on Saraswati. What amused him was the description of the goddess as quarrelsome and possessing a fiery temper. She was also said to possess a strongly independent will and to not be very obliging to the male gods. Could his Saraswati, with her deliberate, precise speech and her aura of serenity, also possess a fiery temper? If so, she kept it well hidden. He tried to picture her picking a quarrel or losing her temper, but he just couldn't do it. Not because she was too sweet or too feminine—she was none of those—rather, he couldn't conceive of any person or any situation capable of ruffling her feathers. But there was no doubt that she was highly independent and that she maintained a marked reserve around men that probably had something to do with some sort of vow of celibacy she had taken. No, obliging to the male gods she certainly was not.

But what most interested him about the goddess was the subtle symbolism behind her imagined existence. Unlike Kali, that denizen of the unconscious—dark, fierce, and terrible, too mysterious for words—Saraswati hovered just beyond the horizon like a luminous sea ready to bathe us in its brilliance. She was the goddess of knowledge, words, and music. She dressed in white, reflecting the light of her fair skin, rode a white swan, and carried no weapon other than a book and a vina, ancient precursor to the violin. Students offered her flowers and fruits before sitting for their exams, and musicians lit incense in front of her image before they practiced their instruments or stepped on stage for a concert. But as Rodrigo was slowly discovering, the gods and goddesses were symbols that began within the temporal bounds of history, only to be wrested from their moorings by humans pondering the mysteries of the universe, and set to work to explain what they found there. Saraswati had begun life as a river that flowed through Western India in the early days of her civilization. The Indus Valley civilization had grown up on her banks and then migrated when she began drying up in the fourth millennium BC. Before the river disappeared, she was chosen for one last task in the mythology of the day, a task that signaled a turning point in the beliefs of her people. She was asked to transport *agni*, the sacrificial fire, to the sea where it would then pass out of the world of men. The sea was their symbol for the ocean of consciousness. By transporting the sacrificial fire to its depths, it symbolized their moving from external rituals to the internal spiritual disciplines that would lead them to enlightenment. By the third millennium, the original Saraswati had become a memory and a myth. It now existed only in the internal world as a symbol for the flow of consciousness within the human being, a migration from the world of spiritual ignorance to the sea of enlightened consciousness. This was the true knowledge and it was encapsulated in one word: *om*, the sound of silence, the cosmic drum from whose primordial vibration the creation arose, and the source of all mantras.

No wonder artists and intellectuals revered her. She was the goddess that Rodrigo would have put on his altar had he been born into a Hindu family. He set his book face down on his chest, still open to the faceplate of the chapter, a full-color depiction of the goddess in a radiant white gown, as beautiful in the painting as he would have drawn her in his imagination. His Saraswati was neither fair of skin nor beautiful, as he judged beauty in a woman, but as he drifted off into a long and pleasant reverie, the brilliance of her mind made her seem just as radiant as the goddess in the picture. As he relived some of her comments from that morning, he could see her teaching her circle of students, but instead of watching her from his seat on the grass, he was now high above them, nearly of a height with the top branches of the banyan tree. She was wearing a white sari now, rather than her usual pale saffron, and everyone else, himself included, seemed but insubstantial shadows flitting at the edge of the light that radiated from her regal figure. The world of philosophy that she was drawing him into was beginning to appear just as attractive, just as creative, as the best fiction that had fired his mind and peopled his mental landscape with heroes since his earliest days. And she was the center of the circle, the source for the wild cornucopia of thoughts that had set his world spinning. There are many types of beauty, he thought, just before he drifted off into sleep. Maybe the most interesting and lasting beauty is the one that is most difficult to see with the naked eye.

When Rodrigo awoke the next morning, his book was lying beside him on the bed. It was well before dawn, but he didn't notice the hour or think to look at his watch. Flush with excitement, all he could think of was the dream from whose waters he had just arisen. He reached for his computer in the dark without being fully aware of what he was doing. As the screen lit up, he barely saw it, his mind still submerged in another place and another time.

Rishikesh
10/18
4:07 AM

I saw her again this morning, the water girl. It was in the courtyard and she was more beautiful than I remembered. But let me start at the beginning, or rather from the first thing I was aware of when I awoke.

I was lying in my bed in my little temple room. I was having trouble sleeping, but it wasn't because I was frustrated, as I had been the last time. Rather, I was too excited to sleep. I simply couldn't stop thinking about the girl. I had seen her that afternoon in the courtyard behind the temple, in the same spot where I had seen her the first time. I was walking through the gardens, conversing with the goddess in my mind, more or less along the same lines as in my previous dream, lamenting how alone I was in this place where no one understood me. But in the back of my mind I was wondering if I might by chance see her there. This thought kept distracting me; whenever I heard some rustle in the hedges, I would look over my shoulder to see if it was her. Then at some point I felt the presence of someone behind me. I turned around and there she was, balancing an empty earthen jar on her hip. It was a shock to see her. I felt acutely self-conscious, though I did my best to hide it. My greeting was deliberately cold, in an effort to regain my composure. It was the tone one used with the servants in the temple as a matter of course. But inside, my heart was beating wildly; in fact, it made me a little angry to see how little control I had over my emotions. She returned my greeting and stood there quietly with her eyes respectfully lowered. Was she waiting for me to say something? I couldn't tell. All I knew was that I felt awkward in her presence. She wasn't your typical low-caste servant, that much I already knew. There was an intelligence in her eyes that I had rarely come across and a quiet, confident, almost regal bearing that seemed so out of place in a person of her station. The silence made me uncomfortable, so I told her that I had appreciated the comment she had made the other day. Her point had been a good one. The sound of my voice made it easier for me to go on. I asked her out of curiosity if she had heard those ideas in the discourse of some spiritual teacher. She smiled and told me that her father had taught her to read when she was a young girl; she had been studying the scriptures more or less on her own ever since.

This surprised me. Even many Brahmin women were illiterate. I had assumed all low-caste women were. Even if some were not, it was hard to imagine any of them studying scripture. I must have said something to that effect, because she asked me if I thought that women had less right to study the scriptures than men, or were less capable of understanding them. There was something in her tone that annoyed me. It was somehow disrespectful, almost as if she were deliberately trying to challenge me. But I didn't react. I replied as politely as I could, saying something about the role of women as enjoined by the scripture, more especially women from the non-Brahmin castes. But she scoffed at this. She told me that the atman within all of us had no caste. Caste belonged to the body and to the culture. Then she quoted the Bhagavad Gita: "A wise man, a pundit, sees all as the same, whether a learned Brahmin or a cow, an elephant, a dog or an outcaste." Had I forgotten this? Was I also unable to see the atman inside her like the rest of the world who remained lost in the dream of maya?

I was stunned by her words. Part of me was angry that a low-caste woman, a servant, should have the temerity to talk to a high priest of the temple in this way. But at the same time, I was thrilled to hear words of spiritual conviction and insight from the most unlikely of sources. Were they just words? Or could it be that her conviction was born of inner experience. The possibility excited me. I don't know how conscious I was of this at the moment, but later, when I was lying on my bed, I couldn't stop thinking about it. She had that look, the eerie sense of inner calm and strength that I associated with yogic adepts. But could this be? It didn't seem possible. I don't remember what I said in reply, but I remember that she quoted another verse from the Gita: "He who experiences the unity of life sees his own self in all beings, and all beings in his own self, and looks on everything with an impartial eye." We started discussing the meaning of the verse. I began to explain some point of philosophy, humoring her a bit. After all, I was a priest. This was my domain, my turf, my country. But she was one step ahead of me, quoting from other esoteric texts as easily as I could, if not more so. I was astounded. I became so excited that I had to make a conscious effort to keep that excitement out of my voice. But at the same time, I started growing worried that somebody might see us. It was one thing to exchange a word or two with a female servant or to give some instructions. But to linger there in a public place and have an open conversation? It wasn't done, no matter how spiritual the topic. Soon my paranoia increased so much that I broke off our discussion, despite its having reached its most interesting point. She was saying that women had an advantage when it came to spiritual practices in the Kali Yuga because devotion was more natural to women. Men were more dominated by their intellect and thus less adept at matters of the heart; and in this age of spiritual darkness, the heart was the surest path to realization. How could I, who worshipped the goddess and placed flowers at the feet of Kali every day, not see the advantages she had given her daughters, whom she loved equally but to whom she revealed more of her secrets, knowing that they had been unfairly disadvantaged by society?

I almost turned and fled at that point, not knowing how to answer her, worried that if I stayed even a minute longer someone would see us and think the worst. Finally, I made some excuse and disappeared into the temple. But all that night I lay in bed, exhilarated, thinking about our encounter and the things she'd said. How could I even think to sleep? I had not had such a stimulating conversation for as long as I could remember. I had finally met someone who could appreciate my thoughts and insights and challenge me at the same time. But she was a low-caste servant and even worse—a woman. The irony was so thick I could taste it. Would I ever get the scope to sit down and converse with her as I pleased? Never! Had she been a man and a Brahmin, she would have instantly been the best and brightest of my students, but as a low-caste woman she could never be my student. She would have to die first and be reborn as a male child in a Brahmin family. What cruel sport this was! The Divine Mother had heard my prayers and had answered them, but in her inscrutable whimsy, she had placed the answer far enough out of reach that I could never profit by it. All I could do was to look on from a distance and know what I was missing. And yet, there she was, toiling in the temple courtyard each morning, filling the earthen jars with water from the well and tending to the plants. The very idea was enough to rob me of my sleep.

Now that I am at my computer, remembering my dream, I remember also that she was beautiful. Dark, freshly oiled skin; long, luxuriant black hair; deep, intelligent eyes. In my dream I was so conscious of her caste, so conscious of being a priest, that I don't think I ever once looked at her as a man looks at a woman, a beautiful, alluring woman. But now that I am back to being who I am, there is no escaping that thought. She reminds me of Ambika as I have pictured her. She has that same boldness and a similar beauty. But unlike Ambika, she seems so enticingly real that I can hardly wait to see her again. And yet she is a creation of my subconscious. That seems hard to fathom at this moment. Just as hard to fathom is the meaning behind her appearance—or should I say, her apparition. Can it have something to do with Saraswati? It is true that I am fast becoming enamored of Indian spiritual philosophy. Could it be that I am in some way mixing up the philosophy with the philosopher? Maybe in this respect, I am becoming more and more like my dreamed alter ego. Saraswati is not beautiful (as perhaps my subconscious mind would like her to be, thus the deliberate makeover), but she has a mind that surprises and challenges me. O my waking self, beware of projection! Think! The very qualities that I feel are missing in Saraswati the person mysteriously show up in this subconscious creation. She is warm, she is beautiful, she meets my priestly self when he is alone in the temple gardens. What exactly is my fictive hero up to? Is this water girl the symbolic figure of what I instinctively feel is missing in my life, gradu-ally taking shape in this dreaming drama that continues to unfold like a daytime serial, sent to me from my subconscious's version of central casting? The artistic and now spiritual companion that Beth could never be? Perhaps, but as with any drama, I won't know until the play is ended. The best authors always withhold their strongest card until the very end. Why should my subconscious be any different? In the meantime, be careful not to project onto real life and its flesh-and-blood characters what your dreaming self desires.

It was only when Rodrigo sat for his morning meditation in the main hall that it occurred to him how odd it was that he could remember so clearly the two verses of the Bhagavad Gita that the water girl had recited during his dream. He owned a copy of the Gita and had read parts of it, especially the chapters on meditation and the different yogas, but had he been asked to paraphrase a single verse, or even part of one, he would have been unable to do so. And yet his imaginary water girl had, as sure in her recitation as he was in quoting his favorite lines of Western poetry, and as an imagined priest, he had recognized those verses word for word. After yoga class, he stopped by his room to pick up his copy of the Gita and brought it with him to breakfast. As usual, he was the first to enter the dining hall. Taking advantage of the tardy appearance of his fellow classmates, he flipped through it, verse by verse, as he nibbled at his meal, until he located the two passages the water girl had quoted. They were exactly as he remembered them from his dream, down to the order of the words. Here was incontrovertible proof of the power of the subconscious. He had read those passages, no doubt, but his conscious mind could never have remembered them weeks after a single cursory reading. But his subconscious had remembered. It had waited for the right moment to work them into the fabric of his dreams. He had read in one of his yoga books that the subconscious mind retained every impression that passed through the gates of the senses and stored them in its infinitely efficient library. Obviously, these yogis knew what they were talking about when it came to the workings of the human mind. Now, if only his conscious mind could be that creative, that retentive. Then he'd really be a writer.

There was no philosophy class that morning, so Rodrigo was able to spend those hours revising the latest scene in his book, endeavoring to accentuate the interplay between his two principal characters and the unspoken subtext, careful lest it get lost behind the philosophy. He thought a lot about the final line he had written, the hint he had left there about Ambika's secret ambitions and her father's role in fostering them. He had, in fact, only a vague idea of what those ambitions might be. Her love for her country and the fact that she was the subject of a colonial power pointed him in a certain direction, but exactly what shape they would take and what role they would play in the book were not yet known to him. He wondered now if this had been a hint left there by his subconscious, consciously unplanned but already thought out at a level he was not aware of. It was a suspicion that would not let him alone. The idea that there might be a creative energy within him that he was hitherto unaware of, working intelligently and purposefully toward ends of its own, fascinated him. It opened up a world of possibilities. He began to wonder if many of the great works of art that he had been weaned on might, in fact, have been confections of the subconscious or even unconscious minds of their creators that had somehow erupted into consciousness, rather than conscious creations of master craftsmen, unlooked for and perhaps never fully comprehended by the mind that had acted as their conduit and given them their final form. What would it mean to find out that you were more a host than anything else, with only a thin illusion of control to cling to? It was something he would have to watch for, just as he was now watching and waiting to find out what would happen in his dreams. He had still not fully come to grips with the undeniable fact that he was dreaming in sequential fashion, his subconscious mind slowly weaving a causal story rather than merely tossing disconnected or imaginary fragments of his life into a psychic soup. He had never heard of this happening to anyone, but on the other hand, he didn't see any reason why it should not. His subconscious had already shown itself to be more powerful than he could have imagined. What was so difficult, then, about picking up the thread from a previous dream and continuing the story it had started?

He was still pondering these questions when he went down to the dining hall for lunch. As he walked past the office, he noticed Bhagavati and Saraswati talking just outside the open doorway. They exchanged greetings and Saraswati called him over with a wave of her hand.

"Rodrigo, it's good you happened by. Do you have a copy of the Bhagavad Gita?"

"Yes," he said, momentarily startled by the question.

"Good. Bring it to class with you this coming Monday. We are going to start studying the Gita. Wednesdays and Fridays will still be the Yoga Sutras, but from now on Mondays will be the Gita. What version of the Gita do you have? Does it have a commentary?"

"It's Shankaracharya's commentary."

"That'll do. If you can, read the first two chapters over the weekend. And bring any questions you have."

As Rodrigo made his way toward the dining hall, he wondered about the import of this encounter. Had his subconscious known about it, too? Could it in some way see into the future as well as the past? Had it been getting him ready for the Gita, his weekend preparatory reading already foreseen by his sleeping self? He could call it a coincidence, but hadn't Saraswati said in her class on samskara that there was no such thing as coincidence, only an endless chain of cause and effect? As he entered the dining hall, Georg and Ely greeted him with a friendly wave. He did not mention to them what had happened but merely took his place in the chain of cause and effect and told them to get ready to start studying the Gita on Monday.

16

S ARASWATI FELT A SPECIAL fondness for her worn and weathered copy of
Ramanuja's commentary on the Gita. The glue in the binding was yellowed
and cracked, the pages were falling out in clumps, and she had long since
had the original paperback cover replaced with a plain red-cloth cover at a Delhi
bookbinder. But to her it was more beautiful than the best leather-bound volume
in Swamiji's private collection. This dilapidated, unassuming book, one that any
library would have relegated to the reclamation bin years ago, had accompanied
her faithfully throughout the long spiritual odyssey that had been her life. It had
received her tears and congratulated her on her triumphs. It had been there to
offer her solace and wisdom when there was no solace or wisdom to be found.
It was in the pages of Ramanuja's graceful and poetic commentary that she had
learned to understand bhakti, the yoga of devotion—not merely as a philosophy
but as the one practice from which all her other practices drew their sustenance.
She had added other copies of the Gita to her collection since—in Sanskrit, Hindi,
and English—but this was the one volume she always came back to whenever she
felt a need to return to the roots of what she considered to be her spiritual life.

It had been her father's copy. He had begun reading to her from it when she
was five, and ever since she had never failed to experience a rising tide of emotion
whenever she read the opening chapters. As a girl, she had been able to picture
Krishna holding the reins of the chariot while her father read, the Lord's bluish
skin radiant like the noonday sky, a peacock feather in his hair and a royal diadem
above his brow. While she hadn't been able to understand Krishna's teachings
at that tender age, his figure in her mind was the one memory from childhood
that she recalled before all others. He was the one she had called upon for guidance from her bed at night, and as she grew older, she had never failed to see
his hand behind the vagaries of fate that might have leveled her had he not been
there to protect her.

One summer night when she was eight, she awoke to see a flash of lightning
illuminating her bedroom window, which overlooked the family's small paddy field.
For one hesitant breath, the gently swaying paddy looked like a forest of molten
gold waving in the wind. The light winked out, the paddy field disappeared, and

moments later there came a thunderclap so loud the walls around her shook. In her mind, she associated that terrible sound with the roar of the fantastic demons that roamed through the bedside tales her father would tell her, most of them drawn from the Puranas, the colorful myths that had paid court to the Hindu imagination for more than thirty centuries. Though she knew these tales were only tales, no more real than the images in her mind, she shuddered with terror at the sound, imagining the great demon Rahu bearing down on their little village, ready to flatten their simple thatch roof with one mighty thunderclap of his tail, but instead of running to her parents in the next room, she knelt down before the little altar by her bedstead and prayed to the image of Krishna that her mother had placed there. She folded her hands and asked the cowherd god to save her, promising him that if he did, she would dedicate her life to his service. As if in answer, the winds subsided. The great lashing tongues of rain withdrew and the night grew calm. Her trembling ceased and she was filled with an unquestioning assurance that Krishna had heard her prayers. The Lord of Vrindavan had taken her under his protection. From that day forward, she considered herself his ward, safe from whatever evils the world might set against her.

This assurance was reaffirmed six years later when she entered the Mother's Benares ashram for the first time, one week before her fourteenth birthday, brought there by her ailing father who had been a lifelong devotee of the saint, and by her mother who followed her father in everything with the devout stubbornness of a traditional Hindu wife. Even now, she could remember the Mother's face exactly as she had seen it on that day, alone with her in her room. The saint was seated on a low wooden cot covered by a batik sheet decorated with elephants and chariots; Saraswati sat on a thin bamboo mat on the floor in front of her. The Mother, who had seemed the incarnation of sweetness the few times she had seen her as a child when she had accompanied her parents to Delhi for one of the Mother's infrequent visits there, now appeared more like an ancient queen, terrible and mighty, surpassingly beautiful despite her aged body. Short in stature, she seemed like a giant at that moment, filling the room with her towering presence. Her eyes blazed and the trembling young woman could not stop staring at her, as if the sage's gaze held her captive with its magnetic force and would not let her go until she had offered up her innermost secrets. Several long moments passed before the Mother's musical voice broke the spell and that remote, unearthly visage became transformed into a warm, earthy smile. "So, my daughter, finally you have come. I have been waiting a long time. The world has been waiting a long time. It is expecting great things from you. Are you ready now to fulfill your promise?"

Saraswati did not know what to make of the Mother's words. She could not speak, not even to say yes, so transfixed was she by the Mother's gaze, but she felt a thrill pass through her when she heard the Mother say that she had been waiting for her; and though her lips could not form the words, her entire being cried out that she was ready to do whatever the Mother asked. The saint smiled and passed her hand lightly over Saraswati's brow. "Fix your eyes on the welfare of the world, daughter; you will do great work for humanity. But never forget who is acting. Always remember Krishna's words from the Gita: 'Though the sage sees, hears, touches, smells, eats, moves, sleeps and breathes, he knows the Truth; he knows that it is not he who acts.'" The Mother then initiated Saraswati into yogic meditation. When the initiation was finished, she patted her on the cheek and said, "Now that you are initiated, the time has come for you to begin fulfilling your vow. Do you remember that night, the night you promised Lord Krishna that if he saved you from the storm you would become his servant? Today he has delivered you into my charge, and it is my charge to you to remember your vow. You will not forget?"

She had not forgotten. On that day, the tears wetting her eyes as she fought the shock of the Mother's omniscience, she had felt Krishna's presence in the room, as real as the Mother's, two ancient smiles looming over her from the precipice of her own heart. More than twenty years had passed since that day, but every time she fingered the Gita's pages or asked her students to read its verses, she remembered her guru's smile that morning and the presence of Krishna beside her, one hand on his bamboo flute, the other resting on the Mother's shoulder. She had become a yogi, as the Mother had instructed, but that vow still held her captive, having fixed her destiny at an age when her village friends were still collecting dolls.

Saraswati took a last, fond look at the opening few chapters and reviewed her lecture once more in her mind. Then she reluctantly put her childhood copy of the Gita back on the bookshelf and took down a copy of Juan Mascaro's English translation, the one she invariably recommended to her students. It had neither the Sanskrit text nor any commentary, but it was written in a sonorous, poetic prose that came as close as any translation she knew of to the grandeur of the original. Of the Sanskrit, she had no need. She had long since committed the original text to memory, as she had done with the Yoga Sutras, the Guru Gita, and the other ancient texts by which she ordered her life.

She put Mascaro's translation into her bag along with a printout of her lecture notes and then prostrated before the picture of the Mother on her altar, as she always did before leaving her room. As she stepped out of her door and looked up, she saw that the sky was overcast, unusual for late October, especially at this hour. The monsoon rains had arrived late that year and now, on the other side of the river, the fag end of the monsoon was getting ready to fling itself against the mountains with a final desperate heave. Finding its way barred, it flung its last angry drops against the flat concrete roofs of Rishikesh, causing a few street merchants to pause and look up at the sky, muttering a few incautious imprecations before they caught themselves and touched their palms to the crown of their heads in an instinctive obeisance to Varuna, god of the winds and the rain. While they readied their plastic coverings and continued to draw the attention of the passersby to their wares with an understated gentility that would have gone unnoticed in Delhi, Saraswati passed underneath the shisham tree in the courtyard in front of her room and headed down the walkway toward the rear of the ashram where her students would be waiting. The few scattered drops grew more frequent and more insistent and caused her to hurry her gait. When she reached the back lawn, she could see that her students had already taken shelter on the veranda of the yoga hall. As always, she would have much preferred to hold class outside on the lawn, but she comforted herself with the thought that this would probably be the last time they would be forced indoors until the following June.

Once the class was settled at one end of the large hall, Saraswati, following her usual predilection, began with a historical overview.

"Today we are going to begin studying the Bhagavad Gita. We will continue studying the Yoga Sutras on Wednesdays and Fridays, but since there are many parallels between the two books, I wanted to begin working on the Gita as well since it will help us to better understand the Yoga Sutras. First, let us begin with a little history.

"*Bhagavad* means 'God' and *gita* means 'song.' The Bhagavad Gita, then, is the 'Song of God.' The text is set in the form of a dialogue between Lord Krishna and his disciple Arjuna on the eve of the great battle of Kurukshetra, a battle that would decide the future of India. The battle of Kurukshetra was a historical battle. It took place approximately 3500 years ago, by our best reckoning, and both Arjuna and Krishna were historical figures. Krishna was a great yogic master who was revered by many as an incarnation of God; Arjuna was a prince and his disciple. The text, however, is highly symbolic. We need to consider it principally as a work of spiritual literature, rather than as any kind of historical document. Most yogis and many historians believe that this conversation between Krishna and Arjuna did indeed take place, but the person who wrote the Bhagavad Gita, Veda Vyasa, was not physically present there to record it, though he was a contemporary of theirs. Rather, with a firm understanding of literary license, he borrowed that historical situation and used it as the setting for a didactic work, a poetic exposition of the teachings of Lord Krishna. Vyasa is revered in India as the greatest writer of antiquity. He was India's Homer, if you will, however his works were, and are, much more influential in Southeast Asia than Homer's works ever were in the West. Veda Vyasa was the author of the eighteen principle Puranas, the defining works of Indian mythology, which he wrote as instructional texts for the masses. He was also the author of a number of lesser works, but his masterpiece was the *Mahabharata*, a verse epic that tells the story of a dynastic struggle in the India of his day that culminated in the Kurukshetra war. The *Mahabharata* as a whole is a very diverse book. It deals with geography, history, warfare, religion, morality, and many other subjects. The Bhagavad Gita is just one small section in this voluminous work, but it is considered by many to be Vyasa's greatest achievement, the jewel in his crown, so to speak. It is considered, along with the Yoga Sutras, to be among the greatest works of Indian spiritual philosophy and one of the world's greatest spiritual classics, but unlike the Yoga Sutras, it is also very much a literary work, and we must bear this in mind because it is this literary license that allows Vyasa to add the symbolic richness that helps make the Bhagavad Gita the classic that it is.

"Now, let us turn to the first chapter in which Vyasa sets the stage for the ensuing dialogue."

Saraswati handed her copy of Mascaro's translation to Marlena, who was sitting just to her left. She had them go around the circle, each reading aloud a few verses, until they had completed the first chapter, "The despondency of Arjuna."

"Now let us take a closer look at the chapter. Those of you who brought your own copies can open them now. As you can see in the first couplet, Vyasa begins with a framing device; he employs a narrator, whose name is Sanjay. Sanjay, as we have learned earlier in the *Mahabharata*, is the advisor to King Dhritarashtra. The king is blind, so Sanjay narrates for him the course of the war. When the Bhagavad Gita opens, we are on the eve of the deciding battle. Sanjay describes for the king the two armies arrayed on either side of the plain of Kurukshetra. One is led by prince Duryodhana, the eldest of Dhritarashtra's hundred sons; the other is captained by his nephew, prince Yudhisthira, the eldest of the five Pandava brothers. It is an internecine conflict, a struggle for the throne between two branches of one family. Sanjay surveys the field, names the principle participants, describes the blowing of the conch, which heralds the coming conflict, and then relates for the king how Arjuna asks Krishna to pull up his chariot between the two armies so that he can better see those with whom he is about to do battle. Krishna, the great spiritual master, is a noncombatant, but he has agreed to be Arjuna's charioteer."

As she said this last sentence, Saraswati raised one hand to emphasize her point, something she rarely did. She was more animated than usual, feeling once again the gathering magic of Vyasa's poetry, that sense of beauty, symmetry, and philosophical depth that she considered unparalleled among all works of spiritual literature.

"As Arjuna surveys the field, he sees his kinsmen arrayed against him: his cousins, the Kauravas, who are determined to take the throne from his brother Yudhisthira, along with his friends and former teachers who are supporting his cousins' claim. Seeing this, he loses heart. He throws down his weapons and tells Krishna he will not fight. Better to die, he says, than to slay his kinsman, even if that battle be righteous. And there ends the first chapter. The stage is now set for Krishna's teachings, which will take the form of a long dialogue between guru and disciple, seventeen chapters long. But before we hear what Krishna has to say, let us pause to understand the symbolism that Vyasa uses to set up his work.

"Who is Dhritarashtra, the blind king? *Rashtra* in Sanskrit means 'structure' or 'framework'; *dhrita* means 'that which has been held.' *Dhritarashtra*, therefore, means 'that which holds together the structure.' We are human beings. Our structural framework is this body and what holds it together is the mind. But our mind without Sanjay is blind. The word *sanjay* means 'conscience' or 'power of discrimination.' The mind, bereft of the power of discrimination, becomes blind. Thus, it depends upon its advisor, Sanjay, to understand what is going on between the two warring parties. And who are these two warring parties? On one side we have the Kauravas, the sons of Dhritarashtra. The word used here is *mamakah*, literally 'the men on my side.' And who are on the side of the mind. Who are its agents? They are the ten motor and sensory organs through which the mind perceives and acts in this world. There are a hundred brothers because these ten organs can each function in ten directions: the four cardinal points, the four intermediate points, above, and below. Those are the Kauravas. On the other side, we have the Pandavas. The root verb *pand* means 'the attainment of spiritual knowledge,' the realization of 'I am Brahma,' 'I am consciousness,' 'I am the atman, the soul.' The five Pandavas, therefore, represent the five stages of spiritual development, which correspond to the first five chakras. When a spiritual aspirant reaches the sixth chakra, she realizes her spiritual identity; she realizes her oneness with the Divine. So on one side you have the life of the senses, which pulls you toward the material world; on the other side you have the urge to achieve spiritual illumination, which pulls you toward consciousness. There is a war going on within each human being between the spiritual and the material, the animal and the divine, and it is only through the power of discrimination that you can see what is happening. And where does this battle take place? The very first line of the Gita tells us. *Dharmakshetre kurukshetre*. It takes place in *dharmakshetra* and *kurukshetra*. *Dharmakshetra* literally means 'field of spirituality.' *Dharmakshetra* is the human body. Where are the ten sensory and motor organs found? In the human body. In order to practice spirituality, in order to meditate, you require a human body. And the human body functions within *kurukshetra*, 'the world,' 'the field of battle.' *Kuru* means 'to do' in imperative mood. We are put in this world to act. We cannot exist without acting. This world is the field of action.

"So this is the situation: The blind mind, tied to the world through the sensory and motor organs, asks its conscience to tell it what is going on. Its conscience explains that within the human being there is a battle taking place between its worldly desires or attachments and its thirst for spiritual liberation. Faced with the enormity of the struggle, unwilling to slay his kinsmen, who represent his worldly desires and attachments, Arjuna becomes despondent. He decides to give up the fight. But Arjuna made a wise choice before arriving at the field of battle. He asked Krishna to be his charioteer. Krishna is the Divine Consciousness. And Krishna will not let him abandon the fight. First he will inspire him to battle, and then he will teach him how to win that war and achieve spiritual enlightenment."

Again Saraswati passed her copy of the Gita to Marlena and had them read the seventy-two couplets of the second chapter. As she listened in silence to the verses rolling by in their English translation, she was conscious of the Sanskrit original, whose echoes she heard in her mind even more clearly than she heard the translation being read aloud by her students. The words she heard and her own memories filled her with admiration for Vyasa's poetry. How she would have loved to have been alive at that time, to have been able to listen to Vyasa recite his own verses around a winter fire, to have been a student of the greatest of all bards. She had read or listened to these verses hundreds of times over the years, and they never grew old but rather increased in majesty as her mind grew in its ability to appreciate them. In her mind they needed no explanation.

It was indeed the Song of God, a divine music that flooded the heart even when the intellect was unable to comprehend its meaning. When the recitation was over, she gathered her thoughts, cognizant of the fact that while the Gita needed no explanation, it was her duty to try and give it one. This was the promise she had given to Krishna as a young girl and reaffirmed before the Mother as she had neared the beginning of adulthood. It was why the Mother had sent her to Rishikesh, though it was the last place she had wanted to go.

"When Krishna exhorts Arjuna to cast off his faintheartedness, Arjuna replies that he is overcome by grief, confusion, and helplessness. He sees no way out. He does not mention fear but it is implied. We all know this state. We have all experienced it in one form or another. We see it around us all the time: depression, despondency, a feeling of helplessness. The great temptation is to give up. But the spirit within us does not allow us to do that. It calls to us and exhorts us to take up arms against our weaknesses, as Krishna does with Arjuna. For many people, perhaps most people, the spiritual path begins here, when the darkness becomes deepest, when the soul cries out in its suffering and its despair. It is at that moment that the Lord reaches out in the darkness and offers his hand. He hears the cries of his children and answers them. It is at that moment that we hear the song of our soul, the *bhagavad gita*. It is the whisper of the promise of dawn at the end of the dark night. It is then that the human being begins to search for a way out of her suffering. And it is there that Krishna begins his teachings. Remember the passage from the Brihadaranyaka Upanishad that we chant before we begin arati: *Asato ma sat gamaya, tamaso ma jyotir gamaya, mrityor ma amritam gamaya.* Lead us from untruth to truth, from darkness to light, from death to immortality. The Bhagavad Gita is the answer to that prayer.

"Now the teachings start, and they start in much the same place as the Yoga Sutras, though in a much more poetic manner. Think back to the first chapter, third sutra: 'Then a man abides in his real nature, the atman.' Here in the second chapter, or second discourse, Krishna tells Arjuna that he is the immortal self, the atman, and neither this body nor this mind. 'The self is not born', he tells him, 'nor does it ever die. Unborn, eternal, unchangeable and primeval, it is not slain when the body is slain.' The Gita was composed six hundred years before Patanjali, and it was a major influence on the Yoga Sutras, as we will see more and more as we go along. After Krishna tells Arjuna the secret of who he is, that he is spirit, eternal and undying, Krishna instructs him not to grieve over the objects and attachments of the world. They are all transitory, he tells him. What is born must die and what is gained must be lost. This is the way of nature. The wise do not grieve over this because they know they are the eternal spirit, the unchanging awareness that witnesses the ever-changing manifestations of the world. And so they remain in peace, having crossed, as Krishna says, 'the mire of delusion.'" She picked up her book and read. 'When the mind stands firm and steady in the self then one attains yoga. Be then a yogi, Arjuna.'"

Saraswati allowed time for a couple of questions and then asked them to read aloud the forty-three couplets of the third chapter. Though she intended to make this chapter the focus of their next class on the Gita, she wanted to prepare their minds for what would be a lengthy and important discussion.

"The first point Krishna makes to Arjuna in this chapter is that nothing can be gained by inaction. The world is bound by action and so a yogi acts, but she transforms her action into yoga by learning to act without attachment. This is the art or practice of karma yoga. In verse thirty-one, Krishna says, 'those who constantly practice this teaching with faith and without caviling are liberated from the effects of their actions.' In other words, they no longer accrue samskara. Georg, you asked this question last week: how can we free ourselves from the bondage of samskara? Patanjali gives us the answer in the language of yogic psychology: 'The identification of our consciousness with our mind and the objects of experience is ignorance. When this identification ceases then ignorance vanishes and the experiencer becomes liberated.' The Gita says the same thing in different words: 'Action is effected in all cases by the energies of nature; he whose mind is deluded by egoism thinks, "I am the doer."' Normally we are under the delusion that we are in control of our lives, at least until a strong wave comes and threatens to capsize our boat. When this happens we may be beset by doubt, but as long as we stay afloat it doesn't last very long. Everything we do, we do under the assumption that we are working to achieve some outcome and that we have some control over that outcome. If we get the results we want, we feel happy; if we don't, we get depressed or angry or frustrated. Most people live their lives in this fashion right up until the moment of their death. But both Krishna and Patanjali tell us that this is an illusion, an illusion that perpetuates our bondage. Everything that happens in this world is a simple play of nature, a clash of energies governed by the law of cause and effect. As long as we remain identified with our mind and our ego, then we remain under the illusion that we can control this play of energy, but actually our ego is part of that play, no more in control of where it is going than an unmanned boat tossed by the waves of a stormy sea. When you learn to act without attachment, as Krishna counsels us, then you break this identification. You free yourself from the fundamental ignorance of the ego. You realize that you are not your thoughts but the consciousness that witnesses them. When you are free from ego, then you are free from the bondage of action; you no longer create samskaras. We are going to discuss this in greater detail next time, along with the other points raised in this chapter, but I want to leave you with one last thought to ponder. Many people, at least in India, when they think of a yogi, they think of someone sitting in a cave doing nothing. Nothing could be further from the truth. A yogi knows better than anyone else the value of action; she also knows that the greatest actions are those that are free from attachment and desire. It is only then that the actions of a person attain perfection, because then they are guided by the dictates of the soul rather than by the selfish desires of the ego. The true yogi does not avoid acting in this world, but she acts from a place of freedom, and for that reason her actions, as Christ rightly put it, have the power to move mountains."

Saraswati glanced again at her watch. They had gone five minutes over. For a moment, she felt piqued that there was no time for further questions, but then she became aware of her reaction and chided herself for being attached to the outcome, reserving an inward smile for the Mother. Krishna's teachings were sublime but she knew she still had a long road to walk before she mastered them. Her continued frustration over the fact that she was still here in Rishikesh, rather than back in Benares with the Mother, was another testament to just how far she had to go. It was one of those attachments that had dug its roots so deep into her soil that she wondered if she would ever get them out. Every time the familiar urge to do something greater with her life spilled over to her conscious mind and did battle with her carefully cultivated serenity, she had to remind herself that it was the Mother's wish that she was here. Though that reminder invariably brought with it an instant softening in her heart, the frustration still lingered—sometimes for minutes, sometimes for hours—like a faint jangling music from a distant neighborhood that cannot be turned off but only ignored. It was there now, she noticed, as she collected her notes and her copy of the Gita and began walking back toward her room. Every time she read or taught this chapter, it stirred afresh these same feelings, the nagging conviction that her continued stay in Rishikesh was a kind of forced idleness, that the work that she had been born to do was waiting for her in the outside world, a world to which her access pass had been revoked. Had not the Mother told her that her destiny was to do some great service to humanity? Then why was she still here? Of course, she knew it was an attachment, that such thoughts had no foundation in reality, that her philosophy did not support them, but that did not make them go away, even after all this time.

Reluctantly, she wrested her attention from her thoughts and acknowledged the chatty conversation of Kadambi and Kiran, who were walking on either side of her, just ahead of Rodrigo and Georg whom she could hear conversing in soft voices behind her. They were sisters, up for the day from Dehra Dun. Their father was an important supporter of the ashram, owner of a large software development company that had moved from Delhi to the more favorable hill climate and lower taxes of Uttaranchal. They had been quiet during the class, but now that it was over, their natural talkativeness spilled over with the added force of its artificial damming. It had been her duty to take care of them this morning and she had done the best she could, knowing how important their family was to the financial health of the ashram. She would have to spend more time with them in the afternoon, but thankfully they had a special luncheon with Swamiji that would buy her a well-earned respite. They were not bad girls, but she had limited patience for conversations that centered around the Indian entertainment industry and only rarely found the somewhat firmer ground of politics or economics, what to speak of spirituality. Especially now, when these feelings were on her again.

After she reached the office and handed them off to Bhagavati, she noticed Rodrigo standing patiently to one side, apparently waiting to talk to her. She felt herself stiffen and once again she became annoyed. That accursed reaction again! It was absolutely time she got rid of it. She sent out a silent plea to the Mother, and as if in response, she felt her tension lessen. Making a conscious effort to smile, she walked over to Rodrigo and asked him if he were waiting to talk to her.

"I do have a question, if you have a minute or two."

"Of course. What is it?"

"I wanted to ask this question in class but there wasn't time. What I was wondering was if it were true that women have a natural aptitude for devotion that makes it easier for them to make rapid spiritual progress in the Kali Yuga. I was thinking that men in general must have a more difficult time because they are more dominated by their intellect, while women are more in tune with their emotions."

Once again Rodrigo's question caught her by surprise. "Did you read that someplace?" she asked, hoping to gain a few seconds, enough for an answer to descend.

"Not exactly, no. It just sort of came to me. I guess it's been bothering me a little because I've always been an intellectual. I've made a career out of it, in fact. Lately, I've been thinking that this might actually work against me when it came to developing devotion."

"I wouldn't worry about it," Saraswati answered, trusting the first response that came to her mind. "Men and women make equally good devotees. It depends on their sincerity more than anything else. Being a simpleton is not going to help if you're not sincere, and being an intellectual is not going to work against you if you are. The truth is, the intellect can be of great help in the spiritual path. We'll get to that when we start talking about jnana yoga, the yoga of knowledge. The one danger with the intellect is that it can contribute to the development of ego. As long as you don't allow your ego to grow, you'll be all right. Just remember what Vivekananda said: 'The mind makes a great servant but a poor master.' It is an interesting idea, though. Being a woman, I almost wish it were true, but unfortunately, I've never seen any evidence of that. Nor do I think that you'll find any Indian scripture that agrees with you on this point."

"Not even the Tantras or the Devi Shastra?"

"Have you been reading the Devi Shastra?" she answered, surprised by the reference.

"Sort of. A little bit."

"And the Tantra also, I suppose. I see. Well, I'm not an expert in the Tantras or the Devi Shastra but I have studied them and to the best of my knowledge the answer is no."

When Saraswati finally made it to her room and sat for her noon meditation, she had a difficult time concentrating. Rodrigo's question kept bothering her. It was clear to her that his question carried overtones of speculation rather than insight, but the more she tried to meditate, the more the suspicion kept nagging her that she might actually agree with him. It was not an intellectual agreement— her philosophical training told her that the answer was no, could be nothing but no—but the feeling would not be put to rest, not even by the soothing syllables of her mantra or by the smiling image of the Mother in her mind, the same as the one on the altar in front of her. Rodrigo had touched a nerve. She lived in a chauvinistic country, a country that oppressed its women at the same time that it claimed to put them on a pedestal. For years she had seen that same chauvinism in the one place she would have never thought to find it: in its spiritual communities and its spiritual traditions. That was one of the reasons she felt proud that when it had come time for Krishna to appear to her in the form of a guru, he had come to her as a woman. Her philosophical principles would never allow her to claim that women were more privileged in spiritual matters than men, the Mother would never allow it, but her heart, which had always rallied to the side of justice, told her emphatically that if devotion did come easier to women, after all that her sex had had to endure in both the material and the spiritual worlds, then it would only be just. Would not the Lord, who was the embodiment of justice, give his daughters something with which to balance the scales? But then she remembered that she was a woman and that in many ways she had always had a harder time with bhakti yoga than with jnana yoga, despite knowing that bhakti was the true foundation of her practice. She had always felt more at home with knowledge and the bright glint of her mind as it honed itself toward a point than with the devotional practices that she performed every day and the turbulent waters they often stirred. Perhaps this was proof of the answer she had given him, though her heart remained dubious. She got up from her meditation before she could fully consider the implications of this proof: if she was more at home with the path of knowledge, then what would have to be buried in her psyche to account for it?

17

OR RODRIGO, IT WAS a revelation to discover that the Bhagavad Gita was not only one of the world's great spiritual treasures, but that it could also be considered a work of historical fiction. It reminded him that any great work of fiction needed to be built on the same foundation as any great work of history: the search for the truth. And what was the truth of his work of historical fiction that was slowly seeing its edifice raised? This was what he was still trying to discover. He had pieced together several scenes. The story had a flow, a profluence; it was headed somewhere. But that somewhere was not yet clear to him, despite the fact that his climax was known, fixed within the boundaries of recorded fact. Now, instead of proceeding directly to the next major scene, Le Gentil's visit to the astrologer, Rodrigo decided to introduce a narrative section sprinkled with several scene fragments, ostensibly dealing with the construction of the observatory, which was now getting underway, but in fact designed to allow him to explore the true nature of his two principal characters and their relationship with each other. He had a distinct feeling that if he wanted to better understand his story, he had to better understand his characters. They were the beating heart of what he was trying to write. Whatever truth there might be in his fiction, he would find it in them or he would not find it at all.

As he worked his way into this narrative section, he deliberately kept any discussion of astrology out of it, but he did allow Ambika to ask Le Gentil a number of questions about his design for the observatory and how it would facilitate his work. He had not known what those questions would be until he actually sat down to write, but they emerged effortlessly with an almost total disregard for his lack of knowledge about astronomy. He had done some research, but as he saw it, it wasn't enough to account for the perspicacity of her questions. While his analytic mind wondered about the role his subconscious was playing in the process, the rest of his attention was drawn by Ambika. She seemed less and less a conscious creation of his mind and more and more a living, breathing presence walking freely in his imagination and making her own decisions. Slowly he slipped into what was fast becoming for him a waking dream. His eyes were open, but he went long stretches with little or no awareness of who or where he was. The computer and his fingers over the keyboard grew transparent as he peered through them into a place that felt more real than imagined. There he saw Ambika and Le Gentil walking through the construction site, the ruins of a former mansion poised on an unpopulated hilltop about a kilometer outside of Pondicherry. There was a smattering of wind-stunted trees that offered no obstruction of the heavens and wide tracks of stubbly pasture worn into grooves by the hoofs of native cattle. Looking behind them, the couple could see the red roofs of the French colonial houses edging toward the ocean; in front of them stretched the dark, fertile plains of the Deccan peninsula. Both his characters were walking under their own power now, heedless of the eye that watched them, and their sparring repartee sprang from their own concerns, their own fears, their own conscious and half-conscious desires, rather than from any deliberate manipulation on his part. It was, in fact, not much different than the dreaming he did at night, though he did not reflect on this or even make that association. All he knew was that his characters fascinated and surprised him, and that he found himself watching and wondering as he waited to see what would happen next.

What did happen was that in the intervening days before his meeting with Ambika's astrologer-astronomer, Le Gentil began to feel a sense of camaraderie with his attractive young assistant that he had never felt before with any woman. As they walked around the site and gave directions to the workers, Ambika translating his instructions with the same tone of frantic reprobation that she knew he would have adopted had he been able to speak the language, he found himself sharing with her his theories and his experiences in astronomy, natural history, physics, geography, and navigation, no longer feeling surprised to hear intelligent answers that spurred him in directions he might not have taken on his own. Female companionship in his experience had always been more about satisfying his carnal pleasures and less about companionship, but he had never met a woman like Ambika. She added a natural inquisitiveness to her bright, agile mind, and her confidence in herself and her rich cultural heritage gave their conversations a quality he had rarely encountered before: unpredictability. Even the brightest of his colleagues at the Academy of Science had rarely surprised him. For years now, his greatest intellectual stimulus had come from books, from masters of the sciences and the arts long dead and thus incapable of answering his queries whenever any of their ideas puzzled him or became a point of contention. But Ambika was a living, constant challenge who spoke French better than many of his university classmates who had gone on to the careers of moneyed indolence required by their titles, or else entered the military and set out bravely to subjugate those parts of the world that weren't already subjugated by the English. The fact that she was a woman, a young and beautiful woman, lent to the situation an air of mystery and complication. There were certain parts of his adventures that he had to judiciously leave out of his tales of past exploits, notably the amorous conquests that would have so greatly amused and impressed his colleagues. Indeed, he had begun to feel uncomfortable with his current conquests as well, worried what she might think of him if she found out.

Ambika, for her part, was used to carrying on stimulating, thought-provoking discussions with both men and women. She would not have fully understood his surprise, because she had yet to fully understand his culture, a deficit she was aware of and intent on remedying. She asked seemingly innocuous questions with a view to gaining a better insight into his European psychology and carefully filed away his answers in numbered compartments in her already-teeming mind. Every disparate bit of information had its utility, and the fact that Le Gentil was so well versed in so many different fields gave her an endless scope to go on probing and learning. He was a vain man. She had seen that at the outset. But only in matters of little importance, as she increasingly recognized. When it came to knowledge, he emptied himself of his accumulated preconceptions with a rapidity that astounded her, so eager was he to free space for new information and new understanding. His hunger for knowledge easily equaled her own, and this slowly gained for him a respect in her eyes that he could not have gained otherwise. That he was attractive never occurred to her. His being French, denizen of a barbaric, warring land, made him a kind of primitive savant, but still a primitive. But his love for knowledge made her begin to look forward to each day together just as much as he did, though for different reasons.

By the time Rodrigo finished this section, Ambika and Le Gentil had attained the unspoken complicity he'd hoped for. She was on her way to becoming his best friend, his foil, and the woman he dreamed about when he discretely entered the best of the brothels frequented by Europeans after dinner with the Governor-General or had one of these women secreted to his house late at night. He was the most interesting of the French imperialists she'd met and the only one with a mind broad enough to perhaps one day appreciate the true worth of the people they thought it their God-given right to rule. Their conversation picked up each morning where it had left off the evening before, enlivened by the reflections that each had made during the night, and the hours spent apart began to seem like interludes in a single, preordained journey whose destination they had not bothered to ascertain.

It was only when Rodrigo put the final touches to this chapter that he became aware of the odd similarities between his waking fictive dream and the sleeping one. The two women were kindred spirits who looked across divides of culture and caste and beckoned their male counterparts to undertake a journey that they would not have undertaken otherwise. One of his fictive heroes was already well on his way; the other could only wait for fate to tip its hand. The first was easy enough for Rodrigo to accompany, for there he still retained some illusion of control. The second was beginning to unnerve him; at times it even left a slightly acrid flavor of foreboding in his mouth. The difference was that Le Gentil was a character in his imagination, for all his independent ways, while Rodrigo *was* the priest. It was his own sense of self that was making its way through the underworld of his subconscious. He felt the effects of those sleeping episodes far more deeply, as if he were leading two lives, the waking and the dreaming, both of equal import, since both were facets of the same search for identity. He had a clear sense that nothing that happened in those dreams was within his control. And yet he was the dreamer. Whatever mistakes he made there were his mistakes; whatever prejudices he evoked were his prejudices. He did not know if he would even enter that particular dreamed world again, an uncertainty that sometimes bothered him as he walked by the river or struggled with his meditation, but what bothered him even more was the uncertainty over what he would do there if he did.

18

WITH THE HELP OF Le Gentil's journals and his own research on Indian astrology and astronomy, Rodrigo started writing what he envisioned would be a critical chapter, the one in which the pendulum would start swinging in favor of the world's oldest culture and the girl who secretly saw herself as its champion. Ambika had arranged the meeting in the professor's house, a modest but comfortable single-story, brick-and-tile construction on the outskirts of Ville Noire, the Indian section of Pondicherry; it was situated on the same road that led to her family's estate, another two kilometers distant. She had been in the house numerous times with her father, who had shared a long and intimate friendship with the professor since their student days. Professor Sandip had been present at her birth and had drawn up her horoscope, which her father kept carefully preserved in a hidden safe along with her mother's gold jewelry and other family heirlooms. She had never seen the horoscope, but its details were well known to her, having been referred to many times by both her father and the professor. She still hoped that one day she would learn enough about Indian astrology to be able to interpret it for herself, but time was something she rarely had enough of, despite being the child of eternity.

It was just after nine when she followed Le Gentil into his carriage after exchanging a complicit glance with the driver, a young man she had known since childhood who took orders from her father and carefully concealed his knowledge of both French and English from the colonizers. The professor was waiting for them at the gate when they arrived. He received Le Gentil with the humility due the luminary of a conquering power, but once the three of them were seated on bamboo mats on the floor of his study among his books and his instruments, his attitude underwent a subtle but perceptible change. Le Gentil had thought of proposing a challenge, one that would be as much a test of Ambika's claims as it would the professor's astronomical prowess. After exchanging a few pleasantries, he told the professor that he had heard of the ability of Indian astronomers to calculate lunar eclipses. Would he be willing to calculate one for him? The professor agreed with a confident smile that contained no trace of the effusive humility that had been so evident in the courtyard in front of his house. Le Gentil watched in fascination as the professor calculated the eclipse he proposed, with all the preliminary elements, in a mere forty-five minutes, and with an exactness that could not have been exceeded. It was a feat no Western astronomer could have matched. His persistent doubts vanished in a moment's excitement. Like a schoolboy fresh from his first experience of the wonders of science, he asked the professor if he would teach him his methods. When Professor Sandip consented to give him one hour a day, six days a week, Le Gentil asked him how long it would take him to learn how to calculate a lunar eclipse using his methods. The professor smiled. "If you are intelligent," he told him, "and if you work at your lessons with the required diligence, then you may be able to learn in six weeks." It would take him all of those six weeks to master the necessary calculations and even longer to learn how to calculate solar eclipses; the fact that Indian astronomers had been able to develop their methods without the aid of telescopes would remain a continual source of wonder for him until long after he had left the Indian subcontinent.

But what impressed Le Gentil most about that first meeting with the professor, and what was even more unexpected than encountering methods of astronomical calculation far in advance of anything he had ever come across, was the clear and demonstrable proof that astrology, if not a science, was at the very least an art form that in the right hands bordered on magic. It was Ambika who turned the conversation to astrology, afraid that the two scientists would remain so wrapped up in their mathematical interchange that they would forget the reason she had brought them together, a reason that was admittedly clear only to her. When Le Gentil expressed his skepticism with a disdainful look and an impatient remark, the professor returned Ambika's smile and asked Le Gentil if he knew the time of his birth. He did: 7:10 AM on September 12, 1725, at Coutances, just off the west coast of Normandy.

"Allow me to make some calculations," he told the Frenchman, "and then we will see if you have the same attitude when I am done." The elder man, his hair going from gray to white in marked contrast to his smooth, vigorous skin, got up and pulled down a large atlas from his bookshelf along with an ephemeris. He unrolled a sheaf of papers with the diagram of the lunar houses already sketched out in a precise, elegant hand and smoothed one of them out on the floor in front of him. With practiced fluidity, he began annotating the vacant chart, consulting his books with a narrowed brow before adding each additional symbol. Ten minutes later, he sat upright and peered down at the completed horoscope. He was silent for a full five minutes, nodding periodically and lifting his eyebrows as if he had seen something particularly interesting or surprising; once or twice, he pointed toward one and then another of the symbols as if he were trying to figure out the connection between them. Then he smiled, fixed Le Gentil with a sudden, forceful gaze, and started speaking.

"Your father did not have much money, but he had a sacrificing nature, and he did all he could to further your education. He died when you were twenty. Your mother, I see, was much younger than your father, but she died more than twelve years before he did. Your relationship with her was purely affective, and you have idealized her in your mind ever since."

The professor spoke as if he were reading from a book. After that first gaze, he barely looked at Le Gentil, seemingly unaware of the look of shock on the astronomer's face.

"I see that you have enjoyed relatively good health, with the exception of your liver. You had an extended sickness at the age of seven, quite serious, that lasted several months. There were some questions about your survival. A weakened liver was at fault and this has stayed with you, but due to the stoutness of your overall constitution, it has not proved to be too serious a problem. I see another extended sickness about seven years ago, for similar reasons, but of a shorter duration. You should avoid beef in your diet. It will have dangerous consequences for your eyesight and your overall health if you continue eating it past the age of forty-five. Your chart closes at the age of sixty-seven. The cause of death will be an illness due once again to a weakened liver."

The professor moved on to a description of Le Gentil's personality traits that fit him far better than he was comfortable admitting, and from there to a brief list of romantic liaisons that caused both he and Ambika to blush. At this point, the professor looked up with an air of surprise that he visibly tried to conceal. "You will marry a woman with wealth far greater than your own at the age of fifty and you will have one daughter. It will be a happy marriage, but the most important woman in your life will be the woman you leave behind. You will be separated physically by a great distance, but you will continue to communicate throughout your lives. This is a connection that has been carried over from your previous life, and it will be carried over to the next. There is something more in your chart concerning this relationship, but I am not confident to interpret it quite yet. I will have to think about it some more and consult some other texts. It is quite unusual. Perhaps we can talk about it some other time, on one of your study visits. I will only say that this relationship will be the focal point of both your destiny and hers; the two are inextricably entwined."

After regaining his former disinterested air, the astrologer touched on a few more topics before he finished up with a description of Le Gentil's professional life.

"Your professional career is divided into two halves by two great disappointments, one that has already passed and one which is due to arrive next year. Due to these disappointments, you will lose everything you have gained up until now, including all your economic possessions. You will be presumed dead by those closest to you, and in fact these occurrences will mark the death of your former self and your relationship with those persons. While this will seem to you at first a tragedy, it is in fact a divine dispensation that will free you from a heavy karmic debt. Everything that you lose, you will regain manyfold, and the last part of your life will be the happiest and most productive, despite a lingering attachment. Now I can see that you have some questions."

Le Gentil, who was unnerved by the candor and the accuracy of the reading, had been fighting to regain his composure ever since the professor's opening pronouncements. "How were you able to know when my parents died?" he exclaimed. "No one in these seas could have possibly known; I have never told anyone. Can you actually see that in my chart?"

"It is rather complicated, much like our methods of calculating lunar and solar eclipses, but in short, it has to do with the placement of the sun and the moon in your chart, and in your case with Venus as well, since Venus is your ruling planet and was sitting on the horizon at the moment of your birth. Each of the major setbacks and triumphs of your life are closely associated with transits of the planet Venus, especially those events that have to do with the love of women and their role in your life. In your case, those are the truly significant events in your life. The major changes that you have gone through, and especially those that you will go through, all come through the agency of women and are represented in your chart by movements of the planet Venus and its related aspects. In poetic language, we would say that you are a plaything of the goddess."

The professor smiled and wiped a few beads of sweat from his forehead with a white linen handkerchief. "There are worse fates I could think of. Much worse."

"Then you actually can read all these events in a person's chart?"

"Yes, certainly."

"It doesn't seem possible, but I am a man who believes what he sees with his own eyes. Can you teach me this as well?"

It was the professor's turn to look surprised. "It is a very involved science. How much you can learn depends to a great extent upon how much time you can dedicate. Aptitude and willingness are not enough. But yes, if you are willing to devote the time, I can teach you."

"I have one question. Call it a doubt, if you will. Everything you said about my past was perfectly accurate. But what about the future events? Do the Hindus consider them preordained? Is there any escape, for example, from the fate you have predicted for me?"

"This is a delicate question. Our sages teach us that everything that happens to us is a result of the law of cause and effect. What the common people call 'fate' is simply the lawful unfolding of action and reaction, cause and effect. We are subject to the consequences of our previous actions, and from that there is no escape, though the precise form those consequences will take is not always so easy to predict. What I can tell you from long experience is that almost everyone's life unfolds in more or less exact accordance with the map that Providence has drawn for him in the skies at the moment of his birth. The one exception I have seen is with highly elevated souls—saints, if you will. For some reason, the more elevated a person becomes, the less their chart seems to correspond to their life. It is as if they become so elevated they can no longer be described, not even by the heavens. But for us ordinary mortals, the word 'fate' is an apt enough term. It refers to the events and the challenges we draw as our lot in life this time around. It is how we react to those events and those challenges that determines the growth of our character, and thus what we will have to face in the next life."

Ambika was pleasantly surprised that Le Gentil had proved so flexible, to the point that he was not only willing to accept the efficacy of Indian astrology but was in fact eager to learn. Her estimation of him was growing rapidly; it was not far from reaching the point where it would begin to cloud her otherwise clear vision. But no one was more surprised than Rodrigo. He had not been aware that Le Gentil would be studying Indian astrology until the moment the words came out of his character's mouth. With each passing day, he was growing more and more fond of his unpredictable protagonist. Le Gentil had begun life as a confirmed rake with a brilliant mind and a streak of courage that would send him across the oceans for nearly a decade in a search for fame and scientific adventure, despite the well-documented dangers. But he was proving that there was more to him than Rodrigo had first realized. Was Le Gentil changing? Was he growing? Or had he always had this in him, wanting only the fair winds and fragrant soil of the Coromandel coast and the enchanting smile of its favorite daughter to bring it to the surface. These were some of his thoughts as he brought the chapter to a close, not recognizing how blurred the line was becoming between the life of his imagination and the life lived out of doors.

It was after Rodrigo finished revising this important chapter that he had the next in the series of dreams that was occupying much of his attention when he wasn't writing or studying. Bathed in a damp sheen of warring emotions, he bolted upright, reached for his computer on the night table, and began typing feverishly.

Rishikesh
10/26
4:32 AM

Another temple dream and again the emotions are so strong it makes me wonder if the more important part of my life were not the one lived in sleep. At the center of these emotions is the same girl, though she did not even put in an appearance this time. As I remember, I had asked my assistant to bring me some information about her: her caste, her family situation, whatever he could discover about her history. It was a delicate request since there was every chance it would raise some sort of suspicion in his mind, and I knew that any doubts or suspicions he had would surely make their way back to the temple elders. He was a close-lipped, somewhat surly young fellow who owed his allegiance to the elders who had appointed him rather than to me, though he made every effort to make it appear otherwise, especially since he knew as well as I that I would be high priest one day, and that from that day forward his livelihood would depend entirely on me. So I made a pretense of being displeased with something she had done. I knew this would pique his interest in the task as well as allay any doubts he might have over why I would make such an unusual request. I remember waiting and fretting for him to make his report. I had not seen her since our meeting in the gardens, but since then I had not stopped thinking about her. Who was she? How could someone with such a brilliant mind be working as a servant in the temple? I had begun fantasizing about her while I paced back and forth in my room or on the open rooftop above, trying to convince myself that my initial fears were ill founded. She was actually from a poor Kshattriyan family, perhaps even a Brahmin family, forced to accept menial labor due to her family's extreme poverty. Vain hopes, these, but it was as if something irremediable had been released in me, a demon I refused to label as desire but instead rationalized as compassion for a spiritually gifted soul caught in a difficult karmic predicament. But I had not totally lost my senses. I was still beset by the fear that the worst of my suspicions would prove true, that she would be a Dalit, an untouchable, with whom any further conversation would be out of the question.

I remember trembling when my assistant knocked on my door and told me he had brought the information I'd requested. What an effort it took to keep my face calm and impassive! I had to make it seem like it was a matter of no importance, while all the while my heart was clamoring for the news. I asked him to wait one moment while I finished an important letter. Actually, I wasn't writing a letter at all, but I forced myself to move my quill for a minute longer, keeping my eyes fixed to the page until I had mastered my trepidation and hardened my features. Finally I looked up and asked him to tell me his news, hoping that an air of impatience on my part would let it be known that I was more interested in returning to my work than in the contents of his report. The first thing he told me was the girl's caste. It was as I had feared: she was a Chamar, one of the untouchable castes. She could fill the water jars and tend the plants but not hand water directly to any of the temple residents. Her mere touch would defile even the most sinful of Brahmins and force him to take recourse to ritual purification. No one knew the social strictures better than I. When I heard this, my blood froze and my grip tightened around my pen, but I kept any expression from my face by an act of will. He told me that her mother was dead; she supported her invalid father through her meager earnings at the temple. They lived in a one-room shack in a section of town restricted to the tanning caste to which she belonged, a dirty place that gave off a foul odor day and night, one I knew by reputation without ever having been there. It was a brief report, but he added one last bit of information that sliced through me like a cold knife. He said she had a bad reputation among her people for making offensive statements and speaking disrespectfully to members of the upper castes. When he finished, he asked me if I wanted to bring a complaint against her. It was all I could do to keep a tremor from my voice as I told him that I would wait to see if there were any further infractions. After all, it was a minor matter and there was her invalid father to consider. After he left, I went to the mirror to see if there was any unnatural pallor in my face. There was none I could notice, but I could feel my blood growing thin, as if it were draining out of my body, and a noticeable weakness in my limbs. My reaction angered me. Why should I let myself be so disturbed over an untouchable woman from whom I could not in good conscience even accept a glass of water without incurring a grievous sin? But even then I could not stop thinking about her and the things she'd said. It was then that I woke up, bathed in sweat, my peace of mind in tatters, convinced that the gods of Olympus were warring inside me.

Now, as I lean back against my ashram pillow, I see that nothing has changed, despite my transit from the dream world to the waking. My hands are clammy, I feel a cold fear in my chest, and at the same time I am aware of an irresistible need to see her again—if only to tell her that I cannot see her or talk to her anymore. And yet she is a phantom, a dream wraith, a fictional product of my subconscious that will continue to haunt me if I don't splash cold water on my face and remember who and where I am. I must take some deep breaths and try to discover the meaning of this madness, but now it is time to go to the main hall for my morning practice.

6:45 AM

I have a few minutes before yoga class with which to write. Meditation was difficult, almost impossible at first. What a struggle I had, trying to shake off the aftereffects of the dream, to slough off these emotions and keep myself from spending that time trying to decipher its meaning. But after an hour and a half of chanting and clinging to my mantra, I feel much calmer. The moment I opened my eyes after meditation, the emotions and the intensity seemed to dissipate almost entirely, though they had been present throughout my meditation. And now, with a somewhat dispassionate eye, I can write these thoughts:

What exactly the dream means, I do not and perhaps cannot know. But I have my suspicions. I suspect it was triggered by Saraswati's class on the Gita. When I came to Rishikesh I was sick at heart. I can admit that now, though I wasn't ready to then. I was bitter toward Beth, bitter toward life in general, perhaps, but I was not able or willing to recognize my own unhappiness. Now that things have gotten better (thanks in large part to my yogic practice), I can safely say that that was the lowest point in my life, the rock bottom that Arjuna faced on the fields of Kurukshetra. Saraswati's explanation of Arjuna's predicament rang as true as anything I have ever heard. It was that pain that got me started on the spiritual path, I know it now. The pain is not entirely gone, of course, nor can I claim that I have entirely forgiven Beth, but now that the pain is fast disappearing, I can admit that many, or perhaps most, of the mistakes were mine. The truth is, my mistakes in this life have been legion, Beth or no Beth. This leads me to believe that I am searching for an idealized relationship in the world of my subconscious, in the hope that I may thereby remedy the mistakes I've made, that I might now learn the lessons I could not when faced with the armies of my attachments and my fears and my desires. I am a long way still from that unencumbered plain, as my fictive self has made quite clear by the sweat he left on my brow, by the fever in my limbs and the fear in my heart, by his crushing disappointment in discovering that the object of his desire is untouchable and thus unreachable. When will I be rid of this pain for good? When will I be able to watch it dance away on the outgoing waves without any rancor in my heart? Perhaps when I am able to fully forgive Beth—and in the process, fully forgive myself. Maybe then I will find the secret of non-attachment and be able to watch this little life of mine—and the great one that surrounds it—as a play of consciousness, as Saraswati tells us we must do if we want to find freedom. Until then, at least I know that this is what I want. That must count for something, this awareness of the cage that holds me captive and this longing for the freedom that lies beyond its bars. But now I must run or I will be late for yoga class. Amrita will not have a heart attack if I am not there, but it is entirely possible that she might, in fact, miss me.

It was Georg's idea to start a study circle that would meet on the two weekday mornings that Saraswati did not hold class. Marlena and Ely both agreed and the next day at lunch they asked Rodrigo if he'd like to join. His immediate thought was for the hours he would lose from his writing, but he had already gotten used to writing in the afternoon on his class days, and the adjustment allowed him to fall into a regular routine that suited his academic need for order. It also reinforced his sense that he was a resident student in a Himalayan university specializing in spirituality and esoteric studies. Mornings he attended class and afternoons he wrote, followed by a constitutional stroll by the riverside, all bookended by his morning and evening practice of yoga, chanting, and meditation. Evenings he studied the texts that continued to accumulate by his bedside. The food was excellent, the company was pleasant, and the chance to throw himself into what was essentially the study of his self was exactly what his soul had been crying for. He was aware of elephants camping out in his living room and the heavy cleaning duties that went with it, but a man can make peace with the most incongruous of house pets once he accepts the fact that they are not going anywhere, at least not anytime soon.

By this time, they had already begun studying the second chapter of the Yoga Sutras. When they told Saraswati about their study circle, she agreed to guide them and started assigning extra reading and discussion topics; they, in turn, began formulating group questions for her classes. Rodrigo, despite his relative lack of experience in spiritual matters, gradually started taking the lead role in their little circle, aided by his years of experience as a university professor, his insatiable hunger for knowledge, and his long-cultivated stamina for the written page—increasingly rare in an age dominated by formulaic movies, docudramas, and television. Georg was happy to cede that privilege and in fact turned over many of his questions to Rodrigo, whom he openly admired for his willingness to search the burgeoning library by his bed for answers to his queries.

The sutras that followed the section on samskara focused on the phenomenon of consciousness becoming identified with the objects of experience, the fundamental ignorance that prevented the witnessing consciousness from becoming aware of its divine nature. This was a topic they all found fascinating because it brought into relief the differences between the Western and yogic approaches to psychology. Rodrigo was surprised to discover that Marlena was a Jungian psychologist who lived and practiced in Geneva. Though she rarely spoke without prompting, she did in fact have much to say, and on this topic they kept her well supplied with questions. Rodrigo learned that Jung had devoted a good deal of time to studying Indian spiritual philosophy and esoteric texts and had been greatly influenced by them in the development of his theories, and in some cases, even in his therapeutic techniques. But though she was a Jungian psychologist, Marlena was not impressed by Jung's understanding of what he read, as she made clear in a number of trenchant comments one morning under the banyan tree.

"Jung didn't understand the human mind half as well as he thought he did, and not a tenth as well as Saraswati. How could he? He never meditated. You know, he actually counseled people not to do meditation. Can you believe it? He claimed it wasn't suited to Western culture. In many ways, he was typical of the person who thinks he understands his subject better than anyone else but doesn't know the one subject that really counts: himself. Which is a strange thing, when you consider that psychology is the study of the human mind, and the only mind we can properly observe is our own. But Jung never seemed to understand that. Neither he nor any of the other leading psychologists of the twentieth century were adept in the one art that trains you to observe your mind. It's actually kind of hard to believe, when you really think about it."

They were going over the sutra they had discussed in class the day before: "Pain is caused by false identification of the experiencer with the object of experience; it may be avoided." Animated comments flew back and forth in rapid succession, but eventually all eyes fell on Marlena. For her, the crux of the difference between Western and yogic psychology was encapsulated in this sutra.

"The work of psychoanalysis, in the simplest terms possible, is to uncover the repressed or unconscious traumas and complexes that interfere with our sense of well-being and motivate us to act in unhealthy ways. If a person can make that unconscious material conscious through psychoanalytic techniques—free association, dream analysis, whatever the technique may be— then the person can analyze it, with the help of her therapist, and free herself from its influence. As a result, the psyche can be reintegrated and return to a normal, healthy ego functioning. At least that's the theory."

Marlena closed her eyes for a moment, and it seemed to Rodrigo as if a dark shadow passed across her face. "For example, say your father molested you when you were a child. You repress the memory. It's now trapped in your unconscious and this hidden trauma continues to poison your conscious life. You are unable to trust men, you have panic attacks for no observable reason, you feel a sense of bitterness toward the world that you can't get rid of. But if you can recover that memory and process it, then the trauma is released; the symptoms go away and you achieve mental health. It's the basic premise of Western medicine. You treat the cause and the symptoms disappear. The only problem is that in many cases it just doesn't work; or when it does work, it works very slowly. I know people who've been in therapy for twenty years, and twenty years later they are still fundamentally unhappy. I've spent a long time thinking about this. I've had to ask myself, just how much good are we doing our patients if they are still unhappy after years of therapy and tens of thousands of Euros? That's part of why I got into meditation and yoga in the first place. I know most psychologists won't agree with me, but I always felt there was something fundamentally wrong with this model. I just didn't know what it was until I came across Patanjali and yoga psychology. The problem, as I understand it now, is that even though a person is able to work through a certain complex or uncover a certain trauma, they still remain identified with their emotions and experiences and thought patterns, repressed or otherwise. That's where Patanjali was the real genius, not Jung. You can go on dealing with complex after complex—we might as well call it samskara—and you never get to the end of it. There's just too much stuff in our psyche to try to clean it out piecemeal like that. What's worse, you're creating new ones all the time—new samskaras, new wounds, new complexes. It's a never-ending story. That's when I realized, *mon dieu*, the problem is not the content of our minds—it's our relationship to that content, the way we deal with it. The real problem is that we identify our sense of self with that content. *I* hate my father, *I* can't forgive him for what he did to me. No you don't, not really. You only think you do because you don't understand your own I. That's the real problem. We don't understand who we really are. What is it Saraswati is always saying, I think but I am not my thoughts? The whole problem with Western psychology is that it doesn't deal with this fundamental ignorance. If anything, it reinforces it. We get fixated on the thought 'I was molested by my father' instead of training ourselves to be aware that it's just a thought—that's all our memories and experiences are, thoughts—and all thoughts are transitory, whether they recur or not. They don't define who we are. That's where the teachings of yoga are so much more profound and effective. You train yourself to identify with the awareness that is witnessing those thoughts. It's pure genius. In our Western arrogance, we think that psychology is a completely new science. Freud invented it and his disciple Jung corrected his mistakes. Nonsense. Yoga psychology has been around for thousands of years. We need to study their findings about human consciousness and integrate them into our work, instead of going off trying to reinvent the wheel. Think about it. If you can break your identification with your thoughts, then you automatically free yourself from your traumas and complexes, no matter how many you have. That is real freedom. But you tell this to just about any university-trained Western psychologist and they'll give you some *merde* about this being 'a regression to a primitive state of ego development' or 'an undifferentiated state of primary narcissism.' Hell, I would have said the same thing myself a few years ago, but it's total *merde*. As long as Western psychologists continue to give primacy to the ego instead of recognizing a spiritual reality beyond the ego, they're going to continue going around in circles and never reach the center."

Marlena had grown indignant by now. She had a fervor in her voice that Rodrigo had not heard before, and she was gesticulating in an expressive manner that he found difficult to reconcile with her typical French reserve.

"Recently, I've been thinking that all this focus on our neuroses and past traumatic experiences can actually reinforce them in subtle ways. I've seen this in my patients. They relive a past anguish, it releases the same hormones into their bloodstream, and they end up identifying even more strongly with the very thoughts they are trying to get rid of. 'I am a person who was molested by my father.' It becomes part of their sense of identity, and this can be almost as destructive as the original event."

"Anyhow, from the standpoint of yoga philosophy," Georg interjected, "that traumatic event is a result of the person's samskaras. It may be the immediate cause of whatever he's going through, but really he is suffering due to his own past actions. Until he exhausts that samskara, he has no choice but to go through it. It's not just going to go away."

"Georg, if I tell that to one of my patients, I'm probably going to walk out of my office with my office chair on my head—if I can walk at all."

Georg shifted his bulky frame uncomfortably on the grass. "I understand that. You'd be out of a job if everyone understood about samskara. All I'm saying is that the person is paying for what they've done in the past, and no amount of psychotherapy is going to change that."

"I think this is one question we can put on our list for Saraswati," Rodrigo broke in, endeavoring to head off any possible flare-up before it got out of hand.

"Why don't we do that," Marlena said, without looking at Georg but without releasing the defiant look that was on her face. "Anyhow, my main point was that Western psychology mostly concentrates on the past and the role it plays in forming our present dispositions, complexes, and neuroses. Yoga is more practical. It concentrates on disciplining our mind in the present moment, learning to control it and observe it. I think we need to blend the two approaches. Western psychology has made a lot of progress in our understanding of the mind, but it needs to add the spiritual dimension. Fortunately, there are a number of spiritually minded psychologists nowadays who are doing interesting work in this area."

"Like yourself, for instance?" Ely queried. "Are you using any meditation or yogic techniques in your practice?"

"Not yet. I don't feel confident enough yet. First I have to get better in my own meditation; I have to understand it better and see how I deal with the material that comes up. It's a lot like working in a private clinic, only I am both the patient and the doctor. I have to gather experience as I go. But I'm working on things that I should be able to work into my practice in the future. Plus, I'm studying what other like-minded psychologists are doing. But it has to start with me. The more I learn about how to deal with my own mind, the better I'll be able to help my patients."

"Well, when you do, let me know, Ely said. "I'll recommend you to my friends. It seems like half the people I know are in therapy, and the other half should be."

From there the talk turned to past lives and eventually to dreams. Everyone wanted to know what Marlena had to say about dream interpretation, none more so than Rodrigo, though he didn't venture any of his own dreams as examples. Ely, on the other hand, had plenty of dreams to discuss. She wanted to know what it meant when she dreamed she was flying, if the people she didn't recognize in her dreams were people she was destined to meet, and if it were possible to control one's dreams like Carlos Castaneda claimed in his books. She had tried looking at her hands while she dreamed but had yet to succeed; she suspected it had something to do with too much seafood in her diet. Of course, Castaneda ate meat and she didn't, but this didn't bother her. She had Indian blood and came from the same country he did, so if anything, she had it in her genes. Marlena had not read Castaneda and couldn't come up with many answers for her, other than some of the traditional interpretations offered by Freud and later disputed by Jung. In the end, they decided to bring the question to Saraswati, which suited Rodrigo since he had been hoping to talk to her about it for some time now.

The next day's class on the Yoga Sutras had plenty of scope for questions. One of the first ones on their list was the question about dream interpretation.

"Yoga recognizes two types of dreams," Saraswati answered, "the ordinary dream and the supramental dream. The ordinary dream, as I mentioned last week, is basically a discharge of nervous energy by the subconscious mind. The impressions stored in the subconscious, real or imagined, reappear in a disjointed or at times a fantasy-like stream. Such dreams are not considered of much importance in yoga since the content of those dreams is just the content of the subconscious. Of course, they reflect the preoccupations and desires of the dreamer, whatever samskaras are active in her life at the time, and in that sense they have meaning and can be interpreted; however, you won't find much reference to them in the yogic texts. A yogi doesn't need to interpret her dreams to understand her samskaras or desires. She is already well acquainted with them through her practice. Moreover, the more advanced the yogi, the less she dreams, since there is less nervous energy to discharge. Of course, if you are not so familiar with your samskaras, then dream interpretation could perhaps help you to understand them. The supramental dream, however, is more interesting, because it arises from the deeper layers of the mind. Ordinarily, a person does not have access to the all-knowing causal or unconscious mind due to the constant agitation of the conscious and subconscious layers. Sometimes in deep sleep, however, when the subconscious and conscious minds become calm, a wave from the causal mind can vibrate the subconscious and give rise to a different kind of dream that reflects the omniscience of the causal mind. A person dreams that there is going to be an earthquake in such and such place, or that someone they know is going to die. And the next day it happens exactly as they dreamed. This is one type of supramental dream. It's sometimes called a prophetic dream. Suppose a man goes to a temple to pray to the goddess to cure his son, whom the doctors have given up for dead. He falls asleep in front of the idol and sees a vision of the goddess in his dream. She shows him a certain plant and tells him how to prepare a medicine from its leaves. When he wakes up, he remembers the dream, he prepares the medicine, and, lo and behold! his son is cured. He thinks the goddess has answered his prayers, but actually this knowledge was already inside him. It came from his causal mind. He just didn't have access to it before. Remember, there is only one causal mind, and it is the repository of all knowledge. In this case, due to his grief, he achieved a temporary concentration that opened a brief portal into those deeper layers. The knowledge he was looking for made its way into his subconscious and took the form of a dream. He sees a vision of the goddess because those are the impressions stored in his subconscious from this life, in this case an imaginary image. Had he been a Christian, he would have seen the Mother Mary. These are all cases of supramental dreams."

Rodrigo raised his hand. "So if I had a dream, and in that dream I saw something or learned something that I couldn't possibly have seen or known, and then later on I find out it's true, does this mean that while I was dreaming I came in contact for some time with the causal mind?"

"If it is not a subconscious impression that you've forgotten, then yes. In that case, some material from the causal mind surfaces during the dream state and makes its way into the subconscious where it is then assimilated according to the impressions that are stored there."

A few minutes later, Marlena raised the question that had been the subject of their mild dispute the previous day.

"The theory of samskara is no excuse for a lack of compassion," Saraswati said firmly. "A knowledge of the law of cause and effect helps us to take responsibility for our own predicament and to understand the importance of right action, since our destiny depends on it. But if we use that philosophy to justify thinking that a person who is suffering is getting what she deserves, then we are only rationalizing our own selfishness; if we do, we create for ourselves the worst possible type of samskara. Rather, you should think that it is my samskara to be in a position to help that person, and hopefully it is that person's samskara to receive my help and benefit from it. A yogi sees everything as an expression of one Divine Consciousness, and a devotee personifies that Consciousness as the beloved. It is your beloved, your very own self, who is suffering. The only acceptable human response is to do whatever is within our power to alleviate that suffering. If it is truly her samskara to suffer—which is something we can never know—then our help may fail, but our hope is that her samskara is to see her suffering end through our intercession.

"I don't mean to imply that any of you lack compassion, but I want you to be aware of this so you can avoid it in yourselves and fight against it when you see it in others. We live in a world full of injustice. People are dying of starvation not a hundred kilometers from where we sit. Every minute a child dies because it doesn't receive the medical attention that most people wouldn't think twice about giving their pets. If we don't do whatever is within our means to alleviate suffering and end injustice, then we are responsible for what happens, just as much as if we had taken the food out of their mouths ourselves. Everything is connected in this world by the web of cause and effect. If we don't use our God-given capacity to alleviate the suffering we see around us, then we will have to pay the price for closing our eyes. We are not only responsible for our actions; we are responsible for our inaction as well. A true yogi is always ready to act for the welfare of the world and all its creatures, knowing that in this lies her own welfare. For we are the world and its creatures. If we turn our eyes from the world, we turn our eyes from our own self. Think about this, because we will talk about it again on Friday. The next sutras concern the eight limbs of ashtanga yoga, and these eight limbs begin with the ten principles of yoga ethics."

19

SARASWATI WAS HAPPY THEY had asked that question. If they hadn't, she would have brought it up herself in their Friday class. Too many spiritualists used the law of karma as an excuse for their lack of social conscience, a jarring absence that never failed to rouse her sense of indignation. All too often it was the sons and daughters of well-to-do families, who sang the glories of their spiritual heritage but failed to lift a finger to help the millions of their disadvantaged countrymen who were every bit the image of the Divine before which they laid their ritual offerings. It was especially important to her that her students would not number themselves among them. She simply couldn't abide people who professed to love humanity but didn't seem to care much for human beings. Perhaps the fact that her students were westerners and relatively new to the spiritual path would work to their advantage. Less bad habits to unlearn. Sometimes it seemed that seven thousand years of spiritual culture could be just as blinding as it was edifying.

It was late afternoon now and she was seated on the flat second-story roof above her room, preparing the coming class on yoga ethics, those principles of right action without which no spiritualist could hope to progress on the path of illumination. The rustling canopies of two tall pipal trees draped her figure in a comfortable shade. The air was cooler now but she was not quite ready to move out of the shadow. One more month and she would be using this late-afternoon hour to soak up the healing warmth of the winter sun, but that welcome delight was still weeks away. From where she sat facing the Ganges, her eyes traveled downriver past the receding mountains toward the plains of Northern India, sequestered just beyond the haze of the horizon. Her native village lay over that horizon, 170 kilometers in a straight line from where she sat, halfway between Meerut and Delhi. Barely a hundred families in carefully tended mud-and-thatch cottages encircled by a grid-like tapestry of wheat fields, vegetable gardens, and scraggly pastureland for the cows and goats. A sky so huge she used to stare at it in the mornings as she walked to school and wonder if it ever came to an end. Until she saw her first city, she never imagined that anything could be as imposing as that sky.

A class on the ethical principles necessary to true spiritual progress would have seemed puzzling to many of the lifelong residents of her village. Wasn't this how any human being needed to live if he wanted to survive and be happy? some of them might have said. And they would have been right, growing up in a traditional rural community where the wisdom of their ancestors had been fed to them for breakfast along with their chapatis. Not that the Kali Yuga had failed to spread its clouds over the countryside as well, but it was one place where the simplest lessons from earlier eras had not completely faded from human memory. Difficult times were always only one bad harvest away, and no one needed to be taught that a family's key to survival was the community they helped to support. Nothing could have been more natural for her while growing up than to see her parents taking some portion of their meager stores to a neighbor who had fallen short of wheat, or helping them to re-thatch their roof. Nor could she ever forget her fond memories of working alongside her neighbors in their fields during harvest time, joining in the songs with which they greeted the rising sun and seeing them return the favor without her father ever needing to ask. Somehow that community spirit—for her a reflection of the innate spirituality of Indian village life—had not survived the migration to the cities. How is it, Mother, that modern living seems to rob us of our compassion so easily, so effortlessly? Have we become so enamored of our own creations that we have forgotten that we are ourselves a creation, a sprig in the tree of nature? Have we become so outward looking that we are no longer able to look into the hearts of our neighbors and recognize that our own heart is beating there? They were questions she had asked herself many times and always the same answer came ringing into her mind with the Mother's accents: "It is not their fault; how could anyone be expected to resist the times we live in? It is your duty to help them, to teach them, to awaken their dormant humanity."

Now, as on other occasions, she was thankful she had grown up where she had, in a simple village where a good supply of rice and flour in the pantry and the respect and affection of one's neighbors were all the riches a person could wish for. As she gazed out from her rooftop, she could feel the relentless motion of India's cities hidden behind the hazy curtain of the horizon, a blind, unforgiving force that bled its citizenry of their humanity by forcing them into a life pitilessly contrary to their spiritual nature. Nowhere was this more in evidence than in the nation's capital, that monolith of avarice and exploitation that she had called home for the better part of fourteen years. To her it sometimes seemed that the entire ego of man had coalesced into this one point on the globe, determined to prove once and for all the power of its mighty fist. If anyone were to ask her to give some proof that humanity had entered the Kali Yuga, she need only ask them to spend a day or two in Delhi.

She had learned that lesson firsthand when she won her scholarship to a presti-gious girl's college in the capital, one of five annual seats offered to impoverished village girls. She had been seventeen then, brimming over with her youthful spiritual idealism, almost entirely gleaned from books and her one magical stay within the protective confines of the Mother's ashram. The reckless pace of the city and the preoccupations and desultory habits of its disaffected youth had come nowhere close to exerting any influence over the dirt paths that she walked every day between her house and the houses of her friends and neighbors in the surrounding villages that formed the limits of her horizon. It was a rude shock, then, when she began to see her life for the first time through the lens of the urbanized middle class to whom the villages were an exotic remnant of an India long buried, relegated to the dusty confines of history and an occasional, uncomfortable excursion to the ancestral home of one's paternal grandparents. The mutual cooperation she had taken for granted in her childhood was nowhere to be found, and her own helpful advances were more often than not looked at with a doubtful eye. Whereas she had grown up sharing what little she had with her friends, her college classmates and hostel mates competed for everything: grades, social attention, front circle tickets for the latest Amitabha Bachchan movie. They had an insatiable hunger for the latest fashions, the coolest gadgets, the newest vehicle. Those who rode bicycles envied those who rode mopeds; those who rode mopeds openly dreamed of getting a car. For a young woman to whom three good saris seemed like a luxury, and who had thought a four-kilometer walk through the fields to the municipal high school a blessing, since she had classmates who walked twice that, the whirl of desire that surrounded her in her college and in the city made her dizzy, and the ubiquitous overtones of intolerance reddened her ears. When she first walked down the corridors of the sprawling Victorian-style campus and into the spacious lecture halls where half the conversations were in English, despite English being no one's mother tongue, she felt as if she had arrived in a foreign country. And in truth she had. India's poverty-stricken villages were a distant reality to her classmates, and she was a hopeless innocent who, they insisted, would never learn to cope with the real world if she didn't get in step with the times—an indoctrination her studiously disdainful classmates were reluctantly willing to bestow.

How had she ever made it all the way to college without becoming aware of this gaping divide? Looking back, it seemed a kind of minor miracle, one she would be forever grateful for. During her sophomore year in high school, she read Swami Vivekananda for the first time; in rapid succession, she devoured the seven volumes of his collected works that lay gathering dust on a shelf of the school library. Vivekananda not only fired her growing passion for the yogic practices she had recently begun, his writings also awoke in her a revolutionary ardor that seemed as natural as sleeping out under the stars on a cot during the long summer nights when the sky cooled enough to make her memories of the rampaging daytime sun pleasanter than they really were. The swami's voice had sounded like a trumpet from out of those weathered pages, calling her to the aid of India's destitute and exploited masses toiling under the same fierce sun that she knew so well. As she reflected on his proud bearing and the regal, shining countenance captured in the black-and-white photo on the cover, she began to see visions of herself coming to the rescue of her less-fortunate countrymen, striding across India as she pictured him doing, helping them to shoulder their burdens and filling them with the inspiration of the soul, even as she helped them to throw off the chains of the body. But never once during all this time did she see herself as a member of the toiling masses. They inhabited an India she had never seen, far from the simple but comfortable village life that had sheltered her throughout the seventeen years before her scholarship changed forever the world she lived in. It was only after she moved into her hostel and began to see herself through her classmate's eyes that she discovered that she was one of the toiling masses herself, and that her new companions had little compassion, either for them or for her. It had not only been a shock but an affront to her dignity, a deluge of cold water in the face that woke her up to the thousand social indignities that crowded round her, clamoring for an attention they rarely got. It was then, by her own reckoning, that her vague, dreamlike idealism began its rapid metamorphosis into a sharply defined, concrete indignation at the injustice that derived its sustenance from the society in which she lived.

Now if she could only pass that on to her students. If she could only show them that this was as much a part of growing a spiritual conscience as sitting for meditation. Maybe then the fact that the Mother had sentenced her to a peaceful life teaching philosophy in a wealthy Himalayan ashram—a place seemingly as far removed from the injustices of the world as any place could be—would not prevent her from making a difference. In her youth she had dreamed of following in Vivekananda's footsteps like his English disciple Sister Nivedita, who became famous as both a revolutionary-minded social worker and a saint. Sitting here on a rooftop in Rishikesh was not her idea of blazing a trail for justice, but even here the world turned on the same axis. She had a debt to pay in answer to her karma, but it need not stop her from doing what she could to dispel the storm clouds that were gathering on the horizon.

20

BY NOW PREPARATIONS WERE underway for the celebration of Diwali, the festival of lights. The local temples were being cleaned and decorated. Small pavilions were springing up in different locations to house the image of the goddess Lakshmi, the goddess of wealth and fortune in whose honor the town would soon be ablaze with the lights of thousands of flickering lamps. As Rodrigo took his late afternoon walk, he could feel the excitement in the air. It crackled like a discharge of kinetic energy from the concourse of devout Indians who considered it a privilege worthy of heaven to spend Diwali in the holy city of Rishikesh, where they would commemorate the beginning of a new year and celebrate fresh hopes for the future. As he walked along the river, he peered into the temples and pavilions, his own excitement growing as he saw the half-hidden images of the goddess being preened and primped by her devotees. For the past week, he had been busy devouring the books on Hindu culture and religious rituals that Saraswati had recommended, his hunger fed by a growing sense that what was taking place around him was as much an inner event as an outer one. His dreams, his studies, the roots that were sinking imperceptibly into Himalayan soil, were all conspiring to convince him that the rhythms of the life that surrounded him were his rhythms, that the mountains that cast their afternoon shadows over his strolling feet were his mountains. The more he relaxed into the unfolding of his days, the more natural everything seemed, and sometimes the thread that connected him to his previous life seemed as tenuous as the sun's reflection on the silent waters that were preparing to slip off into the anonymity of the night.

His dreams had also become a part of his daily landscape. Saraswati's lucid explanation a few days earlier had provided the context his mind had been waiting for. Within moments, he had become convinced of what he had already suspected: his were not ordinary dreams. He had seen things he should not and could not have seen, things he was now sure he had never come across before. Her words had removed the doubts and the confusion and replaced them with the conviction that the ocean of the unconscious had been rocking him to sleep, and that each time he rose to his feet in the temple grounds, clothed in the thin garments of a

Brahmin priest, he was dripping water from one of its overflowing waves. After class, he had gone up to her and asked her if she could recommend some books on Hindu culture, especially concerning Brahmins, caste relations, and the history of Kali worship. She was a perceptive woman. She asked him if he had been having any unusual dreams, and his evasion of the question had sounded as weak in his ears as his legs customarily felt after sitting cross-legged for close to an hour in meditation. Fortunately she didn't press him on it, though he knew from the piercing quality of her look that he had not fooled her. Instead, she wrote out a sizable list of titles that might be available in Rishikesh. Those that he had found had proved as informative as she had promised. Many of the small details from his dreams that he had glossed over in his journal now became intelligible. They made it clear beyond any possibility of a doubt that his imaginary temple was situated somewhere in a dreamed Bengal, and that his alter ego was a Barendra Brahmin with all the peculiarities typical to that caste. These were not generic details, strung together haphazardly by his subconscious, but a swell of knowledge that had washed into his dreamscape from a source beyond the borders of his tiny mind. They were things one only came across in Bengal, some in a Bengal that had long since disappeared, and the precision of the details reinforced his now-firm belief that the all-knowing unconscious mind was slipping missives into the soporific brew of his dreams.

It was from these readings that Rodrigo got the idea for his next scene. Diwali, he discovered, was celebrated on the same night as Kali Puja, a festival peculiar to Bengal and the Bengali people. He would have dearly liked to see Le Gentil attend a Kali Puja, but there was no such festival to be had in Pondicherry, and Ambika's family resisted any temptation on his part to give them a Bengali ancestry. Diwali it would have to be, so he read as much as he could about it until he felt more excited about Diwali's immanent arrival than he had felt about Christmas in many a year.

At the same time that Rodrigo was growing increasingly interested in Indian culture, Le Gentil was going through a similar process. His conversations with Ambika after his meeting with the professor were now marked by an insatiable curiosity to know what other riches India might have to offer his wide-ranging mind. He had been born in a time when the ideal image of a scientist was still someone who was as well versed in as many different branches of the sciences as possible and interested in them all. There was no mania for specialization as of yet, no pervading misconception that the world was too unwieldy for one person ever to become adept at more than a single discipline, no raised eyebrows when a scientist cultivated the arts as assiduously as the sciences, or vice versa, though those days were already gestating in the womb of an incipient globalization of thought. He was free to wander through the fascinating backwaters of anthropology and natural history without ever feeling that he was betraying his credo as an astronomer. And wander he did, as far afield in Pondicherry and the surrounding areas as his carriage and Ambika would take him.

After one short excursion to the ruins of an ancient temple, Le Gentil asked

Ambika if she knew of any upcoming religious festival that she could take him to see. When she informed him that the entire city, with the exception of the European section, would soon begin preparations for Diwali, arguably the most important festival of the year, Le Gentil immediately became enthused. Over the following days, as he observed the decorations rapidly going up in Ville Noire, his curiosity mounted about the alien religion to whom the festival belonged. What little he had seen of the religion of the Hindus seemed comparatively primitive to him, a curious mixture of idol worship and exotic superstitions that appeared incongruous when juxtaposed with the scientific acumen and extraordinary achievements of their astronomers. But then he had to ruefully admit that many of his own Christian beliefs came into direct conflict with his scientific training. In fact, the stubborn refusal of the clerical community to adjust church doctrine to the latest scientific findings had been for years an irksome reality that he had learned to live with but never appreciate. Copernicus had not dared to publish his thesis for fear of reprisals from the church, a well-justified fear. Though the church had eventually accepted that the earth was a satellite of the sun and not the stationary center of the universe it had long insisted it to be, each accommodation of scientific theory had been a grudging one, and usually decades or even centuries delayed. So he was not much surprised by his observation, only a little dismayed to see the same unflattering dichotomy at work in an alien culture a half a world away. What this said about the human race, he preferred not to consider. But with his natural bent for anthropology, a discipline he considered essential to the development of any true and well-rounded scientist, he remained curious to learn about the beliefs of the Hindus and how they impacted their culture.

Two days before Diwali, he asked Ambika to take the carriage through Ville Noire before heading out to the observatory for his regular inspection of the ongoing construction. He had the carriage stop in front of a huge pavilion that was going up at one end of a large open field that lay in between two crowded neighborhoods. Separate groups of children were playing on the stubbly grass and a shepherd was leading a ragged flock of goats past the pavilion and out toward the fields outside of town. They got down from the carriage and walked over to where the workmen were tying together the large bamboo poles, some of them a full forty feet in length, with a rapidity and dexterity that made him nod his head in appreciation. Out of long habit, he found himself making mental notes of their technique and asking himself questions for later investigation about the tensile strength, durability, growing cycle, and climatic necessities of the bamboo they were using. All of this would go into his journal that evening when he sat down at his desk with a candelabrum and a fresh quill, his favorite part of the day, a time for reflection and deep thought after the normal hours of intense activity and unfettered curiosity. In the meantime, Ambika walked quietly beside him, answering his occasional question and noting his observations in the notebook that she was never without.

It was only after they had reached the observatory and completed their daily rounds of the construction that Le Gentil and Ambika picked up their ongoing conversation, turning their attention from the outside world to their apprehension of it. Le Gentil wanted to know about Diwali, as much as Ambika could tell him, and she had come prepared, by now thoroughly accustomed to the barrage of questions that ensued whenever Le Gentil's sight fell upon something that incited his curiosity. She had even taken the precaution of talking to her father and the family priest about the origins and significance of the festival, knowing she could use their help to satisfy this unusual white man and his insatiable thirst for knowledge. As they unpacked the food basket and arranged their lunch on the outspread blanket, Ambika began relating the history of Diwali, including some details that were as new to her as they were to Le Gentil.

"Diwali was originally a folk festival dedicated to the worship of the goddess Lakshmi, the goddess of wealth and fortune. It began as a way of thanking the goddess for her blessings at the end of the harvest season, which traditionally falls on the new moon in the month of Ashvin—that can be anywhere from mid-October to mid-November in the Gregorian calendar. But over time, it grew to take on a much more elaborate meaning. What started as a one-day festival grew into five days, and each day has a separate, unique significance; in fact, these were actually different festivals that gradually got absorbed into Diwali. Here in the south, we generally call it by its original name, Dipavali, which means 'festival of lights.' In its present form, Dipavali day, the day of the new moon, commemorates the day Lord Rama, the god-king, returned from his fourteen years of exile in the forest. On that night, the new moon night in Ashvin, the residents of Ayodhya received Rama and his queen Sita by lighting rows of lamps to illuminate their way to the city.

"However, like most religious festivals in India, Dipavali has its roots in a mystic symbolism that was our ancient sages' way of translating the highest concepts of spiritual philosophy into a language the common people could understand. On the morning of Dipavali, Indian families begin cleaning their houses. If you go to my house, you'll see my mother on her hands and knees scrubbing the floors, even though she has servants to do that work the rest of the year. The idea is that with these simple gestures we imitate the deeper housecleaning of the spirit that is a necessary prerequisite to all mystic or spiritual endeavor. Once the housecleaning is complete, we begin preparing the lamps. When night falls on Dipavali, you'll see thousands upon thousands of lamps everywhere you go—in every window, on every veranda, in the streets, in the fields, and especially in the pavilions and temples where they've set up the images of the goddess. The city is beautiful beyond belief, but so is every village on Dipavali night. These lights symbolize the illumination of the spirit toward which all true devotees point their lives. In the earthen homes of our peasants and farmers, you'll see candles or simple clay lamps, and in the mansions of the great landowners and businessmen, you'll see the finest silver lamps burning camphor, but it is the same light; it shines the same on everyone. All night long the devotees take their offerings and lay them before the image of the goddess in the hope that the light that illuminates her image will continue to illuminate their spirit for the rest of the coming year."

"Are they really aware of this symbolism?"

"Some are; many are not. But it doesn't matter. They all feel it, even if they can't verbalize what they feel. It's in their blood. It's in the soil, the water, the air. You'll feel it, too, when you experience it firsthand."

After Ambika sketched a brief outline of the story of Rama, she told him about her great-uncle, who was still spoken of in awed tones in Pondicherry among the penitents who had known him, though he had died more than a decade earlier. Every year, it was said, he would fast for the two weeks leading up to Diwali, spending most of the night in silent meditation. Then on Diwali night the goddess Lakshmi would appear to him in white robes and give him instructions that he would follow throughout the year. It was said that he could see into the future and read the innermost thoughts of any man that came before him, even thoughts the person himself was not aware of.

Le Gentil found the history of Diwali interesting. He especially enjoyed Ambika's brief but colorful account of the epic fantasy the *Ramayana*, with its army of monkeys doing battle with the demons and helping Rama to rescue his kidnapped wife. But he laughed at this story of a mysterious uncle that seemed typical of the religious superstitions of this complex but credulous culture.

"But you are a Christian, Ambika. Surely you don't lend any credence to such tales."

Ambika smiled, thinking to herself how even a little arrogance could make fools of the most intelligent of men, a character trait that seemed to cross cultural boundaries as easily as sunlight through a window.

"You have seen an eclipse predicted with methods you didn't know existed before you came here, and now you are learning how to do it yourself. Your former ignorance about those methods did not negate their validity or stop people from using them. Some people consider the prediction of an eclipse to be magic, but, as you well know, it is science. Do you deny the possibility that there may be a psychic science far beyond what you are aware of? Ignorance is pardonable, Monsieur Guillaume, but it is no excuse for close-mindedness. Are you forgetting so quickly what you have learned of our astrology?"

It was the first time Ambika had addressed him by his first name, tempered as it was by the addition of "Monsieur," and the unexpected familiarity made the caustic nature of her reproach even more piercing. He swallowed his immediate response and looked at her with a deliberate effort to maintain the open mind that he prided himself on. Slowly he forced the next words from his throat, a place they seemed reluctant to vacate.

"I can admit the possibility of a psychic science beyond what I am aware of, but I have seen such types of claims in my own country. We have no shortage there of spiritists and occultists. And what I have seen of such claims falls somewhere between laughable and cleverly disguised charlatanism. So forgive me my incredulity. It is not without foundation. Was your uncle an astrologer, then?"

Ambika shook her head. "No, not in the sense you mean, though he may have been versed in astrology. He was a master of a far greater science." Ambika fell silent for a few moments, staring off into the distance as if she were sorting through her memories. Then she looked at him with her familiar look of quiet, defiant confidence. "We have no shortage of charlatans in my country either, and I have seen my share. But fool's gold owes its allure to the existence of real gold. I knew my great uncle and he was no charlatan."

Le Gentil took another bite of bread and cheese. He chewed thoughtfully, feeling Ambika's eyes on him.

"Are there masters of this psychic science you speak of still living?"

"There are."

"Will you take me to meet them, then?"

Ambika smiled. "I will, though not yet. There is no use going completely unprepared. If a student comes to you to talk of astronomy, you would expect him to have at least a basic understanding of the subject. The persons I will take you to see are masters of the human mind and human consciousness, far greater than any you have ever met. You should know something about the subject before you go there."

Le Gentil felt himself stiffen at her remark, but he knew enough of Ambika by now to know that these were not empty words he was hearing, and the aura of attraction that surrounded this inexplicable woman persuaded him to give her the benefit of any doubt, despite his natural misgivings and justifiable skepticism.

Rodrigo, however, did not share any of Le Gentil's reticence. A surge of excitement swept through him as he realized, suddenly and unexpectedly, that Ambika was going to take Le Gentil to meet a yogic master. A gap had opened, and into that space rushed a host of un-envisioned possibilities. It occurred to him once again that he had no real idea where his story was leading him—if it could even be called "his" story. But rather than become a cause for trepidation, the yawning chasm in front of him filled him with a liberating sense of adventure. The story was going somewhere. The fact that he didn't know where that was only made the voyage that much more interesting. He withdrew his hands from the keyboard and set them on his lap as he looked out the window toward the mountains. A sense of calm settled over him. He took his mind back to the interviews and diary entries he had read by famous writers who claimed that at some point their characters took over the story, wresting the reins from the supposed author. He smiled. This had always seemed a quaint notion to him, a poetic way of paying respect to the creative process, perhaps, but nothing more. But for several weeks now his own experience had been telling him otherwise. The more he worked, the more Ambika and Le Gentil ceased to be cardboard cutouts that he moved across the fertile plains of his imagination. More and more, they appeared to him as real people with minds and destinies of their own. It was an uncanny feeling but comforting. In some way, it absolved him of any responsibility for their lives, except in the mundane sense of bringing their intentions, feelings, and actions into as sharp a relief as possible, like an interpreter who improves the speaker's language so that his meaning might not be misconstrued, or a photographer who airbrushes a portrait to bring out the luster in a person's skin that the original photo had failed to capture. His duty was to work as responsibly, as authentically, and as carefully as he could, out of respect for what was taking shape on the screen in front of him, out of respect for his characters, for their lives and for the lives of those who might one day read their story and see their own story reflected there. The unknown possibilities that lay before Ambika and Le Gentil, possibilities that could only become conscious through the medium of the narrative, were the same possibilities that his own life was rushing toward. In this way, his characters were leaving their mark forever on the course that his own feet would take.

But for now, Rodrigo would have to remain patient and stay the course. There was no leaping ahead to find out what destiny had in store for him. He still had a scene to finish—Diwali night—and after that some transitional scenes before he could meet up with the yogi whom Ambika was planning to introduce to Le Gentil.

He was in the middle of working through the Diwali scene when the new moon night arrived, a fortuitous sequence of events, since he could feel his lack of religious experience slowing him down. There was a special Dipavali arati celebrated that evening in front of the Shiva statue that lasted well into the night, the ghat decorated with hundreds of small lamps whose power waxed as the night enfolded them. A special *puja*, or worship, was performed for the goddess Lakshmi just after nightfall; it was followed by a concert of Indian classical music with flute and tabla that brought tears to Rodrigo's eyes. As the music lifted its mystic overtones into the night, a parade of tiny earthen lamps released by unseen hands floated downriver behind the musicians, their flickering lights dancing as if they could hear the music and could not resist its enchantment. Never before had Rodrigo heard music so beautiful and never in such an idyllic setting. Amrita, who had sat next to him during the concert, told him afterward that the best Indian musicians were known to enter into states of yogic trance while they performed, uniting their minds with the Divine Consciousness through intense, prolonged concentration and the ethereal beauty of their art. Rodrigo did not doubt it. He was a novice but he could feel the transport of that music, and there had been a few fleeting moments during the concert when he had felt the distant approach of something that he could only describe as spiritual ecstasy.

Shortly before midnight, he met up with Amrita, Marlena, and Ely. Together they spent the next few hours going from pavilion to temple to pavilion along with thousands of other pilgrims, laying offerings before the various images of the goddess and joining in the chants as best they could. Amrita was their guide. She explained not only the rituals but how to commune with the goddess in their minds while they performed them. After thirty minutes in the first pavilion, Rodrigo felt so at home with the revelry and its underlying currents of devotion that it was as if he had grown up with an image of the goddess on his nightstand and a stick of burning incense soothing him to sleep. The carefree nature of the wandering pilgrims and the constant music reminded him more of an all-night jazz festival than any solemn religious rite, but it was precisely this unbounded quality coupled with the mystic overtones of the Himalayan night that left such an indelible impression in his heart. It was after four in the morning when he reached his room, drunk with a tranquil euphoria that seemed more propitious than anything he had ever known. He had no thoughts of his transgressions or his failed dreams when he fell asleep. The world floated into existence like colored mist from a cauldron of joy and all he could see in front of him was a luminous river of possibilities. For once, Rishikesh was asleep in the hours after dawn, submerged in its dream of the goddess, while Rodrigo found himself plunged in a very different dream pledged to the worship of a very different goddess who was at that moment surfeited with the offerings of her devotees in a land far to the east known as Bengal.

Rishikesh
11/2
9:55 AM

I was not expecting to find my way back to the temple this morning, or even hoping to do so, considering that I was going to bed at the hour that I have been having these dreams, the hour before dawn, but maybe I should have been prepared after a night spent worshipping the goddess. And not just any night—Diwali night, or rather Kali Puja in the language of my dream.

In my dream it was the following night, the night after Kali Puja, and I was leading a procession through the streets of town along with the other priests. We had begun in the temple grounds, where a large pavilion had been erected to shelter the life-size clay image of the goddess. I was dead tired because I hadn't slept the night before, but I was riding a wave of euphoria. All that previous night and on into the morning, the townspeople had poured into the temple grounds to perform the ritual worship and request a boon from the mistress of the night. I had spent those hours by the feet of the goddess, performing the rites and receiving the offerings. It had been exhilarating to see the devotion in their eyes and hear the tremor in their voices; to know that I was their priest, the one who enabled them to commune with the goddess; to feel her pleasure as she watched her faithful servant carry out his duties.

Despite the exhaustion, I had been floating on a sea of devotion all day, except for a couple of excruciating hours in the early morning when I had to go to a nearby field to preside over the ritual sacrifice of goats. Fortunately, I remember only a brief flash of this, for even though I was clearly used to it, I found it difficult to bear. Now the closing portion of the puja was about to begin. The image was placed in a specially decorated palanquin set on the shoulders of a group of acolytes while

I presided over the ceremonial preparations for her journey. A kirtan band was playing as we started out the gate. I was leading the way, the other priests by my side, and the goddess right behind us. The entire town was waiting, thronging both sides of the street. The music was deafening: drums, cymbals, conch shells, everyone chanting in unison. It was raucous, intoxicating. People were literally reeling in the streets, dancing, turning wild circles, jumping with their heads thrown back and lifting their arms to the night sky like madmen. I wanted to do the same but I couldn't; as the lead priest in the procession, I had to maintain the expected decorum. We marched to the edge of the river accompanied by thousands of drunken madmen, though there was not a drop of alcohol in anyone's veins. There I presided over the ritual immersion of the image, reciting the ancient mantras to extract the soul of the goddess and free her once again to merge with the infinite space that surrounds us. Then I sat and watched with a sense of deep satisfaction as her now-lifeless image soaked up the water and sank out of sight. A great shout went up and then everyone dispersed—to sleep, I assume—but I stayed there and meditated on the impermanence of life.

The ritual immersion seemed to me a perfect analogy of incarnate life. What was the goddess but a simple clay figure veiled by bright clothes and jewels? I had performed the ceremony that instilled in that clay figure her unseen soul, bringing the image to life as I installed her on her altar in the pavilion. Now, a few days later, I had consigned her lifeless figure to the universal waters to which all living things return. What was our body but a slightly larger clay figure that lived a few more days but ended up in the same place, with our soul gone to wherever it came from? Perhaps this is what our sages had been alluding to when they devised this ceremony and imbued it with the rich symbolism that so few people understood. And thus, as the goddess is eternal and omnipresent, regardless of the time she remains confined to her clay image, our soul is also equally eternal and omnipresent. These were my thoughts as I sat there and meditated, fully cognizant of myself as the Mother's representative. But then another thought, more immediate and earthbound, pushed aside my spiritual reverie. I remembered that before the Kali Puja had begun, our temple had been challenged to a scriptural debate by another, more prestigious temple. I had been selected by the elders to represent us. The excitement of Kali Puja had pushed it to the back of my mind, but now that the puja had ended, it came rushing back to the forefront with a force that robbed me of my tranquility. The debate was fast approaching, and though I was proud of my scriptural knowledge, I was fearful that I might be defeated in public and lose prestige in the eyes of those whom I was working so hard to impress. At the same time, it was the opportunity I had been waiting for. This was my chance to establish my reputation outside the confines of the temple and the community that worshipped there. If I won the debate, then the news would spread among my Brahmin peers, even to places where I had never been. I would thenceforth enjoy a certain renown in the public eye, something I had long wished for. That was my feeling when I woke up, part of me still looking out over the water to where the image had disappeared, another part of me waking up to the yellowed walls of my ashram room.

Now that I am myself again, scrunched over my computer, legs still under the covers (though who exactly this self is, is increasingly open to question), I am somewhat in awe of the contemplative nature of my dreaming self, and a bit dismayed that I lack the same qualities in real life. In my dreams I am an accomplished meditator—it shows in the depth and quality of my thoughts as I watched the clay image sink out of sight—but in the waking state I am a novice to the interior life. I have been having a series of extraordinary dreams, yet I have thus far failed to decode the cipher that conceals their hidden meaning. In truth, I have mostly just enjoyed them like I might enjoy a night out at the cinema, apart from a few hurried reflections at the end of each journal entry. But were I to stop and reflect deeply on my current experience, where would it lead me? When these dreams first began, I marveled that I was dreaming in sequence and even supposed that it might be the novelist in me leaking over into my dreams. Now such thinking seems fanciful and simplistic. What's worse, it ignores the most important question: what are my dreams trying to tell me? Were I now my dreaming self, dreaming the dreams of the dreamer, it would be the first question to come to mind and the last I would leave unanswered. Perhaps I can learn something from my alter ego and make a concerted effort to decipher the language of these dreams and the teachings they mean to communicate. The first thing that draws my attention is their extraordinary sequential nature. A story is unfolding as I sleep and the unconscious mind is the weaver of this tale—for how else could it be so rich in details that I would otherwise have no way of knowing? Why is my unconscious mind choosing the story form for its unsolicited eruptions? Can it be because there is meaning in a story that goes far beyond the disparate details that compose it? A story's primary meaning cannot be found in scene and detail. It emerges from the way that story unfolds over time, and from the arc that the characters within it describe as they submit to or defy the forces presented them by that imagined universe (the reflected image of the actual universe). My priest is moving in a certain direction. He has no choice since he is caught within the machinery of the story form. He is changing as he goes along. Perhaps it is those changes that my unconscious is pointing me toward. Maybe the situation and the uncanny, inexplicable details are simply scene and setting, nothing more, the external trappings that serve only to give form to an internal journey. It is this journey I should be looking at. I had not considered this. My priest is ambitious, but his is not an ordinary worldly ambition. He is seeking spiritual knowledge, no matter how much his ego might sully his quest. And now a test is coming up of that knowledge. I think Saraswati would say that he is seeking himself, and that knowledge is his path to the one he seeks. I am going through a similar process, hence this may be my unconscious's way of guiding me through that process, though in my dreams I am much further along than I am in real life. As to the nature of that guidance, I do not yet feel confident enough to say, but from now on I intend to pay much closer attention.

Over the next few days, Rodrigo finished sketching out the Diwali scene. Though Le Gentil was far more skeptical and far less knowledgeable about the religious festival than Rodrigo had been, his main character ended up enjoying his night of sacred revelry at least as much as his creator, if not more. Some of that had to do with his beautiful companion, who guided him through the rituals and translated for him when he insisted on sitting next to the priest in the pavilion and talking to him while the aged Brahmin accepted the offerings of the devotees and facilitated their communication with the goddess whose celestial presence he zealously conducted into the world of material form. The priest was rightfully annoyed with this pale-skinned intruder who in the centuries before the arrival of the Europeans would have been considered a demon by some and a curiosity by others, and in neither case allowed to disturb the sanctity of the puja. Times had changed, however. The Brahmin was prudent enough to indulge an influential member of a conquering race, despite the disgust he carefully concealed when Le Gentil attempted to shake his hand. Ambika was careful to preface her translation of the astronomer's questions with an apology for his barbaric behavior and a clear intimation that the governor would be grateful for his forbearance. Since she and her father were well known to him, it was an easy transition to a running commentary from the priest's lips that lasted well into the night.

While Le Gentil was oblivious of the various undercurrents flowing through their conversation, he was alert to every nuance of the priest's explanations; he left that night knowing more about Dipavali and its symbolism than any European alive. It was also the first time that Le Gentil had seen Ambika in her native element, severed by the night and the thronging crowd of her countrymen from the colonial Christian veneer she wore so adroitly during the hours that the sun hung in the sky. She wore her hair loose, flowing over the thin folds of her sari like a horse's mane whipping in the wind, and the sight of her performing the ritual movements and chanting the unfamiliar mantras with such unabashed delight made it seem like the goddess herself had stepped down from her pedestal and breathed her life force into this dark-skinned beauty from the Coromandel coast. Even when she was translating for him, laughter wafted from the musical syllables of her speech like the overtones of a high-pitched gong escaping into the darkness. This woman, who was always under such control as she navigated her daily course through the hard interiors of French colonial society, now appeared as wild and unfettered as any barefoot washerwoman singing gaily by the river's edge, slapping her clothes against the bare surface of the boulders and frightening the dirt into submission with a joyful thwack-thwack-thwack. Details that had gone unnoticed now took on meaning: the slight stridency that crept into her voice whenever she talked about matters concerning her native culture; her secretiveness when he asked her about her family or her life after hours; the deference with which the other servants treated her, entirely different from the eager-to-please submission they showed their Western bosses. This was the part of her she kept hidden from the people she appeared to emulate. By the time the first traces of dawn began to reveal lineaments of the horizon floating far out above the ocean's edge, he had realized that what he saw during the day was merely a garment she wore to conceal her nakedness, just as the image of the goddess hid herself behind her fine human clothes. Knowing this made her appear even more attractive to him. Who does not feel the lure of mystery when it wraps itself in a human form?

Looking back, Le Gentil would point to that night as the turning point in his relationship with his young assistant, the night the goddess reached out through her and cast a spell over him that would not recede until long after his ship had departed from the South Indian shore. Yet the reality was otherwise. The attraction had been building since the day he had first set eyes on her in the Governor-General's office, and the explanation for it could be summed up in a single word: destiny. Though the more Rodrigo looked at it, filtering his imagined story through the burgeoning prism of a yogi's insight that turns the white light of day into the colors that compose it, a better word would be *samskara*. He could not yet see the forces of destiny that had brought these two characters together in his mind, but a growing instinct told him that it could only be through a long chain of cause and effect. The more independent they became, the more the shadow of an unseen history trailed behind them. If he could uncover it, then maybe he could better see where the winds of their samskaras were blowing them. It was a curious thought, but not to his eyes, not any longer, not now that he was learning that the mind was not a simple book whose pages he turned as he wished but rather a surging sea whose vast depths lay beyond his ken, and whose wind-whipped waves spun his little boat as its giant will willed.

21

S ARASWATI HAD ALWAYS BEEN fond of November. As a child growing up on the plains of Northern India, it had been the last balmy month before the severity of December and January sent her running for her blankets as soon as the sun dipped toward the horizon. Poised between the scorching winds of late summer and the inevitable mid-winter cold wave that would take its toll among the elderly and the infirm, November was like an interlude between the two acts of a yearly play: the extremes of heat and cold that nature imposed as a necessary condition on those who wished to accept her bounty. Here in Rishikesh, however, winter arrived early and left late. November was anything but balmy. As the sun's light spent less and less time moving across the dial, shortening the days, a chill wind began to blow across the face of the mountains, carrying away the last of the summer's warmth. The morning haze above the river deepened and the early morning fog became a constant companion to the schoolchildren who wrapped themselves in sweaters and scarves as they made their solitary march through the nearly deserted streets to their school buildings. It was only when the mid-morning sun cut through the fog and began to warm the marble ghats and concrete roofs that the street merchants began unwrapping their wares, ready to cast a familiar veil of activity over the reflective solemnity of this temple town huddled in the shadows of the Himalayas. The pilgrims would start appearing, descending from their ashrams and their hostels in pursuit of the material suste- nance they needed to maintain their spiritual quest. But once the sun fled from the sky, the town would quickly and quietly return to its protective cocoon. Nothing more would be seen or heard after that except for the winter wind whipping down from the mountains, until the first plaintive notes of the morning chants rose above the river, only to fade again like the light of a false dawn.

Afternoon was the time of day that Saraswati reminded herself how much she depended on the sun—her and the rest of the earth's inhabitants. Each afternoon, she would ascend to the roof above her room to rescue whatever warmth she could from the setting sun before it disappeared for the better half of its diurnal cycle. She would sit there with her books, delving into the mysteries of spiritual phi- losophy, until the shadows of the mountains enveloped her and sent her running for cover to the insulated warmth of her first-floor room. On this afternoon in late November, she was leaning back in her fraying lawn chair, her eyes brooding over a leather-bound copy of Shankaracharya's *Crest Jewel of Discrimination*. The sun shone directly in her face, making her pale saffron sari appear diaphanous in its crisp autumnal light. A second lawn chair stood at a cross angle to hers, waiting for Rodrigo to join her for a private study session. Skipping briefly over the introduction, she started reading the verses of the opening chapter, savoring Shankaracharya's elegant Sanskrit as she intoned the lines to herself in the same cadence that one heard in Indian ashrams. She paused after the fifth verse, struck once again by the sobering power of its simple but profound pronouncement: "Who could be more foolish than the man who has achieved the difficult attainment of a human body but still neglects his true good?"

Wasn't this the root source of all our problems, Mother, this seemingly willful disregard of our spiritual being in favor of the mad worship of the ego that makes beggars of us all? She felt disheartened sometimes to see how securely ignorance ruled the world, how everyone had to pay the price for it, the enlightened as well as the benighted. The enlightened even more so, since they were aware of what a paradise the earth would be if only its people would remove the dark veil that clouded their eyes and realize that they were all one family moving toward a single destination. A familiar sadness revisited her as she sat gazing past her book into the shadow-hidden destiny of the human race, sadness for the loss of what could be. It was not a personal sadness. She had the Mother's company to sustain her, her beloved guru who lived in her mind, answering her thoughts, guiding her footsteps even while she slept. She had drunk from the founts of spiritual ecstasy and knew that every day of living brought her one day closer to the heart of the Divine, where she was destined to lay her ego to rest for eternity. The earth she walked was already nestled in the shadows of paradise. But what of the rest of humanity who labored under a different shadow, the crushing, oppressive shadow of self-interest, greed, exploitation, and ignorance? This was the greater sadness that followed her as she walked. And all of it so appallingly unnecessary, no matter what her philosophy told her. There was simply no excuse, no justification, for the tragedies that human beings inflicted upon each other, no matter how intricately woven the chain of cause and effect, no matter how surgically precise its cut.

She thought back to when this sadness had first forced itself upon her conscious awareness. It had been the second of the two great shocks that confronted her when she left the protective surroundings of her village—little more than a girl who had convinced herself she was a woman—for the gaping maw of Delhi and its twelve million half-digested souls. The first had been her sudden intrusion into the upper-class society of her college and the subsequent discovery that she was little more to her classmates than an unwashed, uncultured, inconsequential peasant who had lucked into her admission through the dubious means of an academic scholarship. The second was the discovery that her unwelcome existence in her hostel was a world of privilege unto itself when compared to the vast urban underclass that she had never before encountered in the flesh. Choked by her alien's loneliness—a feeling that was virtually nonexistent in her village, where everyone felt at home inside of everyone else's house—she ran for refuge to Swami Vivekananda's writings and the Mother's exhortations to serve the suffering, volunteering to work in a school for tribal girls in a slum area on the outskirts of Delhi, seven kilometers and two crowded buses from her hostel—seven kilometers that felt more like seventy, so drastic was the shift from one world to the other. The conditions were shocking. A warren of ramshackle huts and garbage-infested gutters surrounded the dilapidated concrete mausoleum that served as both a schoolhouse and a hostel for the nearly one hundred girls who would have still been begging in the streets had they not been rescued by the idealistic nun who had started the home. The neglect and humiliation that these destitute, low-caste girls had to face on a daily basis, some of it from their own community who could not see why girls should be educated at all, left her so emotionally exhausted at times that her tears seemed superfluous, if not egregious. The sheltered ignorance of her own childhood began to seem shameful to her, but that was nothing compared to the incongruity of her student life. The frivolity and petty melodramas of her classmates contrasted so violently with the tragic earnestness of these young girls that every time she stepped on campus she could feel the outrage stalking her like a pair of pitiless panther eyes, reminding her constantly of those sober-eyed girls who had learned at a desperately young age the menace that life could be and had still dared to be tortured by hope, a hope that only their remaining innocence could sustain. The only solace she found from her calamitous emotions was in her meditation and in the two visits the Mother paid to the capital during her student years. Both times she had a chance to cry openly in the Mother's presence and feel the soothing touch of her wrinkled hand on her brow. She had grown worried that she was becoming emotionally unstable, losing her bearings in a world where everyone else seemed to be growing saner the more she lost her way. Why was she so deeply affected when nearly everyone else her age seemed oblivious to the contradictions, untroubled by the weight of such persistent injustices? Until the Mother explained to her that it was simply an outpouring of compassion that had broken loose once the conditions holding it back had been removed. "Once awoken," the Mother counseled her, "compassion is more powerful than an unbridled river; it will take time to learn how to harness it. For a while, you will have to suffer through rough waters. But don't lose heart; the waters will settle. This is simply your destiny shaking off the effects of its long sleep. The compassion has been there all along, but it is your meditation and the unfolding of your samskara that has finally set it free." She had never forgotten the Mother's final words to her on the second of her two visits: "When you discover your heart beating in the breast of every living creature you see, then you will understand why the devotee's sorrow is as deep as their bliss and just as worthy."

The Mother had been right, as she always was. Saraswati had learned to harness it, though it had taken her more years than she had expected and far more pain than she could have ever imagined at that young age. The unbridled river had eventually become a steady current, the greater part of it carefully concealed. The raging feelings had been tempered by time and experience, fired into an enduring resolve that had still not found the outlet she required to satisfy its calm but insistent demands. The ambit of her awareness had continued to expand as more and more of the iniquities of life were revealed to her increasingly observant eyes, but never again would the poignant confusion be as great as it had been during those difficult months when she first opened her heart to the tragedy of life and allowed it to overwhelm her.

Saraswati reluctantly pulled her mind back to the *Crest Jewel of Discrimination* and forced herself to concentrate on the next verse. "People may quote the scriptures, make sacrifices to the gods, perform actions and pay homage to the deities, but there is no liberation without recognizing the oneness of one's own true being—not even in the lifetimes of a hundred Brahmas." Yes, Mother, she must never forget. It was not enough to recognize the tragedies and the injustice. It was not even enough to fight against them. There was no escape from suffering until one opened one's eyes to the Divine Spirit from which all things arise. Not as a single human being, not as a culture fighting to lift itself from the quagmire of poverty and corruption. That was why she was here, why her guru had sent her. There was no way out of the darkness until it could be illumined by a spiritual consciousness, and she would have to do her part to light those lamps. At least there were some lights aglow on the horizon, the most unlikely of people sometimes, people like Rodrigo who were waking out of the dream of material ignorance. Her hopes for the future lay in people like him. Whenever she chafed at the exile that the Mother had imposed on her, she tried to remember that even if she were not, for the time being, on the front lines, she was helping to train people who would be. It was a responsibility worthy of the vow she had taken. She could not and would not let the Mother down.

Saraswati's reverie was interrupted by the sound of footsteps coming up the stairs. She closed her book and stood up to welcome Rodrigo, once again feeling the unaccounted-for nervous tension that his presence seemed to inspire in her. At least it seemed to be gradually disappearing. She was thankful for that. Hopefully a couple of face-to-face conversations would be all it would take to banish it forever.

The first thing she did after he had taken his seat was to ask him how his meditation was progressing, having been reminded once again, as the Mother reminded her each and every day, that it was the one thing that most mattered, the one sure means to channel into this world the light that would heal it of its sorrows.

"It's a struggle, to be perfectly honest," Rodrigo replied. "It's by far the most difficult thing I've ever attempted, but I'm keeping at it, morning and evening without fail, sometimes at night also before I go to bed. I can't claim that I've developed much concentration, but at least my stamina is increasing. In the beginning, it was hard for me to sit for even five minutes. I couldn't keep my mind or my body still at all. Now I'm sitting for at least forty-five minutes and sometimes as long as an hour."

Saraswati was gratified to hear this, but it did not surprise her. She could see the meditative discipline in the way he carried himself, so different from the unsettled and troubled aura that had hung over him when he had joined her class a few months earlier. There was a quiet surety in him now that she could see growing, almost by the minute. The intellectual arrogance she had once detected behind his careful speech had since been swallowed up by an insatiable thirst for spiritual knowledge that reminded her of her teenage years when she had first met the Mother and seen the glories of the spirit reflected in a human countenance. Though her instinct and her experience assured her that he was in no need of advice concerning his meditation—his own internal voice would show him the way far more deftly than she ever could—she offered a few words of caution, just to emphasize what he would surely discover without any help from her. She nodded slowly as she spoke, remembering her own difficulties in years past—and those that still remained.

"Of course, it is true. There is no more difficult endeavor than trying to tame the mind. Fortunately, what is really important in the initial stages is not so much the concentration we achieve, but how sincerely and how hard we work to achieve it. It is the effort we put into our meditation that ultimately clears the debris from our mind. Deep concentration is the fruit of long, painstaking internal work, and there are no shortcuts. I see a lot of beginners come through here, and unfortunately most of them seem more interested in accumulating experiences and seeing lights and visions than in discovering the self. When they realize how hard it really is, most of them give up. They want something for nothing, like almost everyone else in this society, but you can't achieve self-knowledge without paying the price in hard work and sacrifice. The spiritual path is for the brave at heart, and I don't see many with that kind of courage. But I don't blame them. Sometimes I wonder how anyone can keep their meditation going in this world we live in."

Saraswati allowed her voice to trail off into an audible sigh that reflected the lingering sadness that edged the corners of her mind.

"Well, that's certainly true for me," Rodrigo said. "But surely you are beyond all that?"

Saraswati stifled a laugh. "I'm not sure I know exactly what you mean by 'all that,' but whatever 'all that' is, I am certainly not beyond it. In some ways, I think it actually gets more difficult the further along you go, especially once you can no longer absolve yourself with the excuse of ignorance."

A pensive look appeared on Rodrigo's face. "I guess what I mean is that sometimes I feel like my mind is such a mess, and then I look at you and you are so calm and so centered. I can only imagine what that's like. No matter how much I meditate, I still can't seem to put my attachments behind me. Sometimes it doesn't seem to matter what it is. It can even be the weather. There's always something to knock me off balance and disturb whatever little peace I can manage. Then I come to class and it doesn't seem like even a hurricane could blow you off center."

Saraswati paused before she answered, looking off at the mountains turning various shades of gold and auburn as they fell under the influence of the descending sun. "Sometimes, the problem with making some progress on the spiritual path is that the Lord just whips up a bigger hurricane for you once he realizes that the little ones are not having the desired effect."

"I'm not quite sure I understand what you mean. I can't imagine you ever getting angry, for instance."

Saraswati smiled. "Oh, I get angry, believe me."

"Really?"

"No need to be surprised. I'm not past that yet. It's different than it used to be, though. It's not so personal anymore. It's not so much about me as about what I see happening in the world around me. That's what meditation does. It loosens the bonds of the ego. Instead of being so self-centered, as we all are when we start off, Krishna becomes the center. The Lord and his creation."

"But then what is there to be angry about?"

Saraswati felt something stiffen inside her, the old indignation that no longer flared up in hot, uncontrolled gusts but now burned steadily like an oil-fed flame. She turned her head slightly and looked him directly in the eye. "Injustice, poverty, exploitation. The thousand iniquities that are all around us, whether we see them or not. The more your meditation deepens, the more you feel everything around you as part of your inner self. You start coming in contact with an ever-present ocean of peace and bliss, and it is everything the sages say it is and more, but there is also an ever-present ocean of sorrow in the minds of living beings, and I, for one, sometimes find it very difficult to separate the two." She leaned back in her chair and turned her gaze once more toward the mountains. "Do you know much about the situation of women in my country?"

"Not really. I've read a little but I don't have any firsthand knowledge."

"When a woman gets married in my country, the common blessing is 'may you be the mother of a hundred sons.' The blessing leaves out what everyone knows: no one wants a daughter. If a girl manages to escape female infanticide or selective abortion, both still very prevalent in India, then what she has to look forward to is a lifetime of discrimination, especially if she lives in a village like two-thirds of our people do. She can look forward to being poorly educated—if she goes to school at all—and to being sent out to work in the fields or as a servant in somebody's house at an age when girls in other countries are still playing with dolls. She'll grow up malnourished while her brothers are given the lion's share of the food—eighty percent of females in this state suffer from anemia, and in places like Bengal it's worse. When she grows up—or more likely, before she grows up—she'll be married off as soon as the family can find someone willing to take her. That is, provided they can raise the dowry. If they can't, then she'll probably become a spinster and then she will be lucky if she doesn't starve. Or if the dowry is too small, she runs the risk of dying in a kitchen fire or another kind of dowry-related death. If she is fortunate, and the dowry is sufficient, she can look forward to working twice the hours that her husband does with no independent income, and in many cases she will be beaten for her troubles. India has the highest rate of domestic violence in the world and no one dares speak out about it, especially women, because they know what will happen to them if they do. And what do our beloved scriptures say about this? I quote: 'In childhood a female must be subject to her father, in youth to her husband, when her lord is dead to her sons; a woman must never be independent.' The *Manu Samhita*, our Hindu social code. And god forbid her husband dies before she does and leaves her a widow. Then it only gets worse. There is a blessing in the Hindu tradition: 'may you die before your husband.' Have you heard it?"

Rodrigo shook his head.

"Most people assume that it refers to the great love Indian women have for their husbands, that they couldn't bear to go on living without them. Actually the blessing is to save them from a fate worse than death: that of being a widow in this society, shut away and looked upon like a pariah until you mercifully breathe your final breath."

"Is it still that bad? I saw a movie about that, just recently, but I thought things had changed."

"Things are changing, at least in the urban areas—or rather, in the well-to-do sections of those urban areas—but slowly, much too slowly. I grew up in a village, though I was lucky enough to be an only child. Sometimes I get the feeling that we might as well turn back the calendar a thousand years for all the good the new laws have done us once you get outside the bigger cities. Old prejudices die hard anywhere but especially in an Indian village. We are very traditional in our villages, very resistant to change; it's hard to overcome thousands of years of tradition with a few pamphlets from Delhi and a couple of high-sounding speeches on the floor of parliament."

Saraswati could hear the calm, dispassionate tone in her voice, the product of many thousands of hours of meditation and the expansive understanding of life's complexities that the ancient scriptures had given her, but the smoldering remains of her youthful outrage were still there, reminding her not only of where she had been but also of where she was going.

"Of course, the exploitation of women in my country is only one of a thousand social injustices. I only use it as an example, one I am quite familiar with, but I don't mean to imply that it is any greater or more important than any other. I could just as well talk about the malicious poverty my people have to endure or the endemic corruption in government and business that perpetuates their poverty. My point is that as the ego diminishes and the heart opens, you start to feel other people's suffering as your own, and the desire awakens to do whatever you can to remove that suffering. It's a natural part of spiritual growth. But sometimes it seems we are powerless to do anything. That's where my anger comes from. It's not just the indignation that people should have to suffer but this seeming inability to do anything about it. All is in the Lord's hands, of course. It is his play, and the highest realization is to surrender completely, but it is only natural to want to be the instrument of his desire and see it coincide with your own—which, after all, he has planted in your breast. Anyhow, we should get to your questions. We are supposed to be talking about the Upanishads."

Saraswati's unguarded venting caught her by surprise. She had been expecting a lively but equable discussion on esoteric matters with an intelligent and intriguing student, but there was something about Rodrigo, something she couldn't place her finger on, that made her feel almost impelled to give free reign to some of the passionate feelings she ordinarily kept such a close watch on, knowing with a visceral, instinctive certainty that they would have been misconstrued by her fellow ashram dwellers. It was not that he inspired her confidence, though she did feel sure that whatever she told him would remain between the two of them, despite this being their first private conversation of any import; rather, there was something about him that set her on edge, like a piece of flint that rubbed her just enough to set the fires within her burning. He was not discourteous or egotistical or spiritually unrefined—indeed, in the nearly three months she had known him, he had come so far that she had to completely revise her initial impression of him. There was simply something in his aura that impinged upon her own and catapulted her almost immediately into a state of heightened alertness whose antecedent she could not discover. Perhaps it was only a growing sense of the strong spiritual samskaras he so obviously possessed. There was something almost frightening as well as exhilarating to see someone open so fast and so hungrily to the desire for spiritual knowledge that lies sleeping inside us all. She knew as well as anyone the dangers associated with any rapid ascent, and the mere fact that he was her student, resolutely and adamantly her student, meant that her samskaras were in some way entwined with his, though to what extent she could not devise, a fact that made her feel vaguely uneasy. The winding dance of samskara, when it wraps itself around another's separately slithering thread, invariably becomes fraught with pitfalls, a happening so commonplace that it makes it seem as if danger and desire are the twin themes of the dance. At least it had always appeared that way to her inward eye, ever since she had made up her mind in her last year of college that she would follow in Nivedita's footsteps and channel all her passion into a spiritual struggle against injustice, a decision that she felt confident would save her from the quagmire of personal desire that seemed to swallow up nearly everyone around her. But she had learned the hard way that samskara was not something she could run away from. Or rather, she had learned that whenever she did run, it had a way of biting her in the back with redoubled force, as if it considered it a personal affront whenever anybody tried to deny its existence. Samskara was a creature best tamed head on; this was the reason she had made what was for her the unusual gesture of inviting Rodrigo to her rooftop sanctuary to help him with his studies.

The passage they turned to in the *Isopanishad* made Saraswati smile with a sense of cosmically choreographed irony. It had everything to do with her initial venting, and since she had no idea that he would bring up this passage for discussion, she considered it a humorous shake of the Mother's finger, advising her that she should press on with her concerns, that now was the divinely appointed hour to bring them to this young man's ears. In college it had been her favorite passage from the Upanishads, one she would chant under her breath for solace whenever she saw how self-centered many of her fellow spiritual seekers could be: *Andham tamah pravisanti ye'vidyamupasate/tato bhuya iva te tamo ya u vidyayam ratah.* "Into deep darkness fall those who worship the immanent; into even deeper darkness fall those who follow the transcendent." It was a verse that had often been misunderstood, plagued by faulty translations and even faultier thinking. For her, it had always seemed simple and straight to the point. Those who concentrated only on spirituality and neglected the material world would be felled one day by their willful neglect. For willful it was. A materialist knew no better, though they were sure to suffer for their ignorance as the first half of the couplet implied. But when a spiritualist with an awakened consciousness neglected the material world and the responsibilities that went hand in hand with incarnate life, then that neglect was not a product of ignorance, easily excused and pitied, but a willful abdication of responsibility, the consequences of which were far graver. To her surprise, it took only a few words from her for Rodrigo to see where she was going.

"So in other words, the more you become aware of your material responsibilities, and that includes alleviating the suffering of others to the extent that you are able, the stronger the samskara you create if you fail to live up to those responsibilities."

"Exactly. In order to do meditation you require a human body. The fact that you have a human body and live on a physical planet implies a debt to society and to the environment. Without parents to nurture you, you would not survive a week. Without the food the farmers grow and the merchants who bring it to market, you would starve to death. Those same farmers depend on the implements the craftsmen make. Every day of our existence we depend upon the society that nurtures us, however little we realize it, and that society depends on the water, light, soil, and air that the earth provides. All of this presupposes a debt, a debt that can never be fully repaid as long as we have a human body. You can make an excuse for someone who lives their life in complete ignorance, if they fail to honor that debt. But for a yogi to do that? Someone who is aware of what she owes, who is aware of the rampant injustice that is a result of two-legged ignorance walking the earth? Well, that is inexcusable. There is a cosmic law to take care of such a willful refusal of one's duty. The higher you climb in awareness, the greater the consequences of your actions, just as the higher you climb on a ladder, the greater the consequences if you fall. If a materialist blinded by ignorance fails to help an old blind woman cross the street, she will create a negative samskara for herself, to be sure, but it won't be that grave. If a spiritually elevated person does it, she may be born as a blind monkey in her next life."

Saraswati joined Rodrigo in his laughter, but for her the exaggeration was meant in all seriousness. She had felt this backlash from the cosmic arbiter in her own life, and she wished to spare anyone who was willing to listen from having to suffer the same lesson. Rodrigo, she could see, was a willing listener, but more significantly, he seemed to have an intuitive grasp of subtle spiritual ideas, and indeed a general intuitive understanding, that eclipsed that of people who had been meditating far longer. The dream or dreams that had obviously rocked his sense of self, and which he had been so reluctant to reveal, were a clear indication that his was no ordinary spiritual samskara. He was not a dabbler who would go home happy with a little peace of mind and the security of knowing that goodness resided in his heart. She was convinced that, like her, he would not remain satisfied until he had gained access to the furnace that rumbled inside him and liberated its light and its warmth to illumine his interior world. She would have dearly loved to ask him about his dreams. If he had been visited by a supramental dream, it might go a long way toward confirming what she suspected about him. Might not the infinite unconscious mind be churning its hidden waters inside him and liberating in carefully regulated doses the knowledge that he had gained in previous lives, lives perhaps spent meditating among these same Himalayan slopes? Could it be adding long-buried memories to the fanciful mix of his imagination, stirring him to find his path once again and finish what he could not the previous time through? When they ended their study session and she told him that they could continue one or two afternoons a week, if he liked, as she found time, she did it knowing that much of this would come clear to her eventually. That thought by itself was enough to send a slight chill through her body that had nothing to do with the crisp November air.

22

RODRIGO WAS NOW SPENDING most of his time immersed in his spiritual practices and his study of Indian philosophy, apart from the few hours he devoted each afternoon to his book. With each passing class, his admiration for Saraswati grew. She no longer seemed cold to him but rather indecipherably remote, wrapped in thoughts whose airy depths separated her from the mass of common humanity. She was a paragon in his eyes, but her virtue lay beyond her, in the spaces to which her mind traveled, the same spaces where he hoped to one day accompany her. But to have any chance at all, he had to study and he had to meditate, and so these two activities became the focus of the day that rose with the sun to greet him. It had been several weeks now since he had revisited his Bengali temple. The absence didn't bother him, however, no matter how much he looked forward to that next dream and the heightened sense of the interior life that invariably accompanied it. Despite the long hiatus, he felt confident that he was not done dreaming this alternate reality, so confident that he took it as a test of patience, a willingness to wait for the familiar heavy breathing of samskara after a necessary lull in the winds. Nor did he attach overmuch importance to the plodding steps of his narrative, now that his anxiety over the prospects of becoming a great writer had subsided into a simple recognition of his limitations. What interested him most now was the steady progress he seemed to be making into the labyrinths of his subconscious and unconscious minds, and the way the ancient Indian sages reached out through their cryptic language and forced him into an interior seeing that would not have been possible a few scant months before. Saraswati was the compass that kept him on course, but increasingly he found himself conversing directly with yogic masters long dead as he made his way down the pathways of his mind; for every question, there seemed to be a reply waiting for him from out of a mouth long since silenced by the relentless passage of time, though he could not always understand their answers and often brought them to his teacher, who sometimes expressed surprise at the unexpected twists his inquiring mind took.

A couple of days after their first private session, Rodrigo awoke to find himself returning from a land and a consciousness that were as much his own as the ones he abdicated each night when he fell asleep. This time the surfacing from one reality to another was filled with a heady sense of anticipation, as if he had drained an effervescent alcoholic brew that lightened his awareness of the present moment enough to send him floating toward the horizon and a bevy of alluring shapes that held in their insubstantial forms the promise of his imagined future. It was not yet dawn, but the glorious sense of homecoming he felt seemed to illumine the room even more than the bluish glow from his laptop screen as he sat up and began to record the details of his dream.

Rishikesh
12/1
4.10 AM

At last, a belated return to the bowers of Bengal. I was wondering when my dreamed self would show his face again—though I never actually see his face, this alternate version of my own. Who knows, perhaps if I can one day look upon his face in a mirror, then I will discover the secret of these dreams. But as to the details, this is the dream as I remember it:

I am sitting in the courtyard on one of the stone benches placed there at intervals between the bowers and the walkways. It is a secluded place, to the rear of the main temple, a place where I often come to imbibe the solitude and go for pensive walks where no one will disturb me. This time I have much to think about. The debate is approaching faster than I care to admit and I do not feel ready. I have heard of the priest they are sending. I know of his reputation; it is the kind of reputation I would like to have one day but can only earn by going through ordeals like this and proving my worth in front of discerning eyes. Troubled by my thoughts, I sense a presence. I become aware of a perfume in the air, an earthy human fragrance mixed with the pungent odors of mustard oil and sesame. I know this scent. The first flare of it in my nostrils pierces my heart. I turn and there she is, the water girl in her threadbare sari, her shoulders bared by the rolled-back sleeves of her bodice, her long black hair tied into a single luxuriant braid that falls to the small of her back. Only a second passes before we speak, but in that second I notice everything about her, details that I feel like I am seeing for the first time and which I am afraid I will never be able to banish from my mind: the proud arc of her forehead and the two small beads of sweat that hover there, glistening in the late afternoon sun that filters through the overhanging leaves of a mimosa tree; her strong, calloused feet, supported by two firm arches like twin bridges straddling the Ganges, each crowned by a trio of golden ankle bells that seem to laugh at the way they were able to creep up on me so silently; the single hand balancing an empty earthen jar on her hip—a defiant, supple hand, a looming, boisterous hip; and last and most of all, two incandescent obsidian eyes that pin me to their gaze.

When she speaks, the spell is not broken but only prolonged. She tells me that she has heard of the debate. She knows this priest; she has attended several of his debates in the past. She is sure of what he will say and how I can defeat him. She sits down on the edge of the bench, not so near as to violate temple decorum but not so far that I cannot feel her fragrance enveloping me like an unseen mist, or sense the warmth of her body just before it dissipates into the leafy atmosphere. With a clear and simple logic, she starts to outline his favorite theses, the ones he has spent a lifetime honing and inevitably introduces into any debate. She tells me how she has rebutted them in the privacy of her mind; this sparks a dialogue between us so rich it feels like it must be criminal. It reminds me that I am talking to a Chamar from whose hand I cannot accept so much as a glass of water without being defiled. The threat of someone observing us hangs over me, not because there is anything in the scriptures that prevents a priest from talking to such a woman at a distance of more than a meter but simply because it will plant a doubt in their minds, and doubts have a way of transforming themselves into rumors that can then rage out of control like any untamed fire. But the richness of our conversation, the thrill it gives me to see the brilliance of her arguments, a brilliance that easily rivals my own, the undisguised warmth of her youthful, redolent body barely contained by the worn cotton of her sari—all these things keep me from giving in to my misgivings. The conversation continues as if time were suspended, until the mist swirls and the dream begins to lose substance. As it does, an old ache returns with redoubled force, the blinding certainty that I have discovered a kindred soul imprisoned in a body that precludes us from ever having any reasonable human concourse. But this cannot stay my excitement. With this dark angel's help I will win this debate; my rise to the reputation and the position I deserve will be all but assured. The dream winks out, my waking consciousness returns (reluctantly, more reluctantly than ever before), but the euphoria, the anticipation, and the ache remain.

Now that the dream is recorded, I must bathe and go to the main hall for meditation. But first some final, rapid reflections:

I have no doubt that through these dreams my unconscious is driving me onward. But to where and to what end? The story continues to unfold, its internal logic is slightly more exposed, but I fumble when I try to explain it to myself. The easy explanation points toward my private tutorial with Saraswati. She is teaching me, guiding me, and thus her reflection appears in my dream as this prescient water woman who leads me down philosophical pathways that I would not have found without her help. But there is more here than meets the dreamer's eye. These dreams have an internal logic of their own that seems more and more independent of my waking life the more I am exposed to them. My dreamed self is locked into a quest for spiritual knowledge. It is the same quest that my waking self is engaged in, only my dreamed self is much further along than its waking counterpart. For this reason, it may be that he can give me the guidance I need, the backward look down the road I am now traveling, and through that glance communicate the knowledge I will need to navigate its pitfalls. In my dream, my thirst for knowledge is mixed with an ambition (dare I call it unholy?) for fame and position and the power that goes with them. It is no secret that these are obstacles one must face in any walk of life if one has set one's eyes on success. Why should it be any different in spiritual life? I do not feel the attraction of these things now, perhaps because I am a novice and only a few steps removed from the emotional gutter, but it would be foolish to assume that I will not have to face them one day. It seems that my unconscious mind in the guise of my fictive hero is warning me to be ready, to be alert, to marshal my strength for a battle that is surely coming. And then there is this unpriestly attraction for the girl out of whose mouth this knowledge has come. Have I not already been laid low by my inability to relate in a healthy way to the opposite sex and to my own romantic and sexual desires? Should I not assume that I will be put to this test again and again until I learn that lesson? Or is that test already on my doorstep? When I first met Saraswati, I did not think that she was a woman I could ever be attracted to. She was too plain looking, too cold, too remote, too unapproachable, too much a product of her culture and her philosophy. Now I am not quite so sure. Though I do not feel any kind of romantic or physical attraction, I must admit that I find her fascinating. I have never met a woman with a mind so agile and so profound; moreover, if our private session is any indication, there is much more passion in her than meets the eye—or rather, than she allows to meet the eye. If this dream is truly my unconscious's way of leading me down the path toward self-knowledge, then an earthly attraction may be looming. I had best be ready for that battle. I can already see the clouds gathering in the sky above the temple grounds. Does this mean they will soon appear in the sky above Rishikesh? And will I be ready if they do?

Throughout the month of November, Rodrigo had continued to work his way slowly through his narrative. It had taken longer than he had hoped to lead Le Gentil to his first meeting with an Indian sage, for the simple reason that he was not doing the leading. Ambika had a mind of her own, fully formed out of the indecipherable interplay between his conscious, subconscious, and unconscious minds, and she refused to take Le Gentil there until she had determined he was ready. In the meantime, she peppered him with short verbal fusillades that tested his understanding of spiritual doctrine, both Christian and Hindu, subjects in which she was nearly as well versed as he was in astronomy. Her intention was not only to prepare him for his meeting with the sage, as she had alluded to earlier, but to stretch his mind to the point where he would be able to see her culture from an entirely different vantage point, one that would not only lead him to appreciate its depths but would throw a new light on his own life and his own culture. As they oversaw the construction of the observatory, rising slowly from the ruins of Monsieur Dupleix's mansion like a sleepy-eyed phoenix yawning itself awake amid the ashes of a former life, or leisurely explored the surrounding areas in the Governor-General's carriage, she never allowed their conversations to stray too far down the pathways of astronomy or anthropology or natural science before she forced them to intersect once again with the unique understanding of the human mind and the human spirit that was the Koh-i-Noor in the crown of Indian civilization.

Though Le Gentil was astute enough to realize that he was becoming a cleverly disguised reclamation project, their discussions were lively and thought provoking enough that he didn't mind. In many ways, these discussions took him back to his youth as a young clergyman, before he had fallen under the spell of Professor Delisle and exchanged his studies of the heavens for those of the night sky.

It had been a time of great debate in French ecclesiastical society, especially among the younger, more curious members of the Church who passed banned or frowned-upon manuscripts among themselves as if they were magic elixirs to be handled with extreme caution. Madame de Guyon's *A Short and Easy Method of Prayer*, Archbishop François Fénelon's *Treatise on the Existence of God* and *Maxims of the Saints of the Interior Life*, Cornelius Jansen's *Augustinus*. Though both the Roman Catholic Church and the French Monarchy had condemned the Quietist and Jansenist movements, their mysticism-flavored brands of Catholicism still counted many followers among the French populace. Le Gentil had a firsthand experience of that popular fervor as a child when his father took him and his mother, then gravely ill, to the grave of Abbé François de Paris in the parish cemetery of St. Medard in Paris. In the five years following the abbé's death, stories had been filtering back to Coutances of the miraculous cures experienced by penitents visiting the saint's tomb: cancerous tumors, blindness, paralysis, arthritis, deafness—all banished by an unseen hand. Hundreds of such cases had been reported, all supposedly verified by numerous witnesses and attributed to the abbé's saintly powers. When they arrived at the cemetery, they found a crowd of more than one thousand people gathered there—a crowd, they were told, that remained there day and night, all year long, as the devout sojourned from all over France to partake of the healing vibrations—and the less devout, simply to see the show. For a show it was. The seven-year-old Guillaume did not know what to make of the hundreds of men, women, and children whom he saw twisting and writhing on the ground in front of the tomb like circus contortionists temporarily deprived of their wits. The local people called them *convulsionaires*. They were said to be immune from physical pain or injury, and the more devout among them had been seen levitating in broad daylight, reading minds, and performing other feats of spontaneous clairvoyance. The family remained there for several days but his mother did not recover. When she died shortly afterward, he felt a backlash of anger at the claims of the Jansenists, who he had believed would bring his mother back from the threshold of death, but he never forgot that scene. His anger had since matured into a scientifically supported skepticism, but in the back of his mind he had never been able to undo the doubt: How could something that thousands of people had claimed to have witnessed over and over again be entirely without fundament?

It was during his youthful discussions with his fellow novitiates that he began reading David Hume, who had written *A Treatise on Human Nature* in Anjou only a few years earlier. Hume so impressed him that he went on to read everything he had written. Along the way he came across a passage in his *Philosophical Essays* that reinforced those doubts: "There surely never was so great a number of miracles ascribed to one person as those which were lately said to have been wrought in France upon the tomb of Abbé Paris. Many of the miracles were immediately proved upon the spot, before judges of unquestioned credit and distinction, in a learned age, and in the most eminent theatre that is now in the world." If the champion of empiricism could keep such an open mind when faced with phenomenon that the sciences could not explain, then he had best do the same. Years had gone by since he had thought about such matters, but now he was once again reminded of Hume's words and the importance of keeping an open mind.

The doors and windows of the observatory were in the process of being installed when Ambika informed him that she had arranged a meeting with the sage for the following Saturday, the day after he was scheduled to vacate his temporary dwelling in Ville Blanche and make the observatory his permanent home. Five days later, on a misty early morning in late July, after celebrating his first successful night in his new dwellings—as close in appearance to a French country manor as he could hope for in this foreign land—he wrapped a light cotton shawl around his shoulders, his only concession to native fashion, and ducked into his carriage where his young assistant was waiting for him with a thermos of steaming jasmine tea. This unexpected offering helped to revive his sedentary spirits, still groggy from the early hour and the thwarted desire to spend his first morning in his new quarters reclining in a chair with his favorite books. He sipped his tea silently as the carriage rumbled off into the darkness and listened to Ambika school him on protocol for the upcoming interview with the sage, who, he was happy to hear, was proficient in English, thus obviating the need for his translator's intermediation. "You must not interpret this as a license to interrupt the swami," she added. "It is considered an insult to interrupt a holy man when he is speaking. You must remember that the swami is doing you a great favor by granting you a private audience—a great honor, in fact. In my country, sages do not bow at the feet of kings; kings bow at the feet of sages."

The carriage journey lasted more than two hours, winding upward into the forested hills northwest of the city, until they came to a narrow path that had to be navigated on foot. The final ascent reminded Le Gentil of Greece: both the ascent of Mount Parnassus in ancient times to query the Delphic oracle and the tales of hidden monasteries in the southern mountains where modern-day Christian monks were reputed to carry on that same tradition under the blessings of the orthodox church. The ascending trail paralleled the musical waters of a mountain stream until it opened into a wide, grassy knoll. Several airy wooden buildings were huddled together at the center of the clearing; these were surrounded by well-tended gardens and thick groves of banana and papaya.

A pair of bare-chested acolytes who were tending the gardens led them to the back veranda of one of the buildings where the swami was waiting for them. He was reclining on a wooden cot, his dark body naked except for a thin white dhoti drawn up to his knees, a necklace of fine corrugated rudraksha beads, and a thick shock of graying hair that fell to his shoulders. Beside him, a wooden table was laden with baskets of fruits and nuts and a pot of yoghurt. Ambika had told him that the swami was around eighty years of age, but if that were so, then he was extraordinarily well preserved. Left to his own judgment, Le Gentil would have guessed that he was still in his fifties. The vigor he exuded and the luster of his nearly unwrinkled skin bespoke a radiant health that could not be explained by the pure mountain air and the traditional vegetarian diet. That, by itself, was a testament to the healing graces of yoga that Ambika had mentioned, as Hume would have recognized had he seen it with his own eyes.

The swami greeted Ambika with some words in Tamil and a broad smile and then switched to English; the warmth in his voice suggested that he was greeting an old and trusted friend. "Will you eat now or do you first wish to take a bath?" There was no introduction, no formalities, just a large welcome and the swami's singular affability that included Le Gentil within its ambit. He had a feeling that it would have included anyone who appeared, regardless of whether the swami had known them for a few seconds or a lifetime.

While they breakfasted, the swami maintained a steady flow of light conversation, asking Ambika for news about the various members of her family and quizzing Le Gentil about France, his travels, and his impressions of South India. Le Gentil was impressed by his fluency and his lively interest in what were essentially mundane topics. There was a humorous, vibrant gleam in his eye that never dimmed, as if all that he heard both amused him and incited his curiosity. Le Gentil was not quite sure what he had expected, but it was not this. The youthful but aged sage seemed as if he would have been at home in any company and with any topic. He seemed anything but the reclusive hermit one might have imagined.

Once the attendant had cleared away the meal, the swami abruptly changed the topic of conversation.

"Ambika has told me that you have shown some interest in the *brahma vijnana*, the intuitional science as taught by our ancient sages."

"I have. She has been teaching me some of your philosophy these past weeks. What little I've learned, I've found fascinating. Metaphysics and philosophy seem to be favorite pastimes in your culture."

"Spirituality has been the focus of Indian culture for thousands of years. Philosophy has its place in spiritual life, but the *brahma vijnana* is first and foremost a practical science, the science of self-realization or God realization. You are a scientist. You must understand the difference between theory and practice. Theory must follow the observation of fact for it to have any lasting validity. Spiritual science is no different. You perform your experiments in the laboratory of your body, mind, and spirit until you are able to perceive the truth behind their existence and their relationship to one another. Then, if you wish, you can describe those experiments so that others may replicate your results in their own laboratories. Otherwise, theories have a way of being disproved or superseded. Did your Western astronomers not at one time theorize that the world was flat?"

"They did," Le Gentil answered, rising to the occasion. "But there are facts that are beyond our powers of observation. In order to determine the truth, we have no alternative but to apply our intellect and our powers of deduction and inference."

"That may be true to some extent in the world of physicality, although even there, there is ample scope for debate; however, in the interior world, the world of human consciousness, there is nothing that is beyond our powers of observation."

The swami began tracing for him in philosophical language the journey that the meditating mind takes until it comes in contact with the Divine Spirit, which otherwise remains hidden behind the vagaries of thought. The lucidity of his explanation at once startled and captivated him. Never before had he heard spiritual realities described in a way that maintained perfect consonance with scientific logic and observable perceptions, albeit perceptions that were difficult for him to grasp. Within minutes, he felt his initial resistance and habitual skepticism falling away, swept aside by the swami's unassuming, friendly manner and his astute and articulate observations. The simplicity of his dress and his surroundings began to take on the feel of a curtain whose sole purpose was to hide this man from the eyes of the world, a curtain he had agreed to lift for a brief interlude. He spoke with a precision that Le Gentil had rarely encountered in anyone, and the flow of logic that ran behind his thoughts seemed as steady and as sure in its course as any of Europe's greatest rivers. In contrast to Ambika, he got the distinct impression that the swami was not trying to convince him of anything. He was simply using his words to give the astronomer a look into his mind. Much of what Le Gentil saw there was too subtle for him to apprehend, but that did not stop him from appreciating the beauty of the vistas he was being shown. He was glad for Ambika's coaching, without which he would have understood little, but it only took him a few minutes to realize that she had only given him the barest rudiments of the language the swami spoke.

Heedful of Ambika's admonishment not to interrupt the sage, Le Gentil waited for appropriate moments to ask his questions; on the strength of those questions, the conversation, such as it was, shifted direction into unseen territory like the waters of a river rounding a thickly wooded bend. Remembering his experience with the Jansenists, he asked the swami several questions about miraculous events and the supernatural faculties of the mind. The swami answered patiently, explaining the subtle mechanisms he deemed responsible for such phenomena, but he seemed to look upon such questions as nothing more than a child's curiosity. After each question, he turned the conversation back toward the pursuit of a spiritual truth that lay far beyond all such trifling manifestations, as if they were simply gaudy colors in a kaleidoscope whose only purpose was to distract the viewer from the far greater beauty of the natural landscape from which those colors were drawn. The conversation turned to religion, both the Hindu and the Christian. When Le Gentil expressed his reaction to the idol worship he had seen, the swami impressed upon him the necessity of having the tolerance to allow people to worship at the level of their native understanding, pointing out that idol worship was merely an early stage in the human being's relationship with the Divine, one that could be seen in the history of all cultures, and that each stage existed in order to prepare the mind for the following stage. All religious belief, the swami contended, regardless of culture, is little more than a child's conception of the world they think they cannot see, a conception that goes on expanding until one is able to relate directly with the Divine within oneself, an unmediated connection between self and soul, at which point all external considerations and differences fall away.

"It may be difficult for many religious people to hear, but there comes a time in the spiritual growth of any human being when he realizes that temples and churches are nothing more than stone and wood, and that many of our cherished religious beliefs are little more than figments of man's imagination. The only true temple is the human body and the world that nurtures that body. Look around you." The swami made an expansive gesture with his arms, as if he were reaching out to embrace the encircling forest with its canopy of bright blue sky. "Every time you open your eyes, you are gazing on the face of God. But before you can see his face in the creation, you must first learn to perceive his existence within yourself. Not believe. Perceive. The moment a human being realizes through direct experience that God dwells within the temple of the human body, he realizes that every expression in this universe is the image of God. At that moment his bondages vanish; he becomes free."

Le Gentil felt a shiver of recognition when the swami looked at him and told him that first he had to perceive his own soul before he could know the truth of incarnate life. Recognition of what, he could not say—a glimpse of the truth that lay behind the swami's words, it seemed, as if for a moment he had stood on a mountain and looked out at the ocean of space that at all other times remains veiled from sight. But he was unable to sustain such a vista. Soon the scientist in him again asserted itself. Unable to reconcile such heights of human thought with the seeming backwardness and impoverishment of the country that had attained them, he expressed his misgivings to the sage about the discord he had witnessed between material neglect and spiritual pursuit.

"Don't be fooled by the lack of wealth you see here," the swami told him, "or the lack of material progress. We Indians have never been much interested in such things. Our greatest souls understood long ago that the only lasting achievement is God realization. All other achievements are brought to naught by the pitiless hand of time. Our sages reached the heights of spiritual understanding, and they have passed that knowledge down to us over many millennia through an unbroken line of illuminated masters. But you are right in one respect: our single-minded dedication to spiritual truth has led to an imbalance in our society, and much unnecessary suffering has resulted from this imbalance. It is up to us to correct this, and we will. Ambika is one of those in whom we have high hopes in this regard. Though I have never been out of India, I know enough of European culture to respect the advances you have made in the material sciences and to also know that you suffer from an equal but opposite imbalance. You have a scientifically advanced but a spiritually benighted society. But this imbalance will also correct itself in time. The pendulum always swings back to the other side. Nature takes care of this. There will come a time, not so far off, when your society will suffer a backlash against this single-minded pursuit of material knowledge and the spiritual ignorance that inevitably results from it. A time will come when your young people will start coming to this country—not to plant tea and steal its gold, as they do now, but to sit at the feet of its sages. And our young people will go to your countries, but for very different reasons."

As the sun peaked in the sky and started edging its way toward early afternoon, Le Gentil began noticing within himself a buoyancy devoid of the usual restless, excited energy that possessed him whenever he became fascinated by his work or a stimulating conversation or Ambika's intoxicating presence. The more he listened to the swami, the quieter his mind grew. Soon he had no more questions. The sense of peace he felt began to draw his attention even more than their conversation. At some point, he became aware that what he was feeling did not have its center within him but seemed to be emanating from the aura of the sage sitting a scant meter away. One glance at Ambika was enough to see that she was in the same almost trance-like state, gazing up at the swami's beautifully chiseled face with a look of rapt attention that he otherwise might have mistaken for infatuation, had he not realized that he had the same look on his own face. He looked again at the swami and saw a look of serenity and fathomless comprehension that now seemed impossible to mistake, though it had taken him a couple of hours and a radically quieted mind to notice. Even the swami's body entered into the enchantment, emanating a fragrance that intoxicated his senses, though he was sure it was not any perfume but just the natural fragrance of his body. By the time the swami ended their session, the astronomer was hardly listening any longer to the sage's words. Rather, he was paying attention more to the silent space behind them. Even when the swami retired to his room for meditation and they were served lunch on the veranda, they ate in silence, both of them unwilling to return so quickly to the world of mundane considerations.

Le Gentil spent most of the return journey lost in his thoughts, replaying in his mind his conversation with the swami and turning again and again with wonder to the buoyant, peaceful feeling that had invaded him, even while he watched it slowly slip away as the rumbling, jolting gait of the carriage pulled him back toward the tempestuous climate of modern civilization. Some of his thoughts were directed toward Ambika, sitting silently beside him as the carriage rattled homeward. He believed he understood now why she was so proud of her culture, a pride she did not voice but could not dissimulate no matter how hard she tried. She was not learning about Western culture, he now suspected, because she wanted to become a convert to something vastly superior, but rather because she recognized the deficiencies of her own culture and wanted to remedy them. In her heart, she was convinced that the soul of India was the soul of the world, and in the wake of his meeting with the swami, Le Gentil found it difficult to disagree.

When Rodrigo emerged from the long afternoon session in front of his computer, he felt a sympathy with his character that ran much deeper than the fondness of a creator for his creation. He felt as if they were both emerging from the same experience, the same trance-like state. They were brothers in their travails, both plunged into a strange new world, slipping and sliding as they tried to get their bearings, struggling to assimilate their experience into their rapidly opening minds. Rodrigo had never met anybody like this sage, though he had felt his presence and heard his melodious words in his mind talking to a rapt Le Gentil and Ambika as clearly as if he had also been sitting there. He supposed that his imaginary sage was a mixture of the pujya swami and Saraswati, but there was more to his experience than he could explain, a suspicion of reality that could not be translated into the language of the imagination. It did not occur to him that it might be a memory, long erased by the transition from one life to the next. He did not suppose that it might be a type of altered perception, such as the swami had explained to Le Gentil. But he did wonder if it might be the voice of his unconscious reaching out to him, gaining direct access to his mind rather than through the gateway of his dreams, using this portal to communicate to him certain truths that had been hitherto locked away in a cosmic vault inaccessible to his conscious awareness.

This thought so entranced him that he was hardly aware of anything but his internal reverie as he grabbed a shawl and headed down the stairs. Though the beginning of arati was only minutes away, he began walking briskly in the direction of Ram Jhula, instinctively feeling the need to let his mind run its course before he took part in the devotional singing and sat for his evening practices. He wrapped his shawl around his shoulders to ward off the growing winter chill and walked with his hands crossed in front of his chest, hidden beneath the thin woolen folds. He kept his eyes lowered, barely aware of the passersby, trusting his instincts to keep him from any unwarranted collision while he trailed eagerly after the inward flight of his thoughts like a young boy scurrying after a runaway kite. The sound of the sage's voice continued to echo in his mind, but it was not the sonorous melodies that attracted his attention and beckoned him onward but some vague intuition of the spiritual truths that those words embodied. It was the ideas and not the words that called him now, like a low trumpet sounding unseen from over a distant ocean. Without being aware of it, his feet took him past the little temple just to the left of the Ram Jhula Bridge where a small group of pilgrims was milling about outside, looking in on the beginning of the evening worship. His pace slowed. As he followed the swiftly moving lights of his thoughts, his ears took in the ringing of the bells and the rhythmic intonation of the mantras being chanted by the temple priest. A sudden wash of irritation dampened the edges of his spirit. Without realizing it, he stopped moving. While his eyes gazed unseeing past the bridge and out over the river, that small hidden corner of his attention fastened onto the mantras and started criticizing the nameless, unseen priest for reciting them incorrectly. Gradually he lost the train of his thoughts, the vague lights disappearing into an interior darkness; all his attention became focused on the mispronounced syllables and faulty rhythms that blasphemed against his years of study and single-minded devotion to the goddess.

These unlettered, so-called Brahmins, he thought, the harsh bent of his criticism now entirely focused on the scene in front of him. They prattle the sacred mantras for money and never give a thought to how they are offending the gods. They care more for the sound of coins clinking in their copper plate than for the divine resonance of the mantras that sustain the three worlds and bring the listener into the presence of the Holy Mother. That is, they *would* bring the listener into her presence if this son-of-a-donkey excuse for a Brahmin did not butcher the ancient verses. Involuntarily, he started intoning the mantras himself in a soft, melodious voice, the rhythms rising and falling in the same precise cadences that the ancient sage Yajnavalkya had pronounced when he had composed them thousands of years earlier, the same verses that the temple priest was intoning in a voice that sounded like a donkey's braying to his ears. For a few moments, he felt an impulse to enter the temple and take over the recitation himself, though he knew it would not do for someone in his position to stoop to such measures in public. He would wait. He would take the priest aside later, scold him, and then inspire him to do better, to bring the true reverence to his worship that his position as the representative of the deity demanded. So much ignorance, he thought, among us whose job it is to remove the veil of ignorance. Closing his eyes, he vowed to himself that if the devi permitted, he would pledge himself to removing the ignorance of his fellow Brahmins so that they might rise up and become a wave to wash away the ignorance of his country.

At that moment an odd feeling overcame him. He opened his eyes and looked around, disoriented, as if he had suddenly found himself in a strange place without realizing how he had gotten there. He blinked his eyes several times, trying to catch his bearings like a man caught in a spell of vertigo, the world in front of him blurred and indistinct. Then he recognized where he was. He heard the bells and the mantras of the temple and smelled the incense wafting upward in thin fingered plumes of whitish smoke, but now they had the familiar feel they had each day when he walked past the temple on the way to Ram Jhula. With a momentary shiver, he realized that he had been dreaming on his feet, revisiting the queer sensation of living in two realities at once that he felt whenever he woke out of his temple dreams. He could still feel the priestly ego within him, the unquestioned conviction that he was the master of Hindu lore, the mild irritation at the supposed missteps of the temple priest, the presence of the devi never far from his dedicated mind. At the same time he knew who he was: Rodrigo, with his habitual insecurities, his nascent spirituality, and the characters of his novel roaming his mind as the devi did the mind of the priest. His waking consciousness had fully reasserted itself, yet he still knew that the priest recited the mantras incorrectly while he, his dreaming self, had repeated them with the sureness and unshakeable conviction of long practice. A chill eddy caused him to wrap his shawl tighter around his shoulders. Shaking off his disquieting reverie, he started walking back briskly in the direction of the ghat, feeling a sudden pull to join the arati. Though he could still feel the jolt of the experience tingling in his arms and legs, he did not want to think about it. Not yet. It was something akin to fear that made him turn his attention away and speed up his gait, wanting only to lose himself in the singing and thereafter let his meditation take him as far away as it could from the place he had just been. He knew the questions would follow him wherever he went—there was no escaping them—but until they forced his hand, he wanted no part of them. There were forces at work in his life, rolling like a boulder down a jagged mountain, and he had no wish at this moment to glance back and see them bearing down on him.

23

*I*T WAS THE DAY after Christmas and Rodrigo did not have much appetite. Considering how much he had eaten of the special Christmas dinner the night before and the stomachache that followed, he thought it prudent to pay heed to what his body was telling him. Instead of going to the dining hall after evening meditation, he decided to go for a walk along the river, electing to go in the opposite direction from Ram Jhula. The night was mostly overcast, unusual for that time of year. Only a few stars found their way through the dim gray shapes to shine their feeble light on the mostly silent city. Though his mind remained quiet in the aftermath of his meditation, Rodrigo was wary of the sleeping consciousness that had until recently only appeared in his dreams. He watched for any sign of its unwarranted presence as he walked, like a strolling constable alerted to reports of unwanted elements within the city limits. The narrow, unlit street was deserted. The black waters of the river glided silently beside him, throwing off silver glints as its rippling current reacted to the starlight that fell softly on its surface. The rolling waters sounded faintly like music. Again he felt the presence of an unseen force rolling him down the corridors of his life. Even his decision to walk along the river instead of going to dinner seemed choreographed by an unseen hand that loomed brooding and reflective beyond the canopy of cloud and star. When he had gone about a kilometer, he stopped and gazed into the darkness above the river, his black shawl wrapped tightly around him, blending with the night shadows.

As he stood there, he made a conscious effort to listen for the river's voice. Three days earlier he had read Hermann Hesse's *Siddhartha*. He had been enthralled by Hesse's tale of the young Brahmin who bore the same name as the Buddha and rode it to a similar end, so enthralled that he had read it all in one evening and then reread it the following day. Siddhartha's determined, tempestuous dalliance with Kamala reminded him of Beth and gave him hope that the mistakes he had made were the mistakes he had had to make in order to weary of his material life and turn back to the spiritual life that he could not remember ever having known. Siddhartha's apprenticeship with Vasudeva made Rodrigo realize that the river had become for him both a teacher and a friend. He did not let a single day go by without taking a long walk along its banks or spending time gazing into its ceaselessly moving waters. He was not aware of having heard its voice, as Siddhartha had, the voice of wisdom, the voice of life, but he had for some time now looked upon the river as a symbol of the spiritual reality that could not be seen but which flowed incessantly through his life, carrying him onward toward the sea. But maybe that was as much a part of the river's voice as the mystic syllable om that Siddhartha had heard, speaking to Rodrigo in images that carried him out of his mundane thoughts and into the questing self that now marked his most passionate moments. Maybe he had been listening to that voice all along without realizing it, even on that second morning in Rishikesh, nearly five months earlier, when he had set a blank sheet of paper in its waters to be taken by the current.

It was late when Rodrigo made it back to his room. He reread the last chapters from *Siddhartha* once again, reciting aloud the scene depicting Siddhartha's final illumination in a soft voice as if he were intoning mantras that had been translated from Sanskrit into German into English. When he finally put aside the book, he remembered again his odd experience in front of the temple a few weeks earlier. For a brief moment he felt uneasy. Was it possible that his dreams had become so powerful that for a few minutes they had wrested control of his waking mind? Merging, however briefly, his destiny with that of the imaginary figure that haunted his sleeping hours? He remembered the sensation he had felt immediately afterward, as clearly as if he had just experienced it, that feeling of being alive in two worlds at once, of inhabiting a mind that was his yet not his. As he lay down to sleep, he remembered the Taoist sage Chuang Tzu's famous dream, and for the first time he wondered, without any facetiousness, just who was dreaming who.

Rishikesh
12/27
4:15 AM

Since that episode in front of the Ram Jhula temple a few weeks ago, I've been wondering when another dream would come. I've been wondering if my temporary loss of identity was like the early warning signs that some epileptic patients get before they have a seizure. But for several weeks now, I have been spared that haunting, enthralling journey into another self—until this morning. Once again, when I awoke from sleep, I could feel my priestly consciousness reluctantly relinquishing control of the reins, but this time the dream had nothing to do with faulty mantras. It was all about the girl.

I was sitting on a wooden platform in the temple grounds that had been erected for the occasion of the debate. Sitting on the platform with me was a priest from a temple in a neighboring district. He was quite famous, and the fact that he was there at all was a matter of great prestige—not only for me but for the entire temple and the surrounding community. The grounds were terribly crowded. People were sitting on the lawn in front of the platform, rubbing knees and elbows; many more were standing to the sides and at the back. The other priest wore a white dhoti and the sacred thread, as I did. He cut a striking figure: perfectly erect posture, lightly bronzed skin, a beautifully balanced intonation that made me envious. There was also a hint of arrogance—or so I thought—an aura of confidence when he spoke that made it clear that the answers he gave were definitive, that there could be no calling into question their validity. This contrasted with my own lack of confidence. I was unsure if I even belonged on the same stage with him. But then I saw her standing at the back with a small group of poorly dressed women, her beauty so striking that she looked as if she belonged to a different race. I had been watching for her before the debate began, afraid that she might not be there, afraid that she would. The more the minutes dragged by without seeing her, the more anxious I became. But the moment I saw her my confidence rose. Then the moderator gave a signal, the crowd hushed, and the first question was read.

As the guest he answered first. He spoke beautifully, but as the debate advanced, I slowly realized that the arguments he was using to support his theses were the same arguments she had said he would use, almost word for word. I kept glancing over at her in growing astonishment. This was exactly what I had prepared for, using the rebuttal ideas she had proposed and which I later refined in my own way. At the time, I had considered it primarily an exercise, but now I saw that I could have had no better preparation. Her foresight both amazed and thrilled me. As the debate went on, I could see that I was gaining an advantage; soon this became clear from the audience's enthusiastic response to my arguments and my rebuttals. Each time I looked at her my confidence grew. They were only quick glances—I could not risk anything more—but they were enough to feel her eyes willing me on, feeding me with their slow fire, helping me to refocus my energy and sharpen my thoughts. Soon I realized I was winning, and winning decisively. My elation spread wings; as it did, I could feel her gaze steadying me, preventing me from losing my focus or becoming overconfident.

When the debate ended, both the judges and the audience declared the outcome in my favor. The other priest accepted his defeat graciously and offered some words of praise that fell on my ears like music from the seventh heaven. But all through the final formalities and the congratulations, I could feel her presence linked to mine as if there were an invisible thread binding us together. I could feel her elation accompanying my own, reverberating in my soul, a calming presence, proud and defiant. I had to fight the urge, the ridiculous urge, to rush through the crowd and embrace her to show my thanks. The very thought of it burned my cheeks, and yet I could not stop thinking about her while I protested modesty before the effusive praise I was receiving from the elders and the prominent town members. The last thing I remembered before I woke up was her two eyes in the distance, burning into me like live coals, searing me with a warmth that felt more pleasurable than the joy of having won the debate and earned such favor in the eyes of my contemporaries.

I am fully awake now but my blood is still racing. Every fiber in me seems to be chanting "what a woman!"—so spiritual, so intelligent, so defiant, and yet unattainable. I can feel the priest's desire clamoring and clutching for my attention, and I have to caution myself that this is his desire, not mine. But what sense does that make? Who else is he, if not me? My thoughts go to Saraswati, who is not nearly as beautiful as the woman I conjure up in my dreams but every bit as spiritual and undeniably real. I do not desire her the way my dreamed self desires the water girl, but then I remind myself that he is not fully conscious of his desire. It is only after I awaken to my real self that I recognize what he could not. Is the same thing happening to me without my conscious knowledge? The same desires, the same fears? Although in this case I am the outcaste, the foreigner, the one denied access to the inner sanctum. Or is this dream simply one further sign that the clouds are gathering, that my desires are arraying their forces on the other side of this divide between my waking and sleeping lives, preparing to cross its poorly guarded borders and challenge me to battle on my own soil? The last couple of days I've been disturbed again by thoughts of Beth. Maybe Christmas nostalgia had something to do with it. I no longer harbor any anger toward her that I am aware of but rather a sense of guilt that tears at me like a knife. My own failings are by far the hardest to swallow—I can scarcely remember hers. My selfishness, when I remember it, burns like lye on an open wound. I remember things I said then and can scarcely bear to hear them now as they repeat themselves unmercifully in my memory. A slammed door, a stubborn coldness nursed along to the point of pride, a string of unkind words. Even worse: the way I justified it all to myself on the grounds that her failings forced me to act that way. Now I know why they say memory is a curse. The failings of others mean little to an aware mind. It is our own failings that crucify us. And now in dream I am headed headlong into the same desire that brought out the worst in me so short a time ago and sent me scurrying to India in an effort to hide out from my shortcomings. Who knows what will happen, but just the thought of falling in love again makes me weak with trepidation. Will I fail this time as well? Will the same weaknesses rear their ugly head? Or will I have the strength to overcome them? And even if "this time" is not now, I suspect my dreams are telling me that it is coming, sooner or later. It probably matters little if it is Saraswati or someone else. It is what is inside me that will either do me in or free me, no matter who the other person is.

Not a comforting thought.

In the days that followed, Rodrigo began to recognize how blurred the line between devotion and attraction was becoming. His admiration for Saraswati was growing rapidly, as was his recognition of the enormous impact she was having on the unfolding of his spiritual life. At the same time, he was finding it increasingly difficult to separate his image of the divine love he was searching for in his devotional practices from his image of the teacher who was helping him to travel there. Yet until he had tried to decipher the meaning of his most recent dreams, he had never thought about her in romantic tones. If he had been asked if he felt attracted to her as a woman, he might have scoffed at the insinuation. But since his latest dream, he could not see her or think about her without being aware of that possibility and the confusion it added to his life. Indeed, at times he wondered if he were only entertaining the idea of falling in love with her because it seemed like a convenient explanation for his dreams.

Inevitably, the same half-conscious dilemma found its way into his writing where he could reflect upon it with a clarity he was incapable of summoning when he was away from his computer. Perhaps it was because his characters did for him what he could not do on his own: they enacted his struggles on a stage where it was possible for him to witness what was going on without becoming attached. The light of awareness, which in his personal life was not yet capable of reflecting its own image without losing itself in the drama, lit up the stage of his imagination and revealed to him his own consciousness as it wrestled with the ropes that bound it. Though the luminous images that lived and grew within the borders of his inner world seemingly acted of their own volition and led him into places he had never been before, they were still facets of his consciousness. Each step his characters took revealed to him the motions of his mind as he had never been able to see them before; each word they exchanged led him deeper into the hidden chambers of the self. Though he had little idea where his characters were going or what they would say when they got there, it was only because he had little idea where *he* was going or what he would say when he got there. His life was still a mystery to him, and he began to suspect that his characters had an important role to play in deciphering that mystery. And so, as Rodrigo spent his free hours peering into the screen of his computer, he paid close attention to what his characters were doing, to what they said and what they left unsaid, knowing that each subtle nuance in the unfolding of their story had something to say about the unfolding of his. Shortly after Le Gentil and Ambika returned from their visit to the sage, they began a series of excursions to the coastal lands north of Pondicherry to catalogue the flora and fauna of that region. Rodrigo had not planned these excursions, but he treated them as an inescapable part of his own journey, as if he had been forced into the same carriage and cautioned not to interrupt his characters while they were speaking.

The expeditions began as day trips, but now that the observatory was finished, they soon evolved into more extended excursions as the two explorers roamed farther and farther afield. Typically they brought with them their driver, Le Gentil's household servant, and sufficient supplies to last them until they got back. As had become their habit, the two of them kept up a running conversation during their trips that sustained itself on a curious mixture of Indian and French cuisine and increasing doses of laughter. As Le Gentil knelt to examine unfamiliar species of plants and animals, and Ambika recorded his observations in her florid and immensely readable hand, he taught her the scientific method and detailed the advances that Western civilization had made in the various sciences, beginning with Aristotle and ending with his own discoveries on the Isle de France and Madagascar, where he had spent the better part of the previous eight years entertaining himself with botanical, zoological, geological, and anthropological research. Though Le Gentil was not unaware of the contributions made by other cultures in these fields, he had alarmingly little knowledge of India's place in world history. Ambika did her best to enlighten him, something Le Gentil enjoyed even more than teaching her what he considered to be the best of his culture: its voracious appetite for scientific achievement. They were both well aware that their conversations were as much a dialogue between two civilizations as a meeting between two human beings. This not only became the axis around which their conversations revolved but the source of much of their laughter, as each in turn discovered absurdities in the other's way of looking at the world, often things they would have never noticed had they not had the unique opportunity of looking through each other's eyes. She made fun of his Eurocentricity and he returned the favor, pointing out that India had a several-thousand-year head start in considering itself to be the center of the civilized world. Together, they understood that neither way of looking at the world constituted a whole truth; they were simply separate facets of a constantly revolving prism. At the center of that prism, the nucleus of its refracted light, shone the spiritual understanding of a race that could not be divided by culture if it were to claim to be a repository of the truth.

One afternoon at the observatory, the topic of conversation turned to spirituality, as it had more and more often in the weeks since their visit to the swami. This time Le Gentil insisted that for all the undeniable wisdom and saintliness of the sage and the marvelous teachings she had been exposing him to in India's sacred texts, none of it could be considered universal truth if it were not echoed in the teachings of all elevated souls, regardless of culture. For once Ambika agreed with him. As they leaned back in their armchairs on the veranda, looking out over Le

Gentil's newly planted gardens where the first shoots of summer spinach were poking their glistening green tips above the damp earth, he began reminiscing about his days as an abstracted young clergyman and the raging debates over Christian doctrine and obscure texts that had served to entertain him and his fellow novitiates during the idle evening hours they all looked forward to after a long day of work and study. He told her about his encounters with the mystic Spaniards Teresa of Avila and Juan de la Cruz; the far more accepted and orthodox but deeply devotional Francis de Sales; the controversial banned writings of the Quietists and the Jansenists that still had such a hold on the French imagination; and the unbelievable tales from *The Lives of the Saints* that seemed uncannily similar to the tales Ambika had related of Indian fakirs and yogis.

That evening, Ambika went to the Governor-General's library and searched for the names Le Gentil had mentioned, some of whom she was already familiar with. She found several of them gathering dust on the shelves—she was sure that Juan de la Cruz's works had not been opened since she had read them as a teenager—and these she borrowed with the Governor-General's hearty permission. For the next two nights, she stayed up late pouring over them with a renewed sense of awe, realizing what she seemed to have forgotten, that the mystic spirit that hung over her land like a thin haze bathed in the brilliance of the Indian sun was also alive, though better hidden, in this strident continent to the north that seemed so intent on subjugating the world and her peoples. The following day, she and Le Gentil left for a three-day trip up the Coromandel coast. She brought the books with her. Once they had set up their makeshift camp, she extracted them from her travel bag to the great surprise of her companion. They spent the next three nights reading out passages to each other by the light of the kerosene lantern and debating their meaning, before she retired to the other side of the hasty partition that separated their bodies but not their minds or their voices.

Though it was late summer and there was no need of a fire, the energy that crackled around them produced its own kind of heat. By now Le Gentil was aware that he was in the process of falling in love. As he lay down to sleep on the last night of their trip, he gazed up at the stars in the nearly cloudless sky and listened for the sound of her breathing on the other side of the partition, modulating slowly into the soothing rhythms of sleep. It was not a mere passion that engaged him, he realized, like so many others he had experienced in his four decades, fleeting gusts of emotion that could not survive the clear sun of a new scientific challenge. This was a slow fire that was beginning to consume his soul. He no longer felt any restlessness when he was with her but only when they were apart. When they were together, the world seemed to slow in its orbit until it came to a virtual standstill in the moment. In her presence his ambitions failed him; the tide that was sweeping his embattled and enthusiastic continent from one protracted war to another passed by unnoticed. Even the joyful cataloguing of new discoveries in the natural sciences became not an end but a means to engage them both in the other's company. All these were unmistakable signs that what had never before happened in his life was now on the verge of becoming a reality. The miracle of love—which he had never known and thus never missed, for how can one miss what one has never felt—was now throwing its soft and spreading mantle over his peacefully reclining form.

An image entered his mind of Ambika on his arm entering the reception hall of the Academy of Sciences to celebrate his election to the post of Permanent Secretary. He smiled involuntarily. She was wearing a powder blue sari and her luxurious raven hair hung down to the small of her back. In the company of those pale, corseted wives with their sallow complexions, her dark beauty and colorful shimmering dress shone with an elegance that could not be matched. He allowed the next thought to form, as natural as it was unprecedented. She had entered the hall as his wife, and for all the condescension that flowed from those supercilious faces, there was an unmistakable odor of surrender in the room, for who among them could compete with Ambika, either in intelligence or in beauty. It was just a dream, he had to tell himself, an unthinkable, unrealistic, though perfectly enjoyable dream. Could he ever think of bringing home a native wife and introducing her into upper-class French society? It had never been done. Surely he would not dare be the first, knowing full well all that he would be putting at risk. Or could he? The dream had already dropped its seed into the fertile meadows of his constantly expanding mind. Every new day they passed together would only pour more sunlight and moisture into that hungry, absorbent soil. Who knows where it would lead? Already he could not look at her without feeling a connection as binding as the straps that secured the trunks in which he kept what were, up until now, his most cherished possessions: his instruments and his journals.

He could not be sure that she returned his feelings. As always, she continued to maintain her habitual reserve in matters of propriety. He could only remember two times that she had even pronounced his first name. But the rapidity with which she opened up parts of her psyche to him that had hitherto remained carefully concealed gave him confidence that she was not immune to the rushing current that had taken hold of his heart. He felt sure that the waters that were now sweeping him away would soon unloose her from her moorings. After that, no one would be able to predict where their destiny would lead them.

The next morning, shortly before they were due to start heading back to Pondicherry, they were standing on a promontory overlooking the Coromandel coast, a desolate, windswept area that stood some thirty meters above a rock-strewn beach. On the previous day, Le Gentil had discovered a species of mollusk attached to the sheer cliffs that bore a remarkable similarity to a mollusk found on the Normandy coast. After they had spent some time investigating its habitat and interaction with its environment, Ambika pointed out to him a pair of red-billed hornbills that were preening themselves among scraggly tufts of marsh grass. "I have heard that the hornbill mates for life," she told him, as she fastened her flying hair with a ribbon.

"There are a surprising number of birds which do," he replied. "It seems to be an inborn instinct, not only in mammals but in the lower creatures as well.

Intelligence does not seem to factor into it. Probably just as well. Who knows what the future of the human race would be if it did?"

Ambika clasped her arms under her breasts and followed his gaze out over the open sea where the blue waters of the Bay of Bengal danced lightly under a cloudless sky. "And is intelligence then the reason the Monsieur has never taken a wife?"

Le Gentil immediately sensed the trap that lay concealed in her words, pronounced with a gentle innocence that, he was quite sure, was as deliberate as it was pleasing to his ear. He adopted the same tone, knowing it would convey more than his words. "Only in the sense that I have dedicated my life to science, not wishing to disrespect the gifts God has given me. Thus I have had little time to pursue such a noble vocation as marriage."

"Then you do consider it noble?"

"I do. As you well know, marriage is considered a sacrament in the Christian faith, and I honor it as such. If I have not celebrated that sacrament yet, it is because I am fully aware that it should not be entered into lightly. One must be ready to dedicate time and effort and the entirety of one's heart. Anything less would be to disrespect our Maker, and I would not do that."

"Is it not possible to be both a dedicated scientist and a successful husband? Or wife?"

"Certainly. But it is not an easy feat, not if one wants to truly succeed at both vocations, especially when you are young. A real maturity is required, if not in both parties, then at least in one. I like to think that I am now capable of that which I might not have been when I was in my twenties or thirties."

A look of satisfaction passed swiftly across Ambika's face, a look he barely caught out of the corner of his eye as they both continued to look out over the vaguely restless sea. "Perhaps when you have recorded the Venus transit and published your journals?"

"Perhaps. I like to think so, but I also know that these things are in God's hands, as much as we may like to think otherwise."

Ambika smiled. "This is true, of course, but is not man through his actions a participant in God's work?"

"He is. It stands to reason that this is also true when it comes to the question of a man taking a wife. And in Hindu society, how are such matters looked upon? Your people marry at a younger age than mine do, I've noticed. They tell me that almost all marriages here are arranged marriages."

"You forget that I am Christian."

Le Gentil turned and feigned a look of astonishment. "Indeed, I had forgotten! But then I believe there are some Christians who never stop being Hindu."

Ambika's eyes crinkled in amusement. "That may well be. Who can say? But is there really so much difference between the two?

"No," Le Gentil answered, more soberly now, all traces of playfulness disappearing from his voice. "I am starting to be convinced that there is not, not nearly as much as we are led to believe. In fact, the difference may be as little as the difference in the angle from which we are both seeing the same ocean. After talking to the swami, I have started to think that religion is entirely a man-made institution, and that the men that make them would do well to realize that. To be honest, Ambika, I think I was always of this opinion. I just never gave it so much thought before. Now that I have, I suspect the closer men get to the truth, the closer they get to each other. All men."

"And all women."

They both laughed, having had this conversation before. Le Gentil had already surprised Ambika with his conviction that women in his country would one day attain equal status with men, and even more so by telling her that he would consider it an achievement and a blessing long overdue. In this, she had found in him an ally equal to the most enlightened of her country's sages.

Rodrigo remembered that conversation, almost as surely as if he had written it himself. Yet he hadn't. There was no mention of it in any of his writings, and he was sure he had never even thought about it before. Yet it was there in Ambika and Le Gentil's memories, as clear to him as it was to them: the surprise and the mutual laughter that had followed, laughter over the follies of men and women; her long narration about the place of women in Indian society, and his excited curiosity that spilled over in the form of numerous questions; her translating for him sections from the laws of Manu and feeling his indignation as her own. Rodrigo looked up from his computer. He thought back to his conversation with Saraswati on the roof above her room, her indignation and her quotation from the *Manu Samhita*. He had not read the *Manu Samhita*, but he had come across references to it in his readings these past few months. But this did not explain his memory of Ambika and Le Gentil's conversations. He could remember what they remembered, as if he were peering into their minds and watching their thoughts take shape as the moment unfolded. Their memories were independent of his conversation with Saraswati or any of the references he had passed over without noting. They were far deeper, far more detailed, far more interesting. Again he had the uncanny feeling that his characters were independent creatures with lives of their own, much of which was unknown to him and only gradually being revealed as he witnessed their story enacting itself in the theater of his mind.

A brief shiver passed through him as he remembered his fleeting loss of identity outside the temple. Once again, he had the feeling that he was emerging from a dream in which he was a spectator who had forgotten where and who he was. The spell had been broken but his reemergence, he knew, was only temporary. Ambika and Le Gentil were waiting just below the surface of his consciousness, waiting to draw him back into the drama of their separate and irremediably intertwined lives. Did those lives continue on without his knowledge while he attended to matters in the realm of his normal consciousness? Or did it require his inward eye peering into the world of their story to wake them from their sleep? And where did he disappear to when they began walking and talking of their own accord, making him forget that he was there also, watching them?

He blinked his eyes and folded shut his laptop, shaken by the notion that his identity was losing the firm footing it had always enjoyed. The notion that he was a dreamed character, as Chuang Tzu and a parade of Chinese and Indian sages both before and after him had claimed, ceased to be a quaint but thought-provoking idea. He felt it implant itself in the center of his being, which then began to waver and grow translucent like a holographic image projected into the center of the room. He was looking at himself, and yet there was no one there to look at, just particles of light wrapping themselves around an idea that threatened to vanish at any moment. They trembled and shone, vibrating in unison with the space around them, joining themselves to an immense tapestry as insubstantial and as infinite as moonlight flooding an open field. The enduring sense of identity that had fastened him to the earth like the strong roots of an ancient oak cleaving the soil was gone. It had not dissolved; it had simply never been, vanished in the infinite space between one moment and the next. In its place remained a spaciousness, a consciousness that he could only describe as endless and eternal.

The several seconds in which this vision transpired were independent of time. The awareness that witnessed them lay suspended, and the passage from one moment to the next seemed like a journey between borders so remote they were only a rumor. But the seconds did pass. A sudden gust of fear buffeted him like a burst of wind flinging open the shutters of a window. The fear of disappearing, the fear of losing himself once and forever. He closed his eyes instinctively and felt that emotion roiling in his stomach. He clung to it with welcoming arms, as if to the rescuing embrace of familiarity. Then he opened his eyes again, and both he and the room were just as they had been when he had looked up from his computer and sighted the sky above the mountains outside his window. He felt a tremor in his hand. He held it up and looked at it and was astonished to see that it was solid. He looked at the sky outside and saw and felt its radiance. He was back, made solid again by this re-entrance into time, but the same unseen force was there that he had sensed while walking along the river. Once again, he could feel it rolling him down the corridors of his life, and the conviction came over him that there was nothing he could do to stop it.

When Rodrigo reached Saraswati's roof the next afternoon, he could still feel traces of his experience from the previous day. Part of him was aware that the two of them were nothing more than two shadows, dancing to the shifting movements of the light. A breeze ruffled their clothes and he felt instinctively the same unseen and impersonal force behind it, propelling both of them toward ends it kept scrupulously hidden. Obediently, he took his seat, alert to the wind at his back.

Saraswati folded shut her book. "Well then," she said, "should we continue where we left off in our last session? If I remember correctly, we had just finished discussing the layers of the mind and we were about to start discussing the chakra system."

The sound of her voice was enough to silence the misgivings in Rodrigo's heart. Her rootedness and the steady modulations of her speech reminded him that in her presence the world made sense. The sun that warmed them shone not on any insubstantial quavering of light but on the promise that had begun to fill his future. Soon they were immersed in a discussion of yogic physiology that went far beyond any of the books Rodrigo had read on the subject.

She started off by explaining that the word *chakra* meant "wheel" or "vortex." In yoga, it was used to refer to the seven subtle energy centers situated along the spinal column from the coccyx to the crown of the head. According to the ancient sages, these energy centers resembled lotuses; they used the word *chakra* because at the center of the "lotus" the energy revolved in a circular fashion, thus creating a type of vortex. From the center of each vortex, energy radiated out in different directions and then returned, thus forming figures or loops that resembled lotus petals. These petals, as well as the centers of the chakras, were of different colors and emitted different sounds due to the difference in the frequency of their respective vibrations, something that was true of every manifestation in the universe, whether matter or energy, perceptible or not. These colors, sounds, and shapes had been carefully recorded by yogis who were able to perceive them in their meditation. When Rodrigo asked her if it were actually possible to perceive the chakras, she assured him it was and that he would perceive them himself once he acquired the requisite subtlety of mind through his daily practice. But what most surprised and intrigued him was her assertion that each petal controlled a different mental propensity.

"Each petal is actually energy vibrating at a different frequency. That energy or that vibration expresses itself in our mind as the different mental propensities: anger, affection, hope, hate, and so on. Do you remember the second sutra?"

"*Yogashcittavrttinirodha.*"

"Very good. So you've been keeping up with your memorization, then?"

"As you instructed."

"Excellent. So, the *vritti*s are our mental propensities; if you remember, they are what occupy the mind, thus the use of the word *vritti*. There are fifty of them, each controlled by a different chakra: four by the first chakra, six by the second, ten by the third, twelve by the fourth, sixteen by the fifth, and two by the sixth. Naturally, propensities controlled by the same chakra vibrate at a similar frequency. Irritation or anger, for example, is controlled by the third chakra, specifically by one petal of that chakra. Hatred is also a *vritti* of the third chakra, as is fear. In other words, the third chakra controls the heavy emotions we share with the other higher mammals. Aggression, competition, fear—these are expressions of third chakra propensities. You know how in photography you start with three fundamental colors and by mixing them together in varying degrees you can create millions of colors of every shade imaginable? Okay. Now imagine a palette with fifty fundamental colors. By mixing those colors in varying intensities you get the infinite variety of human thought and emotion. Now in order to progress spiritually, one has to be able to bring the different *vritti*s under control. Someone who has not conquered hatred or anger cannot achieve enlightenment. If you know which *vritti* is out of balance or out of control, and you know which chakra controls that *vritti*, then by doing practices specifically designed for that chakra you can bring the *vritti* under control and accelerate your progress. Think back to the sutra, but now translate it as 'yoga is control over the *vrittis* of the mind.' All the practices of yoga, to one extent or another, are designed to help us purify, strengthen, and balance the chakras, starting with the postures you do each morning. Each of them works on specific chakras."

"Even though they are physical exercises?"

"Actually, the asanas should rightly be called physico-psychic exercises. Each of the chakras is associated with certain glands and nerve plexuses. The third chakra, for example, corresponds to the solar plexus. The adrenal glands are in this area, the pancreas, and so on, and these glands secrete the hormones that are responsible at a physiological level for the third-chakra *vrittis*. The asanas work by exerting pressure on the glands. They balance the hormone secretion, which in turn balances the energy of the chakra, which in turn helps us to control our mind. That brings me to my next point: everything in our existence is inter-related. The physical body, our vital energy, mind, consciousness—they are all different levels of the same existence, different vantage points, you could say. We know from studying modern physics that solid objects are actually composed of minute particles vibrating in space. Those particles—the electrons and neutrons and so forth—are themselves just patterns of energy. From one vantage point your chair is solid. From another it's mostly space with a few minute particles occupying that space. And from another it's a web of energy. But that's where modern physics stops. The yogic sages went even further, much further. They discovered that this web of energy that we call the universe is actually mind in what you can call condensed or transmuted form; and mind is in turn a trans-muted form of consciousness. You take water and freeze it; it becomes ice. Heat it and it becomes vapor. But it is still the same substance, whether it is an ocean of ice or water or vapor. The primordial substance of this universe is conscious-ness. So to return to the chakras, they are the controlling centers of the energy flow that makes up our microcosmic existence. Their physical counterparts are the nerve plexuses in our spinal cord and brain, and the associated glands. Their mental counterparts are the *vrittis*. Say you get angry. At the physical level, the adrenal glands in the abdomen start secreting certain hormones into your bloodstream. At the energetic level, that petal in that chakra gets activated and starts to vibrate at a certain frequency. At the mental level, you feel angry and you lose your capacity to think properly. It's all one process, but it occurs at dif-ferent levels of our existence."

Rodrigo furrowed his brow, struggling to place this new information in the context of all that he had studied up until then. "How does this all relate to samskara?" he asked.

"Samskara activates the *vrittis*. Remember the principle: the subtle manifesta-tion is always the cause of the cruder one. The subtle cause is samskara. First the samskara gets activated. The external conditions activate the samskara but obvi-ously the samskara has to be there, otherwise there won't be any reaction. If you have a samskara to get angry under certain conditions, you will. If you don't, you won't. The samskara activates the *vritti* at the respective chakra, which activates the glands, which secrete the hormones, which stimulate the nervous system. Obviously samskara and *vritti* is a two-way street. You work on exhausting your samskaras so the *vritti* does not get activated or go out of control, and you work on controlling the *vritti* so that you don't create further samskaras."

Saraswati folded her hands and placed them in her lap. She leaned back in her chair, her dark eyes shining. "Do you see how perfectly it all fits together?"

For the next forty-five minutes, she took him through each of the chakras and all fifty petals while he copied into his notebook the shapes, colors, sounds, and *vritti*s associated with each. She asked him to begin memorizing them, for he would need to remember them when he began practicing more advanced meditation techniques. The certainty with which she said this surprised him. If he had not mistaken her tone of voice, she was telling him quite matter-of-factly that it was not a question of if but of when. Not that Rodrigo hadn't already been thinking about it. He had read with fascination the complicated techniques described in several of his books—chakra visualizations and other esoteric practices for forcibly raising the kundalini. The dream that he could eventually become an advanced yogi had already taken root in his psyche, but he had not dared practice any of these procedures on his own, seeing how difficult they appeared and having been warned against learning techniques from books by both the swami and Saraswati. Apprehensive, lest her words prove too good to be true, he made an effort to keep the excitement from his voice as he asked her about it.

"When do you think I might be ready to start learning these advanced techniques? Will you teach me?"

Saraswati was quiet for a minute, her eyes half-closed, while Rodrigo awaited her answer with something of the suspense he had felt in earlier years while waiting to hear if a story he had submitted for publication had been accepted.

"That will be up to Swamiji, though I may also teach you some things if he so wishes. Either way, I don't think it will be long. He's due back from tour at the end of next week. I'll talk to him about it when he gets back. There is one other thing I wanted to talk to you about. In the first week of February, a Tibetan master, Kulya Rimpoche, is coming to Rishikesh to conduct a three-week meditation intensive. I did the same intensive twelve years ago, the last time he was in Rishikesh, and it was a fantastic experience, very rigorous but very powerful. It's based on three-year intensives that the masters from his lineage conduct from time to time in Tibet. You spend most of the day in sitting meditation, broken up at intervals by periods of walking meditation. Once a day you have a short interview with the Rimpoche; he asks you about your practice and gives you some guidance. He may also teach you some specific meditation techniques, it depends. And each evening he gives a talk. Apart from that, the intensive is conducted in complete silence. I remember when I did it, people were saying that it was worth a year's meditation on your own; based on my experience I would have to agree. When I heard he was coming, I thought of you. It would be difficult, of course, but after seeing the progress you've made in the few months you've been here at the ashram, I think it would do wonders for you."

"Do you really think I'm ready for it?"

Saraswati nodded her head solemnly. "I do."

That was all Rodrigo needed to hear. "If you think I should do it, then I'll do it."

"I'm glad to hear it," Saraswati said, visibly pleased. "You'll have to train for it, start sitting longer hours, control your diet, but I'll help you with that. It's going to be held in a *dharmasala*, a traveler's lodge for spiritual pilgrims, about twenty miles upriver, but your room will be waiting for you here when you get back. There is one more thing, though. I understand you're a writer. Amrita tells me you've been working on a novel while you've been here, is that right?"

"That's right. I'm also a professor of literature at the University of North Carolina, but I'm on sabbatical at the moment. I'm using it to finish my novel."

Rodrigo started telling Saraswati about his writing. To his surprise, she seemed almost eager to listen. She even asked him a few questions about the stories he had published and what it was like trying to teach and write at the same time. Rodrigo got somewhat carried away, but after a few minutes he restrained himself. He ended by describing the experience he had after completing the last scene and commenting on how much his spiritual practices were beginning to affect his writing. "Indeed," he said, "I think they've completely altered the course of my novel."

"I don't doubt it," Saraswati said, looking at him quizzically. "The more you meditate, the more you can access the higher layers of the mind, and they are the source of creative inspiration. Actually, there is a very close link between the practice of the arts and the practice of spirituality. But it seems you've already discovered that. Hopefully, we'll get a chance to talk about it some time. But what I wanted to say is that you won't be able to write while you're there. The only things you can bring are your clothes, toiletries, sleeping gear, and a mat. All your time during those three weeks goes into your meditation. But it's still more than a month away. You'll get a lot done in the meantime, and I suspect you'll find that the intensive will do as much for your writing as a year spent in front of your computer."

24

SARASWATI WAS PLEASED THAT Rodrigo had decided to take part in the intensive. She had almost forgotten her earlier uneasiness and now considered him to be her protégé, though she did not explain it to herself in those terms. Rather, she told herself that he was the most promising westerner she had seen in a long time, perhaps ever. In fact, she had never come across anyone who had made so much progress in so little time. It was her duty, both to him and to the Mother, to guide him as long as he continued to look to her for guidance. Recommending the intensive was simply a way of carrying out her duty.

That evening, after a long meditation and a tiny dinner, she removed the slim volume of the Rimpoche's teachings from the shelf above her bed. It had been a long time since she had looked at it. She took a cloth and carefully wiped off the faint accumulation of dust that clung to its edges. Then she opened it fondly to the Rimpoche's picture. His aged smile brought out her own and transported her back to that landmark experience, and from there to the troubled years that preceded it.

She had graduated from college three years earlier, a difficult transition fraught with confusion and self-doubt as the challenges she had faced during her four years in college were compounded by the necessity of deciding what she was going to do with her life. The most important of these decisions was forced upon her without any warning three days after her graduation. Her parents had made the trip to Delhi to attend the graduation ceremony, the first time they had been to the capital since the day they had brought her to school four years earlier. After the graduation, they took a hotel in the Chandni Chowk area of Old Delhi with plans to spend the following day exploring the old and new capitals with their daughter as their guide. The next morning, they spent several hours strolling up and down the wide avenues of New Delhi. They stopped under the imposing arch of India Gate to eat peanuts they bought from a street-side vendor and again in front of the Lok Sabha, where her father peered fixedly into the faces of everyone who entered and left to see if he could catch a glimpse of the men and women who were misgoverning the country and doing such injustice to the sacred memory of Jawaharlal Nehru, with whom he had once shaken hands in a Meerut rally. They took lunch in a South Indian restaurant in Connaught Place, her mother fascinated by the continual stream of white faces that poured along the circular walkway of this thriving commercial district ducking in and out of shops and speaking languages whose syllables she had never heard before. After they left the restaurant and its pungent aromas, her mother paid a visit to a fashionable sari shop with pale mannequins in the window draped in costly, silk-embroidered saris, while her father inexplicably whisked her away to a bookstore. The three tourists met up again an hour later to take a bus back to Old Delhi. When Saraswati asked her mother about the package swinging from her elbow in a plastic shopping bag, her mother gave her a coy smile and told her that it was "just a little something."

They spent the rest of the afternoon and part of the evening in Old Delhi strolling among the fabled remnants of the Mughal Shahs. Most of that time was spent inside the magnificent Lal Quila, the red fort, where the opulent Mughal esthetic had reached its zenith in the first half of the seventeenth century. Still in the trance of the past, they boarded a bus the next day to Agra to tour the Taj Mahal, the first time any of them had seen the world's most famous mausoleum, constructed by the emperor Shah Jahan in memory of his dead wife, the incomparably beautiful Mumtaz. Afterward they visited the Agra Fort, two and a half kilometers distant, where Shah Jahan's son Aurangzeb had imprisoned his father after seeing his grief-stricken sire empty half the royal coffers to build the Taj and then announce his plans to build a second mausoleum for himself just across the river, in effect threatening to deprive the pitiless Aurangzeb of his patrimony. The proposed mausoleum was never completed. Shah Jahan spent the last eight years of his life pining for his long-dead wife in a five-by-eight cell in the eastern tower from whose one small window he could look out at the Taj on the mist-laden banks of the Yamuna. It was in this tower that the three of them stood to watch the sun complete its fiery descent over the western bank of the river and reflect, in her father's words, on the fleeting, transitory nature of incarnate life, which glistens for a moment like a drop of dew on a leaf and then is gone with the first glance of the morning sun.

The next day they traveled back to their village. Her parents were in high spirits, as high as she had ever seen. The following morning she discovered why. After breakfast her mother cleared the table and went to the family chest while her father looked on. She brought forth the package she had declined to talk about two days earlier and drew from it a piece of fabric that she laid out on the table. It was a beautiful gold-and-red, hand-embroidered silk sari that rustled as softly as a whisper, as fine as any she had ever seen. "It is your bridal dress," her mother told her, tremulous with emotion. Saraswati froze in a jolt of stunned recognition, realizing in that brief moment that her place in life was just as circumscribed as that of the Dalit girls whom she had been teaching to defy the imposition of a society that strove with all its might to deny them their real worth. Her mother interpreted her shock as a paroxysm of joy and started telling her nervously about the marriage arrangements they had completed the day before they left for her graduation. The groom was the son of the village headman in a nearby village. He was an educated young man, having just completed a master's degree in business administration, and would soon be assisting his father in managing the family holdings, which were said to be quite extensive. Did she remember the boy? They had met once, before she went away to college, the night they attended the Chat festival in that village. The father, who was an honest man, had not demanded a large dowry, as he by rights could have. Between her jewelry and the sale of their small plot of land on the edge of the village, they had managed to raise the money. The boy and his family would be coming over for lunch so the two young people could get acquainted. With a nervous smile, her mother added that the date for the wedding had been fixed by the astrologer for Saturday.

What her mother mistook for joy was in fact a kind of horror. Saraswati was only barely aware of the incredulous smile that was frozen on her face. But when she finally recovered her composure, she found that she could not blame her parents. Nor could she justify her anger at them. They were only doing what they felt best for her, adhering to a path that had been burned into their genes by thousands of years of tradition. It was inconceivable to them that she would not marry if she were given the chance, just as it was inconceivable to every other parent of an unmarried twenty-one-year-old daughter in a traditional Hindu family. Arranged marriages were still *de rigueur* in Indian rural life, and it was rare, almost unheard of, for a daughter to refuse the groom her parents had chosen for her. Had she been four years younger, unmarked by her experiences in the capital, she probably would have swallowed her anxieties and accepted their decision without a word of objection. Her mother would have consoled her and counseled her about her fears, having passed through the same experience herself at the age of sixteen. She would have drawn for her a rosy picture of the happiness that marriage to a good man from a good family would bring. But those four years had marked Saraswati as indelibly as the sun that had tempered her dark skin since birth. They had awakened samskaras that might have remained sleeping for many years had she remained in her village and thus been saved from the haunting, capricious challenges that had dogged her steps from the day she first stepped on campus.

One samskara that had remained dormant during her teenage years was awakened during the first months of her college life: she would not marry. She would never yoke herself to a man, never give up her freedom. Deep inside her had grown a distrust of men and all that came with living in a rigidly patriarchal society. Had she been more observant, she would have noticed that that distrust had been there since the beginning of her teenage years when the immature attentions of the village boys would turn her insides cold. For every upper-middle-class girl who considered herself emancipated from the strictures of Hindu society, there were fifty village girls like her—low-caste girls, poor girls, uneducated girls— who would be second-class citizens or worse their entire lives, simply because generations of men had deemed it so. And the first step to slavery, she knew, was accepting the domination of a husband.

She did not waste any time in telling her parents that they could cancel the lunch. She would not marry this boy or any boy. She offered no explanations. Her voice was cold and implacable, the resolve welling in her with surprising rapidity. Her father became furious and her mother, unable to understand her obstinacy, made no effort to restrain him. The rift between them could not be breached in one night, but that one night was all they had. Saraswati left the next morning for Delhi and did not return for over three years, writing only infrequently to let them know she was well but without offering any details about her life. When she finally did return on a visit of conciliation, she came back to a relationship that was irrevocably changed. The woman she had become was someone her parents barely recognized, an adult who had been their child but who knew that to be just a memory in a river of memories that had already flowed out of sight.

Now, from the clarity of her Himalayan solitude, she thought of the three years that followed the rupture with her parents as her descent into maya, the lost years when she broke free from her spiritual moorings only to find herself swept out to a sea of high waves and foggy horizons—though she knew in truth that those turbulent waters were nothing more than the other side of the Mother's smile.

When she reached Delhi, she went straight to the Dalit hostel where she had been volunteering three afternoons a week for nearly all her college life. Sister Vandana was happy to give her a room for as long as she needed. With her money running thin, she started answering ads in the morning and helping afternoons in the hostel. One morning, she saw an ad for a secretarial position on the staff of Women Against Injustice, one of the leading human-rights organizations in India. She had seen them on more than one occasion marching in the streets of Delhi: strident women in simple saris holding placards and shouting slogans. The founder of the organization, Vimala Krishna, had appeared at her college once and given a lecture on the politics of poverty that had moved her to tears and elicited a surprising standing ovation from her otherwise apathetic classmates. The moment she saw the ad her heart began to race. She had no desire to be a secretary but every wish to find a job that would mean more to her than just earning a paycheck. She drew a thick circle around the ad and wasted no time in boarding a bus for South Delhi where the WAI offices were located. When she reached there, she was stunned to find herself within minutes on the other side of a desk from Vimala Krishna herself. The Oxford-educated, fifty-two-year-old activist and author was wearing an emerald green sari; she had her hair tied up into a bun and sported the red dot in the middle of her forehead that announced to the world that she was a married woman. But there any similarity with the typical Indian housewife ended. Her very first words—which had nothing to do with Saraswati's typing skills or prior experience—transported the wide-eyed young woman into a world of social activism that she had only seen in the provocative articles that sometimes appeared in the *Hindustan Times*.

"Do you know why I am in Delhi today? Yesterday we got word that Monsanto has filed a patent for a variety of wheat they stole from our Indian farmers. Can you imagine how absurd that is? Filing for a trade-related intellectual-property-rights patent for something that has been gifted to us by nature? Did these seeds just pop out of their heads and fall to the ground and sprout? You know, in their hands the seed of life becomes the seed of death. If they win their patent, then our farmers will have to buy their seeds from Monsanto. In less than two hundred years of corporate capitalist agriculture we have gone from a natural biodiversity of over eight thousand food crops to eight; and now Monsanto and two other companies are at war with humanity for control of the world's seed bank. These people will stop at nothing to take the seeds from the hands of the farmers. Do you know what happens when they get control? The cost of production escalates and crop prices fall. Our farmers are being starved out of their own lands because they can't afford the seeds and chemicals that Monsanto forces them to buy. And what does Monsanto tell the world? 'The green revolution will eliminate poverty.' The green revolution that they have engineered and which is making our farmers poorer every year and making Monsanto richer. My dear girl, poverty comes from systems of dispossession, the same systems that Monsanto is trying to force on us and the rest of the countries of the south. People are poor because they've appropriated their resources. People are dying because they've taken away their water and taken away their land. There isn't a single man or woman on this planet who isn't capable of earning their livelihood—if they had the resources available to them. Well, I'll tell you now. Today we are going into court and we are going to fight that patent and we are going to block that patent, no matter how long it takes. We are not going to let Monsanto continue destroying the livelihood of our farmers."

All this before she had even asked Saraswati her name. And all said with a benevolent smile that would have done any grandmother proud.

The job paid little, barely enough to live on, but when Vimala Krishna offered it to her, she jumped at the opportunity. They started her out as a simple secretary, but with her education, her youthful energy, and her innate fearlessness, she soon became an indispensable member of the WAI field staff, traveling all over North India, from Punjab to Bengal, documenting abuses and helping the more experienced staff members to organize campaigns. Her fluent, polished English and incisive prose attracted notice, as did her degree. She had switched to journalism from English literature in her second year of college, without quite understanding why, other than the fact that she preferred reading newspapers to novels, but when she saw her first article published in the WAI journal two months after her return to Delhi and then reprinted two weeks later in the *Hindustan Times*, she knew that destiny had shown its hand. That first article led to another and then to another, each of them characterized by qualities she had not known she possessed: a sarcastic wit and an inborn ability to rally people to a cause with a well-turned phrase. Though she saw little of Vimala Krishna, the older woman encouraged her in her efforts whenever they met or talked on the phone. She began sending Saraswati on specific assignments, wherever a piece of investigative journalism was indicated that could help WAI in their campaigns. She also explained to her why she had chosen those initials for her organization, pronounced exactly like the English word *why*. "The what," she told her, "is important. People have to know what is going on before they can fight against it. But the why is even more important. If we don't come to grips with what makes one group of human beings exploit another, then we will never come to the end of it; there will always be a new injustice to fight right around the corner. If we don't discover the why behind the arrogance of domination, colonialism, patriarchy, and reductionism, then we will never be able to give them up. Always remember to ask that question when you are writing your articles. You don't always need to answer it. Just ask the question. The people themselves will find the answers if you show them where to look. Then there is a chance that what we do will make a real difference in people's lives. Not just a temporary difference, a lasting difference. Maybe even a permanent difference."

Three months after she joined WAI, she was able to move into her own apartment in South Delhi. Two months later, WAI sent her to Haridwar to begin organizing a movement against the diversion of water from the Upper Ganga Canal to Delhi, where the water supply was under threat of privatization because of pressure from the World Bank. It was the first time she had ever been given responsibility of any real magnitude. Rather than cause her any trepidation, however, the challenge excited her. How many women in her culture ever came close to such an opportunity? After a series of difficult meetings with local politicians, she wrote an inflammatory pamphlet that she distributed personally to the local farmers who depended on that water for irrigation. She asked them to pass it on to whomever they could. The pamphlet quickly spread all over the region and was the basis for a series of articles that she was able to get published in newspapers from Haridwar to Kanpur. In little more than six weeks, the reaction from the local agricultural community forced the politicians to adopt the same slogan she had popularized through her pamphlet: *ma ganga bikri nahin ho jayga*, the Mother Ganges is not for sale.

The sense of empowerment she felt was intoxicating. A better world was possible, and she was one of those who would make sure it came to pass. Vimala Krishna and the other senior members of WAI agreed. Her salary was increased, she was given a new position—public relations secretary—and they agreed to let her concentrate on women's issues whenever there were no other pressing campaigns that needed her attention. In effect, she became what she had trained to become without ever seriously thinking she would: an investigative journalist, one whose mere presence on the scene became a cause of concern for vested interests, aware that any exploitation or abuses she witnessed, especially when they concerned women, would likely become a focus of the reading public.

Thinking of those three years reminded her of the story the Mother had told her disciples about maya the day after her initiation. Had the Mother been looking into her future as Saraswati sat there by the edge of the dais in the first flush of devotion? Very likely. The parallels were obvious.

A teenage disciple of a forest sage asked the master to explain to him about maya. When the disciple could not understand his explanation, the master sent him to the river to fetch a bucket of water. The boy dutifully took his bucket and set out down the forest path to the river. There he met a young maiden, the daughter of the local raja, who had gone there to bathe. The two young people struck up a conversation. A mutual attraction sprung up and she invited him to pay a short visit to the palace. That short visit turned into an overnight stay, the overnight stay into a love affair. Soon they were married, had children of their own, and eventually he became king when his wife's parents died. Life was good to him, so good that he completely forgot his youthful apprenticeship in the forest. One day, his kingdom fell under attack by a neighboring kingdom. His forces were soon routed. After a tongue lashing from his wife, who berated him for endangering her father's legacy, he was forced to flee to the forest to save his life, the same forest he had left many years earlier to fetch a bucket of water for his master. As the defeated and saddened king entered deeper and deeper into the forest, he started to feel a sense of familiarity. He had been there before, he was sure, but he could not remember when. Those memories were lost now in the fog of the past. He happened upon a path and began to follow it. With each step the sense of familiarity grew, until he emerged into a clearing and saw his master sitting there in the same spot where he had left him more than twenty years earlier. "Where is my water?" the master asked. Suddenly it all came back to him. The years he had spent falling in love, siring children, governing a kingdom, and fleeing that kingdom in shame and in panic, now seemed to him nothing more than a dream, as ephemeral and as fleeting as any dream that disappears into the shadows the moment one awakens from sleep. "Now do you understand?" the master asked. "That is maya."

Saraswati had laughed and laughed when the Mother came to the end of the story. She had told it beautifully, and the ending had come as a total surprise, even though, as the climax neared, she could feel the same sense of inexplicable familiarity that the disciple felt as he walked through the forest. The lesson remained imprinted on her psyche along with the beguiling smile the Mother sported when she came to the end of the story, but somehow she had forgotten it once she returned to Delhi and started falling in love with her successes as a WAI journalist, working for all the right causes but forgetting that the Mother had sent her to the river to bring back a bucket of water. As her notoriety increased and her confidence blossomed, her passion and her fervor for each of the many causes that demanded her attention gradually shunted aside the spiritual ideal-ism that had carried her buoyantly through her teenage years and into her early twenties. Her meditation sessions gradually became brief respites in a hectic daily schedule, more from force of habit than anything else. The intervals between them grew further and further apart until she no longer considered herself a meditator but only someone who managed to sit still a few times a month with her eyes closed to breathe in a little of the taste of life and gather the energy and will to go on. The less she meditated, the more her mind grew restless with the thousand impressions she was witness to, the seemingly endless litany of woe and injustice that made her burn with indignation, even as it brought tears to her eyes. Instead of looking to Vivekananda and Nivedita as her heroes, she began seeing herself as a female Bhima wielding the mighty mace of her pen to fell the enemies of mankind—the rich, the arrogant, the greedy, the pitiless and compassionless. But Bhima did not have Vivekananda's shining eyes or Nivedita's faith in the hands of Providence. Saraswati began having trouble sleeping, harassed by thoughts of the work yet undone, grieved by memories of the things she had seen and turned over in her head a hundred times as she tried to convert those images into words in the hardbound notebook she carried with her wherever she went. Many of her nights in the capital were spent on a bench in her office after typing until well into the morning. Not infrequently, she would get up a couple of hours later and return to the computer to relieve herself of the sights and sounds that would not let her sleep. Though she continually told herself that nothing could be more meaningful than the life she was leading, the happiness of her childhood, which had never completely abandoned her during her difficult years in college, faded and vanished without her notice. A slow, imperceptible depression started seeping into the unguarded recesses of her mind, like a thin fog rising in the hour before dawn that remains to mask the sun. It was as if the long momentum of her earlier years had run out. What was left in its place was a growing despondency that she held back by sheer force of will and the constant distractions of the heartfelt struggle that gave her no time or motive to examine what was happening inside her. But when this irrepressible tide grew strong enough, its insistence could no longer be ignored. She could feel it in her stomach and in the sudden shafts of fear that flew at her out of the night when she walked the dimly lit streets of Delhi after a public meeting or lay down on her bench in the office, listening against her will to the groaning of the water pipes and the shrill creaking of the corrugated tin roof when the wind gusted and swirled.

Late one morning, a few days before Holi, the festival of colors, she was squinting into her word processor when she heard the Mother's name mentioned from the other side of the office. Her ears perked up and her fingers stopped moving. These were not people who took an interest in spiritual figures, but for some reason they were discussing a public kirtan organized by a counsel of religious leaders to commemorate the birth of Mahaprabhu, the great Vaishnava saint, a day that coincided with the Holi festival. She had not seen the Mother in four years. Beset by a sudden feverish anxiety, she walked over to where they were sitting and asked them about the kirtan. Her colleague could not remember the details—she had seen the announcement in a newspaper the day before—but she thought it interesting that a well-known saint would be participating in a public kirtan on Holi. There were newspapers in the office but Saraswati felt a need to escape. She slipped out of the office and went downstairs to the nearest newsstand where she bought copies of all three leading dailies. She sat down on the bench in front of the newsstand and searched hungrily through them until she found the announcement in the calendar section of the *Times of India*. The Mother and seven other religious leaders would be leading a twenty-four-hour kirtan in the ballroom of a large hotel about a mile from the airport, beginning Saturday evening.

When Saturday evening arrived, Saraswati found herself sitting on the floor in a back corner of the ballroom, hunched up between the wall and a modestly overweight Punjabi couple who sat on a blanket with their three young children, munching savories and cautioning them with upraised fingers to sit still. For the next half hour she watched the hall fill up, waiting for the Mother to appear on the wooden dais at the front. The rich scent of incense and the inviting sounds of the musicians tuning their instruments brought back memories of her visits to the Mother's ashram. There had always been kirtan around the Mother, and she always associated the poignancy of those meetings with the raucous, rhythmic chanting she had first grown to love as a child during religious festivals when the villagers would stay up all night swaying to the thrumming of the *dolak*, sending their voices out into the night to the gods that they were sure would hear them and be pleased with their devotion.

At ten minutes to eight, the Mother arrived with a small retinue dressed in the traditional white cotton, every one of them known to her. The sight of the Mother and the devotees who had once pronounced Saraswati's name with fondness brought tears to her eyes. Sadness welled up inside her. She thought of her parents whom she hadn't seen for three years, though they lived a mere three hours from the city by bus. Her pride caught in her throat like an ugly tumor and she felt ashamed. Then the music started. The loudspeakers made the wall next to her reverberate. Nearly two thousand voices joined themselves to the musicians, and the flood of sound assaulted her ears like the trumpets of an invading army. As she struggled with her emotions, she fell back into the familiar chants with the surety of a habit lost but not forgotten, but not even the sacred syllables could lift her out of the sadness that pressed in on her from all sides and made the room seem far smaller than it was. An hour later, the Mother and her retinue rose to leave, exiting by a back door to the rear of the dais. Her departure brought a fresh sense of anguish to Saraswati. The closing of the door seemed symbolic, the ending of a hope that had been too faint for her to notice. She closed her eyes and dropped her head to her hands, trying to fight off the music, which began to throb in her temples like the onset of a migraine. A couple of minutes later, she felt someone touch her on the shoulder. She looked up to see Revati standing over her, a diminutive, dark-skinned Bihari woman who had been with the Mother since childhood and rarely left her side.

"Mother wants to see you. She's waiting outside in the parking lot."

Saraswati hurried after Revati to where the Mother was standing by the side of her car, surrounded by a small crowd of devotees. She bent down to touch the saint's feet, the tears thick in her eyes, and received the Mother's blessing, a weathered hand pressed lightly to the crown of her head accompanied by the words *shubhamastu.*

"Daughter, I am leaving now for Haridwar. I will be there for two days. Come and see me. It has been too long; you must make up for lost time."

The Mother's words sounded in Saraswati's ears like the voice of her own conscience. She left the following morning for Haridwar. Though it was the beginning of March and the chill wind off the Ganges in the early morning stiffened her bones, it seemed like the onset of summer to her. The frost that had encrusted her heart was thawed by the Mother's presence. Though the aged saint never once mentioned her giving up her spiritual practices, Saraswati felt remorse driving her like a whip. She joined in the collective meditations morning and evening, and whenever she couldn't be with the Mother, she passed her time in a relentless, unforgiving effort to control her body and her mind with the yogic techniques she had willingly abandoned. After seeing the Mother off for Benares, she returned to Delhi and requested a one-month leave of absence for health reasons. Following the Mother's suggestion, she decided to spend that month in Rishikesh, meditating and recovering her spiritual life. The Rimpoche arrived in Rishikesh three days after she did. She signed up for the intensive on the spot, sure that this was why the Mother had suggested she go there, and followed him upriver to the secluded ashram where he would conduct the three-week program.

Saraswati knew very little about Tibetan Buddhism at the time. She had read a couple of books by the Dalai Lama while she was in college and a copy of the biography of Milarepa that a friend had given her as a graduation present. But the suffering of the Tibetan people was well known to her, and their defiant faith in their religion and their spiritual teachers despite decades of exile and Chinese oppression was all she needed to know about the authenticity of their practice. She looked upon the intensive as an opportunity to make up for the time she had lost; the enforced nature of the intensive routine was exactly what she needed to return her to the habits she had once had. But the intensive turned out to be much more than a regimented routine of meditation and silence. She had not counted on the Rimpoche's presence when she signed on, but it was his presence that made the difference. He was a small, wiry man in his early seventies with thin, round-rimmed glasses, leathery skin cured and tanned by the immense altitudes of his childhood and the closeness of the Tibetan sun, and a frank, open, almost childlike smile that masked the iron will and taskmaster severity that characterized his relationship with his disciples. In her first private session, he scolded her for abandoning her practice for so long and cautioned her that she should consider her pride to be a venomous snake that would rob her of her life if she did not cut it off at the head. He taught her a meditation technique to practice alongside what she had been taught by the Mother; and lo, her pride did rear up like a cobra and spit its venom directly in her face. Every day the Rimpoche asked her about it, and every day she recounted her struggles in an increasingly humble and distraught voice. On the eleventh day, he taught her a second technique and told her to will herself not to lose her concentration when her struggles reached their apex, not even when she was sleeping. Though by the fifteenth day she was weary beyond belief and frayed to distraction by the crowd of internal weaknesses that fell upon her like dragons from a medieval Tibetan painting, she willed herself to keep fighting. Two days before the intensive ended, she locked herself into lotus posture and remained awake all night in meditation. One hour before the four o'clock gong rang to call the meditators from their cells to the morning practice, the inner voices quieted and she felt her individuality dissolve in a flood of feathery soft effulgence that could have been the moon peering through her window had it not been a new moon night, the darkness so complete at that hour that not even the few stars that slanted through the window could pierce the impermeable fastness of her room. She remained lost in that state until the gong sounded and she became aware again of her ego, floating in a sea of silence, preparing to make its journey back into the world.

The memories of those three weeks and that first taste of spiritual ecstasy were still strong in her mind when she noticed the chill piercing through her sari. She got up and went to the window to close the shutters. A glance at her watch showed that it was nearly midnight. She had been reminiscing about her past for the better part of two hours. It had been a long time since she had revisited those years—she did not ordinarily give in to nostalgia—but there were times when the Mother sanctioned taking a backward glance down roads already traveled. This, she felt, was one of those times. The lingering emotions that played in her stomach, the slight nervous tension that she had grown unused to, told her that those samskaras were not dead yet. There was a reason she was still here. As she got ready for bed, her mind filled with an expanding image of the ashram: its fragrant courtyards, the high walls that surrounded them, and the mountains beyond. For all her chafing at the bit, she knew that those walls protected her not only from the outside world but from her own samskaras—the obvious reason why the Mother had sent her there. She might be in exile but she knew it was warranted. Maya was a difficult ocean to cross. She had to learn how to handle those waves before she could return to the outside world.

As she lay down, she thought back to the experience Rodrigo had described for her. From his description, it did not appear to be the true dissolution of the ego that happens in deep meditation, but it did seem to be—incredibly so—a genuine glimpse of that state. He had not even been meditating at the time. He had just gotten up from an afternoon's writing. In fact, he had only been meditating at all for a handful of months. How was this possible, Mother? How does a novice and a westerner have such a profound experience with so little preparation? For a moment, she felt something akin to a mixture of awe and apprehension. She was used to new meditators having powerful experiences in the beginning stages of their practice. There was even a word for it in yoga philosophy: *samvit shakti*, those brief openings of the mind that serve to inspire the seeker to keep moving along what is a very difficult path. But normally, these were relatively superficial experiences that only seemed powerful because the new aspirant had nothing to compare them to. This was different. There was nothing superficial about it and no pretense involved, from what she could see. His was an authentic glimpse of what every yogi longs for but finds so difficult to achieve, even after years of practice: the falling away of the ego, the touch of divine grace that reveals to us what our deepest self has never forgotten—that we are just a drop in an ocean of consciousness, the drop that is the ocean.

She wondered if he even realized how profound his experience was. Probably not. He also had nothing to compare it to. No amount of philosophy can truly prepare you for the encounter with the self when it first happens. Could this be the source of the disquiet she had felt around him a few months earlier, the intuitive recognition of his unusual nature? She remembered Inayat Khan's *The Art of Music* and his exploration of the close connection between spiritual meditation and artistic creation. It was something she had thought about often during her college days, how single-minded creative pursuit could engender spiritual states. Something similar must have happened to him. But even then, it could not have happened unless the way had already been prepared. She had no doubts anymore that powerful past-life samskaras were leading him down the spiritual path. She was his guide for the moment and the principle witness to the unfolding of his spiritual life, but she was no more responsible for what he was experiencing than she was for the wind at his back.

Whatever doubts remained in her mind about Rodrigo had more to do with her own samskaras than with his.

25

RODRIGO HAD LONG FELT a special connection with Tibet, ever since his senior year in high school when the Chinese police brutally put down a peaceful demonstration in Lhasa, killing at least thirteen people and wounding hundreds more. The images he saw in the newsreels and the clandestine photos smuggled out by Western onlookers conveyed to him a strange blend of the exotic and the tragic. He loved the high cheekbones and colorful robes that reminded him of American Indians, but he shuddered to see innocent citizens running in terror from the Chinese bullets. Curious about this culture of which he knew little or nothing, he read avidly the articles that were then appearing in the newspapers and periodicals. They educated him on the history of the Chinese invasion and occupation of Tibet, but the one thing none of them explained was why the Chinese would want to be there in the first place—other than to back up a spurious claim that Tibet was historically part of China. What did they have to gain in those inhospitable mountains where, as far as he could see, the Tibetan people had to be heroic to be able to thrive under conditions that would make the rest of humanity cower?

The demonstrations continued all through his senior year and into his freshman year in college. Periodically, the Chinese Armed Police would open fire on the peacefully demonstrating crowds, adding to the fatalities and the wounded and deepening the world's mistrust of the so-called "People's" Republic. At that time everyone he knew—his classmates, friends, and family—was aghast at the stories and pictures coming out of China. The idea that such brutality and oppression could still be going on in the world's most populous country, thirteen years after the death of Mao Zedong and the end of the Cultural Revolution, astounded and angered him. He was young and not very serious as a rule, but it was hard not to take this seriously. How could such things be happening, just across the ocean from where he was growing up? Could people really be that stupid, that twisted, that cruel?

In March of his freshman year, reports of new atrocities surfaced as Lhasa went up in flames and hundreds of protesters were gunned down by Chinese police. Three months later, just after finals week, with most of the campus still in a swoon from the post-finals parties, he woke up to news of the Tiananmen

Square massacre: thousands of peaceful demonstrators shot dead in the heart of Peking in front of the government tanks and the eyes of the world. The parties stopped, as if cold water from across the globe had been thrown in everybody's face. Those students who still remained on campus either walked the quads in silence or else remained glued to their TV sets, well aware that most of the dead and wounded were students not much different than themselves, young men and women barely out of their teens who might have also been spending their time partying had they not felt their lives unbearably circumscribed by an oppressive, totalitarian regime.

All that summer and into the fall, he followed the news from that region almost as faithfully as he followed the *New York Review of Books*. When finals week rolled around again in December and the networks carried the Dalai Lama's Nobel Peace Prize Acceptance Speech, he stood up in his dormitory lounge and cheered. The other students, who were occupying the sofas and easy chairs, enduring the news as they waited for the Lakers–Magic game to come on, let out a few obligatory laughs, but the merriment lasted no more than a few scant seconds. All of them knew that the Dalai Lama deserved that prize as much as anyone ever had, after all that he and his people had been through.

His interest in Tibet had continued throughout his academic life. Five years before taking his sabbatical, he had agreed to become an advisor for the Chapel Hill chapter of Students for a Free Tibet, a volunteer position he took quite seriously and which gave him a great deal of satisfaction. Yet for all his interest in Tibet, he had never taken the time to learn much about Tibetan Buddhism. Now, it seemed that his connection with that embattled but dignified country was coming full circle. He had taken part in their political struggle; now it was time for him to take part in their spiritual practices.

He began his preparations for the intensive by buying several books on the history and practice of Tibetan Buddhism that Saraswati had recommended, including one on the Kagyupa lineage to which the Kulya Rimpoche belonged. He discovered that Tibetan Buddhist practice was a branch of Buddhist Tantra and thus bore many similarities to the various schools of Hindu Tantra he had already read about. The very word tantra, whenever he saw it or heard it pronounced, conjured up an indefinable air of mystery and allure. Adding to this air of intrigue was the fact that the priest in his dreams was a worshipper of Kali, one of the principal Tantric deities. Some of the esoteric practices he read about seemed incredibly intricate, involving a plethora of mantras and mystic symbols and a host of gods, goddesses, and demiurges. In some cases, they seemed more like the practice of magic than spirituality. Among the books Saraswati recommended were a pair by Alexandra David–Neel, the first Western woman ever to enter Tibet and the first to become an ordained lama. The tales she told were almost too fantastic to believe: yogis who seemed more like sorcerers, holding contests to see who could melt more snow with the heat they generated through a special technique called *tumo*; running as fast as horses for days without stopping through the practice of *lung gom-pa*, wind meditation; training in telepathic communication. Yet David–Neel seemed as trustworthy a source as one could find, a crusty, pragmatic, intrepid French woman who would not believe what she had not seen with her own eyes, a woman of such resolve that she crossed the Himalayas on foot into the Tibetan plateau at a time when that land was forbidden to foreigners. That feat alone, along with managing to become a lama by passing herself off as a man, seemed to him in many ways the equal of the feats of sorcery she had witnessed during her travels.

Even more fantastic was the *Life of Milarepa*. The eleventh-century Tibetan saint had learned the black Tantric arts as a young man—not with any spiritual intent, but because he wanted to revenge himself on an evil uncle who had dispossessed his family and virtually enslaved him and his mother after his father's death. Milarepa used the incantations he learned to bring down the stone roof of his uncle's house during a party, killing more than thirty people. When this became known, he was forced to flee the district. Overcome by remorse, he began searching for a spiritual teacher who could help him to expiate his bad karma and achieve spiritual liberation. His search led him to Marpa, who accepted him as his disciple. Instead of initiating him, however, Marpa put him to work building a stone house. When the house was nearing completion, Marpa asked him to tear it down and rebuild it in a different spot. This repeated itself four more times over the course of several years. Despairing of ever getting initiation, Milarepa sought out a different guru, but when that proved fruitless, he returned to Marpa and received initiation through the intercession of Marpa's wife. After his initiation, Marpa revealed that he had purposely put Milarepa through such travails in order to burn off the heavy burden of evil karma that he had kept secret from everyone. Had he finished the last house, he would have exhausted that samskara and achieved liberation very quickly; since he hadn't, he would have to perform rigorous spiritual practices for many years.

Rodrigo loved the story, both for its literary value and for the hope it gave him that his own struggles, present and future, could be a means of overcoming his burden of bad karma. The idea that there could exist mantras capable of conjuring up terrible storms and bringing down the roof of a house, thus fulfilling man's dream of controlling nature directly with his mind, seemed both a fanciful notion right out of ancient mythology, with its wizards and fateful enchantments, and a sure indication that the world was not as circumscribed as his twentieth-century Western upbringing had led him to believe. But far more important was the hope Milarepa's story gave him that he could overcome his past through hard work. Milarepa had nearly ruined his body by building and tearing down stone houses; afterward, he retired to a Himalayan cave and spent years in intense meditation, struggling with internal demons far worse than any Rodrigo harbored. The ordeals he passed through were monumental but he came out of it a saint. To what extent the man and the legend had intermingled, he could not know, but the lesson remained the same. If Rodrigo were willing to pay the price in hard work and sacrifice, then he could become the person he now longed to become. That willingness was the true measure of the man.

Though his own practices in no way resembled the arduous discipline that Milarepa followed when he retired to the Himalayan caves in a single-minded pursuit of liberation, Rodrigo began to feel a sense of kinship with the great Tibetan sage. Two days after he agreed to participate in the intensive, Saraswati presented him with a routine she had designed for him. It consisted of longer sessions of sitting meditation, gradually increasing in length over the month of January; twice-daily asanas, including certain postures specifically designed to improve his physical ability to sit; and a week-long cleansing fast followed by strict dietary restrictions to help him get ready for the austere rations of the intensive that would serve to free up for meditation the energy that normally went into digestion. He found the new routine exacting and often exhausting, but it gave him a sense that he was following the same trail up the mountain that Milarepa had followed more than nine hundred years earlier.

One afternoon, Rodrigo brought the book along with him to his private session, aware of its presence in his knapsack like a hidden talisman. This time they met in the secluded courtyard in front of Saraswati's room. It was a crisp January morning, cloudless, as it had been for the past few weeks. Rodrigo had taken to wearing a fur-lined jacket in the mornings and evenings to ward off the chill wind that blew off the river. Saraswati had an orange woolen shawl wrapped snugly around her shoulders.

"Would you mind if we walked by the river for a while?" she asked. "I'd like to get some sun."

Rodrigo followed her through several shaded courtyards and out the side gate of the ashram, which opened onto the river about forty meters west of the Shiva statue. As they emerged into the afternoon sunshine, Rodrigo opened his jacket to let in what felt like a sumptuous warmth. He caught the distant scent of baking bread from one of the shops back up the road and heard the ringing of the bell in the small temple above the ghat. Emboldened by the brisk afternoon air and the familiar sights and sounds that now seemed as much a part of the feeling of home as any in his past, he asked Saraswati what she thought about the ready acceptance the Tibetans seemed to have for tales of magic and supernatural powers.

"I think it shows that Tibetan culture is not so divorced from fundamental spiritual realities as are most other cultures. India is much the same as Tibet in this respect, especially rural India. We are taught from childhood that there is much more to the world than what we can see with our eyes or touch with our hands or understand with our intellect. Unfortunately, the more we fall under the influence of Western civilization, the more we forget that this material reality is only the shadow of a spiritual reality. Things that a materialist, with the typical arrogance of the materialist, assumes are impossible, a spiritualist knows are quite possible. Which is not to say they are necessarily any more interesting."

"Do you think it is actually possible that a person can create a storm with mantras, like Milarepa was supposed to have done?"

"Of course. The mind is capable of anything. Gaining control over matter is just one of the feats it is capable of. The mind is not bound by the limitations of the three material dimensions. It can see into the past and into the future just as readily as it can see into the present, and it can certainly impact directly on matter. You can call it magic or supernatural power, if you wish, but the fact is, these are all natural phenomena. The mind and its powers are just as much a part of nature as a mountain or a river; the difference is that the mind is much more subtle than matter, and it's precisely because it is so subtle that learning to harness its powers is such a monumental challenge. For that reason such powers are very rare. It's only natural that most people are unacquainted with them. The ordinary person will likely never come in contact with anyone who has such powers, but if you think they don't exist or that such things are impossible because you haven't seen them with your own eyes—well, that is nothing short of foolishness. All these so-called supernatural powers have been minutely catalogued in the yogic texts, and there are innumerable examples throughout history of yogis who have mastered them. But then, you are already aware of this. What is the title of the third chapter of the Yoga Sutras?"

"Powers."

"Literally, *siddhi*s, or occult powers. Occult because they are hidden. In Tibet and India, the day-to-day lives of our common people are still steeped in the traditions of our great spiritual teachers, so people haven't forgotten that these things exist, even if they haven't seen them with their own eyes. In the West, from what I understand, most people would laugh at you if you tried to convince them that a person could control the weather with their mind or see into the future or materialize an object out of thin air."

"Pretty much."

"Maybe in some respects they're better off that way. People are too easily fascinated by such things. Who wouldn't want to be able to control the elements? Think of it. It's every child's dream. Point your finger and stop the rain. But what a waste of energy! Once one of Ramakrishna's disciples told him about a sadhu who had acquired the power to walk on water after thirty years of a certain rigorous yogic practice. Ramakrishna's comment was, 'What folly! Can this power take him one step nearer to God? For three paisa, a boatman would have taken him across the river in his boat.' That's pretty much the attitude that most spiritual masters have toward these things. Why would you waste your time trying to develop occult powers when you could be using that same energy to achieve enlightenment? It's pure folly. That's one of the reasons you almost never see spiritual masters displaying their powers in public. It sets a bad example. Anyhow, you won't have to worry about such things in the intensive. That's not the kind of Tantra the Rimpoche is going to be teaching you. He's going to be teaching you the real Tantra."

"The real Tantra?"

Saraswati paused and pointed at a flock of birds that was wheeling above the river in a graceful collective pirouette that seemed as if it had been painted into a vast canvas framed by the gray shadows of the mountains. They stopped and watched silently for a minute or two before she picked up the thread of the conversation.

"The natural tendency of water is to flow downward in accordance with the law of gravity. If you want it to flow upward you must apply force. There is no other way. The human mind also follows a natural law, the law of evolution. If it is left on its own it will continue to evolve, but evolution is a very slow process. If you want to accelerate that movement, you have to apply force. In other words, you have to expend effort. This is the underlying spirit of Tantra. *Tan* means 'dullness' or 'ignorance,' and *trae* means 'to liberate.' Tantra is that which liberates you from ignorance, that which leads you to illumination. This is impossible without effort—prodigious, monumental effort. The Tantric doesn't want to wait hundreds of lifetimes to achieve enlightenment, so she approaches life like a battle. Here the enemy is ignorance, all the mental weaknesses, complexes, and fears that stand between us and our goal. Armed with her practices, the Tantric picks up the sword of discrimination and sets out to slay her enemy, and she doesn't rest until the battle is won. At least that's a poetic way of describing it. The main thing in Tantra is that you don't avoid obstacles or challenges; rather, you seek them out because you know that it is only by overcoming these obstacles that you can reach your goal. If you are afraid of something, then go right it at until you overcome that fear. If greed is your problem, then look for opportunities to be generous. Give until it hurts and then keep giving until it doesn't hurt any more. Face your demons and challenge them outright. The Rimpoche is all about that. He points out your weaknesses and challenges you to have the courage to defeat them. Your meditation is the battlefield and your practices are your weapons. There is nothing easy about the Tantric approach, but there's no denying that it's the fastest way to liberation. You've seen the great Tibetan paintings of the different demons like Mara and so forth? Well, in Tantra you go looking for those demons and you do it with a smile on your face. In Western mythology you might compare it to a knight riding out in search of a dragon. It's the ultimate adventure, the making of the knight. It requires great courage and great perseverance, but if you succeed, then you win the ultimate prize: the lady of illumination."

Rodrigo remembered that talk whenever his legs ached that month or his mind rebelled against the strictness of his new regime. He told himself that such difficulties were nothing compared with those he would face when he joined the intensive, and that those would be nothing compared to what Milarepa had faced or the Buddha underneath the Bo tree. But that did not make them any the less difficult. Saraswati had not only put him on a rigorous schedule, she watched over him with great attention to make sure he followed that schedule to the letter of her law. His reward for all this effort was twofold: the satisfaction of seeing the progress he was making under her direct and exacting tutelage, and the chance to spend hours with her in spiritual conversation. Though many of these hours were spent either on the roof above her room or on a bench in the courtyard below, she sometimes joined him on his afternoon walks, transforming a time he had formerly dedicated to reflection or daydream into an extension of his studies. Free time became a rare commodity, but he found that the lack of idleness was not a burden but a blessing.

The more time they spent together, the more curious Rodrigo became about Saraswati's personal life, but he was careful not to voice any unwarranted questions, instinctively respecting the unspoken line she drew between her personal life and her function as a spiritual teacher. One afternoon, he was surprised to see her waiting for him on the bench in front of her room wearing a white sari. He had never before seen her wearing anything but the saffron sari that he accepted as the symbol of a renunciant. Unable to restrain his curiosity, he asked her about it, eliciting a light smile.

"My saffron saris are drying at the moment. I ran out of clean ones and had to wash them all this morning. All two of them, that is."

"And you're allowed to wear a white sari, then?"

Saraswati looked amused by the question. "I wear what I choose to wear, Rodrigo. I am not a sannyasi. I try to follow the sannyasi lifestyle, it's true, but that's my personal choice. Wearing the saffron sari makes it easier for me to maintain that discipline, but up until this point I haven't taken initiation into any sannyasi order."

This was a revelation for Rodrigo. He had assumed that she was a female monk, similar to the swami and the other monks who inhabited the ashram or walked the streets of Rishikesh, male and female alike. He would have liked to ask more about that choice but she had forthwith changed the subject. This one granule of information was as much as he had learned of her personal life in the four months he had known her, nor had she ever asked him about his, other than querying him about his writing on that one occasion. It felt a little strange, spending so much time with someone he knew so little about without ever once touching on personal matters. He had learned through his own experience as a teacher that no matter how much he tried to keep his relationships with his students strictly professional, the more time he spent with them, the more the artificial barriers between teacher and student dissolved, as if both time and proximity were powerful solvents. He had often reflected on this, eventually realizing that despite the fact that his students came to him to learn what he knew and they did not, there was no escaping the fact that he and they were simply fellow creatures sharing a slice of the insoluble mystery of life frozen into a few moments in time. But studying with Saraswati was unlike anything he had ever experienced, either as a teacher or as a student. He still had no idea what she thought about him. He liked to think that they were drawing closer to each other, but in some ways she was as distant as anyone he had ever known. From where he sat, she appeared almost bereft of ego, as if her personal life had never existed. Or if it had, then she scarcely remembered it and no longer gave it any attention, so rooted did she seem in the spiritual reality of the moment. Perhaps the thawing he felt of what had once seemed a deliberate aloofness on her part was only an illusion that he was creating with his writer's predilection for drama, the beginning of a story between them no more substantial than the story he was living out through his characters whenever he sat down before his computer to write. She was, in short, an enigma to him, a puzzle he felt instinctively intent on solving without knowing if he would ever have the opportunity to do so.

Despite the fact that Saraswati's personal history was little more to him than a thin mist, Rodrigo gradually became aware of aspects of her personality that were not in evidence when she was teaching class. She could be witty, even bitingly sarcastic, especially when their talks touched on any kind of social injustice, even the small iniquities that generally went unnoticed to all but the most observant of eyes. She did not smile often, but when she did, it was a smile of genuine warmth, sometimes radiating a cheerfulness that felt irrepressibly infectious in contrast to her normal tranquil but serious air. On rare occasions her smile turned ironic, but only when she reflected on spiritual paradoxes that invariably escaped Rodrigo's comprehension, or when she was pointing out the subtle injustices and ethical inconsistencies that human beings too often willingly embraced by covering them with a pale veneer of social orthodoxy. Despite her tranquil, deliberate demeanor and the thoughtfulness that always resided in her eyes, he could sense a fire in her that she kept carefully hidden. He did not think of it as passion, though he had seen it nearly reach that pitch when she talked to him of the injustices against women in her country and the righteous anger she claimed she possessed but which he had never seen. It felt to him more like an iron will that was not cold and unyielding but rather fueled by a secret inner furnace, a source of strength she cultivated assiduously for the day when she would need its heat for the task she had set out for herself. He assumed that task to be the quest for enlightenment, but there were times when he suspected that the truth was not that simple, that she was a being who was not only spiritually elevated but more complex than he imagined.

His brilliant but resolutely reserved teacher was a frequent topic of conversation among the little group of students who frequented her classes on a regular basis. As could be expected, those who also lived at the ashram did not fail to notice how much individual attention she was giving Rodrigo. She also sat for short individual sessions with them on occasion, and they would seek her out at times when they had some pressing doubt or problem, but such meetings were relatively rare and thus in great contrast to the amount of time she was now dedicating to Rodrigo. The subject came up one day at lunch when Georg remarked that the American seemed to have been elevated to a position of favor, quoting the biblical phrase "the last shall be first" with light but good-natured sarcasm. It was some ten days after Saraswati had told him about the intensive and Rodrigo was quick to explain the nature of their arrangement.

"I'd like to think that it might continue after I get back from the intensive but I know better. She's being conscientious, that's all. She suggested I take part in the intensive, so she has to prepare me for it. Anyhow, I'm enjoying the attention while it lasts. You know, if anyone else wants to sign on for the intensive, I bet you'll get the same treatment. Any takers? Anybody want to join me?"

Georg threw up his hands. "No thanks, maestro. These fat legs of mine would probably fall off if I had to sit as long as she is making you sit."

Ely and Marlena, who was getting ready to return to Switzerland, and the two newer students who were sitting with them all had similar reactions. But they were curious to hear more about their talks and the regimented discipline he was following. When Rodrigo told them that she was not actually a sannyasi, although she wore the saffron robes, they were uniformly surprised. That was when Marlena offered a piece of information that radically altered Rodrigo's perception of his teacher.

"I heard she used to be some kind of radical journalist."

"You're kidding," Rodrigo said, not quite able to believe what he was hearing.

"I was pretty surprised myself, but yes, it seems so. I got to know this Indian family that was staying here a couple of months ago. Nice people—except for the husband; he was a little overbearing. Overweight, too. But his wife was an angel. I was eating dinner with them one evening and he started complaining about Saraswati. It seems she had made trouble for some of his business friends with her articles. According to him, she had cost them lots of money by getting the public up in arms about their business practices. He went on and on about why they were harboring a socialist in a spiritual ashram. He even said something to the swami about it; naturally it didn't do him any good. After they left, I tried asking her about it, but you can guess what she told me: 'The past is just a dream, Marlena. If you want to wake up, you have to let the dream go.' And then, of course, she changed the subject."

"Typical Saraswati," Georg remarked. "Everybody's got a past, but I doubt you'll ever get her to show any interest in hers."

"Have you guys ever read Carlos Castaneda?" Ely chimed in. "I remember his teacher, Don Juan, telling him about the importance of erasing personal history. He says that when other people know your personal history they pin you down with their thoughts. They create an image of who you are based on your past and that limits your freedom. Maybe that's what she's doing. Maybe she's trying to erase her past so that those samskaras don't box her in."

"Well, if you are going to live in the present," Marlena said, "then you can't go around dwelling on the past. It makes perfect sense. She may be taking it to an extreme, but maybe that's what it takes."

Rodrigo did not offer his opinion, but everyone else agreed that Saraswati must be following a similar type of discipline, yet another indication, as they saw it, that the perennial philosophy could be found wherever one went, regardless of culture. For his part, Rodrigo was too surprised by this unexpected piece of information to give the rest of the conversation more than his superficial attention. The ensuing discussion was as lively as ever but he spent most of it occupied with his thoughts. The more he thought about it, the more he felt sure that what Marlena had said was true. It would explain Saraswati's unexpected interest in his writing—the only time she had ever shown any interest in his personal life. It would also explain the passion—if he could call it that—that she showed whenever she talked about social injustice in India. There was an intensity about her in those moments that never surfaced when she was talking about spirituality, the subject to which she confined most of their conversations. Those were the moments when she had felt most human to him, most accessible. Obviously they were things she had not simply read about; they were things she had seen with her own eyes and then written about. But if so, then what had happened to make her give up that life and retire to a Himalayan ashram? That was the question he would have loved to have answered. If there had indeed been a time that she had lived as immersed in the world as he, following a kindred profession, then there was much more to this woman than had met his eye. Such a radical change in lifestyle did not simply arise out of nothing. There had to be a story behind it, most likely a fascinating story. Now that Marlena had alerted him to this all-important detail from her past, he would be on the lookout for any chance to bring it into their conversations. If the interest she had shown in his writing and the intensity she displayed when talking about social problems were any indication, it was a samskara that was not completely buried, no matter how serious her efforts might be to erase her past. It also gave them one more thing in common, though somehow he doubted she would see it that way.

Despite Saraswati's cheerful observation that he would have plenty of time for his writing in the month leading up to the intensive and thus would hardly miss the three weeks that he would have to do without, the arduous schedule and their frequent talks left very little time for his novel. In truth, that entire month felt much more like a spiritual intensive than a writing sabbatical. Even when he was not performing his spiritual practices, attending her classes, or completing the reading assignments she gave him, the challenges he faced in his practices and the subtle spiritual ideas that he was trying to digest continued to preoccupy his mind. He was surprised how much energy his meditation required. The supposition that sitting still for a number of hours each day would be a most refreshing and relaxing activity afforded him a rueful laugh. The truth was, it took enormous effort to wrestle with his mind for long periods of time. Often he arrived at breakfast feeling ravenously hungry after two hours of determined struggle in his morning meditation, and as the days went by he felt his desire for food noticeably increasing. When he brought this development to Saraswati's attention, wondering if he were actually burning calories through his mental effort or if his desires were just running away with him, all she said was, "Don't worry about it. It's normal; it'll pass. The important thing is to maintain your discipline." The diet she had imposed limited how much he could eat almost down to the mouthful. She forbade him tea and excursions to any of the numerous vegetarian restaurants in Rishikesh that were such a delight to the normal spiritual traveler. He was also on his honor to report to her any slippage in his dietary regime. Whenever he thought of adding something prohibited to his tray during mealtimes, the thought of having to admit his lapse to her was an effective deterrent, but it did not make the discipline any easier to follow, and at times the thoughts that most disturbed his meditation were images of succulent dishes that churned his stomach with gastric juice and left his mouth wet with saliva.

With all his frustrations that month, especially those connected with his recalcitrant stomach, it was little wonder that in the few hours he did find for his writing, his characters prepared a banquet for his mind that would have done justice to his wildest fantasies. He took this as a sign of compassion on their part toward their unseen creator. Often the sights and smells of those South Indian dishes called to him as he wrote even more than the mantras he was trying to ride toward liberation. It was Ambika and Le Gentil's way of helping to see him through difficult times, he decided, and he was grateful for their intervention.

The event in question was Ambika's invitation to Le Gentil to dine with her and her family on their estate just south of the city. For the astronomer, who had no dietary restrictions to trouble his eighteenth-century mind, the primary source of both his anxiety and his excitement was the thought that Ambika's invitation signaled a turning point in their relationship. He knew that it could have been simple courtesy on her part, a function of the Indian tradition of hospitality. It could have been curiosity on the part of her parents to meet her exotic employer, who had almost certainly been the source of much laughter and perplexity in their family discussions. And indeed, it was her father who had extended the invitation through his daughter. However, Le Gentil knew Ambika too well by now to think that she had nothing to do with it. If she had not suggested the invitation, then at the very least she had fanned her parents' curiosity with what she had told them—and perhaps even more so with what she hadn't. He knew her parents to be wealthy, well-educated, upper-class Indians. Having raised such an educated and astute daughter, they would have undoubtedly seen through some of her maneuverings, reading in her speech and her mannerisms signs that there was more to their relationship than she was letting on. This would have led them to decide that they wanted to see for themselves what she had left unspoken. Added to this were Le Gentil's fears about what her parents would think of him. Would they consider him a barbarian, unfit for their daughter? Surely the thought of a possible marriage to this famous foreigner would have occurred to them, even if it had not yet occurred to her. Would they see this dinner as an opportunity to size him up as a possible suitor, or would they have already decided against him because of his European origin and see it as a means of scouting the enemy, in case they had to take action against him in the eventuality that what had already occurred to them occurred to her as well and met with a favorable response? These unvoiced concerns left Le Gentil somewhat on edge in the week leading up to the great event. He even fretted in Ambika's presence over what he would wear, days before the actual dinner, a show of indecision he had never displayed before, proud as he was of his tailored Parisian dress and the cutting figure he drew whenever he looked himself up and down in the full-length mirror that he had had installed in his bedchambers.

Though she did her best not to show it, Ambika was nearly as anxious about the dinner as he was. It had indeed come as a surprise to her when her father had extended the invitation in a tone of voice that made it clear that it was a summons rather than a request; however, she had already been thinking about the possibility—the necessity, rather—of introducing him to her parents, knowing that such an eventuality could not be put off indefinitely. Her father's invitation had simply settled the matter. She told Le Gentil about it the next day and got his immediate assent, noticing, as she did, the look of alarm in his eyes that she hoped was not a reflection of what she was feeling. The invitation was for a week from Saturday at six o'clock, ten days hence, leaving just enough time for her to worry herself to distraction. Perhaps this was part of her father's intention. She had been feeling more and more worried about the amount of time she was spending with Le Gentil. Not because there was any impropriety in the arrangement. She had been placed there by the governor, whom—as everyone well knew—she had a duty to please for the sake of her people. Whatever duties were incumbent upon her to fulfill the necessities of that post would be sanctioned by all but the most malicious of tongue waggers. What worried her was what her parents would think, specifically her father, despite the fact that he had groomed her to fulfill the role she was now fulfilling, forcing her to become a Christian when it was the last thing she would have agreed to had she had a choice in the matter. Would her father suspect that she was forgetting herself and her duty, developing an undue sympathy for this westerner that could undermine their plans for her in their moment of need? What worried her even more—though she hesitated to admit it, even to herself—was the secret knowledge that any such suspicion on his part would be well-founded. Her only hope was to convince him that she was merely playing a role, cultivating this familiarity with a consequential Frenchman as a useful tool in the furtherance of her duty. She was less than confident, however, that she could pull it off. Her father was extremely perceptive, and even if she could keep her own feelings sufficiently well hidden, she knew very well that Le Gentil could not.

Ambika arrived at the observatory late Saturday morning to finish up some work they had left pending on the previous day and to coach the astronomer in the finer points of etiquette when dining with a Hindu family. She also gave him some last-minute advice on how to win over her father. "He is something of what you might call a militant Hindu," she warned him, "especially when it comes to what he considers the superiority of Indian culture and Indian religion. If you can avoid getting in any arguments with him, then half the battle is won. I won't ask you to concede his points. I know how much good that would do. But if you can just listen attentively and tell him that you'll think over carefully what he's said, then I'm sure he'll be impressed. He seems to be convinced that all Europeans are supremely arrogant." Ambika raised her eyebrows with this last remark.

"Don't worry," Le Gentil replied. "It shouldn't be too hard. I've had plenty of practice with his daughter."

Ambika flashed an indulgent smile. "Judging by how you've fared with his daughter, I think you'll do well to keep quiet on most subjects. My father is a lot cleverer than I am. I wouldn't want to have to nurse your ego back to health afterward."

"*Touchée, ma belle.* I'll do my best to make a good impression. But if I may ask, why are you so uptight about this dinner?"

Ambika looked at him with an air of incredulity. "They're my *parents.*"

It was one idea that needed no cross-cultural translation.

When their carriage pulled into the Iyer estate early that evening, the head of the family was standing outside the front door of the manor house to receive them, his wife and two other children poised demurely behind him. Tall for an Indian, his slim figure and proud, angular features reminded Rodrigo of a dark-skinned Roman patrician. When the carriage halted, the doctor walked over and opened the door. After assisting his daughter to the ground, he greeted Le Gentil with his hands folded to his chest. There was no handshake. In a thickly accented but perfectly understandable French, he asked Le Gentil if he would like to take a short stroll around the estate while there was still light and the women were getting the table ready for dinner. The cautionary look on Ambika's face when he accepted the offer reminded him to let the older man do the talking.

It was a sprawling estate of more than five hundred acres fronted by a long row of close-set coconut palms. Two lush rows of large bottle palms lined either side of the flagstone path that ran from the gate to the house, a large two-story sixteenth-century mansion of more than twenty rooms, bordered on all sides by carefully tended flower beds and ornamental shrubs. The spacious two-acre lawn in front of the house sheltered shade trees of varying sizes and a large circular flower garden with wicker benches and tables at its center under a lattice-work trellis wreathed with flowering vines.

His host brought him first to the flower garden where he pointed out a number of rare specimens that Le Gentil had never seen before and which immediately aroused his curiosity.

"I will send some seedlings back with you from my nursery. I have many species of flowers and other plants that are available nowhere else in the province. Horticulture is a hobby of mine, you see. Or perhaps, I should better call it a passion."

From there the doctor led him out back where a spacious orchard stretched out on either side of the dirt road that wound its way through the rest of the estate. In the distance, he could see several hundred acres of tilled land. Most of these fields were green with crops of various sizes divided into large square sections set off by borders of raised dirt; other fields were being prepared for planting. The nursery occupied a half-acre clearing in the middle of the orchard where workmen were busy tending the thousands of seedlings that were laid out in neatly ordered rows, some enjoying the protection of a large wood-frame shade house, others laid out on racks in the open sun. On the other side of the orchard, he saw a number of small cottages that he assumed were servants' quarters.

Dr. Iyer motioned toward the orchard and the fields beyond with a panoramic sweep of his left hand. "This estate began as a commercial plantation. My great-

great-grandfather had a number of such plantations. He was a merchant but he made most of his fortune through land holdings and agriculture. He passed it on to my great-grandfather, who built the manor house and moved here with his family. It has since come down to me. I am a doctor of Ayurveda myself, but I have inherited the family love for agriculture." He turned and smiled. "As well as the dependence on the money it brings in."

As they started walking toward the nursery, the doctor asked Le Gentil if he were familiar with Ayurveda."

"Not really, but your daughter has told me a little bit about it. It sounds quite interesting."

"I have studied something of your Western medicine," the doctor continued with a dismissive air. "To be honest, it seems rather primitive to me in comparison to Ayurveda, although perhaps that is merely a reflection of the youth of your culture."

Le Gentil bristled for a moment, but he remembered Ambika's advisory warning. Glad that her father had not been looking at him, he replied, "To be sure, I have thought so myself on the few occasions when I have been forced to take recourse to one of our doctors. I have had the good fortune, though, of not falling sick since I have been in your country, nothing that required a doctor at any rate, but should it so happen, I shall be certain to consult an Ayurvedic physician as well. Ambika has told me that you have a well-known clinic in the city. Who knows, perhaps you will see me there one day."

The doctor looked at him fixedly; his eyes narrowed slightly. The intensity of his gaze reminded Le Gentil of Ambika's but with much more force. For a few uncomfortable moments, it felt like the probing of a doctor's scalpel. "Yes, my clinic is in the part of town that I am told you refer to as 'Ville Noire.' You are welcome there, but let us hope there will not be any need."

They took a short tour of the nursery where the doctor gave orders to one of the workmen to prepare some seedlings and send them up to the house when they were ready. On their way back, they stopped under a medium-sized fruit tree with which Le Gentil was not familiar. The doctor plucked one of the unusual-looking purple fruits and cut it open with a pocketknife that he pulled from the pocket of his shirt. The soft, succulent, cream-colored flesh was a delight equaling any fruit the astronomer had ever tasted. "It's a mangosteen," the doctor told him. "My father planted it, the first of its kind in India. When we make it available to the markets, it fetches a very high price. I will send some back with you for your table." The doctor gave a shout and then some instructions to the workman who appeared a few moments later. Then they entered the house through a back door.

As soon as Le Gentil entered the dining room, a rich array of aromas assaulted his senses. The crackling sound of frying ghee could be heard in the adjoining kitchen where Ambika's mother was giving instructions to a pair of maidservants. Dr. Iyer pulled out a chair for his guest on one side of the long mahogany table that dominated the center of the dining room. They were quickly joined there by Ambika, her mother, and her younger sister and brother. Indrajit was sixteen, a slim, mahogany-skinned boy with a laughing expression and the restless energy of his age. His sister Ambuja was three years younger, a perfect image of what Ambika must have been at her age, with the same luxurious black hair and the promise of a coming beauty that would dazzle men's eyes and turn otherwise dark-skinned women green with envy. She was, however, surprisingly silent, a trait that distinguished her from her sister. It did not take long for Le Gentil to conclude that she took after her mother, a short, rounded woman who despite her curious eyes and avid attention spoke little during the course of the evening. Ambika clearly had been fashioned after the image of her provocative and supremely self-assured father, perhaps a function of being the oldest child, eight years older than her brother whose character seemed to fall somewhere in between the two parents.

Ambika's father completed the introductions, which had been interrupted at their arrival, and then called for the maidservants to start serving the meal. They emerged from the kitchen with platters of fresh dosas and fried breads, which they began serving onto the large silver plates that were set out in front of each chair. They followed this up with sambar and coconut chutney and then tiny servings from a wide array of different curries, gradually filling up the plates in a perfectly symmetrical fashion until each seemed more a work of art than a meal. It was a feast for Le Gentil's eyes as well as his nose, but for Rodrigo it was a feast for his mind. As his fingers danced lightly over the keyboard, his mind regaled itself with the kind of meal he promised himself he would have as soon as he arrived back in Rishikesh after the intensive, remembering the one South Indian restaurant he had noticed and willing it to the kind of perfection he was seeing on the Iyer dinner table.

The food was a delight for the astronomer as well, a myriad of delicately spiced dishes that far surpassed anything in his experience, either in Asia or in the far-less-ambitious dining rooms of his native France, a fact he readily admitted to his hosts without the slightest reticence. He still held firm to his belief, however, that the desserts would not prove a match for the truffles, cakes, and pastries of the best Parisian confectioners, but until that moment arrived, he gave verbal witness to the truth that his taste buds proclaimed. Nevertheless, his main attention was reserved for Ambika's father and the steady stream of conversation that proved to be the meal's main course.

Dr. Iyer began the evening by inquiring politely about Le Gentil's work and what life was like in his native France, but he soon turned the conversation into a cultural comparison that left no doubts as to where his bias lay.

"I have been told that the average Frenchman, in fact the average European, only takes bath once a month, and often not at all during the winter months. As a physician, it makes me wonder what it is that makes your people display such a flagrant disregard for the human body. Is it simply ignorance of the benefits of regular hygiene, or does it have something to do with Christian belief, perhaps an underlying conviction that through sickness and suffering they will gain easier entrance to the so-called kingdom of heaven? I have heard of the self-flagellation that is practiced by some of your monks. Is this done with a similar intention, a kind of collective self-flagellation?"

This was uttered without the slightest trace of sarcasm; however, the astute astronomer had seen this same facility in the doctor's less-adept daughter, who always in the end betrayed the humor that she did her best to conceal. Taking his cue from those conversations, he did his best to answer back in the same tone of voice.

"It is true that the great piousness of our common people induces them to seek out sufferings when perhaps they could be easily avoided, in the interest of making their souls more pleasing to heaven, but with the rapid advance of science in my country such practices are becoming a thing of the past. It is sad in one sense, since when something is gained, something is also lost, but this is also inevitable. I myself have learned to bathe every day without fail, but then I am a scientist—I lack the piousness that many of our simpler folk have."

For the first time, Le Gentil saw in his host the slight hint of a smile. He could not be sure, but he had the vague suspicion that it was the smile of someone who had just stooped down to pick up the gauntlet, having been hoping for precisely that opportunity.

"Yes, you are very right. Our sages have taught us this also. For everything one gains in the relative world, one must also lose something. I have often wondered what the French and the British stand to lose by expending so much effort to gain their colonies and expand their empires. But you are in perhaps a much better position to comment on that than I."

Out of the corner of his eye, Le Gentil caught Ambika's insistent stare. Her intention could not have been clearer had she mouthed the words "avoid getting in any arguments…just listen." He was careful not to make direct eye contact with her as he nodded sagaciously, buying a few precious seconds to gather his thoughts before he replied.

"I am a scientist not a politician, so I can't claim to understand what ramifications it may have in the political arena, but it may mean that Europe will have to one day concede her preeminence in the sciences as she opens her doors to the contributions and insights of other cultures. But are not such gains and losses all part of a greater dialectic that ignores the temporary or local imbalance in the service of a collective purpose?"

Le Gentil flashed a wry smile at Ambika as he noticed the telltale flush of pride in her cheeks. The doctor took off his wire-rimmed glasses and wiped the lenses deliberately. When he put them on again, he nodded with a complacent, generous air.

"Yes, there is a greater dialectic, as you put it, in the forces of history. But if our sages are right in their claim that the ultimate destiny of man is perfect freedom, then that collective movement must be a movement toward a collective freedom. Can freedom be attained through the practice of slavery?"

The doctor's tone had deepened in gravity. Le Gentil felt the chill in the air. He realized that the conversation had reached the edges of a frontier he had best not cross. "My immediate reaction is to say no," he said, "but I think this is something I would have to reflect upon carefully before I would feel confident enough to venture an opinion. The point you make is a profound one, and I have always thought that profound ideas cannot be understood without adequate reflection. At least not by me."

Ambika took advantage of the pause to change the subject. She began telling her father of a discussion she and Le Gentil had recently had about the relationship between the three doshas of Ayurveda and the concept of the four humors that had dominated European medicine since it was first propagated by Hippocrates in Ancient Greece but which had lately fallen into controversy. She could sense that her father was annoyed with her ploy, almost certainly assuming that she was coming to her employer's defense, but he displayed no outward sign of irritation as he smoothly launched into a brief but precise explanation of the doshas, followed by a trenchant disquisition on the weaknesses of the Greek system. While he did concede that both were founded on similar ideas, the Greek system, in his estimation, did not demonstrate anywhere near the scientific precision of the Indian system of *prakruti* and *vikruti* in its apprehension of the subtler workings of the human organism; nor could European physicians boast of anything approaching the exhaustive clinical history that Indian doctors had at their disposal.

It was a topic that allowed Dr. Iyer to put on display his vast knowledge and penetrating powers of analysis in his chosen field, something he was inordinately and unapologetically proud of. This is what Ambika was counting on, since it bought for Le Gentil a welcome reprieve. It also kept her father's acutely perceptive eyes off her for a time, a respite she welcomed as well, since she could already sense her father's suspicions settling on her as he continued to watch her out of the corner of his eye while he conversed with Le Gentil. She wondered uncomfortably how much she had given away about her relationship with her employer, a relationship her father was sure not to countenance if he became aware of how close they had become.

The conversation continued for more than two hours, rounding from one topic to another but always finding its way back to international politics and the clash of cultures between the colonizers and those who, in her father's words, had "the unenviable fortune of being the recipients of their beneficence." To her surprise and undying gratitude, Le Gentil showed a self-control and a good sense she had not thought possible. Every time her father baited him into a discussion that would allow him to argue from a position of unsuspected strength, Le Gentil demurred to his "better judgment and wider knowledge" in the subject; or else he creased his brow into an expression of intense interest and told the older man that he would have to reflect upon it at length before he would be able to give any kind of intelligent answer. As she had hoped—without really believing it would come to pass—her father showed himself increasingly at ease and increasingly impressed with his charming and intelligent guest. The arrogant and ill-bred European—which his father considered to be the only species of European to be found, at least on Indian soil—did not put in an appearance that night. While her father appeared almost disappointed at first that his table was turning into a conference room rather than a battlefield, by the end of the evening he exuded genuine warmth and appeared to be truly enjoying himself. The only truly dangerous moment occurred early in the evening when her father maneuvered the conversation into the treacherous waters of religious intolerance. The sweets had just arrived—rice pudding, fragrant with the scent of cardamom and fresh cashew nuts, both from the estate, as was virtually everything on the menu that night, a fact her father skillfully pointed out with a careless, understated aside; banana fritters; and a variety of Indian sweetmeats, made ever the more palatable by the chilled coconut water with which they were served. The Frenchman tasted each of the sweet dishes in turn, extolling their virtues, and then launched into a long description of the wonders of the Parisian confectioner: varieties of chocolates unmatched anywhere in the world, peerless pastries, and cakes so enchanted it was said that a man need only taste them once to gain a memory that would see him happily through a lifetime of dried bread and moldy cheeses.

"I have heard that food is practically a religion in Paris," her father said, after listening to this long litany of praise in the name of the Parisian confectioner. "I should like to taste your Parisian chocolates one day and these enchanted cakes you speak of with their impossible-to-pronounce names. I would only hope that the prelates in this world of Parisian sweets show more tolerance for the culinary tastes of other lands than your Christian fathers do for the beliefs and practices of non-Christian cultures."

Le Gentil blinked his eyes, still smiling, as he was jerked out of his imaginary world of Parisian delights with a rapidity that left him unable to respond.

"India has distinguished itself for countless centuries," the doctor continued, "as a land of religious tolerance. Our sages have taught us that any slight to another's religion is an insult to our own. We have learned this lesson and welcomed all of the world's religions on our soil with open arms. They thrive here. When the Christians were still persecuted in the West, they flourished here in India, only a few years after Christ was crucified by his own people. My own daughter wished to embrace the Christian faith and I did not oppose her. Yet for a people who profess to love their neighbor as themselves, your Christian fathers show a remarkable intolerance for anyone who professes religious ideas that do not come out of their Bible—or out of their own mouths."

Le Gentil gathered his wits. Before Ambika could step in he gave an answer that immediately lightened the atmosphere at the dinner table and reminded everyone again of the magic cakes that were indeed nearly as good as he made them out to be.

"I assure you, Dr. Iyer, our confectioners are far more tolerant than our priests. They have to be. The happiness of our people and their own sustenance depends on it, while the only thing we depend on our priests for is our misery."

By the time Ambika and her parents saw Le Gentil to his carriage, she was feeling positively radiant, glowing with the conviction that he had made a conquest of her father. This was more than she could have hoped for. Once the carriage had disappeared out the gate and could be heard rattling in the distance behind the tall line of coconut palms that swayed ghostlike in the advancing moonlight, Dr. Iyer tapped his daughter on her shoulder and asked her to accompany him to the flower garden for a short chat. He still seemed to be in high spirits, but Ambika felt like a prisoner whose reprieve has just been overturned.

The sky was nearly cloudless but the moon, only three days from full, hid the light of all but the strongest of stars. Only Venus shone forth in her full glory, lying close to the horizon like an observant eye surveying the earthly landscape, attuned to the beauty that all other eyes missed. Ambika noticed her there as she sat down and was grateful for her presence. Venus's soothing light seemed to fall on her like a protective shroud, veiling her from the probing eye of her father and filling her with its womanly power. Whatever her father might do, she felt secure in the knowledge that her destiny was her own. Not only Le Gentil's fortune but her own as well was inextricably linked to the queen of the night sky, a protectress who was known to watch over her attendants, as any regal lady would.

"Ambika," her father began, once they were settled and she had turned a silent and inquisitive eye toward him, "it is late so I will get straight to the point. Your astronomer was a pleasant surprise. He is far more than I expected. He must have been Indian in his previous birth. A Malabar, most likely. However…" He sighed audibly before continuing. "An unseemly intimacy has sprung up between you and him. You did your best not to let this be known, I know, but it is not something you were able to hide, at least not from me. I saw the way you looked at him and especially the way he looked at you. In this respect, he was a true barbarian with no ability to keep his feelings from his face. You, however, were only somewhat more adept than he, and that in itself shows how far this thing has gone. I have entrusted you with a great responsibility. Our motherland is depending on you and a handful of others who have the capacity, the means, and the position to be able to alter the dreadful course of oppression that our people have been subjected to. Will you throw it all away because of a weakness that you have been warned against? Will you denigrate all that we have worked for because you've allowed the emotions of a teenage girl to run riot in the body of a twenty-four-year-old woman? Had I known this would happen, despite all your training, I would have married you to an Iyer Brahmin years ago, whatever the cost to our plans." Dr. Iyer took off his glasses, wiped the lenses deliberately with a handkerchief, and put them back on. "There is still time for that. It can be arranged in a matter of days. It seems I may have to have a talk with the governor about a change in your fortunes and your availability for this work that he has given you."

Ambika felt a brief chill pass through her, but rather than surrender to the greater will of her father, as she had done throughout her life, she felt a fire flare up inside her—not a wayward brush fire, a product of mischance and quickly out of control, but a tempered flame that she directed to her will. She directed it now at her father in a voice that was cold in tone but which generated immense heat by the force behind it.

"You may do as you wish. It makes no difference. I have pledged my life to the freedom of my people and I will fulfill my pledge by whatever means at my disposal, until the last breath I take. In this respect, what you say or do makes no difference to me. It is *my* work and it is my word. I will tell you now and I will tell you only once—mark it well. No one can stop me from fulfilling my pledge, not the governor, not this Frenchman." She paused to look her father directly in the eye, the fire all but consuming her now. "Not even you."

Her father leaned back and looked at her, his eyebrows furrowed, a slight frown etched into his face. He was silent for a full two minutes. Finally the frown disappeared and his habitual mastery returned. "So be it. I will think over the matter. Now it is late. You should get some rest."

While Ambika did not yet realize it, with her words she had made the decision that would decide the course of her destiny. If Venus could have smiled so that human beings could see, then all Pondicherry would have seen her smiling that night and wondered what human folly had delighted her so.

Rodrigo passed most of that month without returning to his temple grounds. He continued to keep his journal, however, preserving in its pages those dreams that attracted his attention, a number of them throwing some unexpected or fragmented light on the spiritual journey he was taking. In one such dream, he was sitting under the banyan tree with Saraswati listening to her discourse on a passage he had read the night before and failed to understand. Her explanation cleared up his confusion, as it almost invariably did in real life; when he awoke, he found that what he remembered of her dreamed discourse made perfect sense; the passage was now intelligible. He thought about telling her but decided against it. She would have immediately dismissed any suggestion that they had actually communicated during those night hours, meeting in astral space to continue his apprenticeship, as he had read about in one of his books. She would have simply pointed out what she had already pointed out before: that this was another example of his unconscious mind transmitting the knowledge that had been sleeping inside him all along.

Though none of these dreams had the power, the immediacy, or the haunting prophetic quality of his sojourn through the life of a Bengali priest in the service of Mother Kali, Rodrigo was not appreciably disappointed with the hiatus. His daily life with its confusion of spiritual setbacks and conquests had started to so absorb his interest that he did not miss that other life that he lived at times with his body hidden beneath the cover of a blanket. He still remembered the girl, the sheen of her ebony skin, the intensity of her eyes, the defiant air that surrounded her like a protective shield, but even with his idealized image of the life of the imagination, a dreamed woman was no match for Saraswati, who was never far from his thoughts, even during his meditation when the whole purpose was to banish her along with the rest of the phenomenal world. Then, six days before the intensive was to begin, he awoke in the hour before dawn bathed in sweat and filled with a sense of longing that he remembered all too well, for it had never completely disappeared.

Rishikesh
1/29
4:15 AM

The temple grounds, the priest, the longing—they are all just as I had
left them. I had wondered if the dreams might have stopped, but they
were only dormant, as I have been dormant my entire life. Sitting up
on my bed now, with my computer beneath my fingers, I can still see
the scene before my eyes, as if by peering into the darkness of my unlit
room I can see clear through to another world. Though I can feel the
ashram around me, piercing through the fog of my mind, drawing me
back from where I have just been and where a part of me longs to stay,
my inward eye can still see my temple sanctuary. I know I cannot fight
this return for long, but while I can still see, I can record where I have
been and in that way keep it alive, even after the coming dawn has
banished the last of my nighttime shadows. And so:

I am sitting in my little room, staring into the painted eyes of the small
idol on my altar, feeling the devi's presence reaching out to me, enveloping me in her warm embrace. It is she, the devi, who has come to me in
the body of this Dalit woman, a gift to remind me that the goddess lives
in all, that I had forgotten this fact and grown prideful in my priestly
garb. The moment this thought arises, I can feel the devi's smile telling
me that I have at last understood. Tears fall. I light a stick of incense and
wave it in front of the idol, which has become for me a living presence.
Exalted, I close my eyes and pray to the devi to lift me up into her light.
I repeat the mantra she has gifted me, and on its wings I catch a flash of
her eyes, and beyond them a sea of effulgence. When I come out of my
meditation, I know what I must do. I must honor this manifestation of
the Divine Mother as I must honor all her manifestations: in truth and
with humility. I call for my assistant, but the moment he enters my room
I tremble, for I remember that I am a priest on earth, and on earth there
are dangers I cannot lose sight of. I must be careful. With my voice as
dispassionate as I can make it, I mention the Dalit woman who brings
water for the temple, the one he had once brought me information about.
He looks at me without blinking; his face betrays no emotion. Proceeding
cautiously, I tell him that a poor but pious woman has given a donation
to the temple and asked me to use it to help someone who is worse off
than she. I tell him that I was thinking of the old man, her father, who is
sick and infirm and has no one to care for him while his daughter works
all day at the temple for wages that barely enable them to survive. The
alms of this pious woman are enough to hire a young girl to look after
the old man and ease his sufferings. Could he arrange this? My assistant
nods his head slowly. As you wish, he tells me. But did I see him raise his

eyebrow for a moment, as if in judgment, as if in silent suspicion. This fear bites at me but I put it out of my mind by an act of will. It is only my fear that makes me think I see this, and my fear is what the devi has pledged to burn out of me. I hand him some rupees and instruct him to make the arrangements, to pay the girl monthly for as long as the money lasts. After that, if there is any further donation, I will let him know. There is no need for him to mention who has given the offering. He need only say that it is a gift from the temple. That should be enough to silence any suspicions he might have. Despite the deception, she will know who has sent this present. There is a bond that unites us, one to the other. I can feel it still, as I felt it during the debate. She is a kindred soul in the body of a woman from whom I must forever keep a distance but a distance that is only of the body, not of the spirit. She will know this and she will know that I know. The dream ends with me alone in my room in front of the idol, thanking her for this gift of herself in the form of this woman who has enabled me to win the debate and silence the lonely cries of my heart. I am exhilarated by the thought of what I have done and by the knowledge that she will know who has sent this gift. And then my heart is rent with longing. The longing follows me into my ashram room and into the cold light of the last stars peeking in through my window.

A dim light is starting to make its presence felt in my room as the moment draws near to head to the hall for meditation. As I look back at my dream from the perspective of my waking self, it seems that the story does not end, neither the one lived down below in my secret sleeping consciousness, nor the one lived up here where the light shines over Rishikesh and follows Saraswati and I as we walk. Does any story ever really end? As the girl prepared my priestly self for the debate, Saraswati is preparing me for my encounter with the Rimpoche—and with myself. It is not only the intensive she is training me for. She is guiding me down the pathways of my spiritual life. I have so much to thank her for, things for which words can never be enough. In the dream, it seems that I have expressed this gratitude with a secret gift. And in real life? How can I best show my gratitude? I believe that the gift she would most appreciate would be for me to throw myself body and soul into this intensive and emerge from it a better man, worthy of the precepts she is teaching me. Will she know that this is a gift I give to her? Perhaps not. One cannot expect dreams and waking life to entirely coincide. Let it go unnoticed then. One day she may realize her place in my heart. I can wait. Is patience not a virtue? Of the longing I will not speak. It is there and it is acknowledged. Perhaps, after all, it is a worthy adversary. She would consider it so.

26

THE SITE FOR THE intensive was a musty, decaying dharmasala built in the middle of the nineteenth century by a wealthy Indian prince as a resting place for spiritual pilgrims making their way upriver to Badrinath, Kedarnath, and other pilgrimage sites in the Himalayas. It was a concrete monolith typical of the era. A large hall occupied most of the first floor, while the second floor consisted of small cell-like rooms on either side of a central corridor; both stories had wrap-around verandas supported by thick round pillars. It stood some thirty meters above the Ganges on a small wooded bluff from where the swift rapids could be heard at any time of day or night rushing past a cluster of boulders that jutted out from the near bank. These boulders had long been a favorite of wandering monks, who would sit on them after their morning ablutions and send their minds into the great unknown.

Rodrigo arrived in the late afternoon in a bus provided by the local chapter of the Tibetan Society, sponsors of the intensive, to transport the twenty-one participants and the five staff persons who would be taking care of the cooking and cleaning. Each participant was assigned one of the tiny, cold, dimly lit cells on the second floor and asked to attend a brief orientation. The Rimpoche arrived a couple of hours later in a cavalcade of cars flying Tibetan flags and blowing horns. There was a colorful, boisterous ceremony to receive him, after which he gave a short talk in the main hall, welcoming the participants and giving some basic instruction in the practice of meditation. After the talk, the Rimpoche and his translator retired to a small suite of rooms adjacent to the main hall, leaving the retreatants free for the night, the only free time they were to enjoy for the next three weeks.

Rodrigo took a short walk by the river after dinner and retired to his room early, thinking it prudent to stock up on sleep while he still could. He was in a good mood; his apprehension about the difficult discipline he was facing was lessened by the calming sounds of the Ganges, strong and unperturbed in its ancient course, and the magnificence of the moonless sky, rising up from the treetops like the dome of an immense cathedral with its dark fresco of fragmented clouds and blazoned stars. As he lay back on the thin mattress of his wooden cot and drew his blanket over him, he thought about the Rimpoche and the impish smile he had adopted while talking about the importance of maintaining mindfulness in one's meditation. His first impression was that of a kindly old man, weathered and worn down by age and the chill eroding winds of the Tibetan plateau. He had moved slowly and deliberately as he entered and left the hall, but he had shown no signs of fading quite yet, despite being in his early eighties. Nor was there any trace of the fierce disciplinarian Saraswati had told him about, just a beaming countenance that seemed to cast an equal light on everyone there. But she had already been through the intensive and he had yet to begin. If she had mentioned it, it was because he had best be prepared.

The thought of Saraswati made him wonder just how much he would miss his enigmatic teacher in the coming three weeks, miss their conversations and their walks by the river, miss her watchful eye that seemed to provide the ballast he needed whenever his discipline began to falter. To the extent that he did, he would know just how far his attachment had grown. He did not harbor any illusions that she would miss him, but he recognized with gratitude just how much she had given of herself to get him ready for his coming ordeal.

That morning after class, she had invited him to do noon meditation with her on the banks of the Ganges, one last chance to prepare his mind before he left to go upriver. They left the ashram shortly before noon and begun walking leisurely in the direction of Lakshman Jhula until they reached the tiny cottage where Swami Sivananda had performed his meditation in the days when he had been a simple sannyasi in search of realization. Rodrigo had passed by it many times. Of late, he had sometimes paused and paid silent reverence to the memory of the saint who had been the soul of Rishikesh for more than four decades during the middle of the twentieth century. But it had never occurred to him that it might be possible to go inside and meditate there. Thus his surprise when Saraswati stopped and called out from the creaky iron gate. Moments later, an orange-clad, shaven-headed monk opened the door of the cottage and waved for them to come in. Rodrigo was delighted at the unexpected opportunity. As he passed across the threshold, he felt a hush come over him, as if he were entering into hallowed space. The front room of the cottage was empty, except for a couple of bamboo mats and a small altar underneath the window on which rested a simple photo of Sivananda in a metal frame. A vase next to the photo held several newly cut flowers and a faint scent of incense lingered in the air. After the monk disappeared into the back room, Saraswati whispered that they had half an hour. Then she touched her head to the floor in front of the altar and sat down in the full lotus posture.

It was Rodrigo's first chance to meditate with his teacher. She never joined the collective sessions in the ashram but instead preferred to do her meditation in the seclusion of her room. He took a few moments to admire her perfectly erect posture and the look of profound absorption that appeared on her face as soon as she closed her eyes. Then he closed his own and began to search for the elusive thread of his mantra. For some reason, he found it much easier than usual. He quickly lost awareness of his surroundings, and it was only when he heard Saraswati whisper in his ear that their time was up that he realized how deep his concentration had been. Once they were outside the gate, she queried him about his experience.

"It was wonderful," he told her. "I don't know why, but for some reason my mind was really quiet today. For once it felt like what I imagine meditation should feel like."

"That was why I wanted to bring you here. Great saints leave their vibrations in the places they meditate. The higher their realization, the greater the vibration. Swami Sivananda meditated in this hut for many years before his disciples convinced him to move across the river to the ashram they built for him. That's the reason your meditation was so deep. You had help."

They started back in the direction of the ashram, but Saraswati turned off the path at the first set of steps that led down to the gleaming white sands on the riverbank. They found some boulders near the water and sat down to watch the current gliding slowly and serenely toward town. After a few minutes silence, she started telling him the story of Buddha and the Bo tree.

"Sometimes I try to imagine the determination he must have had, vowing not to end his meditation until he had achieved enlightenment. Seven days and seven nights he sat there under the Bo tree without getting up from his seat. He almost collapsed from weakness and near starvation. Then a girl from a nearby village, Sujata, came by and left him some sweet rice. That humble offering gave him the strength to continue. On the seventh day, all his mental demons, his remaining attachments and doubts and fears, massed together for one final attack, but he wouldn't allow anything to weaken his resolve or cause him to turn aside from his vow. He was ready to die rather than get up from his seat without achieving enlightenment. According to the story, it was in the hour before dawn, with the light of a single star on his brow, that he broke through. All his past lives flashed before his eyes and he entered into nirvana. The Tibetan literature says that at the moment the Buddha broke the cycle of birth and death, the gods wept and came to offer him flowers. I don't know about the gods, but it's certainly true that the people of India wept and offered him flowers when they found out he had achieved the goal that all human beings seek. They still do. One realized soul does more for this planet than a legion of philanthropists and social reformers, no matter how well intentioned they may be."

Saraswati turned and looked at him with an expression that might have done the Buddha proud, a mixture of benevolence and iron determination. "You will need something of the Buddha's resolve to get through this intensive," she said. "But I don't doubt that you will find it. It's there inside you."

Now, lying on his bed in the dharmasala, accompanied by the quiet sounds of the river down below and the faint light of the few stars visible through his window, Rodrigo found it hard to conceive of that kind of effort, whether the Buddha's or his own. The very idea didn't seem quite real as he let himself drift off into sleep. Of all the dreams men dream, this was the one most difficult to understand. But then, he had only to cross the barrier of sleep before he would have the opportunity to find out firsthand the price that must be paid for freedom.

At four AM the morning gong sounded. By four thirty, everyone was in the main hall and at their meditation cushions, where they remained until seven thirty, motionless except for the small readjustments of posture that were permitted them. For those whose heads nodded, there was a monitor patrolling the room with a birch switch, a young, bright-faced monk in wine-red robes who grinned like a cherub at all hours of the morning and night and seemed to thoroughly relish the sound of his switch as it whooshed through the air and rebounded off the shoulder or thigh of a wavering meditator, bringing him back to life with a shock of recognition and an ounce of pain. At seven thirty, the gong sounded and everyone got up from their meditation cushions and started walking in a counterclockwise circle around the room with their heads bowed as they contemplated their footsteps in the eternal attention of the mindful state. Some leeway was given to the wobbling efforts to get up of those whose legs had fallen asleep while their minds remained in contemplation, but if they delayed too long to join the mindful snake winding itself around the room, the young monk with his cherub's smile gleefully helped them on their way with a cheerful thwack or two on the offending legs. Fifteen minutes later they sat again, until the nine o'clock gong called them to breakfast, which was served on the veranda amid the chill winter winds and in sight of the rushing waters of impermanence. They walked, ate, and suffered in silence. The only words permitted in this retreat were those spoken by the Rimpoche, unless in direct conversation with him, but after four and a half hours practice, all Rodrigo wanted was his hot soup and barley meal and a chance to stretch his legs.

At 9:40, the gong called them back to their meditation cushions. Twenty minutes later Rodrigo felt a tap on his shoulder. He opened his eyes to see the hall monitor pointing him toward the Rimpoche's room. It was ten o'clock, time for his individual session with the master, the first of the daily sessions during which the Rimpoche would guide the progress and practice of his students.

It was only mid-morning but Rodrigo already felt as if he had been put through an oil mill, squeezed and pressed until all his vital juices had been extracted. He lifted himself up onto his unsteady legs and walked over to the Rimpoche's room. The door was open. Inside, the Rimpoche was sitting on a low wooden cot covered with a thin mattress and a black cotton sheet. He was dressed in his monk's robes and was wearing the same kindly, almost childlike smile with which he had welcomed the participants during the ceremony the evening before. His translator was sitting on the ground to one side of the cot, a thick-jowled, thick-limbed monk in his late twenties who looked more Indian than Tibetan and who watched him enter with wary, close-set eyes that seemed to convey more than a touch of condescension. Rodrigo knelt down and bowed his head before the Rimpoche as he had been instructed; when he straightened up again, he looked at the old man with nervous expectation. It was then that he began to notice those aged eyes boring into him, as if the saintly old monk were examining his thoughts and the lifetimes of misdeeds that had brought him to this point. The Rimpoche looked at him for more than a minute without saying anything. The smile gradually faded from his face and his look changed to one of immense authority and severity. Finally, he turned his head to his translator and muttered a few words in Tibetan. Then he turned back to Rodrigo, who had been growing more and more uncomfortable under the intensity of that gaze, and continued to watch him with the same penetrating, probing look while the translator explained a meditation technique that the Rimpoche wanted him to practice. When he was done, the Rimpoche addressed him through the translator. "Do you have any questions?"

Rodrigo shook his head.

"The purpose of this meditation," the Rimpoche continued, "is to develop compassion for all living beings. You should direct it especially toward those people whom you have made suffer in this life. You will know whom I mean. If you practice it sincerely, it will begin the process of erasing the destructive karma you have created by your selfish actions."

The Rimpoche shook his head disapprovingly. As he did, Rodrigo felt a sense of power beat against him like waves against a sea wall during the onset of a storm. "You have based your life on selfishness. This must end. Today." When the translator finished translating this final word, the Rimpoche spoke again but this time in slow, measured English, his voice gravelly and stern. "Selfishness. Understand? No more." He paused and then repeated the words "no more" a second time. This time the tone was softer but the words seemed to crack like thunder in Rodrigo's ears; he could feel tears welling in the corners of his eyes. Then the Rimpoche dismissed him with a peremptory wave of his hand.

When Rodrigo returned to his meditation cushion, he was shaking, not from any weakness in his legs but from a feeling similar to the one he had felt months earlier at the Kunjapuri temple: an acute awareness of the magnitude of his transgressions. The intensive, which had begun as an exciting though daunting adventure, now took on the character it would maintain for the remainder of those three weeks: that of a great fist pounding against his ego, implacable and unrelenting. That evening in his discourse, the Rimpoche told the story of a Buddhist monk whose master had put him through such severe trials that up until the day of his enlightenment he felt as if he were carrying the weight of a fifty-kilo stone on his back. Rodrigo knew that he carried a similar stone: his ego. On that first day, he could have sworn that his stone weighed far more than fifty kilos, so heavy in fact that when he laid down to sleep that night, he wondered how it was even possible to breathe.

The following morning, the Rimpoche dismissed him after less than two minutes with another peremptory wave, but not before fixing him with the same cyclonic gaze that had made his entrails quaver. "Go. Meditate," he told him. "Burn away your selfishness before it consumes you." Rodrigo's legs were on fire from the

long morning session, but his mind burned even more fiercely. All through the
morning and most of the previous day, he had been practicing the compassion
meditation, alternating it with short sessions of his regular practice. He had
begun by cultivating compassion toward himself as he had been instructed. That
had been difficult enough, considering how he had felt when he came out of the
Rimpoche's room that day. But then the practice got far more difficult. One by
one, he began reliving the acts of selfishness that had dotted the course of his
relationships and his career, gradually working his way backward into memories
long forgotten. Acts of unkindness, many of them unconscious at the time, came
rushing back into his mind with stunning clarity, along with the anguish they had
occasioned, the anguish that had gone unperceived by him at the time, or which
he had ignored or glossed over. Holding the image of those persons in his mind,
he absorbed the shock of their neglected feelings and began directing the compassion toward them that he had withheld in the past. "May you be happy, may
you be at peace, may you be secure and free from enmity." Over and over again,
he struggled to offer his love in the form of a luminous cloud, fighting, as he did,
with the heavy feelings of remorse that assailed him every time he remembered
how he had acted. Often his own heart worked against him, stubbornly reluctant
to extend compassion, peace, and security to those for whom he had secretly
nursed a longstanding resentment. His unwillingness to let go of what were often
imaginary slights pained him, but he stuck to the practice with a determination
that gave him hope that he might one day succeed at overturning what he now
saw to be a well-cultivated, lifelong habit of selfishness.

As the days passed, he began extending that cloud of compassion to those he
felt had wronged him at one point or another in his life, beginning with Beth and
traveling back through his school days and into his childhood. As the residues
of bitterness and anger slowly melted away, he was often shocked to see that he
had also wronged them, in thought if not in deed, drunk on the wine of his secret
vengeance. He began to perceive that his actions and theirs were entangled in a
web of contradictions and causality, and that neither of them could be absolved
from the consequences of their actions until the ignorance that bound them to
their suffering could be bathed in the light of compassion and understanding.
From there, the cloud extended outward in ever-widening circles, even to public
figures whom he had never met but whom he blamed for worsening the world he
lived in: toward the Chinese bureaucrats who had sent their soldiers into Tibet,
toward the sitting American president who had recklessly and heartlessly invaded
Iraq, toward the leader of the Islamic Mujahideen who had sent his hijacked planes
into the twin towers in New York. Images of death and destruction filled his mind.
It seemed to him a terrible vow that he should seek to extend compassion to the
people who had loosed this scourge upon the earth, people whom he had long
thought of as monsters. But he forced himself to recite the words that were designed
to sow compassion in his heart: they were also seeking their own happiness as
all creatures do, however misguided their ways; they were also unknowingly on
the path to enlightenment, fighting through the darkness of their minds and

hearts until they could one day come into the light. The more he repeated those words—words that at first seemed empty, almost irresponsible, an abdication of his moral imperative—the more they began to take on meaning, at first merely the possibility that such tragedy might be part of a greater design, then, slowly, a growing certainty that all suffering flowed on to a higher purpose.

The results of these efforts left him emotionally and physically drained. The meditation, which was designed to arouse compassion for all sentient beings, not only aroused compassion—it also unleashed a flood tide of remorse and opened him up to all the bitterness, the selfishness, the resentment, and the despair that he had carefully locked away behind secret doors he had never meant to open. His closed eyes often filled with tears while he sat on his cushion in the meditation hall, never more so than one evening, seven days into the intensive, when the sadness he had felt at his mother's death returned with an intensity he had not remembered feeling even in the days that followed her passing. For more than two hours sobs racked his breast; it was all he could do to remain motionless on his cushion instead of running from the room in an effort to escape the pain.

It had been years since he had dwelt on that terrible episode in his life. Somehow he had managed to shut it away in a darkened corner of his mind, and there it had lain to trouble him no more—until his meditation had finally unearthed it from its hidden tomb. This time he could not repress the memory; there was no longer anywhere for him to hide. His meditation and his mindfulness forced him to keep his inner eye open and absorb all the sorrow that had lain there unattended for so many years. As he watched her frail figure grow weaker in her suffering and then move no more, he realized how much he lamented that he hadn't told her how much he loved her. She must have known, but the young and self-absorbed boy he had been had left those words unspoken, and what had remained of his omission was a secret, silent guilt. He let the waves of this guilt wash over and through him, forcing himself to observe the pain and acknowledge it for what it was: his legacy and a worthy teacher. The guilt was followed by anger, anger at his mother for having abandoned him, a feeling he had never been aware of until that moment but which—as he recognized in a flash of insight—had been there all along, coloring his perceptions and feeding the vague feelings, never completely suppressed, that he had been victimized by life. It was the same anger, he realized, that he had felt at Beth when she told him she was leaving, a feeling that had been born when he was twelve and that had continued to hold him in its grip ever since. Then another layer seemed to fall away. He saw himself keeping Beth at a distance, his heart possessed by a stubborn coldness, unwilling or unable to open, and in that man he saw a boy's face unconsciously trying to protect himself by closing his heart, trying to save himself from the pain of being abandoned by this woman who was for him all women, as his mother had been all women, not realizing that the wall he built for protection was the same wall that would keep her out and cause her to abandon him as surely as if he had willed it all along. When he saw his own youthful face and realized that fear and pain was at the root of all his failed relationships, he opened himself up fully to his tears and carried them to his room that night.

Those tears were still present when he stepped into the Rimpoche's room the next morning, seemingly clouding his vision but actually laying him bare for the teaching that had been waiting to enter his previously impervious heart. For the first time since their initial private session, he saw the Rimpoche smile—not the childlike smile he had witnessed then, but a smile of satisfaction that let him know that the venerable monk had been waiting for those tears all along.

"Now you are ready to begin letting go," the Rimpoche said, nodding his head slowly. "Before you can be free of your suffering, you must first learn to embrace it. You must embrace it so that you can embrace the suffering of all living beings and help them with their burdens. Now that you have begun to accept your suffering, you must learn how to let it go." He turned toward his translator and spoke in a steady stream of guttural Tibetan syllables, his voice leaping from one tone to the next with the precision of a master instrumentalist. When he finished, the translator turned his head back toward Rodrigo and began conveying instructions for a meditation technique that he was to practice in his room for one hour each night before he went to sleep. It was called "the meditation of the great void" and its purpose was to free the conditioned consciousness from its attachment to the traces left behind from past thoughts and actions. "Learn to release your past into the great void and you will find that you are and have always been free," the Rimpoche added. "It is in that emptiness that you will see the Buddha's smile."

It was, however, the Rimpoche's smile that Rodrigo saw at that moment, a smile etched so deeply into his face that it seemed as if it had been there for all eternity and would never pass away. "Now go," he said. "Meditate on compassion and release your experience into the void." This time he did not wave his hand to dismiss Rodrigo; he merely lowered his half-closed eyes a fraction of an inch to signal that their session was over.

In the days that followed, Rodrigo leaned on the Rimpoche's words like a blind man leans his hand on the shoulder of the person who is leading him across the street. He could not see where he was going, but he trusted the Rimpoche to guide him. The swirling panorama of disgraceful events from his past continued to parade in his mind, sweeping him along in their tide of remorse, but the anguish gradually diminished and he found that he could extend compassion to himself with steadily increasing ease, as well as to the people he had wronged and those who had wronged him. His mind began to grow lighter, and into its lambent atmosphere began to appear acts of kindness that had been extended to him, often unnoticed at the time, revealing that the light of compassion had been shining on him for as far back as he could remember. They were followed by his own acts of kindness, some tinged with selfish motives but many that were not. The same eternal force that had motivated the Buddha to vow to renounce nirvana in order to free all beings from suffering was also at work in him, hidden within the marshlands of his mind but still flowing steadily, wearing its course into the landscape in the sure knowledge that it would one day become a river from which all could drink. At night he practiced the meditation of the great void, and while he did not succeed in letting go of the myriad samskaras that held him in thrall like a web of finely wrought chains, he felt himself growing in spaciousness. A faint glow began to surround his memories and the emotions that raged alongside them, a distant luminescence that seemed to hold all his turbulent inner world in its comforting embrace.

As his mind grew in spaciousness, he was able to witness its workings for short periods of time, as if he were a spectator in a vast theater filled with shifting land-scapes and an ever-changing cast of characters. These interludes would not last long. The strident music would strike up again. His mind would be captured by the rushing tide of thoughts like a man cruelly abducted from his country home and shackled to a slave train on a forced march through the countryside. But every time he lost his way, he found it again. Back and forth he went, oscillating between the witnessing consciousness and the slavish attraction of his desires. Every time he became aware of where his thoughts were taking him, he made an effort to pull back, stepping off the stage against the will of his ego and back into the audience. It was a fierce and constant struggle that began when the first gong sounded in the morning and continued until the blessed forgetfulness of sleep overtook him in his tiny cell at night.

The longer the struggle continued, the more conscious he became of his desires. He saw how they raged furiously from morning until night like a forest fire burn-ing out of control, from the simple need to scratch an itch, or relieve the pain in his legs by shifting their position, to desires that seemed so deeply rooted he could not separate them from his sense of who he was: his longing for artistic greatness and the renown that would follow in its wake; the overwhelming need to see himself completed in the love and companionship of a woman, which had transferred itself from Beth to his dreamed water woman to Saraswati. Between these two overwhelming, dictatorial desires and the simplest needs of the body swirled an infinite web of other desires, twisting and intertwining themselves in endless loops that wrapped around him like chains of fire and held him fast in the earthly dungeons of his ego. He saw his selfishness now for what it was: a mad obsession with the fulfillment of his own desires coupled with a near total disregard for the sufferings of others. He saw the roots of his anger springing from thwarted desire and his depression as the weight of his longings becom-ing impossible to bear. Desires that had seemed so attractive and so necessary before, began to feel painful now, as he saw how they clouded his awareness and pulled him slavishly where they willed. Fanciful dreams of publishing his novel to critical acclaim and popular approbation sent his mind reeling in a paroxysm of superficial delight. He saw himself accepting a literary prize, giving a speech to a rapt audience about the genesis of his book, enjoying the avid attention of their eyes, hearing in their questions their acknowledgement of him as a literary master. But then the light of his consciousness would flood back in. He would suddenly become aware of the shallowness of this dream and the gluttony of his ego, surfeiting itself on the imaginary adulation of others. And then the pain would follow, the pain of being trapped in his ego, in his selfishness, cut off from the blissful, compassionate light of consciousness. He would release that pain and for a few moments his spirit would breathe the clear air of freedom, seeing his desires for what they were—mere mirages—but then Beth's image would rise up and he would hear her muttering sweet endearments, or he would begin wondering what Saraswati thought of him, and off his mind would go racing once again, maddened in its pursuit of these strange phantoms until the voice of consciousness could make itself heard through the din, and again he would pull back and wonder at the fearful power of desire.

Midway through the retreat, the Rimpoche began a series of talks on *prajna*, transcendental insight, which comes not as words or images but as a direct, naked apprehension of reality that falls like a thunderbolt, illuminating the landscape that had hitherto been veiled in the shadows of ignorance. "It is an experience," he said, "that cannot be put to the service of the ego, because when it comes in contact with delusion it burns it to ashes, as lightning burns to ashes whatever it strikes." Perhaps there was some budding measure of *prajna* in what Rodrigo was experiencing. His delusion was still there, inescapable, at times overwhelming, but he was learning to see into it and beyond it to the ground of what was real and lasting and not merely ephemeral. Early in the third week, the Rimpoche asked him to describe what he had learned during his meditation about the workings of his mind. While Rodrigo shared his observations, the old man's faint and tranquil smile seemed to illuminate the room, while his eyes used that light to peer into Rodrigo's soul. "You have witnessed what the Buddha witnessed twenty-six centuries ago," the Rimpoche told him when he concluded his short recitation, "and what all the Buddhas before and after him have witnessed. You have seen the first two of the four noble truths. 'There is suffering. The origin of suffering is desire.' Now you must meditate on the third noble truth." Rodrigo had not thought about the four noble truths during all those long hours of meditation, yet they were the first of the Buddha's teachings and the rock upon which Buddhism had been raised.

"The end of suffering is attained by *nirodha*," the Rimpoche continued, "the cessation of clinging and desire." His words fell like a revelation so simple and so clear that he could not understand how he had not seen it before. The same word Patanjali had used, *nirodha*, the same path in different robes.

"How can we cut off desire?" he asked.

"It is not sufficient to cut it off," the Rimpoche answered, "for it immediately grows back again. You must bring it up by the roots. In order to do that, you must be able to see through to the ground from which desire arises. Look there. When you have seen into its source, come and tell me what you see."

Try as he might, Rodrigo could not follow his desires to their source, though at times he had a vague intimation that if he could just quiet his mind enough he would see the ground of their arising. And so he struggled on, fighting like a warrior who knows that he has reached his last battle and that the legacy he leaves behind depends entirely on its outcome. He fought the pain and the stiffness in his body, screaming at him at every hour of the day and night. He fought the furious resistance of his mind, which roared out at every opportunity what a glorious relief it would be if he would just give up. But then he would see the Rimpoche's face among his thoughts and know that he would be there in the evening to remind him why he was making this journey and again in the morning to show him in the flesh the greatness that could live inside a human form. He remembered Saraswati's confident words that he had the will of the Buddha inside him, and he knew he could not let either one of them down. His effort was the gift he wished to give them both, and so he pressed on like a swimmer with his lungs on fire, aching to reach the shore.

In the early morning of the last full day of the intensive, Rodrigo heard the sound of a gong ringing through the bowers of the temple gardens, where he sat dreaming in delirious conversation. The swelling ripples of sound seemed to reverberate outward toward the edges of the vaulted sky. He saw the hanging vines of Indian sky flower and bougainvillea, with their bright red, yellow, and blue flowers, begin to tremble and grow diaphanous. The musky fragrance that perfumed the air around him began to dissipate and fade from his consciousness. He felt himself rising out of his body, gazing back down at himself as he sat on the secluded stone bench, only a scant meter from the fragrant figure of the dark-skinned woman whose mere presence was an intoxication to his senses. He hovered for a few radiant moments, watching the two figures rapt in conversation, until he was racked by a wave of separation and longing. He became aware of tears wetting his cheeks, and then, moments later, of his body lying on the cot of his tiny cell. The breaking of the waters against the boulders below awakened his senses, and in that instant he remembered who and where he was.

The dream was still fresh in his mind when he sat up, the elation and longing still coursing through his veins and his nerve fibers with their electric current. He felt a momentary pang of disappointment that he did not have his computer with him. But then he let the disappointment go, realizing that the dream was lodged in his mind as memory; it would be there for him to recover whenever he needed it. He got up to go to the bathroom and get ready for the morning practice, but from the moment he rose from his bed until the moment he reached his meditation cushion, he moved in a kind of waking dream, barely aware of his movements. The dream images continued to command his attention, and no amount of effort could enable him to pull his mind back into the present.

It had been morning; he had been waiting for the girl in the temple gardens, knowing that she would come sooner or later to fill the large earthen vessels with water and tend to the plants that were under her care. He became aware of her approach by the sound of her ankle bells rustling melodiously to the fluid rhythms of her gait and by her fragrance, a sensuous mix of the sesame oil she rubbed on her body and the frangipani she wore in her hair. Then the earthen vessel she balanced on her head with one upraised hand became visible floating above the hedges, nestled on the matted strands of her rich black hair. Moments later, she turned the corner and he could see that she was wearing a smile she had reserved for him alone—she had sensed his presence as he had sensed hers. She paused for a moment and looked at him, the large water pot motionless on her head. Gladness shone in her face and a sense of majesty that filled him with awe. She put down the water pot without taking her eyes from his. Then she folded her hands to her chest in greeting. With a naturalness that belied the vast chasm between their social positions, she sat down on the bench beside him, their bodies turned at forty-five degree angles so they could see into each other's eyes without having to sit face to face. She thanked him for his gift, never once questioning that it came from him and from him alone. As she spoke, his mind soared, as if her words had transported him out of his earthly existence. He thanked her for her help in the debate, his speech hesitant at first, then gaining surety as her gaze filled him with confidence. At her gentle insistence, he began talking about his dreams for the future: the reforms he wished to bring to the temple once he became high priest, his adoration for the devi, his determination to be a pure vessel in her service, his search for the esoteric understanding hidden in the sacred scriptures. She listened quietly, with eyes that took in everything he said and more; and then, gradually, softly, but without a hint of timidity, she told him of her wish to help him in his endeavors, in whatever small way she could, sharing his hope that he might one day realize his dreams. Her quiet declaration overwhelmed him; he could see that she had noticed, but despite his pride he did not mind. In the silence that surrounded their words a pact had been sealed; thenceforth nothing could be hidden. The conversation went on far longer than he thought was prudent, but he could not bring himself to break it off. Her words blended into a musical wash of sound; every minute fraction of his senses became alive with the intoxicating nearness of her presence. He felt an ecstasy approaching that was not merely of his mind but of his body as well. Then the gong swelled in his ears and the longing and the separation grew until he thought it would drown his existence.

Throughout the morning practice, Rodrigo struggled with his desire as he had never struggled before. It was not merely a powerful distraction but a live presence that seemed to reach down into the roots of his soul, a longing that had woken up from a dream and now claimed its rightful place at the center of his world. Every time he tried to pull his mind free, the girl's musky mixture of frangipani and sesame wafted through the closed room in which he sat. Her shining black eyes swam in his mind like twin pools of liquid light reflecting back to him the beauty he was struggling vainly to renounce. Her laughter mocked him and beckoned him in turn. Try as he might, she would not leave him. The hours between his dream and breakfast passed like a final judgment on all that had come before, sapping what energy he had left and bringing him to the borders of despair.

When the gong sounded, however, and he reached the veranda, the hot soup and the roiling waters of the Ganges brought a welcome relief. For a few minutes his mind remained quiet. He gazed upon the wooded slopes on the far bank with the thankfulness of a prisoner who has just been liberated from solitary confinement and is looking for the first time in years on the verdant glories of nature. But his reprieve was short-lived. As soon as he sat on his meditation cushion again and closed his eyes, he saw with profound dismay that the landscape within was still racked by the interminable storms of desire.

By the time he entered the Rimpoche's room for his final meeting with the Tibetan master, Rodrigo was at the end of his powers. The kingdom of desire that flourished inside him seemed so vast, so entrenched, so heedless and self-absorbed, that he could not imagine how anyone could come to the end of his samskara and thus free himself. For a brief moment, he caught a glimpse of how monumental the Buddha's accomplishment had been; he felt like prostrating on the floor and paying homage to that incomparable sage who had conquered the armies of desire that hold man in thrall and thus stepped off the unending wheel of birth and death. As he bowed his head before the Rimpoche for the last time, it seemed as if the weight of this impossible task bore his head toward the earth, while the man before whom he bowed had been placed there by unseen powers to remind him of the overwhelming heroism of those who had succeeded. When he straightened up, he saw the Rimpoche observing him with beaming, tranquil eyes. His smile seemed so full of compassion that Rodrigo could feel something inside him melt and give way. He could not wrest himself from that gaze, nor had he any wish to, for those eyes seemed not only to penetrate into him but beyond him, into the great void that holds the whirling dust of planets and stars in its silent, eternal stare.

"Do you have any last questions?" the Rimpoche asked.

"What is the path to freedom?" Rodrigo blurted out in perplexity, surprising himself with this unpremeditated question.

The Rimpoche's smile broadened. "You are already free. You are just not aware of it. The awareness from which you witness your world is the freedom you seek."

As he walked out of the room and back into the meditation hall, Rodrigo felt certain that eons still lay between him and the Rimpoche's simple statement of truth.

That night Rodrigo was so exhausted, he fell asleep as soon as he reached his room, without making any attempt to perform his night meditation. He awoke a couple of hours later from a dream that seemed to rekindle the hope that had faded to the barest of a whisper during his long struggle that day. In the dream, he had been sitting on the concrete platform just outside the Kunjapuri temple compound. Instead of lying down, as he had done in real life, he was sitting with his eyes closed performing the meditation of the great void. His mind was calm and spacious. The Himalayan range seemed to shimmer and tremble like luminescent shadows beyond his closed eyes. As he was meditating, he heard the sound of ankle bells, a melodious rustle gliding through the open spaces of his mind. He opened his eyes and saw a young woman in a sky blue sari walking along the path up toward the temple, the same woman he had seen at the temple some six months earlier. She looked at him, smiled, and then dropped her eyes demurely and continued walking. He got up obediently and followed silently behind her. When she disappeared into the temple, he followed her in. The girl watched him enter and then turned and pointed. There, hovering a few feet above the altar, was a life-size image of Mother Kali—not a stone or wooden image but a living, breathing presence, her eyes blazing like black stars in the firmament, her four arms rippling in an aureole of air, her bare feet painted red with henna. Overwhelmed by the devi's presence, he prostrated on the ground in front of her. When he got up to his knees, he saw that there were flowers in his hands. Instinctively, he held them out to the Mother. Petals of different colors began to stream forth from his palms and swirl in the space in front of her. He saw the Mother smile at his offering. Then the room began to spin, revolving faster and faster until it finally disappeared. Instead of the four walls of the temple sanctuary, he now looked out on an infinity of stars. Around these stars revolved planets, and on these planets walked living creatures of all sizes and shapes. A inexplicable sadness welled up in his heart, the sadness he had carried with him all the years of his life, but this sadness was more than mere sorrow: it was the glue that connected him to each of these living creatures; through his sadness he lived in them and felt what they felt. Realizing this, he heard the devi's voice bathing him gently like the light of stars, compassionate, radiant, the hearts of all creatures beating within her mother's heart and soothed in their sadness by her mother's love. Then, quietly, the vision faded. He found himself back in the temple room at Kunjapuri, kneeling in front of a stone image of the Mother, pouring out his heart to her. Still dreaming, he heard himself tell her that whatever she wanted from him, it was hers to take. Whatever she wished to give him—whether sadness or joy, pain or pleasure—he would take it gladly and wait for his freedom for however long she wished. Then the room grew dark. The last thing he remembered was the Mother's presence accompanying him on the journey back into his body.

Rodrigo sat up, feeling refreshed and infinitely lighter. He saw by the dim glow of his watch that it was midnight. He crossed his legs, folded his hands, and began to practice the meditation of the great void. As he meditated, he felt his mind gradually expand until it passed beyond the borders of space. Images started appearing in that void, but he watched them float by without any attempt on his part to reach out and capture them or follow them in their course. He saw Beth, her smiling eyes wetted by the tears he had caused her, but the sight of her occasioned neither desire nor regret. He saw Saraswati and felt a cautious tug at his heart, but both her image and the sentiment it aroused floated on and out of sight. Image after image rose and fell in that great space and passed on, accompanied by wispy clouds of emotion, but he remained in the same still place, watching them arise and disappear in turn from his seat in the gallery of the infinite space within him. The words of the Rimpoche came back to him as a flash of insight. He saw that the awareness that witnessed the passage of all these thought forms, so real yet so momentary, was like the space through which the wind and birds pass, untouched and unsullied by their passage. He saw that he was and had always been free, though this freedom did not belong to him, to the ego, which thought itself to be a man and thus suffered the pains of being a man. It was a freedom that could not be called his, for it was free of him as well, free of everything, and yet, for a few precious moments, he was, inexplicably and irrevocably, that awareness.

He did not know how long he remained in that state. But soon his mind grew tired and began to cloud over. When he felt he could go no further, he lay down on his cot and followed his awareness into the land of sleep.

In the morning the participants sat for one final meditation. When the gong sounded, they each bowed in turn before the cherubic monitor and then waited while the kitchen staff prepared the hall for a generous breakfast of fruits, breads, sweets, and yoghurt, in addition to their normal hot soup and barley meal. After breakfast, Rodrigo went down to the river to sit on the rocks and meditate, both by force of habit and by force of will. At ten, he returned to the hall for the closing ceremony. The Rimpoche thanked each of them for their participation and gave the group his blessing. As he was pronouncing his final words, the same cavalcade of cars that had brought him could be heard careening around the bend, flying their Tibetan flags and blowing their boisterous horns. After they had seen the Rimpoche off, the participants remained behind for lunch. Their hosts announced that they had arranged an excursion by jeep to the Nilakantha temple for those who didn't need to get back to Rishikesh right away. Rodrigo went on the excursion, drinking in the marvelous vistas that the climb to the temple afforded and enjoying the heavy feeling in his stomach after three weeks of painfully light rations. Once again, he felt the joy of a prisoner who has been freed from his captivity, gazing upon the mountains as if he were seeing them for the first time, though he knew that this incarceration had not been a punishment but a means to free his soul. As he looked down from the temple to the faraway plains, he reflected back on the seven months he had been in India. He was no longer the man he had been when he'd arrived; something had been freed that had been long imprisoned. He could see his life stretching out before him in the clarity of the high Himalayan air and it no longer worried him or filled him with uncertainty. Though he could not see the exact path his steps would take, he finally felt as if he knew where he was going.

When he made it back to the ashram, it was well after dark. He went to his room to meditate, but rather than break for dinner, he continued his meditation and then fell into a long and apparently dreamless sleep. His last thought before he fell asleep was how much he felt at home—not merely in this place but in his own skin.

27

WHEN THE FINAL SUNDAY of the intensive dawned, radiant and warmer than it had been in months, Saraswati felt a sense of anticipation and excitement bubbling up beneath the surface of her thoughts, unsteadying her mind as she tried to meditate. She had been glad to see Rodrigo go—or so she had thought at the time. The extra tutoring had altered her routine, and she had welcomed the prospect of being able to return her attention to her own studies and practices. The sense of relief, however, proved short-lived. Soon she found herself wondering how he was doing much more than she considered seemly, fretting over the difficulties he must be facing—knowing, as she did, that six months of meditation was far too little preparation for such a difficult intensive—until she began to wonder what had possessed her to send him in the first place. In the sober light of his absence, it seemed like a willful and irresponsible act. The last few days had passed slowly. Too much of her time had been spent wondering how he was getting on and what changes she would see in him when he returned, rather than abiding in the present, as she was normally able to do.

After lunch, she went up to the rooftop with her books and a second chair. Though she knew he would not make it back until mid-afternoon at the earliest, she kept glancing at the courtyard down below each time she heard the sound of footsteps on the concrete path, thinking it might be him on his way to her room, eager to share his experiences, just as she was eager to see the changes in his face that she felt sure would be there. The afternoon passed, and when he did not arrive, she grew more and more unsettled. At four thirty, she left the roof and passed by his room. The heavy padlock was still on the door, so she went out the gate and began walking by the river, thinking it would be nice to surprise him as he crossed the Ram Jhula Bridge and headed down the lane to the ashram, but the arati began and still he did not appear. Nor did he show up during the music, though she craned her neck many times to look for him, as if her attention could hasten his return. Afterward, she went to her room to do her practices, but her mind was troubled. Not only had he not come, she felt strangely disappointed. This could mean only one thing: she had developed an unforeseen attachment. How deep it went, she could not be sure, but she knew she would have to deal with it sooner rather than later, before its roots thickened and it became difficult to extirpate. She was aware how pernicious such attachments could become if left unattended.

Lying on her bed, she thought back to the one time a serious attachment had entered her life and robbed her of her peace, a year after she had seen the Mother in the Delhi kirtan and resumed doing her spiritual practices. She was still working for WAI then, writing articles for the WAI journal that were sometimes reprinted in the city's newspapers and traveling to different parts of Northern India to organize and report on campaigns, but her previous depression had completely disappeared. Though her schedule continued to be hectic and she often felt frazzled by the many demands on her mind and her heart, she had turned into something of a fanatic about her twice-daily meditation—and it was her meditation that sustained her spirits. If she had to work late in the office, she would do it in a corner of the room, even if her colleagues were still typing away at their computers or chatting among themselves. When she was traveling, she would do it on trains and in buses and in railway stations, wherever and whenever she had a chance. When she arrived at her destination, the first thing she did was to inform her hosts that she would need to break for meditation at a certain hour. Whenever the pace of life started to overwhelm her, she would insist on taking leave for a few days and then board the next train to Benares to spend those days with the Mother, soaking up her divine presence and meditating to her heart's content. After a while, her colleagues gave her the nickname Saint Saraswati, though they rarely used it in her presence. She didn't mind, since it reminded her of the true focus of her life, and on at least a couple of occasions she signed office memos by that name to everyone's amusement.

One day, after returning from a trip to Madhya Pradesh to document the progress of a micro-industry project for a rural women's collective, she found a letter on her desk from a reporter whose byline she had seen with regularity in the *Hindustan Times*. It contained his number and a request to call him about the possibility of doing a regular column. The letter was handwritten and had been delivered in person a few days earlier. She called him immediately, and he suggested they meet for dinner that night to discuss his proposal. A few hours later, she found herself in the Alka restaurant in Connaught Place at the appointed hour, sipping tea and waiting for Vikram Singh to arrive. Two years her senior, Vikram liked to be fashionably late, a trait she could never reconcile with the exigencies of being a successful journalist. Yet successful he was, as she soon found out when he began sharing stories of the social dignitaries he had interviewed and then complained that Penguin Books had pushed back the publication date of his first book, a selected anthology of his magazine and newspaper articles written over the past seven years. Vikram was a boyish-looking twenty-seven, a Sikh by birth who did not wear the traditional turban but instead wore his hair slicked back and fashionably long. He wore English-tailored suits, frequented the best restaurants, and never wore a tie, always leaving the top two buttons of his shirt open. He was also devilishly handsome, a fact he was aware of and used to his advantage, both in his professional and his personal lives. When he finally arrived, forty minutes after the hour they had agreed upon, he flashed a mischievous smile and reached out to shake her hand before she had time to offer the more traditional namaste. "Do you realize how good your articles are?" he said, as he sat down. "Brilliant, simply brilliant." Then he launched into a detailed analysis of the Alka's best dishes. When he saw her hesitate over the menu, he told her that the paneer butter masala could not be missed. "And the thali, of course, the thali." Then he called the waiter over with a waggle of his index finger and ordered for the both of them.

It was the beginning of a schoolgirl crush and a long, slow swoon that she never could explain. Though she had on a few occasions felt some passing attraction toward one boy or another during her school days, she had grown up with an innate mistrust of the opposite sex that always overrode whatever attraction she might have felt. The teachings of certain Indian sages about the dangers of sexual desire in spiritual life reinforced that distrust and gave her the intellectual justification for the decision she had made during her college years to remain unmarried, free from the contagion of the second chakra. As a result, she had remained naive to a fault about such matters. The idea that one could have a boyfriend before or without marriage never even occurred to her until she had nearly finished her freshman year and realized that the male friends of some of her classmates were not simply chaste companions. It took her a while to get over her shock, but in time she decided that such things had nothing to do with her, so she learned not to see what was going on. It was only when she started working for WAI that her not-seeing became problematic. She discovered that illicit liaisons were common in village life, though never talked about, and it was always the women that suffered. But they also suffered in their marriages. That was the lot of being poor and being a woman in India. Her indignation with the suffering she saw inflicted on these mostly innocent women by the men around them snuffed out any possibility in her mind of ever becoming emotionally intimate with a man, even on a platonic basis. That was why it was so hard for her to understand what was happening. She was, to put it succinctly, completely smitten.

A dizzying six months followed during which they cut a course through the best restaurants of Delhi, often followed by the theater or a movie if there was no important public event to attend. They argued passionately for hours, often deep into the night. They read out loud to each other, mostly from the books that fascinated him at the moment, but at times from the books that fascinated her. Whenever she left Delhi for her fieldwork, she would literally count the hours until she could board a train back to the capital. Before she arrived, she would call him with the cell phone he had given her as a birthday present and wait breathlessly until he told her where and when they could meet. For the first time in her life she was deliriously happy, though if the truth be told, she was more delirious than happy. Her colleagues were amazed by the transformation, but they chalked it up knowingly and cynically to the magic dust known as "falling in love," as they waited secretly for the same thunderbolt to strike them. Before long she was dreaming of marriage, certain that it was just a matter of time, fretting about the prospect of having children and wondering when she should take him to meet her parents, who she knew would not be able to adjust to the idea that their traditionally brought-up daughter had a boyfriend. She spent hours thinking about exactly what she should tell them, how to cushion the blow, how to deal with the excitement that would follow once they realized that the daughter who would never marry might, in fact, one day give them a grandchild. In the meantime, Vikram made good on his promise. He arranged a meeting with one of the senior editors on the paper, having already recommended her work; two weeks later, she began writing an editorial for the *Hindustan Times*'s Sunday magazine on social issues and social injustices that rapidly became an institution among progressively minded Delhi readers. The *Times* did not shy away from controversy and her column stirred up its fair share. It was not infrequent in the streets and eateries of Delhi to hear someone say that hers was the one column they would not read. The new position more than doubled her tiny income, which was soon increased even more by periodic requests from the editorial staff for special features. Things could not have looked more propitious. Her career was taking off and her heart had finally known what it meant to fall in love, both occurring through the agency of the same dapper, sweet-tongued star of the journalistic world.

As her own name became more well-known, however, and she began meeting people she would not have ordinarily met, she started hearing stories about her beau that were less than flattering. A female reporter from the paper turned up her eyes when Saraswati mentioned him and muttered something about the Indian Don Juan. A friend of hers that had previously worked for WAI told her that he had something of a "reputation." At first, she disbelieved such stories—he had respected her chastity with an unspoken assent that made her assume he attached the same value to it as she did—but she heard such remarks more and more frequently, often in a tone that made it clear that the speaker assumed she knew all about his peccadilloes and therefore condoned them. Finally, she arranged a luncheon with a couple of his women friends on the promise of complete confidentiality. What she heard from them shocked her more than nearly anything she had seen in her four and a half years with WAI. According to them, he had had a string of girlfriends for as long back as they could remember, which had not impeded him from simultaneously dating other women. And yes, this had been going on even after he had started seeing Saraswati. On the verge of tears, her habitual confidence thoroughly shaken, she confronted him about it the following day, making a thunderous declaration that should any of it be true, it would have to stop right away if he wanted to marry her—having decided beforehand that even should it be true, she would forgive him as long as he promised to reform his character. He did not bother to deny her accusations. He simply looked at her sweetly, with a smile that she had lately come to realize reflected more condescension than compassion, and said, "But my dear, I love you for your mind, not your body—not that you have offered me your body. Anyhow, I am not ready for marriage. Surely you must have realized that?" This statement was accompanied by a look of perplexity that made her realize he was telling the truth. Whatever else he might have done, he had never led her on in that respect. The thought of marriage had probably never even entered his mind.

Saraswati was devastated. She cut off all contact with Vikram, returned her cell phone by post, and refused to answer his calls when he rang the office. Those calls did not last long—a matter of days. A week later, she took a month's leave of absence from WAI and went to stay with the Mother in her Benares ashram, where her guru's serene, loving presence and the consolation of her fellow ashramites helped to cure her of the worst of her grief. What remained was mostly anger, which would take another couple of years to die out. While she was there, she sent her column in by post. The first two articles consisted of a two-part series entitled "The Philandering Male." It was greatly appreciated and long remembered by single middle-class women in the capital, and she attributed part of her cure to the bitter invective that she was able to unleash in its pages.

Eventually, between the Mother's sage counsel and the inevitable perspective afforded by time, Saraswati came to see the good that had arisen from her infatuation with Vikram. She had gained a regular income and taken the first steps toward becoming a professional journalist. This proved to be a godsend six months later when her father suffered a stroke and could no longer work. Her parents' savings were meager, and inevitably she became their only means of survival. She resigned her stipend with WAI, something she had been planning on doing anyways, and after spending a month in her village helping her mother nurse him back to some semblance of health and adjust to her new life as a caretaker, she returned to WAI as a part-time volunteer, giving her ample scope to pursue her career as a freelance investigative journalist and essayist who specialized in social causes, especially injustices done to women.

The other, and in her eyes more important, benefit was that her disaster with Vikram allowed her to tear out the last shreds of romantic illusion that had been hiding unknowingly in her heart; with this, she finally put to bed the last of her village-girl naiveté. She had been blindsided by emotions she had never had to deal with before, but it would not happen again. Thanks to Vikram, her unformed idealism had hardened into a more pragmatic recognition that she was human and subject to the universal law of attraction, as well as all the other weaknesses that human beings were prey to. Thanks to him, she knew the warning signs and the dangers of not heeding them. Above all, she recognized the blindness caused by illusion and realized that this could never be a path to the truth.

Propping herself against her pillow, Saraswati laughed out loud at how naive she had once been. She could not harbor any rancor or resentment toward Vikram. After all, it was he who had set her firmly on the path to renunciation. Looking into her heart, she saw none of the blindness that had affected her then, none of the delirium that had felt so intoxicating as it led her down the sure road to suffering. Yes, some measure of attachment had grown in her for her precocious student, but how can one be fully free from attachment in this world of relativity?

Was it even healthy? What mother does not feel attachment for her child? She would not be human if she didn't. Certainly there would come a time when she would be free of all attachment, as she neared the threshold of liberation, but that time was still far away. In the meantime, this was a necessary part of her journey, an inescapable part of being human. What she felt for Rodrigo was simply the natural excitement and justifiable concern of a teacher who sees her pupil blossoming and wants the best for him—and perhaps a bit of the glad recognition that she had met a kindred soul. It would not be natural if she didn't look forward to seeing him again and accompanying him part way on his journey. We all need company on the path. Nevertheless, she promised the Mother she would remain wary. If this attachment ever grew beyond the natural ties of human companionship, she would not be caught in its snares. If such an eventuality came, she would take whatever steps were necessary to keep to her path. Her resolution satisfied her. There was no use in chiding herself anymore. If she was to be a mother to spiritual seekers one day, as her own guru was to her, then she could not make any distinction between man and woman. Her sympathy was for all.

Saraswati glanced at the clock and realized that the staff kitchen was about to close for the night. She got up and hurried out the door, feeling hungrier than usual and justifiably happy at the thought that tomorrow she would see Rodrigo and have a chance to hear about his spiritual adventure.

It was the beginning of March and the weather was changing rapidly. By early April, the summer heat would be upon them and people would begin to look forward to the cooling monsoon rains of early June as they dabbed the sweat from their foreheads with a handkerchief and complained about the nearness of the Himalayan sun. Saraswati, however, loved the heat. Both in the capital and in the village where she had grown up, the pre-monsoon temperatures could reach forty-five degrees. The wind would burn one's skin rather than cool it, and farmers would be in the fields with their bullocks and their ploughs by three thirty in the morning, beginning their day's labor in the dark so they could be safe inside their cool earthen cottages by nine when the sun became so fierce that the sky seemed to be on fire and the ground burned their feet. Rishikesh, by comparison, was a blessed five or six degrees cooler on average. While the town's residents complained of the heat and her merchants closed shop in the middle of the day, Saraswati never ceased to be thankful how cool it was compared to the capital, a mere five hours away. All through the winter, she had spent a good part of her afternoons on the roof soaking up the weak but still potent sun that for her was a sustenance as important as the food she ate. She was on the roof now, waiting for Rodrigo, musing ruefully that as cool as Rishikesh was by comparison with Delhi, it would not be long before she would have to shift her afternoon venue to her room or to the shade of a nearby tree.

He had been in class that morning, but they hadn't had a chance to talk, other than a quick word afterward to confirm their afternoon session. By then, she had controlled the eager anticipation that had bubbled over when she saw him sitting with the other students under the banyan tree and had recaptured her habitual composure. She had enjoyed the class, the introduction to the Bhagavad Gita that she had developed over the last couple of years by synthesizing the ideas of various commentators and adding a fresh perspective of her own, inspired by an offhand comment she had once heard the Mother make. She had an entirely new group of students now, most of them transient guests of the ashram who would be gone in a few days, or at most a week or two, to be replaced by other spiritual seekers for whom her class was a kind of minor tourist attraction. It had been a unique experience, having serious long-term students who looked upon her as more than just a philosophy teacher. She had welcomed it and considered it a kind of training for the life she hoped to lead. But for the time being, that was over. Marlena had gone back to Switzerland a month earlier; Ely was at this very moment on a plane to Argentina; and Georg was in his room getting ready to leave for ten days in Benares and Bodh Gaya before he headed back to Germany. Only Rodrigo was still here, after a three-week absence, but there was no sense in his attending class anymore since he had heard it all before. She would have to suggest it to him. They could continue his studies in private sessions as they had been doing before. He was, after all, something of an adept now, she thought, remembering the glow in his face and the tranquil confidence in his glance that was noticeable even from a distance.

Saraswati's ruminations were interrupted by the sound of Rodrigo climbing the stairs. She put down her book, which she hadn't actually been reading, having been on the same page for the last twenty minutes. Moments later Rodrigo was sitting beside her, his bright eyes beaming with delight, a feeling she found contagious. At her behest, he spent the next hour recounting his three-week odyssey, beginning with his first impressions of the Rimpoche and ending with his visit to the Nilakantha temple and its stunning Himalayan vistas. She felt a chill when he told her of the Rimpoche's initial words to him and the rapid descent it had occasioned into the shadow world of his private phantoms. Her anxious empathy turned to fascination as he described in extraordinary detail his encounter with the mysterious and intricate world of desire, and the witnessing consciousness within which it unfolded, each succeeding session with the Rimpoche spurring his mind to greater and greater depths. Her fascination turned to wonder as he told her of his midnight meditation and the short but earth-shaking taste of freedom he had enjoyed. When he was done with his account, she felt as if she had been on a voyage of her own, her body still vibrating from the undulating waves of emotion that had carried her along as she listened. Neither one of them spoke for more than a minute, as if each of them needed that time to assimilate the weight of his story. What resonated most of all within her during those moments of silence was how similar his final meditation had been to hers when she had done the intensive twelve years earlier. The sense that they were kindred souls enveloped and warmed her like the sun inching closer to the peaks of the nearest mountains.

"I have a confession to make, Rodrigo. After you left for the intensive, I started worrying that maybe I had pushed you into this thing too soon. To be honest, I've never heard of anyone attending one of these intensives after only six months of meditation. It's just not enough preparation—or so I thought—which is why I questioned my judgment in sending you. But it just goes to show: in the end Providence gives us the experiences we need at the moment we need them. You were ready, after all; that much is obvious from your story. It was a heroic effort, Rodrigo. I probably shouldn't say this, but I am proud of you."

Rodrigo blushed slightly with a touch of the humility that she had seen growing steadily in him and which she found so becoming in a man who had once had trouble concealing his arrogance.

"I hardly think of myself as heroic, but it did give me an appreciation for real heroism. When I think of what the Buddha went through, or Milarepa, it's almost impossible to fathom. What I experienced was just a tiny glimpse of what they went through. Now that I have a better idea of what's involved, it's hard for me to ever imagine actually becoming enlightened."

"I feel the same way sometimes. But we'll get there, both of us—one of these lifetimes."

"If I ever do, it will be thanks to you, in large part. I wouldn't have gotten anywhere at all without your help."

Saraswati was used to hearing compliments, and as usual she didn't know what to say, so she changed the subject. "I guess you must be anxious to get back to your writing."

"I can't wait. It's the thing I missed the most. It will also be nice to get back to a regular routine. The last seven weeks have been such a challenge, ever since..."

"Ever since I made life so difficult for you?"

"I suppose that's one way to put it. It has been tough, though God knows, it was exactly what I needed. That reminds me, there is one thing I wanted to ask you about, now that I have the chance. It's about the relationship between discipline and creativity. The one fear I have with all this strict spiritual discipline, apart from not actually having time to write, is that it might stifle my creativity. I was wondering if you had any thoughts about that."

"You don't have the slightest worry in the world, Rodrigo. I've probably had this discussion at least fifty times in the past ten or twelve years. Somehow people seem to think that too much discipline can rob them of their spontaneity or stifle their creativity. I'm not sure what gives them that impression but the opposite is true. I can tell you this from personal experience. What stifles spontaneity and creativity is not discipline; it's anxiety, fear, lack of confidence, shyness, depression, anger, being reactive—any kind of emotional complex. Spiritual discipline frees you from your complexes. When you free your mind from its chains, you naturally free your creativity and your spontaneity. No one is more spontaneous than a saint, because a saint is not chained to the dictates of her ego; no one is more creative than a yogi, since a yogi is tuned into the soul, which is the source of infinite creativity. As long as you are a slave to your emotions and your cultural conditioning, then you can't be free in any true sense of the word, neither spiritually nor artistically.

The only footnote I would add is that authentic discipline is always self-discipline. Discipline can't be merely imposed; otherwise it is not real discipline. Sooner or later, it will generate some kind of adverse emotional reaction. But even then it is not the discipline that binds you; it's the reaction."

For a moment Saraswati thought about sharing some of her own writing experiences, but then she thought the better of it. There was no need to dig into the past for something he was capable of understanding in the present.

"There is another thing I wanted to ask you about," Rodrigo said. "I was reading *Autobiography of a Yogi* before I left and it got me thinking about finding a guru. When I met the Rimpoche, it reminded me of Yogananda's experience when he met his guru, but I didn't get the feeling that the Rimpoche was my master. Yogananda knew right away that Yukteswar was his guru; he even recognized his face from a dream. I didn't feel anything like that. I just felt like the Rimpoche was my teacher for as long as I was there. It was a really important experience, but I'm not sure what it means going forward. So my question is, how do you recognize your guru, assuming you have one? And if you don't, is it really necessary to find one to be able to achieve enlightenment?"

Saraswati had not anticipated the question, but she instinctively felt that it was the right time to discuss something she rarely discussed with her Western students. She started slowly, carefully searching for the right words to explain something that was very difficult to explain and even more difficult to understand.

"I don't think you so much find a guru as the guru finds you. You may remember, that's what happened with Yogananda. His master found him. You must have heard the expression, 'When the disciple is ready, the master appears'? That's generally how it works, even if sometimes it doesn't seem that way on the surface. You can go looking for a guru—a lot of people do—but it's sort of like a blind man looking for someone to guide him across the street. He may be able to sense that someone is there, but actually it's the person who can see who comes up and takes his hand. Personally, I think it's more prudent to work on preparing yourself. Once you are ready, the guru finds you; it's usually as simple as that. As to whether or not it is necessary to have a guru—well, from one point of view it is and from another point of view it isn't, but from the deepest point of view, I think the question is mute. We have a saying in India: God alone is the guru. And God is always guiding us, with or without our knowledge. There is a verse from the *Guru Gita*, I'm sure you've heard it."

Saraswati started chanting the verses that had been her favorite since she had first heard Lata Mangeshkar singing them on an old record: *akhanda mandalakaram, vyaptam jena characharam, tadpadam darshitam jena, tasmai shri guruve namah.*

"I recognize it. I have a couple different recordings of it in my iPod."

"I thought you might. Do you know the meaning? Well, roughly translated, it means 'I bow down to that divine guru who pervades the moving and non-moving in the form of this infinite universe and who shows the disciple the path to liberation.' In India, we attach supreme importance to the guru because the guru shows us the path to liberation. In one of Kabir's poems, he says, 'If both God and the guru are before you, whom should you bow down to first? First you should bow down to the guru because it is the guru who shows you the path.' That's how important the guru is. And it only stands to reason. If we want to master any subject, we need a teacher, the more adept the better, and spirituality is the most difficult of all subjects to master. How can anybody expect to successfully navigate such a difficult path without the help of someone who knows the way? You can try, but it's not exactly the wisest of choices. In the beginning, the guru leads the disciple along the path by teaching her what to do and what not to do. Meditate in this way, behave in that way, eat this, don't eat that. And if the guru is a perfect guru, a *sadguru*, then these teachings lead us unerringly toward the goal, because in the case of the perfect guru, it is Brahma himself who takes the help of that human structure and uses it as a medium to communicate his divine wisdom. That's the reason we revere the physical form of the guru. But that's only the first stage. As we become more elevated, we begin to feel a presence guiding us from within—a voice, if you will, that tells us exactly what we need to do in each and every situation. That presence is God acting as our internal guide. In the beginning, we can't hear this voice, so we depend on the teachings to know what to do and what not to do. But once we start feeling that inner guidance, the relationship becomes purely internal. This is the aspect of God that we call 'guru.' It doesn't depend on an external physical structure. Remember, God alone is the guru. I feel that presence guiding me and I call it my guru; Francis felt it and he called it Christ; Mahaprabhu called it Krishna. But in all three cases, it's the same presence, the same guide, the same guru. So we all have a guru, and it's the same guru for all of us. It just takes different forms in the external world at different times according to our needs."

"And if the guru is not a perfect guru?"

"It doesn't really matter. A master who is not realized can lead you up to the level she has achieved; after that, God will find a different medium through which to guide you. The only danger is that if the teachings are less than authentic, you may be led astray—there is no dearth of charlatans and half-charlatans, well meaning or not, posing as spiritual teachers—but even then it means that it's your samskara to be temporarily led astray and learn an important lesson through that experience."

"And what about you? Do you have a guru—a physical guru, I mean?"

"I do. You've met her."

Rodrigo blinked in surprise. "I've met her? I don't understand. When?"

Saraswati smiled at the look of confusion on his face. "Don't you remember? This was maybe a month before you started attending my class. You were walking along the river about halfway between Ram Jhula and Lakshman Jhula, just a little ways past Swami Sivananda's meditation hut? As I remember, you were walking in the direction of the ashram; the Mother was walking with a group of devotees in the opposite direction. I was one of those devotees."

"Of course! The old lady! The holy woman! She's your guru?"

"She's my guru."

"There was a German woman translating for her. She called her 'the Mother.'"

"That was Premananda. She's one of Mother's earliest European disciples and her first Western sannyasi."

"Wow. I remember that day very well; I'll never forget it, in fact. She asked me if I were lost. At first I thought she was talking literally, like she thought I might be looking for my hotel or something; then I realized that wasn't what she was talking about at all. It kind of shook me up. I knew she was some kind of spiritual teacher; in fact, I remember, she had an almost hypnotic effect over me. I couldn't make much sense of the other things she said, but those words stuck in my head for days. The fact is, I was pretty lost at the time and I knew it, I just didn't much like hearing about it…Wow, what a coincidence!"

"Coincidence! Rodrigo, you forget the teachings. There is no coincidence in this world, only incidence. You know, just before you showed up, the Mother was telling us that the only thing we take with us when we die is our spiritual attainment. However far we advance in this life, we pick up from that point in the next life, so no one should ever entertain the thought that they are too old to start doing spiritual practice or feel regret that they started late in life. There were some older devotees with us, so I thought she was saying this for their benefit. Then she started describing what happens when a yogi dies, how their samskara leads them to a favorable birth so that they can resume their practices from where they left off. She said that with such people there is always a precise moment of awakening that activates their inborn spiritual samskara, though the circumstances that trigger it can be very different. Then—and this is the interesting part—she said that often with such persons it is their destiny to come in contact with a saint or a spiritual master who triggers their dormant spiritual samskaras by giving them a conscious push, thus starting the process of awakening in the new life. It was just as she was saying this that you happened by. I remember very clearly. As soon as she said this, she paused and looked at you. I thought she was waiting for you to go by before she continued. But then she stopped you and asked you if you were lost. I don't call that coincidence. Do you?"

"Probably not."

"That's why I was saying, you don't have to worry about finding a guru or getting the guidance you need. Everything happens at the precise moment it's supposed to happen. Whatever guidance we need is provided at the exact moment we become ready to receive it. In your case, it was the Mother giving you a little push when you needed it. And now here you are. There's a connection there."

"I knew she was a spiritual teacher, but I had no idea she was a guru."

"She is—one of India's greatest, one in a long line of realized masters."

"How long have you been her disciple?"

"She was my parent's guru. The first time they took me to see her, I was only five; I barely remember it. I saw her a few more times as a child after that. It was nice, but I didn't really understand what was going on. She was more like a kind of distant grandmother to me when I was little. We had her picture in the house and we used to go visit her every blue moon and there would be lots of people there and my parents loved her and called her mother; that's mostly what I remember from those days. When I was fourteen, though, they took me to her ashram in Benares to be initiated; I found out later that it had been at her request. My father had taught me some mantras before then, but my parents didn't really meditate much, so neither did I. I didn't really start meditating until I was initiated. Even then, it took me a long time to fully realize that she was my guru—ten years, in fact. Or rather, I knew she was my guru on an intellectual level, but I didn't really appreciate what that meant. It hadn't really sunk in, not completely, not where it really counts—in the heart. That didn't really matter, though, because she had assumed responsibility for me. That's what really counts. She was guiding me all that time, even when I wasn't aware of it, right from my childhood. Who knows, perhaps even before then. She's the reason why I'm here at the ashram, but I'll tell you about that some other time… Well, maybe, we'll see. As a rule, I try to avoid looking backward. As I believe the Mother told you when she met you, God has given us two eyes in the front to look ahead, not behind."

"She did say that, actually. I still remember it sometimes."

"It's one of her favorite sayings. One of mine also."

"Do you think she might also be guiding me in some way?"

"I can't say, Rodrigo. That's between you and her, between you and your higher self. If you ask for my opinion, though, I'd say that for now it's your own past-life samskaras that are guiding you."

"I wonder," Rodrigo said in a cautious tone, as if he were mulling this possibility over in his mind. "All I know for sure is that for now you are guiding me."

Saraswati shook her head. "I'm just a medium, Rodrigo, don't forget that. I started earlier than you in this life, that's all, so I'm sharing with you what I've learned. I have the feeling, however, that you've heard it all before. Just not with this set of ears."

That evening, Saraswati went to the roof to perform her meditation. With the change in the weather, it was no longer uncomfortably cold after the sun went down; she was glad to be able to drink in the freshness of the night while she meditated. Afterward, she remained there for some time, gazing at the stars hanging over the mountains and contemplating the unexpected happenings in her life. Rodrigo's return was still uppermost in her mind, that and his amazing experiences during the intensive. How strange that a Western man with no background in spirituality should have such powerful experiences in so short a time. But the journey between life and death and back again was too mysterious to be understood by the individual human mind. Had the Mother seen his sleeping spiritual samskaras as he passed her on the road and decided to awaken them with a single push of her aged finger? She did not doubt it—not for a single moment. The evidence was overwhelming. Who could he have been in his past life? A yogi was the only answer that made any sense, the only possible answer in a sea of possibilities. The thought that he might be merely retracing steps he had already walked was a humbling one. She had spent years groping her way forward out of the darkness; now here was this unschooled novice racing toward the light with blinding speed, unconsciously intent on regaining his previous spiritual awareness so that he could then begin making fresh progress in this life. For a moment, she felt uncomfortable at the thought that he might overtake her on the path, but then she chided herself for her momentary pettiness. Was the earth not blessed by each soul that awakened on her soil? But what part did she have to play in this headlong race of his toward the light? What was her samskara in all this? How is it that she was his teacher, and maybe soon his friend and confidant? Did you foresee this as well, Mother, when you untied the knot of his samskaras, knowing that it was my samskara to accompany his awakening and play my own part in that drama? If so, then tell me, where will this story lead us?

Saraswati realized that she saw too little of the future to be sure of the course that she was plying; at the same instant, she realized how dangerous it was to be heading upriver without a sure hand at the helm. She needed help and there was only one place she could get it: Benares. The thought excited her. It had been months since she had seen the Mother, months since she had been able to sit at the feet of her guru and listen to the wisdom that flowed unceasingly from her lips. She knew the Mother would not approve of her abdicating her duties without good reason, but now she had the perfect excuse. At the very next opportunity she would go to Benares and put this question directly to the Mother.

By now a chill had started to penetrate through her warm Kashmiri shawl. She wrapped it about her more tightly and got up to go back to her room. She glanced over at the Shiva statue in the near distance, illuminated by a single light. The water of the river lapped black and ancient on either side. A thrill ran through her as she felt the touch of Consciousness around her, a silent, luminous awareness stiller than the night and infinitely alive. For a moment, the statue seemed to come to life, as if, through the magic wand of maya, she had been transported back to the time when Shiva walked the earth and made it sacred with his presence. A laugh escaped her throat, the musical sound of a momentary freedom; for a single instant, she saw how she and Rodrigo were simply strands in a universal weave, the outward fabric of an infinite inward Consciousness. That Consciousness had spun them together—how far back she could not tell—and at some point it would spin them apart again. That was not what mattered. What mattered was the dance. The moment passed and the statue once again became a statue, but she could still hear her laughter trailing after her as her footsteps echoed soft and fragile from the marble steps that led her to her room.

28

T took Rodrigo his return to realize how much a part of the ashram he had become and how much the ashram had become a part of him. It had been dark when he'd arrived from the intensive; he had made it to his room without coming in close contact with a single human soul. But the following day was full of reunions, some with friends he had not known he'd made. When he attended the morning practice, he caught a number of warm, welcoming smiles from ashram residents he had never talked to, some because they didn't speak a word of English. Though all maintained the mandatory silence as they entered the hall and took their seats for the chanting and meditation, that silent communication seemed as expressive as any words could ever be. Their eyes told him they were glad to see him back; that, in turn, let him know that they saw him as a part of their community, his place as natural and as significant in its humble way as that of the pujya swami. One young monk reached out and slapped him playfully on the back as he took his seat on a cushion just behind Rodrigo's and enthusiastically threw himself into the chant that was already bouncing boisterously off the walls. Afterward, as Rodrigo walked to Amrita's class, several members of the ashram staff waved to him or said hello. The guard at the back gate that led out to the yoga hall jumped off his stool and chattered at him enthusiastically in Hindi with a few words of English sprinkled in. Rodrigo shared his smile, doing his best to make it seem as if he understood what he was saying, and then went on to his class where Amrita gave him a generous hug and afterward insisted on walking back with him to hear about the intensive. Passing by the office on his way to breakfast, Bhagavati called out a friendly greeting and told him she was glad to see him back. Two other members of her office staff did the same, clean-shaven young men whose names he still couldn't get straight, dressed in the typical, loose-fitting white cotton dress that he had also adopted. Halfway through breakfast, Georg walked in and their animated conversation lasted right up until Saraswati's class. Georg was leaving in the afternoon, but he insisted that Rodrigo visit him the next time he passed through Europe.

Rodrigo was a bit overwhelmed by all the attention, but it was Saraswati most of all that he was glad to see. When he saw her ambling up the path with her saffron sari and her thoughtful gait, he knew that there was no place else he would rather be. For him the ashram was now the center of the known universe. They spent the afternoon together on her roof and then took a walk by the Ganges before arati, slipping back effortlessly into a routine that for him had become a kind of sacred ritual. When she told him there was no sense in his attending her classes anymore since they would be beginners classes, she suggested in the same breath that they continue their private sessions twice or three times a week as before. In practice, "twice or three times a week" translated to "daily," since Saraswati started joining Rodrigo for his afternoon walks on their off days. Soon he formalized the arrangement by stopping by her room at the same hour each day or waving to her on the roof if she had already gone up, from which point they picked up their conversation from the day before as naturally as if it had never been interrupted.

Rodrigo's mornings, however, were now free. He used them to begin the slow process of rousing his characters from their long sleep. Ambika was the first to wake. He caught her sitting on a wicker chair on the veranda of her family manor house on a similar sunny morning nearly two and a half centuries earlier. She was not surprised by his presence, for she did not notice him, but he was surprised by hers. She had filled out since the last time he'd seen her. The lines on her face were deeper, as if the girl in her was finally making the transition into full womanhood. A half-eaten plate of coconut fritters and papaya slices was lying beside her feet on the smooth white marble, forgotten as she stared out at the flower garden, aware only of her thoughts gaining momentum in the clear, balmy air. She was thinking of her father, aware of his domineering presence inside the house as he got ready to head to his clinic in his three-horse carriage. Ambika would travel with him, getting down at the edge of town from where she would then walk the one kilometer uphill to Le Gentil's observatory residence. A sense of surprise had been simmering in her for some time now as she tried to understand why her father had not talked to the governor to terminate her employment, or, in fact, made any mention of the astronomer and her perceived attachment that she knew he would never condone. If he were going to act, he would have acted already. It was not like him to wait and it was impossible for him to forget. He still remembered slights he had suffered when he was a boy, and he had always found a means to settle accounts with the offenders, even if it had taken him thirty years to do so, a fact she had heard him admit with pride on more than one occasion. No, if he had decided to let things be, it was because he saw an advantage in it. He was a man who calculated every eventuality down to the minutest fraction. But what that advantage was, she could not say, and this preoccupied her, for she knew that any unseen advantage he enjoyed could easily prove a significant disadvantage for her if it remained for his eyes alone to see.

When she finally made it to work that morning, Le Gentil was seated at his desk working at the difficult Hindu methods for the calculation of solar eclipses. Since his first meeting with Professor Sandip, he had been working assiduously at the problems the professor had set out for him; as a result of his efforts, he was gradually gaining a hands-on intimacy with the workings of Hindu astronomy. The astrological postulates that lurked behind the complicated manipulations of figures and equations were still mostly either unintelligible or unknown to him, but the evidence of his eyes had dictated that he keep an open mind about them; every few days he would take some time out to read from the astrological theories of those same Hindu astronomers that so impressed him with their logic, their erudition, and their creative insights into the movements of the heavenly bodies. He knew that their ultimate prize was meaning, and as a scientist who prided himself on the expanding circular ambit of his knowledge, he knew that it would have to be his as well.

As soon as Le Gentil noticed Ambika enter through the open door, he exclaimed in an excited voice that he nearly had it. A few days more, perhaps only a few hours, and he would master the method that the professor had predicted would take him months longer to learn. There was a glow on his face, and she knew right away—because she felt it in her own heart—that his excitement was not merely over mastering the method but because she was there for him to share it with. "I knew all along you'd learn it quicker than the professor would believe," she told him. "But don't let me interrupt you while you're working. I think you've forgotten how much you hate that. And I have my own work to do." Le Gentil laughed a laugh of happy satisfaction, waved his hand, and was quickly absorbed once again in his world of magical figures. Amused by the look of furrowed concentration on his face, Ambika went into the kitchen to boil some water for their tea. When the tea was done, she set a cup unnoticed on a corner of his desk and sat down at her own desk to continue work on the translations, which had now begun to occupy the better part of her time. It was enjoyable work, enabling her to both improve her French and expand her knowledge of the achievements of her countrymen in the fields that most fascinated him. The time passed quickly; before she knew it, Jiddu, Le Gentil's teenage cook and household servant, was calling them to lunch.

Jiddu had known only the rudiments of South Indian cooking when he came to work for Le Gentil, but he was a fast learner and his lack of experience helped him to master the basic French cuisine that Le Gentil insisted on having at his private table. Some of the dishes that the astronomer loved best would have offended an experienced South Indian cook, but Jiddu had the advantage of being free of such prejudices. With Le Gentil's help, he learned to cook meat and foul as well as some of the best Parisian chefs, and though he didn't eat meat himself, he actually felt a sense of regret when Ambika's influence eventually caused Le Gentil to eliminate meat from his table.

Jiddu spoke virtually no French. Most of his instructions came through Ambika; when she was not there, he proceeded from memory and a sometimes comical mistranslation of Le Gentil's gestures and hand signals. He loved to stand near the dining table during lunch with a towel over his forearm, as he had seen in an illustration in one of Le Gentil's books, and listen to the animated though unintelligible conversation between his employer and Ambika, which would often continue till mid-afternoon, first at the table while they made their way leisurely through their food, and then afterward on the veranda, where they would sip Chinese tea and look out over the garden. On this occasion—though he did not know it—the conversation centered on the strange religion of the white barbarians, which the aristocratic Ambika had also adopted to the perplexity and amazement of everyone he knew.

They had just started on their first dish, cream of cauliflower soup, when Le Gentil posed a question that had long been on his mind.

"By the way, I've been meaning to ask you, why did you become a Christian? The more I see how much you love your culture—and its religion, I might add— the odder it seems, especially now that I've met your family."

Ambika knew she could not tell the truth exactly, but she did not want to lie either. How could she tell him that her father had groomed her since childhood to become the ears and eyes of the revolutionary-minded Tamils inside the Governor's administration? She could not—not then and maybe never. But she would lean as far toward the truth as she could, so as to be true to the sentiments that reigned over her heart.

"I was young at the time, quite young, so you might say that I didn't really know what I was doing, but I felt like I was doing it for the good of my people. The Europeans were here and it was clear, even to me, that they were in the process of taking over our country and turning us into a colony. I guess I felt that it only made sense to try to understand our colonizers; what better way to do that than to understand their religion? Or so I thought. I didn't realize then that for most Europeans religion is more of a pastime than a way of life, as it is for us. Anyhow, the only way to understand a religion is from the inside, so I converted and gradually it all started to make sense."

"And your father allowed this?"

"You might be surprised, but he was actually in favor of it."

"And now that you are a grown woman and you know all that you know, what do you think of Christianity now? I know that might seem like a strange question to ask a grown Christian, but I think you know why I ask it."

Ambika nodded and asked Jiddu to serve the main course. She waited until he had cleared away the soup bowls and served the mashed potatoes, vegetables au gratin, and fresh baguette before she continued speaking.

"I don't consider Christianity to be separate from Sanatana Dharma. I look at them rather as different branches of the same tree of wisdom. My land is not a land of one religion but of many. There are so many different gods and goddesses and ways of worshipping them that sometimes I think that every village and even every family has their own religion. But somehow, if you look deeply enough, you'll see that we all essentially believe in the same things, no matter how strange or different they may seem on the surface. Those shared truths are what tie it all together. In Christianity I find the same truths, even if it sometimes appears that they're in hiding, at least from many Christians. You may be surprised, but many Indians consider Christ to have been a great yogi and the equal of our greatest sages, as he showed when he was here."

"What do you mean, when he was here?"

Ambika's tone softened. She looked at him, not with an air of defiance but with the quiet confidence of one who is sure of what she is speaking and willing to share it with someone she trusts.

"You are not a Biblical scholar, Guillaume, I know, but you were once a novitiate in the clergy and you must know that there are eighteen years of Christ's life that are unaccounted for in the New Testament. In Luke we see Jesus in the temple at the age of twelve and the next mention of him says that he became about thirty."

"Yes, of course. What are you implying?"

"Where do you think he spent those years? He spent most of them in India and Tibet. It has been documented, and I have been told by a father from your country that they are aware of this in the Vatican, but they refuse to let it become public knowledge."

Le Gentil's natural tendency was to scoff at any assertion that seemed on the surface to be preposterous, but the look on Ambika's face stopped him. He felt a slight queasiness in his stomach and so put down his fork. "Go on. What do you mean, it's been documented?"

"Jesus's stay here was recorded and those records have been preserved. The story, as documented, goes more or less like this: More than seventeen hundred years ago a young traveler from Palestine reached India in the caravans that used to ply the trade routes between the Middle East and the Indian subcontinent, the routes that are popularly known as the Silk Road. At that time, India was not only the oldest but the most advanced and the richest civilization on earth, as even the proud Chinese admitted. They had been sending their students to our universities for many centuries. But India was not only famous for its riches and its erudition; it was also famous for the wisdom of its spiritual teachers and for the secret practices they taught. Tales of those teachers had reached Jesus through his contact with the Essenes, an ascetic Jewish community, so he traveled to India in search of those teachers. He stayed here for eleven years, first in Kashmir and Tibet and then traveling down through the Gangetic plains until he reached Puri, where he held several famous debates with renowned sages of the day. By that time, he had become an adept in yoga and Tantric practices and a great saint. Summaries of those debates were preserved in the Jagannath temple, along with a history of his travels and his teachings. I have seen those documents. In fact, I have even translated parts of them into Tamil from the Sanskrit originals, though these translations have been kept secret. I have also heard that similar documents exist in a monastery in Lhasa and in another in Ley that record his stays there. When Jesus was ready, he returned to his own people and brought the spiritual teachings back with him. You may not be aware of it, but for the first two or three centuries after his death, there were numerous Christian enclaves devoted solely to the practice of the meditation techniques he taught, mostly in the desert areas around Palestine and into Egypt and Syria. Most of Jesus's original teachings have been lost, but some of them have been preserved in certain places—and India is one of those places."

"I remember now, your father said something about Christianity flourishing in India not long after the death of Christ."

"What my father said was true. The apostle Thomas came here about twenty years after Christ's death. He landed on the Malabar coast, about one hundred leagues from here, and established a Christian community that still exists. It's the oldest Christian community in the world and home to some of Jesus's teachings that have otherwise disappeared, including Thomas's own writings. You probably don't know this, but Thomas also wrote a gospel. I can translate it for you, if you wish. I think you'll find it more interesting than the four canonical gospels. It is far more mystical and in my opinion more representative of Christ's teachings, since he concentrates on what Christ taught rather than what Christ did. It's also the oldest of the existing gospels and the only one that was actually written by an apostle, rather than by one of his followers after his death."

As Ambika continued with her account of the development of early Christianity in South India, Le Gentil began to feel overwhelmed by this reordering of his understanding of history. Though Ambika was a little too proud of her native land and its many contributions to human civilization, there was nothing in her voice or in her eyes to make him suspect that she was holding on to such claims as a way to show that India had a far greater influence on European culture and thought than any European suspected. He could see that she was simply relating what she had learned and found to be true, however colored by her individual sense of pride. And if it were all true? Would it then bring his own Eurocentric world crashing down around him? Hardly. It would merely be an episode in the historical life of Jesus that threw an unexpected but not illogical light on his spiritual development during a critical period of that life that is conspicuously absent from the recorded histories. Le Gentil was, after all, a scientist, and a scientist searches for truth wherever he can find it, even if it doesn't fit the theories he carries with him into his search. It is better to have your eyes open to a truth that bothers you, he thought, than to keep them closed while you cling to a comforting falsehood.

"I should like to see these translations you've made," he said. "In French, of course. These are things that are not taught in the cathedral of Notre Dame."

"It shouldn't take too long. I can have some of them for you by the end of next week."

"It seems I will have to make a more comprehensive study of world history. I had forgotten that the Silk Road passed through India."

"Why is it so many modern European seafarers seem to think they are the first to see the wonders of the Orient?" Ambika said, shaking her head bemusedly. "All modern science has done is to cut down the time it takes to travel from one place to another. It hasn't increased human curiosity. People have been fascinated by faraway lands and other cultures since before recorded history. In the beginning they walked. There is a legend—which may be fact—that Shiva traveled to Europe on a yak. That was nearly seven thousand years ago. It took a lot longer then, but that didn't make travel any less interesting. You must know that the Romans were frequent visitors to India. There was a great deal of trade between our two countries long before the time of Christ. Which reminds me, not far from here are the ruins of a Roman settlement. It was a kind of a trading post, I'm told."

The anthropologist in Le Gentil straightened up and took notice. This was something close at hand and verifiable by his own eyes. "Can you take me there?" he asked.

Ambika's features brightened into a wide smile. "Of course. That's why I mentioned it. We haven't taken a long excursion for a while now. I was thinking that would be a good place. It's about time we saw some scenery other than Pondicherry."

As Rodrigo listened to the conversation unfolding in his mind, he gradually became aware of an unspoken intimacy between his characters that was far more marked than it had been when he had left for the intensive. Their understanding of each other's feelings went far beyond what he remembered. Suddenly he realized, startled, that the tension that had been growing between them was now almost entirely absent. It had been replaced by something else: loyalty, a shared avowal, some sort of secret agreement? He couldn't quite put his finger on it. It was almost as if they preferred that no one know, not even him. Had something happened while he'd been gone? Had they admitted their feelings to each other and found them reciprocated? He didn't think so, but if they had, he knew nothing about it. The only way he had of finding out would be to search through their memories, but rather than do this, he decided to forestall his curiosity and allow the drama to play itself out, spurred by a vague feeling that it would somehow be an invasion of privacy. It was only fitting, he decided. Some things were always better left offstage.

Rodrigo was in the middle of Ambika and Le Gentil's lengthy conversation about Christianity when his dreaming self paid another visit to its temple enclave.

Rishikesh
3/11
4:20 AM

As I wake, I feel a tingling in my spine, a remnant from this latest dream, as if my body were coursing with kinetic energy. Somehow this heightened physical sensation is tinged with fear. Why? Was I afraid in the dream that I would not be able to handle this energy? Or is it because she was with me, because she had led me there and was waiting for me when I came out, because we are now bonded together in some way that I fear I cannot escape? But let me save these reflections for later, lest the dream slip away.

She had told me of a Tantric sage living in the forest about a half-day journey from the temple. What she had learned about spiritual life, she had learned principally from him, and she was sure he could throw light on many of the difficult esoteric questions I was pursuing in my studies of the ancient scriptures. The prospect thrilled me. I decided to leave immediately. I remember traveling into the countryside in some sort of open, horse-drawn carriage, passing smaller and smaller villages until I reached a tiny hamlet at the edge of the forest. I spent the night there and went on foot in the morning, following the directions given to me by the villagers with whom I had spent the night. The sun had risen but the morning star was still visible in the sky. I took it as a good omen—perhaps it was something I had read in one of my Sanskrit books. I followed a long, winding path into the forest until I emerged into a clearing where I saw a couple of thatched huts by the edge of a small stream. There was a large garden to one side with vegetables, banana trees, and papaya. Then I received a shock. There she was, emerging from the smaller hut to meet me. Her hair was wet and was hanging loose down her back. She smiled like I had never seen her smile before, as if she had been set free in this place, released from the bondage of her caste and her sex. Stunned to see her, I asked her how and why she had come. She said that she had arrived in the night. She had thought it best that she introduce me to the sage; otherwise he might not receive me. Then she reached out and took my hand and led me into the larger hut. I should have recoiled at her touch. I remember clearly wondering why I didn't. She was a Dalit and unclean by Hindu law. But her touch felt cool and pleasant, welcoming me into this strange environment.

Inside the hut, the sage was waiting for me. He was sitting on a tiger skin, wearing only a loincloth. His long matted locks fell over his shoulders; his skin glistened from some kind of oil, and there were streaks of ash on his chest and arms. We sat down in front of him on a pair of bamboo mats and he began talking. As he talked, I became aware of a powerful vibration that gave his words a clarity and a force that one did not see in ordinary mortals. I had come with questions, but his answers did not merely satisfy my thirst—they turned everything I knew upside down. He explained the symbolism behind many things that I had long taken for granted, the hidden symbolic source of the rituals I had grown up practicing so dutifully without ever truly understanding. He impressed upon me that the real temple was the human body, and the true deities the energies inside it, the spiritual and psychic energies that the yogi must master if he is to realize the truth he seeks. Then he asked her to go out. I remember that she smiled then—she had been silent throughout—and looked at me with pride. Once she was gone, he told me to sit in meditation posture. He explained that up until then I had only received Vedic initiation. To become a true twice-born, I would have to receive Tantric initiation. He taught me a Tantric practice and then had me meditate in front of him. As I began concentrating, I began to feel energy leaping in my body, shooting up my spine. After some time, he reached out and touched me at each of the four upper chakras: the heart, the throat, between the eyebrows, and at the crown of the head. A tingling sensation spread over my body and this gave me immense pleasure.

When I finally exited the hut, she was sitting on the grass waiting for me; she motioned for me to sit next to her. My head was still spinning. It was almost too much for me: the unexpected initiation, sitting there with her in silence amid the sounds of the forest, the energy coursing in my body. What I remember of the dream ends there—except for one more fragment, which must have been later in the day: I went with her to meditate under a tree at the edge of the clearing. As we meditated, I felt as if we were tied together by a bond I could not escape, and this scared me, almost as if I were sure that I had fallen into some kind of trap.

A strange thought comes to me now as I watch the dream images still swirling in my mind. The scene in the forest appears very much like the scene where Ambika takes Le Gentil to meet the sage. Has that influenced my dream? Has it created the visual backdrop for my subconscious to reuse? It seems logical but my gut tells me no. If anything, it says, that image arose out of my subconscious at that time because this dream was already hiding in its depths. I am not sure if this makes sense, but something inside me seems convinced that this is so. What the dream means, I hesitate to speculate. It would be easy to think that my subconscious is expressing its gratitude to Saraswati, as well as my hidden fear at the closeness that is springing up between us. She led me to the Rimpoche, just as the girl led me to the Tantric in my dream. Perhaps, perhaps. But again my mind rebels. It is not that simple, it insists. These dreams have a life of their own, an irrepressible momentum that will not stop for my facile explanations. It is no mere reflection of my "real" life, the one lived up here at the surface where the sun shines and all seems so evident in its unsuspicious light. The priest is real—or rather I am real in the life that I am leading as a priest in my dream world. I think he would scream at me if I told him that he were merely a reflection of another's life, a recomposition from another's memories. "Look at me," I can almost hear him shout. "My thoughts and emotions are flesh and blood. What is happening to me is beyond my control—and beyond yours. It is the hand of God that is sweeping me along and no one else's. Heaven help me and heaven help us all, for who can know his will." I can almost feel him staring at me now from beyond the shadows with his unyielding priest's stare, arrogant and proud, yet scared. He wills me to respect him. Dare I not?

29

SARASWATI HAD TO WAIT until the swami came back from tour at the end of March before she could put in her request for two weeks' leave to visit the Mother in Benares. By this time, she and Rodrigo were spending all or part of every afternoon together. They had moved their study sessions to the shade of the young pipal tree in her courtyard, where they shared their mutual passion for the truths hidden in their texts, but much of their time was spent walking by the banks of the Ganges, either south away from town to where the encroaching forest quickly plunged them into a solitude that had come down to them unchanged through the centuries, or else north toward the clamor and bustle of Lakshman Jhula and beyond toward the snowcapped peaks where the river was born. She was still leading the way in this journey into the wisdom of India's ancient sages, but at times he pointed her in directions she had never taken before and they went there together. As the days passed, she found it more and more difficult to think of him as her student. Her teacherly eagerness to see him step off the mountain ledge and embrace his flight into the great unknown with outspread arms had quietly morphed into the calmer delight of a shared exploration. There were times when she looked forward more to seeing him than she did to her meditation, a fact she could not dismiss, no matter what label she chose to attach to it. She sometimes worried about this at night when the silence that hung over the ashram afforded her a perspective she did not have during the day, but in the end she always surrendered her feelings to the Mother. The future would be as the Mother willed; her only wish was to be able to surrender fully to the Mother's desire.

The day after the pujya swami arrived, she was able to have a few minutes alone with him in his office. There was nothing unusual in her request, but still, for some reason, she felt nervous asking for the time off, and she knew she could not hide that nervousness from him, no matter how adept she was at hiding it from others. After enduring the searchlight of his eyes for what seemed like endless moments, he arranged for her to take two weeks in late May, without telling her what his eyes had seen. His only comment was a smile, and she could not decipher the worlds of meaning it contained.

It had been a strange odyssey, the journey between her renunciation of Vikram and her arrival in the ashram to be its resident philosophy teacher, a period in her life, like all the other periods in her life, that she had chosen to ignore so that she could keep her mind firmly in the present. But Rodrigo's presence in her life had acted like a magic elixir, thrusting her back into the past in her moments of unguarded solitude. Scenes that had been purposely forgotten kept returning to her mind. She began to catch glimpses of strange shadows of meaning that had until then been hidden by the glare of the Indian sun: the anger she had felt when she left for the Mother's ashram after being deceived by Vikram, furious at herself for having been tricked by the oldest of delusions; the fiery vow she had taken, as the train pulled out of New Delhi station, to dedicate her life to spirituality and the quest to be free from ignorance and attachment. She had felt an overwhelming desire at that moment to be free from the world's snares, once and for all; yet the immediate result of her vow was that her life became even more weighed down by worldly responsibilities. She pushed in one direction and the universe pushed right back—with the Mother's laughter as a backdrop.

After her father's stroke, she, as the only child, had to assume full financial responsibility for her parents, a debt considered as sacred in an Indian family as the pledge between guru and disciple. After she hired a servant for them and assured herself that her mother was ready to assume the full-time care of her father, she returned to Delhi, acutely conscious of the sum she had to send each month to her village home, regardless of whatever other expenses or debts she might have. She had no choice but to actively start seeking other assignments, in addition to her weekly column and the occasional special features they threw her way. See how the Mother weaves her web, she thought, sending her back into maya when all she wanted to do was run! Doors that had once been closed to her now swung open with a huge samsaric grin. The offers multiplied to the point that she got to know the turnings between her newly leased two-bedroom apartment in Greater Kailash, Part Two and the offices of the leading magazines and newspapers in Delhi so well that when she needed to take a taxi or a three-wheeler, she invariably directed the driver which streets to take depending on the hour of the day and the likelihood of traffic. Her volunteer excursions on behalf of WAI became more and more infrequent, and she found herself relying more on the work of her former colleagues for her material rather than on the miles logged by her own two feet. There was no shame in this, she told herself. There was no use documenting the flood of injustices in the country if no one ever heard about them. There were pitiful few reporters in the capital who were willing to take on such issues. It required a grit that few journalists were willing to live with on a daily basis. It was what set her apart—her relentlessness, her stamina, and her disregard for the enemies she might make—not inconsequential in a country where journalists could still disappear or be intimidated into moderating their stance. As a result, her byline started appearing in numerous magazines and newspapers of consequence. Her cell number was entered into the Rolodex of most city editors or pinned to their message board. She carried a laptop at a time when they were still looked upon as a mark of prestige and a portable Dictaphone so that no thought could escape her, carried away by the runaway Delhi traffic or swallowed by the smog. Everything she had thought to run away from had caught her going out the back, except for Vikram, who was nowhere to be seen, though she walked past his book every time she went into a bookstore and skipped over his articles whenever she read the paper.

The most difficult thing she had to deal with was her notoriety. The magic of her name appearing in print seemed to open doors and raise eyebrows wherever she went. There were important parties and events to attend, contacts she needed to cultivate. Calls came not only from editors interested in a story but from a world of intimate strangers who either had an axe to grind or a just cause to espouse to a largely indifferent world. Though she was used to tackling tragedies from all over Northern India, she found that there was injustice and suffering enough in the city to fill all the hours of her day. For a woman whose most significant hours were spent with her eyes closed, trying to submerge the impressions that filled her mind in a sea of non-becoming, it was a challenge to open them again and find that she was a constant object of people's attentions, her ego fêted or criticized or followed into public restrooms with such determination that it was a wonder it did not wrest free from her control and change the locks on her apartment door. She withstood this constant bombardment with the help of two things: the belief that this unsought-after lifestyle was not only her duty to her parents and to her country but a personal crusade for the betterment of mankind; and the strength that her meditation gave her to remember that her goal was not to become somebody but to become nobody, to leave the world a better place without any trace of her ego ever having been there. Beyond this, she also took what measures she could to keep people at arms length, especially men. Though she recognized every day when she looked in the mirror that she was not pretty by any conventional standard, it was not enough to keep her free of suitors. Her name, her growing influence in the city, and the magic of her words, which were consumed on a regular basis by hundreds of thousands of free citizens in both English and Hindi, created an aura around her that attracted men of a certain type—Vikram's type especially, but also thoughtful, civic-minded men who valued her thoughts and her indignant, crusading, compassionate emotions more than the covers of the pulp magazines with their photoshopped images of the latest daytime actress or the newest Miss India. As warm and as sympathetic as she tried to be with the people whose stories lived through her words in the hearts of Delhi's readers, she could be equally as cold with any man who wished to get close to her on a non-professional basis. This earned her a new nickname, which was shared with her by a couple of her female colleagues. No longer Saint Saraswati—though she was just as strict with her meditation, which she now practiced in the privacy of her apartment—she became "the ice queen" among the men she had rebuffed. The women, mistaking her aloofness for haughtiness, had another nickname for her that never did come to her attention: the Mughal princess.

Looking back on the years since Vikram and the strict control she had exercised over her personal life during that time, it came as a wonder to Saraswati to see how much she had changed over the past several months. She already felt closer to Rodrigo than to any human being she had ever known, and the distance was decreasing with dizzying speed. When she endeavored to understand why her mind had taken to exploring the ruins of the past, she discovered that part of the reason was that somewhere inside her she longed to share it with him, just as she longed to hear the story of how he had gotten to this point in his life, and through these shared stories to somehow build a bridge to that imagined time when she had known him in another body. Only a few months ago, she would have scoffed at such thoughts. Now she rebelliously defended them to herself and fought the desire to ask him to show her his work. She even brought out her old articles, carelessly heaped in a pile on the long concrete shelf that stood high above her bedstead where she could barely reach them, and wondered what he would make of them. When she typed out the text of her upcoming classes, as she regularly did on the now-ancient laptop that was the only article of note left over from her old life, still finding it easier to think with its now-sticky keys under her fingers, she would pause over certain lines and wish he were there in the room with her so she could ask him for his feedback. When he talked on their walks, as he sometimes did, of the writers who inspired him or his own efforts with his novel, she listened with a strange, excited energy and then steered the subject back to spirituality as quickly as she could to avoid falling headlong into her old samskaras, which she now understood were far from being extinguished. Moreover, she knew that the day could not be far off when she would show her own work to him.

Once she had confirmed the dates with the Mother's personal secretary and gotten her reservation for the train out of Haridwar, she told Rodrigo of her trip and asked him to take over her classes for those two weeks. He was so taken aback that she couldn't help but laugh at the look of horrified surprise on his face. "Tell me you're kidding" were the words he finally managed to get out, a quaint American expression that she had never used but had always enjoyed. It took a few minutes for her to convince him not only that he was ready but that the very necessity of having to teach those classes would make him ready. She had discovered in her first few months at the ashram that she learned more by teaching classes than she ever had as a student. Fortunately, this was not a novel idea to Rodrigo. His years as a university professor had made him acutely aware of the phenomenon. As soon as he got over his shock, he became enthusiastic about the idea, and they decided to use their afternoon sessions to plan his classes together. The classes would cover the middle chapters of the Bhagavad Gita, containing Krishna's teachings on karma yoga, jnana yoga, and bhakti yoga. Under the shelter of the pipal tree, they began sketching out an outline of the first of the three yogas—karma yoga, the yoga of action—while Rodrigo typed it into his computer. Rather than simply giving him her notes for those classes, she had decided that the exercise of going through it together would be more beneficial.

"Arjuna begins the chapter by asking Krishna, 'If wisdom is the highest ideal, then why do you counsel me to engage in this terrible fight?' 'I am confused,' he says, but he is not only confused—he has lost heart. When he sees what he's up against, his courage fails him. How can he raise his sword against his kinsmen? How can he go to war? It's a natural reaction; we might even think it a reasonable one. Does anyone ever want to go to war? Who wouldn't be scared or have doubts that it was the right thing to do? Here is where I usually remind my students that this is not only symbolic—Krishna is talking about both the internal war and the external war. The internal war is the fight against our own weaknesses, and the external war is all the daily challenges that life presents us with. Krishna's answer to Arjuna is that no one can remain without acting—anyone who thinks they can is deluded. We have to act, if only just to maintain our bodies, and so we must do our duty—we must fulfill our responsibilities. Arjuna is a warrior, so he must fight, but we are all warriors, whether we realize it or not. We are all on the battlefield of life. So Krishna tells him that there is no escaping this struggle; it is our human inheritance. Once we accept that we cannot escape the challenges of being human, then we come to our first philosophical dilemma: Given that I must act and that action is the cause of bondage, how then can I act without binding myself and thereby convert my action into spiritual practice or yoga? Arjuna already knows that actions create reactions—samskaras—and so do your students, but you might want to review briefly with them how samskara works. That will set the stage. You've outlined Arjuna's dilemma, and by extension our own. Once they've understood the predicament, you lead them through the rest of the chapter wherein Krishna teaches us the yoga of action."

Saraswati waited for Rodrigo to finish typing before she continued, impressed with how effortlessly his fingers flew over the keys.

"Krishna starts by saying that whenever action is done without attachment, it creates no fetters. This is the key philosophical point: detachment overcomes ego. When action is done with a sense of ego, it creates samskara; when it is done without a sense of ego, it doesn't, since there is no doer in the sense of a separate, individual agent. If you are fully identified with God or Consciousness when you act, then you can't be identified with your ego; hence your actions will necessarily be in harmony with the Cosmic Will. As Krishna says a little later in the chapter, 'it is only the ignorant man, misled by egotism, who thinks, "I am the doer."' At this point, you may want to stop and initiate a short discussion or take questions. This is usually a very difficult point for beginners to understand: If you have no sense of ego when you act, then there is no one there to accrue samskara. Intellectually we may understand it, but what does it really mean in practice? Most people have never had the experience of acting without ego, so it's difficult for them to understand what that feels like."

"I don't know that *I* understand what that feels like."

"I think you understand it better than you let on. But anyhow, that's the beauty of having to teach the class. You have over a month to work on egoless action, so that when it comes time to teach it, you'll know what you are talking about."

"A month? You want me to become adept in karma yoga in a month?"

Saraswati made no attempt to hide her amusement. "That should be enough, don't you think? It's not like you have any other pressing engagements in the meantime...Anyhow, Rodrigo, you don't need to become an adept. You just need to understand the theory and practice it as diligently as you can in these few weeks. If you do that, then you'll have your moments. They don't have to be long moments or many. You succeed once, even for a few seconds, and you'll know exactly what Krishna is talking about. Then you can teach it, and hopefully they'll also practice and gain their own insight.

"So, back to the chapter. At this point, Krishna begins outlining a method for freeing oneself from the feeling of ego or the feeling of agency: non-attachment to the fruits of one's actions and surrendering one's actions to the Supreme. I usually begin this section by talking about how normally everyone is attached to the results of their actions. For example, if a student takes a test, then she's attached to her grade. She feels elated if she gets a good grade and terrible if she fails. You're a novelist, so I expect you'll come up with more interesting examples; I have a tendency to be too philosophical and intellectual about these things. Anyhow, then I point out that even though we act as if we had some control over the results of our actions, the truth is, we have no control whatsoever. Once the action is complete, the reaction is already set in motion; there is nothing more we can do at that point except to experience the reaction at the appointed time. Our attachment to our grade, for instance, is not going to affect what grade we get; it only affects our inner experience. If you think about it, being attached to the fruits of one's actions is downright foolish. It can't possibly help us in any way; it can only hurt since it robs us of our peace of mind. But I don't tell them this. I usually initiate a discussion at this point, and most of the time they come to that conclusion on their own. If not, I nudge them in that direction. And that leads us to Krishna's next point: do your own duty and do it as perfectly as possible. In other words, if the only thing we can control is our action, then it's only logical to try to make that action as perfect as possible."

"Which will give us the best possible result, if we are attached. If we must create samskaras, at least we should create the best possible samskaras, right?"

"Exactly! If you are unable to free yourself from the ego when you act, then at least you'll be creating a better future for yourself. Krishna alludes to that later in the chapter. So then I talk a little about this aspect of karma yoga, how a yogi strives for perfection in all her actions, from brushing her teeth to taking care of her children to performing her meditation. In order to achieve that perfection, we have to be totally present in the moment. We have to have all our awareness focused on what we are doing, instead of getting caught up in our thoughts. This is what the Buddhists call 'mindfulness.' The only way to achieve perfection in action is through perfect attention or perfect mindfulness."

"You know, that sounds a lot like something I've been reading from the native American tradition, only they use the term 'impeccability.' But I think it's more or less the same idea. Ely gave me a couple of Carlos Castaneda's books before she left. Castaneda's teacher, Don Juan, taught him that a spiritual warrior must strive to lead an impeccable life. His every action must be impeccable if he wants to hunt spiritual power. I have a couple of quotes here that I copied into my computer. Would you like to hear them?"

"Please."

"Here's one I found quite interesting: 'A warrior is in the hands of *power* and his only freedom is to choose an impeccable life.' Nice, huh? Here's another good one: 'The seer who travels into the unknown to *see* the unknowable must be in an impeccable state of being.'"

"Nice. I like that word, 'impeccable.' It fits the mood of karma yoga perfectly. So what happens when a yogi is focused on the action at hand and strives to be impeccable? Only the present moment exists for her. There is no past, no future. The present is the great challenge that she embraces. Perhaps this is what your Don Juan meant when he used the term 'spiritual warrior.' You accept the challenge of attaining mastery over your action without worrying about the result. In this case, 'mastery' is synonymous with 'presence.'

"Then we move on to keeping one's mind focused on the Supreme Self by surrendering one's actions to the Supreme. In verse fifteen, Krishna says, 'In sacrificial action the all-pervading Spirit is consciously present.' In practice, this means that we try to see everything as an expression of God and serve him in whatever form he appears to us. To the extent that we can do this, our mind remains conscious of his presence. Once one of Ramana Maharsi's disciples asked him how he could learn to see everything as God. Ramana's answer was very simple: call everything God. It sounds simple, and it is, but that's part of what makes it so profound. It reduces our experience to the one fundamental unity: the actor, the action, and the object of the action are one. If everything is God, then you are also God. You are not the actor; you are not a separate, independent agent. You are just an instrument. If an old woman comes to you and holds out her begging bowl, then you ideate that God is appearing in front of you in the form of that old woman. The alms you give her are God; the action of giving the alms is God; and you, the instrument through which the Lord gives himself the alms, are also God. The One Consciousness expressing itself through a myriad of different forms. If we can remain aware of this, even to some extent, then everything becomes *lila*, the divine play—Krishna multiplying himself into different forms and dancing the *rasalila* with the *gopis*."

"You know, this reminds me of one of Salinger's short stories. Are you familiar with his work?...Oh, you'll love him, at least his later books. The story is called 'Teddy'; it's about a boy who remembers his past life. Teddy's on a cruise with his family, and this guy comes up to him while he's relaxing on a deck chair and tells him that he's heard a recording of an interview he'd done with some university professors. They get to talking and the guy says that from what I gather you are convinced that you were a holy man in India in your past life but that you somehow fell from grace. The guy is actually a skeptic, but Teddy plays it perfectly cool. He tells him, 'No, no, no, I was just a person making good spiritual progress; I wasn't enlightened or anything. But then I met this woman and I sort of stopped meditating. I wasn't so advanced that I could have gone straight to Brahma when I died. I would have had to be reborn anyhow, but I wouldn't have had to reincarnate in an American body. It's so hard to meditate and lead a spiritual life in America. People think you are a freak if you try.'"

Saraswati laughed. "Is that really true? Is it that difficult to lead a spiritual life in America?"

"It probably was back then. He wrote that more than fifty years ago. I think things have gotten a little better since then, although I'm probably not the right person to ask since I wasn't a meditator until I got here. Anyhow, a little later in the same scene, the guy asks him about his first spiritual experience. He thinks for a minute and then he says, 'Yes, I must have been five or six at the time. My sister was drinking a glass of milk and all of a sudden I saw that she was God and the milk was God. All she was doing was pouring God into God.'"

"Beautiful! That's exactly it. Here, let me make a note of that story." Saraswati had heard of Salinger but she had never read him, an oversight she intended to correct. She opened her notepad and jotted down the titles of the Salinger books that Rodrigo recommended. "You should tell that story in your class," she said. "It's perfect. If you can get them to understand just this one practice, then your work is done."

"Which means that I'll have to understand it first. I guess I'll have to work on it when I'm pouring my tea at dinner tonight."

"And when you are drinking from your water bottle or typing at your computer, and on it goes. Okay, so then we come to the end of the chapter. The last thing Krishna talks about is desire. He calls it 'the great enemy that must be slain in order to reach the goal,' desire being the opposite of detachment. Listen to this line; it reminded me of you when I read it this morning." Saraswati held up her copy of the Gita and started reading in her best dramatic voice. "'As fire is shrouded by smoke, a mirror by dust, and a child by the womb, so is the universe enveloped in desire.'" She put the book down. "It sounds like a description of your experience during the intensive. I think you could just share your story at the end of class and it would be more powerful than any philosophy."

In the afternoons that followed, they continued outlining Rodrigo's scheduled classes. It went faster than Saraswati expected, so they began taking longer walks than usual. She showed him some of the places where she used to meditate when she first came to Rishikesh, and they began stopping for a short meditation before they returned for arati, each time in a different place.

One day, when they were walking on the Sivananda ashram side of the river, Rodrigo pointed to a path that disappeared into the woods and began telling her about the time he had walked back to Rishikesh from the Kunjapuri temple by that path, the day his ego had completely broken down, two days before he had appeared in her class for the first time. She remained quiet as he talked about his marriage, his teaching position at the university, his adoration of different writers and artists, his long-time desire to be a great writer himself. This time she could not bring herself to change the subject. His story felt like a part of herself that she was not aware of. The deeper he went, the quieter she became, each episode resonating inside her like the chords of a symphonic movement in which they were both instrumentalists—he as the soloist; she, striking up a soft accompaniment behind him. The feeling that they were simply catching up on the missing episodes in each other's life seemed incongruent to her mind but perfectly natural to her heart. They had only exchanged words for the first time less than eight months earlier, and she had yet to share any of her present life with him, yet it was a feeling she could not shake. A voice of warning rising out of the numerous texts stored in her brain suggested that this feeling was dangerously close to becoming an obsession, the beginning of the attachment that clouds the mirror of wisdom and enslaves the soul to the ego, but this cautionary voice yielded to her heart's supposition that this altered sensibility was indeed a vague recognition that his was a story she had been accompanying for ages already and which would not be complete without these missing episodes.

On that day, she barely noticed the crossing at Lakshman Jhula, beginning with the long flight of stone steps down to the shops at the foot of the bridge and then across the 140 meters of narrow, swaying suspension bridge, buffeted by the eternal mountain winds that swirled above the river, one hand on the steel-mesh sides to help her keep her balance. On other days, she would invariably stop and look downriver at a tableau of unsurpassed beauty that was at times capable of stopping her heart for a momentary beat. Scores of ashrams and temples clung to the wooded slopes on either side of the foaming, blue-glinting waters, half-hidden by the dark green of the pines and the azure shadows of the mountains, the shimmering, translucent light making it appear that the scene was not quite real but had been painted into existence with the brilliant colors of a master artist's palette. But on this day it all went unnoticed. Other scenes rose up before her eyes: a university lecture hall in a strange and imposing country; the face of a fair-skinned, willowy woman whom she had never seen but whose every feature seemed instantly familiar to her; the lean figure of a dark-haired young man with round-rimmed reading glasses and an angular beauty to his face, leaning over a scattering of books, several of them open, scribbling furious notes in a spiral-bound notebook, an aura of determined passion filling the tiny room. It was only when they had passed Sivananda's cottage and neared Ram Jhula that she became fully cognizant of her surroundings again. Rodrigo had reached his impasse under the tree at Kunjapuri, having retraced his steps and by doing so, shown her the whole shaky edifice of his ego that had had no choice but to come crumbling down, doomed by the apparition of a young woman in a sky blue sari who had evaded his last desperate attempt at salvation and thus sent him spinning off the mountain and down into the depths of his despair.

His openness shocked Saraswati. Though she had heard similar stories of one kind or another told by an assortment of pilgrims feeling their way through Rishikesh, never had she heard one told with such clarity. It was as if his life were a work of fiction that he had fully deconstructed with the help of the Rimpoche and the long hours of meditation, recognizing in its separate parts the elements necessary to the journey of becoming the man he wished to become.

A couple of days later, they sat for meditation on the flat concrete roof of a cottage set into the steep embankment that led down to the river, not far from where Rodrigo had met the Mother. She knew the monk who lived there, an old hermit who could be heard puttering about his cottage at mealtimes amid the rising scent of boiling rice and dal but who was scarcely ever seen. At that hour of the afternoon, the monk was silent. The closest dwellings were far enough away that the only sounds that reached them were muffled echoes that seemed to float in the air, carried along by the river's steady current. When they finished their meditation, she began talking about the time her life had also reached the borderlands of despair, violating her own precept to never look behind. She began by telling Rodrigo that she had once been a journalist. He showed the barest evidence of a smile and nodded, making it clear that this was something he had already known. Then he remained quiet, his eyes fixed partially on her, partially on the wooded slopes framed by the sky behind her. When she told him how the Mother had called her to Haridwar, how she had spent those two days absorbed in the practices she had almost forgotten, his eyes beamed and turned inward, while his smile gladdened the shadows in her heart.

This was two days before she was to leave for Benares. As they walked back for Arati, she felt as if she had crossed a frontier she had not planned on crossing and from which there was no return. She could no longer consider herself his teacher, for all the help she still had to offer. She could only be his friend—and he, hers. It felt like a sigh that she had been holding in for a long time. Now that she had let it out, she felt a sense of relief but also a sense of nostalgia. The role she had played in his life was gone, carried away by the river that rolled inexorably alongside them. Late that night her nostalgia returned. It seemed unbearably precious to her that she had been the one to guide him during the early days of his awakening. But when she felt a lament grow inside her for its ending, she brushed it aside and laughed, realizing, with a surety that lit up the room around her, that this was a part of her life—and his—that could never be lost.

30

R ODRIGO THREW HIMSELF INTO the preparation of his classes with the same fervor and meticulousness that had characterized him throughout his university career. He took the notes he had written up during his afternoon sessions with Saraswati and revised them at night, pouring through his now-substantial library of spiritual books to find examples, quotes, and further ideas that he could introduce into the weave. He limited his work on the novel to the hours before lunch, spurred on by the conviction that this was also a kind of writing he needed to cultivate, though it did not occur to him that it might one day deeply influence the character of his published works. After finishing each class to his satisfaction, he read it aloud in his room, correcting flaws that his spoken voice revealed, and then set to work memorizing them. He found that he enjoyed this as much, if not more, than he had enjoyed preparing his university lectures, lectures he still hoped he could one day develop into a book of literary criticism. Those lectures had served as the basis for most of his published articles, and he knew that recordings of them were regularly passed around among his students.

Despite the enthusiasm he showed for these philosophical writings, it did not interfere with the hours he spent with his characters. That time was sacred; he did not allow it to be interrupted by thoughts intruding from the world outside the one where Le Gentil and Ambika traced their separate but interdependent destinies. As the days passed by that led up to Saraswati's departure for Benares, Le Gentil and Ambika departed on a journey of their own that would last nearly as long. They had decided not merely to visit the ruins little more than a day's journey from the city but to continue on into the interior of the Deccan peninsula where Le Gentil would have a chance to catalogue flora and fauna that could not be seen near the coast and to see more of the indigenous culture, including areas that had yet to feel the heavy imprint of a European presence on their soil. Such a long trip surprised Rodrigo; he had not been expecting it. What surprised him even more was a conversation his two characters had inside the carriage shortly after leaving the outskirts of Pondicherry. Ambika warned the astronomer that the driver was in some way connected to her father and that whatever transpired within reach of his eyes and ears was sure to be passed on. "He understands far more of what we say than you think," she cautioned him. That warning, and the wariness she felt whenever the driver was around, told Rodrigo that their relationship had progressed further than he had imagined. There was a sense of collusion between them that excluded the rest of the outside world, and despite his semi-omniscient eye, he also felt at times that he was violating their privacy by peering in behind the curtains of their seclusion.

When they reached the edge of the ruins the following morning and decamped with their provisions, Ambika suddenly stood up in front of an open bag that she had been rummaging through and exclaimed in a tone of self-reprobation that she had forgotten to pack the flour and the salt. It was an extraordinary and crippling omission, since bread of some kind, even the simple unleavened flat bread that they were limited to on such a trip, was an obligatory part of her employer's diet. With a look of tortured consternation, she ordered the driver to return to the nearest town with the carriage and a small handful of one-rupee coins. At a moderate pace, he would be back at the campsite by nightfall. In the meantime, they would be busy with their excavations. Le Gentil took advantage of this fortuitous omission to order some extra flint, a roll of white muslin cloth, a spare bottle of ink, and some extra goose quills. The driver turned a disgruntled and doubtful eye toward the willful woman who was there for the same reason as he but acted every bit his mistress. Then he shrugged his shoulders and drove off in the rattling carriage, leaving behind Jiddu, who, unlike him, did not understand a word of French. Ambika waited until she had seen him disappear beyond the trees before she allowed herself a sigh of relief.

They began their day by poking through what had obviously been some kind of ancient settlement. It was situated on a small hill at the edge of the forest, about fifteen kilometers from the nearest village. Pieces of quarry stone belonging to the foundations of what had once been dwellings were still visible above ground, enough that Le Gentil was able to sketch some rudimentary floor plans. The ruins covered an area approximately three hundred meters by two hundred meters and appeared to have been surrounded at one time by a boundary wall. He had not seen any sign of this kind of stone construction among the Tamils, but that by itself was no proof that the ruins had not been built by their ancestors. The one indication that suggested the possibility of Roman origin was the remains of a circular foundation on the southern slope that could have belonged to the castellum. Le Gentil had brought with him some tools for excavation: several spades of various sizes, a pickax, and a metal sieve. He started digging in the grassy area enclosed by the possible castellum, while Ambika sifted through the earth and separated anything that looked to be of interest. After he got down several feet, he found a couple of small iron implements that piqued his interest, but there was no way of determining whether or not they were of indigenous origin. The work was tedious and the results uninspiring, but he was used to this, and anyhow archeology was not what was foremost on his mind. When they broke for lunch, his thoughts were mostly on Ambika and the prospect of spending a leisurely afternoon with the woman he loved under the shade of the sturdy banyan tree that towered over one edge of the ruins.

When they were starting on their dessert—dried mango and fresh cashew fruits that they had brought with them from Pondicherry—Le Gentil asked the question that had been on his mind since the previous morning. "So I take it by what you said yesterday that Mahesh understands French. That is surprising to me since he's always made out as if he didn't understand a word I said, unless you translated it for him. Is he here to keep a watch on me or to keep a watch on you?"

Ambika flushed but she didn't bother trying to hide it. She took a deep breath and admitted what she knew she should not be admitting. "By now, I think it's both of us."

Le Gentil nodded pensively. "But originally you hired him—or your father hired him—to keep an eye on me."

"Yes," Ambika replied stiffly, averting her gaze. "It was my father's suggestion."

Le Gentil continued in a thoughtful tone of voice, as if he were more musing to himself. "I see. So he reports back to your father, who, I suppose, does not keep whatever information he receives entirely to himself. And how many Maheshes are there, if I may ask, currently in the employ of French officials in the province? Just between you and me."

Ambika looked directly at him, overcoming the fleeting sense of dishonesty that had made her feel so uncomfortable a few moments before. Their eyes met and the sense of unwavering trust she saw in him transported her beyond any national borders that might have come between them.

"Quite a few. To be honest, there is little that goes on behind French doors that isn't known to us."

"And you are also one of them?"

She hesitated, but only for a moment. "Yes."

Le Gentil shrugged his shoulders and smiled. "Well, that explains a lot. I won't press you with questions you don't want to answer. Just tell me one thing. What is the purpose behind all this?"

"Information is power, Guillaume. I won't lie to you; we hope to be a free nation one day. As we were for so many centuries before the Europeans arrived. There is no way of knowing when and how this information will prove useful, but it will."

"Well, I for one would like to see a free and independent India. Unfortunately, I very much doubt it will happen in my lifetime."

"Nor in mine, but what does that matter as long as I can help to bring it about sooner rather than later."

Sensing her warring emotions, Le Gentil thought it kinder to change the subject. "So tell me more about where we are going from here. Is it true your people worship a mountain because a monkey king once lifted it and carried it to Lanka? You still haven't finished telling me that story you started the other day, what did you call it?"

"The *Ramayana*."

"Yes, the *Ramayana*. So what happened after ...."

Their conversation continued until nearly four o'clock. Le Gentil was surprised at how easily he had turned aside from the revelation that Ambika was not merely the governor's chief translator but the eyes and ears of the Tamils inside the plastered walls of the governor's mansion. No wonder she had seemed reluctant when the governor had given her out on loan. There could not have been much of interest to report while following around an eccentric scientist who spent more time watching the heavens than the colonial subjects of the French crown. But all that was in the past, he knew. Even at a distance of several meters he could feel her heart beating in tandem with his own. Nor did he begrudge her efforts on behalf of her people. He would have gladly done the same had their positions been reversed.

Though he did not have much desire to return to their work, a lifetime of habit would not leave him in peace. Finally, he stretched his legs and suggested they return to their digging. Jiddu had longed since washed the pots and plates in a nearby stream and was curled up on his side, fast asleep, a few meters away under the shade of the same banyan tree. Without disturbing him, they walked back to the excavation site and began toiling away while Le Gentil taught Ambika a pair of songs that had been popular in France the year he'd left. The sun was dipping toward the tree line when Ambika suddenly straightened up and held aloft a small, shiny object that she had separated from the dirt. It was a gold coin with an inscription she could not read. She handed it to Le Gentil without saying anything, her face deliberately impassive. He took out his handkerchief and wiped it off. Then a smile lit up his face. It was a Roman coin, a gold denarius from the first century BC, with the high forehead and furrowed brow of Augustus Cesar looking out at him across a space of nearly eighteen centuries.

"My God!" he exclaimed, "you were right. The Romans were here."

Ambika flashed an impish smile. "Guillaume, you really must brush up on your Roman history. You might want to start by rereading Strabo and Pliny. There are copies in the governor's library. As they both documented in their histories, there was regular trade between India and Rome for centuries before Jesus traveled here. By the time Jesus was born, the Romans had already learned how to sail directly to India via the Red Sea using the monsoon winds. Where do you think Rome got its pearls from and its beryls, its spices and its fine muslin? From South India. Ships used to arrive in the ports of Kerala from Rome nearly every day during high season. In fact, Roman coins were the most popular currency in India at that time, especially here in the south where most of the trade was conducted. Which means, by the way, that it's not so surprising to find a Roman coin here, and it's no proof, by itself, that these ruins are Roman. But if I tell you they are Roman, you can be sure they are."

Le Gentil placed the coin in her hand. "A mistake I will never make again, *cheri*, I promise. Here, you keep it for now."

By the time they heard the sound of the carriage rattling up the path in the gathering dusk, they had pulled from the earth some fragments of Roman pottery, a circular lead ingot, and the remnants of an amphora that had been used to transport either wine or olive oil to India. Ambika's face once again clouded with caution when Mahesh stepped out of the carriage with their provisions, a sight that made Le Gentil feel closer to her than ever. He was thrilled about their findings and content to be in his element, expanding the frontiers of human knowledge, but he was even more content to be sharing his quest with Ambika, who, by the look on her face, was now allied with him against anyone who might come between them. If this were true, then his hopes might not be hopeless after all.

When Rodrigo broke for lunch that day, he had to fight the temptation to skip the meal and continue writing so that he could find out what was going to happen next. He had known that some kind of romance would be brewing, right from the day he had first imagined Ambika standing by the side of the Governor-General's desk with her luxurious jet black hair falling straight down to the small of her back, but now that it was nearly upon him, he could feel his blood quicken and his mind grow bright with anticipation. All his previous ideas of what would or might happen had been rendered superfluous by the actions of his characters. They themselves did not know what would happen, nor could he as he peered into their hearts and saw the uncertainty and the desire bubbling the cauldron from within. His only choice, he realized, was to turn the page and follow them as the words appeared, filling the empty space of his computer screen as they fell out of the sky of his mind and into his fingers. And even this was not a choice, since by now he was just as much a prisoner of his story as Ambika and Le Gentil.

As he closed his computer and went to wash his hands, he felt the anticipation in his mind and his heart and decided that it was better to be the reader than the writer. The reader could refuse to leave his hammock, or lock himself in a room and let his heart rush ahead through the pages of a story until his mind caught up. But a writer had to suffer in slow motion, feeling every emotion like a weighted pendulum thumping against the inner walls of his chest, hearing every footfall as if it were resounding off the hard surfaces of a marble chamber, while the story crawled forward toward its unexpected end, holding him in thrall, at the mercy of his characters and the whimsical nature of time. Writing, he decided, was an exercise that required enormous patience, as well as a good stock of determination and more than a few ounces of courage, all virtues he knew it would do him good to develop.

The night before Saraswati was scheduled to leave, they took a short walk up to Swami Sivananda's cottage and back. When they reached the ashram gate, Rodrigo handed her a hardbound notebook as a present. "In case you have any thoughts on the train and choose to record them for the benefit of humanity."

"Are you trying to stir up my old samskaras?" Saraswati remarked with a smile, and indeed, in a certain sense, that was exactly what he had in mind. When he went to bed that night, he fell asleep thinking about the stories she had shared with him from the days when she had traveled around Northern India for WAI, documenting the fierce injustices that would have otherwise gone unchallenged and bringing them to the attention of the public through the medium of the written word. His own writing seemed so inconsequential by comparison. Saraswati had sought the burning center of the fire, while he had remained all his life on the periphery, warming himself in its glow. Now he was beginning to understand the indignation she displayed when she talked about discrimination against women in her country. How wrong he had been when he had thought her cold and distant, more like a page of philosophy made flesh than a living, breathing person! She was not only full of passion—her passion was drawn from a well of compassion. Her heart had gone out to the people around her that she had seen suffering, and she had chosen to do something about it, unlike so many others, including himself, who shed a few tears when they watched the local or national news and then immediately wrapped themselves back up again in their own lives. He felt like throwing up his fist and shouting, "Long live Saraswati!" She was exactly the kind of person the world needed—more of her and less of him. Just the thought that she was his friend filled him with a sense of pride.

In the morning, when Rodrigo awoke, he felt some of those same feelings, but this time he felt them beating in another's breast that both was and was not his own.

Rishikesh
5/12
4:30 AM

I can still feel her nearness, as if the air were awash with an electric mist. She seems to be under my skin as well, a tingling inside that grows stronger the moment I think of her and see her sitting near me, turning toward me with her panther's eyes, which burn with the fire of her indignation. I can remember every feature in her face and every detail of the dream. These dreams seem to be growing stronger, if that were possible, or else my memory is growing stronger, preserving with its graven colors the experience of my subconscious that seems so real my senses can scarcely believe it didn't actually happen.

We were traveling back from the sage's dwelling. It must have been the day after my initiation. First we walked together through the forest in silence. It was so still and my senses were so acute that I could hear a single leaf rustling in a tree, high above me. But the greater part of my senses was tuned to her presence. Her fragrance was more potent than the damp, musty breath of the forest floor. The rustle of her sari, the chimes of her ankle bells, the whisper of her hair as it swayed from side to side, lightly brushing her back, were all the music my ears wanted to hear. And though I did not look at her directly, her figure out of the corner of my eye danced in front of me like Radha whirling in orbit around Krishna, maddened by his flute. When we reached the village and sat to wait for a conveyance back to town, she began talking of her life, and I slowly began to cry and then to shout without letting the tears reach my eyes or the words my lips. She talked of the madness that infected the society that held her body captive though it would never imprison her mind. "I have seen the spirit that is sheltered inside my body," she told me, "and I know that it is the same spirit that is sheltered within all bodies, man or woman, Brahmin or Dalit, human being, plant, or animal. You cannot paint it or imprison it or cut it with a knife and watch it bleed. Then how is it that women are barely treated better than cattle in our country, declared by the scriptures to be the property of their husbands or their fathers? How is it that a Brahmin is defiled if he takes water from the hand of a Dalit or has to clean his house if her shadow crosses its threshold?" She began telling me of all the indignities she had suffered since childhood, growing up as a Dalit woman in a society that drank intolerance like holy water, growing into adulthood as the only daughter of an infirm father and a long-dead mother. Her indignation burned me like a spray of acid, eating away at my prejudices and my pride. For what could I say to her? She was right. The religion I lived to serve was grand and glorious, but it was also teetering on the edge of madness. I felt strong and secure in my rightful place as a man, a Brahmin, a priest, but what were these privileges when measured against the spirit that hides within our bodies, and at whose expense did they come?

But even as I felt the truth of all that she was saying and the shame it brought me, I knew I could not contemplate giving up these privileges that were so much a part of who I was. Then a thought arose: Could I give them up for her? It was a mad thought, an impossible thought, but her presence was overpowering. Never in my life had I known such a person, such a woman. I, too, if I were to confess, had thought women to be little more than chattel—when I had given them any thought at all. But here was a woman who dominated my senses, whose mind— astoundingly—was easily the equal of my own.

The wagon arrived and we huddled in it with the other villagers. As we neared the town, my fear started to grow, until I could not shut it out any longer from my thoughts. I whispered to her that it was better we not be seen together entering the town. She lowered her eyes and I knew she understood, but as I told the driver to stop and got out, I felt like a coward, like one of those same people who had happily brought our society to the brink of madness with their smug and arrogant smiles. Then I started to wake. The image faded, but still I could feel her presence like electricity crackling against my skin.

So what to make of this dream? These last days I have been thinking a lot about Saraswati's life before she came to the ashram, what she has told me of it. This must have influenced the dream. The parallels are obvious: her indignation over the plight of women in this culture, her concern with suffering and injustice. For some reason, though, I feel the suffering even more deeply when I think of this dreamed girl, who for me is so very real. Is it because she has felt society's foot on her neck since the day of her birth while Saraswati has only seen it on the neck of others? (Though she has the great heart to feel those sufferings as her own and to want—no, to burn—to do something about it.) Beyond this, I don't know what to make of this dream, or of all the dreams that have come before it. My fictive priest—I cannot call him a hero any longer—is being thrown up against it. I can feel his attachment, his pride, his cowardice, and his ego, and it is hard not to think of them as my own (it makes me wince just to think of it). This girl, who has been favored by the goddess of misfortune, seems many times his better. Shall I dream soon that he overcomes these failings, that he shows the courage it will take? I hope so. Is this the challenge my subconscious has laid out for me in my own life, to overcome similar failings that still dwell within me? I cannot think otherwise. But for now, I will let this dream sit and ferment, as I know it will, and see where it leads me when its bubbling brew is ready. And now, with the girl's indomitable image still before me, my thoughts turn to Saraswati. What brought her to the ashram, to a life that seems the polar opposite of the one she had been living? She was once a crusader for social change; now she lives the life of a spiritual recluse up here in these mountains. She has told me nothing of what happened between the time she met the mother in Delhi at the height of her despondency and the time she came to live in the ashram. By my reckoning, there were seven years in between, since she has been here a little over four years by her own account. What transformed this social activist into the woman she is now, who perhaps one day will be a saint? Something inside me is restless to find the answer, and I am convinced it is not mere idle curiosity. I feel sure there is some lesson here for me as well, something that will have a profound impact on my life. Until I find out what that is, I suspect my mind will remain restless.

31

THOUGH THE ASHRAM LOST some of its charm with the absence of Saraswati, Rodrigo's classes demanded so much of his attention that he did not miss her as much as he thought he would. As she predicted, and as his experience had always borne out, his classes proved more of a learning experience than a teaching experience. The challenge of having to explain to others concepts he did not fully understand himself forced him to meditate on those ideas in ways he rarely did when he was merely studying. It was only when he was able to explain them in his own words and come up with examples drawn from his own time and culture that he felt as if he truly understood them. Until he could put those concepts into words of his own choosing, they remained as shadows in his mind, felt but not truly comprehended. He had experienced this before as a university professor, but the concepts contained in the Gita were subtler and far more profound than any of the literary ideas he had made a career of expounding. The deepest truths and loftiest ideals of human psychology were contained in its seven hundred highly condensed couplets, many of them practically unintelligible to a mind that had not made use of the lamp of meditation to explore its hidden landscapes and unexamined motivations. He was still a novice, as he well recognized; he knew it would take a monumental effort on his part to justify the faith Saraswati had shown in him. Fortunately, her thorough outlines of each class, the many hours of preparation he put in, and his own experience of having taken those same classes, paid off to an extent that surprised him. Not only did his students go away with enthusiastic smiles, often plying him with questions on the walk back to his room, he finished each class with a more finely honed set of diagnostic tools with which to analyze and direct his own spiritual practices. On several occasions, a spiritual understanding struck him with the force of revelation during the middle of the class. A strange lucidity illumined his thoughts, revealing the secret import of words he had read or heard many times without ever truly understanding their meaning, as if the horizon had suddenly fallen away, exposing the infinite space that lay beyond it. These were the moments he cherished most, when his words ceased to be the vehicles of an intellectual understanding, like the quantifiable digits of an equation, and became instead luminous symbols of a direct seeing that could not be communicated but only experienced.

Following the sequence contained in Vyasa's masterpiece, Rodrigo spent the first week on karma yoga. These were the classes he spent the most time preparing. They were also the classes that gave him the most satisfaction, since they greatly enhanced his understanding of both his spiritual practices and his writing, which he now conceptualized as a specialized branch of karma yoga. Though he did not have much time to practice the yoga of writing during the two weeks that Saraswati was gone, when he did have time he began each session as Krishna advised, consciously offering his writing to the Supreme Consciousness and trying to remain aware, as he wrote, that he was carefully arranging the stems of a bouquet of words to be laid at Krishna's feet. With the help of his mantra, he tried to remember that his words were Krishna's words, an acoustic expression of the One Spirit, that he was just an instrument through which the wind of the Divine was blowing, like Krishna's flute, which opened itself up to the great master's breath and thus became music. Whenever thoughts appeared in his mind, as they too often did, of an imagined future—seeing his book published and praised, bringing smiles or tears to the faces of thousands of nameless readers—he reminded himself that once his words had taken their final shape, they were no longer his. Only the samskara was his, set in motion by the time spent at his computer, and he would deal with that samskara when it came due. Whether the book sank or swam was not his concern. His only concern was to shape those words into the most perfect of possible shapes, to make them as sure and as true as they could be in the moment that he was shaping them. And when he looked up from his computer and noticed that his time was up, he did his best to leave his writing behind him and concentrate his attention fully on the next task at hand. He did not always succeed at this, but when he did, it brought him a sense of freedom that reminded him of his final magical night at the intensive. He discovered that his worries and anxieties were shadows that could only hide in the half-light of the past or the future, never in the full light of the present. In the present moment they did not exist. All that existed was the glorious challenge that life had placed in front of him and the awareness that within that moment lay the possibility of perfection.

It was not only his writing that Rodrigo tried to turn into yoga but all the activities that made up his day, even the act of brushing his teeth or turning down the covers of his bed. The more he was able to stay in the moment, the more he was able to enjoy the effort to master each of those activities and the more acute his senses became. He noticed each brush stroke, the feel of the bristles on his gums, the places where he needed to expend a few extra strokes to remove some piece of food he ordinarily would not have noticed. At times, the two minutes he spent on his teeth rivaled a Tintoretto painting for the aesthetic pleasure it gave him, a work of art burnished to perfection by the careful, loving hand of an attentive artist. He found that he enjoyed brushing his teeth as much as he had enjoyed standing in the Louvre admiring the canvases of the masters on those regal walls, for there was something in it that could be found in any great work of art: the search for aesthetic perfection. At certain moments, when his mind grew quiet, intent upon the act at hand, he could feel a sense of timelessness enveloping him. It appeared only in brief flashes, but its appearance let him know that it was always there, hidden behind the obsessions of the ego, and that a day would come when it would forever banish the linear motion that up until now had governed his perception of life. It was in these brief moments that he stepped out of his ego and became witness to the dance that his body and mind enacted in the theater of the world. Miraculously, the dance did not rely on him for its movements. Rather, it was in the moment of his absence that the perfection of its choreography became perceptible to the consciousness that inhabited his body. The world moved of its own accord in a breathtaking harmony that could not be dissolved into its separate parts, except by imprisoning himself in the dimly lit cell of his ego. When that moment passed, he would find himself back again in his prison, but as Saraswati had hinted, one glimpse was enough to know exactly what Krishna was talking about. God could not take up residence until you vacated the premises; you had to move out before he could move in. The Rimpoche had said the same thing in different words, words that came back to him now with a force he had not perceived when they had been spoken one evening in the dharmasala hall in front of a gathering of meditation-weary students: "You live in illusion and the appearance of things. There is a reality but you do not know it. When you do, you will see that you are nothing; and being nothing, you are everything."

Rodrigo was sorry to see the classes on karma yoga end, but once he began preparing his lectures on jnana yoga, the yoga of knowledge, a new wave of enthusiasm and understanding swept over him. This was the yoga he was most attuned to, the yoga he had been born to and had begun cultivating by instinct long before he knew of its existence. As he looked back over his life, it was easy to see how he had unknowingly adopted this path. "The wise who have realized the truth shall teach thee wisdom," Krishna had said. He had looked for those sages in every work of literature he had come across since his early childhood, when he used to read under the covers with a flashlight after his mother kissed him goodnight and turned off the light in his room. He found them in the guise of Merlin, who showed him that time was far more fluid than anyone gave it credit for, flowing both ways at once; in the Count of Monte Cristo, who taught him that a man could overcome any obstacle through sheer determination; in Lord Greystoke, who let him know, as the former Tarzan prepared to return to the forests of Africa where he had grown up, that the so-called civilized society in which he lived had lost more than it had gained when it divorced itself from the wonders and wisdom of nature. Much of what he learned about the world, he learned from the writers who spoke to him across the ages through their stories, graduating as the years went by to writers of subtler vision and greater breadth. He fed himself on their ideals and led his life by their precepts, weighing conflicting visions in the light of his own meager experience and gradually discarding ideas that no longer served him. But as Saraswati had pointed out, the danger of accepting an imperfect master as your guide is that you might be led astray, and his own life had borne that out. Most of the values and attitudes that had glutted his ego to the point where it had no option but to come crashing down had been absorbed from the books he'd read, themselves by and large products of the cultural conditioning that he had failed to recognize as a hermetic partition separating him from himself. The enlightened wisdom that was just as much a part of humanity's heritage as the works of its literary masters had failed to reach him, though it had always been there, seeding the soil from which all life grew. Now that he had finally turned his attention toward it, he was amazed to see how omnipresent it was. Some of those same literary masters had drunk from its fount, and they were among the ones who had most moved him and whom he had least understood, though they were few and had mostly gone unrecognized by his youthful eyes.

Shortly after attending Saraswati's first classes on the Gita, some seven months earlier, he had copied out the final verse from this chapter and taped it to the wall above his bed: "Therefore, cleaving asunder with the sword of wisdom the doubts of the heart, which thine own ignorance has engendered, follow the path of wisdom and arise." He began his first class on jnana yoga with that quote and then turned to Saraswati's outline, mindful of his good fortune, knowing that his teacher, true to her namesake, was the personification of the goddess of knowledge. Her first and most important point was that jnana yoga provided the map without which any traveler was bound to go astray. The essence of wisdom lay in the understanding of what to do and what not to do, the ability to discern between the action that leads us toward Consciousness and the action that leads us away. This was all that wisdom asks of you, he told them, the ability to see the path that leads to the Divine. This is what the sages have labored to teach us. It was while he was explaining this point that he was overtaken by one of those moments of lucidity that left him listening to his own words with the same sense of expectation as his students. All at once, he saw that the three paths were not separate paths or different yogas but different phases in the unfolding of one path. The path began with knowledge, for first a yogi must be able to see the landscape and know which is the road that leads to his destination. Then he must walk, trusting his journey to the diligent steps of karma yoga. When his actions and his effort bear fruit, it comes in the form of devotion, for devotion is not a path but the goal, the dawn of love for God on the horizon of the yogi's life, the moment of revelation that accompanies the opening of the spiritual heart. He saw that this was as much true in every step of the journey as it was a description of the path as a whole. Every step requires the wisdom to know what to do and the stamina to do it, so that each action can deepen our compassion and further the opening of our heart. Though Rodrigo could hardly call himself a devotee, he saw in that moment that his long search for knowledge, which had finally matured with his initiation into the spiritual path, had been directed toward a single end, toward the transformation of his course, earthbound nature into the liberating gold of unconditional love.

Rodrigo purposely left bhakti yoga for the last and final class, dedicating most of the two weeks to what he knew best—karma and jnana—trusting that Saraswati would rescue him on her return. Devotion was unfamiliar territory for him. It was not that he had difficulty understanding the concepts—they were the simplest of all. But no collection of words, no matter how clear, could ever explain the taste of a mango, and devotion was something he had never felt. The closest thing he had ever known was the romantic love that he had learned from books before he had felt it stirring from its slumber and wreaking havoc in his life, though recently, both in the intensive and afterward, he had felt something in his meditations that seemed to be waiting to engulf him. He hoped that it was the beginning of devotion, the promised ocean of love that would one day overflow the boundaries of his soul, but at this point he could only hope.

Paradoxically, what rescued him when it came time to teach the class was this same lifelong infatuation with romantic love. The chapter began with Arjuna's question, whether it was better to worship the Divine as the Personal God or the Impersonal God. Krishna's answer was straightforward: "They who fix their attention on the Absolute and Impersonal encounter greater hardships, for it is difficult for those who possess a body to realize me as without one." In his notes, Saraswati had emphasized that it was in fact almost impossible for a human being to love an impersonal entity. "We love our wives, our husbands, our mothers, our children, our friends," she had said. "This comes as naturally to us as breathing. But how can we open our hearts to an impersonal spirit who is beyond our conception? How can we express our sorrows to a being that our mind cannot visualize? So in devotional practice we personalize the Divine, visualizing him or her as our father, our mother, our lover, our friend. In this way, we can turn the natural sentiments of our human hearts toward the being who dwells within us as our Beloved. In worldly love, our sentiments are confined to this person or that person, but when our love ceases to differentiate between one object and another, then emotion becomes devotion; we begin to love the entire creation as the outward aspect of our Beloved—every leaf, every stone, every being that crosses our path. At this point all sorrow ceases, for when our Beloved is the entire creation, then we can never be separated."

While Rodrigo had not yet tasted of this divine intoxication, he had tasted of the delirious wine of romantic love, as they all had, so he began the discussion with readings from the gospels of world literature, quoting from both popular and classical texts to show how deeply rooted the ideal of finding love embodied in the beloved was in the human psyche. As far back as human thought could reach, this had been the primary source of both tragedy and comedy, from simple farce to the most sublime drama. He dipped into the literature of ancient cultures from different corners of the globe—our only access into their inner life—to show that the same theme occurred over and over again. He used examples from contemporary Western culture, which by now had been successfully exported worldwide, not only from books but from movies and popular music. He could see their heads nod and the smiles being passed along from face to face. It wasn't difficult for any of them to understand that people walked from the cradle to the grave in search of love, led onward by the myths of popular culture as if they were following a glowing carrot dangling from a stick. This ideal could not be so ubiquitous if it did not touch something deep within us all, and each of them knew right away from their own experience what that was.

"But why is it?" he asked, "as we munch our popcorn during a good romantic comedy, hiding our tears so that no one sees and then secretly buying the video to watch it again when we feel down, why is it that none of us ever seems to attain that ideal? And we know of no one who has. At best we've heard rumors of someone who has come close. Either our love is unrequited, or we are betrayed, or our partners reveal themselves to be human and thus inherently flawed, and we discover that the happiness we were searching for in our beloved cannot be found there. Why is this?" He should not have been surprised when every single one of them came up with the same answer: Because what we are really searching for is God, our higher self; we were just searching in the wrong place. He should not have been surprised, but he was. It was as if everyone had anticipated what he had planned to say. "A finite love cannot satisfy an infinite desire" was the phrase he had kept in reserve for just that moment, but his words proved superfluous because the same wisdom had erupted spontaneously from everybody's lips. He realized then with a shock just how obvious the answer was. It wasn't anything that required a teacher. It was simply the human experience writ large, something everyone who had lived long enough and begun to turn his gaze beyond the gratification of the ego readily understood. Nothing in the world outside us can satisfy the longing we have. We can only satisfy it by finding the Beloved that lies inside us like an ocean, waiting for us to dive in and lose ourselves in her love. They knew it with their minds and they knew it in their hearts—and so did he.

From there the discussion took off, everyone becoming teacher and student in turn. They talked of how this romantic ideal was actually the urge to know God gradually gathering steam. We search for our beloved in our mothers and then in our fathers, in our friends and then in our lovers, doomed to continue searching until the beloved turns infinite on us and becomes the ocean of creation with its center everywhere and its periphery nowhere, until nothing remains outside us and we realize that we are the Beloved whom we seek. He ended the class by reading from the mystic poetry of Tagore and Kabir, both of whom had borrowed heavily from the language of romantic love—making him wonder how much difference there really was. At the end, no one was looking at him; nor were they looking at each other. They were looking at themselves. He had assumed it would be the most difficult of his classes, the one for which he was the least prepared; it turned out to be the easiest, for what could be easier than to talk about something that everyone already knew. As complicated as his intellect had made the spiritual path appear to be, it was really quite simple, a mere matter of turning inward toward the heart, which lies in wait for our arrival.

Rodrigo had planned to celebrate making it through the last of his classes by treating himself to a meal that night in an excellent Italian restaurant that had recently opened less than a hundred meters from the ashram gate. He was so moved, however, by the collective realization of his students that he lost any desire for a four-cheese pizza or a plate of manicotti. Instead, he ate a light meal in the ashram dining room where he had a chance to share some conversation with several of his students. It was a balmy night, and afterward he went for a walk along the river, clambering down in the moonlight to the warm, white sand that lay glistening under the reflective sheen of a nearly cloudless sky. Though it was barely eight thirty, Rishikesh was virtually silent. A few faint voices reached him over the water. About fifty meters upriver, he could see the shadowy shapes of two monks settling themselves on a pair of large, smooth boulders to perform their evening meditation. The air was scented with the fragrance of Himalayan pine and spruce, seemingly carried to him by the river's current. He leaned back against a small boulder about three meters from the water's edge and started examining the few stars that were strong enough to accompany the nearly full moon on her nightly voyage, cognizant that his astronomer might at that moment be borrowing his eyes to likewise study the wonders of the heavens. No constellations were visible, but he thought he caught several jewels from the diadem of Cassiopeia glowing regally in the western corner of the sky, a few leagues as he reckoned it from the imperious moon.

Inevitably, his thoughts returned to his class. The residual charge from that experience sent his thoughts bubbling along in a sea of devotional musings. Would that he could attain that infinite love that his students had talked about with a certainty that he had also felt but which now escaped him. He was still looking for the girl of his dreams, as the water girl would attest to. Who else was she but that same ghost hiding out in his subconscious in a new form, a shape shifter who thought to elude him with her Merlin magic and her Tantric practices? Every time he pursued these phantoms of his imagination, whether grafted onto a live woman, as in the case of Beth, or not, it had always led him, sooner or later, into a vale of suffering. They had not talked about this side of romantic love in class, what some might call the shadow side, but he was sure Saraswati would say that this was simply the price of trying to make an infinite desire fit into a finite woman. In the Gita, Krishna had said that this maya of his was impossible to surmount unless one fully surrendered to him; this seemed now to be a mere statement of fact. Rodrigo knew himself to be pursued by his inner longings, and he knew that unless he turned those longings toward the Infinite, toward Krishna in whatever form he chose to take, then the shadows of a thousand women would continue to pursue him down the corridors of time and never leave him in peace. He looked up at the moon and saw the feathery wisp of a cloud veil her eyes. Hera never sleeps, he thought. She tempts us with her beauty, with her cosmic coquetry, and maddens us by dancing just beyond our reach, stretching out to us a beckoning, mocking finger, until the day we realize that it is Krishna who is peering through her eyes, waiting for us to decipher her magic and join him on his divan in the depths of space. He turned this conceit over in his mind and decided that there was hope for him after all. Somewhere inside a devotee was waiting to emerge.

Then he remembered that Saraswati would be back in two days. This was a conversation they must have. He would not be so indelicate as to ask her about her romantic illusions and how she had fought through them—if, indeed, she had ever had any. But he could share his own thoughts and challenges. He could tell her about the discussion they had had in class and ask her how she thought it fit into the teachings of bhakti yoga. He remembered that she had once mentioned that among the different ways a devotee can relate to God—as friend, servant, child, parent, or lover—the highest of these and the most difficult to realize was that of lover. It was for this reason that the love between Krishna and Radha was so celebrated in the mystic literature of India. Was this also true in human relationships? And if so, was not the human experience of romantic love a reflection of a higher devotional love? Was it not a parallel experience in the realm of the ego—not a parody but an instinctive training for the day when that love expands to embrace the entire universe? He wondered what she would make of this question. He wondered also what had moved her to dedicate her life to social causes and then to give them up to become a spiritual recluse. For a few moments, he turned over in his mind the idea of what it would be like to have a lifetime to find out. But then he remembered the moon gazing down at him with her Hera smile. The stars around her seemed to laugh, and he knew they were laughing at him and his insistence on chasing phantoms in the dark.

Rodrigo went to bed as soon as he reached his room and fell immediately into a deep and mostly dreamless sleep, a restful slumber that felt well deserved after the concerted mental efforts of the past two weeks. His slumber ended not by waking up to his ashram room but by waking into an early morning dream that was anything but restful. When he woke from this dream, the peaceful, carefree feeling that had accompanied him throughout much of the night had been replaced by a raging fire that seemed to be on the verge of consuming both his body and his soul.

Rishikesh
5/27
3:40 AM

For several minutes after I woke up, I truly did not know where I was. The room was dark but my mind was darker still, clouded by fear, by desire, by the feel of her body against mine banishing every other thought but that of her presence. Even when my eyes finally focused, I found it difficult to believe that I was not still in my priest's alcove, staring at the door through which she had just vanished, not daring to believe what had just happened and not able to think about anything else.

It was late at night. I was alone in my room, having just finished the meditation the Tantric sage had taught me, nearly ready to lie down on my cot and abandon myself to the oblivion of sleep. My mind was a whirl of thoughts as I performed a final prostration in front of the image of the goddess on my altar. So many of the rituals and practices I had taken for granted were not what I had taken them to be. They were only a gateway into something whose existence I had not suspected. The hidden esoteric knowledge that I had been searching for in those ancient, dusty tomes had come to me clothed in the flesh of a forest yogi, a casteless recluse who had no need of books to see the truth. Due to this encounter, my world was changing so fast that my understanding could not keep up.

As I was preparing my bed, I heard the door behind me creak open, so softly I was not sure if that was what I was hearing. I turned and saw a shape standing in the tenuous light that entered in through the open doorway. Then the door closed behind her and the shadows covered her features. The sight was so inconceivable that my mind refused to believe what my eyes were seeing—until she stepped out of the shadows and into the faint starlight that came in through the open window. The shock of what I saw rooted me to where I stood. I must have opened my mouth to say something, or else that shock was visible on my face, for she put a finger to her lips to signal me to be quiet. By then, the electricity was running through me like a wild stallion on an open plain. She moved toward me with soft and silent footsteps. She had a slender, confident smile on her lips, but in her eyes I could see a burning, intoxicated light that was a pure reflection of what I was feeling. When she reached me, I managed to say in a frightened whisper, "What are you doing here!" She put her fingers to my lips with a touch so light it felt as if a feather had brushed them. "Tonight I shall be your devi," she said. I remember her words exactly and how her eyes shone with a strange, otherworldly light when she said them. She told me that she had come to initiate me into a secret Tantric practice that would help me to overcome my shame and my fear. With a naturalness that astounded me, she stepped out of her sari, took my hand, and led me to the bed. My fear leapt at me like a mad dog but it was unable to stop me.

What followed I cannot describe in this journal. She possessed me that night in a way I would not have thought possible. It was not a simple expression of carnal desire but a practice, a symbolic ritual with a meaning that far exceeded its earthly gestures, though within that practice carnal desire raged like a fire that nearly consumed us. We wrestled that desire with conscious intent, seeking to harness its wild power, until the fire burned upward into our brains and downward into the roots of all desire, consuming everything in its path, even passion itself. The world of prejudices that was harbored in my mind was laid bare for both of us to see, and though I instinctively tried to cling to it, I could not hold on. It was swept away by a flood that could not be held back.

When the ritual was over, we did not speak—I, because I could not; she, because she was still lost in the world I had just left. We lay there bathed in a transcendent air that was perfumed with the sweat of our bodies. Finally she got up and put on her clothes. She looked at me, her eyes filled with a tranquil tenderness that nearly overwhelmed me. Her look made me aware of the tears that filled my own eyes. With a graceful gesture, she spooned one of those tears onto her finger and brought it to her lips. Then she brought her hands to her breast to bid me goodbye and disappeared through the doorway as silently as she had come. I stared after her, weak with the memory of my desire and the immediacy of my fear, knowing that I was now on a path from which there was no turning back and over which I had no control. Then the room clouded. Perhaps it was the tears clouding my eyes. When my eyes focused again, I was back in my ashram room, still staring at the door through which she had vanished. Though she was gone, I could feel her presence on my skin, a feeling that holds me prisoner still.

Do I even want to know what this dream means, what it might reveal about the dreamer? How can I reconcile this desire made flesh with my search for an infinite spiritual love, a desire so fierce it will obey nothing that my mind can say to it? At this moment I feel humbled. I recognize that I am growing spiritually, perhaps soon beyond all recognition, but it is just as obvious that I am still tied to the earth by chains that won't let me go. Tomorrow Saraswati returns. What can I say to her? When we sit and talk about devotion, will she sense the presence of such desires in me and recoil instinctively? Can I even talk about such things without feeling that I am a hypocrite, knowing that somewhere deep inside me I want her to possess my body as well as my soul? Perhaps I am too hard on myself. It is a dream, after all. While it may be a true litmus of unfulfilled desire, I have never consciously thought of her in that way. It may also be that she is beyond such things, who can say? though I have heard of elevated yogis who have been tempted by such desires even after years of profound meditation. What I do know is that I have lived a life in which all my spiritual yearnings have been unconsciously channeled into the dream of finding the ideal woman to love. This cannot be turned around in a day or in a year. Was that not the whole purpose of the ritual we performed (assuming for the moment that it was not simply a thinly disguised outlet for carnal desire), the endeavor to harness that primordial biological passion and use its unbridled energy to propel the practitioner beyond the flesh and into the realm of the soul? I am changing for the better, rapidly and undeniably, but I cannot go from animal to divine in one giant leap. There must be stages in between, and this may be one of them. But this is something I will not talk about with Saraswati. I am on my own here. I just hope I know what I'm doing.

When Rodrigo sat in front of his computer after breakfast, he was beset by feelings of trepidation. The dream had left such a strong imprint on his psyche that he was afraid it would induce his writing to go in a direction he did not want it to go. He had been hoping to see a growing spiritual awareness become manifest in Le Gentil; the last thing he wanted was the intrusion of lust as a motivating force. But his characters surprised him, reminding him once again that they had their own path to walk, independent of his own. He was only the witnessing consciousness, a spectator in a theater in which the actors were mostly improvising their lines, sticking only loosely to the script the author had handed them. Fortunately, they were gifted in the art of improvisation.

By then, Ambika and Le Gentil were getting ready to leave their excavations and proceed on the second leg of their journey. They had spent a total of three days at the ruins, camping out at night under the stars and journeying forward on their endless conversation during the day. As they worked, they unearthed other artifacts of Roman origin. None were of any great import by themselves, but taken together they constituted proof of how at home the Romans had been in ancient India. With such close contact, it was unthinkable that Indian ideas and intellectual discoveries had not traveled back to Rome with the Romans and thereby made their way into the currents of Western civilization. This was the topic of discussion when Ambika and Le Gentil finished their last dinner at the campsite, having decided to leave at first light. Their eyes were on the rich canopy of stars above their heads as they spoke in hushed tones, instinctively paying homage to the grandeur that surrounded them.

"When I was a girl and I was studying Alexander's visit to India—well, it wasn't exactly a visit, let's call it an aborted invasion—I read that he had specifically wanted to meet some Indian fakirs and yogis because he had heard strange and miraculous stories about them. I remember thinking that if such stories had reached the emperor's ears, then there must have been people in Greece and Macedonia that knew India quite well and perhaps had even traveled back and forth. Some of them had probably developed a passion for studying the wisdom of our Indian sages; otherwise, how could such stories have reached the emperor? Usually, only a select few who interest themselves in esoteric knowledge know about such things; it stays confined to certain closed circles. And only if the people in those circles were people of influence—scholars, priests, philosophers—could Alexander have heard about the exploits of our sages. And that was centuries before the Romans. We know the Romans came here for commercial reasons, but I suspect it went far beyond that."

"At this point, I think it difficult to assume otherwise," Le Gentil said. He poked at a few embers still smoldering from the fire that Jiddu had used to cook their meal. "If traders came here, it means that explorers came before them, and where there are explorers, there are scientists, often the explorers themselves. There must have been men coming here in search of knowledge in those days, rather than just for spices and pearls. It's only the fact that it was never documented that bothers me. Or perhaps it was and those documents didn't survive the middle ages. You're familiar with the middle ages, I suppose?"

"Of course. There is a reason why they are also called the dark ages. You can't expect much in the way of enlightened knowledge to survive centuries of willful neglect. Especially when the church had total control during those centuries. They had a vested interest in making such knowledge disappear, principally eso-teric knowledge but also any cultural history that displaced Europe as the center of the civilized world. That was how they built up their supremacy, by making everything that challenged it go away."

"For a religious person and a Christian, you seem to take a dim view of the church."

"Was it not Christ who warned us against the blind leading the blind? I don't make the mistake of confusing the church with Christianity, or religion with spirituality. The church is the church, religion is religion, and spirituality is spiritu-ality. Anyway, the past doesn't interest me nearly as much as the future. The more interesting question is, what is going to happen now? Obviously, there was much more contact between India and Europe in ancient times than there has been in recent centuries. Certainly the origins of Christianity were deeply influenced by Hindu and Buddhist thought. Since then our cultures have grown far apart. Now that they've been thrown together again by force—not our force but yours—I wonder what will come of it, other than a lot of misery for my people."

"Are you asking for my opinion?"

"Of course. I'm already familiar with my own."

"Okay. Well, ever since we saw the swami, I've been thinking about many of the things he said. One thing he said that makes more and more sense the better I understand your culture is that India and Europe are both out of balance but in opposite directions. I was thinking about his claim that people in the West would suffer a backlash against materialism and come to India in search of spiritual knowledge. Now that I've been here more than a year and have had a chance to know the Hindu mind, I have to admit that's probably true. It's hard to imagine it happening in my lifetime, but I'm ready to concede that the time will come. But I also think the opposite is true: sooner or later young Indians are going to start emulating the West, because they'll want to have what Europe has. Especially once some Indians have a chance to go to Europe and see firsthand what life is like there. There is a huge difference between an industrialized society like ours and an agrarian society like you have here—on the material plane, I mean. I'm not trying to boast; I'm just relating what I've seen with my own eyes. Europe is far ahead of Asia in most things related to the material world: standard of living, science, education, industry. Our society is full of problems, I won't deny it, and perhaps our culture is a child's culture when compared to yours, but one day in Paris or London would be enough to convince you how much India is missing. I'm starting to understand the emphasis on spirituality that is such a part of your culture, but the material world is also important. Man cannot live by spirituality alone. Once people in India and all over Asia begin to realize how far behind they are in these areas, they are going to want to catch up."

"I don't doubt it. I think it's inevitable, and probably necessary also. The world is changing and we have to change along with it. I just hope we don't lose sight of what's really important in the process. Our culture is what has sustained us through thousands of years of civilization. We may be materially poor, but no country has a richer cultural heritage. We have to find a way to progress materially without sacrificing what is our real strength."

Ambika fell silent. Le Gentil continued to stir the embers of the fire as they both spent a few minutes with their own thoughts. Then she again picked up the thread of their conversation.

"You know, my father predicts that India will be an independent, industrialized nation within a hundred years. He tells me from time to time that we are preparing the way for my grandchildren to be the equal of any citizen of the world."

Le Gentil shook his head. "Your father is an intelligent and strong-minded man, Ambika, but I think he underestimates the military might of the European nations and their readiness to use it. Between France, England, Spain, and Portugal, we've spent the better part of two centuries at war with each other. We shift allegiances every generation or so, but we're always at war with somebody. And we are very good at it, if you permit me the expression. We've turned warfare into an advanced science. If anything, we've become too good at it, too good at inventing deadly weapons and even deadlier strategies for how to use them. And when we are not at war with one another, we are in competition: for colonies, trade markets, we even race each other for scientific achievements. This competition is what has spurred our material advancement the last two centuries or so. Whatever it is, we want to beat our neighbors to it. Now it's Asia. I'm afraid that neither the French nor the English will ever leave India alone. Our countries are in a race to establish their empires, and I think that for our politicians, India and China are nothing more than sources of raw materials and potential markets waiting to be exploited. I should like to live another hundred years. I should like even better to see you live a hundred years and have a chance to know your great-grandchildren. But I'm afraid that what we would see then is an India that is even less free than the India we see today. And likely poorer as well, because whatever wealth it has and whatever wealth it is destined to generate is all headed for the French and British coffers to build more ships, more buildings, more weapons, and more factories. I have no doubts about this, Ambika. This is the open discourse of our leaders, and we—excuse me, they—have the might to carry out their words."

There was a hard edge to Le Gentil's voice now. He was speaking the truth as he saw it, and he saw no advantage in sugarcoating it. But though it was dark, he noticed a glistening at the edges of Ambika's eyes and the shadow of a sorrow that had fallen over her face. He checked himself and softened his tone.

"Of course, I'm just a scientist. What do I know about the future of world politics? Maybe in a hundred years the best telescopes and compasses will come from Indian factories and your grandchildren will be the owners of those factories. And my grandchildren will travel here in the fleetest Indian schooners to buy instruments for their observatory."

Ambika smiled weakly. "Your 'maybe' doesn't sound very convincing. And anyhow I am not convinced. I am very much afraid that you are right and that my father is a well-meaning dreamer who should be glad he will not be around to see the fate of his great-grandchildren … if I ever give him any."

They were both quiet for a few moments.

"I will tell you this, Ambika. It may be longer than we wish before India takes its place as a free and prosperous nation, but if it can produce one Ambika, then the future of India is not only bright, it's assured. It would be a great loss to the world if you didn't have grandchildren. I should dearly love to see them and to have a chance to talk to their grandmother."

"And what would you tell them if you did?"

Le Gentil closed his eyes for a few moments, wondering what he would say to her grandchildren should he ever meet them. When he opened them he had a smile of conviction on his face. "I would tell them that their grandmother was the finest woman I had ever known—and the most beautiful. And that if they wanted to be great men in their own right, then they should try to live up to her legacy. Their country could ask no more of them than that."

The bright sheen over Ambika's eyes glistened even more strongly in the faint starlight that slid past the folds of her sari, casting her slim figure in silver shadows.

"Should I ever have the chance to meet your grandchildren, I would tell them that their grandfather was not only a great scientist, he was a great sage."

Le Gentil smiled wistfully. "What a beautiful thought, Ambika. I only wish it were true."

"It will be. I know it for a fact because I know you, Guillaume. This is your destiny, and there is nothing in this world capable of altering it."

They were silent for a long time after that, both of them looking out at the stars rather than at each other. But their hearts were filled with gladness and with peace, and they felt so close to each other in those moments that not even an intervening ocean of stars could have parted their clasped hands or separated the steadfast beating of their hearts.

It was only after Rodrigo looked up from his computer that he realized that this was the declaration of love he had been waiting for. How could he have not seen it coming? Maybe because it was not the scene he would have written had he planned it. Instead, it was the scene they improvised for themselves. He touched his fingers to his forehead in the Hindu gesture of respect and humility. He would not change a word of it. If this was how they chose to express their love to each other, then they deserved to have it kept that way.

It was late Sunday morning when Rodrigo put the finishing touches to the scene. Saraswati was due back sometime that night. He found himself wishing he could say to her something similar to what Le Gentil had said to Ambika. He thought ruefully that he was a long way from being able to do so, not unless he wished to risk their friendship, but the mere thought of a finite distance made it seem possible to him that such a day might come if he could only remain patient and stay the course. For the rest of the day, he continued to muse off and on about what he would say if he could write that scene as he wished. He would have to be just as subtle as his characters, probably more so. He would have to sound more spiritual than romantic—that would be his only real chance of success. One yogi to another, something so spiritually authentic on the surface that she might even say yes before she realized where he was going. It was such a wonderful fantasy that he managed to keep it going for hours without tiring, rehearsing it in his mind, refining the details and the dialogue, deliberating for long stretches over what would make the perfect setting. Moonlight of course was virtually obligatory. The riverside was his preferred venue. It would have to be after they had meditated together. Their mood would be at its subtlest then, infinitely more susceptible to starlight, moon shadow, and the sweet allure of devotional feelings played out through the divine medium of finite actors rehearsing their eventual union with the Infinite. He told himself after each imaginary rehearsal that it was just a fantasy, but somehow each time he played it through in his mind it came out a little more polished, a little more poetic, a little more possible—until by the time he went for his late afternoon walk, it began to seem almost probable. After all, he was a writer. He had the necessary skills to develop the scene. Given time, he would find the right words. For the rest of his walk, he weighed the power of mantra against the power of poetry. In the end, he decided he would need the power of both. Saraswati was no ordinary girl. She was a goddess in disguise—not merely a namesake—and goddesses were notoriously difficult to please. Or so he had read. But as he well knew, the truth did not easily confine itself to the pages of a book.

32

O N HER WAY BACK from Benares, Saraswati stopped off to see her parents for a few days. As always, she was glad to help them out and keep them company but saddened to see what had become of their lives. The morning that she was due to take the bus back to Rishikesh, she went for a short walk through the village and out to the fields where she used to love to wander as a child. The pre-monsoon sky was the color of slate, a burgeoning presence that caressed her cheeks with its cool, moist breath. As she walked alongside the fields of wheat and sugarcane, rustling lazily in the pregnant air, she remembered the monsoon of her childhood, how it would crack over her head in the early afternoon and send her into paroxysms of delight as its sudden currents of cool air swept across the plains and wiped away in an instant all traces of the stifling summer heat. Minutes later, the heavens would open and send her scurrying for the nearest tree, where she would stand with her neck arched and her tongue outstretched, lapping up the drops that filtered through its leaves, or else enjoy their ticklish feel as they slid across her forehead and down her neck to the small of her back. Her favorites were a pair of aged mangoes about a kilometer north of the village, where the children would often congregate. One or two of the more daring boys would invariably climb into their branches and throw down the inviting yellow fruit for their comrades to feast upon, especially during the afternoon rains when the steady drops that fell from its towering canopy of dark green, dagger-like leaves provided the perfect antidote to the sticky juice that clung to their fingers and the sides of their mouths with a lingering residue of its tart sweetness.

The trees were still there. She was surprised to see hundreds of fruits hanging majestically from their upper branches, having escaped thus far the marauding youngsters who were at this moment nowhere to be seen, undoubtedly shackled to pen and paper in the same grade school in the next village that she had attended. Taking advantage of the morning solitude, she sat down under its spreading branches on a carpet of brown and green leaves that crackled underneath her. From her vantage point under the tree, she could see the fields stretching out below a low-hanging sky to the limits of the horizon, broken only by scattered clusters of trees and the hazy silhouettes of the rooftops that formed her village, a picturesque blend of elegant thatch roofs among which fluttered the morning wash like the distant flags of hundreds of small countries. She allowed herself a brief smile as she remembered the many happy hours she had spent under this tree as a child, taking in the landscape that she so adored and playing with the other village children. There had been unhappy hours as well, their unhappiness now forgotten, the inevitable conflicts with her playmates that now appeared so innocent by comparison with the trials and tragedies she had endured since then. But she had not come to this place to wax nostalgic about her childhood. Ordinarily, she would not have allowed her mind even a short excursion into the past. Whenever she noticed herself slipping into such reveries, she would return to her mantra, its calming syllables rising and falling alongside the waves of her breath, until those thoughts floated away of their own accord and she found herself once more firmly rooted in the present. But on this occasion, she had sought out her favorite childhood tree precisely to turn her eyes toward the past and examine it for lessons that she might have missed. "An occasional backward glance," the Mother had called it, the closest the master ever came to sanctioning any attempt to escape the reality of the present. "An occasional backward glance may be warranted under certain circumstances, when we need to understand its impact on the present, but this should never be confused with the normal human tendency to escape into the past or the future. If you have any doubts, then don't look back." Those words had stayed with her ever since she had first heard the Mother speak them. In her unsteadiest moments, they had helped her to regain some perspective. Now she lowered her eyes and sought the Mother's permission to look back down the road she had traveled. When she felt the familiar caress of her guru's smile, she whose words and example had been her principle primer in the art of internal warfare, she asked her to enlighten her mind about the meaning of the words she had spoken a few days earlier, words she still found difficult to understand, as she had found difficult to understand the stern, inflexible bent of the Mother's eyes that had seemed to border on reproach. She knew from past experience that a day would come when she would fully understand the meaning of those words, when the Mother would lift the veil that covered her eyes, but for now they were obscured by the darkness brought on by her inability to see the path stretching out before her.

It had not always been this way. For the last four years, her path had seemed as clearly defined and as self-evident as a newly paved highway sweltering under the glare of the midday sun. True, for reasons she did not always comprehend, the Mother had chosen to keep her in Rishikesh instead of letting her take the final step toward the fulfillment of what she considered to be her destiny, but she recognized that these four years had been a necessary training period, one she hoped would soon come to an end, though she dared not vocalize that hope in the Mother's presence. As she conceived it, this phase in her life had actually begun during her final year in Delhi, a year in which her life seemed determined to spiral once again out of her control. Twelve months before her arrival in Rishikesh, she had received a call from the managing editor of *India Today*, Southern Asia's most widely read newsweekly, a regular presence in the lives of most educated, English-speaking Indians who professed to be committed to keeping up with events and issues in their native land. She had met him briefly once before, six months earlier, when the weekly had picked up one of her articles and asked her to revise it for its next issue. He had poked his head into her meeting with an assistant editor to let her know how much he had enjoyed reading her articles over the years, an admission that only served to make her nervous. She had been even more nervous when she received his phone call and agreed to meet him in his office, knowing that in all likelihood he was going to ask her to write a major piece for them, something that could conceivably catapult her into the upper echelons of Indian journalism, should the article be well received, thereby opening doors to other national publications.

The editor was a debonair man in his early sixties with graying hair and a direct, concise manner that told more about his forty-plus years as a journalist and a professor than any of the awards sitting on the mantle above his desk. He held out his hand to her and with a relaxed, confident, business-like tone told her that the magazine—long known as a conservative, centrist publication—wanted to hire her as a contributing editor. The Indian people, he explained, especially the educated public that comprised the magazine's principal readership, were increasingly valuing the need for a social consciousness that was not merely political but humanitarian in a country that despite its economic growth and rapidly expanding middle class was still yoked to an enduring tradition of endemic social injustice, continuing poverty, and institutionalized corruption. In his opinion, he knew of no other journalist who was more in tune with the concerns of the common people. Her stories were the kind he wanted to introduce into the magazine, a steady diet of human interest stories that would not only appeal to the magazine's readership but would hopefully go a long way toward alleviating the miseries of the people who appeared in her pages.

It was an appeal she could not resist, the seeming culmination of the years that had begun with her volunteer work in a tribal girl's hostel and blossomed into a steady career as an activist-turned-journalist in the nation's capital and its second most populous city. Her first article appeared a month later, and soon few issues were published that did not include her byline. It was then that she began to realize how naive she had been about the relative fame she had hitherto enjoyed. She had grumbled to her few friends and chafed at the restrictions it had imposed on her inner life, but what she had experienced up until then had been nothing but a light wind ruffling her hair compared to the storm that followed once her name started to be mentioned as one of India's most controversial and well-known journalists, championed by many, idolized by some, and despised by others with a passion usually reserved for corrupt politicians and the coach of the national cricket team.

At first, she resisted the attractions and the onslaughts with the same dogged determination that had seen her through the previous years, accepting the extra effort it required as a small price to pay for the chance to make a much greater impact on the world around her. When she was invited to a national talk show to discuss the issues of the day, she brought her most articulate manner with her and a firm resolution that she would not let the national exposure displace a single hair on her head. She smiled, confined her answers to the short sound bites dictated by the ten-minute format, and shook hands affably with the television staff, who exuded the firm conviction that social issues were as much entertainment as sports or the movie industry. When the wife of India's president, the Burmese-born Usha, invited her to lunch and asked her for advice about several of the welfare projects she was engaged in, she told herself that the first lady was simply a woman with a desire to help, nothing more, no different than the millions of other women throughout the world whose hearts bled when they saw suffering and injustice. She would not let herself be dazzled or misled by the trappings of political power.

But one invitation led to another, one well-known face wanting to talk to her became a second and then a third and a fourth, and gradually her resistance began to waver. She could not help but notice the excitement she felt whenever she interacted with the influential and the famous; the way her mind would be buzzing for hours afterward, still caught in the threads of an experience that hid from her the simple beauty of the present; the way her plans and dreams seemed to multiply faster than she could keep up with; the fact that it became more and more difficult to reach that silence space within her where all of life's tribulations found their resolution, where there were no more questions to be posed or answers to be sought. She was not in danger of falling from the path as she had done seven years earlier—as unsteady as her meditation became, it remained the bedrock of her life—but she could not help but question if the life she was leading was not distancing her from her spiritual goal. Increasingly, she was moving in a circle of fascinating, talented people, yet on those few occasions when she had a chance to spend a few days with the Mother in her ashram, she always felt as if it were only then that she was able to breathe freely. Though she valued her career almost as much as she valued her spiritual life, the closer she came to the pinnacle of worldly success, the more she felt the mud oozing round her ankles.

Gradually, it became clear to her that she lived and worked in a world steeped in spiritual ignorance, and the closer she got to the corridors of power, the more that ignorance seemed to hold sway. She was determined to be an instrument for change, but she did not want to end up like the people with whom she ate lunch or saluted in the halls of Parliament, caught in the snares of their ego and only barely able to keep the emptiness at bay. "This maya of mine is insurmountable," Krishna had said in the Gita, "except for those who take refuge in me." Now that she was living her life close to the center of maya's storm, she was beginning to see firsthand just how insurmountable it was.

As the months passed, she began to view the change in her circumstances as a test. Clearly the Mother was asking her to choose: "There, you have seen all that maya has to offer: the bright lights and the renown, the glow of material success, the allure of power, the subtle intoxication of seeing your ego as an instrument for change. I offer it all to you on a platter. Now choose. Do you want maya or do you want me?" She wanted the Mother; she wanted her soul. When this became clear, she began to realize that she could not continue with the life she was leading. None of the standards by which the world judged success ever made anybody happy, as far as she could see. If anything, these highly successful people with whom she was spending her time were worse off in many ways than the poor village folk she had grown up with or those that she had met during her travels through Northern India, people who often lived in misery but were rarely miserable. The one thing holding her back was the feeling that she was making a difference, but even that she was beginning to question. Several times during that year, she was invited to give lectures to university audiences as a guest of the journalism department. She prepared those lectures with the assiduousness required by the chance to influence large numbers of the young minds who would one day be turning the country in directions yet unimagined, but afterward she couldn't help but feel, despite the generous applause and the flurry of questions, that her passion for meaningful change had fallen on an auditorium full of ears deafened by the clamor of their own minds. She had a readership of more than twenty million souls, more than she could have ever hoped for, but while she looked for signs of the good her work was doing, her colleagues and friends congratulated her with the smiles they reserved for celebrities and then turned back to their lives like prisoners disappearing behind a clanging iron gate, unable or unwilling to separate themselves from the trials of their egos long enough to breathe the air of an honest and enduring empathy.

Her trips to her parent's house also helped to fuel her doubts. She had always admired her father for his sympathy for the sorrows of others and his practical farmer's intelligence, fruit of his long allegiance to the earth. She saw her own social consciousness as an outgrowth of his, tempered by the fires of a far-more-rigorous spiritual discipline. But in the years since his stroke, she had watched him grow more and more insular and irritable, a fact made all the more noticeable by the long intervals between her visits. He had always been an active man. It was not hard to understand how his enforced inactivity grated on him and gradually soured what had been sweet, but in time his preoccupation with his own drama became so jarring to her sensibilities that she began to wonder if it had not been there all along, covered up by his better qualities, which were only able to flourish in the absence of adverse conditions. Her mother was not much different, taking on the martyr's mantle like a shroud of honor, humming a victim's litany to herself while she insisted on doing all the most difficult household and caretaker tasks herself, holding to the conviction that the servant Saraswati paid to do those same tasks was fundamentally incapable of doing them the way they needed to be done. The cheerfulness Saraswati remembered from her childhood was nowhere to be seen. It gave her chills to think that their faith in the Mother had not saved them from a spiritual decline that she considered the worst enemy of old age, something she feared as she feared few things.

But was she so different, really? It was a question that haunted her, especially when she noticed how pronounced her self-absorption had become. Was she not just as caught up in her career as everyone else? Was she not just as attached to her dwindling privacy, to her image of herself as a crusader for social change, a leader and a light in times of darkness? Her own ignorance, so deeply rooted that it was a wonder she could ever step back far enough to recognize its face, seemed to her merely a reflection of the same malady she saw around her everywhere she looked. What kind of realistic change could she hope for when the ignorance that was the root cause of injustice showed no signs of going away? This was the question that most plagued her mind, accentuated by the growing realization of how deeply she was entwined in the world's snares. Could the sorrows that afflicted mankind really be removed if the spiritual ignorance that was their cause remained firmly rooted in the soil? Would they not simply throw out new shoots as soon as conditions allowed? If the malady in the minds of the exploiters remained, would they not simply take their claws elsewhere if one avenue was denied them? Was this not the real enemy, the cloud of ignorance that hung over the hearts and minds of human beings like a monsoon that never broke, never releasing its cooling winds and refreshing rains? How could she think to chase injustice from people's doors if she could not change the mentality that engendered it?

As her doubts grew, she began paying more frequent visits to the Mother's ashram in a concerted effort to keep her spiritual practices from floundering. During one of these visits, Premananda invited her to an evening talk she was giving in a nearby town where the normally reserved and unassuming sannyasi gave literacy classes twice a week. At first Saraswati found the affair rather dull. It was held in a drab, stuffy lecture hall in the local high school where the poor lighting made her feel as if she had entered the anteroom of Hades. The fifty or sixty people who attended, mostly students from Premananda's literacy classes who had brought along friends and family members, seemed particularly unenthusiastic as they trickled in, most of them no doubt attending the talk out of mere politeness. As Premananda began talking in her low-keyed voice, mildly distorted by the thick Teutonic accent she had never lost despite her long years by the Mother's side, Saraswati kept stealing glances at her watch, conscious of the slow crawl of time that was preventing her from getting back to the ashram. It was a simple talk on the importance of meditation and spiritual practices in daily life, nothing she hadn't heard a hundred times before, but as the time crawled by, she began to notice something she had rarely seen in the eyes of the people she talked to in her daily rounds as a well-known Delhi journalist. She wanted to call it inspiration, but she knew that so simple a word could not begin to do justice to what she saw. It was as if lights were going on, one by one, behind windows that had longed been plunged in darkness. There was nothing dazzling or profound in Premananda's words that she could see; on the surface, they seemed almost dull and often labored as the older woman struggled with the difficult syntax and complex grammar of the Hindi language. But it was not the words, she realized, that was lighting those lamps. It was the wisdom they conveyed. Premananda was talking simply and directly from her own experience, sharing without any observable trace of ego the simple lessons she had learned in her years by her guru's side, lessons that would transform her listener's lives and bring them peace and understanding if they could put them into practice.

Midway through the talk, Saraswati suddenly felt as if somebody had dumped a bucket of cold water on her. This is what people really want! she thought. They want to wake the god that sleeps within them; nothing else can bring them the peace they seek! In the end, after all the injustices were removed and their bellies filled, they would still suffer if they could not find rest at the altar of their inner deity. One look at them was enough to know that this simple truth was hidden in every human heart, waiting to be uncovered. Until she could do for them what Premananda was doing, she would simply be another blind woman leading people off the precipice and into a darkness not much different than the one she was leading them out of. In that moment, a sudden illumination flooded her thoughts. She would become a sannyasi! She would follow in the footsteps of Vivekananda and Nivedita! This was the path that had been waiting for her all along!

It did not occur to her that there might be other ways to do what Premananda was doing. The figure in front of her droning on in her Germanic-flavored Hindi was like a figure lifted from the annals of Hindu mythology, a goddess directing her to the path that had been selected for her on the day of her birth. The older woman's saffron sari dazzled her eyes like the purest poetry had never done. She knew in that moment that she would remain restless until the day that she could also wear the saffron robes and offer her former name into the ceremonial fire where it would be at once forgotten, along with the thousand failures of her former life.

The gap between this first blinding flash of inspiration and the day she took her request to the Mother did not prove as easy to negotiate as she thought it would. Her friends looked at her as if she were crazy to even consider such a rash decision, and her ego was tempted to agree with them. "You're under a lot of stress," they told her. "That's all. Take a few weeks off, go to your ashram, and you'll think differently about it when you get back." It seemed like sound, considered advice. People depended on her, from her editor to her readers to the hundreds of people she had yet to meet whose stories were waiting to be told. Was she really prepared to abandon them? Was this not just a means of escaping the burden of responsibility? She had worked hard to achieve a lifestyle that afforded her the luxury of doing what she really wanted to do. Did she truly want to give that up? The concerts, the art exhibitions, the stimulating conversation with some of the brightest minds in Delhi, the chance to keep her finger on the pulse of the nation? And there were her parents to consider. She was their only source of income. She could not become a sannyasi without making some arrangement for their financial security.

But despite the rising tide of reasons to believe that her flash of inspiration was no more than a spark from a loose wire that needed fixing, she persisted in her preparations, driven forward by a voice inside her that would not leave her in peace. "No lasting good will come of your work," it told her, "unless you dedicate yourself to your enlightenment and the enlightenment of others. Only then will you find peace and bring peace to others." Despite her fears and the fears of her friends and colleagues that took the form of well-meaning advice, she tied up one loose end after another until she finally felt ready to ask for a meeting with the managing editor of the magazine to inform him of her decision. To her surprise, he was the one person who did not try to dissuade her. He simply nodded slowly and gravely as she talked, a look of curious wonder in his eyes that gradually turned to one of generous comprehension. When she was done, the former Delhi University lecturer extended his hand to her and told her that he would miss her. "Once you're settled, do let me know where you are," he said. "Perhaps you can still contribute some articles in the future on the state of spirituality in India. Maybe even a blog." She expressed her gratitude to him for all that he had done for her, and then it was over. When she passed through the main doors and into Connaught Place, she stopped for a moment, surveyed the irrepressible flow of pedestrians coursing along the wide circular walkway like the mythological serpent that holds up the earth, and took what seemed to her like one last deep and liberating draft of the electric, smog-laden air.

Two days later, she arrived at the Mother's ashram in Benares with her belongings pared to the bare essentials—what she could fit in two suitcases—and a hope that the master would help her find a suitable means to provide for her parents. Amalina, the ashram secretary, showed her to a dormitory room, and a couple of hours later the Mother called for her. After doing prostration, she knelt in front of the Mother's cot. The Mother inquired about her health and her parents, her ancient eyes crinkling at the corners, expressing a joy so sacred and so boundless that Saraswati felt as if she might dissolve in the aura of her love. But when she gathered her resolve and made her request to be accepted as a monastic disciple, the saint's mood suddenly and unexpectedly turned grave.

"And how exactly do you propose to provide for your parents? You are their only child. You are well aware that this is your responsibility and yours alone."

The Mother's stern tone of voice and the granite cast of her eyes stopped Saraswati from voicing what was really in her mind. She had thought to ask the Mother if she could arrange for the patronage of some rich devotee so that she could devote herself full time to her service, but in the face of the Mother's displeasure she didn't dare. She hesitated, lowered her eyes, and then, faltering, fell back on her other remaining option.

"Mother, I have enough money saved up to support them for at least a year, maybe two. I thought that in the meantime, I could continue to write articles from time to time, maybe with more spiritually oriented content, enough to maintain them while they are still alive."

The Mother's face grew even sterner. Saraswati could feel the chill in the room deepen, despite the early summer heat.

"You cannot keep your feet in two boats. You cannot be both a sannyasi and a journalist at the same time. And do not think that I will ask my householder disciples to support your parents for you. The life of a sannyasi is not an escape from worldly responsibilities. It is the embracing of a greater responsibility: that of all humanity. It is for those who have been freed by their samskara and by the Lord's desire. As long as your parents are alive and you are their only child, it is your responsibility to care for them. It is your duty, and until I release you from that duty, you must accept it."

"But Mother," Saraswati burst out petulantly, "I've made up my mind. I want to be a sannyasi. I want to dedicate my life to your service."

The Mother's eyes flashed like great bolts of lightning exploding against the granite face of a distant mountain. "Willful girl! Will you submit to my will, or will you make the same mistake that led to your downfall in the past? Speak!"

The Mother had scarcely raised her voice, but the terrible change in tone and the indomitable force behind it made Saraswati tremble. Her rebelliousness shriveled before the Mother's fire; tears began to fall silently from the corners of her eyes.

"I am sorry, Mother. Please forgive my words. I will do according to your desire. Should I go back to Delhi?"

"No. In this one respect your intuition has led you true. It is time for you to leave your old life behind, but it is not time for you to become a sannyasi. I will make arrangements for you. In the meantime, stay here and meditate. Incinerate your past in the fire of your meditation."

A few days later, Amalina informed her that the Mother had arranged a job for her as a philosophy teacher in a well-known Rishikesh ashram where the pujya swami was her good friend. It would pay enough to support her parents. When she said goodbye to the Mother a couple of days later, the Mother left her with these words: "Go with my blessing. There you may live like a sannyasi. You may even wear the saffron sari if it pleases you, but never forget that you are not a sannyasi. Remain there until I tell you otherwise."

The transition was easier than she expected. From the very outset, the forested hills and secluded ashrams of Rishikesh were tinged with an aura of adventure. For the first time in a long while, she could walk the streets unrecognized. She had no cell phone in her pocket, and no contact with her past, except for an occasional visit to her parents and the mail that a trusted friend had agreed to forward without disclosing her whereabouts, mail she always found an excuse not to answer. Wary about being recognized, she refused to talk about her past with anyone, even with those who did recognize her, though she soon found that in Rishikesh nearly everyone respected the sannyasi's vow to leave her past behind. She was not a sannyasi, but she cut her hair and donned the saffron sari, and the life she led soon convinced everyone around her that she was, a misconception she did nothing to dispel. When she realized after her first classes how little she actually knew about spiritual philosophy, she accepted it as a challenge from her guru, a test she was determined to pass. She filled her room with yogic texts, brought her questions to the pujya swami whenever she had a chance, and took upon herself the task of mastering the path of jnana yoga in the hopeful conviction that this was the Mother's way of preparing her for her future life as a monastic disciple. And to the extent that she did master those difficult texts, she realized how necessary that preparation was. Determined to be a guide and a light for others, she knew that it was not enough to seek her own realization; she would have to learn how to articulate the path for others, to recast it in a language the lay disciple could understand. This freedom from her past and her wholesale dedication to the study and teaching of spiritual philosophy had such a profound impact on her meditation that one day, not many months after arriving there, she realized that she had never been happier. For the first time in her life, she could say with conviction that the path in front of her was clear and untrammeled. At the end of the path burned the light of liberation, and she felt secure in the knowledge that her efforts to free herself would also enable her to free others.

In these last few months, however, something had changed. For four years her horizons had been free of clouds, but now she could feel a crisis looming, and she knew from past experience that she could not ignore it. Suddenly, as if in answer to the plea that she had put before the Mother when she first sat down under the mango tree, her life seemed to come into focus. The landscape of the past, so difficult to decipher, began to reveal an order that had hitherto gone unnoticed. She saw that her past could be divided into several clearly definable phases, and that each of these phases had culminated in a specific crisis. Each time, her life had radically altered its course, depending on her response to that crisis. When she graduated from college, the weight of social expectation had come careening down upon her. Unprepared for this unforeseen turn of events, she had renounced the idea of ever getting married and had made a clean break with her parents. At the end of her three years with WAI, she had nearly lost her spiritual way, perhaps forever, but the Mother had stretched out her hand and she had clung to it with all the strength of her desperation and climbed out of the quicksand that was threatening to take her under. Six years later, with Vikram safely in her rearview mirror, she had accepted the challenge of journeying to the center of the storm by taking a job with the magazine, and in that journey she had discovered that her true path was renunciation. Now, a similar challenge was testing her will and her readiness to follow through on that decision: Rodrigo. For four years she had been at peace; now once again she was restless—restless to get back to Rishikesh and see him, to walk along the banks of the river and talk with him as she could talk with no one else—of spirituality, of art, of the madness of the world that was waiting to engulf them at the slightest misstep—while her desire to be with him advanced on a steady, unrelenting course, as if the distance between them had no effect whatsoever on its determined intention to lay siege to her life.

There was no longer any doubt in her mind about the magnitude of her attachment. She had gone to Benares to get the Mother's advice on how to navigate a teacher's growing fondness for her student, knowing that he had ceased to be a student and become a friend, the closest she had ever had. But rather than give her advice, the Mother had challenged her to face her fears and finish this samskara, once and for all. Nor had she said it very gently; rather, it had felt more like a rebuke, as if she had been an exasperating child trying her mother's patience. What then was she afraid of? She had been asking herself this question for the past week, groping in the fog for an answer. The Mother's intent was still hidden to her but slowly the mist was parting. If it were true that she was standing at a crossroads, as she now believed she was, then this was the test that would determine the road her life would take. Rodrigo had shown up at this precise moment in her life in order to test her resolve. If she truly wished to become a sannyasi and a spiritual teacher, then she would have to prove she was ready. A sannyasi must be able to love and to guide without letting attachment grow. She must be able to stand free from the snares of the world if she hopes to free others. It was not an easy task, but then she had never expected it to be. The easy answer was to run away, but she had already tried that, as the Mother had clearly hinted at, and the samskara had followed her into another life. Perhaps she had once been in this same position, and instead of taking the path of renunciation, she had run to safety, into the waiting arms of worldly life. It was time, the Mother had told her, to turn and face her fears. So be it. If she wished to don the saffron robes and follow in her guru's footsteps, then she would have to face her samskara head on and defeat it. Thus the Mother's rebuke. She had asked for this challenge. So accept it, once and for all!

Saraswati felt a gust of wind in her face. Like a gentle slap, it seemed to trigger a surge of resolve. Even now, even here, 170 kilometers from Rishikesh, she could feel the samskara curling around her feet like a welcome noose whose silky binding threads caressed her ankles with its sweet promises of surrender. Maya the enchantress, as much male as female. But she would defeat her! With the Mother's help, she would emerge victorious from this challenge, as she always had in the past. As if in answer, the sky darkened, maya growing stone-faced at this challenge to her authority. A few moist drops splattered on a leaf high above her, their faint pattering music filling her with an impulsive need to hike up her sari and run. Under the village rooftops across the fields lay freedom from the torrents that were getting ready to burst above her head. But there was no freedom from the desire whose music was already pouring its fierce, irresistible floodwaters through the riverbeds within her. A single swollen bead of water dropped from a leaf above her onto a brow that was already moist with her own feverish thoughts. She looked up as if she had awakened from a dream and then she did run, aware that the waters of the heavens were fast behind her. But the music followed, and above it rose a singular melody like the cry of a violin arcing high above the orchestra's plaintive chords: In the morning she would see him; in the afternoon they would walk; the dance they had begun together would continue in the shadow of the mountains, while the stars looked on and laughed their silent and inscrutable laugh.

It was after nine at night when Saraswati made it back to her room at the ashram. As she unpacked her bag, she had to fight an impulse to walk through the ashram grounds on the odd chance that Rodrigo might be taking a walk after dinner. As recently as a few weeks ago, she might have looked upon such a thought as a sign of spiritual weakness and done her best to forcibly suppress it. But her heart was now a wild animal straining at its leash. She no longer had the will to keep it caged up.

In the morning, on her way to class, she passed by Rodrigo's room, and for the first time she knocked on his door. It almost seemed like a reckless act to her, this simple sign of friendship, a thrusting open of the doors that had protected her heart for so long with no regard for the consequences. Perhaps it was just the weight of inertia that made it seem so irremediable an act. But it was for her a major step and she knew it, whether he noticed or not. When she saw the surprised smile on his face and felt the warmth of his greeting, all her hesitation vanished. "I don't want to disturb your writing," she told him. "I just wanted to see if you'll be free this afternoon for our walk." When the time was agreed upon and she headed out to the banyan tree for her class, that simple act made her feel lighter and more courageous than she had felt in weeks.

They met shortly before three at the gate of the ashram, each with an umbrella in his hand. After a short consultation, they decided to follow the river past Lakshman Jhula to a secluded spot where they could do a short afternoon meditation, provided the rains held off. As soon as they were out of sight of the ashram gates, Saraswati insisted on hearing how his classes had gone, the long version since they had at least half an hour before they would be clear of town. The story he told, with his writer's eye for detail that she had long since come to appreciate, made her catch her breath at key moments when the simple events of a morning class seemed to compete with the best of Kalidasa's dramas. They walked side by side at a pace that was slower than either of them would have walked had they been alone, meandering down the path like the laziest of streams, oblivious to their surroundings. When Rodrigo talked of the moments of lucidity that had come upon him while he was teaching, like the sun bursting from behind a cloud, how they had shed light on his own experiments in karma yoga, transforming his morning shower into an act of worship, she felt the years slipping away from her, as if the wonder in her eyes were making her younger with every step. She nodded when he came to the classes on jnana yoga, neatly ordering the spiritual path and the universe around it into clearly definable, interwoven segments, and shared with him how dazzled she had been by those same challenges when she'd first arrived at the ashram. By the time he came to his class on bhakti, they were already picking their way down a steep path north of town to a secluded formation of smooth boulders that they had visited on more than one occasion in the past.

It was the perfect spot for a short meditation and an extended discussion that lasted the rest of the afternoon. They had chosen adjoining boulders that jutted out into the water. The light drops of spray on their face and hands were a refreshing antidote to the sun, which made its late summer presence felt despite the lazy mass of clouds that hid it from view. Picking up where they had left off, Rodrigo's storytelling was even more dramatic than it had been during their walk. He carefully built up his lack of confidence in talking about devotion so that when he told her how he had felt when his students showed him that the simple truths of bhakti were known to every human heart that took the time to look within itself, she felt a shock of delight and surprise that she was sure could not have been more gratifying had she actually been there. After he came to his conclusion that the various forms of human love were a preparatory training within the confines of the ego for the divine love that awaits us in the later stages of the journey, he fell silent and looked at her with an unspoken question that hung in the air like the fragrance from an unseen flower. She breathed in that fragrance, letting it fill the pores of her lungs and enliven the blood she felt pumping in her heart, before she tried to find the words that he was waiting for. When she began voicing her own thoughts, she felt as if she had understood something about devotion that she had never understood before, aided by his eyes and his unvoiced thoughts that seemed to give wings to her own.

"It's funny, I was thinking about the exact same thing the last couple of days. Maybe we were picking up on each other's thoughts, I don't know, but it's been on my mind a lot lately. I stopped off to see my parents on the way back from Benares. They're not doing very well, unfortunately, especially my father. He was a farmer—I think I told you that—but since his stroke, the most he can do is sit up in a chair, and he can't even do that without my mother's help. He can't even feed himself properly; somebody has to help him. He doesn't admit it, but these past ten years have turned him bitter, very bitter. I don't know where his faith in God has gone, but it doesn't seem to have survived the stroke. I can understand it, after all he's had to suffer, but it's discouraging to see how easily that faith can be lost when you're really put to the test. That started me thinking about how much we define our lives by what we do rather than who we are. He can't do any of the things he prided himself on all his life, and because of that he seems to feel as if he's lost everything that was meaningful to him. What's scary to me is that I think we're all like that to some extent. These past couple of days I fed him breakfast and then read to him like he used to read to me when I was a child. The whole time I was reading, I couldn't help wondering how I would react if I were in that chair, half-paralyzed, not able to do any of the things that mean so much to me. How much would it change my life if I couldn't teach, if I couldn't use my talents to help humanity but instead had to depend on people to bathe me and feed me? How much would it change yours if you couldn't write? I like to think that I'd accept it as God's will and spend most of my time meditating, that what's really important in my life wouldn't change, but after sitting for a few hours with my father I got a feel for how difficult it would be. It's true that the more I practice, the more I'm able to look on my external life as a passing show, like the scriptures teach us—the more you can abide in the atman, the less it matters what you can or cannot do—but the truth is, I'm still very much attached to what I'm doing with my life and what I hope to do in the future. That got me thinking about the relative importance of our external life. We all have one. We can't simply call it an illusion and leave it at that, no matter what Shankaracharya says or how brilliantly he says it. I started to realize that I've never really fully understood the importance of my external life—from a spiritual point of view, I mean, the cosmic point of view. Krishna didn't come to the earth to abide in the atman. He was already there. He came here to dance. It's his *lila*; there has to be a purpose to it. The Mother always says, 'God doesn't make mistakes.' If the whole world, except for a few highly advanced yogis and saints, define their lives by what they do, then what they do must have as much inherent dignity from a cosmic perspective as the realized consciousness that witnesses it all. Think about it. God created the universe for the sheer dramatic joy of it. You can't discount the drama. What is this universe, other than a vast theater of unsurpassed beauty in which you can watch an infinite number of storylines, all perfectly composed and intricately interwoven? Certainly, the deepest life is the inner life, the movement toward God, the quest for illumination. And the only way we can achieve that is by not getting caught up in the drama to the extent that we forget that we are actors putting on a play for his benefit. But that's just the main plot. It doesn't mean that the subplots are not just as interesting or just as necessary. If we could enjoy the entire drama as Krishna does, as the witnessing consciousness, I think we would see that every aspect of the creation has its own inherent artistic beauty; I think we would see that all the subplots contribute in some important way to the denouement of the play. As spiritualists, we need to remember that we are actors, no doubt, but we also need to appreciate the whole scope of the drama; otherwise we miss the point.

"So then my question was, how do all the subplots contribute to the main plot? If the point of the drama, the premise of the story, from the individual's standpoint, is to attain freedom so that we can merge back into the witnessing consciousness and enjoy the drama from the box seats as Krishna does, then how does this endless number of storylines contribute to that plot? Actually, I was thinking of you at that moment; I was trying to explain it to myself as a writer might. And then it occurred to me that it's through the subplots that we learn our lessons. It is there that we make our mistakes, hone our skills, find out what it's like to become attached and then have to struggle to become detached. It's the arena in which we work on ourselves. And the arena in which we work on developing devotion is relationships. It's practice for the main event, but it's also more than that, because who else are we relating to if not to God? He is all there is, whether we realize it or not. So in that sense, developing a relationship with God is just a matter of becoming more aware of what is. The person you fall in love with doesn't cease to be God just because you're too asleep to realize it. It's the same dance; it's just a matter of what name you give it. The question is not just whether you are able to develop devotion for God; the question is, can you love another person with a totally open heart—no artificial barriers, no self-interest, no ego? How can we possibly love God self-lessly with all our heart if we can't love another human being selflessly with all our heart? The real question is, can you love? Not whom you love. So yes, I agree with you one hundred percent. I think that through our relationships we expand our capacity to love. We keep practicing with other living beings until our love becomes infinite, and then we call it devotion. Of course, by the time we get to that point, we already know that it's God we're in love with, no matter what form he takes."

Saraswati was sure she was blushing but she couldn't help it. Her words had both embarrassed and inspired her. She wasn't so much embarrassed that she had said this in front of Rodrigo but that she had said it at all. It wasn't like her to speak in this way, not about love or even about devotion. But something inside her was changing, struggling to break free like the first trickle from a dam that is getting ready to give way. Despite her apprehension, she felt a compulsion to see where the floodwaters would take her.

"It sounds so easy," Rodrigo said, after some moments of silence, "but of course it's not."

Saraswati was thankful for his words; they felt like a temporary reprieve from what had in essence been a thinly veiled admission of her feelings. "No, it's not," she said. "But it is the easiest of the paths and the most enjoyable. Jnana yoga can be pretty dry much of the time. Trust me, I know from personal experience."

"You know, your description reminds me of a movie I saw. I don't think it was meant to be a spiritual movie, but it had a very similar premise. In the movie, the main character's life is actually a TV show, but he doesn't know it. He grows up in this town, supposedly on an island, and he thinks everything is real, but actually it's a gigantic television studio, the whole town. It's a drama; he just doesn't know it. All his friends and everyone in the town are actors, even his wife, and the show is broadcast live twenty-four hours a day, just like the one we're in. Then, when he's about to turn thirty, same age as the Buddha, he begins to realize how unrealistic and choreographed everything seems. He starts dreaming of the outside world and eventually he tries to leave; in other words, he goes searching for the truth. So the producers have to come up with bigger and bigger obstacles to keep him from leaving: his bus breaks down, there's a hurricane, a supposed nuclear melt-down in a nearby town, and so on. Sort of like what the Buddha's father did to keep him from leaving. But nothing stops him. Eventually he escapes, discovers the truth, and the show ends. The audience turns the channel to a different show. One soul achieves liberation, so we congratulate him and turn our attention to the next drama. Actually, there's been a few movies recently based on similar ideas. Maybe it's something in the collective unconscious."

"That sounds like a movie I might like to see, a Hollywood version of the search for enlightenment—the one story that never grows old and never gets boring. It may be a modern movie but the story is as old as the hills: the central plot, the hero's journey, starts with the suspicion that things are not as they seem; you are not who you think you are. Only when you realize this can you then set out to discover who you really are. And the way to do that, of course, is to break your identification with the ego, to realize that you're an actor playing a role. But the other point I was making—I don't know if they make this point in the movie—is that everything the hero learns, she learns by participating in the drama. If she doesn't go through it, then she can't gain the skills necessary to go beyond it. The drama has its importance. It can't be dismissed. You can't simply say, 'oh, it's just a drama; the whole point is to be free.' It's not *just* a drama. It's the life experience we need in order to wake up and earn our freedom. You have to transcend the role, but transcendence is not the same thing as escape. In the ideal spiritual life you still play the role—better than ever, in fact—but at the same time you transcend that role by achieving identification with Consciousness. And who could be a better actor than a soul whose mind is aware of its oneness with God."

"God playing all the parts."

"Exactly. Correct me if I'm wrong, but wasn't Shakespeare an actor as well?"

"He was. In those days most playwrights also acted in their own plays."

"It's no different with a yogi or a devotee. You play your part, but you're just as aware of everyone else's part, and, above all, of the play as a whole."

By this time, the sun had dipped behind the mountains. Twilight would soon be upon them. If they were going to return in time for arati, they needed to leave now, but neither of them felt any inclination to go back. Encouraged by the fact that it hadn't rained, they decided to remain there to perform their evening meditation. By the time they finished, it was dark. Great jagged rents in the clouds let through enough starlight to turn the river from black to a deep, silvery gray. Moonrise was still a couple of hours away, and the nighttime shadows that enveloped them made Saraswati feel as if they had made the transition into a hidden world, a world of impregnable solitude and mystic expectations known only to yogis, unveiled at the hour of twilight to those whose eyes never sleep. Unwilling to leave just yet, they lingered there a while longer. Rodrigo asked her about her experiences with the Mother, and she shared with him experiences that she had never had occasion to share before because she had never had anyone to share them with. The river magnified each of those episodes, revealing contours she had never noticed before, its flowing waters reflecting a symmetry between these experiences that made her see even more clearly how the Mother had been leading her judiciously forward, calling forth the necessary challenges and required inspiration with the perfect timing of a master conductor. When they started walking back, Rodrigo began telling her about the unusual dreams he'd been having. She listened silently as they climbed up the path and began walking down the road toward Lakshman Jhula, immersed in the deep shadows cast by the canopy of branches that blocked their view of the night sky. He talked slowly, with frequent pauses, as if he were reliving those dreams in his mind and stopping at the end of certain segments to take a closer look at those inward images. The solitude helped her to enhance her own vision. She felt as if she could picture exactly what he was seeing, each English phrase rolling through the empty air like the chant of the Bengali priest in some far-off time when life was simpler but still very much the same. When they reached Lakshman Jhula with its brash lights and the discordant sounds of tourists creating their own improvised revelry in a town that had none of its own to offer, Rodrigo changed the subject deftly, in seeming obedience to their surroundings, segueing into a light discussion of his novel and the impact that not only his dreams but all his experience in Rishikesh was having on happenings that were taking place more than two thousand kilometers and a couple of centuries away. Saraswati listened with her mind seemingly alert and curious, but her heart was still caught in the tangle of his dreams, certain that the man who walked beside her, whose life was becoming increasingly entangled with her own, was a volcanic island with the greater part of its mass submerged in a sea of spiritual samskaras. It was this submerged portion that most fascinated her, though it did not entirely escape her that a live volcano could be dangerous—especially the closer one got.

In the weeks that followed, Saraswati and Rodrigo met each day at mid-afternoon and walked with their umbrellas aloft, holding off either the sun or the rain. Traditionally, the pre-monsoon skies of early June would empty their stores in the early afternoon several times a week, a short but voluminous unburdening that sent instantaneous rivulets coursing down the streets and pathways of the town with wild abandon. Then the clouds would recede, satisfied with their handiwork, and the sun would return from its siesta, usually just in time for the couple's walk. If the rains lingered, they would find a café where they could sit and sip tea, or else wander into one of the many ashrams or temples to practice meditation or pour over the spiritual texts that they were now exploring in tandem. But once the rains ended, they would begin walking again, enjoying the vibrant freshness that lingered in the air. Though their conversations still revolved around the texts they were studying, two new strands wove themselves into the empty spaces that had been reserved for them: they shared the stories of their lives, especially Saraswati, who felt as if she were making up for lost time, and they talked of art as if it were a temple erected solely for the worship of the Divine.

"Do you remember when we were talking about the layers of the mind?" she asked him one afternoon while they were discussing art on a concrete bench in the courtyard of the Sivananda ashram, a stone's throw from the library where they sometimes hibernated when the rains arrived unfashionably late. "Well, the first layer of the superconscious mind, the *atimanas kosha*, is where great art is born. I wouldn't call the articles I wrote literature, but I had this experience sometimes when my mind would go into *atimanas kosha* while I was writing. The words would just begin to flow by themselves. It wasn't like writing, really; it was more like a kind of meditation, almost a kind of trance. I just transcribed what I heard, like I was taking dictation from the Cosmic Mind. Sometimes in that state, I wasn't even fully aware of what I had written until I read it afterward. It was quite an experience, when it did happen, and it was by far my best work."

"That used to happen to Mozart, you know. He said that he didn't really compose his pieces. He would just hear music in his head and transcribe what he heard. But how can you say that your articles aren't literature? I think you need to show them to a certain university professor and let him be the judge."

Saraswati hesitated for a moment. She queried the Mother, whose image she pictured floating just above Rodrigo's head, and then agreed with her guru that the time had come. The thought brought with it a sense of relief. "Okay," she said softly, "I'll show them to you tonight. But to return to our discussion, in Sanskrit the usual word for poet or writer is *kavi*. Literally though, *kavi* means 'seer of truth,' a sage, but also what we might call a visionary. The way I see it, true artistic greatness cannot be measured by the amount of craft or skill an artist has but rather by the depth of their insight, their ability to see the truth that is covered by the veil of appearances and to communicate that truth to others by removing that veil. In ancient India, people used to pay the same respect to great writers that they paid to sages, because they considered them sages. And actually, the great writers of antiquity were sages, from Kalidas to Valmiki to Chandidas. The only difference between them and other great teachers is that they were able to convey their vision through the language of drama or epic poetry or whatever forms they chose. It's hard to imagine a greater work of literature than Vyasa's *Mahabharata* or Valmiki's *Ramayana*. Look at how many centuries have passed and still Indian children learn their basic lessons about life and spirituality through these two books. Both of them were great yogis as well as great writers. That, I think, is why their books have lasted for so long."

"There is one American writer who says that there's no real value in reading a book unless the writer is more intelligent than you are. I guess we could just substitute the word 'wiser' and it would be more or less the same thing."

"I know a number of important writers in Delhi. I used to travel in those circles before I came to Rishikesh. All they ever talked about was developing their craft or how talented a craftsman this writer or that writer was. You never heard them talking about developing their vision or their wisdom or their insight, but that's exactly what an artist needs if she wants to be a great artist. Of course, you have to have the craft—being a visionary doesn't make you an artist—but what is the good of being an artist if you have nothing to say? What good does it do anyone? For me, a great artist is someone who is able to lift her mind into *atimanas kosha* and establish a link with the Cosmic Mind and then can transmit that insight to others through the power of her words or her music or her images. For that you have to meditate; you have to cultivate devotion. Of course, some people are born geniuses, but that only means that they did the necessary work in their previous lives. And how many born geniuses do you come across? One a century?"

That evening Saraswati brought a stack of her articles to Rodrigo's room, a selection of what she considered her best work dating all the way back to her university thesis. There was a slight tremor in her hands when she handed them over, as if she were handing them to someone who was set to pass judgment on her life. It was only after she let go of them that she realized that she had been holding her breath. Her unexpected anxiety, however, proved unfounded. When they met the following day, Rodrigo was gushing over how much he loved her work. On his request, she burned her entire collection to a CD, and before the week was up he had finished the last of her articles.

One afternoon, they were walking along a wooded path east of town that wound into the Chilla forest, part of an enormous elephant and tiger reserve where the sightings of these magnificent beasts were becoming exceedingly rare due to the unrelenting encroachment of human beings. Saraswati had been telling him about the ongoing efforts to preserve their habitat by Indian conservationists when he suddenly veered off to tell her how hard it was for him to understand why she had stopped writing.

"If your articles had such an impact on me, I can just imagine how much impact they must have had on Indian readers. I seriously wonder if there's another journalist anywhere in India who's doing work as important as you were doing. And you gave it up, just like that!"

"As I was saying," Saraswati continued calmly, "records show that populations of large animals at the periphery of their range are extremely vulnerable to extinction, That's what's happening in India. Most people know that the Bengal tiger is on the verge of extinction. India has the world's largest population of tigers but there are barely a thousand left in the entire country. But what many people don't know is that the Indian elephant is also in danger of extinction."

"And what about socially conscious journalists? Are they not also in danger of extinction?"

She let out a sigh that she hoped conveyed just the right touch of mild exasperation. "It seems you are not going to let me escape this time. Okay, I'll answer your question. The answer is no. Socially conscious journalists are not in danger of extinction. They may seem like an endangered species sometimes, but they are hardly on the verge of disappearing like our beautiful Bengal tiger. Who are in danger of extinction are writers who are both spiritually and socially conscious. Unfortunately, those are precisely the writers we need the most. When I was still a journalist, the thing that bothered me most about many of the supposedly great writers of our day is how little responsibility they took for trying to guide society in the right direction. Of course, there are some who do, but very few. There are plenty of writers who are good at showing what's wrong with our society but almost none who are able to show us where we should go from here and how to get there. We were talking about what makes for a great writer or a great artist? I think this is the other key point. How much can a writer inspire people to move ahead in their lives? To what extent can she give people the direction they need to lead a better life? I've always thought that the measure of a great book or a great story is that when you finish reading it, you emerge from that experience a better person, a wiser person, a more aware, more conscious person. If not, then why bother reading it? Aren't there better uses we can make of our time?

"The great sages of India were not revered simply because they had achieved a high degree of spiritual realization. People revered them because they dedicated their lives to removing people's ignorance and guiding them along the path of elevation. Or to be more poetic, because they led them out of the darkness toward the light. *Asato ma sat gamaya, tamaso ma jyotir gamaya, mrityor ma amritam gamaya.* That's what we look to a great artist for. Artists and writers have such a profound impact on people's lives and on society in general, but that impact can be for better or for worse. If they heighten people's despair instead of giving them hope and showing them a way out of their despair, if they distract our minds from the important questions of life, then I can't call such persons great artists. How many artists are more concerned with selling books or records than with fulfilling their social responsibility toward their fellow human beings? If anything, I'd rather see such artists become extinct. We can keep a section in the museum for their books so that people can see on display examples of what to avoid in their lives."

This was a sore point with Saraswati but she made no pretense of trying to hide her anger—nor did she see any need to.

"If I had my way, I wouldn't use the word 'artist' at all for such people; I'd invent another word: word-merchants, picture-peddlers, music-mongers? Anyhow, to get back to your original question, what happened with me is that I began to question if I were really making a difference. It's one thing to be able to show what's wrong with the world; that's the easy part. It's important, I know, but it's not enough to see clearly what's wrong if you can't also show what's right and inspire people to have the faith that they can right those wrongs and overcome the obstacles that stand in their way. That's what I wasn't doing—at least, not enough. Gradually, I began to realize that without some degree of spiritual wisdom to go with your social consciousness you can't solve these problems. Most of the time you just exchange one problem for another, and that's not real change. It's just a merry-go-round. The Buddha was able to get off the wheel of birth and death because he could see the truth that governs the universe. You have to have some deep realization of what the purpose of life is before you can know which path to take in whatever situation. I realized that I had a lot of righteous anger and I was able to stir up those sentiments in others because I could write well, but I wasn't able to lead them anywhere worth going. So I left it behind and dedicated myself to developing real wisdom—not just anger mixed with a little compassion and made to pass for wisdom. When I first came here, I thought I was giving it up for good, but I'm not so sure anymore. I look on it now as more of a hiatus. Maybe that's partially your influence. At any rate, when and if the time comes, I will start writing again. But not until I have something worthwhile to say."

"I can understand your reasons, Saraswati, and I respect them, but I don't know that I can fully agree with you. I read your articles and I came out of that experience far more socially conscious than I went in. I feel like a changed human being because I read your articles. I find it hard to believe they wouldn't have the same effect on almost anyone who read them. I think you're shortchanging yourself and your writing. Maybe in the long run you're shortchanging all of us."

"I appreciate your enthusiasm, Rodrigo, and your support, I really do. But this wasn't an impulsive decision. It took me a long time to arrive at it, and I haven't had a single regret since. I made the right choice, and I have faith that time will bear that out."

What Saraswati could not bring herself to reveal just yet was that her decision had not been to stop writing but to become a sannyasi. She had been on the verge of telling him on a couple of occasions, but each time she pulled back at the last minute, as if she had reached a wall whose perfectly smooth face offered no holds with which to climb. She shared everything else of her past that seemed significant with a ravenous appetite that made her realize how hungry she had been for such an opportunity, but she was not yet ready to share this most private part of herself. It was still too bound up with her struggle to come to grips with her attachment. She wanted to trust her heart to tell her when the appropriate moment would be, but her heart, she realized, was an unproven helmswoman. She had depended on her intelligence and on the Mother's words for so long that she hesitated to consign herself to uncharted waters with so inexperienced a guide, though she realized full well that she might not have a choice. The Mother's most recent words in Benares were still revolving in the kaleidoscopic landscape of her thoughts, but their meaning remained submerged within the turbid waters of her heart. If she wished to capture them, she would have to offer herself to those waters, which now pulled at her like a magnet, exhorting her to let go.

33

JUNE ARRIVED FOR RODRIGO like the gale winds that herald the coming of the monsoon. The tentative nature of his relationship with Saraswati before her trip seemed to be nothing more than a memory on her return. With each afternoon walk, it receded further and further into the shadows of his past until he could no longer make out its presence. Whatever reticence there had been in her manner was gone, leaving only the quiet thoughtfulness that lent an aura of profound contemplation to everything she said, though at times a hidden passion blazed forth that surprised him with its sudden, crackling heat. Nowhere was this passion more evident than in her articles, which he read with the slow, excited absorption he had once reserved for Proust and the other masters of fiction who had provided meaning to the foggy interiors of his mind. She was a natural storyteller, but the fact that her stories were real gave them a visceral poignancy that fiction rarely achieved. Though she declined to call them literature, he knew better. While her language was often disarmingly simple, devoid of any linguistic flourish, it was that simplicity that allowed her to reveal the pains and sorrows of India's most neglected citizens without the intrusion of an intervening consciousness to tarnish the effect. There was a beauty and a power in her simple, straightforward descriptions of these people's trials and tribulations—brought on by the seemingly omnipresent machinery of injustice—that would have been negated by any attempt at linguistic color or ornamentation. It was language at its starkest and most immediate, that most gossamer of veils between the reader and the notations of the human heart.

Though he declined to show her his own work-in-progress, bound as he was by the time-honored tradition that enjoined him to maintain sacrosanct the first draft, a tradition she fully endorsed, he discussed his story with her at length, as well as the many experiences brought on by his journey into the living world of the writer's craft. She became visibly excited when he described watching his characters step into the clear air of his imagination, as if that space belonged entirely to them during the time they inhabited it, living and breathing as independent creatures whose only link to their creator was their unconscious need for him to transcribe their experience. To her way of thinking, this was clear proof that his meditation was beginning to lift his art into the hallowed precincts of the superconscious mind, the thousand-chambered palace of yogis and artists where the Divine Presence cavorted with human consciousness and sent its missives into the world of living beings. Early one afternoon, while they lunched together in town, she announced with unimpeachable conviction that the world needed spiritually conscious writers more than it needed literature professors.

"Do you really want to be a literature professor for the rest of your life?" she asked.

"No, of course not. I've always dreamed of becoming a full-time writer one day."

"Then why not start now? Stay here and write. I can arrange a student visa for you through the ashram *gurukul.* All you need is a little money to pay your room and board. I don't think you could find a better place to work on your writing. Look at what's happened since you've been here. Imagine how much progress you would make if you spent another year or two in the ashram."

Saraswati's proposal caught Rodrigo entirely by surprise. His visa was up in six weeks, and the thought of going back to Carolina and teaching classes left a distinctly unpleasant taste in his mouth. Six weeks was an eternity, he told himself. So much could happen between now and then that there was no sense in vacating the present, especially when the present was so much more interesting than the future. But despite his best efforts to the contrary, he had grown more and more aware of the passage of time. Soon he would need to start browsing the online ads for apartments. After that, it would only be a matter of days before he needed to reconfirm his flight and buy a train ticket to Delhi. Soon his old life would be beating at his door, and the sole purpose of his trip—finishing his book—was far from accomplished. But that was not what was bothering him, not really. In the nearly eleven months that he had been at the ashram, he had finally acquired the writer's discipline. One way or another he would continue writing. One way or another he would finish his book. But that was small consolation for the prospect of having to say goodbye to Saraswati, perhaps forever. Though he had told himself many times in these past days that India was only a plane ride away, that he would surely be back soon, that in the meantime the Internet would serve as a lifeline between two writers, he was realistic enough to know that the ocean between them would be more than figurative. How could he face the possibility of an ending to something that seemed like it was only just beginning, especially when that undefined something now seemed like the most important thing in his life? Though he had yet to express his true feelings to Saraswati, he had rehearsed them so often in his mind that it sometimes felt as if he had already said all there was to say. Now that their conversations had taken on a more intimate character, he was convinced that there was no more perfect woman in the world for him. He was a literary romantic who had taken to the saving graces of yogic practice after tasting the intoxication of its philosophy; she was the vessel that had filled him with the wonders of the Orient. He could not say that she was everything he had dreamed of in a woman, simply because he had never dreamed of a woman like her. But having gotten to know her, he could say with conviction that no dreamed female could ever be half the woman she was, neither the water girl of his temple nor Ambika, should either find a way to incarnate into the world. No matter how powerful his imagination, it paled before the woman whom fate had sent to intersect his path.

Rodrigo didn't say much during that luncheon, other than to tell her that he would give it serious thought, but when he got back to his room, his heart was pounding away furiously at the lining of his chest wall, its thumping music forcing him back and forth between the window and the bed, where an open book lay unread despite his best attempts to maintain his regular after-lunch reading. As he paced up and down, he paused from time to time to stare out the window at the phantoms acting out his fantasies in well-ordered riot. He had been in love with Saraswati for a while now, though it was only recently that he had openly declared this to himself. He had since revealed those feelings to her numerous times, but only in the safety of his imagination. On several of these occasions, she had nodded vacantly, her eyes lost in an inward contemplation; then she had looked at him, her lips curving into a tranquil smile, and said, "I have come to that same conclusion myself. It seems to be a mutual samskara." More frequently, she had reached out to take his hand and said, "I love you also, Rodrigo, but as a friend. You will always be in my heart, but my path is a solitary one." The first time he heard this, it brought tears to his eyes, but after repeated rehearsals he accepted his fate graciously and wished her well on her journey. Once she had even thrown her arms around him, wild with glee, an act of girlish abandon so out of character that he never attempted to recreate the scene, realizing that it violated his aesthetic sensibilities. But never, throughout the course of his fantasies, had he truly believed that she might share his feelings. This was the first real intimation that she might. She had asked him to stay; what other sign did he need? True, the world did need a spiritually conscious writer more than it needed a spiritually conscious literature professor, but she had yet to see his writing. She had nothing to judge it by. He lived with his work every day, and he had yet to see any indication that the world needed this particular writer. It might well be that in his case it needed a successful literature professor far more than another failed writer. No, this was personally motivated. She wanted him to stay. He did not need to be a yogi to see that.

By the time Rodrigo left his room to meet Saraswati for their afternoon walk, he had already navigated the precarious backwaters of her suggestion that he give up his profession. It was not an ideal solution. His money would not last forever, and it would be hard to find a similar position should he be forced to go back to teaching once it was gone. Nor could he imagine spending the rest of his life in India. It would be far better to work for a few more years, save up some money, and publish a book or two. Then they would be free. No, the ideal solution was for Saraswati to move to America. Just imagine the good she could do in a place where genuine spiritual teachers were few and far between. With his salary, she wouldn't have to worry about supporting her parents. She could spend her summers in India, even bring her parents to America if she wanted. He might be prepared to stay in India if it came down to a choice between losing her or staying, but the logical solution was to convince her to join him there.

But could he do it? One day earlier, he would have not thought it possible. It was only a fantasy that he had polished within an inch of perfection, never a realistic hope. But one day can be the dividing line between two completely separate worlds—worlds without even a suspicion of the other's existence. He was not so naive to think that he could just ask her and expect a positive response. He would need to prepare the ground, just as he had done so many times in his imagination, but at least now he knew that the soil was fertile. Her heart would need time to make its claims known to her mind. For now the most he could do would be to help it along as subtly as he knew how. He could begin by letting her know that he was serious about exploring the possibility of staying.

That afternoon Rodrigo confined his conversation to the usual topics, but when he sensed Saraswati's aura of expectation, he mentioned in his most subdued manner the email he had received a few days earlier from his lawyer, notifying him that a couple had put in an offer for the house. If all went well, it would be sold within a few weeks and the money divided between him and his ex-wife after fees and taxes had been deducted, whereupon his share would land in his now-depleted bank account. The money to stay in India would soon be no problem. He had already started thinking seriously about her proposal, he told her; he would let her know as soon as he took a decision.

As Rodrigo's mind swirled with the dust of his desire and the insistent winds of Saraswati's disquisitions on art and his future as a writer, he watched the particles settle in the world of *The Venus Transit*, impregnating the comings and goings of his characters with the ethereal traces of a world far into the future. He could not say to what extent the events that followed arose out of the independent destinies of his characters, or how far they were influenced by the yearnings of their real-life descendants, but as he watched Ambika and Le Gentil face the inclement weather of the choices they confronted, he could not help but notice the parallels with his own unfolding predicament. Their trip had gone on longer than planned, their plans having been organically modified when it became clear to both of them that their declarations of admiration and respect were, in fact, declarations of love. Neither showed the hesitation or uncertainty that plagued Rodrigo and lingered like a fine perfume in the places he and Saraswati walked. Ambika and Le Gentil were as clear about their feelings as a summer dream is of its fruitful impermanence. Their future was the only unknown that faced them, and no future, no matter how uncertain or ephemeral, could change the feelings that drew strength from their silence.

Instead of returning directly to Pondicherry after their visit to Thanjavur, the ancient capital of the Chola dynasty, as they had planned, they decided to continue on to Madurai, the capital of the Nayaks, a forty-league trek that would delay their return to Pondicherry by nearly two weeks. Their driver was visibly disturbed by the change in plans. With the help of a series of animated gestures, he described for them the turbulent state of current affairs in that region: since the decline of the Nayaks, the city had become the focus of a three-way power struggle between the local petty kings, known as *palaiyakkarars*; the titular Muslim governor appointed from Delhi, himself a petty sovereign; and the increasingly powerful British East India Company. But neither the surliness of their driver nor the uncertain political landscape did much to sway either Le Gentil or Ambika from their true purpose: the chance to extend their private interlude. Jiddu, moreover, was delighted to be able to continue his adventure. He had walked around Thanjavur in a daze, especially when they took him to the Brihadishwara temple, one of the architectural wonders of the ancient world. Le Gentil fully appreciated his cook's stupefied amazement. Though the astronomer spent the better part of those three days in the Saraswati Mahal Library with his translator by his side, browsing through its thirty thousand palm-leaf and paper manuscripts, some of them of a staggering antiquity, he found time to survey every inch of India's largest temple with its thousands of intricate sculptures and frescoes. Afterward, he declared it to be one of the world's greatest monuments to the powers of the human imagination.

The journey to Madurai took the better part of two days, traveling along the royal road that connected the capital of the Nayaks to the French protectorate of Pondicherry. During the trip, Le Gentil busied himself with an English copy of Megasthenes's *Indica*, a third-century BC account written by the Greek ambassador to the court of Chandragupta, the founding emperor of the Mauryan dynasty and the first ruler to unite the subcontinent. He found it rather tedious, apart from Megasthenes's account of Alexander's request to meet the sage Dandamis and his description of the use of elephants in the various Indian armies, a tactical advantage so overwhelming in the warfare of the day that it was claimed that Alexander abandoned his invasion of India when his advance scouts passed him information that the Gangaridai in Eastern India had a force of four thousand of these well-trained monsters. Far more interesting, however, was Ambika's narration of the life and work of Chanakya, Chandragupta's teacher and prime minister and the real architect of the Mauryan Empire. She could quote portions of Chanakya's *Arthashastra* from memory, the work that had established him as the world's first great economist, statesman, and political strategist, and she wove these passages into her narrative to show how even the most seemingly innocuous episodes from Chanakya's life were shaped by clearly defined and well-thought-out principles, all subordinated to his lifelong goal of creating a unified and well-ordered society throughout the subcontinent. The more he listened, the more impressed he became with the acumen of this ancient political genius whose maxim "Learn from the mistakes of others; you can't live long enough to make them all yourselves" seemed to him to be the essence of practical wisdom. Though Ambika balked at his request to translate the *Arthashastra*—"the original runs over five hundred pages," she told him, her eyes wide with a humorous terror—she agreed to read out to him from the original whenever he was in a mood for statecraft and nation building.

Megasthenes had spent nearly all his time in India at the emperor's palace in Patliputra. The one exception he had made was a trip to Madurai, renowned at the time for its wealth, its magnificent temples, and its fervent guardianship of Tamil culture. Twenty centuries later, it was no longer home to the Pandya dynasty, but from what Le Gentil could see, not much else had changed. Though the British would soon gain an economic stranglehold on the city through their dubious alliances with the *palaiyakkarars*, whose main concern continued to be the taxes they levied, regardless of whether they sent their annual tithes to the European traders or to the Mughal lords at Delhi, little effect of these political stratagems could yet be felt among the local people who wound their way from the markets to the temples at the same leisurely pace they had employed since the days when Megasthenes had sat with them to ascertain the truth of the fabulous tales he had heard: philosopher kings who could disappear into thin air at a whim, and flying ants as big as ferrets who dug up gold from the bowels of the earth and heaped it into piles for their human masters.

They remained there for six days. Ambika took him to meet poets, philosophers, scientists, and priests. They attended a Shiva worship at the Minakshi Sundareswarar temple, whose architectural splendor, they both agreed, surpassed even that of the Brihadishwara temple. They sat through a pair of concerts of classical instrumental music and a scriptural debate between two pundits, which Ambika translated with such meticulous rapidity that Le Gentil left the hall more in awe of her prodigious linguistic powers than of the impressive erudition of the two debaters. Within a day of their arrival, every intellectual and artist of note seemed to have become aware of the presence of the foreign scientist and his attractive translator, beating a constant trail to the lodgings she had found for them in a guest bungalow in the spacious grounds of the Thirumalai Nayakar palace complex, where they had been welcomed like visiting royalty. These conversations with the cognoscenti of Madurai often lasted until the first dim glow of dawn appeared in the open windows, signaling to their visitors that the hour for their morning ablutions had come. Le Gentil found these exchanges so stimulating and so thought provoking that he almost dispensed with sleep altogether, catching short naps in the intervals between one activity and another, though when it came time to make the nearly hundred-league journey back to Pondicherry, both he and Ambika spent the first day of their trip completely oblivious of the rumbling, jolting music of the carriage, both of them plunged in an interminably sound sleep with their shoulders and heads slumped against each other like the entwined images of Shakti and Shiva in the temple grounds where they had stayed.

While each day in Madurai was filled with fascinating and challenging encounters, their most lasting impression came from a visit to the ashram and clinic of Agastha Thirumular Siddhar, a healer and yogi who was one of the principle guardians of Tamil medicine. Ambika prepared Le Gentil for the visit by telling him about some of the impressive cures she had seen over the years, not the least of which was her own experience with a *siddhar* from Coimbatore whom her father had sent for when she contracted a severe case of rheumatic fever as a child. When they arrived at the ashram, the master was sitting on a reed carpet in his clinic, attending to the last of what had been a long line of patients. To either side of the sturdy, bare-chested, middle-aged man sat several young students. On the wall behind him were shelves with hundreds of bottles containing the dried herbs and tinctures that he used as his principle remedies. The last remaining patient was an old, hunchbacked woman with rheumy eyes who complained that she could no longer see anything more than shadows. "That is all there is in this world, mother, only shadows," the siddhar told her. "We are all merely shadows. Why do you wish to have your eyes bewitched yet again by the false colors of maya?" The old woman, however, whimpered pitiably and complained that she could not even cook her food in this condition or gather brush and scraps for the old cow that was like a child to her. The siddhar grunted in seeming annoyance. He told one of his students to bring a certain herbal tincture whose crimson drops he proceeded to splash in the woman's eyes while she let out a pair of high-pitched, staccato yelps. He then fastened a bandage over her eyes and instructed her to keep perfectly still until he told her otherwise. When he removed the bandage some five minutes later, the surprised woman told him that her sight was much improved. She could make out shapes and colors, though everything was still fuzzy and blurred at the edges. He then asked her if she knew where to find a certain plant and instructed her how to make a concoction from its leaves. "Drink it twice a day on an empty stomach, morning and night. Before you go to bed, put a couple of drops of this tincture in each eye and keep them closed for five minutes. In a week, your eyes will be well enough to fill your mind with delusion. Now go, feed your cow. Come back if you repent of having chosen to see too much." He ended his instructions with the traditional siddhar refrain: *aodu pambe*, "dance, cobra, dance." The happy woman staggered out like a newlywed after a night of revelry, her snake-charmed eyes glittering from the tincture he had applied.

During the hour they spent with the siddhar, Le Gentil plied him with questions about his medical practice, while Ambika transcribed those answers into her notebook. Though Le Gentil did not number medicine among the many disciplines he practiced, he had no illusions about its importance among the pantheon of sciences. Since he had come to appreciate the depth of Indian knowledge in this field, he had begun to harbor a secret desire to bring some of their medical secrets back with him to Europe, where the thought of entrusting his life to a doctor was enough to send him into a mild state of panic. Though his friends and colleagues thought him squeamish, he knew it was simply his scientist's ability to recognize how relatively primitive the science of Western medicine was.

"There is no disease that cannot be cured by a person of yogic understanding," the siddhar replied, in answer to one of his questions. "Man has sleeping inside him the power to create universes. Why should he not be able to conquer such a simple thing as disease, which is in essence nothing more than an imbalance between the vital elements? The body, though mortal, is the instrument through which we attain our divine goal. It is our responsibility to enhance its powers in whatever measure we can and to preserve it as long as possible, provided we do not violate the laws of nature." He motioned with his hand to the vast store of herbs and tinctures behind him. "Everything we need to keep our body healthy is provided to us by nature. For every disease, there is a plant growing nearby that can cure it. This is the decree of nature, the counterweight that balances the divine scales of natural law. However, it is our human responsibility to learn how to employ what nature has provided us. This includes the preventive measures that keep our body from falling into a state of imbalance, such as breathing exercises, periodic cleanses, and a sensible diet. This is what the great line of the siddhars has dedicated itself to for many centuries. In our individual practice, we seek oneness with the Divine; in our work, we pledge ourselves to maintaining the purity of the only temple worth visiting: the human body."

After describing at length diverse techniques, from simple cleansing routines designed to strengthen the immune system, to procedures for removing malignant masses from the surface of the brain, he led them into an adjoining room that was filled with a collection of Tamil texts. "This is the accumulated wisdom of the siddhars, at least that part of it that can be confined to books." He pointed to his heart and then to his head. "The rest, the most important part, is in here and in here."

Le Gentil had been impressed by the cure he had seen, but the mere thought of the centuries of Indian medical expertise crowded into that little room excited him as few other discoveries had on his long trip through the Orient. He realized immediately that he had a responsibility to transport that knowledge back to his native land, where rich and common folk alike were still subject to widespread contagions, chronic illnesses, and childhood tragedies that he knew in his heart could be prevented with the proper knowledge and its judicious application. When he asked the siddhar if it would be possible to obtain copies of those texts, the older man fixed him with a gaze that reminded him of a cobra hypnotizing its prey. The yogi's head swayed rhythmically from side to side in an undulating motion, before a slight smile brought it to a halt.

"And what would you do with these texts? You are not a doctor."

"I would get them translated and bring them back to Europe, where this knowledge could be used to save people's lives and alleviate their suffering."

The yogi shrugged his shoulders. "You would do better to bring a siddhar with you, but I doubt you would find one willing to go." Then he nodded his assent. He told Ambika where she could obtain copies of several important texts to bring back with her to Pondicherry and promised that he would allow copies to be made on the premises of any texts she wished, if she could make arrangements for a scribe to come and do the work.

"You have found a treasure trove, Guillaume," Ambika told him after they had left. "I was surprised that he assented so readily. I had always heard that the siddhars guard their knowledge among themselves, only passing it on from master to disciple. Although I do have a suspicion."

"And what would that be?"

"I have my doubts that your Western doctors will pay any serious attention to the theories of some Hindu magicians, as they might think of them. I wonder if that was not what was behind the siddhar's smile."

"You may be right. In fact, I don't doubt it. But somewhere, somebody is bound to pay attention. Somebody will get excited, just as I have. And whether they pass it off as their own knowledge and publish it, or simply use it to treat their patients and cure people who might not have been cured otherwise, it doesn't really matter. Knowledge shouldn't be shut up in little rooms or confined to certain cultures. If I can help put an end to this, I will consider mine a life well lived."

It was on the journey back, after they had both surfaced from their slumber, that he began outlining the plan that would occupy much of the later stages of his life. He would begin by hiring a team of translators to start translating important Indian texts into the principal European languages. No branch of the arts or sciences would be excluded—astrology; mathematics; Indian classical music; medicine; spiritual philosophy; yoga, literature; Chanakya's *Arthashastra* and *Nitishatra*, his treatise on ethics; Lagadha's *Vedanga Jyotish* and Aryabhata's *Aryabhatiya*—wherever a bright and inquiring mind had something important to offer the rest of the human race. With the first of these texts, he would approach scientists, thinkers, and artists in France and elsewhere in Europe, inspiring them not only to a study of the Oriental texts but also to make the trip to India to learn what could not be learned from books, just as the Chinese had been doing for millennia by sending their brightest students and best scholars to Indian universities and ashrams. But he would not stop there. India was not the only ancient culture with a storehouse of treasure to offer humanity. China was waiting at its borders, and other cultures in Asia who were being eyed greedily for their material wealth and commercial potential while their true treasures were lying neglected in dusty volumes and in the minds that kept alive their intellectual, spiritual, and artistic traditions.

Ambika did not need to be asked to offer her help. She saw immediately the enormous potential for breaking down the barriers that divided their cultures and kept her nation in an economic and political thrall from which it might otherwise need centuries of unnecessary suffering to escape. Almost as soon as its gleam became evident in the mind of Le Gentil, she spied its glow on the horizon as one might spy the polestar rising from the gloaming at day's end. She would help him find those texts and guide their translations. They would embark on this journey together, just as they had traveled together to the ancient seat of the Nayaks, and they would leave their success or failure to the hands of destiny, which had woven its wreath and placed it about both their necks. As their carriage approached the outskirts of Pondicherry, Le Gentil dozing by her side, Ambika reflected on the events of the past fourteen months. She thought back to the day she had first gone to Le Gentil's quarters to begin work as his translator. Within days, she had set to work translating Indian astronomical treatises, partly at his insistence and partly at hers. One volume had led to another, one branch of human knowledge to a second and then a third. The work had been going on more or less unabated for over a year, but only now did she realize why. As she thought this, she found herself staring directly into the eyes of Providence and saw that those eyes were smiling back at her—for, of course, it was Providence who had set them both to work and awakened this idea in their minds once it was time for them to become aware of her designs.

The emotive power of Ambika's realization had its effect on Rodrigo as well. He could not help but reflect on his own recent past. Though he still labored under the emotionally persistent delusion that he was the architect of his journey, his intellect had been initiated into a radically different perspective through the auspices of Saraswati's tutorship. Whenever his mind became quiet enough, he thought he could make out clear traces of a divine authorship in the meanderings that had led him to this juncture in his life. But as with Ambika and Le Gentil, whose future he could but dimly make out in the shadows that populated the far reaches of his mind, his destiny remained shrouded by a veil his eyes could not pierce. The supposition that his future was already written—faultlessly composed in a blend of free verse and off-rhymed stanzas by a Divine Mind capable of the most dramatic turns of fortune conceivable—appealed so much to his literary sensibilities that he now accepted it as a truth that had no need of direct perception to establish its claims. He was also a character but in a novel infinitely more complex than his own. He could feel its clear impress on his mind, so much so that he half expected to surprise the divine gaze with one rapid glance behind him, though all he could see were the mountains hovering silent and calm in the still air. His recent conversations with Saraswati had had a telling influence on his consciousness and his work. If all life was a drama and he, a character, then where was this drama leading him? What unforeseen turns were waiting in the scenes to come? What was the premise, the overall design, the all-important climax? These thoughts preoccupied him most whenever he emerged from his writing, acutely aware that he was transitioning from one dramatic space to another, from the world within his mind to the world that enveloped it. Ambika and Le Gentil's destinies were woven together in much the same way that his and Saraswati's were—disparate permutations of the same infinite, brooding Consciousness. But while theirs glimmered on the horizon like a mirage—which, though it deceives, nevertheless gives some indication of the forces that conjure its existence—his own was still hidden by the curvature of the earth's surface, which hides from view the vast panorama of the universe that contains our tiny portion of infinity.

At the end of each morning session, Rodrigo began to feel more and more as if he were getting up after a long meditation. One day, he saw in a flash of comprehension that writing was indeed nothing more than an extended meditation on the human condition. Why are we hungry for stories, he thought? Why do I sometimes hold my breath, wondering what my characters will do next, and then feel surging clouds of glory when they do something I did not expect but secretly hoped for? Why do I fall into a swift melancholy when they disappoint me by taking the easy path that can only lead to suffering, making cowards of us both? In that moment, he realized why he wrote and why he read and why human beings had gathered around campfires before they had dreamed of books: to listen to the stories that make us rediscover our humanity, over and over again. What were those stories but the reflection of our own lives on the wide-mirrored screen of the storyteller's art? Do we not live through the struggles of these characters from the moment they appear within our imagination? Do we not face the same moral choices and pay the same consequences for our failures with our hidden tears and the sorrow that is forced from our hearts? What was it Chanakya said? Learn from other's mistakes? Yes, and from their triumphs also. Learn from them through the stories that reenact the dance we do from one living day to the next. Drink in their wisdom and suffer through their ignorance, which is your ignorance reflected back at you so that you may come to know who you are. Feed on their tales until you realize that you are humanity, that all the glory and sorrow of the human race lives within your breast and taps its rhythmic drumbeats on the resonant soil beneath your feet. Call it a rehearsal for life, if you will, but this *is* life, for where else do we live but within his infinite imagination, as characters feeling our way into the heart of the human predicament.

He thought back once again to something Saraswati had said, that the measure of a story was the extent to which you emerged from its dreamed experience a better, wiser, more compassionate human being. He had thought her criterion rather reductive at the time. He had even cringed a little when he thought how some of the other professors in his department might react should he voice such an opinion. But on further reflection, he decided that it wasn't limiting at all, except in the sense that it demanded an authenticity and humanity from the writer that could not be feigned. If a writer was able to see into the beating heart of the human struggle and was capable of transporting us there, then it mattered little if the experience he offered us was the simple sorrow of a young girl who has lost her favorite doll, or the transports of the Buddha as he sits under the Bo tree and opens his eyes to see the morning star flash upon a world bathed in the light of illumination. What we hunger for is experience. Each little grain feeds our understanding and hastens us on our way. Perhaps even his simple tale of the Venus transit, though he had become increasingly doubtful of its merits, uncomfortably aware of his characters' stubborn refusal to turn their attention toward more spiritually significant matters.

It was at this time that he found a dog-eared copy of Toni Morrison's *Beloved* in a small shop where tourists could trade in their old paperbacks for a few rupees. When he handed it to Saraswati with the thought that she might like it, he quoted from a magazine interview that he had clipped out years earlier and kept in the drawer of his office desk. When asked how she responded to the contention that her characters were larger than life, the Nobel Prize-winning author had replied, "My characters are not larger than life; life is that large." Saraswati looked startled and then broke into a radiant smile. "That's it! That's what a writer needs to do, to show that life is that large. So large, in fact, that we might as well call it infinite.

For what is life, anyhow, but the way God expresses herself in the world of form? Of course, this cannot really be put into words. But we can try."

It was not only in his personal life and in his writing that Rodrigo found himself confronted by the demands that the stories that he lived and wrote placed upon his growing understanding. His dreams were just as insistent. They occurred more frequently now, but the more they came, the more they remained the same. The girl was his—or rather, he was hers—but the glory of their union could not conceal the terror that seemed to be lurking somewhere up ahead.

Rishikesh
6/24
4:05 AM

Longing, delirium, fear. These are the emotions I wake to these days whenever the dream returns, bequeathed to me by my priest in the hour before dawn—a parting gift, I sometimes think, to remind me just how compelling life really is. This time we had arranged to meet in an abandoned building shortly after dusk—a temple, I believe, but long since fallen into disuse. It may have been my suggestion, I'm not sure, but I felt uncomfortable in those surroundings, and so did she. The inner sanctum was bare of any idol. The walls were missing large chunks of plaster. There were animal droppings in the corners, a clump of dried dung near the entrance where a cow had wandered in. We sat on a stone step in a broken doorway looking out over an overgrown field that was sunk in shadow, the wind moaning softly in our ears. But after a few minutes, the electricity generated by her presence and the familiar intoxication of her impassioned ideas made me lose all notion of our surroundings. We could have been in a cave or on a mountain peak surrounded by clouds, for all it mattered. My world quickly dissolved into the sweet misery of my need for her and the fierce, blissful certainty that she was mine, if only for these short, stolen hours that I refused to let end, by shutting out all thoughts of the future. We talked without ceasing, her hand reaching confidently for mine. The devi was real again, more real than she had ever been in all my long years of worship. I remember thinking, Let the world around us dissolve and disappear; let us be clothed in starlight and drink drafts of space until we merge into emptiness. Then we embraced and all my poetic images were forgotten. The hot lava of the earth rushed into us and burned us until nothing was left but the sound of our suffocated breathing. Afterward, gasping for air, we lay there and looked out at the night. She began to talk again, slowly, like a eulogy. Tantric rites, secret teachings, some temple gossip concerning the elders that was circulating among the staff, vague intimations of the future that I was determined not to understand. A few minutes of exhausted joy before the old fear started creeping back like a returning scout with news of the enemy's unrelenting advance: a moment's misstep, an unnoticed breach of caution, the long-feared discovery, the scandal, the disgrace, the loss of everything I had worked my entire life to achieve. A cold shudder passed through me. I knew that it was just my fancy, that we were safe, for the moment, but I also knew that moment had to end. But then I glanced at her beside me, more beautiful than the stars, wiser than the sacred texts, holier than the image of the goddess on my altar. My fear was beaten back, though it did not go willingly. I woke up to see the stars in my room, glimmering where the ceiling should have been, and was. The fear was still there, tugging at the collar of my nightshirt and dampening my pores.

Is this my love for Saraswati, the goddess who is still beyond my reach, refusing to be calm and speak quiet while my plans are busy being laid? Am I afraid that I will not succeed, or am I afraid I will? Is the beauty of this devi who haunts my dreams the beauty that I see hidden inside the live goddess who haunts my daytime hours? The one whose paltry looks are a defense against a world that would otherwise refuse to leave her in peace? It is time I stop thinking in questions or searching for a parallel means of transport to take me toward my goal. It is what it is. The dream is a dream, the story is a story, and I am the priest who must consecrate his existence by accepting his longings and his fears, who must have the courage to do what is right or else pave the way to hell with his duplicitous and ignoble intentions. This, my consciousness, has split into him and her so that I might prove my strength of character. Or, if not to prove it, then to summon it into existence. Be noble, I tell myself. Be just, be compassionate, be honest. Above all, be courageous. Your dreaming heart will pay the price if you are not.

34

RISHIKESH
7/3
4:20 AM

I woke up this morning beset by a powerful sense of foreboding, something very close to undiluted and unrelenting dread. This is not a poetic conceit, something to endow my characters with once I have found the right words to wrap it in, but a tremulous heat that makes it difficult for me to type. It is a paralysis of sorts, though it is passing quickly, the same overheated angst that I felt in my dream when the roof of my life seemed ready to cave in and bury me in its rubble.

I had been asleep, lying in the little bed of my temple room, the dreamer dreaming! of open skies and freedom, when a knocking at my door aroused me. I was filled with terror. Is that the word? No. Shock would be better, followed by the hot flush of uncertainty. She was lying beside me, blissfully asleep in my arms in that narrow wooden cot, which would not have allowed us to sleep any other way. The door began to creak open and a shot of adrenalin-assisted fright rushed through me like an electric current. I bolted out of the bed, covering her with the sheet in one rapid motion, and rushed to the door, which was already a foot open. My assistant was there with a wax candle in his hand, pushing his insolent face into the doorway. I tried to block the open doorway with my body and engage his eyes with mine so that he wouldn't see the figure in the bed behind me, stifling my anxiety with all the willpower I could summon. He told me that he was sorry to disturb me at this hour, but there was an emergency, an important visitor who had just arrived, and he knew he should not disturb the elder priests. It was, of course, my duty. Ordinarily, I would have thought nothing of it, but I was sure that some semblance of anger showed in my face for several moments before I caught myself and reined it in, along with the fright, the awful fright. Had he seen? Would he go straight to the elders once the sun had risen? Was there something I could do to stop him? But no, nothing was certain, and that only made it worse. I told him I would be down as soon as I was dressed. He turned and left with a sly look on his face, but it appeared to be the same sly look that always inhabited that doubtful countenance. When I closed the door, I could sense that she was awake. Thankfully, the sheet was still over her head. That, perhaps, I thought, might be my saving grace. When she removed it, her face was composed. Her naked body glistened in the faint moonlight that slanted in through the open window. I thrust her sari into her hands and whispered in a pleading tone to wait two minutes and then leave by her usual route, taking all care not to be seen and staying as far as possible from the front courtyard where the visitor was waiting. My heart pounded as I watched her wrap her sari solemnly about her body. There was no trace of worry in her movements, no inordinate hurry. Her motions were calm, her face sunk in resolute repose. For a moment, I was awed by her eerie composure, but then I remembered that it was I who had everything to lose, not her. I was caught by a quick flush of anger, but just as quickly her beauty overwhelmed me. All I could do was watch helplessly as she stole out the door and disappeared into the shadows like the goddess that she was, merging into the kingdom of the night. The moment she was gone, my terror rose up and clutched at my throat. I wrapped my dhoti around my waist and picked up the sacred thread from the night table where she always insisted I leave it, unwilling to recognize the caste superiority it represented. I slung it over my shoulder, muttering the Gayatri mantra like a magic incantation to ward off the evil that seemed to be stalking me, and headed down to the temple enclosure where my assistant was waiting for me with the visitor. The last thing I remember was the look he gave me, a certain gleam in his eyes that felt like the cold breath of Yama, the god of death, on my face.

Now, as I get ready to close my computer and take a cold shower before I sit for meditation, I can still feel that clammy breath, though logic tells me that it is only because the room is sticky with the Indian summer. The long-overdue monsoon is getting ready to break, as I am repeatedly told, and the heat is weighing upon everyone like a kitchen furnace that never shuts down. And yet Saraswati is persistently cheerful, seemingly untouched by the heat. I can see her smiling face in my mind, reminding me that this is just a dream; I have no reason to fear. These dreams belong to a different world. They have their own destiny that may be the destiny of my dreaming self but not of the self that walks along the banks of the river in the shadow of the mountains. I will not let this foreboding enter here where the sun can still be felt, despite the clouds that congregate all day in front of the nearest peaks. Sometime in the next few days I will put the question. Then my fate will be decided—or rather, revealed—and no dream can presage what will happen on that day, whatever fears it may reflect. Only then will I see if this passion play is leading me where I think and hope and pray it is. Saraswati ki jay. All glories to the goddess!

The next days passed slowly for Rodrigo as he carefully summoned his courage and fought back any remaining faintness of heart. The full moon was fast approaching, the last that he would see in Rishikesh. Acknowledging its presence as an integral part of his plan, he asked Saraswati if she would like to accompany him for an evening meditation on the banks of the river, under the light of the full moon. She seemed delighted by the prospect and suggested they forego their evening meal so that their stomachs would not keep their minds tied to the earth. And so everything was set, just as he had imagined it would be during so many solitary moments since returning from the Rimpoche's intensive.

That day Rodrigo found it difficult to write. Instead of spending the morning working on his novel, he recorded his thoughts in his journal and then went to sit in a shaded corner of the ghat where he listened to the river and bared his soul to the silent, smiling Shiva, who had become a kind of surrogate spiritual teacher for him, a mute repository of the wisdom he was seeking. The mute visage of the statue seemed to echo his thoughts as he mused over the sundry ways of destiny. So much could change from one day to the next, he thought, from one minute to the next, all hinging on a simple twist of fate. A fallen log is swept along in the current. It lodges on a boulder by the water's edge and remains there all winter long. In the spring, a family of otters uses it to construct its dam, and another season passes. The log becomes a part of the landscape, part of an enduring home. But what if it glances off the boulder and is thrust back out again into the restless waters, tumbling over the falls and carried at length to the sea. It all depends upon the angle at which it strikes. One degree, more or less, and the balance shifts. The weight of the world is forever altered. And yet even that is according to Shiva's desire, his ever-watchful eye guiding the falling log, hefting its rough bole in his watery palm, feeling the impact against his stone self, watching it carried long miles down to a silt bed where its stored sunlight will one day fuel a future furnace.

The sun crept further into a cleft between two brooding banks of cloud and bathed the smooth white shoulders of the statue in a golden effervescence. Rodrigo's eye lingered on the faint smile that he had first seen nearly one year before. He thought back to that day, to the person he had been and to the person he was now. He had dropped a flower into the water then, and the current had shifted imperceptibly, carrying him back to this same place eleven months later, instead of out to the Bay of Bengal, as it might have done, and from there to the Atlantic shores where he might never have dreamed of the person he had now become. Now the current had brought him to the edge of another cataract, a much longer descent that would change more than just his own life. Less than four weeks until his visa expired and only a few hours before he came to the edge of the precipice. Was he ready? His nervousness made him think not, but Shiva's eternally peaceful gaze told him otherwise. The current would take him where Shiva willed. The great god's smile would follow him as he went, watching over him as he slid past boulders, warmed by the midday sun and silvered by the stars at night. Had it ever been any other way?

They met at eight o'clock. He came to her room to get her, as the occasion rightly warranted. They walked quietly out the gate, silenced by the enormous moon that hung directly in front of them, ascending in its slow course from its bed beneath the stars, up into the wide firmament above the mountains where its muted radiance reflected back to them their dreams and hidden aspirations. In the western sky, he could see Venus's quiet presence lightly dappling the nearest peaks, a luminous augury of his coming fortune. It was all he could have wished for. For some minutes, the incomparable beauty above him almost caused him to forget why they had ventured out into the temple of the night.

They passed into the shadows beyond Ram Jhula, neither of them speaking until they had cleared the wooded path and emerged out onto the paved road that marked the approach to Lakshman Jhula. There the presence of other human beings, the commingled voices, the lights burning in the still-open shops, distracted their attention from the goddess above in her nocturnal contemplation. As if in response to this human concourse, they fell back into their usual easy conversation. Some minutes later, they passed the bridge, and soon, the last building, a small, neglected temple, half hidden by the trees that lined the roadside. Here they left the road and followed a narrow path that skirted the edge of the temple's worn stone walls on its way down to the white sands at the river's edge, about two hundred meters from the long, looming shadow of the bridge that seemed to tremble as it lay suspended against the pale luminescence of the night sky. Gradually their conversation ceased and their thoughts grew still. A single glance between them was enough to know that it was time to begin meditating. Wordlessly, they shut their eyes. The passage of time dissolved into a murmuring of the breeze and a lapping of the waters against the boulders on the far shore. For once, Rodrigo's mind was clear of thoughts. What waited for him afterward seemed an eternity away, and an eternity still remained an hour later when the slow chant of Saraswati's voice called him from his meditation.

After they opened their eyes, they spent a few quiet minutes staring out at the moonlight resting on the water like the veil of the goddess draped over the divan on which she reclines. Then Rodrigo's words, pronounced in something like a whisper, filled the space before them like a song coming across the waters from the lips of an unseen singer.

"This morning I had a talk with the Shiva statue down by the ghat. I don't know if you could call it a conversation, exactly—more of a communion, perhaps—but I do believe he spoke to me in some way. A more sober mind would probably tell me that it was just a combination of the wind and my overactive imagination, but

I like to think that it was his voice I heard. I told you about the ritual I invented to inaugurate my novel? It was almost a year ago that I made that offering before the statue. At the time, I thought of it as an offering to the gods of literature, but as I was performing the ritual, I told the statue that I accepted him as the representative of whatever gods or cosmic forces exist in this world. Then I asked him to fill me with his sacred fire. Today it felt like he was welcoming me back as his disciple and showing me through his smile that he had fulfilled my wish. I don't know if I ever mentioned the poem I used to end the ritual. It went like this…"

Rodrigo paused, raised his voice slightly, and intoned the verses as if he were chanting an ancient Sanskrit mantra: "Today the air is clear of everything. It has no knowledge except of nothingness, and it flows over us without meanings, as if none of us had ever been here before, and are not now: in this shallow spectacle, this invisible activity, this sense."

He smiled as he recalled the feeling he had had that morning, the resonance of the poet's words once again filling him with an inexplicable sense of quietude.

"Today, I repeated the ritual—more or less. I used the same poem to empty myself; then I placed my destiny in Shiva's hands. And now I place it in yours. I have a request to make, but before I do, I want you to know that I make it without any expectations. Let it be as Shiva wills."

Saraswati looked at him, her eyes inquisitive but calm. Rodrigo took a deep breath and looked back out over the river as he spoke, allowing his words to wrap themselves in moonlight.

"I was wondering if you had ever considered the possibility of getting married one day, and if so, would you consider being my bride?"

Though he was not looking at her, he could feel her stiffen at the shock. His own breath stopped. His face flushed but his limbs ran cold. Out of the corner of his eye, he could see a tear glistening on her cheek, reflecting the hushed light of the goddess above who watched and waited for her answer. A long minute passed and then another. With each passing moment, he felt his confidence ebbing until it was barely a whisper that could not be heard over the din of his pounding heart. Finally she started to speak; her voice wavered, she stopped, and then started again.

"Rodrigo…there's something I haven't told you. Now I wish I had, but somehow I couldn't; I don't know why. Before I came to Rishikesh, when I decided to give up journalism, I didn't just decide to give up journalism. I decided to become a sannyasi and dedicate my life to the Mother's service. I went to Benares and begged her to initiate me into her order of monastic disciples, but she wouldn't do it because I am my parent's only means of support. This duty is very important in our culture. Instead, she sent me to Rishikesh. She told me I could live the lifestyle of a sannyasi, but I would have to support my parents until she released me from that responsibility. That's why I'm still here. Waiting for her permission to become a sannyasi. I'm so sorry I didn't tell you earlier. I should have, I know, but…well, now you know."

By this time, Rodrigo's heart was tied in knots, an old constriction that had been waiting for an opportunity to reassert itself. He had thought that he had come to the edge of the river without expectations, ready to allow destiny to seek its course, but now that destiny had opted for the course he had most feared, he saw that his disappointment was a bottomless well into which had disappeared his hopes and his desire. He found himself unable to answer her, unable to look at her, unable to bridge the chasm that had opened up between them.

"Say something," she said, finally breaking the long silence.

Rodrigo breathed a sigh and followed it with a painful effort to re-enter the world of the living. "And you still feel this way?" he asked, struggling to get the words out. "You still plan to be a sannyasi, then?"

"It's my destiny, Rodrigo," she replied, her voice fading to little more than a whisper.

Slowly, Saraswati began telling him the story of how she had accompanied Premananda to her talk and realized in a flash of insight what she wanted to do with her life. Rodrigo listened with his head bowed but his heart slowly coming to life as he perceived the beauty of her desire, even as his heart welled with tears.

"I realized that day that nothing can bow a spirit that refuses to be bowed, and no amount of money or social justice can help someone who has lost faith in life and in God. I want to give people that faith, Rodrigo, and I don't think there is any better way to do that, at least for me, than to be a sannyasi in the Mother's service. She is my ideal and I mean to follow in her footsteps."

Saraswati touched him lightly on the hand. "I care about you very deeply, Rodrigo. I think you know that, even if I've never come out and said it. But this is my destiny. I have to follow the path that has been set out for me. I hope you will understand and forgive me for any pain I've caused you."

Rodrigo made no effort to hide that pain, but when he spoke, his voice sounded clearer and stronger than it had a few minutes earlier. "Of course. How could I do otherwise?"

But that was as far as his words could take him.

They walked back into the same silence through which they had come, accompanied by the veiled eyes of the moon and the distant glance of Venus as she continued her sentinel's vigil in the obsidian depths of the western sky. When they parted in the front courtyard, Rodrigo thought he noticed a tremor in Saraswati's hands as she held them to her breast in the traditional gesture. For a moment, he wondered at the pain she might be feeling over his fateful indiscretion. Then she disappeared and he was alone with his sorrow. His eyes filled with tears as he approached the steps to his second-story room. When he reached the landing, he paused for a moment on unsteady feet. A shadow fell across him. He looked up to see a dark cloud hiding the pale face of the moon and others advancing silently across the sky. He remained there and watched with clouded eyes as the stars went out, one by one, until only Venus remained, impossibly distant and impersonal. For a moment, he imagined he heard her laughter blowing by him and ruffling his shirt. Then he went into his room and everything turned black.

PART THREE

DEVI

35

FOR THE FIRST TIME in nearly a year, Rodrigo slept through his alarm. It wasn't until the sun crested the mountains and found its way through his open window that he rubbed his groggy eyes and sat up on the bed. For a few moments he was disoriented. Then he remembered why he felt so poorly and why he was waking up at what had become a strange hour indeed to be opening one's eyes. The morning practice in the main hall had already ended and Amrita's yoga class was about to begin, but he did not regret having missed the former and he had no intentions of attending the latter. He was quite sure, without needing to analyze his feelings, that the company of other human beings would only make things worse. His was not a sorrow that bore sharing. He would nurse it in private, as he had always done, though he hoped he had better results this time. For he was a yogi now, far better prepared for the life of a recluse, even if the motive for his seclusion was not a desire for God realization but the intense sorrow of romantic rejection. He would spend his time meditating and writing. He would meet his demons head on with no excuses, in the full awareness that the source of his sorrow was within him and in no way dependent on the sentiments of a woman who had her own path to walk, her own samskaras to deal with. For the three weeks that remained to him, he would maintain the same course he had been on these many months, the only difference being that he would walk and study alone, in the true condition of the spiritual path in which we are always alone with our Higher Self, no matter how many breathing bodies surround us. It was only prudent under the circumstances that he avoid Saraswati, but this did not mean that he would run from his pain. It only meant that this was one battle he would fight alone. It should be easy enough to arrange. He knew her habits so well by now that he should have little problem turning into a ghost and allowing himself to be carried away by the wind.

Not unexpectedly, Rodrigo found it exceedingly difficult at first to concentrate on his writing, but rather than feel troubled by the marshlands he encountered, he welcomed the challenge. His preoccupation with his characters and their story gradually helped him to shunt aside his preoccupation with his own, less-fruitful drama. Though Ambika's presence in his mind was not nearly enough to make up for the lack of Saraswati's presence by his side, it was enough to fill Le Gentil's world with frequent eddies of joy and holy intimations of an enchanted future. Living vicariously, as he did, through his characters, Rodrigo took strength from their absorption in a world that far antedated his own and used it as a bulwark during his meditations and his walks, when he had no choice but to grapple with the powerful feelings that were mostly held in abeyance by the enchanted atmosphere of his literary wanderings.

On the third day of his self-imposed exile, the long-overdue monsoon broke. The sky became so dark by late morning that if it were not for his watch, he might have sworn it was dusk. Just before noon, the winds swept down from the mountains with a deafening roar that drowned out the sound of his own thoughts. Minutes later the heavens opened and he experienced firsthand the meaning of the word "deluge." When the downpour paused almost an hour later, holding its heavenly breath like a Titan waiting for his minions to slink from their shelters so he can sport with them again, Rodrigo slipped out of the ashram to find water coursing everywhere, rushing merrily down streets and gutters, cascading off rooftops and hillsides, turning his surroundings into a movie set from a biblical epic. He rolled his thin cotton pants above the knees, held his black umbrella aloft like a standard, and marched out of the devastation as if he were marching out of the wreckage of his own life. Gloomy but resolute, he set out in the direction of Lakshman Jhula, until he came to the Italian restaurant where he had once sat with the other students from Saraswati's morning philosophy class and exchanged gossip about their remote and enigmatic teacher, a fitting place, he decided, to sort through the rubble of his shattered dreams.

The second-floor balcony was surprisingly empty. Its only occupant was an Indian teenager in a t-shirt and jeans, who was leisurely mopping up the puddles of water deposited by the rain blowing over the balustrade. Rodrigo took a seat at the same table where he had sat to celebrate Clara's departure. The boy leaned his mop against one of the pillars that supported the overhanging concrete roof and brought him a menu, which he placed wordlessly on the table. It was the third time Rodrigo had been to this restaurant. Though he read through the list of offerings carefully, on the off hope that he might encounter some nectarean dish he had overlooked on his two previous visits, he already had an idea what he would order, and he saw nothing in the menu to persuade him otherwise. It had been a full day since he had eaten, a fact that had almost completely escaped him until a few hours earlier when he had finally identified the pain in his stomach as a ravenous hunger, rather than the more poetic torment of the rejected lover he had assumed it to be. He closed the menu and called for the boy, who pulled a small lined notepad and a stub of a pencil from the back pocket of his jeans and took down the order without a single glance at his patron. As the boy shuffled off and disappeared down the steps to the hidden kitchen from where the musky odor of a wood-burning stove ascended the stairs like incense from a temple, Rodrigo remembered with a rueful grimace how long he had waited for his food on the previous occasion. Adding into his calculations the likelihood that he was the first customer of the day, he calculated that it would not be less than forty-five minutes before his eggplant Parmesan, calzone with homemade mozzarella, and tomato-and-basil soup would be ready. More than enough time for Saraswati's ghost to best him in an ethereal bout of hand-to-hand combat before the food arrived to deaden the impact of her rapier-like thrusts, but even this had the telltale markings of fate all over it. At least his lime juice and seltzer water arrived in short order to provide him with a modicum of sustenance that was denied his ghostly adversary.

While his drink did little to assuage the gnawing demands of his hunger, it helped him face the spectral images that populated his mind, many of which should have been familiar to him. This was not the first time he had been turned down by a woman with whom he had fallen in love, but it was the first time that the woman in question had been his best friend—not that it made it any easier to take: the problem in having become such close friends was the certainty he felt that he would never meet another woman who would understand him as she did or hold in her hand the promise of an intimacy that a mere romantic passion could never approximate. He was no stranger to romance. He had suffered through several pedestrian affairs before Beth. He had watched its idealized appearances on the silver screen with varying degrees of fascination and dismay, hoping to discover there the secrets that might redeem his own failed efforts. He had recreated impassioned scenes from the world's classic novels countless times in the dexterous theater of his imagination. But nothing in his experience could compare with the intimacy that had grown up between him and Saraswati these past few months. No woman he had ever known had possessed more than a pale reflection of her transcendent charms, not even the creations of his own mind, who, before her entrance into his life, had no suitable model on which to drape their insubstantial selves. The thought of enjoying her company for the rest of his life held him fast like a powerful magnet, while the thought of losing her to the pitiless demands of destiny cut into him like a samurai's self-impaled dagger. But that was the price that destiny had exacted. He would not turn his face away from that uncompromising fact. It was not simply her destiny, he knew, that had cheated him, but his own as well. As he looked out over the balustrade at the lustrous sheen of the Himalayan pines just across the road, their brown-and-green spires pointing toward heaven, the thin ribbon of the Ganges peaking out from behind them, he remembered her first class on samskara and the light that had seemed to illumine the musty interiors of his psyche. Nothing without a purpose. Nary a whisper of the wind that is not part of an infinite design. No effect without a cause, and no one to blame for his predicament but his own torpid self, tarrying blind and self-absorbed down the back lanes of his former lives, setting him up for this consummate fall. His mind, with a year of yogic philosophy at its back, told him that he was only getting what he deserved. He had laid the foundations of his presently occurring future with the quarry stone of his previous actions. But his heart was not ready to accede to what his mind so readily grasped. He was here at this table—suffering a self-inscribed tragedy, in a self-imposed exile—because he knew he could not see her without tasting once again that well-meaning rejection, so bitter in his mouth. He knew he could not look upon her face without knowing that his own face betrayed how little progress he had made. He could not accept her destiny gracefully and be happy for her because he was attached; and because he was attached, he was deaf to the unerring whispers of his own destiny. All this he knew, as perfectly as he knew Hamlet's Act Three, Scene One soliloquy, and yet he still could not escape the fires that burned within the walls of his ego's retreat, like an arsonist who forgets to unbolt the door before he commits his disgraceful act and then finds himself trapped within his own designs when the lock is melted by the flames.

Rodrigo went to the top of the stairs and ordered another lime juice and seltzer water, calling down to the boy whom he could see lounging on a chair near the entrance with his eyes glued to a glossy magazine. When he returned to his seat, he recalled sitting around that same table ten months earlier with his fellow students, at a time when his mind was not yet attached but nevertheless mired in an ignorance far deeper than the one in which he now stood. By then, he had already begun to gain some measure of emotional stability, the precursor to a mental calm that now seemed completely and irrevocably lost, but he knew that it had only been the torpid pleasure of remaining in bed, ignorant of the responsibilities that come with being awake. Awakening to consciousness demanded that one face one's sorrows and embrace them without any thought of striking out in search of an easier road. "Pain, when met head on, without any vacillation, contains within it the virtues of a magic elixir, the capacity to transform the mind that longs to remain asleep into one that recognizes the hard-won beauty of waking into full consciousness." When Saraswati first told him this, he had found it difficult to believe that she had ever faced the pains that ordinary mortals face, but now, having covered some of the same road that she had walked, he knew that the branding irons that marked the forehead of the awakened soul were as hot and as fierce as any that burned through skin and seared the flesh. He had rubbed enough of the sleep from his eyes to know that there was no turning back and no turning away. The pain was his legacy to himself, as the light of freedom would be on the day it dawned in his mind, fruit of the efforts he was now making and would continue to make.

As Rodrigo finished his second lime juice and seltzer water, he recalled the last time he had fought through the painful bonds of romantic attachment. It had not been so very long ago. Then he had been able to escape into his cynicism, his anger, and his righteous conviction that he was the victim and Beth the culprit—turbulent emotions that conveniently concealed the imprint of his own hands on those events and temporarily blinded him to a loss that might have otherwise consumed him. That avenue was now closed to him, despite the fact that those impulses were still there, clamoring to be set free. His consciousness would not allow it. The clarity he had gained through ten and a half months of dedicated meditation and spiritual study was like a palmful of smelling salts held to the nose of an unconscious man. It burned his nostrils and refused to let him sleep. The bitterness forced him to open his eyes to the reality in front of him. The only choices left to him were the ones that Saraswati had been instilling in him since the day he first sat down under the banyan tree to participate in her class: He would have to face his fears, knowing that fear was the greatest obstacle and never far from his pain. He would have to accept his attachment for what it was, with no mystic veil draped over it to hide the blemishes, and then work steadily to leave it behind, knowing that the road ahead was only open to those who learned to love without attachment or self-interest. Above all, he would have to keep walking the path, no matter how difficult those steps might be. Saraswati would not have it any other way, and neither would he. Though the idea that henceforth he would have to swallow the bitter with the sweet and honor them both equally seemed more like a tragic complication than a necessary part of the hero's journey, he knew he had no other choice. There comes a point in the journey, he told himself, when the old life, with its unconscious joys and melodramatic sorrows, cannot be recovered.

A sharp pang of nostalgia cut through him as he thought back to the person he had been, that beloved figure from his life story who seemed to be on the verge of being lost forever. Maybe it was okay, he thought, to grieve for the loss of who he had once been, even for a life lived under the shadow of ignorance—but only briefly, as briefly as could be managed. All that was permitted here was a passing sorrow. Soon he would have to fix his eyes up ahead, never to look back. Thinking this, he realized that he was grieving as much for the loss of his dying self as he was for the loss of the dream that had ended with Saraswati's gentle denial. As he looked across the table at the ghosts of his past, he recognized them to be phantoms sustained by the unrequited desires that were the true source of his suffering, insubstantial images of light upon the screen of consciousness and nothing more. He reached out to touch them, but all his hand encountered was a cold emptiness before it recoiled. And into that emptiness fell the greater part of the weight that had been upon his back. He was not quite ready to laugh yet, but he was finally ready to look ahead.

The boy reappeared, balancing a tray of food on one upraised hand. Soon Rodrigo's hunger pangs were gone. His sorrow remained, but there was no longer any residue left of the sharp spasms of intermittent agony that had followed Saraswati's not-unexpected denial of his claim upon her heart. He would nurse that sorrow while it lasted and learn from it what he could. Somewhere deep inside, a voice called on him to follow that sadness and not let it go, to let it lead him inward, into the heart of all living beings, where sorrow sits at the right hand of joy and instructs her in the nuances of the Divine.

It was a voice he knew he could not ignore.

That night Rodrigo dreamed again of his temple retreat. Behind the veiled lids of his eyes, he discovered that the sorrow that weighed upon his waking hours had settled into his sleeping ones. Once he awoke, he recognized that it was only fitting. He could not leave this struggle until he had learned the lessons that had been set out for him to learn. By now, he was aware that the act of falling asleep was only a change of venue, not of substance. Nothing of any real import differed on either side of that shadowy vale.

Rishikesh
7/12
5:10 AM

My worst fears have been realized: I have been found out. Yes, I was only dreaming, but that hardly seems to matter. I am who I am; the fact that I was dreaming does not change that.

This time I was reclining in my room after the noon meal when there came a knock at the door. With a touch of annoyance in my voice, I told whomever it was to come in. Everyone knows I do not like to be disturbed when I am taking rest after my meal. But as soon as I saw the face of my assistant insinuate itself in the open doorway, my annoyance changed to apprehension. For some days, I had been avoiding him as best I could, as if by avoiding him I could hold off the terrible noose that seemed to be swaying portentously above my head. He was overly polite as he entered the room with a sheaf of papers and placed them on my desk, some important documents I needed to sign. His unaccustomed unctuousness made me feel even more uncomfortable, since his politeness had been steadily eroding over the previous months. Something must have ignited it. Knowing him, it could not be an augury of good intentions. While I was perusing those papers, he sat down on the empty chair without waiting to be asked, a small slight that nevertheless thoroughly annoyed me. When I finished signing the papers and handed them to him, he said he wished to make a small request. His words were accompanied by a smile, the kind of smile I have seen from usurers who are getting ready to cheat their clients, those poor souls who, despite knowing that they are likely to be cheated, are in no position to do anything about it. I remained silent, meeting his lack of proper courtesy with some measure of my own. With a voice as oily as clarified butter, he said that his brother who lived in a northern district was sick and needed attending to. He would like to request a short leave from his duties. Of course, he would also need money for his journey and for his brother's care; a hundred rupees should do.

It was a substantial sum, and I said so as coldly as possible, without drawing any attention to the complete and utter impropriety of the request. "I believe this is very little to ask," he told me, "if you take into consideration Your Excellency's delicate position." He then assured me in an apologetic tone, which did nothing to mask his intention, that he would be back at his duties in three weeks, four at the most, as attentive as ever. Both of us were well aware of his unspoken implication: by assuring my prestigious future as the high priest in the temple, he was assuring his own as well. His smile reminded me of the fresh-water crocodiles that I have seen near the banks of the Ganges, vicious creatures that seem to smile at you with their crooked teeth while they wait for you to place an unsuspecting foot in the water and thereby furnish their next meal. There was a malicious gleam in his eye that was far more explicit than any words could have been. I knew right away that he knew everything. More than likely, the incident of the earlier night had only confirmed what he had already suspected, since he betrayed not the slightest hint of shock or surprise. I knew immediately that he would not betray me as long as I acceded to his whims and his desires to lead a comfortable, well-respected life. I realized also that his demands, though far from insubstantial, would never be more than I could manage, since he knew as well as anyone the extent of the power and wealth a person in my position commands. I nodded my head and asked him to come by my room that evening. No more words passed between us. None were needed. It was a tacit agreement that I could live with. I was not about to give up all that I had worked for, and I could sense that with him my position was safe. We needed each other. As much as I might have despised him at that moment, there is a confidence generated by the symbiosis of creatures who live off each other that is hard to find outside the sphere of their mutual, parasitic dependence. Strangely enough, when he went out and I lay down again, my mind was more settled than it had been in days. I was not bothered by thoughts of the girl or fears of a scandal. I fell almost immediately into a satisfied slumber, and it was from that slumber that I seemed to awake in my ashram bed.

Now, as I reflect on this dream in the light of my present trials and tribulations, I feel somewhat disgusted with myself for the crude complacency I showed. My worst fears were swept away with a bribe, with money that was not my own but offered to the goddess by innocent and trusting devotees. And this is the reason for my sound, untroubled slumber! I have no need to look for hidden connections between this dream and my waking consciousness. It reveals the dreamer as he really is—as clear as day, though it be night—selfish, unscrupulous, unabashedly attached to prestige, power, and comfort, for all his spiritual sensibilities and intellectual gifts. If that is my character, at least one aspect of it, stripped to the bone by the x-ray eye of the subconscious mind, and if I am the product of all my past actions, then how can I wonder when I ride into India on a wave of self-inflicted misfortune and finish my sojourn here by getting turned down by the one woman I have truly loved? No cause without an effect, and no effect without a cause. We get what we deserve in this earthly drama. How could I have thought otherwise? I wanted a goddess to be my wife, without ever once stopping to think that if she really were a goddess, what would she want with me?

36

THE LAST FEW DAYS had been, by Saraswati's reckoning, the longest of her life. Four days ago she and Rodrigo had gone to the riverside together to meditate, bathed in the purest mantle of molten moonlight. She had thought it incredibly beautiful. The silence was better than music, and the slow breathing of Rodrigo beside her was better than silence. She had no wish to speak, but when Rodrigo began speaking, she listened to him as she had once listened to the waves on the beach at Konark, within sight of the famous Sun Temple, whose medieval sculptures had embarrassed her with their erotic interpretations of a mystical union. She had found the waves at Konark immensely calming. They were nature's poetry, lapping the shores of the world with their divine syllables. Rodrigo's voice calmed her in the same way, and his words were no less poetry to her ear. But then came the words that had left her in shock, swelling her eyes with tears that she hid by turning her face toward the river and keeping it there while she answered him.

She had never imagined that he might ask her to marry him, though the thought of what it might be like to be married to so spiritual a man had already made its way to the shores of her conscious mind. Prior to the time her parents had tried to betroth her, she had never given any serious thought to marriage, apart from a few fleeting childhood fantasies that soon turned to aversion. She had never found an adequate explanation for her youthful distrust of men, but later, when she had seen the effects of their perfidy, their arrogance, and their selfishness on a daily basis in her travels, she had thought it just as well that she had grown up with this innate inoculation against what was for many a devastating infirmity. The vaccine, however, had eventually worn off. Once Vikram slipped her defenses and exposed her hidden weakness, she had given herself up to elaborate musings about the marriage she felt sure was looming on her horizon. Perhaps the fact that she had allowed her imagination such free rein in that regard had contributed heavily to the bitter disappointment she felt afterward when she discovered that he was little better than the legions of village men who cheated on their wives and made only the barest of efforts to conceal their tracks. Once she let go of her bitterness, she wondered what had ever possessed her to get involved with a man who had no interest in spirituality and no great zeal for social justice. But Rodrigo was nothing like Vikram. He was the first and only man who had ever asked her to marry him, and had she not been committed to becoming a sannyasi, she would have thought him the ideal man with whom to share her life. He was her closest friend, a comrade in all that was important to her, perhaps the only true friend she had ever known—something she would not have thought possible the day he turned down the ashram path to the banyan tree and awakened samskaras she had supposedly cremated, their ashes scattered to the winds. Losing his friendship now, unfairly endangered by the heedless fires of romantic desire, would be an unwelcome tragedy after all that they had been through.

That night, when Saraswati returned from the river, she could not sleep. His question continued to burn inside her as the hours passed and her body tossed and turned. The fires raged until she discovered, to her dismay and her surprise, that her answer had been a reflex, the mere retelling of the past rather than an honest attempt to look unencumbered into the future. She sat up in her bed as the force of her realization banished any possibility of sleep. The glowing dial of her bedside clock showed 2:45 AM Crossing her legs, she took her mind back to her last visit to the Mother. The words that had appeared so enigmatic at the time seemed to gather shape in the darkness of her room. Their edges sharpened until their outlines became clearly distinguishable. Finally, she shook her head and a caustic, muffled laugh escaped her lips. Thirty-six and still a fool! She had gone to the Mother with the idea of finding out how she could best avoid a precarious attachment on the way to a goal she considered as immovable as the Jagannath temple in Puri, which had already withstood the onslaught of ten centuries. But she had forgotten that a woman's desires and her samskaras can sometimes be poles apart. The Mother had been quick to remind her. As soon as Saraswati broached her concerns, the aged saint sat up ramrod straight on her cot. Rapping herself several times on her chest with her closed fist, she said, "Look at me; am I afraid of fear? No, fear is afraid of me. Am I afraid of clash? No, clash is afraid of me." The Mother's unbreakable determination crashed over her like a mighty wave, surging with the weight of her battle-edged words. "What is important," she continued in the same iron tone, "is not where your destiny is leading you, but whether or not you have the courage to meet it. You cannot run from this samskara; if you do, it will follow you into the next life, as it has followed you into this one. It is time for you to stop running and face what you have not been willing to face in the past, regardless of the dangers it entails. But beware: the heart can be a cruel mistress. She will keep you prisoner until you prove to her that you are willing to seek your freedom without sacrificing her love." Unable to comprehend the import of these words, she tried to rephrase her question, but the Mother fixed her with a stare and the question died on her lips. She prostrated and went to the rear balcony, looking out over the marble steps of the bathing ghat down to the banks of the Ganges, the wide, murky waters so different from the same river in Rishikesh, some eight hundred kilometers upstream. There she meditated on the Mother's words, hoping for the light of understanding to pierce through the veil, but a solution to her dilemma seemed no closer than when she had set out for the Mother's ashram several days earlier.

Weeks later, the mist was finally clearing. She could not run from Rodrigo or from her feelings. Whatever the dangers—and she was well aware how quickly the rugged cords of attachment could bind a living soul to the grinding wheel of birth and death—she would have to learn to navigate them, as she had learned to navigate so many other dangers in the past. As would he, though his struggle would perhaps be fiercer, for the swift eddies of romantic desire were seemingly threatening to unmoor his mind, as he had intimated with his proposal that was branded into her consciousness like a mantra that continued to repeat itself on the in-and-outgoing tides of her breath. Did she still want to be a sannyasi? It was a question she would have not dared ask herself before this night. It was, in fact, a question she would have not even thought to ask, so irrevocable seemed her future. But now, in the revealing light of the Mother's words and all that had happened since, she could not be true to her destiny if she did not ask it. The original meaning of the word *sadhu*, "renunciant," was "honesty," and no one could be truly honest if she was not honest with herself. As the glowing dial of her clock crept slowly toward the first blush of dawn, Saraswati sat on her bed and meditated on her desires and her dreams. Before long, the answer came rising up out of her subconscious like a slowly gathering mist: yes, she still wanted to be a sannyasi—but not yet. She now knew that she was not ready and would not be ready until she had lived through her samskara with Rodrigo and imbibed the lessons that were inscribed upon its gradually unfolding petals. This, obviously, was why the Mother had sent her to Rishikesh. She had to mature before she would be ready to don the saffron robes, and her maturation would not be complete until she had walked with Rodrigo the stretch of road that they were meant to walk together. She had been his teacher, and still was, in some ways, but he was also hers. This was a lesson they would have to learn together.

The next afternoon, weary from her sleepless night and the extended struggle with her tempestuous thoughts, Saraswati waited for Rodrigo on the bench outside her room, rehearsing over and over again the words she planned to say to him. When he didn't appear, she passed by his room and was surprised to see the padlock fastened. The thought that he would go for his afternoon walk without her brought on a momentary flash of anger. Could he be trying to punish her for her determination to become a sannyasi? Was he going to let that get in the way of their friendship? Then she realized, chagrined, that he must still be hurting from her refusal to marry him. She was hardly an expert in such matters, having nothing to fall back on for wisdom, other than a few symbolic scenes from the devotional literature on her shelf and the mostly forgotten snatches of conversation from her earlier life that she had barely paid attention to at the time. But she was not entirely without any worldly sense. Obviously, he needed some space to put his emotions back in order. No matter how much progress he had made, he had only been meditating for less than a year. She mustn't forget that.

When Rodrigo didn't show for arati, she thought it just as well, and again, when he was nowhere to be seen on the following day. When he didn't show up for their walk on the third day, however, she began to lose patience. The Mother's words applied to him as much as they did to her. Nothing could be solved by running away, either from her or from his feelings. He must know that their friendship was just as important to her as it was to him. The emotions were not easy on either side, but that did not stop her from showing up for their walk. There were things that needed to be said and telepathy was not the answer. When she passed by his room and saw the padlock announcing his absence, she left the ashram to see if she could find him on one of their usual routes, but there was no sign of him, and the heavy rains of the breaking monsoon soon sent her scurrying back to her room. After arati, she again passed by his room but he was not there. As usual, she went to her room for meditation, but midway through her practice the thought occurred to her that he might have left the ashram. Her stomach went cold, and for the first time in years she felt a sense of panic. She told herself that Rodrigo would never do such a thing, but the thought persisted, making a mockery of her meditation. When her clock showed eight, she got up from her blanket and went down to the office just as the guests were starting to trickle in for dinner. Manu, a tall, thin native of Haridwar who had been on the ashram staff for more than ten years, was seated in front of the computer, deliberately entering some data with his two index fingers. Saraswati asked what seemed like a suitable question about the activities calendar for the coming month, waving hello to some of her students as they passed by the open doorway, her eye attentive for any sign of Rodrigo. Then, as nonchalantly as possible, she mentioned that she hadn't seen Rodrigo for several days. Was he still at the ashram? Manu raised an eyebrow as he looked at her, a gesture that made her feel vaguely uncomfortable. "He's here," he said. "But if you're looking for him, you won't find him in the dining hall. He sent word a few days ago that he was going to be doing a cleansing diet this week, so he wouldn't be taking his meals in the dining hall." Saraswati tried to keep the sense of relief from showing on her face. Obviously, he was doing his best to avoid her, but at least he hadn't done anything more foolish than that.

Now, on the following morning, fresh from her meditation, Saraswati decided that enough was enough. They had things to discuss, lessons to learn that could only be learned together. She respected whatever emotional difficulties he was dealing with, but since when did difficult emotions take precedence over the spiritual companionship that had become such an important part of both their lives? Her morning classes on the previous days had been fuller than they had been in months, but her days had been emptier. She had grown so used to sharing her thoughts and spiritual investigations with Rodrigo, relying on him for the give-and-take that invariably brought out the best in her, that without him her thoughts seemed like the petty carping of a middle-aged housewife. Without the firm anchor of his sea green eyes that seemed to grasp her ideas when no one else could, her thoughts began to drift haphazardly, stubbornly resisting her efforts to secure them. The buoyancy she had felt these last few months was steadily waning, and she knew exactly what to attribute it to. She had become dependent on their friendship in a way that only became conspicuous by its absence. These, she knew, were the dangerous waters that the Mother had alluded to. She had become attached, and attachment had its consequences. But as the Mother had clearly said, this was one battle she could not win by running away—not that that was even an option any longer. They would have to ride their attachment to its predetermined end and take care that they not be thrown by its wild and unpredictable bucking. If she wished to be a true sannyasi one day, and in time, a realized sage, she would need to learn to sublimate these feelings, to drive them upward as one drove the kundalini toward the crown chakra, transforming attachment and conditional love into non-attachment and unconditional love, and a latent passion into active compassion. Rodrigo was not only her best friend; he was her samskara made flesh, a divinely ordained opportunity to emerge victorious in an interior battle that she had run from in previous lifetimes—or else fought, only to be defeated. This time she would be equal to the test. Her heart would not keep her a prisoner. She would prove to the Mother, and to herself, that she could love this man without being overcome by passion or attachment, and without forsaking her vow to serve the Mother in the saffron robes of a renunciant. But she couldn't well achieve this if she didn't see him. It could not be done alone; it was a battle that required two contestants—not him against her, but each against herself on the staging grounds of their relationship.

As soon as her meditation was over, Saraswati went straight to Rodrigo's room, determined to put an end to his seclusion. She was relieved to see that the door was bolted from the inside, cutting off any avenue of escape. She knocked. When he did not answer, she planted herself on the step in front of his door and called out to him as firmly as she knew how. "Rodrigo, I am not leaving here until you let me in, so you might as well open the door." She waited a couple of minutes; when there was no sound from inside the room, she repeated her proclamation and sat down on the step to wait him out. This time she heard a stirring from within. A minute or two later, the door opened and a dour-faced Rodrigo invited her in with a resigned shrug of his shoulders.

The room was in a disheveled state, very unlike him, as she remembered from the one time she had been inside it. The bed was still unmade. From the fresh indentation in the pillow, she guessed that he had still been meditating when she'd knocked. She was not about to excuse herself, however, for disturbing his meditation. She took a seat on the chair in front of his desk, while he sat cross-legged on the edge of his bed.

"You've been avoiding me," she said, unable to keep the accusatory tone from her voice.

Rodrigo shrugged his shoulders once again. "Would you expect any different, after the other night?"

"Yes, I would. I can understand what you're feeling. It's only natural, but you're a yogi now. You have to rise above those feelings—and don't roll your eyes at me. You know the philosophy. This is our samskara; we have to accept it for what it is—both of us have to, myself included. Things can't always be exactly how we'd like them to be. We have to accept that and move on; otherwise, we're just going to suffer for no good reason. Remember what the Mother said: God gave us two eyes in the front of our heads so we can look ahead, not behind. We both have a mission to fulfill in this life, and for me, becoming a sannyasi is part of that mission. But it doesn't mean our relationship is any less important to me than it is to you. Remember what I told you the other day—I don't believe we can truly love God unless we can truly love another human being with all our heart. We just need to learn to do it without attachment and without expectations, that's all."

Rodrigo let out what sounded like a laugh, though the expression on his face was more of disbelief. "That's all? You make it sound so easy."

"I didn't say it was easy. I just meant that it's not hard to understand what we have to do. It's not easy for me, either, but it's not like we have any choice. That's the price we have to pay if we want to become enlightened. There's no easy way around it. So what do you say? Are you ready to move forward now? My room, two thirty as usual?"

Rodrigo threw up his hands in a gesture of mock surrender. "Okay, okay, I give up. I'll be there."

"Good. I'm glad that's over. We have a lot to talk about. I have to start preparing my class now, but I want you to make two photocopies of your passport and visa. I need you to go to the office and leave them with Shankar. Before nine. You'll also need to complete the application forms he has for you. I've already filled in some of the information; all you need to add is your personal data and your signature. He is going to Delhi today and I asked him to drop off your paperwork at the Foreign Registration Office and the Ministry of Home Affairs so we can apply for your research visa. In two weeks you will officially be a visiting scholar. I spoke to a Mr. Rao at the Ministry of Home Affairs, Foreigners Division. It's in Lok Nayak Bhavan. Write down the address." She waited for Rodrigo to get his notebook and a pen. "He's expecting the papers this afternoon—if Shankar gets there before closing—or else first thing tomorrow morning. And he'll be expecting you next week or the week after, before your visa runs out. You have to show up there at least one day before your visa expires for the obligatory interview, so he can complete the application process and give you your new visa. You should also thank the swami, first chance you get. He was kind enough to make a call for me and that was all it took. The rest is just a formality."

37

$\mathcal{A}$FTER SARASWATI LEFT, RODRIGO went down to the office to make the photocopies and fill out the forms, glad that she had forcibly ended his self-imposed seclusion, though he knew it would not be easy to regain the free and intimate camaraderie they had enjoyed before he had overstepped his reach. He spent the rest of the morning working on his book. He had begun sketching out the day of the Venus transit two days earlier—the climatic scene, according to his original plan, though things had changed so much since then that the scene no longer had the same meaning he had originally attributed to it. The final outcome would be up to his characters, and he could only guess what they might do. Two things, however, were certain. One was dictated by Le Gentil's actual journals and the blow that fate had struck from what should have been a cloudless sky on Sunday morning, the fourth of June, 1769. The other was his own mood. He doubted he would ever be in a position better suited to write this scene than he was now. The downward cast of his dreams and the despondency brought on by Saraswati's rejection had prepared him perfectly, as surely as if it had been planned ahead of time by the Cosmic Playwright—as it undoubtedly had.

Le Gentil and Ambika had spent the weeks that followed their belated return from Madurai preparing the observatory for that fateful day. All during the month of May and into early June, the morning skies had been cloudless, a billowing blue ocean that lifted Le Gentil's spirits in a manner similar to the way he felt them lifted whenever he caught a glimpse of Ambika's eyes, those dark, smiling fountains in which he saw reflected the whole of his future, a wide, glorious expanse that was sheltered in her watchful presence. The English at Madras had sent him an excellent achromatic telescope, three feet long, to go along with the fifteen-foot reflecting telescope that he had brought with him. Each evening, he ascended to the observation deck to observe the night sky through both of his priceless treasures. The stars barely twinkled, a token of the pristine clarity of the South Indian skies at that time of year, thankfully free of the persistent haze that made the stars above Paris so inconstant in their light. He was able to see Jupiter in greater detail than he had ever seen it before; with the addition of the achromatic telescope, he was able to witness the emersion of Jove's first satellite with astonishing clarity.

As the day of Venus's transit of the sun approached, his impatience grew. Nine long years he had been in Asia, nearly seventy thousand miles of travel, having set sail on the twenty-sixth of March, 1760, to measure the elliptic conjunction of Venus with the sun. He could still taste the disappointment in his mouth from having failed to record the first transit eight years earlier. At long last his vindication was at hand. Soon he would be able to sail back to France a hero, secure in the knowledge that his name would be written into the annals of scientific achievement for all time to come. But this was not his only coming triumph, for he intended to sail back with an even greater prize: a woman who had no equal, in beauty or in brains, on either side of the globe.

With the sense of timing he considered essential to his work as an astronomer, he invited Ambika to the observation deck for lunch on the day before the transit. That morning, he had instructed Jiddu to set up an awning and gave him precise orders as to the menu, which he tailored specifically to the occasion. Though it was hot, there was a steady breeze coming off the ocean that made it feel quite pleasant. The sight of Pondicherry spread out below them, and the ocean beyond, reflecting the brilliant June sun like a turquoise mirror especially fashioned for a queen, seemed so beautiful to his wandering eyes that the thought of leaving such beauty behind cleaved him with a sharp pang of regret. But fast on its heels, the thought that the Coromandel coast's most precious jewel might be coming with him offered him all the solace he needed. He took Ambika's hand in his own, and with his free hand he pointed toward the eastern horizon, following the sleek lines of the two proud telescopes.

"You see there to the north. That is where Venus will set tomorrow morning, just as the sun is rising to greet her. At a few minutes to seven, she will egress the face of the sun. The timing needs to be measured within a few seconds to give us useful data. If I can measure the conjunction within two seconds, then I will be able to measure the sun's parallax to a precision of 1/40th of an arcsecond, which will provide our distance to the sun with an unprecedented precision of one part in five hundred. Add this to the observations that will take place tomorrow in different parts of the globe by my illustrious colleagues and we will be able to make a precise measurement of the AU, the astronomical unit, the geometric distance from Earth to the sun. It will be one of the greatest achievements of modern astronomy, providing us with a precise and reliable means of measuring astronomical distances."

"And then your work here will be finished?" Ambika asked, the emotion showing in her voice.

"Yes," he answered glowingly. Then he gave a start, realizing what he had just said. "No," he blurted out. "I mean, my astronomical work will be finished but our work will be just beginning. That's what I wanted to talk to you about. Soon now, I will need to be sailing back." He was aware of the single tear that glistened just at the rounded edge of her lustrous cheek, a jewel that only seemed to add to her beauty. "I want you to come with me, Ambika. As my wife, of course. I hope your father will not object. I have not taken the liberty of talking to him without having talked to you first, but for me, yours is the only consent that matters."

At first, Ambika could not think of anything to say. She had been waiting for this moment for some weeks now, knowing that it was a possibility, hoping and praying that he would ask her, and dreading what she might say if he did. From the moment she began fantasizing about the possibility of sailing to France with him, a war had broken out between her desires and her duty. Her father would never agree, but that was the least of it. She had given her promise, not only to him but to herself and to her people, and she feared what might happen if she broke her promise. She feared just as much what might happen if she didn't. She had told herself that it was just an idle fancy, that the Frenchman could never consider marrying an Indian native. She had never heard of such a thing ever happening. But deep in her heart, she knew his feelings as well as she knew her own. Their hearts had begun resonating together through the quiet hours and the hectic, when they were apart as well as when they were together, like perfectly synchronized clocks that go on marking time together no matter how far apart their dials may be. And so it did not come as a surprise when he asked her. It was more like the turning of a page in a story she had already heard from the storyteller's lips. She could not think of anything to say, only because she was still at war with herself. Finally, she did what seemed most expedient. She begged for time.

"Let us wait for a couple of days to talk about this, Guillaume. At least until tomorrow. The transit is too important."

"For me, there is nothing more important in this world," he answered, still overwhelmed by her beauty, which he was now gazing at in the same way that he surveyed the heavens at night—with awe and wonder and a scientist's hunger for knowledge. "But very well. We will wait."

Le Gentil awoke at two o'clock the next morning, his anticipation refusing to allow him to sleep any longer. He heard the sandbar moaning in the southeast, a good omen since it meant the breeze would be coming from that direction, and he knew that the wind from the southeast was the broom of the coast, bringing serenity to the skies. Nervous nonetheless and unable to sleep, he got up from his bed and ascended to the observation deck. As soon as he peaked his head out, he was astonished to see that the sky was completely covered with clouds, especially to the north and northeast where it was already beginning to brighten ever so slightly. A profound calm hung over the land. He felt a sense of doom envelop him. He went back down and lay on his bed, staring at the ceiling, unable to close his eyes. He heard the moan of the sandbar even more distinctly, but now he could hear it clearly coming from the northeast, the worst of all possible omens. After an hour, he got up again to look at the sky. His sense of doom deepened. He repeated his heavy footsteps another hour later. Finally, at five o'clock, he went up to sit on the observation deck and meet his fate.

Meanwhile, several miles away, Ambika woke up after a troubled sleep and rushed to the nearest window. As soon as she saw the sky, her heart sank. She knew then why her sleep had been so troubled. With a heavy heart and a sense of foreboding, she went down to the garden to wait out the sky.

Shortly after five, Le Gentil felt a slight breeze from the southwest that gave him a glimmer of hope, for the sky was somewhat clearer in that direction. If the breeze turned, there was still a chance the sky could clear. For a time, he remained in a state of uncertainty, while the winds turned their attention to the west, then to the northwest, then to the north. They picked up in strength and began to blow with unrepentant fury. The great, motionless clouds that had been hanging in the northeast began to move until they formed a second curtain between his telescopes and the sky. The squall died down around six but the clouds remained. At three minutes to seven, at almost the precise moment that Venus was scheduled to come off the sun, he spied a vague whiteness in the sky that gave him a suspicion of the sun's position, but he could distinguish nothing more through his telescope. The transit was over and he had missed it. His fate had cheated him once again.

Le Gentil sat back down. Only with difficulty did he accept that the transit was over. He picked up his journal to record his experience but his hands shook. A moment later the journal fell from his grasp. He didn't bother to pick it up. Instead, he sat there and stared vacantly into the southeastern sky. At nine o'clock, the clouds thinned and the sun came out in all its brilliance. It would continue to shine unimpeded for the remainder of the day.

Ambika found him some minutes later with his head in his hands, plunged in a dejection from which he would not emerge for the next two weeks. It would have passed earlier, except for the following episode:

The day after the missed transit, Ambika brought a bowl of soup to the fallen astronomer's bed, from where he refused to get up, seeing no good reason to do so. She spent a few futile minutes trying to convince him to return to his work, while he propped himself up and sipped his broth, but to no avail. Then a promising gleam came into his eye.

"There is one thing and one thing only that can make me feel better," he told her. "Tell me that you will marry me and come back with me to France when the time comes."

A cloud passed over Ambika's eyes. She had come to her own decision the night before, aided by the ill omens that had plagued them on the morning of the transit. She had no wish to add a further blow at such a difficult hour, but she could not keep her feelings from her face. There was no longer anything she could hide from this man. He had taken up his lodgings deep within her soul where there were no doors to close and nothing that went unnoticed. She was quiet for a minute. Then she unburdened herself.

"Do you remember what professor Sandip said when he read your chart, about the woman you would leave behind?"

"I've done my best to forget it."

"I've been thinking about this for a long time, Guillaume, long before you asked me, just in the hopes that you might. I want to be your wife. My heart is at peace about that. But I can't leave my country. My fate is tied to my people. For better or for worse, I can't abandon the soil of Mother India until my country is free. There are some things that are more important than the fate of two people."

Her eyes sought the floor but she refused to cry. She had made her choice, the only choice she felt was open to her. For a long time they were silent. Then Le Gentil spoke, his voice falling to a whisper.

"And if I stay in India?"

She looked up, proud and defiant. "Then I will be by your side. But if you leave to follow your destiny, then my heart goes with you, though my body cannot."

Neither Le Gentil nor Ambika shed a tear as they remained wrapped in the silence that united them, their hearts beating in unison, as they had not ceased to do for some time now. There were some tears, however, in Rodrigo's eyes. His characters had shown him the futility of his petty emotions. There were indeed things that were more important than the fate of two people. He had forgotten this but his characters had not. He would take a lesson from them. In the afternoon, he would meet Saraswati and put his petty disappointment behind him. She deserved no less. He thanked his characters, the gods of writing, and the Shiva statue that raised its watchful shadow outside his window. If ever there was a timely therapy, this was it, he thought, prescribed by the Divine Doctor at the moment he most needed it.

38

ARASWATI AND RODRIGO TOOK up their afternoon walks again as if nothing had changed, but in the once closely guarded recesses of her heart, she knew that everything had. Somewhere between his proposal and her belated recognition of her true feelings, a longstanding wall had come down. For the first time in her life, she felt free to give full rein to her emotions; as if in recognition, she found that her grateful heart was now full of language, longing to give voice to the urgings and the joys that had been reined in by the well-meaning efforts of her intellect. The devotional songs that had been a necessary but not always natural part of her spiritual practices now outstripped her meditation and her studies in the impact they had on her consciousness. For the first time in several years, she joined the collective morning practice, drawn irresistibly from the solitude of her room by the intoxicating chants that celebrated the soul's love for the Divine in its myriad forms. The most beloved of these forms was Krishna, the charismatic cowherd who had shepherded her heart's aspirations since childhood; but now, in the light of her overflowing sentiments, she saw him as she had never seen him before: not a distant dreamed figure but a smiling, laughing, bodily presence as close as her own heartbeat. Rodrigo's slender silhouette among the men in the hall made her room seem like a forgotten sepulcher, and sometimes, when she pictured Krishna in her mind as she sang, she saw Rodrigo sitting beside him, enfolded in the youthful god's arms, both of these beloved figures slipping in and out of each other as easily as sunbeams crossing the sky.

The one caveat in this riot of feeling was that she could not yet share openly with Rodrigo how she felt, despite the near declaration she had made in his room. For her part, she was ready. She had been rushing toward the open expression of her sentiments ever since she had knocked on his door and rescued him from his unhappy seclusion. With each succeeding day, her heart fought against her habitual reticence, overwhelming it, brick by brick. But there was more at stake here than just her longing to share her feelings with him. From the moment she had entered his room, she had felt a ring of sorrow radiating from the edges of his aura. His heart was enclosed in a wall of its own, brought on by her unfortunate, half-conscious words. She longed to throw her grappling hooks and tear it down with declarations of affection, but the prudent voice inside her told her she mustn't. She must respect his feelings and allow him time to throw open the gates of his own accord, after learning the lessons that sorrow had come to teach him. And so, while their conversations remained as animated as ever, drawing deep from the wells of the world's storehouse of spiritual and literary lore, there was one topic of conversation they never touched upon. Whenever they skirted its edges, she drew back, unsure how to proceed. As one day folded into the next, it seemed wiser to leave certain things unsaid. She, who had been so good with words for so long, did not trust them now. Instead, she entrusted this mission to a subtler means of communication, hopeful that his heart would be capable of sensing her own heart's whispers and would be able to translate them into a language that she could not yet speak with any fluency. The words would have to come, but in a time and a place of their own choosing.

Early one afternoon, they sought shelter from the rains in the Sivananda ashram library. They found a spot at one end of a long table by the edge of the stacks, as far away from the checkout desk and the few other patrons as they could get. Saraswati took down a copy of the songs of Mirabai from a nearby shelf, and they took turns reading the poems to each other in soft whispers, huddling close together until their temples were almost touching, so as not to disturb anyone. It was as close as she had physically gotten to a man since Vikram. Despite the musty interiors of the library, the familiar vanilla-and-almond aroma of old books only a few feet away, the only fragrance that could hold her attention was the sweet, man-ish incense that wafted from his body, mixing with Mirabai's soft syllables until it seemed as if the Rajasthani saint were composing her odes to the god who sat beside her, attracting her through the senses as he had attracted her through his mind. His nearness intoxicated her. She reveled in it, desire surging in her like a neglected river swelling after the arrival of the monsoon rains. She could hear the chimes of her heart and feel its beat, the irresistible pulse of the tambour marking time for the bhajan singers, who are determined to lose themselves in song. She could smell the sweet fragrance of danger in the air as her habitual control began to give way. When passion comes, she thought, it comes with elephant strides, trampling everything that stands in its way. Who can withstand its thunderous steps? As if on cue, Mira's verse echoed the determined advance of her desire in the soft cadences of Rodrigo's hypnotic voice: "Listen, my friend, this road is the heart opening, kissing his feet, resistance broken, tears all night." She had known tears in these last days, even though they had not made their appearance on her cheeks. She was a woman; some things did not need to be learned afresh in each succeeding life. They were lodged in her racial memories, ancient fires that never cease to burn. She knew that she could lose herself in this man who sat beside her, that one small step would be all that was necessary for her to be carried away by the rampaging river that was straining to flood the landscape within her. It was as if she had come to the edge of a precipice and had dared to look over it at the long fall down. And yet, she was not scared. The danger thrilled her. The sight of the abyss filled her with an aliveness as great as any she had ever known. This was the sacred earthly passion that lent its images to the saint's devotional verses and made up in poetic fervor what it lacked in mystic aspiration.

When Rodrigo extended the book to her again, she stopped him with a gentle touch that lingered even after she quietly told him, "You read. You are the poet and I am your audience." He turned the page and echoed her thoughts once again with the words from a song whose familiar melody seemed to sound softly in the space around them.

"She might not distinguish splendor from filth, but she'd tasted the nectar of passion. She might not know any Veda but a chariot swept her away. Now she frolics in heaven, ecstatically bound to her god. The Lord of Fallen Fools, says Mira, will save anyone who can practice rapture like that."

Out of the corner of her eye, she could see the rain cascading in rivulets down the glazed window above them. The thunderous music of the monsoon had softened to a light patter. A sonorous quietude stole in through the open doorway, turning her thoughts toward the immensity that harbored them. Heaven could be painted in many colors, she thought. Surely this afternoon deserves its place in that gallery, a portrait of the Divine as near to perfection as any portrait could ever be. This man, this feeling, the chariot of his presence in her life sweeping her toward the exultation that she longed for every time she picked up a book of devotional poems or joined in the bhajans at dusk by the river's edge or watched the Mother close her eyes and join the Creator in the infinite halls of space. Was it any wonder that the path of love had always been considered the fastest and the best? If this was danger, then heaven was made for the brave, for how could one turn down love in any form when its appearance was so rare and so dazzling? Again, as if in answer, the poet spoke out of the mouth of the god who whispered to her, even as he tightened his hold upon her heart.

"Do not mention the name of love, O my simple-minded companion. Strange is the path when you offer your love. Your body is crushed at the first step. If you want to offer love, be prepared to cut off your head and sit on it. Be like the moth which circles the lamp and offers its body."

Her eyes opened wider, searching for Mira's gaze behind the veil of centuries, while Rodrigo's voice continued to intone the saint's words without a pause. Was she being simpleminded? Was she ignoring the dangers because the pleasures seemed too sweet to forego? Perhaps, but it was better to have to ask these questions and have her future decided by the answers than to never be faced with them at all. If she was going to renounce the world, its passions and its pleasures, then she should have something to renounce. It is easy to give up something you have never had. There is no heroism in that, no sacrifice, nothing to test the real depths of your character. For the first time in her life, she was realizing what it was like to truly love a man. Vikram had been nothing more than a passing fancy, an ill-conceived attempt to experience something she had not been ready to experience. He had not touched her soul the way Rodrigo did. He had neither fired her deepest aspirations nor challenged her to be better than she was. Her old sense of resolve flared up again. This divine earthly passion was something she had to experience; she was not ready to renounce the world until she did. This was her present destiny, and she would follow it until it released her hold on her, or until there were no more lessons to be learned. Would she have decided to become a sannyasi had she met Rodrigo beforehand and felt what she did now? She could only wonder, but the wondering seemed of little consequence. Providence had withheld that meeting until she had decided on her vocation. There was a reason this was so. The Divine Potter would not fill an unfired vessel. If she was to become a sannyasi, then it would have to be because she had loved and loved well, and looked beyond that love, once and for all, to a higher love where the heart looks upon all creatures alike—not because it is sworn to do so, but because it has chosen to of its own free will.

By now the rain had stopped. Rodrigo looked up and glanced out the window, as if the outward silence had called him from the inward dream. A shaft of the sun's light fell across the table where they sat. "One more poem before we walk?" he asked. Saraswati nodded, not yet willing to break the spell. Rodrigo thumbed through the remaining pages until his index finger paused under a title that seemed to catch his eye: "O my mind." Saraswati leaned back, closed her eyes, and directed her attention to Mirabai's final message for her before they left the shadows of the reading room to rejoin the constant, invisible motion of the outside air.

"Take no pride in the body; it will soon be mingling with the dust. This life is like the sporting of sparrows; it will end with the onset of night. Why don the ochre robe and leave home as a sannyasi? Those who adopt the external garb of a yogi, but do not penetrate to the secret, are caught again in the net of rebirth."

As they got up to leave, Saraswati wondered if Rodrigo had deliberately picked that verse to end the reading. She hoped he had. They pushed open the screen door at the library entrance and emerged into a dappled sunlight that tasted of cloud and smelled of rain. A couple of ochre-robed sannyasis were strolling in the direction of the meditation hall, their hands clasped behind their backs. They smiled as they glanced at the younger couple and then returned to the reflective tones of their quiet conversation. Don't give up, she whispered under her breath as she watched them pass. Until I am completely convinced myself, don't you be.

A couple of days later, Saraswati invited Rodrigo to accompany her for a night meditation by the banks of the river. Heedful of what might still be a difficult memory, she suggested they head south, away from Lakshman Jhula, to a pebbly strip between the water and a group of large boulders. She brought a blanket to cushion their seat from the many small, rough stones, and they sat together, as close as two bodies could get without touching. It was after nine, but the moon, now halfway through its waning phase, had not yet risen. Though the sky was clouded, a small handful of stars peaked out through the gaps in the ruffled curtain. Venus lay on the horizon, so bright that the wispy clouds around her formed a halo of silvery light. When they finished their meditation, Saraswati inched her way toward the subject they had been avoiding, hoping to put to rest the ache she knew was still in Rodrigo's heart.

"Have you ever thought that maybe this isn't the first time we've been together? That we might have known each other in our past lives? Somehow I don't think we could've become this close this fast if it wasn't a continuation of something we started long ago."

"You really think so?"

"I'm sure of it. I gave up questioning that months ago. I wonder sometimes what kind of relationship we might have had, but that kind of knowledge is not usually vouchsafed to us mere mortals. Too bad. There are some important samskaras we are meant to work on together. It might help to know exactly what they were. But that's wishful thinking, I suppose."

Rodrigo picked up a pebble and tossed it into the flowing water. Though the ripples were scarcely visible in the faint evening starlight, she could feel them spreading out over the surface of the water like the ripples of each of the countless actions that had led them to this place in time.

"To be honest, I've never felt this close to anyone in my life," he said, his words igniting a sudden warmth in her heart.

"Me either. That's no accident, you know."

"No, I suppose not. I guess I am curious about the past, but maybe it doesn't matter. Maybe all that matters is that we remain open to the lessons we are meant to learn in this life, whatever they may be."

Saraswati smiled. "Even if they are difficult ones?"

"How about, *especially* if they are difficult ones. Aren't those the ones we learn the most from?"

"They are. They absolutely are."

For Saraswati, Rodrigo's words were a welcome indication that he had put the other night behind him, or was very nearly there. They were partners now on the path, placed side by side to help each other discover the significance of their lives, blooming as spiritual beings in an act of divine cross-pollination to an extent that would not have been possible had they been on their own. She could feel it in her blood and in the whisperings of her heart. This man beside her had set her free to love in a way that she had never been able to before—outside of the worshipful surrender she experienced whenever she was in the Mother's presence or felt her hallowed touch within the precincts of her mind. She had not consented to his proposal of marriage, but she was convinced now that the ties that bound them were far deeper than those that most married couples experienced. They were spiritual ties, a mystic fellowship that went far beyond the attraction they both felt and was undoubtedly the true source of that attraction. It was something so subtle and so deep that she doubted her own parents had ever even imagined such a possibility. She had not yet said this to Rodrigo, but she knew that the conditions were almost ripe for doing so. There was only so long that some things should go unsaid, even if the spirit is sure to know what the mind cannot.

As they got ready to head back, she saw that the clouds had moved away from the face of Venus. When he stood up and helped her to fold the blanket, she could see the full light of that distant orb reflected on his forehead like the crescent moon on Shiva's brow. A shiver ran through her, a sudden glimpse of a majesty that had been hidden from her eyes until then, a fleeting image of a divine being who had stepped out of ancient myths and knowingly wandered into her own uncertain age. How fitting, she thought, that Venus should alight on the brow of this artist who was so close to rediscovering his eternal self. She remembered that in ancient India, Venus had been considered a female deity: Vena, the first of the Gandharvas, patron of the arts. Only later had it become widely accepted that the planet was male. The later sages had named him Sukra, the guardian of the secret of immortality. Male, definitely male, she decided, as if her voice was the only one that mattered. After all, she was Saraswati. If anyone would know, it was she.

39

T HAT NIGHT, RODRIGO DECIDED that it was time to put his disappointment behind him. Though his sadness persisted, like background music in an elevator's steady ascent, he knew he was on his way to where he truly wished to go: toward a more elevated, more enlightened, more compassionate consciousness. There were lessons to be learned in everything, as Saraswati had always pointed out. This was no different. And to tell the truth, he did feel better after their evening meditation. It had not been mere words, what she had said the other day—that this relationship was just as important to her as it was to him. Their talk by the riverside had cleared up any doubts he might have had, despite the absence of romantic overtones. They might not have their hearts synchronized like Ambika and Le Gentil, but he agreed with her—their relationship must have spanned lifetimes. If that were true, then the fact that she wouldn't marry him was just a detail. They still had much to go through together, whether it be now or at some other date far in the unforeseen future. However the drama played out, he knew he would be fine with it in the long run; he knew he could trust the hand of the Divine Playwright to weave him into the plot with the same perfection that he had dedicated to the rest of the creation.

Rodrigo fell asleep that night in a state of quiet but confident reflection, but when he awoke he found his confidence in himself badly shaken.

Rishikesh
7/21
4:05 AM

Is it possible to be two men in one body? No, it is not, and the very thought disheartens me. Is there, then, no escape from the import of my dream? The first thing I felt when I woke up was fear and confusion, as if the walls of the world were closing in on me. Then I remembered the dream and gradually my fear turned to self-loathing, a well-deserved antipathy to my own selfishness. But let me explain:

It was late at night. I had been lying on my cot when the curtain before my door rustled and she appeared, entering as silently as a ghost. There was much I needed to tell her: the fact that we had been found out; the need for extreme discretion; the saving grace that all my extortion-prone assistant wanted was money and privileges, that he also had a position to protect and the best way to protect his position was to protect mine. My head was so full of these thoughts that I barely looked at her as she sat down on the edge of my bed. But when she put a finger to her lips and then to mine, my mind began to calm down. The intoxication of her presence was like an elixir that was both the cause and the cure for all my troubles.

Once I was quiet, she told me that she had important news. I wanted to prattle on, to tell her how glad I was that she was there, despite everything, but something in her eyes bid me halt. She took my hand, and without any preamble she told me she was pregnant. She had taken what precautions she knew, but somehow they had failed. My mind quickly entered into a state of shock. How could this be! How could the devi allow it! In my confusion, I even looked at the idol and muttered some incoherent phrase. My hands began to shake, but she grasped them even more firmly and gradually the tremors ceased. I looked into her dark panther's eyes and saw them blazing with defiant strength. Suddenly I realized that she was neither shocked nor afraid but determined. I had already suspected that she was much stronger than I; this confirmed it. Even now, from the safety of my waking consciousness, I can remember the strength I saw in her eyes. She started talking to me in a confident whisper. "Let us fly from here," she said. "Let us go someplace where no one knows us, where no one can ever point to our caste and tell us what we can or cannot do. Let us raise our child to be a yogi and teach him to never cower before the evils of this society. Come, let us leave these tired walls to those who see nothing wrong with living in a prison and go out to search for God together."

I heard her voice clearly, but the words seemed to be coming through a fog—the fog of my fear and a lifetime of attachment that made me deaf to what she was saying. My mind swirled with images of my misfortune, searching for a means of avoiding what I had long feared. Before I knew what I was saying, I told her that there were certain herbs she could take. I knew of a vaidya who could help her provoke a miscarriage. No one would know. We would be safe. As soon as I said this, her face turned cold. She let go of my hand and pulled back on the bed. For a long minute, she searched my eyes; then I could see the disbelief disappearing behind a mask of icy recognition. "Is that what you want?" she asked. To my utter disgrace, I told her that it was, that there was nothing else I could do, that a man in my position could not give up everything he had worked a lifetime to achieve. "Then you will not leave with me?" she asked. "How could you think that I would?" I answered. "Don't you see how much I have to lose?" She didn't say anything more. She got up and looked at me. There was pity in her eyes. Though light clouds of anger and disappointment lingered there as well, it is the pity I remember best. She folded her hands to her breast and made a move toward the door. Before she could reach it, I pleaded with her not to tell anyone. We would find some other solution. If necessary, she could have the child and I would make arrangements for her expenses. She shook her head sadly. "Don't worry, I won't tell anyone."

I wanted to stop her from leaving, but I was paralyzed, rooted to the bed. And then it was too late. The door had closed behind her. I hung my head, suffocated by my fear, sensing that my life was disintegrating around me. Somewhere among my feelings, there was a small measure of remorse for how I had treated her. Or am I imagining this now to assuage my guilt over the way my dreaming self acted the moment he was put to the test? Either way, it was not my finest hour. Let this be a lesson to me. When real life comes knocking and calls me to the test, may I find a way to defeat my selfishness. If ever I was to say a prayer, it would be this: May I learn the meaning of sacrifice and selflessness before it is too late, before I lose the ability to wake up from these dreams, before I become this priest whom I have just now learned to despise.

Rodrigo had a difficult time getting started on his book that morning. In some ways, the dream had laid him even lower than his thwarted romantic desire. It was an entirely different kind of desolation, one dependent only on his shortcomings for its sustenance. While he knew that in many corners a dream was just a dream—indeed, one short year before, he had been of that mind—he could no longer accept that as an excuse. The study of yogic philosophy had condemned him to a life's penance of full responsibility. If he had acted in such a despicable manner when the vigilance of his conscious mind was lifted, it could only mean that his tendency toward selfishness was still very much alive. With a sudden stab of remorse, he remembered the Rimpoche's words: "You have based your life on selfishness; this must end." It had not ended yet. He was consciously working toward that goal, but the dream reminded him that he was still a long way from fulfilling his promise to the Tibetan master who had left such an indelible impression on his life.

He bowed his head for a moment, letting his forehead come to rest on the edge of his desk. He took a few deep breaths in that position, then raised his head up again and straightened his back, consciously shaking off his timidity with one firm contraction of his erector spinae muscles. This was no cause for despair, he reasoned. Years of egotism, perhaps lifetimes, could not be dealt a fatal blow in a mere year's time. What was required was simple enough, though it would not be easy. He must not relax his efforts until he had achieved all that he could achieve in this lifetime. For a moment, he gazed out the window at the faintly smiling Shiva. The indomitable repose on the statue's face rekindled the fire that had been growing steadily over the past months. He was determined to awaken the dormant divinity within him, even if he had to sojourn through the fires of hell to do so, a hell for which he was the sole architect. He might be just beginning, he told himself, but even the barest of beginnings carries within it the certain promise of the end, just as long as the walker keeps walking. With that, he turned his attention back to *The Venus Transit*, hopeful that Le Gentil would share his determination and do better by Ambika than he had done by his dreamed lover, who was just as beautiful and just as deserving. Fortunately, he had little to worry about in this regard. His characters had no intention of letting him down. While they may have depended on him for their existence, it was they who reached out to console him, giving him all the support he needed and raising once again the question: just how much does the creator owe to his creation?

By the middle of June, Le Gentil had begun to recover from the doldrums that had plagued him ever since a veil of clouds had come between him and what he had assumed to be his destiny. Ambika had remained by his side throughout this time, doing her best to revive his spirits despite being afflicted by the same fateful melancholy. Two weeks after the transit, she arrived at the observatory in the morning to find him at his desk pouring over the upcoming movements of the various planetary bodies. The unexpected sight lifted her spirits, temporarily banishing from her mind the mournful thoughts of a coming separation that she feared would last a lifetime. Not wishing to do anything that might stifle his newfound motivation, she hid her surprise and asked him if he would like a cup of tea, a morning ritual they had indulged in for many months but which had been suspended by the two weeks of worry. Soon she was seated at her desk, busy with her translations of the texts they had brought back with them from Madurai. Over the next few days, they settled back into their old routine. Le Gentil worked mornings at his calculations, fueled by his nighttime perusal of the skies, while Ambika translated and brought to his attention passages that she knew would spark his imagination. In the afternoons, they sat on the veranda and discussed those texts and a thousand other topics with nearly the same verve as always. In July, a French colleague, the astronomer Pierre Antoine Veron, alighted in Pondicherry for a few days' rest on his way to the Moluccas. He spent most of his free hours with Le Gentil, discussing their work and planning for the November transit of Mercury across the sun that Veron proposed to observe in Manila. Yet, despite the renewed activity, there was one topic they didn't discuss, though its presence continued to be felt like an unseen shadow across an open window. Finally, after Le Gentil had seen Veron off on his voyage, Ambika suggested they take a day trip up the coast, ostensibly to gather more material for his journals, though she could see in his eyes that he had divined her hidden intentions.

They set out early the next morning. By mid-morning, they reached a small fishing village about halfway between Pondicherry and Mahabalipuram, where they spent the rest of the morning walking along the coast, gathering samples and filling several pages of Ambika's notebook with the astronomer's annotations. By this time, the fishermen were returning from their day's labor. Ambika sought out the eldest among them, a pair of wiry old men gnarled by time and blackened by the sun but still imbued with a young man's sinews, the stamina to endure long hours at sea, and the patience to wait out nature that was the pride of their profession. They were happy to answer Le Gentil's questions about the habits and qualities of the sea creatures with whom they had spent a lifetime in fruitful symbiosis, embarking on a conversation that lasted the better part of two hours and which covered numerous pages in Ambika's journal. The conversation began by the water's edge where the fishing folk were tying up their boats and continued in a mud-and-thatch hut that belonged to one of their interlocutors, at the edge of the densely packed hamlet. They took a late lunch there, happily served to them on banana leaves by the old man's cherubic daughter-in-law, while her two young children clung to the folds of her sari and peeked out at the curious strangers. When their conversation was over, the woman set out two straw mats on the veranda for them to take rest on, protected from the sun by the wide overhanging roof, before she retired to the cool interiors of the dwelling with the rest of her family.

"It was nice to get away, don't you agree," Ambika said, once they were alone, gazing at the sea some thirty meters distant. "I'm glad that you've been working again, but I thought you could use a change of scenery. You haven't been very happy lately."

"How can I be happy, Ambika, with the choice I'm facing? Either I abandon my life's work, at least the greater part of it, or I abandon the woman I love. Either way, I have everything to lose."

Ambika found it difficult to restrain a tear. "I'm so sorry I put you in this predicament," she said.

Le Gentil sat up abruptly. "Don't think that. Not even for a moment. You are only following your conscience. That is exactly what I want you to do." He reached out and clasped her hand. "I've already told you this, but I'll tell you again—I support your decision one hundred percent. Your willingness to sacrifice your personal desires for the welfare of your people is part of why I admire you so much. I doubt there are many people in this world that have the courage you have, or the selflessness."

"Then you're not angry with me?"

"Angry? No, my love. Never, not even for a moment. How could you even think that? It's just karma, as you call it. If I'm sad, it's because I also have a duty to my people, to the Academy, to the work that God put me on the earth to do, and I fear that duty will take me away from you. The sadness is necessary. I wouldn't be a real human being without it. All these days, I've been weighing the different factors and trying to listen to my heart. I haven't talked to you about it because

I needed to listen and to think. I needed to know what was in my heart before I could share it with you."

Ambika sat up as well. Like Le Gentil, she leaned back against the smooth earthen walls of the hut that showed such obvious care, like everything else in that simple fishing village. "And what does your heart tell you?" she asked.

Le Gentil let out a deep sigh that conveyed as much or more to her than his words. He dropped his head into his hands for a moment and then smiled weakly. "I believe it is God's will, Ambika, that I return to France, at least for a time. There is much yet for me to do, and I don't think I could do a tenth of it if I remained here. Whatever I did here would not have the impact it would have if I were in France. There I believe I can exert a great influence over the minds of many people. There is so much ignorance about the world; I want to remove it, to the extent that I can. Knowledge is the great equalizer. It can make kings out of paupers and restore dignity to people who should never have lost it in the first place. And there is much I can do there to bring our two cultures closer together, as you well know—if we can bring our plans to fruition."

"I feel the exact same way," Ambika told him, her own sadness now replaced by a passionate determination. "I want you to stay, with all my heart, but I was hoping that this would be your decision. I refuse to be selfish about this, and I knew you would not be."

"Then you won't be angry with me?"

"No, my love. Never. You make me proud, now and forever."

They were silent for a couple of minutes, each sheltered within the beating of the other's heart. Then Ambika asked him if he had thought about when he might be leaving.

"In a few months, I should think. My heart will need that long to prepare for the separation. It will also take at least that long to gather the most important manuscripts. I want to take back as many translations with me as I can. In the meantime, we'll make arrangements for sending future translations every few months or so. There's a comet I want to observe in late September, so it wouldn't be before October, at the earliest. Of course, once I do go, I'll expect regular letters from then on. Long ones."

"As will I. And when your journals are published, I want the first copy that heads east."

"If God wills that they be published, then the first copy that comes into my hands will go out on the next ship setting sail for India. And if God favors us, and the work goes well, then on one of those future ships, I will also come."

"I will go to the seashore to look for you. Whenever you are in sight of the ocean, look out over the waters and remember that I am on the other side of the world looking back at you."

Their hands reached for each other as they looked out at the waves lapping gently on the Coromandel shore, and beyond to the horizon where their dreams could be seen sailing in the bluish haze. They were still sitting there with their hands entwined when the sun dropped below the mountains directly behind them, the now-darkened waters hiding the distant sails that they would never cease to think of, all through the long years that awaited them.

As Rodrigo looked in on their silent vigil, he could feel the peace in their hearts reaching out to him from beyond the pages, crossing centuries, bridging the gap that separated him from his creation. He wondered if this was a message from his characters to their creator, a timely and precious gift to bring with him when his own journey took him back across the ocean and into another life. He was still not sure when that would be, for like Le Gentil, there was still much that was left for him to do, but if his characters would not let selfishness stand in the way of the good they could do with their lives, then neither would he. All that was left was to look into his heart like his astronomer had done and follow the instructions written there. There was nothing complex about love. It might speak in whispers, but when it spoke, the clarity could be deafening. He was listening, he whispered to his soul. He was listening.

40

Rishikesh
7/26
4:00 AM

The nightmare continues—though in fairness, I question whether it deserves so harsh a name. Either way, utter disconsolation is its fruit, the tears that come when you recognize that you have lost—through your own stupidity, your arrogance, and your selfishness—the one thing that really matters to you, and that there is nothing you can do about it.

This time I was walking through the streets of the poorest part of town, the area where the Chamars lived, that class of untouchables whose work it is to tan the hides that are later made into our shoes and bags. It was a squalid place and dark. Though it was daytime, it seemed as if the sun could not penetrate the suffocating atmosphere of that dismal shantytown. The strong smell of sulphides assaulted my nostrils, forcing me to hold a cloth over my nose. It was an uncomfortable, almost nauseating feeling, walking down those streets—not only because the environment was so noxious by comparison with the meticulously maintained interiors of the temple grounds, but also due to a certain innate revulsion that I had difficulty suppressing. It was the first time that I, a Brahmin priest of the highest order, had entered such a place, and I knew that the eyes that followed me as I walked were thinking the same thing I was: what was I doing there? What I was doing was searching for the girl's house with a desperation that had finally overcome my resistance. She had not shown up for work for several days now. That, by itself, given the anguish I must have caused her, was understandable. Nevertheless, I had grown worried. Most of my worry, I knew, stemmed from my ongoing fear of what she might do—if she might, after all, tell someone. But I was also ashamed of how I had acted and wanted to make it up to her somehow. Moreover, after several days apart, I was finding the separation profoundly unsettling. Her presence clung to me like a second skin, nearly as familiar and as necessary as my own. I could never leave the temple, I knew that, but the thought of losing her was just as difficult to bear. There had to be a solution, some way to avoid severing our connection—a connection, I now realized, that was deeper than any I had ever had with another human being, or might ever have—but whereby at the same time I would not lose all that I had worked toward since I was a boy learning the mantras from my father's mouth.

So here I was, coming to her, pleading with the devi to help us find a solution that would not involve my utter disgrace. My assistant had given me the directions. He had offered to call a carriage for me but I had declined, and I could see that he really didn't care. He had gotten his money and was about to leave on his trip; I could do what I liked. I followed his directions, and after a few inquiries I found the house. A shack really. You could not call it anything else. The walls were pieced together from odd scraps of wood, every board different from its neighbor. The roof was a few strips of corrugated tin. I was sure there was no bathroom inside, but I didn't dare think about where they went to relieve themselves. There was a makeshift door, a piece of laminated wood rotted at the top. The door was ajar, unlocked. I knocked. When no one answered, I pushed it open, listening to the creak of the unoiled hinges with a mounting trepidation, afraid of what she would say when she saw me. But the single room was empty, except for a simple table, a couple of chairs, and a wooden cot against one wall. A ragged curtain hung from a rod that was suspended from the ceiling, creating a makeshift partition. I called again, then pushed aside the curtain, but there was nothing behind it, just another wooden cot with two of its boards broken. There were no clothes, no utensils, no sign of any living human presence. I was sure I had the wrong house. But then I saw it. It was lying on the table in full view, the only spot of color in that forsaken room. A single white lotus, a flower we had both contemplated in the yogi's small lotus pond after I had been initiated into the Tantric practice. She had told me that it was her favorite flower because it represented the purity of the human soul and the goal of all our journeys, the thousand-petaled lotus at the crown of the head. Its whiteness was a symbol of the truth that we are spirit, unsullied by the man-made differences of caste and creed, class and culture. She had plucked a blossom from the pond and handed it to me. "Do you see how it grows unsullied in the murky waters and the mud? Nothing can disturb its purity. See how the water slides off? We should be like this lotus. Let all the prejudices of the world slide off our backs without allowing the purity of our minds to be disturbed. Let us never forget that no one is Brahmin and no one is Dalit. We are all Shiva's children. We are all groping through the darkness, trying to find our way back to him." The flower was her message to me. Somehow she had known that I would come. She was telling me that I had forgotten, that I had let myself be swallowed up by the quicksands of ignorance. She had left the flower so that I might remember. But she herself was gone.

At that moment, the agony struck like the deity's fist flashing down from the heavens. I stumbled out the door like a man drunk on bad wine. I went up to the nearest neighbor, another shack a few feet away. I banged on the door. An old woman opened it, cross-eyed and suspicious. I asked her where the girl had gone who lived next door with her father. She shrugged her shoulders and told me they had left. The girl had taken her father south in search of better fortune. Or was it north? She could not remember. There was nothing left for them in this place, the girl had said. At that moment, the full weight of what I had done fell on me. I staggered back into the empty shack, clutched the flower in my hand, and wept. I was still weeping when I woke up in a room whose faded walls offered me no consolation.

Now that I am awake, I can no longer shake off the feeling that these dreams are more real than I had imagined. Their full significance is becoming clearer now, and the clarity is like a dagger to my heart. But I must not forget that no one is born a hero or a saint. Saints and heroes also had their inner battles to win, as I have mine. What is a saint, after all, but a villain who has overcome his villainy? What is a hero but a coward who has overcome his cowardice? Let me give myself a chance to overcome my selfishness before I ask the question, who am I? There is still time left to prove that I am better than I was.

On this morning, Rodrigo knew he could not sit before his computer to write. He had more important things to do. The first of these was to sit and think. After breakfast, he went down to the ghat and sat down on one of the upper steps in the shade offered by the small temple where the pilgrims would go to ring the bells after they had laid their flowers in the current in front of the statue. From where he sat, he was hidden from the street. The ghat was empty, and the relative seclusion reinforced the feeling that he had come for a private audience with the father of Tantra, sequestered in his Himalayan haunts. He turned his eyes toward the statue, still tormented by the sense of guilt that had haunted him when he awoke. A feeling of incalculable loss compounded his agony. For some minutes, he nursed his sorrow without thought, without reflection, allowing the tears to run unchecked down his cheeks, heedless of the fact that it had only been a dream. Though the statue's eyes were sunk in eternal contemplation, the ever-present smile was a sign that the god was aware of his tears and loved him for them. Slowly his anguish subsided. His mind grew quiet. The green-and-slate tint of the waters flowing behind the statue in their eternal glide toward the sea pulled his attention inward to where the divine yogi awaited him with his watchful gaze. Though he did not yet know in what physical shape his guru would appear in this life, he could sense that guiding presence within him, drawing him like a magnet down the path that had been prepared for him. With his eyes closed, he bowed his head. Addressing that presence by the name of Shiva, he silently put the question that he had come to ask and followed it with the intonations of his mantra, determined to wait for the master's voice in silence and to be ready when he spoke. The image of the statue's smiling face lingered in his mind. Then another image impressed itself upon his consciousness: the face of an old man blazoned in a mirror. The tears he saw there were the same tears that now glistened on his cheeks. The sorrow that was in the old man's eyes was his own sorrow, but rather than being nourished by a recent agony, it reflected the resignation of an ancient loss that was beyond recovery. He looked long into those eyes. He drank their pain as if it were a potion to rouse him from his sleep. When he had drunk it to its dregs, the image faded and was replaced by an image of himself in priestly garb seated at a simple wooden table in a deserted shack, clutching a white lotus blossom and lamenting his loss with tears that would gather below the desert sands to form a hidden pool of sorrow, waiting for its chance to bubble forth again.

Moments later, Rodrigo opened his eyes and offered his silent thanks to the statue sitting majestically by the water's edge. Though he could not yet put it into words, he knew that this was the answer he had been waiting for. But a still more important question remained. He hesitated to ask it, afraid of what the answer might be. But he had made a vow the previous morning, a promise to himself and to the Rimpoche. It was time to fulfill that promise. He closed his eyes again and spoke his concerns to the image of Shiva, which now floated within his mind, immanent and alive, its eyes gazing directly at him, its smile bringing tranquility to his thoughts. Instead of the river in the background, he saw stars. The slim crescent moon on the god's brow glowed with a pale luminescence like a halo. He had only to wait a moment before the thoughts came tumbling into his mind, faster and faster, with the confident cadences of a Shakespearean sonnet. Minutes later, he jumped up from his seat, his eyes open wide, knowing now exactly what he must do. Had he stopped to observe himself, he might have noticed that the fire that suddenly consumed him was the same fire that had long lit his literary aspirations. There was a poetic rightness to his thoughts, a glimmer of unearthly perfection in the world of form, a single finger pointing toward a moon that cannot be explained, for its true nature is not what we see but that which the perfect symmetry of the moon disguises. But he did not stop for any literary or mystical reflection. He simply folded his hands to his chest in gratitude, thanking the statue and all it represented. Then he slipped on his sandals and went to bring a living consummation to his dreams. Somewhere, separated from him by a chasm of time and space, an old man was waiting to thank him.

His first stop was the Blue Sky Cafe. There he wrote two long emails with instructions to his lawyer and his banker, and a shorter one to the head of his department at the university. Then he went to the telephone room inside the ashram and called both his lawyer and his banker, calling their attention to the emails he had just sent and insisting that they follow his instructions to the letter and without any delay. From there he went to the office to look for Bhagavati. He found her a few minutes later in the ashram clinic, where he made a formal request for a brief audience with the swami. Bhagavati accompanied him back to the office and penciled in an appointment for the next morning. Only then did he give himself permission to relax. He went to his room to grab his umbrella and then went for a short walk before lunch, the tension easing out of him with the melodic precision of a prelude to a baroque fugue.

That afternoon, he and Saraswati went for a walk in the hills east of town, following well-worn mountain paths along the edges of steep crevices and past graceful cottages whose inhabitants leaned back in their wicker chairs to watch the couple pass, as they might watch the flight of a bird or listen to the moaning of the wind in the trees. This time they did not talk of philosophy. They hardly talked of anything at all. Saraswati's eyes were bright with laughter and a girlish joy that made his own heart beat with a similar gaiety, shorn, at least for a while, of its preoccupations. He was aware that this might well be one of the last times he would walk with her, but that only enhanced his appreciation of every minute they spent together that afternoon. Several times, he held her hand to help her navigate some treachery in the path. The touch of her skin imbued him with a confidence that made him feel as if he could hold his own with the sun. Every time she smiled at him—and she smiled virtually every time their eyes met—he could feel his chest swell with pleasure. When she did talk, he listened not so much to the words but to the sound of her voice. It rang like music down the wooded paths that curled among the hills, joining itself to the birdsong and the whispers of the wind in the branches. Time came very nearly to a standstill, moving along so gently that they could hear the sound of Krishna's flute in the forest, brought near to them by this slowing in the river of infinite moments. When they halted their leisurely gait to watch a sparrow carousing on a branch beside its nest, neither of them speaking a word, he realized that the afternoon had already lasted a lifetime. A mantle of thankfulness dropped over him. He could have done no better had they been married and seen their lives carried along by the swift current of the Ganges down a vale of daily concerns. One moment contained in itself all others, he thought, if one could only find the beauty hidden there.

By the time they began their descent toward Muni-ki-reti, it was already evening. The first stars had made their appearance low on the horizon above the wooded slopes across the river; behind them, the purple glow of the descending sun still lingered among the trees. They reached for each other's hand and held on tightly until they reached the street. Only when they saw the pavement looming out of the growing darkness, and heard the harsh, muffled roar of a distant three-wheeler struggling up the hill toward them, did the clamor of Rishikesh finally intrude upon their private space. They unclasped their hands and replaced that temporary union with simultaneous smiles, though neither could see the other's face properly in the gloaming, and began walking briskly down the road until they came to the Ram Jhula Bridge. Only then did Rodrigo let out the sigh that had been suppressed by the magic that had followed them down the forest paths all afternoon. Saraswati asked him which train he would be taking to Delhi. It was an innocent question, fueled by her eagerness to see him back again for an indefinite stay, but it felt like an arrow to his breast. It's funny, he thought, how time can stand still and open a window into eternity. But then the window shuts and you are left once again on the outside looking in through the opaqueness in the glass at a memory of what life could be and had once been. The clarity is lost so quickly, though the memory remains. He wondered then what all yogis have wondered and wonder still: How long before eternity is the only hour I know?

Rodrigo's interview with the pujya swami was scheduled for ten o'clock. At a quarter to ten, he was sitting in the anteroom outside the swami's chambers with a copy of the Bhagavad Gita open to the chapter on karma yoga. Once again, he reminded himself to act selflessly, without attachment to the fruits of his actions. It was not an easy proposition. On the eve of what he hoped would be his greatest triumph, he had found himself wondering if such a selfless act might not convince Saraswati that she should marry him after all. Right up until the moment he fell asleep that night, he had allowed himself to be dragged down the dead-end alleys of what-ifs: What if he invited her to America, to see what it was like, to have a taste of the world before she renounced it for good? What if she agreed to come? It would only be a visit at first, but the calendar would turn over. One month would blend into the next. She would be in no hurry to don the saffron robes. America might intrigue her with its youthful culture, its elegantly stylized materialism, its legions of wide-eyed seekers opening their doors to the promises of yoga. They would continue their walks along the suburban streets of Chapel Hill, take weekend excursions into a natural beauty that would be entirely new to her. And somewhere along the way, somewhere between lunch in an organic restaurant and a lecture she was invited to give in a local yoga center, she would find that she could no longer do without his company—or even if she could, there would be no real reason to. It could happen, he told himself. All it would take would be a casual invitation, a mutual desire, and a small residue of gratitude for being freed to follow her dream, just enough to compel her to accept his invitation. But before he fell asleep, the memory of his recent dreams interrupted, bringing with it the distasteful sensation that he was sinking back into selfishness, and he began to berate himself for having forgotten why he had come to such a decision in the first place.

Now, as he sat waiting for the swami to open his door, he hoped that the weight of the Gita in his hands would banish such thoughts forever.

At two minutes past the hour, Bhagavati entered the anteroom with a cheery smile and knocked on the swami's door. She opened it, exchanged a few words with him, and then told Rodrigo he could go in. Rodrigo closed his book and walked into what was primarily an office, though it also served as the swami's bedchamber, as evidenced by the small bed against one wall, underneath a window that looked out on the swami's private garden. The swami was seated behind a large mahogany desk, half-cluttered with papers. Behind him were a large bookcase and a pair of filing cabinets. With a broad smile, he motioned for Rodrigo to pull up a chair and waited for him to be seated before he asked him how he was doing and how he could help him. Rodrigo found it difficult to get started, despite having rehearsed several times what he was going to say. But once he got going, the words spilled out almost as fast as he could speak them.

"I have a request to make, Swamiji. Saraswati's told me about how she hopes to become a sannyasi once she is released from the responsibility of supporting her parents, and I've decided I want to help her with that. I recently sold my house in the States and split the money with my ex-wife. I'd like to use that money, most of it anyway, to set up a trust fund for her parents. It's a pretty substantial amount. I think it should be more than enough to support them for the rest of their lives; whatever is left over when they are gone could be donated to some service project—I thought you might be able to recommend something. Anyhow, I called my lawyer and my banker yesterday, and I set everything up on that end; they're ready to transfer the money. I was hoping you could assist me to set up the trust fund. I don't have much time—my visa is up in a few days—and I really don't know how to go about doing such a thing. What I was thinking was that maybe it could be some kind of joint account with her name and their names, and maybe your name also as a trustee, plus some written instructions for what happens to the money once her parents are gone. Anyways, that's pretty much what I had in mind. I hope it's not too much to ask."

The swami shook his head pensively. "No, it's not too much to ask. I'd be happy to help, if that's what you've decided to do. But tell me one thing: Why is it you want to do this?"

Rodrigo let out a sigh. "I'm not sure exactly how to explain it, but I guess I feel like I owe her this after all she's done for me. Well, maybe 'owe' is not the right word, but I just feel like I want to do something for her and this is the best way I know how. I don't know if I could even put into words how big an impact she's had on my spiritual life. To be honest, when I first came to Rishikesh, I wasn't really that interested in spirituality."

The swami smiled. "I remember; I remember quite well."

"I guess it was pretty obvious. But that all changed when I started attending her classes. It was like I was asleep and she woke me up. And she's been guiding me ever since. Whatever progress I've made on the path, I owe a good part of it to her. That's a debt I don't think I'll ever be able to repay, but at least I can try."

The swami rested his chin on the back of his hands and peered intently into Rodrigo's eyes. "Are you sure you don't want to take some time to think about this? That's quite a large sum of money. I wouldn't want you to have any regrets later on."

Rodrigo shook his head. "I won't. I've thought about it a lot these last days and I'm quite sure that this is what I want to do. After all, it's just money; it's not that important. What Saraswati has given me is far more valuable. I feel good about this, Swamiji; it's the right thing to do, I'm certain of it. I don't want to sound pompous or anything, but I feel like I have a chance here to be an instrument for God's will, and it feels great to be able to be that instrument. For once."

"I'm glad to hear you say that, Rodrigo. You've come a long way since I first saw you in that garden out there, a very long way, indeed. But as I told you then, you came to India for a reason. It seems now that that reason has been fulfilled."

Rodrigo remembered that day in the garden. Though it had been less than a year ago, it felt more like a memory from another life. He realized suddenly how true the swami's words were and how genuine the warmth they carried. For a brief moment, he recognized his great fortune to be sitting in the swami's office, asking for his help. There was no greater privilege, he thought, than the company of a man whose saintliness smoothed the rough edges of anyone who came in his contact. He did not know what he had done in previous lives to deserve the attention of beings like the Mother, the Rimpoche, and the swami, but whatever the reason, he was grateful, and he would remain grateful for as long as he lived.

"Then you'll help me set up the trust fund?" he asked.

"I will. It has been a boon to have Saraswati here these past few years, but I also feel that it's time she moved on with her life. I'll ask Manu to set up the account. I already have her information and her parents' as well. It shouldn't take more than a couple of days to get the paperwork done. The ashram is a tax-exempt charitable and religious institution. If we set up the trusteeship through the ashram, then you won't lose part of the money to the government. But you said that your visa is up in a few days. I thought you were going to be with us for at least another year, if not longer?"

"I was seriously considering that possibility, but now that I'm going to set up this trust fund, it won't really be an option. My money's going to be tight, and I can't really afford to lose my job. I have a full professorship waiting for me back in the States, and it's unlikely it would still be there if I stayed away another year. That's not the only reason, though. I still have things I need to deal with there and I think it's time I faced them. I'd love to stay—I'm not sure there's any better place in the world than Rishikesh—but I'm starting to feel strongly that I need to go. I guess you could say that my samskaras are waiting for me. I'm sure I'll be back at some point, probably sooner than I think, but for now I feel it's time."

As Rodrigo said this, an image of Le Gentil flashed in his mind. Suddenly, he realized that what had started out of his mouth as an excuse was actually the truth. He had not thought to imitate his fictional astronomer, but their destinies seemed to be once again following a parallel course. The fact was that his destiny lay on the other side of the ocean. Whatever impact he would have on the world, whether through his writing or through the influence he would have on his students, it would have to be made within the confines of his own culture. The language he spoke would find it difficult to cross cultural borders, especially those as far away as India. Perhaps one day, he would learn to speak a universal language that would not lose anything in the translation, but for now he had a responsibility to fulfill to his own people, as Ambika and Le Gentil did—or would, once their story was finally written.

"I did want to make one further request. I've thought about it, and I prefer that Saraswati doesn't know where the money came from. I think it's better that way—for both of us. I was hoping that you could talk to the Mother, explain the situation so that she'll let her become a sannyasi, and then maybe that way Saraswati will think that this was all arranged by you and the Mother."

The swami rubbed his beard and looked at Rodrigo in a way that reminded him of the Rimpoche. Then he smiled, the same mischievous-seeming grin that Rodrigo had first seen in the picture hanging by the entrance to the office.

"I'll talk to the Mother. Four years is a long time to be waiting. And I'll set up your trust fund—but on one condition."

Rodrigo nodded, slightly apprehensive.

"You have to tell her. You have to promise me that you won't leave India without doing so."

It was not what Rodrigo wanted to hear. He tried reasoning with the swami but soon saw the futility of any such attempt. Finally he agreed and thanked him for his help. As he was getting up to go, the swami had one last word for him.

"It's a good thing you are doing, Rodrigo. These are the kind of actions that make a true human being of a man."

"Thank you, Swamiji. I kind of wish it hadn't taken me so long, but at least I'm finally headed in the right direction."

Two days later Manu came to his room with the finished paperwork for the trust fund. All that was left for him to do was to forward the account information to his lawyer. There was also a handwritten note from the swami with two simple lines: "Don't forget your promise. Good luck."

He had not forgotten, but he had availed himself of the chance to wait until the last possible moment. Tomorrow that brief reprieve would come to an end, since he was leaving Rishikesh early the following morning. Saraswati already knew that he was leaving for Delhi; what she didn't know was that he would not be coming back. He now had one more day to gather the courage to tell her.

The next morning, Rodrigo bought some fruits and nuts from the vendors outside the ashram gate so that he could continue writing through the lunch hour and straight up until his afternoon walk with Saraswati. One scene remained to be written: the parting scene between Ambika and Le Gentil. His own parting scene was scheduled for the afternoon. It was his hope that by dedicating the hours until then to his characters, they would enlighten his mind about what to say and provide him with the courage to say it. He began his session by invoking the presence of the guru within him and asking for his guidance. He thought of the Mother and her unforeseen intervention in his life, the Rimpoche and their private meetings, Shiva's image floating in the sky of his mind, all of them swirling together as different aspects of the Divine Presence, the same voice with many faces. After prostrating mentally to each of them, he asked them to speak to him through his characters, as he suspected they had been doing all along. Then he sent his mind backward in time to the Coromandel coast, where a large frigate with three tall masts and furled sails was swaying gently at anchor in Pondicherry harbor.

It was the first of March, 1770. The beach that morning was full of activity. Crates of all sizes containing supplies for the journey were jumbled together on the sand as strong-bodied, bare-chested Tamils, their chocolate skin glistening in the late-winter sun, lifted them into longboats for transfer to the French frigate, the Dauphin. Those passengers and crew members who had family or friends in the French colonial port were busy saying their last goodbyes. Among them, Rodrigo could see two slim figures standing apart from the crowd, speaking with subdued voices, though no one else on that boisterous morning was paying any attention to their private leave-taking. His mind hovered at a distance, not quite making out the words but clearly aware of the poignancy in their faces, until the strength of their emotions pulled him into their experience, bridging the chasm between the observer and the observed.

Le Gentil was still weak from his last illness, but he and Ambika had both known for some weeks now that it was time for him to go. He had first gotten sick at the end of September while observing the comet, a daily fever that he neglected despite her insistent preoccupation and which forced him to remain in bed while the ship in which he had secured passage set sail. Again, at the end of December, the same fever returned, this time accompanied by dysentery and sharp pains in his stomach; again, he was forced to remain in Pondicherry, despite having reserved passage on an outgoing vessel. Both times, he wryly told Ambika that his subconscious mind had arranged the illness because it knew he wasn't ready to leave. His subconscious was very intelligent, she told him. It had saved her the trouble of slipping some herbs into his tea that would have provoked the same result. Now, though he was still convalescent, they both knew it was time.

They had come early to the harbor and remained on the beach until the last of the ship's longboats was ready to return. The ship's mate, who had been supervising the loading of the supplies, called to Le Gentil to make haste and finish his goodbyes. They were due to set sail within the hour and Le Gentil needed to be aboard. Faced with the prospect of their imminent separation, the astronomer found himself grasping for a few more minutes, desperate for any means of staving off the anguish of their parting.

"Why don't you come with us in the longboat, my love? A couple of the harbor boats will be transporting the last of the crates. You can go back with one of them."

Ambika squeezed his hand and felt her love radiating out to him through her tears. "You know, I have never been in a boat. I have never been to sea."

"Then come, if only to spend a few more minutes together. Let me spend my last minutes in India by your side."

Ambika smiled sadly. "It's better I don't. If I take one step off the soil of Mother

India, just one, I will never return. I will follow you to the ends of the earth. No," she said, summoning her courage from the vast stores that had been gifted to her, "I have made a vow that I will not leave India until my country is free. I am a prisoner here, a prisoner to my duty, to my country, to my samskara."

Le Gentil could no longer restrain his tears. They coursed down his cheeks in glistening rivulets to join his barely audible sobs. Ambika rubbed his hands. She passed her palm over his cheeks and wiped his tears, the smile widening on her face.

"You know, Guillaume, in my land we believe that a man does not live one life but many lives; he keeps coming back until he achieves perfection. This is not the first time we have been together, and it will not be the last. I hope that you will return in this life so that I can be by your side. I will go to the seashore every day to watch for you. But if you cannot, I have faith that I will find you in the next life. And if I have difficulty finding you, then I know that you, Guillaume Joseph Hyacinthe Jean Baptiste Le Gentil, will surely find me."

He leaned over and kissed her. Then he stepped into the boat. As the oarsman pulled, he remained standing in the stern, gazing at his beloved, their eyes fixed on one another until their figures were only small shapes in the distance. When he reached out for the rigging and climbed onto the frigate, his eyes remained on her, though by then she was just a small wisp of color on a distant shore. Once on deck, he stood at the bulwark, watching her standing motionless in the distance, knowing that she was watching him as she would continue to watch him through all the years to come, both of them fully cognizant of the fact that sight was not an obstacle where the heart was concerned. The anchor was weighed, the sails unfurled. But Le Gentil remained oblivious to everything but the glimmer of her sari on the shore and the image in his mind of her long, lustrous hair hanging loose over her shoulders, sheltering the bright beacons of her eyes. Soon the timbers moaned and the deck began to pitch as the wind caught the sails and pulled him out into the grandeur of the ocean. It was only when he could no longer see her that he let his eyes rest upon all that he was leaving behind. The shore became a faint amber line receding toward the horizon. Above it the clouds billowed in a sky that seemed to rest on a bed of eternity. As the ocean spread around him, rimming his life with its azure swells, he felt a sense of peace descend upon him, wiping away the anguish that had up until then fastened its grip upon his heart. Her hand was still held fast in his. Their hearts continued to beat in unison with a secret power that not even the ocean could overcome. Finally, after nine long years, he was going home, but he was not going alone.

Like Ulysses, Le Gentil's journey still had long leagues and many challenges to go. He would not make it back to France for eighteen months, and then only after passing numerous trials that included terrible storms, one shipwreck, and yet another war. Once in France, he found that his relatives had declared him dead and robbed him of his estates. He had also been deprived of his precious seat at the Academy. In the end, however, he would overcome these obstacles and leave a legacy that would make his countrymen proud, as he had hoped he could. He would die a happy man—happy, most of all, because he had his eyes set on what lay beyond this life. And what lay beyond this life was Ambika.

Though Rodrigo's fingers ceased to move, he continued to peer through the backlit screen into the landscape of another time and place. Slowly that scene receded, as if he were pulled back by some unseen force into his own place and time. He offered no resistance, but as he became aware once again of his identity and his surroundings, he had the uncanny feeling that what he had witnessed had not taken place within his own imagination but within the imagination of the guru to whom he had offered his hesitant prayers. He had simply done his best to write down what he had seen. Finally, he reached out and closed the laptop. He had finished the first draft of his novel. Strangely, he felt no elation, no relief, no sense of triumph; he gave no thought at all to the significance of the moment. All that remained in his consciousness was the final line, still echoing faintly in his ears, as if he could hear Le Gentil's parting thoughts as the old astronomer lay peace-fully on his deathbed. No, it was not over, he thought. All he needed was a little patience. Not ordinary patience, but the patience of a yogi, the ability to wait a lifetime, knowing how little difference there really is between an hour and a life. If Le Gentil could show that kind of courage, then so could he.

It was two o'clock when he finished writing. He took a few minutes to eat the fruits and nuts he had purchased that morning. Then he grabbed his umbrella and started for the door. The rain, which had begun to hurl thick, thudding drops at his window a quarter of an hour earlier, was falling with the full force of the North Indian monsoon. As he stepped out onto the second-story balcony and locked his door, he heard two sharp cracks of thunder. As if in answer, the sky darkened even further. A single stern gust of wet air blew down the balcony toward the river. The cool rush of wind in his face gave him a surge of energy. He opened his umbrella, hunched his shoulders, and descended the stairs like a soldier going out to battle, braving the staccato onslaught of the downpour with some of the same courage he knew he would need to be able to tell Saraswati he was leaving.

41

SARASWATI WAS WAITING FOR Rodrigo on the veranda in front of her room. Knowing that it would be a while before they could venture out, she had placed a couple of chairs in front of her door and beside them a pitcher of water and two glasses. Open on her lap was a copy of the *Narada Bhakti Sutras* that she had unearthed from her library, earmarking several passages for them to take a look at. It was one of those passages that she was looking at now as she waited for Rodrigo to arrive: "Devotion is far greater than the paths of action, knowledge, or yoga, for it is the fruit of these practices." For years, she had been so caught up in her pursuit of spiritual knowledge that she had never properly appreciated this simple but fundamental truth. Until now. Once again she had Rodrigo to thank—or rather the passionate feelings that he had unleashed in her with his poet's sensibility and his lotus eyes. Their most recent conversations had all revolved around devotion. Even when they were silent, as they had mostly been on their last, magical excursion through the hills east of town, their eyes had been as voluble as eyes could be, discoursing with every glance on the mysteries of the heart and the glories of love in all its myriad manifestations. When their hands had reached out for each other, as they had often done that afternoon, she had felt a physical shock that reminded her of the kundalini energy snaking up her spinal column in transports of profound meditation. Krishna's life had been celebrated in the annals of her country's spiritual traditions not as a transcendent presence gracing the uncomprehending pathways of a planet but as the staging ground for the richest of all human dramas: the divine dance between two incarnate souls, love transforming itself into lover and beloved so that it can thereby fulfill its self-appointed destiny. Can love ever reach its apex if it does not find expression in the world that we inhabit? Is that not why the Lord created this world, so that he could fall in love with his created beings and have them fall in love with him? Had he not become Rodrigo so that she could finally know what it was to throw open the doors of her heart as wide as they could go? Had she not seen her lungs filled with the Mother's divine breath so that Rodrigo could know what it meant to have his heart burst open and flood the lowlands of his soul? There could be no other answer to this unanswerable question. The creation was the fulfillment of the Lord's desire, his last eternal wish, a single, endless chance to know himself through the act of love before he once again withdrew into the infinite ocean of eternal rest. Was there any doubt, then, that the path of the heart was the greatest of all paths, the jewel in Krishna's crown? This was what she was waiting to tell Rodrigo. They were words she might have gone a lifetime without discovering if he had not come along as the embodiment of her destiny, words that once intoned could never be put to rest, for they would go on sounding throughout eternity as the abiding music of creation. Perhaps she had waited so long to tell him how she felt because she had taken that long to understand this. What is important is not where your destiny is leading you, the Mother had told her, but whether or not you have the courage to follow it where it leads. Hers had taken a turn she could never have imagined, but now that her course had unexpectedly and irrevocably changed, she was ready to follow it to the end, no matter where it led her. Your will, Mother, she told herself, turning her eyes inward toward the Mother's unfathomable gaze. Your will, not mine—though perhaps one day, I will be able to truthfully say that your will and mine are one.

A few minutes later, Rodrigo arrived with his umbrella held aloft and his sandals splashing through the puddles that seemed to spring up fully formed the moment the rains began. As he passed through the sheer sheets that poured off the eaves and battered the hedges at the edge of the veranda, she felt as if he were entering her private sanctuary, set off from the outside world by a living curtain of water whose scudding sounds refused to let any rude noises enter to disturb the privacy of their twin voices. She was grateful for the rain, for the things she wanted to say were so private that only the universe should hear.

Soon they were deep into the *Bhakti Sutras*, letting the ancient sages give voice to the feelings that were now so palpable between them. They moved effortlessly from one sutra to the next, their imagination alive with the images that leapt off the pages, calling them forward into the ecstatic lands they were both yearning to visit. Finally, as the rain gradually relaxed its determined efforts, she began watching for the right moment to take the leap from the universal dance of devotion that they were discussing to the dance they were dancing with each other, the dance whose steps were being taught them by a wing-footed, Cheshire-grinning destiny who had interlaced their arms and sent them spinning across the dance floor. But this fateful goddess had yet one more twist to add that caused Saraswati to temporarily lose her balance.

"There is something I need to tell you," he said. "After reading those verses, now seems like the perfect time. I just hope I can find the right words."

There was a note of hesitation in his voice that gave her pause. She fell quiet and waited for him to go on.

"I've been thinking a lot lately about what you said that night at the river, how you wanted to become a sannyasi. I was so blinded by my own desire at the time that I couldn't appreciate what you were trying to tell me. But now I can. I think you'll be a great sannyasi, if that's what you decide to do with your life. And you are absolutely right. The world needs a dedicated sannyasi a lot more than it needs a dedicated journalist. I have no business trying to stand in your way, not if I feel about you the way I do. Rather, I should be doing everything I can to help you fulfill your dreams. So then I thought, what if I *could* help? What if I could remove the obstacle that's standing in your way? Wouldn't that be the right thing to do, the only thing?"

"I don't understand. What are you talking about?"

"I guess I should just come right out with it, then. I went to the swami the other day and asked him to help me set up a trust fund for your parents. Remember, I told you a couple of weeks ago that my house was finally sold and I was getting part of the money? Well, I used that money to set up the trust fund. The paperwork was finished two days ago. You and the swami are the trustees. Your parents can access the money directly, but there's a limit on how much they can take out each month. If they want to go over that limit in any given month, then they have to get either your signature or the swami's. Past a certain amount they'll need both—like if they need to remodel the house or something. As long as there are no major unexpected expenses, it should easily last them the rest of their lives. Whatever is leftover afterward will go to the service project of your choosing. And one more thing: the swami agreed to talk to the Mother about it. If everything goes according to plan and the Mother agrees, as the swami thinks she will, then you'll soon be a free woman. Maybe even within a few days. There will be nothing standing between you and your dreams. The swami told me that he will be sorry to see you go, but he understands that it is time for you to move on."

Saraswati's eyes began to fog over. Her initial shock was followed by a hot flare of anger and then by a powerful sense of betrayal. An image of Vikram flashed in her mind, an image that she associated with a lifelong caution against the perfidy of men. Irrational or not, she didn't care. Making no effort to bridle her anger, she said in her most caustic tone of voice, "You're telling me that you set up a bank account for my parents, without even talking to me about it?"

Rodrigo appeared bewildered. "But isn't this what you've been dreaming about for four years: your freedom?"

Only now did Saraswati notice the sting of tears in her eyes, brought on by her anger and her confusion. "Do you think you can buy my freedom like this?" she lashed out again. "Is that how it's done? Do you think you can just plan my life like that without consulting me first?"

"Of course not. I just wanted to help. I wasn't even going to tell you about it. I wanted you to think that the swami or some devotee of the Mother had arranged it, but the swami insisted I tell you before I leave."

Saraswati saw the look of genuine shock in Rodrigo's face and realized instantly that she had stepped over an invisible line, a line she should never have even approached. "I'm sorry, Rodrigo," she said, reining in her emotions as best she could, ashamed of what she had said and suddenly afraid of the possible repercussions. "I shouldn't have said that. I don't know what came over me, I really don't, but I certainly didn't mean what I said. Please, accept my apologies."

"That's okay; don't worry about it. I guess it must be kind of a shock, huh?"

"It is, a very big shock, though perhaps not in the way you mean it. I just…I don't know." She looked down at the floor, not knowing what to say. Then again she looked up at him, clutching at an unlikely hope. "And if I don't accept?"

"It's already done," he replied softly. "The account's set up; the money's been wired."

"I see." Saraswati took a deep breath, willing herself to a calm she did not feel. "Well, if it's done, it's done. Tell me again, why are you doing this?"

"I had thought that would be obvious. Isn't the highest devotion when you love the Lord not because it gives you pleasure but because you want to give him pleasure? Love is love, whether it is love for God or for God in the form of the woman you love. If you really care about somebody, then you want to make that person happy, that's all. Why shouldn't I be able to do something for you? Plus, it's not such a big deal. It's only money."

Of course, he was right. What could she say, other than to acknowledge how great a sacrifice he had made on her behalf? The tears still stung her eyes but there was no longer any anger to trace them to. "There is no way I can thank you, Rodrigo. I don't know what to say. You have a great heart. I already knew that but this only proves it even more. It's your head I have to question now. Wasn't that practically all the money you had? There are other ways to help without going to such an extreme. You could have lived here for the rest of your life on that money." Suddenly, something he said earlier took on ominous overtones. "Wait a second. Didn't you say that the swami insisted you tell me before you left?…But you're just going for a day or so to pick up your visa. What would a day or two matter? You are coming back in a couple of days, aren't you?"

Rodrigo lowered his eyes for a couple of seconds. When he lifted them again, she could see tears glistening at their edges. A sudden foreboding left an icy chill where moments before there had been passion and heat.

"Actually, I'm not. I'm leaving for the States tomorrow. My flight is at midnight. I'm not going to have the money to stay, at least not for as long as it would take to be able to support myself as a writer. I need to keep my job for the time being, and to do that, I need to go back. But there's more to it than that. My samskara is there; my work is there, at least for now. I can't ignore that. And anyway, you're not even going to be here. To be honest, that was the only reason why I even considered staying."

"You don't know that, Rodrigo. You may think I'm free to go. I might even think it, but it's not that simple. It doesn't matter what you or I think. What matters is our samskara. I can't see into the future any more than I can see what's going on on the other side of the galaxy. And what about your writing? How are you going to be a full-time writer if you have to teach?"

By now the shock had traveled to her stomach where it left a sinking sensation that she refused to identify as panic.

"I may not be able to be a full-time writer for a while, but that doesn't mean I'm going to stop writing. I may not have as much time, but whatever time I do have, I'm going to use it to write. It's what I do. After you, it's what I most care about in this world. That much at least I've learned about myself since I've been here. I don't know if my writing is any good or if it's ever going to be worth reading—all I have to offer is who I am, and I have a long way to go before there's any real wisdom there—but I'm not going to stop as long as I can still breathe and move my fingers. What comes of it is up to the Lord. I'm not going to worry about that part of it. No attachment to the fruits of one's actions, right?"

She shook her head. "With or without attachment, you're going to be a great writer. I know it."

"I hope that proves true, Saraswati, but you know, you haven't actually read anything I've written."

"I know your desire and I know your mind. That's all I need to know." Her voice grew fainter now, as if she barely had the strength to voice the question that was foremost in her heart. "And what about us? What happens to us? Does this mean that after tomorrow I won't see you any more?"

His face lit up with a smile. "I like to think that it's not a question of whether or not we'll see each other again, but rather of when. Honestly, I find it impossible to believe that I won't be back. I'd be leaving too much of myself here. Who knows, I may become like Ron and spend my summer vacations in India, to get my regular spiritual bath, as he puts it. Of course, you probably won't be in Rishikesh anymore, but wherever you are, I'll come and visit, you can be sure of that, just as long as it's allowed and you tell me it's okay. I don't know what the Mother will say about it, but I simply can't imagine not seeing you again. In the meantime, there's email and telephones and video chats. We're both writers, aren't we? We can make our conversations virtual instead of physical. Any time you want to talk on the phone, just email me a time and a number and I'll call. But if you ask me whether or not we still have a samskara together? Well, I have no doubt whatsoever."

There was no mistaking the conviction in his voice. Whatever anger or feelings of betrayal she might have felt, they had no existence or justification outside of her own jumbled thoughts. He was only doing what made sense to him after an act of sacrifice that would mark them both for the rest of their lives. They were quiet for several minutes, staring out at the rain, which by now had thinned to a gentle patter on the leaves, the hedges, and the puddles, a musical cadenza that seemed to be leading them steadily back toward the outside world.

"Would you like to start walking now?" Rodrigo asked. "The rain's just about stopped and we've been sitting for a long time?"

For once, she could not look forward to their walk. What was the use of sending her body if her mind was a prisoner of the future, too acutely conscious that in a few dwindling hours Rodrigo would be leaving Rishikesh, not knowing when, if ever, he would return? "I think I'll pass this time, Rodrigo, if you don't mind. I'd like to be alone for a while. Anyhow, I'm sure you have a lot of things to take care of before you go. What time are you leaving?"

"Six thirty. My train's at eight but I want to give myself plenty of time. I reserved a taxi at Muni-ki-reti for six forty-five."

"Then come and get me at six. I'll walk over with you. We can say our goodbyes then."

"Okay. At least we can cross the bridge together one last time."

Saraswati shook her head vehemently. "Don't say 'last,' Rodrigo. Please. Don't use that word. We'll just be crossing the bridge one more time. Neither you nor I know how many times we still have to cross that bridge together. Only God knows."

Saraswati watched Rodrigo until he disappeared around a corner. Then she went into her room, lay down on her bed, and began to cry the tears that she had held in for so many years. She could not tell if they were tears of sorrow or tears of joy, though she guessed that they were both, in proportions that varied as different images flowed through her mind: the Mother, whom, it appeared, she might soon be joining, as she had so often dreamed of; her parents in their lonely house, taken down by their years; Rodrigo, walking along the banks of the Ganges in the rain, his brow glistening with an interior light that no cloud could mask; Krishna in his celestial chariot, presiding over all matters, great or small, in the court of human destiny. Why had she reacted with anger when Rodrigo told her what he had done? It was a selfless act, an act born out of love, a sacrifice as potent and as sacred as any the ancient sages had conducted to propitiate the gods. Why had she felt betrayed, when what he had done was as great an act of fealty as a man could pay to a woman who has rejected his hand in marriage? There were things buried in her past whose shadows still stalked her, though she tried in vain to make out the shapes that cast them. But what of it? What of the past when destiny rolls us so inexorably toward the future? Let the bones of the past rot and merge with the dust that the winds carry up to heaven. Our only business is with the present, our only duty to let it guide us toward the future. Two eyes in the front of your head, the Mother had always said. Then let her pay heed to her guru's words. Once again, her destiny had led her to an unexpected bend in the road. This time she would not resist. It was nothing more than the Lord's wind at her back. All she had to do was to open her arms and let them be wings, so that she might glide with the currents that his divine breath sent forth.

Slowly her tears subsided. Like the rain misting outside her window, they brought a refreshing coolness to her mind. Her inner voices grew quiet, until she no longer remembered why she had been crying. Whatever may have gone awry in her soul now felt right, in harmony with the weather that freshened as the afternoon wore on. Her tears had washed her clean, as if she had gone out in the rain without her umbrella, lifted up her arms, and surrendered to the heavens. A smile crept over her face, though she had no mirror there to make her aware of it. It is not over, she thought. These things are never over until your samskara says they are, whatever he or she might think. Neither of them would be free until the Divine Arbiter released them. No matter how far they ran, their samskaras would drag them back again, until they had learned the lessons they were destined to learn together. She, for one, had had enough of running. She thought back to that night by the river. A few ill-considered words from her mouth had been enough to send him spinning off into space, and her into a future she was no longer sure she wanted. A lesson well-taken. She would have to be much more careful in the future where her words and her actions were concerned. This was not a child's game, this dance of theirs, this life. The next time he reached out his hand to carry her across the dance floor, she would be ready and willing to listen to the whispers that come from the land beyond the ego. But in the meantime, the dance continues. Tomorrow is just another step on the bridge to eternity. We will walk across Ram Jhula as we have always done, knowing that whatever route we take, it will bring us back to the place from where we started. There will always be another bridge to cross, Rodrigo. And after that another, and then another. Take my hand and let us steady each other as we go.

42

ODRIGO PARTED FROM SARASWATI that afternoon with an uneasy feeling in the pit of his stomach. Why had he waited until the last minute to tell her about his decision? Residual cowardice? A farewell gift from his now-departed priest? Had he not betrayed her confidence in him by not sharing his thoughts and his plans with her from the moment their vapors had emerged, clouded and triumphant, from the furnaces of his subconscious? At the very least, he would have saved her the shock that he knew to be the cause of her unwillingness to walk with him that afternoon, a walk he had been greatly looking forward to, as much as he had dreaded the emotional land mines of their immanent leave-taking that would have surely been its principal theme. Perhaps in some respects it was just as well. Though he had already packed his bag and mailed his books the day before, he had other goodbyes to say that deserved his just attention. Saraswati had been perfectly right about that.

His first stop was the office where he said goodbye to Bhagavati and the other members of the staff. For some reason, Bhagavati appeared quite certain that he would be back the following summer; she even promised to reserve the same room for him with its unguarded view of the Shiva statue, shadowed by the mountains. The swami had left that morning for Almora, but she assured him that his goodbyes would reach him the moment he returned. From there, he searched out all the sundry faces that had made the ashram so much his home during these last months, from the jovial guard at the back gate whom he could not escape chatting with in his nearly non-existent Hindi every time he passed that way, to the smallest of the cherubic monks who looked upon their novitiate as an extended childhood romp. His last stop was Amrita's room, where he found her lying on her bed reading a book and listening to a Bob Marley CD on her portable boombox. When she heard the news that he was leaving, she was not only surprised but visibly concerned. "Have you told Saraswati?" she asked in a faintly accusatory tone. "I can't imagine she'll be too happy about it." Reluctantly, he was forced to tell her about the trust fund and why he had changed his mind about staying. Amrita listened without interrupting his brief explanation, but she wasn't shy about expressing her opinion once he had finished. "Do you really think you're doing the right thing? It's a wonderful gesture, taking care of her parents like that, but that's no reason for you to be leaving. I know how little money it takes to stay here. Are you sure you're not just running away?" Though he did his best to justify himself, the skeptical look on her face made it clear that she remained unconvinced. They parted with a long and somewhat tearful California hug, but despite the effusive farewell, he could feel the unspoken criticism at his back as he waved to her one last time and headed for the ashram gate.

There were still two hours to go before dark. The rain had stopped while he was making his rounds, charging the atmosphere, as it always did, with an invigorating freshness. He thought of taking one last walk through town to bid farewell to the various places that had become so familiar to him, so laden with significant memories, but as he reached the Ram Jhula Bridge and paused to decide which route to take, he remembered his visit to Kunjapuri almost a full year earlier. Drawn by the memory of those Himalayan solitudes, he looked up at the distant peak where the temple lay hidden from his naked eye. When he had made the ascent the year before, he had not yet begun to meditate. Mired in the morass of a terrible dejection, he had been aware of the vast beauty that surrounded that secluded symbol of the Hindu faith, but he had failed to appreciate it. Now he was a different man, a semblance, perhaps, of the man he had hoped he could become on that afternoon when he descended into the darkness of utter despair under the shade of a courtyard tree. Perhaps now he would be able to appreciate that beauty. Perhaps now he would be able to enjoy the temple solitude as a yogi would—absorbed in profound contemplation. This was his final day in the Himalayas. Why not take advantage of a final chance to sit at the top of the world and look out at the creation from a vantage point not much different from the Creator's own? Inspired by the thought, he hurried across the Ram Jhula Bridge and hired a taxi from Muni-ki-reti to take him to the temple. He told the driver that he wanted to stay until after dusk so that he could meditate there, and promised him an extra two hundred rupees for the wait, a sum that inspired the driver almost as much as the thought of his upcoming meditation inspired him.

Forty minutes later, Rodrigo was standing at the foot of the stairs that led up to the temple, watching the sun hover in the western sky not far from the horizon, flooding the Gangetic plains with a golden light and turning the Ganges into a thin ribbon of silver winding its way through a turquoise haze. He remained there for several minutes, letting his eyes wander freely from one end of the atmosphere to the other, listening to the faint chime of unseen voices from the half-hidden village on the slopes below him and inhaling in deep drafts the spicy fragrances of mountain wildflowers and Himalayan pine. Then he slowly ascended the 408 concrete steps with a growing sense of reverence, a humble recognition that he was climbing into a sacred space high above the clamor of the world. He kept his hands pressed to his stomach, elbows in, his eyes half closed, walking as he thought a monk might walk, turning that ascent into a conscious meditation. When he passed the golden lions who jealously guarded the entrance to the temple enclosure, he turned back for one last look at the world from which he had come and then passed under the archway into a secluded space dedicated to the mysteries that the world below ignored or at best looked up at with a vague, uncertain fascination.

After making a short circuit of the grounds, which were empty of pilgrims at this late hour, he passed through the small opening in the back wall and went to sit on the concrete platform where he had looked upon the high Himalayas for the first time. They were still there, more majestic than he remembered them, massive rocky spires stretching toward heaven with the same silent gestures they had used to communicate with human beings throughout the million-year history of that transitory race. He felt their shadows fall on him as he looked from peak to peak, the vast panorama receding into a distant haze that grew imperceptibly dimmer with every passing moment. The solitude and the silence engulfed him. He felt their pressure forcing his private thoughts back toward the unknown seas whence they came. How was it possible to cling to the uncertain mooring of the ego, this vapid shadow of purloined thought, in the face of such immensity? Of what significance were these limited, garish desires when set against the backdrop of the planet's loftiest heights? Undoubtedly, it was this that had brought the first yogis to these lonely peaks to pursue their meditations. Or perhaps it was the sight of such a canvas—so beautiful, so redolent of infinity—that had made them yogis in the first place. Rodrigo wanted to close his eyes then and there and give himself up to the immensity that bore down upon him. But he had already chosen his seat for evening meditation. Or rather, it had been chosen for him, predetermined by the unseen forces that had led him off the precipice one afternoon in late August when the leaves had begun to fall, decorating the temple grounds with the crepitating song of their afterlife. Obedient to the play of destiny, to its meticulous attention to setting and detail, he went back into the temple grounds and sat down under the twin spreading shade trees where his ego had broken down the last time he had ascended to these heights.

From his seat under one of the trees, the mountains were still visible, though much of their bulk was now hidden by the sparse vegetation behind the back wall and the three small buildings that fronted it: the temple with its conical spire and its orange-and-white-striped columns; the gazebo, enclosed with wire mesh, where a silent blue Shiva peered out at him, wearing a garland of snakes around his neck and a crescent moon in his hair; and a third building, its purpose unknown to him, with its orange doors and windows shut tight, as if it also were locked in silent contemplation. He took in the scene around him, gazing for a moment through the open doorway into the temple interior where he could see the shadow of the priest sitting before the hidden image of the goddess in whose honor the temple had been built. Then he closed his eyes, bowed before the image of Shiva that had come to preside over his innermost thoughts, and began his meditation.

Slowly the confines of his limited existence began to give way. His mind opened up into an ocean deeper and more luminous than the Himalayan sky that had absorbed his attention a short while before. His mantra, with its sonorous accents, pulled him inward like a magnet, drawing his attention away from the thoughts that danced like kites in the sky of his mind, caught in a willful breeze. Then he heard the rustle of ankle bells coming from deep inside him, a distant music that called to him with unimaginable beauty. He felt that music tug at his heart, threatening to burst it open from the sheer joy it exuded. It grew louder and seemed to surround him until he was sure he was hearing it with his physical ears as well. Almost against his will, he opened his eyes. It was twilight now, the world sinking deep into shadow. But even then there was no mistaking what he saw. Leaning against a column on the veranda of the temple was the same girl he had seen that day, just before his existence had dissolved into tears. She was wearing the same sky blue sari, one leg crossed in front of the other, the toes of that foot barely touching the ground, the ankle bells clearly visible below the drape of her cloth. She was smiling at him, the same bewitching smile that he had never quite forgotten, beckoning him with her eyes, the light of her dark face radiating out toward him as if it were the light of Venus shining through the thin mountain air in the hour after dusk.

For one interminable moment he felt paralyzed. The whirling motion of his mind came to a standstill. His eyes were unable to tear themselves from this inexplicable figure who held his gaze as if she were dreaming him and had fallen in love with her creation. Then she laughed, her laughter ringing through the twilight sky so clearly that it seemed to be skipping from one mountain to the next. Suddenly, as if the spell were broken, he felt his eyes close. There, in the space within his mind, he saw her gradually coming into focus, her skin luminous in the dark, her eyes glowing like two emeralds reflecting the light of a runaway fire. Her eyes caught his gaze and he felt himself losing consciousness of everything but the radiant mosaic of her face and the gentle smile that was beauty itself wrapped into the only form that could hold it. Then her face began to change. Her features gradually metamorphosed into the features of his mother as he remembered her from his childhood, gazing at him with a look of such fondness that his small heart could not contain the love it felt. But the eyes remained the same, the same two jewels glowing in the night with the light of a thousand fires. The face changed again. He saw his aunt opening the pages of a book and beginning to read to him, stirring his mind with heroic images in which he saw himself striding across strange and beautiful lands. His child's face looked up into her eyes and saw the same light, the same unbearable love, the same twin jewels shining in the depths of space. Again her features metamorphosed. He saw Beth setting challenges he was not yet ready to meet, lovingly putting into place the next pieces of the puzzle that was describing his destiny. The light that played across her face shifted and Saraswati's face emerged, reaching out to him across the gaping chasm that separated one life from the next, calling on him to finish the journey that he had begun so many lifetimes ago. Again and again the face changed. He saw his teachers, his childhood companions, his enemies and his friends, the women he had loved and the women who had loved him, populating this life and those that came before it. Men and women both, but always the same eyes, the same eternal witness to the changing weather of his heart, gazing at him with a love that had never wavered through all the forgotten episodes of his days.

One by one, the faces passed in front of his inner eye, faster and faster, until they became a river of faces flowing through his existence, looking at him through the same set of eyes, the laughing eyes of the goddess who had never let him out of her sight since the moment of his birth and the many births before it. The river flowed into an ocean, its borders expanding until its shores disappeared from sight. He heard her laughter filling the space around him, the music of the universe surrounding him with its infinite song. Then he saw that he himself was a note in that song, a wisp of color in the devi's dream. Her laughter became his own, for what was he but a thought in the mind of the goddess. She indeed was dreaming him and everything that surrounded him: the temple, the mountains, the clamor on the plains, the tilt of a planet as it rushed through space, the countless dramas with which she kept herself entertained. She was sporting with him as she sported with all that she created. Her smile had descended upon him the moment he had looked back to see who it was who was dreaming him into existence.

Caught in the widening gyre of eternity, he lost awareness of everything but the devi's smile, which stretched outward until it dissolved into a spreading sea of love. How long he remained afloat in that sea he did not know, nor did it matter, for time ceased to exist in the borderless lands of her smile. Then, slowly, his rapture receded. The devi withdrew into her dance. But as he watched her go, he knew that she could conceal herself from him no longer. From now on, wherever he looked, he knew he would catch a glimpse of her eyes hiding behind the folds of her veil. When he opened his own eyes again, twilight had turned to night. His driver was waiting. The demands of the world could not be ignored. He had a journey to continue, a journey that he now knew would bring him back to these mountains, back to the ancient hand that had first pointed him on his way. With a prayer of thanks that he knew would be heard even before his mind could speak it, he bowed down and touched the Mother's feet. Moments later, he felt her hand upon his head. Only then did he get up, grateful for the blessing that had been his, long before he had awakened from his sleep.

Acknowledgments

The analysis of the Bhagavad Gita in chapter 16 was inspired by a discourse of Shrii Shrii Anandamurti entitled "Dharmakshetra and Kurukshetra."

The following quote, which appears in chapter 31, is paraphrased from a quote attributed to the Kalu Rimpoche: "You live in illusion and the appearance of things. There is a reality but you do not know it. When you do, you will see that you are nothing; and being nothing, you are everything."

About The Author

Devashish holds an MFA in fiction from San Diego State University. He divides his time between Ananda Kirtana, a spiritual community in the Brazilian countryside, and his farm in Puerto Rico, where he has a yoga center and a tropical-fruit plantation.

9 781881 717096